P9-DXI-741

PELICAN BOOKS

THE GREEK MYTHS
VOLUME TWO

Robert Graves was born in 1895 at Wimbledon, son of Alfred Perceval Graves, the Irish writer, and Amalia von Ranke. He went from school to the First World War, where he became a captain in the Royal Welch Fusiliers. His principal calling is poetry, and his *Selected Poems* have been published in the Penguin Poets. Apart from a year as Professor of English Literature at Cairo University in 1926 he has since lived by writing. His bibliography published in 1965 credits him with 114 heterogeneous books; but the total is now 120. His historical novels include: *I, Claudius*; *Claudius the God*; *Sergeant Lamb of the Ninth*; *Count Belisarius*; *Wife to Mr Milton*; *Proceed Sergeant Lamb*; *The Golden Fleece*; *They Hanged My Saintly Billy*, and *The Isles of Unwisdom*. He wrote his autobiography, *Goodbye to All That*, in 1929. His two most discussed non-fiction books are *The White Goddess*, which presents a new view of the poetic impulse, and *The Nazarene Gospel Restored* (with Joshua Podro), a re-examination of primitive Christianity. He has translated Apuleius, Lucan and Suetonius for the Penguin Classics, and compiled the first modern dictionary of Greek mythology, *The Greek Myths*. He was elected Professor of Poetry at Oxford in 1961. He has made his home in Majorca since 1929.

ROBERT GRAVES

THE GREEK MYTHS

VOLUME TWO

PENGUIN BOOKS

Penguin Books Ltd, Harmondsworth, Middlesex, England
Penguin Books Inc., 7110 Ambassador Road, Baltimore, Maryland 21207, U.S.A.
Penguin Books Australia Ltd, Ringwood, Victoria, Australia

—

Specially written for Penguin Books
First published 1955
Reprinted 1955
Reprinted with amendments 1957
Revised 1960
Reprinted 1962, 1964, 1967, 1969, 1971, 1973

—

Copyright © Robert Graves, 1955, 1960

—

Made and printed in Great Britain by
Cox & Wyman Ltd, London, Reading and Fakenham
Set in Monotype Bembo

CONTENTS OF VOLUME TWO

105.	OEDIPUS	9
106.	THE SEVEN AGAINST THEBES	15
107.	THE EPIGONI	21
108.	TANTALUS	25
109.	PELOPS AND OENOMAUS	31
110.	THE CHILDREN OF PELOPS	40
111.	ATREUS AND THYESTES	43
112.	AGAMEMNON AND CLYTAEMNESTRA	51
113.	THE VENGEANCE OF ORESTES	56
114.	THE TRIAL OF ORESTES	64
115.	THE PACIFICATION OF THE ERINNYES	70
116.	IPHIGENEIA AMONG THE TAURIANS	73
117.	THE REIGN OF ORESTES	80
118.	THE BIRTH OF HERACLES	84
119.	THE YOUTH OF HERACLES	90
120.	THE DAUGHTERS OF THESPIUS	95
121.	ERGINUS	97
122.	THE MADNESS OF HERACLES	100
123.	THE FIRST LABOUR: THE NEMEAN LION	103
124.	THE SECOND LABOUR: THE LERNAEAN HYDRA	107
125.	THE THIRD LABOUR: THE CERYNEIAN HIND	110
126.	THE FOURTH LABOUR: THE ERYMANTHIAN BOAR	113
127.	THE FIFTH LABOUR: THE STABLES OF AUGEIAS	116
128.	THE SIXTH LABOUR: THE STYMPHALIAN BIRDS	119
129.	THE SEVENTH LABOUR: THE CRETAN BULL	121
130.	THE EIGHTH LABOUR: THE MARES OF DIOMEDES	122
131.	THE NINTH LABOUR: HIPPOLYTE'S GIRDLE	124
132.	THE TENTH LABOUR: THE CATTLE OF GERYON	132
133.	THE ELEVENTH LABOUR: THE APPLES OF THE HESPERIDES	145
134.	THE TWELFTH LABOUR: THE CAPTURE OF CERBERUS	152
135.	THE MURDER OF IPHITUS	158
136.	OMPHALE	162
137.	HESIONE	168
138.	THE CONQUEST OF ELIS	175
139.	THE CAPTURE OF PYLUS	182
140.	THE SONS OF HIPPOCOÖN	185
141.	AUGE	186

CONTENTS

142. DEIANEIRA   190
143. HERACLES IN TRACHIS   195
144. IOLE   199
145. THE APOTHEOSIS OF HERACLES   200
146. THE CHILDREN OF HERACLES   207
147. LINUS   212
148. THE ARGONAUTS ASSEMBLE   215
149. THE LEMNIAN WOMEN AND KING CYZICUS   223
150. HYLAS, AMYCUS, AND PHINEUS   227
151. FROM THE SYMPLEGADES TO COLCHIS   232
152. THE SEIZURE OF THE FLEECE   236
153. THE MURDER OF APSYRTUS   241
154. THE *ARGO* RETURNS TO GREECE   244
155. THE DEATH OF PELIAS   250
156. MEDEA AT EPHYRA   253
157. MEDEA IN EXILE   256
158 THE FOUNDATION OF TROY   259
159. PARIS AND HELEN   268
160. THE FIRST GATHERING AT AULIS   278
161. THE SECOND GATHERING AT AULIS   290
162. NINE YEARS OF WAR   295
163. THE WRATH OF ACHILLES   305
164. THE DEATH OF ACHILLES   313
165. THE MADNESS OF AJAX   321
166. THE ORACLES OF TROY   325
167. THE WOODEN HORSE   330
168. THE SACK OF TROY   336
169. THE RETURNS   346
170. ODYSSEUS'S WANDERINGS   354
171. ODYSSEUS'S HOMECOMING   369

INDEX   377

Map showing the sites mentioned in text

THE GREEK MYTHS

VOLUME TWO

OEDIPUS

Laius, son of Labdacus, married Iocaste, and ruled over Thebes. Grieved by his prolonged childlessness, he secretly consulted the Delphic Oracle, which informed him that this seeming misfortune was a blessing, because any child born to Iocaste would become his murderer. He therefore put Iocaste away, though without offering any reason for his decision, which caused her such vexation that, having made him drunk, she inveigled him into her arms again as soon as night fell. When, nine months later, Iocaste was brought to bed of a son, Laius snatched him from the nurse's arms, pierced his feet with a nail and, binding them together, exposed him on Mount Cithaeron.

b. Yet the Fates had ruled that this boy should reach a green old age. A Corinthian shepherd found him, named him Oedipus because his feet were deformed by the nail-wound, and brought him to Corinth, where King Polybus was reigning at the time.[1]

c. According to another version of the story, Laius did not expose Oedipus on the mountain, but locked him in a chest, which was lowered into the sea from a ship. This chest drifted ashore at Sicyon, where Periboea, Polybus's queen, happened to be on the beach, supervising her royal laundry-women. She picked up Oedipus, retired to a thicket and pretended to have been overcome by the pangs of labour. Since the laundry-women were too busy to notice what she was about, she deceived them all into thinking that he had only just been born. But Periboea told the truth to Polybus who, also being childless, was pleased to rear Oedipus as his own son.

One day, taunted by a Corinthian youth with not in the least resembling his supposed parents, Oedipus went to ask the Delphic Oracle what future lay in store for him. 'Away from the shrine, wretch!' the Pythoness cried in disgust. 'You will kill your father and marry your mother!'

d. Since Oedipus loved Polybus and Periboea, and shrank from bringing disaster upon them, he at once decided against returning to Corinth. But in the narrow defile between Delphi and Daulis he happened to meet Laius, who ordered him roughly to step off the road and make way for his betters; Laius, it should be explained, was in a chariot and Oedipus on foot. Oedipus retorted that he acknowledged no betters except the gods and his own parents.

'So much the worse for you!' cried Laius, and ordered his charioteer Polyphontes to drive on.

One of the wheels bruised Oedipus's foot and, transported by rage, he killed Polyphontes with his spear. Then, flinging Laius on the road entangled in the reins, and whipping up the team, he made them drag him to death. It was left to the king of Plataeae to bury both corpses.[2]

e. Laius had been on his way to ask the Oracle how he might rid Thebes of the Sphinx. This monster was a daughter of Typhon and Echidne or, some say, of the dog Orthrus and the Chimaera, and had flown to Thebes from the uttermost part of Ethiopia. She was easily recognized by her woman's head, lion's body, serpent's tail, and eagle's wings.[3] Hera had recently sent the Sphinx to punish Thebes for Laius's abduction of the boy Chrysippus from Pisa and, settling on Mount Phicium, close to the city, she now asked every Theban wayfarer a riddle taught her by the Three Muses: 'What being, with only one voice, has sometimes two feet, sometimes three, sometimes four, and is weakest when it has the most?' Those who could not solve the riddle she throttled and devoured on the spot, among which unfortunates was Iocaste's nephew Haemon, whom the Sphinx made *haimon*, or 'bloody', indeed.

Oedipus, approaching Thebes fresh from the murder of Laius, guessed the answer. 'Man,' he replied, 'because he crawls on all fours as an infant, stands firmly on his two feet in his youth, and leans upon a staff in his old age.' The mortified Sphinx leaped from Mount Phicium and dashed herself to pieces in the valley below. At this the grateful Thebans acclaimed Oedipus king, and he married Iocaste, unaware that she was his mother.

f. Plague then descended upon Thebes, and the Delphic Oracle, when consulted once more, replied: 'Expel the murderer of Laius!' Oedipus, not knowing whom he had met in the defile, pronounced a curse on Laius's murderer and sentenced him to exile.

g. Blind Teiresias, the most renowned seer in Greece at this time, now demanded an audience with Oedipus. Some say that Athene, who had blinded him for having inadvertently seen her bathing, was moved by his mother's plea and, taking the serpent Erichthonius from her aegis, gave the order: 'Cleanse Teiresias's ears with your tongue that he may understand the language of prophetic birds.'

h. Others say that once, on Mount Cyllene, Teiresias had seen two serpents in the act of coupling. When both attacked him, he struck at them with his staff, killing the female. Immediately he was turned into a woman, and became a celebrated harlot; but seven years later he happened to see the same sight again at the same spot, and this time regained his manhood by killing the male serpent. Still others say that when Aphrodite and the three Charites, Pasithea, Cale, and Eurphosyne, disputed as to which of the four was most beautiful, Teiresias awarded Cale the prize; whereupon Aphrodite turned him into an old woman. But Cale took him with her to Crete and presented him with a lovely head of hair. Some days later Hera began reproaching Zeus for his numerous infidelities. He defended them by arguing that, at any rate, when he did share her couch, she had the more enjoyable time by far. 'Women, of course, derive infinitely greater pleasure from the sexual act than men,' he blustered.

'What nonsense!' cried Hera. 'The exact contrary is the case, and well you know it.'

Teiresias, summoned to settle the dispute from his personal experience, answered:

> 'If the parts of love-pleasure be counted as ten,
> Thrice three go to women, one only to men.'

Hera was so exasperated by Zeus's triumphant grin that she blinded Teiresias; but Zeus compensated him with inward sight, and a life extended to seven generations.[4]

i. Teiresias now appeared at Oedipus's court, leaning on the cornelwood staff given him by Athene, and revealed to Oedipus the will of the gods: that the plague would cease only if a Sown Man died for the sake of the city. Iocaste's father Menoeceus, one of those who had risen out of the earth when Cadmus sowed the serpent's teeth, at once leaped from the walls, and all Thebes praised his civic devotion.

Teiresias then announced further: 'Menoeceus did well, and the plague will now cease. Yet the gods had another of the Sown Men in mind, one of the third generation: for he has killed his father and married his mother. Know, Queen Iocaste, that it is your husband Oedipus!'

j. At first, none would believe Teiresias, but his words were soon confirmed by a letter from Periboea at Corinth. She wrote that the sudden death of King Polybus now allowed her to reveal the circumstances of Oedipus's adoption; and this she did in damning detail. Iocaste then hanged herself for shame and grief, while Oedipus blinded himself with a pin taken from her garments.[5]

k. Some say that, although tormented by the Erinnyes, who accused him of having brought about his mother's death, Oedipus continued to reign over Thebes for a while, until he fell gloriously in battle.[6] According to others, however, Iocaste's brother Creon expelled him, but not before he had cursed Eteocles and Polyneices – who were at once his sons and his brothers – when they insolently sent him the inferior portion of the sacrificial beast, namely haunch instead of royal shoulder. They therefore watched dry-eyed as he left the city which he had delivered from the Sphinx's power. After wandering for many years through country after country, guided by his faithful daughter Antigone, Oedipus finally came to Colonus in Attica, where the Erinnyes, who have a grove there, hounded him to death, and Theseus buried his body in the precinct of the Solemn Ones at Athens, lamenting by Antigone's side.[7]

1. Apollodorus: iii. 5. 7.
2. Hyginus: *Fabula* 66; Scholiast on Euripides's *Phoenician Women* 13 and 26; Apollodorus: *loc. cit.*; Pausanias: x. 5. 2.
3. Apollodorus: iii. 5. 8; Hesiod: *Theogony* 326; Sophocles: *Oedipus the Tyrant* 391; Scholiast on Aristophanes's *Frogs* 1287.
4. Apollodorus: iii. 6. 7; Hyginus: *Fabula* 75; Ovid: *Metamorphoses* iii. 320; Pindar: *Nemean Odes* i. 91; Tzetzes: *On Lycophron* 682; Sosostratus, quoted by Eustathius: p. 1665.
5. Apollodorus: iii. 5. 8; Sophocles: *Oedipus the Tyrant* 447, 713, 731, 774, 1285, etc.
6. Homer: *Odyssey* xi. 270 and *Iliad* xxiii. 679.
7. Sophocles: *Oedipus at Colonus* 166 and scholiast on 1375; Euripides: *Phoenician Women, Proem*; Apollodorus: iii. 5. 9; Hyginus: *Fabula* 67; Pausanias: i. 20. 7.

*

1. The story of Laius, Iocaste, and Oedipus has been deduced from a set of sacred icons by a deliberate perversion of their meaning. A myth which would explain Labdacus's name ('help with torches') has been lost; but it may refer to the torchlight arrival of a Divine Child, carried by cattlemen or shepherds at the New Year ceremony, and acclaimed as a son of the goddess Brimo ('raging'). This *eleusis*, or advent, was the most important incident in the Eleusinian Mysteries, and perhaps also in the Isthmian (see 70. 5), which would explain the myth of Oedipus's

arrival at the court of Corinth. Shepherds fostered or paid homage to many other legendary or semi-legendary infant princes, such as Hippothous (see 49. *a*), Pelias (see 68. *d*), Amphion (see 76. *a*), Aegisthus (see 111. *i*), Moses, Romulus, and Cyrus, who were all either exposed on a mountain or else consigned to the waves in an ark, or both. Moses was found by Pharaoh's daughter when she went down to the water with her women. It is possible that *Oedipus,* 'swollen foot', was originally *Oedipais*, 'son of the swelling sea', which is the meaning of the name given to the corresponding Welsh hero, Dylan; and that the piercing of Oedipus's feet with a nail belongs to the end, not to the beginning, of his story, as in the myth of Talus (see 92. *m* and 154. *h*).

2. Laius's murder is a record of the solar king's ritual death at the hands of his successor: thrown from a chariot and dragged by the horses (see 71. *1*). His abduction of Chrysippus probably refers to the sacrifice of a surrogate (see 29. *1*) when the first year of his reign ended.

3. The anecdote of the Sphinx has evidently been deduced from an icon showing the winged Moon-goddess of Thebes, whose composite body represents the two parts of the Theban year – lion for the waxing part, serpent for the waning part – and to whom the new king offers his devotions before marrying her priestess, the Queen. It seems also that the riddle which the Sphinx learned from the Muses has been invented to explain a picture of an infant, a warrior, and an old man, all worshipping the Triple-goddess: each pays his respects to a different person of the triad. But the Sphinx, overcome by Oedipus, killed herself, and so did her priestess Iocaste. Was Oedipus a thirteenth-century invader of Thebes, who suppressed the old Minoan cult of the goddess and reformed the calendar? Under the old system, the new king, though a foreigner, had theoretically been a son of the old king whom he killed and whose widow he married; a custom that the patriarchal invaders misrepresented as parricide and incest. The Freudian theory that the 'Oedipus complex' is an instinct common to all men was suggested by this perverted anecdote; and while Plutarch records (*On Isis and Osiris* 32) that the hippopotamus 'murdered his sire and forced his dam', he would never have suggested that every man has a hippopotamus complex.

4. Though Theban patriots, loth to admit that Oedipus was a foreigner who took their city by storm, preferred to make him the lost heir to the kingdom, the truth is revealed by the death of Menoeceus, a member of the pre-Hellenic race that celebrated the Peloria festival in memory of Ophion the Demiurge, from whose teeth they claimed to have sprung. He leaped to his death in the desperate hope of placating the goddess, like Mettus Curtius, when a chasm opened in the Roman Forum (Livy: vii. 6); and the same sacrifice was offered during the War of the 'Seven Against Thebes' (see 106. *j*). However, he died in vain;

otherwise the Sphinx, and her chief priestess, would not have been obliged to commit suicide. The story of Iocaste's death by hanging is probably an error; Helen of the Olive-trees, like Erigone and Ariadne of the vine cult, was said to have died in this way – perhaps to account for figurines of the Moon-goddess which dangled from the boughs of orchard trees, as a fertility charm (see 79. 2; 88. 10 and 98. 5). Similar figurines were used at Thebes; and when Iocaste committed suicide, she doubtless leaped from a rock, as the Sphinx did.

5. The occurrence of 'Teiresias', a common title for soothsayers, throughout Greek legendary history suggested that Teiresias had been granted a remarkably long life by Zeus. To see snakes coupling is still considered unlucky in Southern India; the theory being that the witness will be punished with the 'female disease' (as Herodotus calls it), namely homosexuality; here the Greek fabulist has taken the tale a stage further in order to raise a laugh against women. Cornel, a divinatory tree sacred to Cronus (see 52. 3 and 170. 5), symbolized the fourth month, that of the Spring Equinox; Rome was founded at this season, on the spot where Romulus's cornel-wood javelin struck the ground. Hesiod turned the traditional two Charites into three (see 13. 3), calling them Euphrosyne, Aglaia, and Thalia (*Theogony* 945). Sosostratus's account of the beauty contest makes poor sense, because *Pasithea Cale Euphrosyne*, 'the Goddess of Joy who is beautiful to all', seems to have been Aphrodite's own title. He may have borrowed it from the Judgement of Paris (see 159. *i* and *3*).

6. Two incompatible accounts of Oedipus's end survive. According to Homer, he died gloriously in battle. According to Apollodorus and Hyginus, he was banished by Iocaste's brother, a member of the Cadmean royal house, and wandered as a blind beggar through the cities of Greece until he came to Colonus in Attica, where the Furies hounded him to death. Oedipus's remorseful self-blinding has been interpreted by psychologists to mean castration; but though the blindness of Achilles's tutor Phoenix (see 160. *l*) was said by Greek grammarians to be a euphemism for impotence, primitive myth is always downright, and the castration of Uranus and Attis continued to be recorded unblushingly in Classical textbooks. Oedipus's blinding, therefore, reads like a theatrical invention, rather than original myth. Furies were personifications of conscience, but conscience in a very limited sense: aroused only by the breach of a maternal taboo.

7. According to the non-Homeric story, Oedipus's defiance of the City-goddess was punished by exile, and he eventually died a victim of his own superstitious fears. It is probable that his innovations were repudiated by a body of Theban conservatives; and, certainly, his sons' and brothers' unwillingness to award him the shoulder of the sacrificial victim

amounted to a denial of his divine authority. The shoulder-blade was the priestly perquisite at Jerusalem (*Leviticus* vii. 32 and xi. 21, etc.) and Tantalus set one before the goddess Demeter at a famous banquet of the gods (see 108. *c*). Among the Akan, the right shoulder still goes to the ruler.

Did Oedipus, like Sisyphus, try to substitute patrilineal for matrilineal laws of succession, but get banished by his subjects? It seems probable. Theseus of Athens, another patriarchal revolutionary from the Isthmus, who destroyed the ancient Athenian clan of Pallantids (see 99. *a*), is associated by the Athenian dramatists with Oedipus's burial, and was likewise banished at the close of his reign (see 104. *f*).

8. Teiresias here figures dramatically as the prophet of Oedipus's final disgrace, but the story, as it survives, seems to have been turned inside-out. It may once have run something like this:

> Oedipus of Corinth conquered Thebes and became king by marrying Iocaste, a priestess of Hera. Afterwards he announced that the kingdom should henceforth be bequeathed from father to son in the male line, which is a Corinthian custom, instead of remaining the gift of Hera the Throttler. Oedipus confessed that he felt himself disgraced as having let chariot horses drag to death Laius, who was accounted his father, and as having married Iocaste, who had enroyalled him by a ceremony of rebirth. But when he tried to change these customs, Iocaste committed suicide in protest, and Thebes was visited by a plague. Upon the advice of an oracle, the Thebans then withheld from Oedipus the sacred shoulder-blade, and banished him. He died in a fruitless attempt to regain his throne by warfare.

106
THE SEVEN AGAINST THEBES

SO many princes visited Argos in the hope of marrying either Aegeia, or Deipyla, the daughters of King Adrastus, that, fearing to make powerful enemies if he singled out any two of them as his sons-in-law, he consulted the Delphic Oracle. Apollo's response was: 'Yoke to a two-wheeled chariot the boar and lion which fight in your palace.'

b. Among the less fortunate of these suitors were Polyneices and Tydeus. Polyneices and his twin Eteocles had been elected co-kings of Thebes after the banishment of Oedipus, their father. They agreed to reign for alternate years, but Eteocles, to whom the first term fell, would not relinquish his throne at the end of the year, pleading the evil disposition shown by Polyneices, and banished him from the city. Tydeus, son of Oeneus of Calydon, had killed his brother Melanippus when out hunting; though he claimed that this was an accident, it had been prophesied that Melanippus would kill him, and the Calydonians therefore suspected him of having tried to forestall his fate, and he was also banished.

c. Now, the emblem of Thebes is a lion, and the emblem of Calydon, a boar; and the two fugitive suitors displayed these devices on their shields. That night, in Adrastus's palace, they began to dispute about the riches and glories of their respective cities, and murder might have been done, had not Adrastus parted and reconciled them. Then, mindful to the prophecy, he married Aegeia to Polyneices, and Deipyla to Tydeus, with a promise to restore both princes to their kingdoms; but said that he would first march against Thebes, which lay nearer.¹

d. Adrastus mustered his Argive chieftains: Capaneus, Hippomedon, his brother-in-law Amphiaraus the seer, and his Arcadian ally Parthenopaeus, son of Meleager and Atalanta, bidding them arm themselves and set out eastward. Of these champions, only one was reluctant to obey: namely Amphiaraus who, foreseeing that all except Adrastus would die fighting against Thebes, at first refused to go.

e. It happened that Adrastus had formerly quarrelled with Amphiaraus about Argive affairs of state, and the two angry men might have killed each other, but for Adrastus's sister Eriphyle, who was married to Amphiaraus. Snatching her distaff, she flung herself between them, knocked up their swords, and made them swear always to abide by her verdict in any future dispute. Apprised of this oath, Tydeus called Polyneices and said: 'Eriphyle fears that she is losing her looks; now, if you were to offer her the magic necklace which was Aphrodite's wedding gift to your ancestress Harmonia, Cadmus's wife, she would soon settle the dispute between Amphiaraus and Adrastus by compelling him to come with us.'

f. This was discreetly done, and the expedition set out, led by the seven champions: Polyneices, Tydeus, and the five Argives.² But some say that Polyneices did not count as one of the seven, and add the name of Eteoclus the Argive, a son of Iphis.³

g. Their march took them through Nemea, where Lycurgus was king. When they asked leave to water their troops in his country, Lycurgus consented, and his bond-woman Hypsipyle guided them to the nearest spring. Hypsipyle was a Lemnian princess, but when the women of Lemnos had sworn to murder all their men in revenge for an injury done them, she saved the life of her father Thoas: they therefore sold her into slavery, and here she was, acting as nursemaid to Lycurgus's son Opheltes. She set the boy down for a moment while she guided the Argive army to the drinking pool, whereupon a serpent writhed around his limbs and bit him to death. Adrastus and his men returned from the spring too late to do more than kill the serpent and bury the boy.

h. When Amphiaraus warned them that this was an ominous sign, they instituted the Nemean Games in the boy's honour, calling him Archemorus, which means 'the beginner of doom'; and each of the champions had the satisfaction of winning one of the seven events. The judges at the Nemean Games, which are celebrated every four years, have ever since worn dark robes in mourning for Opheltes, and the victor's wreath is plaited of luckless parsley.[4]

i. Arrived at Cithaeron, Adrastus sent Tydeus as his herald to the Thebans, with a demand that Eteocles should resign the throne in favour of Polyneices. When this was refused, Tydeus challenged their chieftains to single combat, one after another, and emerged victorious from every encounter; soon, no more Thebans dared come forward. The Argives then approached the city walls, and each of the champions took up his station facing one of the seven gates.

j. Teiresias the seer, whom Eteocles consulted, prophesied that the Thebans would be victorious only if a prince of the royal house freely offered himself as a sacrifice to Ares; whereupon Menoeceus, the son of Creon, killed himself before the gates, much as his namesake and uncle had leaped headlong from the walls on a previous occasion. Teiresias's prophecy was fulfilled: the Thebans were, indeed, defeated in a skirmish and withdrew into the city; but no sooner had Capaneus set a scaling-ladder against the wall and begun to mount it, than Zeus struck him dead with a thunderbolt. At this, the Thebans took courage, made a furious sally, killing three more of the seven champions; and one of their number, who happened to be named Melanippus, wounded Tydeus in the belly. Athene cherished an affection for Tydeus and, pitying him as he lay half-dead, hastened to beg an infallible elixir from her father Zeus, which would have soon set him upon his feet again. But Amphiaraus hated Tydeus for having forced the Argives to march and, being sharp-witted, ran at Melanippus and cut off his head. 'Here is revenge!' he cried, handing the head to Tydeus. 'Split open the skull and gulp his brains!' Tydeus did so, and Athene, arriving at that moment with the elixir, spilt it on the ground and retired in disgust.

k. Only Polyneices, Amphiaraus, and Adrastus now remained of the seven champions; and Polyneices, to save further slaughter, offered to decide the succession of the throne by single combat with Eteocles. Eteocles accepted the challenge and, in the course of a bitter struggle, each mortally wounded the other. Creon, their uncle, then took command of the Theban army and routed the dismayed Argives. Amphiaraus fled in his chariot along the banks of the river Ismenus, and was on the point of being thrust between the shoulders by a Theban pursuer, when Zeus cleft the earth with a thunderbolt and he vanished from sight, chariot and all, and now reigns alive among the dead. Baton, his charioteer, went with him.[5]

l. Seeing that the day was lost, Adrastus mounted his winged horse Arion and escaped; but when, later, he heard that Creon would not permit his dead enemies to be buried, visited Athens as a suppliant and persuaded Theseus to march against Thebes and punish Creon's impiety. Theseus took the city in a surprise attack, imprisoned Creon, and gave the dead champions' corpses to their kinsfolk, who heaped a great pyre for them. But Evadne, Capaneus's wife, seeing that her husband had been heroized by Zeus's thunderbolt, would not be parted from him. Since custom demanded that a lightning-struck man should be buried apart from the rest, and his grave fenced off, she flung herself on the general pyre, and was consumed alive.[6]

m. Now, before Theseus's arrival at Thebes, Antigone, sister of Eteocles and Polyneices, had disobeyed Creon's orders by secretly building a pyre and laying Polyneices's corpse upon it. Looking out of his palace window, Creon noticed a distant glow which seemed to proceed from a burning pyre and, going to investigate, surprised Antigone in her act of disobedience. He summoned his son Haemon, to whom Antigone had been affianced, and ordered him to bury her alive in Polyneices's tomb. Haemon feigned readiness to do as he was told but, instead, married Antigone secretly, and sent her away to live among his shepherds. She bore him a son who, many years later, came to Thebes, and took part in certain funeral games; but Creon, who was still King of Thebes, guessed his identity by the serpent mark on his body, borne by all descendants of Cadmus, and sentenced him to death. Heracles interceded for his life, but Creon proved obdurate; whereupon Haemon killed both Antigone and himself.[7]

1. Hyginus: *Fabula* 69; Euripides: *Phoenician Women* 408 ff., with scholiast on 409; *Suppliants* 132 ff.; Apollodorus: iii. 6. 1.

2. Aeschylus: *Seven Against Thebes* 375 ff.; Homer: *Odyssey* xi. 326 ff. and xv. 247; Sophocles: *Electra* 836 ff. and Fragments of *Eriphyle*; Hyginus: *Fabula* 73; Pausanias: v. 17. 7 ff. and ix. 41. 2; Diodorus Siculus: iv. 65. 5 ff.; Apollodorus: iii. 6. 2–3.

3. Aeschylus: *Seven Against Thebes* 458 ff.; Sophocles: *Oedipus at Colonus* 1316; Pausanias: x. 10. 3.

4. Apollodorus: i. 9. 17 and iii. 6. 4; Hyginus: *Fabulae* 74 and 273; Scholiast on the *Argument* of Pindar's *Nemean Odes*.

5. Aeschylus: *Seven Against Thebes* 375 ff.; Euripides: *Phoenician Women* 105 ff. and 1090 ff.; Diodorus Siculus: iv. 65. 7–9; Apollodorus: iii. 6. 8; Hyginus: *Fabulae* 69 and 70; Scholiast on Pindar's *Nemean Odes* x. 7; Pausanias: ix. 18. 1; Ovid: *Ibis* 427 ff. and 515 ff.

6. Hyginus: *Fabulae* 273; Apollodorus: *loc. cit.*; Euripides: *The Suppliants*; Plutarch: *Theseus* 29; Isocrates: *Panegyric* 54–8; Pausanias: i. 39. 2.

7. Sophocles: *Antigone, passim*; Hyginus: *Fabula* 72; Fragments of Euripides's *Antigone*; Aeschylus: *Seven Against Thebes* 1005 ff.; Apollodorus: iii. 7. 1.

*

1. Apollo's lion-and-boar oracle will have originally conveyed the wisdom of forming double kingdoms; in order to prevent political strife between the sacred king and his tanist, such as brought about the fall of Thebes (see 69. *1*). But the emblem of Thebes was a lion, because of the lion-bodied Sphinx, its former goddess; and the emblem of Calydon was a boar, probably because Ares, who had a shrine there, liked to adopt this disguise (see 18. *j*). The oracle has therefore been applied to a different situation. Shields with animal devices were regularly used in early Classical times (see 98. *3* and 160. *n*).

2. The mythographers often made play with the syllable *eri* in a name, pretending that it meant *eris*, 'strife', rather than 'plentiful'. Hence the myths of Erichthonius (see 25. *1*) and Erigone (see 79. *3*). Eriphyle originally meant 'many leaves', rather than 'tribal strife'. Hesiod (*Works and Days* 161 ff.) says that Zeus wiped out two generations of heroes, the first at Thebes in the war for Oedipus's sheep, the second at Troy in the war occasioned by fair-haired Helen. 'Oedipus's sheep' is not explained; but Hesiod must be referring to this war between Eteocles and Polyneices, in which the Argives supported an unsuccessful candidate for the throne of Thebes. The cause of a similar dispute between brothers was the golden fleece, for which Atreus and Thyestes contended (see 111. *c–d*); its possession set the owner on the throne of Mycenae. Also, Zeus had golden-fleeced rams on Mount Laphystium, which seem to have been the royal insignia of neighbouring Orchomenus and which caused much blood-shed (see 70. 6).

3. Hypsipyle ('high gate') was probably a title of the Moon-goddess's, whose course describes a high arch across the sky; and the Nemean Games, like the Olympian, will have been celebrated at the end of the sacred king's term, when he had reigned his fifty lunar months as the Chief-priestess's husband. The myth preserves the tradition that boys were sacrificed annually to the goddess, as surrogates for the king; though the word *Opheltes*, which means simply 'benefactor', has here been given a forced sense: 'wound about by a serpent', as though it were derived from *ophis*, 'serpent' and *eilein*, 'to press together'. Neither does *Archemorus* mean 'the beginning of doom', but rather 'original olive stock', which refers to cuttings from Athene's sacred olive (see 16. *c*), presumably those used in the Games as crowns for the victors of the various events. After the disasters of the Persian War, the use of olive was discontinued at the Nemean Games in favour of parsley, a token of mourning (scholiast on Pindar's *Argument to the Nemean Games*). Parsley was unlucky, perhaps because of its notoriety as an abortificient – the English proverb has it: 'parsley grows rank in cuckolds' gardens.' It grew rank in the death-island of Ogygia (see 170. *w*).

4. Tydeus's gulping of Melanippus's brains is reported as a moral anecdote. This old-established means of improving one's fighting skill, introduced by the Hellenes and still practised by the Scythians in Classical times (Herodotus: iv. 64), had come to be regarded as barbarous. But the icon from which the mythographers deduced their story probably showed Athene pouring a libation to Melanippus's ghost, in approval of Tydeus's action. The lost epic of the *Seven Against Thebes* must have closely resembled the Indian *Mahabharata*, which glorifies the Maryannu soldier-caste: the same theme of kinsman pitted against kinsman occurs, the conduct of the fighters is nobler and more tragic than in the *Iliad*, the gods play no mischievous part, suttee is honoured, and Bhishma, like Tydeus, drinks his enemy's blood (see 81. *8*).

5. Amphiaraus's end provides yet another example of the sacred king's death in a chariot crash (see 71. *a*; 101. *g*; 105. *d*; 109. *j*, etc.). The descent of Baton ('blackberry') to Tartarus in his company seems to be told to account for the widespread European taboo on the eating of blackberries, which is associated with death.

6. Evadne's self-immolation recalls the myth of Alcestis (see 69. *d*). Relics of a royal cremation found in a bee-hive tomb at Dendra near Mycenae suggest that, in this particular instance, the king and queen were buried at the same time; and A. W. Persson believes that the queen died voluntarily. But they may both have been murdered, or died of the same illness, and no similar Mycenaean burial is reported elsewhere.

Suttee, in fact, which seems to have been a Hellenic practice, soon went out of fashion (see 74. *8*). Lightning was an evidence of Zeus's presence, and since 'holy' and 'unclean' mean much the same in primitive religion – the tabooed animals in *Leviticus* were unclean because they were holy – the grave of a man struck by lightning was fenced off, like that of a calf that has died of anthrax on a modern farm, and he was given heroic rites. The graveyard near Eleusis where the champions are said by Pausanias to have been eventually interred, has now been identified and opened by Professor Mylonas. He found one double burial surrounded by a stone circle, and five single burials; the skeletons, as was customary in the thirteenth century B.C., to which the vase fragments are attributable, showed no signs of cremation. Early grave-robbers had evidently removed the bronze weapons and other metallic objects, originally buried with the bodies; and it may have been their finding of two skeletons in the stone circle, and the anomaly of the circle itself, which suggested to the people of Eleusis that this was the grave of Capaneus, struck by lightning, and of his faithful wife Evadne.

7. The myth of Antiope, Haemon, and the shepherds seems to have been deduced from the same icon as those of Arne (see 43. *d*) and Alope (see 49. *a*). We are denied the expected end of the story: that he killed his grandfather Creon with a discus (see 73. *p*).

107

THE EPIGONI

THE sons of the seven champions who had fallen at Thebes swore to avenge their fathers. They are known as the Epigoni. The Delphic Oracle promised them victory if Alcmaeon, son of Amphiaraus, took command. But he felt no desire to attack Thebes, and hotly disputed the propriety of the campaign with his brother Amphilochus. When they could not agree whether to make war or no, the decision was referred to their mother Eriphyle. Recognizing the situation as a familiar one, Thersander, the son of Polyneices, followed his father's example: he bribed Eriphyle with the magic robe which Athene had given his ancestress Harmonia at the same time as Aphrodite had given her the magic necklace. Eriphyle decided for war, and Alcmaeon reluctantly assumed command.

b. In a battle fought before the walls of Thebes, the Epigoni lost Aegialeus, son of Adrastus, and Teiresias the seer then warned the

Thebans that their city would be sacked. The walls, he announced, were fated to stand only so long as one of the original seven champions remained alive, and Adrastus, now the sole survivor, would die of grief when he heard of Aegialeus's death. Consequently, the Thebans' wisest course was to flee that very night. Teiresias added that whether they took his advice or no made no odds to him; he was destined to die as soon as Thebes fell into Argive hands. Under cover of darkness, therefore, the Thebans escaped northward with their wives, children, weapons, and a few belongings, and when they had travelled far enough, called a halt and founded the city of Hestiaea. At dawn, Teiresias, who went with them, paused to drink at the spring of Tilphussa, and suddenly expired.

c. That same day, which was the very day on which Adrastus heard of Aegialeus's death and died of grief, the Argives, finding Thebes evacuated, broke in, razed the walls, and collected the booty. They sent the best of it to Apollo at Delphi, including Teiresias's daughter Manto, or Daphne, who had stayed behind; and she became his Pythoness.[1]

d. Nor was this the end of the matter. Thersander happened to boast in Alcmaeon's hearing that most of the credit for the Argive victory was due to himself: he had bribed Eriphyle, just as his father Polyneices did before him, to give the order to march. Alcmaeon thus learned for the first time that Eriphyle's vanity had caused his father's death, and might well have caused his own. He consulted the Delphic Oracle, and Apollo replied that she deserved death. Alcmaeon mistook this for a dispensation to matricide and, on his return, he duly killed Eriphyle, some say with the aid of his brother Amphilochus. But Eriphyle, as she lay dying, cursed Alcmaeon, and cried out: 'Lands of Greece and Asia, and of all the world: deny shelter to my murderers!' The avenging Erinnyes thereupon pursued him and drove him mad.

e. Alcmaeon fled first to Thesprotia, where he was refused entry, and then to Psophis, where King Phegeus purified him for Apollo's sake. Phegeus married him to his daughter Arsinoë, to whom Alcmaeon gave the necklace and the robe which he had brought in his baggage. But the Erinnyes, disregarding this purification, continued to plague him, and the land of Psophis grew barren on his account. The Delphic Oracle then advised Alcmaeon to approach the River-god Achelous, by whom he was once more purified; he married Achelous's daughter Callirrhoë, and settled on land recently formed by the silt of the river, which had not been included in Eriphyle's ban. There he lived at peace for a while.

f. A year later, Callirrhoë, fearing that she might lose her beauty, refused Alcmaeon admittance to her couch unless he gave her the celebrated robe and necklace. For love of Callirrhoë, he dared revisit Psophis, where he deceived Phegeus: making no mention of his marriage to Callirrhoë, he invented a prediction of the Delphic Oracle, to the effect that he would never be rid of the Erinnyes until he had dedicated both robe and necklace to Apollo's shrine. Phegeus thereupon made Arsinoë surrender them, which she was glad to do, believing that Alcmaeon would return to her as soon as the Erinnyes left him; for they were hard on his track again. But one of Alcmaeon's servants blabbed the truth about Callirrhoë, and Phegeus grew so angry that he ordered his sons to ambush and kill Alcmaeon when he left the palace. Arsinoë witnessed the murder from a window and, unaware of Alcmaeon's double-dealing, loudly upbraided her father and brothers for having violated guest-right and made her a widow. Phegeus begged her to be silent and listen while he justified himself; but Arsinoë stopped her ears and wished violent death upon him and her brothers before the next new moon. In retaliation, Phegeus locked her in a chest and presented her as a slave to the King of Nemea; at the same time telling his sons: 'Take this robe and this necklace to Delphic Apollo. He will see to it that they cause no further mischief.'

g. Phegeus's sons obeyed him; but, meanwhile, Callirrhoë, informed of what had happened at Psophis, prayed that her infant sons by Alcmaeon might become full-grown men in a day, and avenge his murder. Zeus heard her plea, and they shot up into manhood, took arms, and went to Nemea where, they knew, the sons of Phegeus had broken their return journey from Delphi in the hope of persuading Arsinoë to retract her curse. They tried to tell her the truth about Alcmaeon, but she would not listen to them either; and Callirrhoë's sons not only surprised and killed them but, hastening towards Psophis, killed Phegeus too, before the next moon appeared in the sky. Since no king or river-god in Greece would consent to purify them of their crimes, they travelled westward to Epirus, and colonized Acarnania, which was named after the elder of the two, Acarnan.

h. The robe and necklace were shown at Delphi until the Sacred War [fourth century B.C.], when the Phocian bandit Phayllos carried them off, and it is not known whether the amber necklace set in gold which the people of Amathus claim to be Eriphyle's is genuine or false.²

i. And some say that Teiresias had two daughters, Daphne and Manto. Daphne remained a virgin and became a Sibyl, but Alcmaeon begot Amphilochus and Tisiphone on Manto before sending her to Apollo at Delphi; he entrusted both children to King Creon of Corinth. Years later, Creon's wife, jealous of Tisiphone's extraordinary beauty, sold her as a slave; and Alcmaeon, not knowing who she was, bought her as his serving-girl but fortunately abstained from incest. As for Manto: Apollo sent her to Colophon in Ionia, where she married Rhacius, King of Caria; their son was Mopsus, the famous soothsayer.³

1. Diodorus Siculus: iv. 66; Pausanias: ix. 5. 13 ff., ix. 8. 6, and ix. 9. 4 ff.; Hyginus: *Fabula* 70; Fragments of Aeschylus's and Sophocles's *Epigoni*.

2. Apollodorus: iii. 7. 5–7; Athenaeus: vi. 22; Ovid: *Metamorphoses* ix. 413 ff.; Pausanias: viii. 24. 8–10 and ix. 41. 2; Parthenius: *Narrations* 25.

3. Apollodorus: iii. 7. 7, quoting Euripides's *Alcmaeon;* Pausanias: vii. 3. 1 and ix. 33. 1; Diodorus Siculus: iv. 66.

*

1. This is a popular minstrel tale, containing few mythic elements, which could be told either in Thebes or Argos without causing offence; which would be of interest to the people of Psophis, Nemea, and the Achelous valley; which purposed to account for the founding of Hestiaea, and the colonization of Acarnania; and which had a strong moral flavour. It taught the instability of women's judgement, the folly of men in humouring their vanity or greed, the wisdom of listening to seers who are beyond suspicion, the danger of misinterpreting oracles, and the inescapable curse that fell on any son who killed his mother, even in placation of his murdered father's ghost (see 114. *a*).

2. Eriphyle's continuous power to decide between war and peace is the most interesting feature of the story. The true meaning of her name, 'very leafy', suggests that she was an Argive priestess of Hera in charge of a tree-oracle, like that of Dodona (see 51. *1*). If so, this tree is likely to have been a pear, sacred to Hera (see 74. *6*). Both the 'War of the Seven Against Thebes', which Hesiod calls the 'War of Oedipus's Sheep', and its sequel here recounted, seem to have preceded the Argonautic expedition and the Trojan War, and may be tentatively referred to the fourteenth century B.C.

TANTALUS

The parentage and origin of Tantalus are disputed. His mother was Pluto, a daughter of Cronus and Rhea or, some say, of Oceanus and Tethys;¹ and his father either Zeus, or Tmolus, the oak-chapleted deity of Mount Tmolus who, with his wife Omphale, ruled over the kingdom of Lydia and had judged the contest between Pan and Apollo.² Some, however, call Tantalus a king of Argos, or of Corinth; and others say that he went northward from Sipylus in Lydia to reign in Paphlagonia; whence, after he had incurred the wrath of the gods, he was expelled by Ilus the Phrygian, whose young brother Ganymedes he had abducted and seduced.³

b. By his wife Euryanassa, daughter of the River-god Pactolus; or by Eurythemista, daughter of the River-god Xanthus; or by Clytia, daughter of Amphidamantes; or by the Pleiad Dione, Tantalus became the father of Pelops, Niobe, and Broteas.⁴ Yet some call Pelops a bastard, or the son of Atlas and the nymph Linos.⁵

c. Tantalus was the intimate friend of Zeus, who admitted him to Olympian banquets of nectar and ambrosia until, good fortune turning his head, he betrayed Zeus's secrets and stole the divine food to share among his mortal friends. Before this crime could be discovered, he committed a worse. Having called the Olympians to a banquet on Mount Sipylus, or it may have been at Corinth, Tantalus found that the food in his larder was insufficient for the company and, either to test Zeus's omniscience, or merely to demonstrate his good will, cut up his son Pelops, and added the pieces to the stew prepared for them, as the sons of Lycaon had done with their brother Nyctimus when they entertained Zeus in Arcadia.⁶ None of the gods failed to notice what was on their trenchers, or to recoil in horror, except Demeter who, being dazed by her loss of Persephone, ate the flesh from the left shoulder.⁷

d. For these two crimes Tantalus was punished with the ruin of his kingdom and, after his death by Zeus's own hand, with eternal torment in the company of Ixion, Sisyphus, Tityus, the Danaids, and others. Now he hangs, perennially consumed by thirst and hunger, from the bough of a fruit-tree which leans over a marshy lake. Its waves lap against his waist, and sometimes reach his chin, yet whenever he bends down to drink, they slip away, and nothing remains but the black mud at his feet; or, if he ever succeeds in scooping up a handful of water, it slips through his fingers before he can do more than wet his cracked lips, leaving him thirstier than ever. The tree is laden with pears, shining apples, sweet figs, ripe olives and pomegranates, which dangle against his shoulders; but whenever he reaches for the luscious fruit, a gust of wind whirls them out of his reach.[8]

e. Moreover, an enormous stone, a crag from Mount Sipylus, overhangs the tree and eternally threatens to crush Tantalus's skull.[9] This is his punishment for a third crime: namely theft, aggravated by perjury. One day, while Zeus was still an infant in Crete, being suckled by the she-goat Amaltheia, Hephaestus had made Rhea a golden mastiff to watch over him; which subsequently became the guardian of his temple at Dicte. But Pandareus son of Merops, a native of Lydian or, it may have been Cretan, Miletus – if, indeed, it was not Ephesus – dared to steal the mastiff, and brought it to Tantalus for safe keeping on Mount Sipylus. After the hue and cry had died down, Pandareus asked Tantalus to return it to him, but Tantalus swore by Zeus that he had neither seen nor heard of a golden dog. This oath coming to Zeus's ears, Hermes was given orders to investigate the matter; and although Tantalus continued to perjure himself, Hermes recovered the dog by force or by stratagem, and Zeus crushed Tantalus under a crag of Mount Sipylus. The spot is still shown near the Tantalid Lake, a haunt of white swan-eagles. Afterwards, Pandareus and his wife Harmothoë fled to Athens, and thence to Sicily, where they perished miserably.[10]

f. According to others, however, it was Tantalus who stole the golden mastiff, and Pandareus to whom he entrusted it and who, on denying that he had ever received it was destroyed, together with his wife, by the angry gods, or turned into stone. But Pandareus's orphaned daughters Merope and Cleothera, whom some call Cameiro and Clytië, were reared by Aphrodite on curds, honey, and sweet wine. Hera endowed them with beauty and more than human wisdom; Artemis made them grow tall and strong; Athene instructed them in every known handicraft. It is difficult to understand why these goddesses showed such solicitude, or chose Aphrodite to soften Zeus's heart towards these orphans and arrange good marriages for them – unless, of course, they had themselves encouraged Pandareus to commit the theft. Zeus must have suspected something, because while Aphrodite was closeted with him on Olympus, the Harpies snatched away the three girls, with his consent, and handed them over to the Erinnyes, who made them suffer vicariously for their father's sins.[11]

g. This Pandareus was also the father of Aëdon, the wife of Zethus, to whom she bore Itylus. Aëdon was racked with envy of her sister Niobe, who rejoiced in the love of six sons and six daughters and, when trying to murder Sipylus, the eldest of them, she killed Itylus by mistake; whereupon Zeus transformed her into the Nightingale who, in early summer, nightly laments her murdered child.[12]

h. After punishing Tantalus, Zeus was pleased to revive Pelops; and therefore ordered Hermes to collect his limbs and boil them again in the same cauldron, on which he laid a spell. The Fate Clotho then re-articulated them; Demeter gave him a solid ivory shoulder in place of the one she had picked clean; and Rhea breathed life into him; while Goat-Pan danced for joy.[13]

i. Pelops emerged from the magic cauldron clothed in such radiant beauty that Poseidon fell in love with him on the spot, and carried him off to Olympus in a chariot drawn by golden horses. There he appointed him his cup-bearer and bed-fellow; as Zeus later appointed Ganymedes, and fed him on ambrosia. Pelops first noticed that his left shoulder was of ivory when he bared his breast in mourning for his sister Niobe. All true descendants of Pelops are marked in this way and, after his death, the ivory shoulder-blade was laid up at Pisa.[14]

j. Pelops's mother Euryanassa, meanwhile, made the most diligent search for him, not knowing about his ascension to Olympus; she learned from the scullions that he had been boiled and served to the gods, who seemed to have eaten every last shred of his flesh. This version of the story became current throughout Lydia; many still credit it and deny that the Pelops whom Tantalus boiled in the cauldron was the same Pelops who succeeded him.[15]

k. Tantalus's ugly son Broteas carved the oldest image of the Mother of the Gods, which still stands on the Coddinian Crag, to the north of Mount Sipylus. He was a famous hunter, but refused to honour Artemis, who drove him mad; crying aloud that no flame could burn him, he threw himself upon a lighted pyre and let the flames consume him. But some say that he committed suicide because everyone hated his ugliness. Broteas's son and heir was named Tantalus, after his grandfather.[16]

1. Pausanias: ii. 22. 4; Scholiast on Pindar's *Olympian Odes* iii. 41; Hesiod: *Theogony* 355, with scholiast.

2. Pausanias: *loc. cit.*; Scholiast on Euripides's *Orestes* 5; Pliny: *Natural History* v. 30; Ovid: *Metamorphoses* ii. 156; Apollodorus: ii. 6. 3.

3. Hyginus: *Fabula* 124; Servius on Virgil's *Aeneid* vi. 603; Diodorus Siculus: iv. 74; Tzetzes: *On Lycophron* 355.

4. Plutarch: *Parallel Stories* 33; Tzetzes: *On Lycophron* 52; Pherecydes, quoted by scholiast on Euripides's *Orestes* 11; Hyginus: *Fabula* 83; Pausanias: 111. 22. 4.

5. Lactantius: *Stories from Ovid's Metamorphoses* vi. 6; Servius on Virgil's *Aeneid* viii. 130.

6. Hyginus: *Fabula* 82; Pindar: *Olympian Odes* i. 38 and 60; Servius on Virgil's *Aeneid* vi. 603 ff.; Lactantius: *loc. cit.*; Servius on Virgil's *Georgics* iii. 7; Tzetzes: *On Lycophron* 152.

7. Hyginus: *Fabula* 83; Tzetzes: *loc. cit.*; Ovid: *Metamorphoses* vi. 406.

8. Diodorus Siculus: iv. 74; Plato: *Cratylus* 28; Lucian: *Dialogues of the Dead* 17; Homer: *Odyssey* xi. 582–92; Ovid: *Metamorphoses* iv. 456; Pindar: *Olympian Odes* i. 60; Apollodorus: *Epitome* ii. 1; Hyginus: *Fabula* 82.

9. Pausanias: x. 31. 4; Archilochus, quoted by Plutarch: *Political Precepts* 6; Euripides: *Orestes* 7.

10. Antoninus Liberalis: *Transformations* 36 and 11; Eustathius and Scholiast on Homer's *Odyssey* xix. 518; Pausanias: x. 30. 1 and vii. 7. 3.

11. Pausanias: x. 30. 1; Scholiast on Homer: *loc. cit.*; Homer: *Odyssey* xx. 66 ff.; Antoninus Liberalis: *Transformations* 36.

12. Homer: *Odyssey* xix. 518 ff.; Apollodorus: iii. 5. 6; Pherecydes: *Fragment* p. 138, ed. Sturz.

13. Servius on Virgil's *Aeneid* vi. 603; Pindar: *Olympian Odes* i. 26; Hyginus: *Fabula* 83; Scholiast on Aristides: p. 216, ed. Frommel.

14. Apollodorus: *Epitome* ii. 3; Pindar: *Olympian Odes* i. 37 ff.; Lucian: *Charidemus* 7; Ovid: *Metamorphoses* vi. 406; Tzetzes: *On Lycophron* 152; Pausanias: v. 13. 3.

15. Pindar: *loc. cit.*; Euripides: *Iphigeneia Among the Taurians* 387.

16. Pausanias: iii. 22. 4; Apollodorus: *Epitome* ii. 2; Ovid: *Ibis* 517, with scholiast.

*

1. According to Strabo (xii. 8. 21), Tantalus, Pelops, and Niobe were Phrygians; and he quotes Demetrius of Scepsis, and also Callisthenes (xiv. 5. 28), as saying that the family derived their wealth from the mines of Phrygia and Mount Sipylus. Moreover, in Aeschylus's *Niobe* (cited by Strabo: xii. 8. 21) the Tantalids are said to have had 'an altar of Zeus, their paternal god, on Mount Ida'; and Sipylus is located 'in the Idaean land'. Democles, whom Strabo quoted at second hand, rationalizes the

Tantalus myth, saying that his reign was marked by violent earthquakes in Lydia and Ionia, as far as the Troad: entire villages disappeared, Mount Sipylus was overturned, marshes were converted into lakes, and Troy was submerged (Strabo: i. 3. 17). According to Pausanias, also, a city on Mount Sipylus disappeared into a chasm, which subsequently filled with water and became Lake Saloë, or Tantalis. The ruins of the city could be seen on the lake bottom until this was silted up by a mountain stream (Pausanias: vii. 24. 7). Pliny agrees that Tantalis was destroyed by an earthquake (*Natural History* ii. 93), but records that three successive cities were built on its site before this was finally flooded (*Natural History* v. 31).

2. Strabo's historical view, however, even if archaeologically plausible, does not account for Tantalus's connexion with Argos, Corinth, and Cretan Miletus. The rock poised over him in Tartarus, always about to fall, identifies him with Sisyphus of Corinth, whose similarly perpetual punishment was deduced from an icon which showed the Sun-Titan laboriously pushing the sun-disk up the slope of Heaven to its zenith (see 67. 2). The scholiast on Pindar was dimly aware of this identification, but explained Tantalus's punishment rationalistically, by recording that: 'some understand the stone to represent the sun, and Tantalus, a physicist, to be paying the penalty for having proved that the sun is a mass of white-hot metal' (scholiast on Pindar's *Olympian Odes* i. 97). Confusingly, this icon of the Sun-Titan has been combined with another: that of a man peering in agony through an interlace of fruit-bearing boughs, and up to his chin in water – a punishment which the rhetoricians used as an allegory of the fate meted out to the rich and greedy (Servius on Virgil's *Aeneid* vi. 603; Fulgentius: *Mythological Compendium* ii. 18). The apples, pears, figs, and such-like, dangling on Tantalus's shoulders are called by Fulgentius 'Dead Sea fruit', of which Tertullian writes that 'as soon as touched with the finger, the apple turns into ashes.'

3. To make sense of this scene, it must be remembered that Tantalus's father Tmolus is described as having been wreathed with oak, and that his son Pelops, one of whose grandsons was also called Tantalus (see 112. *c*), enjoyed hero-rites at Olympia, in which 'Zeus's forester' took part. Since, as is now generally agreed, the criminals in Tartarus were gods or heroes of the pre-Olympian epoch, Tantalus will have represented the annual Sacred King, dressed in fruit-hung branches, like those carried at the Oschophoria (see 98. *w*), who was flung into a river as a *pharmacos* – a custom surviving in the Green George ritual of the Balkan countryside, described by Frazer. The verb *tantalize*, derived from this myth, has prevented scholars from realizing that Tantalus's agony is caused not by thirst, but by fear of drowning or of subsequent immolation on a pyre, which was the fate of his ugly son Broteas.

4. Plato (*Cratylus* 28) may be right when he derives *Tantalus* from

talantatos, 'most wretched', formed from the same root, *tla*, 'suffering', or 'enduring', which yields the names of Atlas and Telamon, both oak heroes. But *talanteuein* means 'to weigh out money', and may be a reference to his riches; and *talanteuesthai* can mean 'to lurch from side to side', which is the gait of the sacred king with the lame thigh (see 23. *1*). It seems, then, that Tantalus is both a Sun-Titan and a woodland king, whose worship was brought from Greece to Asia Minor by way of Crete – Pandareus is described as a Cretan – in the mid-second millennium B.C., and reimported into Greece towards its close, when the collapse of the Hittite Empire forced wealthy Greek-speaking colonists of Asia Minor to abandon their cities.

5. When the mythographers recorded that Tantalus was a frequent guest on Olympus, they were admitting that his cult had once been dominant in the Peloponnese; and, although the banquets to which the gods invited Tantalus are carefully distinguished from the one to which he invited them, in every case the main dish will have been the same umble soup which the cannibalistic Arcadian shepherds of the oak cult prepared for Wolfish Zeus (see 38. *b*). It is perhaps no coincidence that, in Normandy, the Green George victim is called 'Green Wolf', and was formerly thrown alive into the midsummer bonfire. The eating of Pelops, however, is not directly connected with the wolf cult. Pelops's position as Poseidon's minion, his name, 'muddy face', and the legend of his ivory shoulder, point rather to a porpoise cult on the Isthmus (see 8. *3* and 70. *5*) – 'dolphin' in Greek includes the porpoise – and suggests that the Palladium, said to have been made from his bones (see 159. *3* and 166. *h*), was a cult object of porpoise ivory. This would explain why, according to the scholiast on Pindar's *Olympian Odes* i. 37, Thetis the Sea-goddess, and not Demeter, ate Pelops's shoulder. But the ancient seated statue of Mare-headed Demeter at Phigalia held a dove in one hand, a dolphin (or porpoise) in the other; and, as Pausanias directly says: 'Why the image was thus made is plain to anyone of ordinary intelligence who has studied mythology' (viii. 43. 3). He means that she presided over the horse cult, the oak cult, and the porpoise cult.

6. This ancient myth distressed the later mythographers. Not content with exculpating Demeter from the charge of deliberate man-eating, and indignantly denying that all the gods ate what was set before them, to the last morsel, they invented an over-rationalistic explanation of the myth. Tantalus, they wrote, was a priest who revealed Zeus's secrets to the uninitiated. Whereupon the gods unfrocked him, and afflicted his son with a loathsome disease; but the surgeons cut him about and patched him up with bone-graftings, leaving scars which made him look as if he had been hacked in pieces and joined together again (Tzetzes: *On Lycophron* 152).

7. Pandareus's theft of the golden mastiff should be read as a sequel to Heracles's theft of Cerberus, which suggests the Achaeans' defiance of the death curse, symbolized by a dog, in their seizure of a cult object sacred to the Earth-goddess Rhea (Tantalus's grandmother), and conferring sovereignty on its possessor. The Olympian goddesses were clearly abetting Pandareus's theft, and the dog, though Rhea's property, was guarding the sanctuary of the annually dying Cretan Zeus; thus the myth points not to an original Achaean violation of Rhea's shrine, but to a temporary recovery of the cult object by the goddess's devotees.

8. The nature of the stolen cult object is uncertain. It may have been a golden lamb, the symbol of Pelopid sovereignty; or the cuckoo-tipped sceptre which Zeus is known to have stolen from Hera; or the porpoise-ivory Palladium; or the aegis bag with its secret contents. It is unlikely to have been a golden dog, since the dog was not the cult object, but its guardian; unless this is a version of the Welsh myth of Amathaon ap Don who stole a dog from Arawn ('eloquence') King of Annwm ('Tartarus') and was by its means enabled to guess the secret name of the god Bran (*White Goddess* pp. 30 and 48–53).

9. The three daughters of Pandareus, one of whom, Cameiro, bears the same name as the youngest of the three Rhodian Fates (see 60. *2*), are the Triple-goddess, here humiliated by Zeus for her devotees' rebellion. Tantalus's loyalty to the goddess is shown in the stories of his son Broteas, who carved her image on Mount Sipylus, and of his daughter Niobe, priestess of the White Goddess, who defied the Olympians and whose bird was the white swan-eagle of Lake Tantalis. Omphale, the name of Tantalus's mother, suggests a prophetic navel-shrine like that at Delphi.

10. The annual *pharmacos* was chosen for his extreme ugliness, which accounts for Broteas. It is recorded that in Asia Minor, the *pharmacos* was first beaten on the genitals with squill (see 26. *3*) to the sound of Lydian flutes – Tantalus (Pausanias: ix. 5. 4) and his father Tmolus (Ovid: *Metamorphoses* ii. 156) are both associated in legend with Lydian flutes – then burned on a pyre of forest wood; his ashes were afterwards thrown into the sea (Tzetzes: *History* xxiii. 726–56, quoting Hipponax – sixth century B.C.). In Europe, the order seems to have been reversed: the Green George *pharmacos* was first ducked, then beaten, and finally burned.

109

PELOPS AND OENOMAUS

PELOPS inherited the Paphlagonian throne from his father Tantalus, and for a while resided at Enete, on the shores of the Black Sea, whence he also ruled over the Lydians and Phrygians. But he was expelled from Paphlagonia by the barbarians, and retired to Lydian Mount Sipylus, his ancestral seat. When Ilus, King of Troy, would not let him live in peace even there, but ordered him to move on, Pelops brought his fabulous treasures across the Aegean Sea. He was resolved to make a new home for himself and his great horde of followers,[1] but first to sue for the hand of Hippodameia, daughter of King Oenomaus, the Arcadian, who ruled over Pisa and Elis.[2]

b. Some say that Oenomaus had been begotten by Ares on Harpina, daughter of the River-god Asopus; or on the Pleiad Asterië; or on Asterope; or on Eurythoë, daughter of Danaus; while others call him the son of Alxion; or of Hyperochus.[3]

c. By his wife Sterope, or Euarete, daughter of Acrisius, Oenomaus became the father of Leucippus, Hippodamus, and Dysponteus, founder of Dyspontium; and of one daughter, Hippodameia.[4] Oenomaus was famous for his love of horses, and forbade his subjects under the penalty of a curse ever to mate mares with asses. To this day, if the Eleans need mules, they must take their mares abroad to mate and foal.[5]

d. Whether he had been warned by an oracle that his son-in-law would kill him, or whether he had himself fallen in love with Hippodameia, is disputed; but Oenomaus devised a new way to prevent her from ever getting married. He challenged each of Hippodameia's suitors in turn to a chariot race, and laid out a long course from Pisa, which lies beside the river Alpheius, opposite Olympia, to Poseidon's altar on the Isthmus of Corinth. Some say that the chariots were drawn by four horses;[6] others say, by two. Oenomaus insisted that Hippodameia must ride beside each suitor, thus distracting his attention from the team – but allowed him a start of half an hour or so, while he himself sacrificed a ram on the altar of Warlike Zeus at Olympia. Both chariots would then race towards the Isthmus and the suitor, if overtaken, must die; but should he win the race, Hippodameia would be his, and Oenomaus must die.[7] Since, however, the wind-begotten mares, Psylla and Harpinna, which Pelops's father Ares had given him, were immeasurably the best in Greece, being swifter even than the North Wind;[8] and since his chariot, skilfully driven by Myrtilus, was especially designed for racing, he had never yet failed to overtake his rival and transfix him with his spear, another gift from Ares.[9]

e. In this manner Oenomaus disposed of twelve or, some say, thirteen princes, whose heads and limbs he nailed above the gates of his palace, while their trunks were flung barbarously in a heap on the ground. When he killed Marmax, the first suitor, he also butchered his mares, Parthenia and Eripha, and buried them beside the river Parthenia, where their tomb is still shown. Some say that the second suitor, Alcathous, was buried near the Horse-scarer in the hippodrome at Olympia, and that it is his spiteful ghost which baulks the charioteers.[10]

f. Myrtilus, Oenomaus's charioteer, was the son of Hermes by Theobule, or Cleobule; or by the Danaid Phaethusa; but others say that he was the son of Zeus and Clymene. He too had fallen in love with Hippodameia, but dared not enter the contest.[11] Meanwhile, the Olympians had decided to intervene and put an end to the slaughter, because Oenomaus was boasting that he would one day build a temple of skulls: as Evenus, Diomedes, and Antaeus had done.[12] When therefore Pelops, landing in Elis, begged his lover Poseidon, whom he invoked with a sacrifice on the seashore, either to give him the swiftest chariot in the world for his courtship of Hippodameia, or to stay the rush of Oenomaus's brazen spear, Poseidon was delighted to be of assistance. Pelops soon found himself the owner of a winged golden chariot, which could race over the sea without wetting the axles, and was drawn by a team of tireless, winged, immortal horses.[13]

g. Having visited Mount Sipylus and dedicated to Temnian Aphrodite an image made of green myrtle-wood, Pelops tested his chariot by driving it across the Aegean Sea. Almost before he had time to glance about him, he had reached Lesbos, where his charioteer Cillus, or Cellas, or Cillas, died because of the swiftness of the flight. Pelops spent the night on Lesbos and, in a dream, saw Cillus's ghost lamenting his fate, and pleading for heroic honours. At dawn, he burned his body, heaped a barrow over the ashes, and founded the sanctuary of Cillaean Apollo close by. Then he set out again, driving the chariot himself.[14]

h. On coming to Pisa, Pelops was alarmed to see the row of heads nailed above the palace gates, and began to regret his ambition. He therefore promised Myrtilus, if he betrayed his master, half the kingdom and the privilege of spending the bridal night with Hippodameia when she had been won.[15]

i. Before entering the race – the scene is carved on the front gable of Zeus's temple at Olympia – Pelops sacrificed to Cydonian Athene. Some say that Cillus's ghost appeared and undertook to help him; others, that Sphaerus was his charioteer; but it is more generally believed that he drove his own team, Hippodameia standing beside him.[16]

j. Meanwhile, Hippodameia had fallen in love with Pelops and, far from hindering his progress, had herself offered to reward Myrtilus generously, if her father's course could by some means be checked. Myrtilus therefore removed the lynch-pins from the axles of Oenomaus's chariot, and replaced them with others made of wax. As the chariots reached the neck of the Isthmus and Oenomaus, in hot pursuit, was poising his spear, about to transfix Pelops's back, the wheels of his chariot flew off, he fell entangled in the wreckage and was dragged to death. His ghost still haunts the Horse-scarer at Olympia.[17] There are some, however, who say that the swiftness of Poseidon's winged chariot and horses easily enabled Pelops to out-distance Oenomaus, and reach the Isthmus first; whereupon Oenomaus either killed himself in despair, or was killed by Pelops at the winning-post. According to others, the contest took place in the Hippodrome at Olympia, and Amphion gave Pelops a magic object which he buried by the Horse-scarer, so that Oenomaus's team bolted and wrecked his chariot. But all agree that Oenomaus, before he died, laid a curse on Myrtilus, praying that he might perish at the hands of Pelops.[18]

k. Pelops, Hippodameia, and Myrtilus then set out for an evening drive across the sea. 'Alas!' cried Hippodameia, 'I have drunk nothing all day; thirst parches me.' The sun was setting and Pelops called a halt at the desert island of Helene, which lies not far from the island of Euboea, and went up the strand in search of water. When he returned with his helmet filled, Hippodameia ran weeping towards him and complained that Myrtilus had tried to ravish her. Pelops sternly rebuked Myrtilus, and struck him in the face, but he protested indignantly: 'This is the bridal night, on which you swore that I should enjoy Hippodameia. Will you break your oath?' Pelops made no reply, but took the reins from Myrtilus and drove on.[19] As they approached Cape Geraestus – the southernmost promontory of Euboea, now crowned with a remarkable temple of Poseidon – Pelops dealt Myrtilus a sudden kick, which sent him flying head-long into the sea; and Myrtilus, as he sank, laid a curse on Pelops and all his house.[20]

l. Hermes set Myrtilus's image among the stars as the constellation of the Charioteer; but his corpse was washed ashore on the coast of Euboea and buried in Arcadian Pheneus, behind the temple of Hermes; once a year nocturnal sacrifices are offered him there as a hero. The Myrtoan Sea, which stretches from Euboea, past Helene, to the Aegean, is generally believed to take its name from Myrtilus rather than, as the Euboeans insist, from the nymph Myrto.[21]

m. Pelops drove on, until he reached the western stream of Oceanus, where he was cleansed of blood guilt by Hephaestus; afterwards he came back to Pisa, and succeeded to the throne of Oenomaus. He soon subjugated nearly the whole of what was then known as Apia, or Pelasgiotis, and renamed it the Peloponnese, meaning 'the island of Pelops', after himself. His courage, wisdom, wealth, and numerous children, earned him the envy and veneration of all Greece.[22]

n. From King Epeius, Pelops took Olympia, and added it to his kingdom of Pisa; but being unable to defeat King Stymphalus of Arcadia by force of arms, he invited him to a friendly debate, cut him in pieces, and scattered his limbs far and wide; a crime which caused a famine throughout Greece. But his celebration of the Olympian Games in honour of Zeus, about a generation after that of Endymion, was more splendid than any before.

o. To atone for the murder of Myrtilus, who was Hermes's son, Pelops built the first temple of Hermes in the Peloponnese; he also tried to appease Myrtilus's ghost by building a cenotaph for him in the hippodrome at Olympia, and paying him heroic honours. Some say that neither Oenomaus, nor the spiteful Alcathous, nor the magic object which Pelops buried, is the true Horse-scarer: it is the ghost of Myrtilus.[23]

p. Over the tomb of Hippodameia's unsuccessful suitors, on the farther side of the river Alpheius, Pelops raised a tall barrow, paying them heroic honours too; and about a furlong away stands the sanctuary of Artemis Cordax, so called because Pelops's followers there celebrated his victories by dancing the Rope Dance, which they had brought from Lydia.[24]

q. Pelops's sanctuary, where his bones are preserved in a brazen chest, was dedicated by Tirynthian Heracles, his grandson, when he came to celebrate the Olympian Games; and the Elean magistrates still offer Pelops the annual sacrifice of a black ram, roasted on a fire of white poplar-wood. Those who partake of this victim are forbidden to enter Zeus's temple until they have bathed, and the neck is the traditional perquisite of his forester. The sanctuary is thronged with visitors every year, when young men scourge themselves at Pelops's altar, offering him a libation of their blood. His chariot is shown on the roof of the Anactorium in Phliasia; the Sicyonians keep his gold-hilted sword in their treasury at Olympia; and his spear-shaped sceptre, at Chaeronea, is perhaps the only genuine work of Hephaestus still extant. Zeus sent it to Pelops by the hand of Hermes, and Pelops bequeathed it to King Atreus.[25]

r. Pelops is also styled 'Cronian One', or 'Horse-beater'; and the Achaeans claim him as their ancestor.[26]

1. Apollonius Rhodius: *Argonautica* ii. 358 and 790; Sophocles: *Ajax* 1292; Pausanias: ii. 22. 4 and vi. 22. 1; Pindar: *Olympian Odes* i. 24.

2. Servius on Virgil's *Georgics* iii. 7; Lucian: *Charidemus* 19; Apollodorus: *Epitome* ii. 4.

3. Diodorus Siculus: iv. 73; Hyginus: *Fabula* 250; *Poetic Astronomy* ii. 21; Scholiast on Apollonius Rhodius: i. 752; Pausanias: v. 1. 5; Tzetzes: *On Lycophron* 149.

4. Hyginus: *Poetic Astronomy* ii. 21; *Fabula* 84; Pausanias: viii. 20. 2 and vi. 22. 2; Lactantius on Statius's *Thebaid* vi. 336; Diodorus Siculus: *loc. cit.*

5. Plutarch: *Greek Questions* 52; Pausanias: v. 5. 2 and 9. 2.

6. Apollodorus: *Epitome* ii. 4; Lucian: *Charidemus* 19; Pausanias: v. 10. 2, v. 17. 4 and vi. 21. 6; Diodorus Siculus: iv. 73.

7. Apollodorus: *Epitome* ii. 5; Lucian: *loc. cit.*; Pausanias: v. 14. 5; Diodorus Siculus: *loc. cit.*

8. Servius on Virgil's *Georgics* iii. 7; Tzetzes: *On Lycophron* 166; Lucian: *loc. cit.*; Hyginus: Fabula 84; Apollodorus: *loc. cit.*

9. Pausanias: viii. 14. 7; Apollonius Rhodius: i. 756; Apollodorus: *loc. cit.*

10. Apollodorus: *loc. cit.*; Pindar: *Olympian Odes* i. 79 ff.; Ovid: *Ibis* 365; Hyginus: *Fabula* 84; Pausanias: vi. 21. 6–7 and 20. 8.

11. Hyginus: *Fabula* 224; Tzetzes: *On Lycophron* 156 and 162; Scholiast on Apollonius Rhodius: i. 752; Scholiast on Euripides's *Orestes* 1002; Pausanias: viii. 14. 7.

12. Lucian: *Charidemus* 19; Tzetzes: *On Lycophron* 159.

13. Pindar: *Olympian Odes* i. 65 ff. and i. 79; Apollodorus: *Epitome* ii. 3; Pausanias: v. 17. 4.

14. Pausanias: v. 13. 4 and 10. 2; Theon: *On Aratus* p. 21; Scholiast on Homer's *Iliad* i. 38.

15. Hyginus: *Fabula* 84; Scholiast on Horace's *Odes* i. 1; Pausanias: viii. 14. 7.

16. Pausanias: vi. 21. 5 and v. 10. 2; Scholiast on Homer's *Iliad: loc. cit.*; Apollonius Rhodius: i. 753.

17. Apollodorus: *Epitome* ii. 7; Tzetzes: *On Lycophron* 156; Apollonius Rhodius: i. 752 ff.; Pausanias: vi. 20. 8.

18. Pindar: *Olympic Odes* i. 87; Lucian: *Charidemus* 19; Diodorus Siculus: iv. 73; Apollodorus: *loc. cit.*

19. Apollodorus: *Epitome* ii. 8; Scholiast on Homer's *Iliad* ii. 104; Pausanias: viii. 14. 8; Hyginus: *Fabula* 84.

20. Strabo: x. 1. 7; Sophocles: *Electra* 508 ff.; Apollodorus: *loc. cit.*;
    Pausanias: viii. 14. 7.
21. Hyginus: *Poetic Astronomy* ii. 13; Pausanias: *loc. cit.* and viii. 14.
    8; Apollodorus: *loc. cit.*
22. Apollodorus: *Epitome* ii. 9; Diodorus Siculus: iv. 73; Thucy-
    dides: i. 9; Plutarch: *Theseus* 3.
23. Pausanias: v. 1. 5; v. 8. 1 and vi. 20. 8; Apollodorus: iii. 12. 6.
24. Pausanias: vi. 21. 7 and 22. 1.
25. Pausanias: v. 13. 1–2; vi. 22. 1; ii. 14. 3; vi. 19. 3 and ix. 41. 1;
    Apollodorus: ii. 7. 2; Pindar: *Olympian Odes* i. 90 ff.; Scholiast
    on Pindar's *Olympian Odes* i. 146; Homer: *Iliad* ii. 100 ff.
26. Pindar: *Olympian Odes* iii. 23; Homer: *Iliad* ii. 104; Pausanias:
    v. 25. 5.

*

1. According to Pausanias and Apollodorus, Tantalus never left Asia
Minor; but other mythographers refer to him and to Pelops as native
kings of Greece. This suggests that their names were dynastic titles taken
by early Greek colonists to Asia Minor, where they were attested by hero-
shrines; and brought back by emigrants before the Achaean invasion of
the Peloponnese in the thirteenth century B.C. It is known from Hittite
inscriptions that Hellenic kings reigned in Pamphylia and Lesbos as early
as the fourteenth century B.C. Pelopo-Tantalids seem to have ousted the
Cretanized dynasty of 'Oenomaus' from the Peloponnesian High Kingship.

2. The horse, which had been a sacred animal in Pelasgian Greece long
before the cult of the Sun-chariot, was a native European pony dedicated
to the Moon, not the Sun (see 75. *3*). The larger Trans-Caspian horse
came to Egypt with the Hyksos invaders in 1850 B.C. – horse chariotry
displaced ass chariotry in the Egyptian armed forces about the year 1500
B.C. – and had reached Crete before Cnossus fell a century later. Oenomaus's religious ban on mules should perhaps be associated with the death
of Cillus: in Greece, as at Rome, the ass cult was suppressed (see 83. *2*)
when the sun-chariot became the symbol of royalty. Much the same
religious reformation took place at Jerusalem (2 *Kings* xxiii. 11), where
a tradition survived in Josephus's time of an earlier ass cult (Josephus:
Against Apion ii. 7 and 10). Helius of the Sun-chariot, an Achaean deity,
was then identified in different cities with solar Zeus or solar Poseidon,
but the ass became the beast of Cronus, whom Zeus and Poseidon had
dethroned, or of Pan, Silenus, and other old-fashioned Pelasgian god-
lings. There was also a solar Apollo; since his hatred of asses is mentioned
by Pindar, it will have been Cillaean Apollo to whom hecatombs of

asses were offered by the Hyperboreans (Pindar: *Pythian Odes* x. 30 ff.).

3. Oenomaus, who represented Zeus as the incarnate Sun, is therefore called a son of Asterië, who ruled Heaven (see 88. *1*), rather than a similarly named Pleiad; and Queen Hippodameia, by marriage to whom he was enroyalled, represented Hera as the incarnate Moon. Descent remained matrilinear in the Peloponnese, which assured the goodwill of the conservative peasantry. Nor might the King's reign be prolonged beyond a Great Year of one hundred months, in the last of which the solar and lunar calendars coincided; he was then fated to be destroyed by horses. As a further concession to the older cult at Pisa, where Zeus's representative had been killed by his tanist each mid-summer (see 53. *5*), Oenomaus agreed to die a mock death at seven successive mid-winters, on each occasion appointing a surrogate to take his place for twenty-four hours and ride in the sun-chariot beside the Queen. At the close of this day, the surrogate was killed in a chariot crash, and the King stepped out from the tomb where he had been lurking (see 41. *1* and 123. *4*), to resume his reign. This explains the myth of Oenomaus and the suitors, another version of which appears in that of Evenus (see 74. *e*). The mythographers must be mistaken when they mention 'twelve or thirteen' suitors. These numbers properly refer to the lunations – alternately twelve and thirteen – of a solar year, not to the surrogates; thus in the chariot race at Olympia twelve circuits of the stadium were made in honour of the Moon-goddess. Pelops is a type of lucky eighth prince (see 81. *8*) spared the chariot crash and able to despatch the old king with his own sceptre-spear.

4. This annual chariot crash was staged in the Hippodrome. The surrogate could guide his horses – which seem, from the myth of Glaucus (see 71. *a*), to have been maddened by drugs – down the straight without coming to grief, but where the course bent around a white marble statue, called the Marmaranax ('marble king'), or the Horse-scarer, the outer wheel flew off for want of a lynch-pin, the chariot collapsed, and the horses dragged the surrogate to death. Myrtle was the death-tree, that of the thirteenth month, at the close of which the chariot crash took place (see 101. *1*); hence Myrtilus is said to have removed the metal lynch-pins, and replaced them with wax ones – the melting of wax also caused the death of Icarus, the Sun-king's surrogate – and laid a curse upon the House of Pelops.

5. In the second half of the myth, Myrtilus has been confused with the surrogate. As *interrex*, the surrogate was entitled to ride beside the Queen in the sun-chariot, and to sleep with her during the single night of his reign; but, at dawn on the following day, the old King destroyed him and, metaphorically, rode on in his sun-chariot to the extreme west, where he was purified in the Ocean stream. Myrtilus's fall from the

chariot into the sea is a telescoping of myths: a few miles to the east of the Hippodrome, where the Isthmian Games took place (see 71. *b*), the surrogate 'Melicertes', in whose honour they had been founded, was flung over a cliff (see 96. *3*) and an identical ceremony was probably performed at Geraestus, where Myrtilus died. Horse-scarers are also reported from Thebes and Iolcus (see 71. *b*), which suggests that there, too, chariot crashes were staged in the hippodromes. But since the Olympian Hippodrome, sacred to solar Zeus, and the Isthmian Hippodrome, sacred to solar Poseidon, were both associated with the legend of Pelops, the mythographers have presented the contest as a cross-country race between them. Lesbos enters the story perhaps because 'Oenomaus' was a Lesbian dynastic title.

6. Amphion's entry into this myth, though a Theban, is explained by his being also a native of Sicyon on the Isthmus (see 76. *a*). 'Myrto' will have been a title of the Sea-goddess as destroyer, the first syllable standing for 'sea', as in Myrtea, 'sea-goddess'; Myrtoessa, a longer form of Myrto, was one of Aphrodite's titles. Thus Myrtilus may originally mean 'phallus of the sea': *myr-tylos*.

7. Pelops hacks Stymphalus in pieces, as he himself is said to have been treated by Tantalus; this more ancient form of the royal sacrifice has been rightly reported from Arcadia. The Pelopids appear indeed to have patronized several local cults, beside that of the Sun-chariot: namely the Arcadian shepherd cult of oak and ram, attested by Pelops's connexion with Tantalus and his sacrifice of a black ram at Olympia; the partridge cult of Crete, Troy, and Palestine, attested by the *cordax* dance; the Titan cult, attested by Pelops's title of 'Cronian'; the porpoise cult (see 108. *5*); and the cult of the ass-god, in so far as Cillus's ghost assisted him in the race.

8. The butchering of Marmax's mares may refer to Oenomaus's coronation ceremony (see 81. *4*), which involved mare-sacrifice. A 'Cydonian apple', or quince, will have been in the hand of the Death-goddess Athene, to whom Pelops sacrificed, as his safe-conduct to the Elysian Fields (see 32. *1*; 53. *5* and 133. *4*); and the white poplar, used in his heroic rites at Olympia, symbolized the hope of reincarnation (see 31. *5* and 134. *f*) after he had been hacked in pieces – because those who went to Elysium were granted the prerogative of rebirth (see 31. *c*). A close parallel to the bloodshed at Pelops's Olympic altar is the scourging of young Spartans who were bound to the image of Upright Artemis (see 116. *4*). Pelops was, in fact, the victim, and suffered in honour of the goddess Hippodameia (see 110. *3*).

THE CHILDREN OF PELOPS

In gratitude to Hera for facilitating her marriage with Pelops, Hippodameia summoned sixteen matrons, one from every city of Elis, to help her institute the Heraean Games. Every fourth year, ever since, the Sixteen Matrons, their successors, have woven a robe for Hera and celebrated the Games; which consist of a single race between virgins of different ages, the competitors being handicapped according to their years, with the youngest placed in front. They run clad in tunics of less than knee length, their right breasts bared, their hair flying free. Chloris, Niobe's only surviving daughter, was the first victrix in these games; the course of which has been fixed at five-sixths of the Olympic circuit. The prize is an olive wreath, and a share of the cow sacrificed to Hera; a victrix may also dedicate a statue of herself in her own name.[1]

b. The Sixteen Matrons once acted as peace-makers between the Pisans and the Eleans. Now they also organize two groups of dancers, one in honour of Hippodameia, the other in honour of Physcoa, the Elean. Physcoa bore Narcaeus to Dionysus, a renowned warrior who founded the sanctuary of Athene Narcaea and was the first Elean to worship Dionysus. Since some of the sixteen cities no longer exist, the Sixteen Matrons are now supplied by the eight Elean tribes, a pair from each. Like the umpires, they purify themselves, before the Games begin, with the blood of a suitable pig and with water drawn from the Pierian Spring which one passes on the road between Olympia and Elis.[2]

c. The following are said to have been children of Pelops and Hippodameia: Pittheus of Troezen; Atreus and Thyestes; Alcathous, not the one killed by Oenomaus; the Argonaut Hippalcus, Hippalcmus, or Hippalcimus; Copreus the herald; Sciron the bandit; Epidaurus the Argive, sometimes called the son of Apollo;[3] Pleisthenes; Dias; Cybosurus; Corinthius; Hippasus; Cleon; Argeius; Aelinus; Astydameia, whom some call the mother of Amphitryon; Lysidice, whose daughter Hippothoë was carried off by Poseidon to the Echinadian Islands, and there bore Taphius; Eurydice, whom some call the mother of Alcmene; Nicippe; Antibia;[4] and lastly Archippe, mother of Eurystheus and Alcyone.[5]

d. The Megarians, in an attempt to obliterate the memory of how Minos captured their city, and to suggest that King Nisus was peaceably succeeded by his son-in-law Megareus, and he in turn by his son-in-law, Alcathous, son of Pelops, say that Megareus had two sons, the elder of whom, Timalcus, was killed at Aphidnae during the invasion of Attica by the Dioscuri; and that, when the younger, Euippus, was killed by the lion of Cithaeron, Megareus promised his daughter Euaechme, and his throne, to whoever avenged Euippus. Forthwith, Alcathous killed the lion and, becoming king of Megara, built a temple there to Apollo the Hunter and Artemis the Huntress. The truth is, however, that Alcathous came from Elis to Megara immediately after the death of Nisus and the sack of the city; that Megareus never reigned in Megara; and that Alcathous sacrificed to Apollo and Poseidon as 'Previous Builders', and then rebuilt the city wall on new foundations, the course of the old wall having been obliterated by the Cretans.[6]

e. Alcathous was the father of Ischepolis; of Callipolis; of Iphinoë, who died a virgin, and at whose tomb, between the Council Hall and the shrine of Alcathous, Megarian brides pour libations – much as the Delian brides dedicate their hair to Hecaerge and Opis; also of Automedusa, who bore Iolaus to Iphicles; and of Periboea, who married Telamon, and whose son Ajax succeeded Alcathous as King of Megara. Alcathous's elder son, Ischepolis, perished in the Calydonian Hunt; and Caïlipolis, the first Megarian to hear the sorrowful news, rushed up to the Acropolis, where Alcathous was offering burnt sacrifices to Apollo, and flung the faggots from the altar in token of mourning. Unaware of what had happened, Alcathous raged at his impiety and struck him dead with a faggot.[7]

f. Ischepolis and Euippus are buried in the Law Courts; Megareus on the right side of the ascent to the second Megarian Acropolis. Alcathous's hero-shrine is now the public Record Office; and that of Timalcus, the Council Hall.[8]

g. Chrysippus also passed as a son of Pelops and Hippodameia; but was, in fact, a bastard, whom Pelops had begotten on the nymph Astyoche,[9] a Danaid. Now it happened that Laius, when banished from Thebes, was hospitably received by Pelops at Pisa, but fell in love with Chrysippus, to whom he taught the charioteer's art; and, as soon as the sentence of banishment was annulled, carried the boy off in his chariot, from the Nemean Games, and brought him to Thebes as his catamite.[10] Some say that Chrysippus killed himself for shame; others, that Hippodameia, to prevent Pelops from appointing Chrysippus his successor over the heads of her own sons, came to Thebes, where she tried to persuade Atreus and Thyestes to kill the boy by throwing him down a well. When both refused to murder their father's guest, Hippodameia, at dead of night, stole into Laius's chamber and, finding him asleep, took down his sword from the wall and plunged it into his bedfellow's belly. Laius was at once accused of the murder, but Chrysippus had seen Hippodameia as she fled, and accused her with his last breath.[11]

h. Meanwhile, Pelops marched against Thebes to recover Chrysippus but, finding that Laius was already imprisoned by Atreus and Thyestes, nobly pardoned him, recognizing that only an overwhelming love had prompted this breach of hospitality. Some say that Laius, not Thamyris, or Minos, was the first pederast; which is why the Thebans, far from condemning the practice, maintain a regiment, called the Sacred Band, composed entirely of boys and their lovers.[12]

i. Hippodameia fled to Argolis, and there killed herself; but later, in accordance with an oracle, her bones were brought back to Olympia, where women enter her walled sanctuary once a year to offer her sacrifices. At one of the turns of the Hippodrome stands Hippodameia's bronze statue, holding a ribbon with which to decorate Pelops for his victory.[13]

1. Pausanias: v. 16. 2–3.
2. Pausanias: v. 16. 3–5.
3. Apollodorus: iii. 12. 7; ii. 5. 1 and ii. 26. 3; *Epitome* ii. 10 and i. 1; Hyginus: *Fabulae* 84 and 14; Scholiast on Pindar's *Olympian Odes* i. 144.
4. Scholiast on Euripides's *Orestes* 5; Apollodorus: ii. 4. 5; Plutarch: *Theseus* 6; Diodorus Siculus: iv. 9. 1; Scholiast on Homer's *Iliad* xix. 119.
5. Tzetzes: *Chiliades* ii. 172 and 192; Scholiast on Thucydides: i. 9; Apollodorus: *loc. cit.*
6. Pausanias: i. 43. 4; i. 41. 4–5 and i. 42. 2.
7. Pausanias: i. 42. 2 and 7 and i. 43. 4; Apollodorus: ii. 4. 11.
8. Pausanias: i. 43. 2 and 4; i. 42. 1 and 3.
9. Scholiast on Pindar's *Olympian Odes* i. 144; Hyginus: *Fabula* 85; Plutarch: *Parallel Stories* 33.
10. Apollodorus: iii. 5. 5; Hyginus: *Fabulae* 85 and 271; Athenaeus: xiii. 79.
11. Scholiast on Euripides's *Phoenician Women* 1760; Plutarch: *Parallel Stories* 33; Hyginus: *Fabula* 85; Scholiast on Euripides's *Orestes* 813.
12. Hyginus: *loc. cit.*; Plutarch: *loc. cit.*; Aelian: *Varia Historia* xiii. 5.

13. Hyginus: *loc. cit.*; Pausanias: vi. 20. 4 and 10.

*

1. The Heraean Games took place on the day before the Olympic Games. They consisted of a girls' foot race, originally for the office of High-priestess to Hera (see 60. *4*), and the victrix, who wore the olive as a symbol of peace and fertility, became one with the goddess by partaking of her sacred cow. The Sixteen Matrons may once have taken turns to officiate as the High-priestess's assistant during the sixteen seasons of the four-year Olympiad – each wheel of the royal chariot represented the solar year, and had four spokes, like a fire-wheel or swastika. 'Narcaeus' is clearly a back-formation from Athene Narcaea ('benumbing'), a death-goddess. The matrons who organized the Heraean Games, which had once involved human sacrifice, propitiated the goddess with pig's blood, and then washed themselves in running water. Hippodameia's many children attest the strength of the confederation presided over by the Pelopid dynasty – all their names are associated with the Peloponnese or the Isthmus.

2. Alcathous's murder of his son Callipolis at the altar of Apollo has probably been deduced from an icon which showed him offering his son as a burnt sacrifice to the 'previous builder', the city-god Melicertes, or Moloch, when he refounded Megara – as a king of Moab also did (*Joshua* vi. 26). Moreover, like Samson and David, he had killed a lion in ritual combat. Corinthian mythology has many close affinities with Palestinian (see 67. *1*).

3. The myth of Chrysippus survives in degenerate form only. That he was a beautiful Pisan boy who drove a chariot, was carried off like Ganymedes, or Pelops himself (though not, indeed, to Olympus), and killed by Hippodameia, suggests that, originally, he was one of the royal surrogates who died in the chariot crash; but his myth has become confused with a justification of Theban pederasty, and with the legend of a dispute about the Nemean Games between Thebes and Pisa. Hippodameia, 'horse-tamer', was a title of the Moon-goddess, whose mare-headed statue at Phigalia held a Pelopid porpoise in her hand; four of Pelops's sons and daughters bear horse-names.

III

ATREUS AND THYESTES

S OME say that Atreus, who fled from Elis after the death of Chrysippus, in which he may have been more deeply implicated than Pelops knew, took refuge in Mycenae. There fortune favoured him. His nephew Eurystheus, who was just about to march against the sons of Heracles, appointed him regent in his absence; and, when presently news came of Eurystheus's defeat and death, the Mycenaean notables chose Atreus as their king, because he seemed a likely warrior to protect them against the Heraclids and had already won the affection of the commons. Thus the royal house of Pelops became more famous even than that of Perseus.[1]

b. But others say, with greater authority, that Eurystheus's father, Sthenelus, having banished Amphitryon, and seized the throne of Mycenae, sent for Atreus and Thyestes, his brother-in-law, and installed them at near-by Midea. A few years later, when Sthenelus and Eurytheus were both dead, an oracle advised the Mycenaeans to choose a prince of the Pelopid house to rule over them. They thereupon summoned Atreus and Thyestes from Midea and debated which of these two (who were fated to be always at odds) should be crowned king.[2]

c. Now, Atreus had once vowed to sacrifice the finest of his flocks to Artemis; and Hermes, anxious to avenge the death of Myrtilus on the Pelopids, consulted his old friend Goat-Pan, who made a horned lamb with a golden fleece appear among the Acarnanian flock which Pelops had left to his sons Atreus and Thyestes. He foresaw that Atreus would claim it as his own and, from his reluctance to give Artemis the honours due to her, would become involved in fratricidal war with Thyestes. Some, however, say that it was Artemis herself who sent the lamb, to try him.[3] Atreus kept his vow, in part at least, by sacrificing the lamb's flesh; but he stuffed and mounted the fleece and locked it in a chest. He grew so proud of his life-like treasure that he could not refrain from boasting about it in the market place, and the jealous Thyestes, for whom Atreus's newly-married wife Aerope had conceived a passion, agreed to be her lover if she gave him the lamb [which, he said, had been stolen by Atreus's shepherds from his own half of the flock]. For Artemis had laid a curse upon it, and this was her doing.[4]

d. In a debate at the Council Hall, Atreus claimed the throne of Mycenae by right of primogeniture, and also as possessor of the lamb. Thyestes asked him: 'Do you then publicly declare that its owner should be king?' 'I do,' Atreus replied. 'And I concur,' said Thyestes, smiling grimly. A herald then summoned the people of Mycenae to acclaim their new king; the temples were hung with gold, and their doors thrown open; fires blazed on every altar throughout the city;

and songs were sung in praise of the horned lamb with the golden fleece. But Thyestes unexpectedly rose to upbraid Atreus as a vain-glorious boaster, and led the magistrates to his home, where he displayed the lamb, justified his claim to its ownership, and was pronounced the rightful king of Mycenae.[5]

e. Zeus, however, favoured Atreus, and sent Hermes to him, saying: 'Call Thyestes, and ask him whether, if the sun goes backward on the dial, he will resign his claim to the throne in your favour?' Atreus did as he was told, and Thyestes agreed to abdicate should such a portent occur. Thereupon Zeus, aided by Eris, reversed the laws of Nature, which hitherto had been immutable. Helius, already in mid-career, wrested his chariot about and turned his horses' heads towards the dawn. The seven Pleiades, and all the other stars, retraced their courses in sympathy; and that evening, for the first and last time, the sun set in the east. Thyestes's deceit and greed being thus plainly attested, Atreus succeeded to the throne of Mycenae, and banished him.[6]

When, later, Atreus discovered that Thyestes had committed adultery with Aerope, he could hardly contain his rage. Nevertheless, for a while he feigned forgiveness.[7]

f. Now, this Aerope, whom some call Europe, was a Cretan, the daughter of King Catreus. One day, she had been surprised by Catreus while entertaining a lover in the palace, and was on the point of being thrown to the fishes when, countermanding his sentence at the plea of Nauplius, he sold her, and his other daughter Clymene as well, whom he suspected of plotting against his life, as slaves to Nauplius for a nominal price; only stipulating that neither of them should ever return to Crete. Nauplius then married Clymene, who bore him Oeax and Palamedes the inventor.[8] But Atreus, whose wife Cleola had died after giving birth to a weakly son, Pleisthenes – this was Artemis's revenge on him for his failure to keep the vow – married Aerope, and begot on her Agamemnon, Menelaus, and Anaxibia. Pleisthenes had also died: the cut-throats whom Atreus sent to murder his namesake, Thyestes's bastard son by Aerope, murdered him in error – Thyestes saw to that.[9]

g. Atreus now sent a herald to lure Thyestes back to Mycenae, with the offer of an amnesty and a half-share in the kingdom; but, as soon as Thyestes accepted this, slaughtered Aglaus, Orchomenus, and Callileon, Thyestes's three sons by one of the Naiads, on the very altar of Zeus where they had taken refuge; and then sought out and killed the infant Pleisthenes the Second, and Tantalus the Second, his twin. He hacked them all limb from limb, and set chosen morsels of their flesh, boiled in a cauldron, before Thyestes, to welcome him on his return. When Thyestes had eaten heartily, Atreus sent in their bloody heads and feet and hands, laid out on another dish, to show him what was now inside his belly. Thyestes fell back, vomiting, and laid an ineluctable curse upon the seed of Atreus.[10]

h. Exiled once more, Thyestes fled first to King Thesprotus at Sicyon, where his own daughter Pelopia, or Pelopeia, was a priestess. For, desiring revenge at whatever cost, he had consulted the Delphic Oracle and been advised to beget a son on his own daughter.[11] Thyestes found Pelopia sacrificing by night to Athene Colocasia and, being loth to profane the rites, concealed himself in a near-by grove. Presently Pelopia, who was leading the solemn dance, slipped in a pool of blood that had flowed from the throat of a black ewe, the victim, and stained her tunic. She ran at once to the temple fish-pond, removed her tunic, and was washing out the stain, when Thyestes sprang from the grove and ravished her. Pelopia did not recognize him, because he was wearing a mask, but contrived to steal his sword and carry it back to the temple, where she hid it under the pedestal of Athene's image; and Thyestes, finding the scabbard empty and fearing detection, escaped to Lydia, the land of his fathers.[12]

i. Meanwhile, fearing the consequences of his crime, Atreus consulted the Delphic Oracle, and was told: 'Recall Thyestes from Sicyon!' He reached Sicyon too late to meet Thyestes and, falling in love with Pelopia, whom he assumed to be King Thesprotus's daughter, asked leave to make her his third wife; having by this time executed Aerope. Eager for an alliance with so powerful a king, and wishing at the same time to do Pelopia a service, Thesprotus did not undeceive Atreus, and the wedding took place at once. In due course she bore the son begotten on her by Thyestes, whom she exposed on a mountain; but goatherds rescued him and gave him to a she-goat for suckling – hence his name, Aegisthus, or 'goat-strength'. Atreus believed that Thyestes had fled from Sicyon at news of his approach; that the child was his own; and that Pelopia had been affected by the temporary madness which sometimes overtakes women after childbirth. He therefore recovered Aegisthus from the goatherds and reared him as his heir.

j. A succession of bad harvests then plagued Mycenae, and Atreus sent Agamemnon and Menelaus to Delphi for news of Thyestes, whom they met by chance on his return from a further visit to the Oracle. They haled him back to Mycenae, where Atreus, having thrown him into prison, ordered Aegisthus, then seven years of age, to kill him as he slept.

k. Thyestes awoke suddenly to find Aegisthus standing over him, sword in hand; he quickly rolled sideways and escaped death. Then he rose, disarmed the boy with a shrewd kick at his wrist, and sprang to recover the sword. But it was his own, lost years before in Sicyon! He seized Aegisthus by the shoulder and cried: 'Tell me instantly how this came into your possession?' Aegisthus stammered: 'Alas, my mother Pelopia gave it me.' 'I will spare your life, boy,' said Thyestes, 'if you carry out the three orders I now give you.' 'I am your servant in all things,' wept Aegisthus, who had expected no mercy. 'My first order is to bring your mother here,' Thyestes told him.

l. Aegisthus thereupon brought Pelopia to the dungeon and, recognizing Thyestes, she wept on his neck, called him her dearest father, and commiserated with his sufferings. 'How did you come by this sword, daughter?' Thyestes asked. 'I took it from the scabbard of an unknown stranger who ravished me one night at Sicyon,' she replied. 'It is mine,' said Thyestes. Pelopia, stricken with horror, seized the sword, and plunged it into her breast. Aegisthus stood aghast, not understanding what had been said. 'Now take this sword to Atreus,' was Thyestes's second order, 'and tell him that you have carried out your commission. Then return!' Dumbly Aegisthus took the bloody thing to Atreus, who went joyfully down to the seashore, where he offered a sacrifice of thanksgiving to Zeus, convinced that he was rid of Thyestes at last.

m. When Aegisthus returned to the dungeon, Thyestes revealed himself as his father, and issued his third order: 'Kill Atreus, my son Aegisthus, and this time do not falter!' Aegisthus did as he was told, and Thyestes reigned once more in Mycenae.[13]

n. Another golden-fleeced horned lamb then appeared among Thyestes's flocks and grew to be a ram and, afterwards, every new Pelopid king was thus divinely confirmed in possession of his golden sceptre; these rams grazed at ease in a paddock enclosed by unscaleable walls. But some say that the token of royalty was not a living creature, but a silver bowl, on the bottom of which a golden lamb had been inlaid; and others, that it cannot have been Aegisthus who killed Atreus, because he was only an infant in swaddling clothes when

Agamemnon drove his father Thyestes from Mycenae, wresting the sceptre from him.[14]

o. Thyestes lies buried beside the road that leads from Mycenae to Argos, near the shrine of Perseus. Above his tomb stands the stone figures of a ram. The tomb of Atreus, and his underground treasury, are still shown among the ruins of Mycenae.[15]

p. Thyestes was not the last hero to find his own child served up to him on a dish. This happened some years later to Clymenus, the Arcadian son of Schoenus, who conceived an incestuous passion for Harpalyce, his daughter by Epicaste. Having debauched Harpalyce, he married her to Alastor, but afterwards took her away again. Harpalyce, to revenge herself, murdered the son she bore him – who was also her brother – cooked the corpse and laid it before Clymenus. She was transformed into a bird of prey, and Clymenus hanged himself.[16]

1. Scholiast on Euripides's *Orestes* 813; Thucydides: i. 9.
2. Apollodorus: ii. 4. 6 and *Epitome* ii. 11; Euripides: *Orestes* 12.
3. Apollodorus: *Epitome* ii. 10; Euripides: *Orestes* 995 ff., with scholiast; Seneca: *Electra* 699 ff.; Scholiast on Euripides's *Orestes* 812, 990, and 998; Tzetzes: *Chiliades* i. 433 ff.; Pherecydes, quoted by scholiast on Euripides's *Orestes* 997.
4. Apollodorus: *Epitome* ii. 11; Scholiast on Euripides's *Orestes* 812; Scholiast on Homer's *Iliad* ii. 106.
5. Tzetzes: *Chiliades* i. 426; Apollodorus: *loc. cit.*; Scholiast on Homer's *Iliad* ii. 106; Euripides: *Electra* 706 ff.
6. Apollodorus: *Epitome* ii. 12; Scholiast on Homer: *loc. cit.*; Euripides: *Orestes* 1001; Ovid: *Art of Love* 327 ff.; Scholiast on Euripides's *Orestes* 812.
7. Hyginus: *Fabula* 86; Apollodorus: *Epitome* ii. 13.
8. Lactantius on Statius's *Thebaid* vi. 306; Apollodorus: iii. 2. 2 and *Epitome* ii. 10; Sophocles: *Ajax* 1295 ff.; Scholiast on Euripides's *Orestes* 432.
9. Hyginus: *Fabulae* 97 and 86; Euripides: *Helen* 392; Homer: *Iliad* ii. 131, etc.
10. Tzetzes: *Chiliades* i. 18 ff.; Apollodorus: *Epitome* ii. 13; Hyginus: *Fabulae* 88, 246, and 258; Scholiast on Horace's *Art of Poetry*; Aeschylus: *Agamemnon* 1590 ff.
11. Apollodorus: *Epitome* ii. 13–14; Hyginus: *Fabulae* 87–8; Servius on Virgil's *Aeneid* ii. 262.
12. Athenaeus: iii. 1; Hyginus: *loc. cit.*; Fragments of Sophocles's *Thyestes*; Apollodorus: *Epitome* ii. 14.
13. Hyginus: *loc. cit.*; Apollodorus: *loc. cit.*
14. Seneca: *Thyestes* 224 ff.; Cicero: *On the Nature of the Gods* iii. 26 and 68; Herodotus of Heracleia, quoted by Athenaeus: 231 c;

Eustathius on Homer's *Iliad* pp. 268 and 1319; Aeschylus: *Agamemnon* 1603 ff.

15. Pausanias: ii. 16. 5 and ii. 18. 2–3.
16. Parthenius: *Erotica*; Hyginus: *Fabulae* 242, 246, and 255.

★

1. The Atreus-Thyestes myth, which survives only in highly theatrical versions, seems to be based on the rivalry between Argive co-kings for supreme power, as in the myth of Acrisius and Proetus (see 73. *a*). It is a good deal older than the story of Heracles's Sons (see 146. *k*) – the Dorian invasion of the Peloponnese, about the year 1050 B.C. – with which Thucydides associates it. Atreus's golden lamb, withheld from sacrifice, recalls Poseidon's white bull, similarly withheld by Minos (see 88. *c*); but is of the same breed as the golden-fleeced rams sacred to Zeus on Mount Laphystium, and to Poseidon on the island of Crumissa (see 70. *l*). To possess this fleece was a token of royalty, because the king used it in an annual rain-making ceremony (see 70. *2* and *6*). The lamb is metaphorically golden: in Greece 'water is gold', and the fleece magically produced rain. This metaphor may, however, have been reinforced by the use of fleeces to collect gold dust from the rivers of Asia Minor; and the occasional appearance, in the Eastern Mediterranean, of lambs with gilded teeth, supposedly descendants of those that the youthful Zeus tended on Mount Ida. (In the eighteenth century, Lady Mary Wortley Montagu investigated this persistent anomaly, but could not discover its origin.) It may also be that the Argive royal sceptre was topped by a golden ram. Apollodorus is vague about the legal background of the dispute, but Thyestes's claim was probably the same as that made by Maeve for the disputed bull in the fratricidal Irish *War of the Bulls*: that the lamb had been stolen from his own flocks at birth.

2. Euripides has introduced Eris at a wrong point in the story: she will have provoked the quarrel between the brothers, rather than helped Zeus to reverse the course of the sun – a phenomenon which she was not empowered to produce. Classical grammarians and philosophers have explained this incident in various ingenious ways which anticipate the attempts made by twentieth-century Protestants to account scientifically for the retrograde movement of the Sun's shadow on 'the dial of Ahaz' (2 *Kings* xx. 1–11). Lucian and Polybius write that when Atreus and Thyestes quarrelled over the succession, the Argives were already habitual star-gazers and agreed that the best astronomer should be elected king. In the ensuing contest, Thyestes pointed out that the sun always rose in the Ram at the Spring Festival – hence the story of the golden lamb – but the soothsayer Atreus did better: he proved that the sun and the earth

travel in different directions, and that what appear to be sunsets are, in fact, settings of the earth. Whereupon the Argives made him king (Lucian: *On Astrology* 12; Polybius, quoted by Strabo: i. 2. 15). Hyginus and Servius both agree that Atreus was an astronomer, but make him the first to predict an eclipse of the sun mathematically; and say that, when the calculation proved correct, his jealous brother Thyestes left the city in chagrin (Hyginus: *Fabula* 258; Servius on Virgil's *Aeneid* i. 572). Socrates took the myth more literally: regarding it as evidence of his theory that the universe winds and unwinds itself in alternate cycles of vast duration, the reversal of motion at the close of each cycle being accompanied by great destruction of animal life (Plato: *The Statesman* 12–14).

3. To understand the story, however, one must think not allegorically nor philosophically, but mythologically; namely in terms of the archaic conflict between the sacred king and his tanist. The king reigned until the summer solstice, when the sun reached its most northerly point and stood still; then the tanist killed him and took his place, while the sun daily retreated southward towards the winter solstice. This mutual hatred, sharpened by sexual jealousy, because the tanist married his rival's widow, was renewed between Argive co-kings, whose combined reigns extended for a Great Year; and they quarrelled over Aerope, as Acrisius and Proetus had done over Danaë. The myth of Hezekiah, who was on the point of death when, as a sign of Jehovah's favour, the prophet Isaiah added ten years to his reign by turning back the sun ten degrees on the dial of Ahaz (2 *Kings* xx. 8–11 and *Isaiah* xxxviii. 7–8), suggests a Hebrew, or perhaps a Philistine, tradition of how the king, after the calendar reform caused by adoption of the metonic cycle, was allowed to prolong his reign to the nineteenth year, instead of dying in the ninth. Atreus, at Mycenae, may have been granted a similar dispensation.

4. The cannibalistic feast in honour of Zeus, which appears in the myth of Tantalus (see 108. *c*), has here been confused with the annual sacrifice of child surrogates, and with Cronus's vomiting up of his children by Rhea (see 7. *d*). Thyestes's rape of Pelopia recalls the myth of Cinyras and Smyrna (see 17. *h*), and is best explained as the king's attempt to prolong his reign beyond the customary limit by marriage with his step-daughter, the heiress. Aerope's rescue from the Cretan fishes identifies her with Dictynna-Britomartis, whom her grandfather Minos had chased into the sea (see 89. *b*). Aegisthus, suckled by a she-goat, is the familiar New Year child of the Mysteries (see 24. 6; 44. *1*; 76, *a*; 105. *1*, etc.).

5. The story of Clymenus and Harpalyce – there was another Thracian character of the same name, a sort of Atalanta – combines the myth of Cinyras and Smyrna (see 18. *h*) with that of Tereus and Procne (see 46. *a*). Unless this is an artificial composition for the theatre, as Clymenus's unmythical suicide by hanging suggests, he will have tried to regain a

title to the throne when his reign ended, by marrying the heiress, technically his daughter, to an *interrex* and then killing him and taking her himself. Alastor means 'avenger', but this vengeance does not appear in the myth; perhaps the original version made Alastor the victim of the human sacrifice.

112

AGAMEMNON AND CLYTAEMNESTRA

SOME say that Agamemnon and Menelaus were of an age to arrest Thyestes at Delphi; others, that when Aegisthus killed Atreus, they were still infants, whom their nurse had the presence of mind to rescue. Snatching them up, one under each arm, she fled with them to Polypheides, the twenty-fourth king of Sicyon, at whose instance they were subsequently entrusted to Oeneus the Aetolian. It is agreed, however, that after they had spent some years at Oeneus's court, King Tyndareus of Sparta restored their fortunes. Marching against Mycenae, he exacted an oath from Thyestes, who had taken refuge at the altar of Hera, that he would bequeath the sceptre to Agamemnon, as Atreus's heir, and go into exile, never to return. Thyestes thereupon departed to Cythera, while Aegisthus, fearing Agamemnon's vengeance, fled to King Cylarabes, son of King Sthenelus the Argive.[1]

b. It is said that Zeus gave power to the House of Aeacus, wisdom to the House of Amythaon, but wealth to the House of Atreus. Wealthy indeed it was: the kings of Mycenae, Corinth, Cleonae, Orneiae, Arathyrea, Sicyon, Hyperesia, Gonoessa, Pellene, Aegium, Aegialus, and Helice, all paid tribute to Agamemnon, both on land and sea.[2]

c. Agamemnon first made war against Tantalus, King of Pisa, the son of his ugly uncle Broteas, killed him in battle and forcibly married his widow Clytaemnestra, whom Leda had borne to King Tyndareus of Sparta. The Dioscuri, Clytaemnestra's brothers, thereupon marched on Mycenae; but Agamemnon had already gone as a suppliant to his benefactor Tyndareus, who forgave him and let him keep Clytaemnestra. After the death of the Dioscuri, Menelaus married their sister Helen, and Tyndareus abdicated in his favour.[3]

d. Clytaemnestra bore Agamemnon one son, Orestes, and three daughters: Electra, or Laodice; Iphigeneia, or Iphianassa; and Chrysothemis; though some say that Iphigeneia was Clytaemnestra's niece, the daughter of Theseus and Helen, whom she took pity upon and adopted.[4]

e. When Paris, the son of King Priam of Troy, abducted Helen and thus provoked the Trojan War, both Agamemnon and Menelaus were absent from home for ten years; but Aegisthus did not join their expedition, preferring to stay behind at Argos and seek revenge on the House of Atreus.[5]

f. Now, Nauplius, the husband of Clymene, having failed to obtain requital from Agamemnon and the other Greek leaders for the stoning of his son Palamedes, had sailed away from Troy and coasted around Attica and the Peloponnese, inciting the lonely wives of his enemies to adultery. Aegisthus, therefore, when he heard that Clytaemnestra was among those most eager to be convinced by Nauplius, planned not only to become her lover, but to kill Agamemnon, with her assistance, as soon as the Trojan War ended.[6]

g. Hermes, sent to Aegisthus by Omniscient Zeus, warned him to abandon this project, on the ground that when Orestes had grown to manhood, he would be bound to avenge his father. For all his eloquence, however, Hermes failed to deter Aegisthus, who went to Mycenae with rich gifts in his hands, but hatred in his heart. At first, Clytaemnestra rejected his advances, because Agamemnon, apprised of Nauplius's visit to Mycenae, had instructed his court bard to keep close watch on her and report to him, in writing, the least sign of infidelity. But Aegisthus seized the old minstrel and marooned him without food on a lonely island, where birds of prey were soon picking his bones. Clytaemnestra then yielded to Aegisthus's embraces, and he celebrated his unhoped-for success with burnt offerings to Aphrodite, and gifts of tapestries and gold to Artemis, who was nursing a grudge against the House of Atreus.[7]

h. Clytaemnestra had small cause to love Agamemnon: after killing her former husband Tantalus, and the new-born child at her breast, he had married her by force, and then gone away to a war which promised never to end; he had also sanctioned the sacrifice of Iphigeneia at Aulis – and, this she found even harder to bear – was said to be bringing back Priam's daughter Cassandra, the prophetess, as his wife in all but name. It is true that Cassandra had borne Agamemnon twin sons: Teledamus and Pelops, but he does not seem to have intended any insult to Clytaemnestra. Her informant had been Nauplius's surviving son Oeax who, in vengeance for his brother's death, was maliciously provoking her to do murder.[8]

i. Clytaemnestra therefore conspired with Aegisthus to kill both Agamemnon and Cassandra. Fearing, however, that they might arrive unexpectedly, she wrote Agamemnon a letter asking him to light a beacon on Mount Ida when Troy fell; and herself arranged for a chain of fires to relay his signal to Argolis by way of Cape Hermaeum on Lemnos, and the mountains of Athos, Macistus, Messapius, Cithaeron, Aegiplanctus, and Arachne. A watchman was also stationed on the roof of the palace at Mycenae: a faithful servant of Agamemnon's, who spent one whole year, crouched on his elbows like a dog, gazing towards Mount Arachne and filled with gloomy forebodings. At last, one dark night, he saw the distant beacon blaze and ran to wake Clytaemnestra. She celebrated the news with sacrifices of thanksgiving; though, indeed, she would now have liked the siege of Troy to last for ever. Aegisthus thereupon posted one of his own men in a watch-tower near the sea, promising him two gold talents for the first news of Agamemnon's landing.

j. Hera had rescued Agamemnon from the fierce storm which destroyed many of the returning Greek ships and drove Menelaus to Egypt; and, at last, a fair wind carried him to Nauplia. No sooner had he disembarked, than he bent down to kiss the soil, weeping for joy. Meanwhile the watchman hurried to Mycenae to collect his fee, and Aegisthus chose twenty of the boldest warriors, posted them in ambush inside the palace, ordered a great banquet and then, mounting his chariot, rode down to welcome Agamemnon.[9]

k. Clytaemnestra greeted her travel-worn husband with every appearance of delight, unrolled a purple carpet for him, and led him to the bath-house, where slave-girls had prepared a warm bath; but Cassandra remained outside the palace, caught in a prophetic trance, refusing to enter, and crying that she smelt blood, and that the curse of Thyestes was heavy upon the dining-hall. When Agamemnon had washed himself and set one foot out of the bath, eager to partake of the rich banquet now already set on the tables, Clytaemnestra came forward, as if to wrap a towel about him, but instead threw over his head a garment of net, woven by herself, without either neck or sleeve-holes. Entangled in this, like a fish, Agamemnon perished at the hands of Aegisthus, who struck him twice with a two-edged sword.[10] He fell back, into the silver-sided bath, where Clytaemnestra avenged her wrongs by beheading him with an axe.[11] She then ran out to kill Cassandra with the same weapon, not troubling first to close her husband's eyelids or mouth; but wiped off on his hair the blood which had splashed her, to signify that he had brought about his own death.[12]

l. A fierce battle was now raging in the palace, between Agamemnon's bodyguard and Aegisthus's supporters. Warriors were slain like swine for a rich man's feast, or lay wounded and groaning beside the laden boards in a welter of blood; but Aegisthus won the day. Outside, Cassandra's head rolled to the ground, and Aegisthus also had the satisfaction of killing her twin sons by Agamemnon; yet he failed to do away with another of Agamemnon's bastards, by name Halesus, or Haliscus. Halesus contrived to make his escape and, after long wandering in exile, founded the Italian city of Falerii, and taught its inhabitants the Mysteries of Hera, which are still celebrated there in the Argive manner.[13]

m. This massacre took place on the thirteenth day of the month Gamelion [January] and, unafraid of divine retribution, Clytaemnestra decreed the thirteenth day a monthly festival, celebrating it with dancing and offerings of sheep to her guardian deities. Some applaud her resolution; but others hold that she brought eternal disgrace upon all women, even virtuous ones. Aegisthus, too, gave thanks to the goddess who had assisted him.[14]

n. The Spartans claim that Agamemnon is buried at Amyclae, now no more than a small village, where are shown the tomb and statue of Clytaemnestra, also the sanctuary and statue of Cassandra; the inhabitants even believe that he was killed there. But the truth is that Agamemnon's tomb stands among the ruins of Mycenae, close to those of his charioteer, of his comrades murdered with him by Aegisthus, and of Cassandra's twins.[15]

o. Menelaus was later informed of the crime by Proteus, the prophet of Pharos and, having offered hecatombs to his brother's ghost, built a cenotaph in his honour beside the River of Egypt. Returning to Sparta, eight years later, he raised a temple to Zeus Agamemnon; there are other such temples at Lapersae in Attica and at Clazomene in Ionia, although Agamemnon never reigned in either of these places.[16]

1. Hyginus: *Fabula* 88; Eusebius: *Chronicles* i. 175–6, ed. Schoene; Homer: *Iliad* ii. 107–8 and *Odyssey* iii. 263; Aeschylus: *Agamemnon* 529; Pausanias: ii. 18. 4; Tzetzes: *Chiliades* i. 433 ff.
2. Hesiod, quoted by Suidas *sub* Alce; Homer: *Iliad* 108 and 569–80.

3. Apollodorus: iii. 10. 6 and *Epitome* ii. 16; Euripides: *Iphigeneia in Aulis* 1148 ff.

4. Apollodorus: *loc. cit.*; Homer: *Iliad* ix. 145; Duris, quoted by Tzetzes: *On Lycophron* 183.

5. Homer: *Odyssey* iii. 263.

6. Apollodorus: *Epitome* vi. 8–9.

7. Homer: *Odyssey* i. 35 ff. and iii. 263–75.

8. Euripides: *Iphigeneia in Aulis* 1148 ff.; Sophocles: *Electra* 531; Pausanias: iii. 16. 5 and ii. 16. 5; Hyginus: *Fabula* 117.

9. Hyginus: *loc. cit.*; Aeschylus: *Agamemnon* i. ff. and 282 ff.; Euripides: *Electra* 1076 ff.; Homer: *Odyssey* iv. 524–37; Pausanias: ii. 16. 5.

10. Aeschylus: *Agamemnon* 1220 – 1391 ff., 1521 ff. and *Eumenides* 631–5; Euripides: *Electra* 157 and *Orestes* 26; Tzetzes: *On Lycophron* 1375; Servius on Virgil's *Aeneid* xi. 267; Triclinius on Sophocles's *Electra* 195; Homer: *Odyssey* iii. 193 ff. and 303–5; xi. 529–37.

11. Sophocles: *Electra* 99; Aeschylus: *Agamemnon* 1372 ff. and 1535.

12. Aeschylus: *loc. cit.*; Sophocles: *Electra* 445–6.

13. Homer: *Odyssey* xi. 400 and 442; Pausanias: ii. 16. 5; Virgil: *Aeneid* vii. 723; Servius on Virgil's *Aeneid* vii. 695; Ovid: *Art of Love* iii. 13. 31.

14. Sophocles: *Electra* 278–81; Homer: *Odyssey* iii. 263; xi. 405 and vi. 512 ff.

15. Pausanias: ii. 16. 5 and iii. 19. 5; Pindar: *Pythian Odes* i. 32; Homer: *Iliad* iv. 228.

16. Homer: *Odyssey* iv. 512 ff. and 581 ff.; Tzetzes: *On Lycophron* 112–114 and 1369; Pausanias: vii. 5. 5.

*

1. The myth of Agamemnon, Aegisthus, Clytaemnestra, and Orestes has survived in so stylized a dramatic form that its origins are almost obliterated. In tragedy of this sort, the clue is usually provided by the manner of the king's death: whether he is flung over a cliff like Theseus, burned alive like Heracles, wrecked in a chariot like Oenomaus, devoured by wild horses like Diomedes, drowned in a pool like Tantalus, or killed by lightning like Capaneus. Agamemnon dies in a peculiar manner: with a net thrown over his head, with one foot still in the bath, but the other on the floor, and in the bath-house annexe – that is to say, 'neither clothed nor unclothed, neither in water nor on dry land, neither in his palace nor outside' – a situation recalling the midsummer death, in the *Mabinogion*, of the sacred king Llew Llaw, at the hands of his treacherous wife Blodeuwedd and her lover Gronw. A similar story told by Saxo Grammaticus in his late twelfth-century *History of Denmark* suggests that

Clytaemnestra may also have given Agamemnon an apple to eat, and killed him as he set it to his lips: so that he was 'neither fasting, nor feasting' (*White Goddess*, pp. 308 and 401). Basically, then, this is the familiar myth of the sacred king who dies at midsummer, the goddess who betrays him, the tanist who succeeds him, the son who avenges him. Clytaemnestra's axe was the Cretan symbol of sovereignty, and the myth has affinities with the murder of Minos, which also took place in a bath. Aegisthus's mountain beacons, one of which Aeschylus records to have been built of heather (see 18. 3), are the bonfires of the midsummer sacrifice. The goddess in whose honour Agamemnon was sacrificed appears in triad as his 'daughters': Electra ('amber'), Iphigeneia ('mothering a strong race'), and Chrysothemis ('golden order').

2. This ancient story has been combined with the legend of a dispute between rival dynasties in the Peloponnese. Clytaemnestra was a Spartan royal heiress; and the Spartan's claim, that their ancestor Tyndareus raised Agamemnon to the throne of Mycenae, suggests that they were victorious in a war against the Mycenaeans for the possession of Amyclae, where Agamemnon and Clytaemnestra were both honoured.

3. 'Zeus Agamemnon', 'very resolute Zeus', will have been a divine title borne not only by the Mycenaean kings, but by those of Lapersae and Clazomene; and, presumably, also by the kings of a Danaan or Achaean settlement beside the River of Egypt – not to be confused with the Nile. The River of Egypt is mentioned in *Joshua* xv. 4 as marking the boundary between Palestine and Egypt; farther up the coast, at Ascalon and near Tyre, there were other Danaan or Achaean settlements (see 69. *f*.).

4. The thirteenth day, also observed as a festal day in Rome, where it was called the Ides, had corresponded with the full moon at a time when the calendar month was a simple lunation. It seems that the sacrifice of the king always took place at the full moon. According to the legend, the Greek fleet, returning late in the year from Troy, ran into winter storms; Agamemnon therefore died in January, not in June.

113

THE VENGEANCE OF ORESTES

ORESTES was reared by his loving grand-parents Tyndareus and Leda and, as a boy, accompanied Clytaemnestra and Iphigeneia to Aulis.[1] But some say that Clytaemnestra sent him to Phocis, shortly before

Agamemnon's return; and others that on the evening of the murder, Orestes, then ten years of age, was rescued by his noble-hearted nurse Arsinoë, or Laodameia, or Geilissa who, having sent her own son to bed in the royal nursery, let Aegisthus kill him in Orestes's place.[2] Others again say that his sister Electra, aided by her father's ancient tutor, wrapped him in a robe embroidered with wild beasts, which she herself had woven, and smuggled him out of the city.[3]

b. After hiding for a while among the shepherds of the river Tanus, which divides Argolis from Laconia, the tutor made his way with Orestes to the court of Strophius, a firm ally of the House of Atreus, who ruled over Crisa, at the foot of Mount Parnassus.[4] This Strophius had married Agamemnon's sister Astyochea, or Anaxibia, or Cyndragora. At Crisa, Orestes found an adventurous playmate, namely Strophius's son Pylades, who was somewhat younger than himself, and their friendship was destined to become proverbial.[5] From the old tutor he learned with grief that Agamemnon's body had been flung out of the house and hastily buried by Clytaemnestra, without either libations or myrtle-boughs; and that the people of Mycenae had been forbidden to attend the funeral.[6]

c. Aegisthus reigned at Mycenae for seven years, riding in Agamemnon's chariot, sitting on his throne, wielding his sceptre, wearing his robes, sleeping in his bed, and squandering his riches. Yet despite all these trappings of kingship, he was little more than a slave to Clytaemnestra, the true ruler of Mycenae.[7] When drunk, he would leap on Agamemnon's tomb and pelt the head-stone with rocks, crying: 'Come, Orestes, come and defend your own!' The truth was, however, that he lived in abject fear of vengeance, even while surrounded by a trusty foreign bodyguard, never passed a single night in sound sleep, and had offered a handsome reward in gold for Orestes's assassination.[8]

d. Electra had been betrothed to her cousin Castor of Sparta, before his death and demi-deification. Though the leading princes of Greece now contended for her hand, Aegisthus feared that she might bear a son to avenge Agamemnon, and therefore announced that no suitor could be accepted. He would gladly have destroyed Electra, who showed him implacable hatred, lest she lay secretly with one of the Palace officers and bare him a bastard; but Clytaemnestra, feeling no qualms about her part in Agamemnon's murder, and scrupulous not to incur the displeasure of the gods, forbade him to do so. She allowed him, however, to marry Electra to a Mycenaean peasant who, being afraid of Orestes and also chaste by nature, never consummated their unequal union.⁹

e. Thus, neglected by Clytaemnestra, who had now borne Aegisthus three children, by name Erigone, Aletes, and the second Helen, Electra lived in disgraceful poverty, and was kept under constant close supervision. In the end it was decided that, unless she would accept her fate, as her sister Chrysothemis had done, and refrain from publicly calling Aegisthus and Clytaemnestra 'murderous adulterers', she would be banished to some distant city and there confined in a dungeon where the light of the sun never penetrated. Yet Electra despised Chrysothemis for her subservience and disloyalty to their dead father and secretly sent frequent reminders to Orestes of the vengeance required from him.¹⁰

f. Orestes, now grown to manhood, visited the Delphic Oracle, to inquire whether or not he should destroy his father's murderers. Apollo's answer, authorized by Zeus, was that if he neglected to avenge Agamemnon he would become an outcast from society, debarred from entering any shrine or temple, and afflicted with a leprosy that ate into his flesh, making it sprout white mould.¹¹ He was recommended to pour libations beside Agamemnon's tomb, lay a ringlet of his hair upon it and, unaided by any company of spearmen, craftily exact the due punishment from the murderers. At the same time the Pythoness observed that the Erinnyes would not readily forgive a matricide, and therefore, on behalf of Apollo, she gave Orestes a bow of horn, with which to repel their attacks, should they become insupportable. After fulfilling his orders, he must come again to Delphi, where Apollo would protect him.¹²

g. In the eighth year – or, according to some, after a passage of twenty years – Orestes secretly returned to Mycenae, by way of Athens, determined to destroy both Aegisthus and his own mother.¹³

One morning, with Pylades at his side, he visited Agamemnon's tomb and there, cutting off a lock of his hair, he invoked Infernal Hermes, patron of fatherhood. When a group of slave-women approached, dirty and dishevelled for the purposes of mourning, he took shelter in a near-by thicket to watch them. Now, on the previous night, Clytaemnestra had dreamed that she gave birth to a serpent, which she wrapped in swaddling clothes and suckled. Suddenly she screamed in her sleep, and alarmed the whole Palace by crying that the serpent had drawn blood from her breast, as well as milk. The opinion of the soothsayers whom she consulted was that she had incurred the anger of the dead; and these mourning slave-women consequently came on her behalf to pour libations upon Agamemnon's tomb, in the hope of appeasing his ghost. Electra, who was one of the party, poured the libations in her own name, not her mother's; offered prayers to Agamemnon for vengeance, instead of pardon; and bade Hermes summon Mother Earth and the gods of the Underworld to hear her plea. Noticing a ringlet of fair hair upon the tomb, she decided that it could belong only to Orestes: both because it closely resembled her own in colour and texture, and because no one else would have dared to make such an offering.[14]

h. Torn between hope and doubt, she was measuring her feet against Orestes's foot-prints in the clay beside the tomb, and finding a family resemblance, when he emerged from his hiding place, showed her that the ringlet was his own, and produced the robe in which he had escaped from Mycenae.

Electra welcomed him with delight, and together they invoked their ancestor, Father Zeus, whom they reminded that Agamemnon had always paid him great honour and that, were the House of Atreus to die out, no one would be left in Mycenae to offer him the customary hecatombs: for Aegisthus worshipped other deities.[15]

i. When the slave-women told Orestes of Clytaemnestra's dream, he recognized the serpent as himself, and declared that he would indeed play the cunning serpent and draw blood from her false body. Then he instructed Electra to enter the Palace and tell Clytaemnestra nothing about their meeting; he and Pylades would follow, after an interval, and beg hospitality at the gate, as strangers and suppliants, pretending to be Phocians and using the Parnassian dialect. If the porter refused them admittance, Aegisthus's inhospitality would outrage the city; if he granted it, they would not fail to take vengeance.

Presently Orestes knocked at the Palace gate, and asked for the master or mistress of the house. Clytaemnestra herself came out, but did not recognize Orestes. He pretended to be an Aeolian from Daulis, bearing sad news from one Strophius, whom he had met by chance on the road to Argos: namely, that her son Orestes was dead, and that his ashes were being kept in a brazen urn. Strophius wished to know whether he should send these back to Mycenae, or bury them at Crisa.[16]

j. Clytaemnestra at once welcomed Orestes inside and, concealing her joy from the servants, sent his old nurse, Geilissa, to fetch Aegisthus from a near-by temple. But Geilissa saw through Orestes's disguise and, altering the message, told Aegisthus to rejoice because he could now safely come alone and weaponless to greet the bearers of glad tidings: his enemy was dead.[17]

Unsuspectingly, Aegisthus entered the Palace where, to create a further distraction, Pylades had just arrived, carrying a brazen urn. He told Clytaemnestra that it held Orestes's ashes, which Strophius had now decided to send to Mycenae. This seeming confirmation of the first message put Aegisthus completely off his guard; thus Orestes had no difficulty in drawing his sword and cutting him down. Clytaemnestra then recognized her son, and tried to soften his heart by baring her breast, and appealing to his filial duty; Orestes, however, beheaded her with a single stroke of the same sword, and she fell beside the body of her paramour. Standing over the corpses, he addressed the Palace servants, holding aloft the still blood-stained net in which Agamemnon had died, eloquently exculpating himself for the murder of Clytaemnestra by this reminder of her treachery, and adding that Aegisthus had suffered the sentence prescribed by law for adulterers.[18]

k. Not content with killing Aegisthus and Clytaemnestra, Orestes next disposed of the second Helen, their daughter; and Pylades beat off the sons of Nauplius, who had come to Aegisthus's rescue.[19]

l. Some say, however, that these events took place in Argos, on the third day of Hera's Festival, when the virgins' procession was about to begin. Aegisthus had prepared a banquet for the Nymphs near the horse-meadows, before sacrificing a bull to Hera, and was gathering myrtle-boughs to wreathe his head. It is added that Electra, meeting Orestes by Agamemnon's tomb, would not believe at first that he was her long-lost brother, despite the similarity of their hair, and the robe he showed her. Finally, a scar on his forehead convinced her; because once, when they were children together, chasing a deer, he had slipped and fallen, cutting his head upon a sharp rock.

m. Obeying her whispered instructions, Orestes went at once to the altar where the bull had now been slaughtered and, as Aegisthus bent to inspect its entrails, struck off his head with the sacrificial axe. Meanwhile, Electra, to whom he presented the head, enticed Clytaemnestra from the palace by pretending that, ten days before, she had borne a son to her peasant husband; and when Clytaemnestra, anxious to inspect her first grand-child, visited the cottage, Orestes was waiting behind the door and killed her without mercy.[20]

n. Others, though agreeing that the murder took place at Argos, say that Clytaemnestra sent Chrysothemis to Agamemnon's tomb with the libations, having dreamed that Agamemnon, restored to life, snatched his sceptre from Aegisthus's hands and planted it so firmly in the ground that it budded and put forth branches, which overshadowed the entire land of Mycenae. According to this account, the news which deceived Aegisthus and Clytaemnestra was that Orestes had been accidentally killed while competing in the chariot race at the Pythian Games; and that Orestes showed Electra neither a ringlet nor an embroidered robe, nor a scar, in proof of his identity, but Agamemnon's own seal, which was carved from a piece of Pelops's ivory shoulder.[21]

o. Still others, denying that Orestes killed Clytaemnestra with his own hands, say that he committed her for trial by the judges, who condemned her to death, and that his one fault, if it may be called a fault, was that he did not intercede on her behalf.[22]

1. Euripides: *Orestes* 462 and *Iphigeneia in Aulis* 622.
2. Aeschylus: *Agamemnon* 877 ff. and *Libation-bearers* 732; Euripides: *Electra* 14 ff.; Pindar: *Pythian Odes* xi. 17, with scholiast.
3. Apollodorus: *Epitome* vi. 24; Euripides: *loc. cit.* and 542 ff.; Aeschylus: *Libation-bearers* 232.
4. Euripides: *Electra* 409–12; Sophocles: *Electra* 11 ff.; Pindar: *Pythian Odes* xi. 34–6.
5. Hyginus: *Fabula* 117; Scholiast on Euripides's *Orestes* 33, 764, and 1235; Euripides: *Iphigeneia Among the Taurians* 921; Apollodorus: *Epitome* vi. 24; Ovid: *Pontic Epistles* iii. 2. 95–8.
6. Euripides: *Electra* 289 and 323–5; Aeschylus: *Libation-bearers* 431.
7. Homer: *Odyssey* iii. 305; Euripides: *Electra* 320 ff. and 931 ff.; Sophocles: *Electra* 267 ff. and 651.
8. Euripides: *Electra* 33, 320 ff. and 617 ff.; Hyginus: *Fabula* 119.
9. Euripides: *Electra* 19 ff., 253 ff., and 312 ff.
10. Hyginus: *Fabula* 122; Ptolemy Hephaestionos: iv, quoted by Photius p. 479; Euripides: *Electra* 60–4; Aeschylus: *Libation-bearers* 130 ff.; Sophocles: *Electra* 341 ff., 379 ff. and 516 ff.
11. Apollodorus: *Epitome* vi. 24; Aeschylus: *Eumenides* 622 and *Libation-bearers* 269 ff.
12. Sophocles: *Electra* 36–7 and 51–2; Euripides: *Orestes* 268–70; Aeschylus: *Libation-bearers* 1038.
13. Homer: *Odyssey* iii. 306 ff.; *Hypothesis* of Sophocles's *Electra*; Apollodorus: *Epitome* vi. 25.
14. Aeschylus: *Libation-bearers*.
15. Aeschylus: *ibid.*
16. Aeschylus: *ibid.*

17. Aeschylus: *ibid.*
18. Hyginus: *Fabula* 119; Aeschylus: *Eumenides* 592 and *Libation-
    bearers* 973 ff.
19. Ptolemy Hephaestionos: iv, quoted by Photius p. 479; Pausanias:
    i. 22. 6.
20. Euripides: *Electra.*
21. Sophocles: *Electra* 326 and 417 ff.; 47–50 and 1223, with scholiast.
22. Servius on Virgil's *Aeneid* xi. 268.

1. This is a crucial myth with numerous variants. Olympianism had
been formed as a religion of compromise between the pre-Hellenic
matriarchal principle and the Hellenic patriarchal principle; the divine
family consisting, at first, of six gods and six goddesses. An uneasy
balance of power was kept until Athene was reborn from Zeus's head,
and Dionysus, reborn from his thigh, took Hestia's seat at the divine
Council (see 27. *k*); thereafter male preponderance in any divine debate
was assured – a situation reflected on earth – and the goddesses' ancient
prerogatives could now be successfully challenged.

2. Matrilinear inheritance was one of the axioms taken over from the
pre-Hellenic religion. Since every king must necessarily be a foreigner,
who ruled by virtue of his marriage to an heiress, royal princes learned to
regard their mother as the main support of the kingdom, and matricide
as an unthinkable crime. They were brought up on myths of the earlier
religion, according to which the sacred king had always been betrayed
by his goddess-wife, killed by his tanist, and avenged by his son; they
knew that the son never punished his adulterous mother, who had acted
with the full authority of the goddess whom she served.

3. The antiquity of the Orestes myth is evident from his friendship for
Pylades, to whom he stands in exactly the same relation as Theseus to
Peirithous. In the archaic version, he was doubtless a Phocian prince who
ritually killed Aegisthus at the close of the eighth year of his reign, and
became the new king by marriage to Chrysothemis, Clytaemnestra's
daughter.

4. Other tell-tale traces of the archaic version persist in Aeschylus,
Sophocles, and Euripides. Aegisthus is killed during the festival of the
Death-goddess Hera, while cutting myrtle-boughs; and despatched, like
the Minos bull, with a sacrificial axe. Geilissa's rescue of Orestes ('mountaineer') in a robe 'embroidered with wild beasts', and the tutor's stay
among the shepherds of Tanus, together recall the familiar tale of a royal
prince who is wrapped in a robe, left 'on a mountain' to the mercy of wild
beasts, and cared for by shepherds – the robe being eventually recognized,
as in the Hippothous myth (see 49. *a*). Geilissa's substitution of her own

son for the royal victim refers, perhaps, to a stage in religious history when the king's annual child-surrogate was no longer a member of the royal clan.

5. How far, then, can the main features of the story, as given by the Attic dramatists, be accepted? Though it is improbable that the Erinnyes have been wantonly introduced into the myth – which, like that of Alcmaeon and Eriphyle (see 107. *d*), seems to have been a moral warning against the least disobedience, injury, or insult that a son might offer his mother – yet it is equally improbable that Orestes killed Clytaemnestra. Had he done so, Homer would certainly have mentioned the fact, and refrained from calling him 'god-like'; he records only that Orestes killed Aegisthus, whose funeral feast he celebrated jointly with that of his hateful mother (*Odyssey* iii. 306 ff.). The *Parian Chronicle*, similarly, makes no mention of matricide in Orestes's indictment. It is probable therefore that Servius has preserved the true account: how Orestes, having killed Aegisthus, merely handed over Clytaemnestra to popular justice – a course significantly recommended by Tyndareus in Euripides's *Orestes* (496 ff.). Yet to offend a mother by a refusal to champion her cause, however wickedly she had behaved, sufficed under the old dispensation to set the Erinnyes on his track.

6. It seems, then, that this myth, which was of wide currency, had placed the mother of a household in so strong a position, when any family dispute arose, that the priesthood of Apollo and of Zeus-born Athene (a traitress to the old religion) decided to suppress it. They did so by making Orestes not merely commit Clytaemnestra to trial, but kill her himself, and then secure an acquittal in the most venerable court of Greece: with Zeus's support, and the personal intervention of Apollo, who had similarly encouraged Alcmaeon to murder his treacherous mother Eriphyle. It was the priests' intention, once and for all, to invalidate the religious axiom that motherhood is more divine than fatherhood.

7. In the revision patrilocal marriage and patrilinear descent are taken for granted, and the Erinnyes are successfully defied. Electra, whose name, 'amber', suggests the paternal cult of Hyperborean Apollo, is favourably contrasted with Chrysothemis, whose name is a reminder that the ancient concept of matriarchal law was still golden in most parts of Greece, and whose 'subservience' to her mother had hitherto been regarded as pious and noble. Electra is 'all for the father', like the Zeus-born Athene. Moreover, the Erinnyes had always acted for the mother only; and Aeschylus is forcing language when he speaks of Erinnyes charged with avenging paternal blood (*Libation-bearers* 283–4). Apollo's threat of leprosy if Orestes did not kill his mother, was a most daring one: to inflict, or heal, leprosy had long been the sole prerogative of the White Goddess Leprea, or Alphito (*White Goddess*, Chapter 24). In the sequel,

not all the Erinnyes accept Apollo's Delphic ruling, and Euripedes appeases his female audience by allowing the Dioscuri to suggest that Apollo's injunctions had been most unwise (*Electra* 1246).

8. The wide variations in the recognition scene, and in the plot by which Orestes contrives to kill Aegisthus and Clytaemnestra, are of interest only as proving that the Classical dramatists were not bound by tradition. Theirs was a new version of an ancient myth; and both Sophocles and Euripides tried to improve on Aeschylus, who first formulated it, by making the action more plausible.

114

THE TRIAL OF ORESTES

THE Mycenaeans who had supported Orestes in his unheard-of action would not allow the bodies of Clytaemnestra and Aegisthus to lie within their city, but buried them at some distance beyond the walls.[1] That night, Orestes and Pylades stood guard at Clytaemnestra's tomb, lest anyone should dare rob it; but, during their vigil, the serpent-haired, dog-headed, bat-winged Erinnyes appeared, swinging their scourges. Driven to distraction by these fierce attacks, against which Apollo's bow of horn was of little avail, Orestes fell prostrate on a couch, where he lay for six days, his head wrapped in a cloak – refusing either to eat or to wash.

b. Old Tyndareus now arrived from Sparta, and brought a charge of matricide against Orestes, summoning the Mycenaean chieftains to judge his case. He decreed that, pending the trial, none should speak either to Orestes or Electra, and that both should be denied shelter, fire, and water. Thus Orestes was prevented even from washing his blood-stained hands. The streets of Mycenae were lined with citizens in arms; and Oeax, son of Nauplius, delighted in this opportunity to persecute Agamemnon's children.[2]

c. Meanwhile, Menelaus, laden with treasure, landed at Nauplia, where a fisherman told him that Aegisthus and Clytaemnestra had been murdered. He sent Helen ahead to confirm the news at Mycenae; but by night, lest the kinsmen of those who had perished at Troy should stone her. Helen, feeling ashamed to mourn in public for her sister Clytaemnestra, since she herself had caused even more bloodshed by her infidelities, asked Electra, who was now nursing the afflicted Orestes: 'Pray, niece, take offerings of my hair and lay them on Clytaemnestra's tomb, after pouring libations to her ghost.' Electra, when she saw that Helen had been prevented by vanity from cutting off more than the very tips of her hair, refused to do so. 'Send your daughter Hermione instead,' was her curt advice. Helen thereupon summoned Hermione from the palace. She had been only a nine-year-old child when her mother eloped with Paris, and Menelaus had committed her to Clytaemnestra's charge at the outbreak of the Trojan War; yet she recognized Helen at once and dutifully went off to do as she was told.[3]

d. Menelaus then entered the palace, where he was greeted by his foster-father Tyndareus, clad in deep mourning, and warned not to set foot on Spartan soil until he had punished his criminal nephew and niece. Tyndareus held that Orestes should have contented himself with allowing his fellow-citizens to banish Clytaemnestra. If they had demanded her death he should have interceded on her behalf. As matters now stood, they must be persuaded, willy-nilly, that not only Orestes, but Electra who had spurred him on, should be stoned to death as matricides.

e. Fearing to offend Tyndareus, Menelaus secured the desired verdict. But at the eloquent plea of Orestes himself, who was present in court and had the support of Pylades (now disowned by Strophius for his part in the murder), the judges commuted the sentence to one of suicide. Pylades then led Orestes away, nobly refusing to desert either him or Electra, to whom he was betrothed; and proposed that, since all three must die, they should first punish Menelaus's cowardice and disloyalty by killing Helen, the originator of every misfortune that had befallen them. While, therefore, Electra waited outside the walls to execute her own design – that of intercepting Hermione on her return from Clytaemnestra's tomb and holding her as a hostage for Menelaus's good behaviour – Orestes and Pylades entered the palace, with swords hidden beneath their cloaks, and took refuge at the central altar, as though they were suppliants. Helen, who sat near by, spinning wool for a purple robe to lay as a gift on Clytaemnestra's tomb, was deceived by their lamentations, and approached to welcome them. Whereupon both drew their swords and, while Pylades chased away Helen's Phrygian slaves, Orestes attempted to murder her. But Apollo, at Zeus's command, rapt her in a cloud to Olympus, where she became an immortal; joining her brothers, the Dioscuri, as a guardian of sailors in distress.[4]

f. Meanwhile, Electra had secured Hermione, led her into the palace, and barred the gates. Menelaus, seeing that death threatened his daughter, ordered an immediate rescue. His men burst open the gates, and Orestes was just about to set the palace alight, kill Hermione, and die himself either by sword or fire, when Apollo providentially appeared, wrenched the torch from his hand, and drove back Menelaus's warriors. In the awed hush caused by his presence, Apollo commanded Menelaus to take another wife, betroth Hermione to Orestes, and return to rule over Sparta; Clytaemnestra's murder need no longer concern him, now that the gods had intervened.[5]

g. With wool-wreathed laurel-branch and chaplet, to show that he was under Apollo's protection, Orestes then set out for Delphi, still pursued by the Erinnyes. The Pythian Priestess was terrified to see him crouched as a suppliant on the marble navel-stone – stained by the blood from his unwashed hands – and the hideous troop of black Erinnyes sleeping beside him. Apollo, however, reassured her by promising to act as advocate for Orestes, whom he ordered to face his ordeal with courage. After a period of exile, he must make his way to Athens, and there embrace the ancient image of Athene who, as the Dioscuri had already prophesied, would shield him with her Gorgon-faced aegis, and annul the curse.[6] While the Erinnyes were still fast asleep, Orestes escaped under the guidance of Hermes; but Clytaemnestra's ghost soon entered the precinct, taking them to task, and reminding them that they had often received libations of wine and grim midnight banquets from her hand. They therefore set off in renewed pursuit, scornful of Apollo's angry threats to shoot them down.[7]

h. Orestes's exile lasted for one year – the period which must elapse before a homicide may again move among his fellow-citizens. He wandered far, over land and sea, pursued by the tireless Erinnyes and constantly purified both with the blood of pigs and with running water; yet these rites never served to keep his tormentors at bay for more than an hour or two, and he soon lost his wits. To begin with, Hermes escorted him to Troezen, where he was lodged in what is now called the Booth of Orestes, which faces the Sanctuary of Apollo; and presently nine Troezenians purified him at the Sacred Rock, close to the Temple of Wolfish Artemis; using water from the Spring of Hippocrene, and the blood of sacrificial victims. An ancient laurel-tree marks the place where the victims were afterwards buried; and the descendants of these nine men still dine annually at the Booth on a set day.[8]

i. Opposite the island of Cranaë, three furlongs from Gythium, stands an unwrought stone, named the stone of Zeus the Reliever, upon which Orestes sat and was temporarily relieved of his madness. He is said to have also been purified in seven streams near Italian Rhegium, where he built a temple; in three tributaries of the Thracian Hebrus; and in the Orontes, which flows past Antioch.[9]

j. Seven furlongs down the high road from Megalopolis to Messene, on the left, is shown a sanctuary of the Mad Goddesses, a title of the Erinnyes, who inflicted a raging fit of madness on Orestes; also a small mound, surmounted by a stone finger and called the Finger Tomb. This marks the place where, in desperation, he bit off a finger to placate these black goddesses, and some of them, at least, changed their hue to white, so that his sanity was restored. He then shaved his head at a near-by sanctuary called Acë, and made a sin-offering to the black goddesses, also a thank-offering to the white. It is now customary to sacrifice to the latter conjointly with the Graces.[10]

k. Next, Orestes went to live among the Azanes and Arcadians of the Parrhasian Plain which, with the neighbouring city formerly called Oresthasium after its founder Orestheus, son of Lycaon, changed its name to Oresteium. Some, however, say that Oresteium was formerly called Azania, and that he went to live there only after a visit to Athens. Others, again, say that he spent his exile in Epirus, where he founded the city of Orestic Argos and gave his name to the Orestae Paroraei, Epirots who inhabit the rugged foothills of the Illyrian mountains.[11]

l. When a year had passed, Orestes visited Athens, which was then governed by his kinsman Pandion; or, some say, by Demophoön. He went at once to Athene's temple on the Acropolis, sat down, and embraced her image. The Black Erinnyes soon arrived, out of breath, having lost track of him while he crossed the Isthmus. Though at his first arrival none wished to receive him, as being hated by the gods, presently some were emboldened to invite him into their houses, where he sat at a separate table and drank from a separate wine cup.[12]

m. The Erinnyes, who had already begun to accuse him to the Athenians, were soon joined by Tyndareus with his grand-daughter Erigone, daughter of Aegisthus and Clytaemnestra; also, some say, by Clytaemnestra's cousin Perilaus, son of Icarius. But Athene, having heard Orestes's supplication from Scamander, her newly-acquired Trojan territory, hurried to Athens and, swearing-in the noblest citizens as judges, summoned the Areopagus to try what was then only the second case of homicide to come before it.[13]

n. In due course the trial took place, Apollo appearing as counsel for the defence, and the eldest of the Erinnyes as public prosecutrix. In an elaborate speech, Apollo denied the importance of motherhood, asserting that a woman was no more than the inert furrow in which the husbandman cast his seed; and that Orestes had been abundantly justified in his act, the father being the one parent worthy of the name. When the voting proved equal, Athene confessed herself wholly on the father's side, and gave her casting vote in favour of Orestes. Thus honourably acquitted, he returned in joy to Argolis, swearing to be a faithful ally of Athens so long as he lived. The Erinnyes, however, loudly lamented this subversal of the ancient law by upstart gods; and Erigone hanged herself for mortification.[14]

o. Of Helen's end three other contradictory accounts survive. The first: that in fulfilment of Proteus's prophecy, she returned to Sparta and there lived with Menelaus in peace, comfort, and prosperity, until they went hand in hand to the Elysian Fields. The second: that she visited the Taurians with him, whereupon Iphigeneia sacrificed them both to Artemis. The third: that Polyxo, widow of the Rhodian King Tlepolemus, avenged his death by sending some of her serving women, disguised as Erinnyes, to hang Helen.[15]

1. Pausanias: ii. 16. 5.
2. Euripides: *Orestes*.
3. Homer: *Odyssey* iii. 306 ff.; Apollodorus: *Epitome* iii. 3; Euripides: *ibid*.
4. Euripides: *ibid*.
5. Euripides: *ibid*.
6. Hyginus: *Fabula* 120; Aeschylus: *Libation-bearers* 1034 ff. and *Eumenides* 34 ff., 64 ff., and 166–7; Euripides: *Electra* 1254–7.
7. Aeschylus: *Eumenides* 94 ff., 106–9, and 179 ff.
8. Asclepiades, quoted by Scholiast on Euripides's *Orestes* 1645. Aeschylus: *Eumenides* 235 ff. and 445 ff.; Pausanias: ii. 31. 7 and 11.
9. Pausanias: iii. 22. 1; Varro, quoted by Probus on Virgil's *Eclogues* i. 4, ed. Keil; Lampridius: *Life of Heliogabulus* vii. p. 809; Libanius: xi. 366d.
10. Pausanias: viii. 34. 1–2.
11. Euripides: *Orestes* 1645–7 and *Electra* 1254 ff.; Pausanias: viii. 3. 1; Stephanus of Byzantium *sub* Azania; Strabo: vii. 7. 8.

12. Scholiast on Aristophanes's *Knights* 95; *Acharnanians* 960; *Parian Chronicle* 40 ff.; Tzetzes: *On Lycophron* 1374; Aeschylus: *Eumenides* 235 ff.; Euripides: *Iphigeneia Among the Taurians* 947 ff.

13. Apollodorus: *Epitome* vi. 25; Pausanias: viii. 34. 2; Aeschylus: *Eumenides* 397, 470 ff., and 681 ff.

14. Euripides: *Iphigeneia Among the Taurians* 961 ff.; Aeschylus: *Eumenides* 574 ff., 734 ff., and 778 ff.; *Etymologicum Magnum* p. 42: *sub* Aiōra.

15. Homer: *Odyssey* iv. 561; Ptolemy Hephaestionos: iv.; Pausanias: iii. 19. 10.

*

1. The tradition that Clytaemnestra's Erinnyes drove Orestes mad cannot be dismissed as an invention of the Attic dramatists; it was too early established, not only in Greece, but in Greater Greece. Yet, just as Oedipus's crime, for which the Erinnyes hounded him to death, was not that he killed his mother, but that he inadvertently caused her suicide (see 105. *k*), so Orestes's murder seems also to have been in the second degree only: he had failed in filial duty by not opposing the Mycenaeans' death sentence. The court was easily enough swayed, as Menelaus and Tyndareus soon demonstrated when they secured a death sentence against Orestes.

2. Erinnyes were personified pangs of conscience, such as are still capable, in pagan Melanesia, of killing a man who has rashly or inadvertently broken a taboo. He will either go mad and leap from a coconut palm, or wrap his head in a cloak, like Orestes, and refuse to eat or drink until he dies of starvation; even if nobody else is informed of his guilt. Paul would have suffered a similar fate at Damascus but for the timely arrival of Ananias (*Acts* ix. 9 ff.). The common Greek method of purging ordinary blood guilt was for the homicide to sacrifice a pig and, while the ghost of the victim greedily drank its blood, to wash in running water, shave his head in order to change his appearance, and go into exile for one year, thus throwing the vengeful ghost off the scent. Until he had been purified in this manner, his neighbours shunned him as unlucky, and would not allow him to enter their homes or share their food, for fear of themselves becoming involved in his troubles; and he might still have to reckon with the victim's family, should the ghost demand vengeance from them. A mother's blood, however, carried with it so powerful a curse, that common means of purification would not serve: and, short of suicide, the most extreme means was to bite off a finger. This self-mutilation seems to have been at least partially successful in Orestes's case; thus also Heracles, to placate the aggrieved Hera, will have bitten off the finger which he is said to have lost while tussling with the Nemean Lion

(see 123. *e*). In some regions of the South Seas a finger-joint is always lopped off at the death of a close relative, even when he or she has died a natural death. In the *Eumenides* (397 ff.) Aeschylus is apparently disguising a tradition that Orestes fled to the Troad and lived, untroubled by the Erinnyes, under Athene's protection on silt land wrested from the Scamander and therefore free from the curse (see 107. *e*). Why else should the Troad be mentioned?

3. Wine instead of blood libations, and offerings of small hair-snippings instead of the whole crop, were Classical amendments on this ritual of appeasement, the significance of which was forgotten; as the present-day custom of wearing black is no longer consciously connected with the ancient habit of deceiving ghosts by altering one's normal appearance.

4. Euripides's imaginative account of what happened when Helen and Menelaus returned to Mycenae contains no mythical element, except for Helen's dramatic apotheosis; and Helen as the Moon-goddess had been a patroness of sailors long before the Heavenly Twins were recognized as a constellation. Like Aeschylus, Euripides was writing religious propaganda: Orestes's absolution records the final triumph of patriarchy, and is staged at Athens, where Athene – formerly the Libyan goddess Neith, or Palestinian Anatha, a supreme matriarch, but now reborn from Zeus's head and acknowledging, as Aeschylus insists, no divine mother – connives at matricide even in the first degree. The Athenian dramatists knew that this revolutionary theme could not be accepted elsewhere in Greece: hence Euripides makes Tyndareus, as Sparta's representative, declare passionately that Orestes must die; and the Dioscuri venture to condemn Apollo for having prompted the crime.

5. Orestes's name, 'mountaineer', has connected him with a wild, mountainous district in Arcadia which no King of Mycenae is likely to have visited.

6. These alternative versions of Helen's death are given for different reasons. The first purports to explain the cult of Helen and Menelaus at Therapne; the second is a theatrical variation on the story of Orestes's visit to the Taurians (see 116. *a–g*); the third accounts for the Rhodian cult of Helena Dendritis, 'Helen of the Tree', who is the same character as Ariadne and the other Erigone (see 79. *2* and 88. *10*). This Erigone was also hanged.

115

THE PACIFICATION OF THE ERINNYES

IN gratitude for his acquittal, Orestes dedicated an altar to Warlike Athene; but the Erinnyes threatened, if the judgement were not reversed, to let fall a drop of their own hearts' blood which would bring barrenness upon the soil, blight the crops, and destroy all the offspring of Athens. Athene nevertheless soothed their anger by flattery: acknowledging them to be far wiser than herself, she suggested that they should take up residence in a grotto at Athens, where they would gather such throngs of worshippers as they could never hope to find elsewhere. Hearth-altars proper to Underworld deities should be theirs, as well as sober sacrifices, torchlight libations, first-fruits offered after the consummation of marriage or the birth of children, and even seats in the Erechtheum. If they accepted this invitation she would decree that no house where worship was withheld from them might prosper; but they, in return, must undertake to invoke fair winds for her ships, fertility for her land, and fruitful marriages for her people – also rooting out the impious, so that she might see fit to grant Athens victory in war. The Erinnyes, after a short deliberation, graciously agreed to these proposals.

b. With expressions of gratitude, good wishes, and charms against withering winds, drought, blight, and sedition, the Erinnyes – henceforth addressed as the Solemn Ones – bade farewell to Athene, and were conducted by her people in a torchlight procession of youths, matrons, and crones (dressed in purple, and carrying the ancient image of Athene) to the entrance of a deep grotto at the south-eastern angle of the Areopagus. Appropriate sacrifices were there offered to them, and they descended into the grotto, which is now both an oracular shrine and, like the Sanctuary of Theseus, a place of refuge for suppliants.[1]

c. Yet only three of the Erinnyes had accepted Athene's generous offer; the remainder continued to pursue Orestes; and some people go so far as to deny that the Solemn Ones were ever Erinnyes. The name 'Eumenides' was first given to the Erinnyes by Orestes, in the following year, after his daring adventure in the Tauric Chersonese, when he finally succeeded in appeasing their fury at Carneia with the holocaust of a black sheep. They are called Eumenides also at Colonus, where none may enter their ancient grove; and at Achaean Cerynea where, towards the end of his life, Orestes dedicated a new sanctuary to them.[2]

d. In the grotto of the Solemn Ones at Athens – which is closed only to the second-fated, that is to say, to men who have been prematurely mourned for dead – their three images wear no more terrible an aspect than do those of the Underworld gods standing beside them, namely Hades, Hermes, and Mother Earth. Here those who have been acquitted of murder by the Areopagus sacrifice a black victim; numerous other offerings are brought to the Solemn Ones in accordance with Athene's promise; and one of the three nights set aside every month by the Areopagus for the hearing of murder trials is assigned to each of them.[3]

e. The rites of the Solemn Ones are silently performed; hence their priesthood is hereditary in the clan of the Hesychids, who offer the preliminary sacrifice of a ram to their ancestor Hesychus at his heroshrine outside the Nine Gates.[4]

f. A hearth-altar has also been provided for the Solemn Ones at Phlya, a small Attic township; and a grove of evergreen oaks is sacred to them near Titane, on the farther bank of the river Asopus. At their Phlyan festival, celebrated yearly, pregnant sheep are sacrificed, libations of honey-water poured, and flowers worn instead of the usual myrtle wreaths. Similar rites are performed at the altar of the Fates, which stands in the oak-grove, unprotected from the weather.[5]

1. Pausanias: i. 28. 5–6; Porphyry: *Concerning the Caves of the Nymphs* 3; Euripides: *Electra* 1272; Aristophanes: *Knights* 1312; Aeschylus: *Eumenides* 778–1047.
2. Euripides: *Iphigeneia Among the Taurians* 968 ff.; Philemon the Comedian, quoted by scholiast on Sophocles's *Oedipus at Colonus* 42; *Hypothesis* of Aeschylus's *Eumenides*; Pausanias: vii. 25. 4; Sophocles: *Oedipus at Colonus* 37 and 42–3.
3. Hesychius *sub* Deuteropotmoi; Polemon, quoted by scholiast on Sophocles: *loc. cit.* and 89; Pausanias: i. 28. 6; Scholiast on Aeschines's *Against Timarchus* 1. 188c; Lucian: *On the Hall* 18; Aeschylus: *Eumenides* 705.
4. Hesychius *sub* Hesychidae.
5. Pausanias: i. 31. 2 and ii. 11. 4.

*

1. The 'hearts' blood' of the Erinnyes, with which Attica was threatened, seems to be a euphemism for menstrual blood. An immemorial charm used by witches who wish to curse a house, field, or byre is to run naked around it, counter-sunwise, nine times, while in a menstrual condition. This curse is considered most dangerous to crops, cattle, and children during an eclipse of the moon; and altogether unavoidable if the witch is a virgin menstruating for the first time.

2. Philemon the Comedian did right to question the Athenian identification of the Erinnyes with the Solemn Ones. According to the most respected authorities, there were only three Erinnyes: Tisiphone, Alecto,

and Megaera (see 31. g), who lived permanently in Erebus, not at Athens. They had gods' heads, bats' wings, and serpents for hair; yet, as Pausanias points out, the Solemn Ones were portrayed as august matrons. Athene's offer, in fact, was not what Aeschylus has recorded; but an ultimatum from the priesthood of Zeus-born Athene to the priestesses of the Solemn Ones – the ancient Triple-goddess of Athens – that, unless they accepted the new view of fatherhood as superior to motherhood, and consented to share their grotto with such male underworld deities as Hades and Hermes, they would forfeit all worship whatsoever, and with it their traditional perquisites of first-fruits.

3. Second-fated men were debarred from entering the grotto of the Underworld goddesses, who might be expected to take offence that their dedicated subjects still wandered at large in the upper world. A similar embarrassment is felt in India when men recover from a death-like trance on their way to the burning ghat: in the last century, according to Rudyard Kipling, they used to be denied official existence and smuggled away to a prison colony of the dead. The evergreen oak, also called the kerm-oak, because it provides the kerm-berries (cochineal insects) from which the Greeks extracted scarlet dye, was the tree of the tanist who killed the sacred king, and therefore appropriate for a grove of the Solemn Ones. Sacrifices of pregnant sheep, honey, and flowers would encourage these to spare the remainder of the flock during the lambing season, favour the bees, and enrich the pasture.

4. The Erinnyes' continued pursuit of Orestes, despite the intervention of Athene and Apollo, suggests that, in the original myth, he went to Athens and Phocis for purification, but without success; as, in the myth of Eriphyle, Alcmaeon went unsuccessfully to Psophis and Thesprotia. Since Orestes is not reported to have found peace on the reclaimed silt of any river (see 107. e) – unless perhaps of the Scamander (see 114. 2)– he will have met his death in the Tauric Chersonese, or at Brauron (see 116. 1).

116

IPHIGENEIA AMONG THE TAURIANS

STILL pursued by such of the Erinnyes as had turned deaf ears to Athene's eloquent speeches, Orestes went in despair to Delphi, where he threw himself on the temple floor and threatened to take his own life unless Apollo saved him from their scourgings. In reply, the Pythian priestess ordered him to sail up the Bosphorus and northward across the Black Sea; his woes would end only when he had seized an ancient wooden image of Artemis from her temple in the Tauric Chersonese, and brought it to Athens or (some say) to Argolis.[1]

b. Now, the king of the Taurians was the fleet-footed Thoas, a son of Dionysus and Ariadne, and father of Hypsipyle; and his people, so called because Osiris once yoked bulls (*tauroi*) and ploughed their land, came of Scythian stock.[2] They still live by rapine, as in Thoas's days; and whenever one of their warriors takes a prisoner, he beheads him, carries the head home, and there impales it on a tall stake above the chimney, so that his household may live under the dead man's protection. Moreover, every sailor who has been shipwrecked, or driven into their port by rough weather, is publicly sacrificed to Taurian Artemis. When they have performed certain preparatory rites, they fell him with a club and nail his severed head to a cross; after which the body is either buried, or tossed into the sea from the precipice crowned by Artemis's temple. But any princely stranger who falls into their hands is killed with a sword by the goddess's virgin-priestess; and she throws his corpse into the sacred fire, welling up from Tartarus, which burns in the divine precinct. Some, however, say that the priestess, though supervising the rites, and performing the preliminary lustration and hair-cropping of the victim, does not herself kill him. The ancient image of the goddess, which Orestes was ordered to seize, had fallen here from Heaven. This temple is supported by vast columns, and approached by forty steps; its altar of white marble is permanently stained with blood.[3]

c. Taurian Artemis has several Greek titles: among them are Artemis Tauropolus, or Tauropole; Artemis Dictynna; Artemis Orthia; Thoantea; Hecate; and to the Latins she is Trivia.[4]

d. Now, Iphigeneia had been rescued from sacrifice at Aulis by Artemis, wrapped in a cloud, and wafted to the Tauric Chersonese, where she was at once appointed Chief Priestess and granted the sole right of handling the sacred image. The Taurians thereafter addressed her as Artemis, or Hecate, or Orsiloche. Iphigeneia loathed human sacrifice, but piously obeyed the goddess.[5]

e. Orestes and Pylades knew nothing of all this; they still believed that Iphigeneia had died under the sacrificial knife at Aulis. Nevertheless, they hastened to the land of the Taurians in a fifty-oared ship which, on arrival, they left at anchor, guarded by their oarsmen, while they hid in a sea-cave. It was their intention to approach the temple at nightfall, but they were surprised beforehand by some credulous herdsmen who, assuming them to be the Dioscuri, or some other pair of immortals, fell down and adored them. At this juncture Orestes went mad once more, bellowing like a calf and howling like a dog; he mistook a herd of calves for Erinnyes, and rushed from the cave, sword in hand, to slaughter them. The disillusioned herdsmen thereupon overpowered the two friends who, at Thoas's orders, were marched off to the temple for immediate sacrifice.[6]

f. During the preliminary rites Orestes conversed in Greek with Iphigeneia; soon they joyfully discovered each other's identity, and on learning the nature of his mission, she began to lift down the image for him to carry away. Thoas, however, suddenly appeared, impatient at the slow progress of the sacrifice, and the resourceful Iphigeneia pretended to be soothing the image. She explained to Thoas that the goddess had averted her gaze from the victims whom he had sent, because one was a matricide, and the other was abetting him: both were quite unfit for sacrifice. She must take them, together with the image, which their presence had polluted, to be cleansed in the sea, and offer the goddess a torchlight sacrifice of young lambs. Meanwhile, Thoas was to purify the temple with a torch, cover his head when the strangers emerged, and order everyone to remain at home and thus avoid pollution.

g. Thoas, wholly deceived, stood for a time lost in admiration of such sagacity, and then began to purify the temple. Presently Iphigeneia, Orestes, and Pylades conveyed the image down to the shore by torchlight but, instead of bathing it in the sea, hastily carried it aboard their ship. The Taurian temple-servants, who had come with them, now suspected treachery and showed fight. They were subdued in a hard struggle, after which Orestes's oarsmen rowed the ship away. A sudden gale, however, sprang up, driving her back towards the rocky shore, and all would have perished, had not Poseidon calmed the sea at Athene's request; with a favouring breeze, they made the Island of Sminthos.[7]

h. This was the home of Chryses, the priest of Apollo, and his grandson of the same name, whose mother Chryseis now proposed to surrender the fugitives to Thoas. For, although some hold that Athene had visited Thoas, who was manning a fleet to sail in pursuit, and cajoled him so successfully that he even consented to repatriate Iphigeneia's Greek slave-women, it is certain that he came to Sminthos with murderous intentions. Then Chryses the Elder, learning the identity of his guests, revealed to Chryses the Younger that he was not, as Chryseis had always pretended, Apollo's son, but Agamemnon's, and therefore half-brother to Orestes and Iphegeneia. At this, Chryses and Orestes rushed shoulder to shoulder against Thoas, whom they succeeded in killing; and Orestes, taking up the image, sailed safely home to Mycenae, where the Erinnyes at last abandoned their chase.[8]

i. But some say that a storm drove Orestes to Rhodes where, in accordance with the Helian Oracle, he set up the image upon a city wall. Others say that, since Attica was the land to which he had been instructed to bring it, by Apollo's orders, Athene visited him on Sminthos and specified the frontier city of Brauron as its destination: it must be housed there in a temple of Artemis Tauropolus, and placated with blood drawn from a man's throat. She designated Iphigeneia as the priestess of this temple, in which she was destined to end her days peacefully; the perquisites would include the clothes of rich women who had died in childbed. According to this account, the ship finally made port at Brauron, where Iphigeneia deposited the image and then, while the temple was being built, went with Orestes to Delphi; she met Electra in the shrine and brought her back to Athens for marriage to Pylades.[9]

j. What is claimed to be the authentic wooden image of Tauric Artemis may still be seen at Brauron. Some, however, say that it is only a replica, the original having been captured by Xerxes in the course of his ill-fated expedition against Greece, and taken to Susa; afterwards, they add, it was presented by King Seleucus of Syria to the Laodicaeans, who worship it to this day. Others, again, loth to allow credit to Xerxes, say that Orestes himself, on his homeward voyage from the Tauric Chersonese, was driven by a storm to the region now named Seleuceia, where he left the image; and that the natives renamed Mount Melantius, where the madness finally left him, Mount Amanon, that is 'not mad', in his memory. But the Lydians, who have a sanctuary of Artemis Anaeitis, also claim to possess the image; and so do the people of Cappadocian Comana, whose city is said to take its name from the mourning tresses (*comai*) which Orestes deposited there, when he brought the rites of Artemis Tauropolus into Cappadocia.[10]

k. Others, again, say that Orestes concealed the image in a bundle of faggots, and took it to Italian Aricia, where he himself died and was buried, his bones being later transferred to Rome; and that the image was sent from Aricia to Sparta, because the cruelty of its rites displeased the Romans; and there placed in the Sanctuary of Upright Artemis.[11]

l. But the Spartans claim that the image has been theirs since long before the foundation of Rome, Orestes having brought it with him when he became their king, and hidden it in a willow thicket. For centuries, they say, its whereabouts were forgotten; until, one day, Astrabacus and Alopecus, two princes of the royal house, entering the thicket by chance, were driven mad at the sight of the grim image, which was kept upright by the willow-branches wreathed around it – hence its names, Orthia and Lygodesma.

m. No sooner was the image brought to Sparta, than an ominous quarrel arose between rival devotees of Artemis, who were sacrificing together at her altar: many of them were killed in the sanctuary itself, the remainder died of plague shortly afterwards. When an oracle advised the Spartans to propitiate the image by drenching the altar with human blood, they cast lots for a victim and sacrificed him; and this ceremony was repeated yearly until King Lycurgus, who abhorred human sacrifice, forbade it, and instead ordered boys to be flogged at the altar until it reeked with blood.[12] Spartan boys now compete once a year as to who can endure the most blows. Artemis's priestess stands by, carrying the image which, although small and light, acquired such relish for blood in the days when human sacrifices were offered to it by the Taurians that, even now, if the floggers lay on gently, because the boy is of noble birth, or exceptionally handsome, it grows almost too heavy for her to hold, and she chides the floggers: 'Harder, harder! You are weighing me down!'[13]

n. Little credence should be given to the tale that Helen and Menelaus went in search of Orestes and, arriving among the Taurians shortly after he did, were both sacrificed to the goddess by Iphigeneia.[14]

1. Apollodorus: *Epitome* vi. 26; Euripides: *Iphigeneia Among the Taurians* 77 and 970 ff.; Hyginus: *Fabula* 120.
2. Euripides: *Iphigeneia Among the Taurians* 32; Scholiast on Apollonius Rhodius: iii. 997; Eustathius: *On Dionysus* 306; Apollodorus: *Epitome* vi. 26.
3. Herodotus: iv. 103; Ovid: *Pontic Epistles* iii. 2. 45 ff.; Apollodorus: *Epitome* vi. 26; Euripides: *Iphigeneia Among the Taurians* 40 ff. and 88 ff.
4. Diodorus Siculus: iv. 44. 7; Sophocles: *Ajax* 172; Pausanias: i. 23. 9; Servius on Virgil's *Aeneid* ii. 116; Valerius Flaccus: viii. 208;

Ovid: *Ibis* 384 and *Pontic Epistles* iii. 2. 71; *Orphic Argonautica* 1065.

5. Euripides: *Iphigeneia Among the Taurians* 784 and 1045; Ovid: *Pontic Epistles* iii. 2. 45 ff.; Herodotus: iv. 103; Hesiod: *Catalogue of Women*, quoted by Pausanias: i. 43. 1; Ammianus Marcellinus: xxii. 8. 34.

6. Hyginus: *Fabula* 120; Apollodorus: *Epitome* vi. 27.

7. Ovid: *Pontic Epistles loc. cit.*; Hyginus: *loc. cit.*; Euripides: *Iphigeneia Among the Taurians* 1037 ff.

8. Hyginus: *Fabulae* 120 and 121; Euripides: *Iphigeneia Among the Taurians* 1435 ff.; Hyginus: *Fabula* 121.

9. Apollodorus: *Epitome* vi. 27; Euripides: *Iphigeneia Among the Taurians* 89–91 and 1446 ff.; Pausanias: i. 33. 1; Tzetzes: *On Lycophron* 1374.

10. Pausanias: i. 23. 9, iii. 16. 6 and viii. 46. 2; Tzetzes: *loc. cit.*; Strabo: xii. 2. 3.

11. Servius on Virgil's *Aeneid* ii. 116 and vi. 136; Hyginus: *Fabula* 261.

12. Pausanias: iii. 16. 6–7.

13. Hyginus: *Fabula* 261; Servius on Virgil's *Aeneid* ii. 116; Pausanias: *loc. cit.*

14. Ptolemy Hephaestionos: iv, quoted by Photius: p. 479.

*

1. The mythographers' anxiety to conceal certain barbarous traditions appears plainly in this story and its variants. Among the suppressed elements are Artemis's vengeance on Agamemnon for the murder of Iphigeneia, and Oeax's vengeance, also on Agamemnon, for the murder of his brother Palamedes. Originally, the myth seems to have run somewhat as follows: Agamemnon was prevailed upon, by his fellow-chieftains, to execute his daughter Iphigeneia as a witch when the Greek expedition against Troy lay windbound at Aulis. Artemis, whom Iphigeneia had served as priestess, made Agamemnon pay for this insult to her: she helped Aegisthus to supplant and murder him on his return. At her inspiration also, Oeax offered to take Orestes on a voyage to the land reclaimed from the river Scamander and thus help him to escape the Erinnyes; for Athene would protect him there (see 115. 4). Instead, Oeax put in at Brauron, where Orestes was acclaimed as the annual *pharmacos*, a scapegoat for the guilt of the people, and had his throat slit by Artemis's virgin-priestess. Oeax, in fact, told Electra the truth when they met at Delphi: that Orestes had been sacrificed by Iphigeneia, which seems to have been a title of Artemis (see 117. 1).

2. Patriarchal Greeks of a later era will have disliked this myth – a version of which, making Menelaus, not Orestes, the object of Artemis's

vengeance, has been preserved by Photius. They exculpated Agamemnon of murder, and Artemis of opposing the will of Zeus, by saying that she doubtless rescued Iphigeneia, and carried her away to be a sacrificial priestess – not at Brauron, but among the savage Taurians, for whose actions they disclaimed responsibility. And that she certainly did not kill Orestes (or, for the matter of that, any Greek victim) but, on the contrary, helped him to take the Tauric image to Greece at Apollo's orders.

3. This face-saving story, influenced by the myth of Jason's expedition to the Black Sea – in Servius's version, Orestes steals the image from Colchis, not the Tauric Chersonese – explained the tradition of human throat-slitting at Brauron, now modified to the extraction of a drop of blood from a slight cut, and similar sacrifices at Mycenae, Aricia, Rhodes, and Comana. 'Tauropolus' suggests the Cretan bull sacrifice, which survived in the Athenian Buphonia (Pausanias: i. 28. 11); the original victim is likely to have been the sacred king.

4. The Spartan fertility rites, also said to have once involved human sacrifice, were held in honour of Upright Artemis. To judge from primitive practice elsewhere in the Mediterranean, the victim was bound with willow-thongs, full of lunar magic, to the image – a sacred tree-stump, perhaps of pear-wood (see 74. 6), and flogged until the lashes induced an erotic reaction and he ejaculated, fertilizing the land with semen and blood. Alopecus's name, and the well-known legend of the youth who allowed his vitals to be gnawed by a fox rather than cry out, suggest that the Vixen-goddess of Teumessus was also worshipped at Sparta (see 49. 2 and 89. 8).

5. Meteorites were often paid divine honours, and so were small ritual objects of doubtful origin which could be explained as having similarly fallen from heaven – such as the carefully worked neolithic spearheads, identified with Zeus's thunderbolts by the later Greeks (as flint arrows are called 'elf shots' in the English countryside), or the bronze pestle hidden in the head-dress worn by the image of Ephesian Artemis. The images themselves, such as the Brauronian Artemis and the olive-wood Athene in the Erechtheum, were then likewise said to have fallen from heaven, through a hole in the roof (see 158. k). It is possible that the image at Brauron contained an ancient sacrificial knife of obsidian – a volcanic glass from the island of Melos – with which the victims' throats were slit.

6. Osiris's ploughing of the Tauric Chersonese (the Crimea), seems forced; but Herodotus insists on a close link between Colchis and Egypt (ii. 104), and Colchis has here been confused with the land of the Taurians. Osiris, like Triptolemus, is said to have introduced agriculture into many foreign lands (see 24. m).

AEGISTHUS's son Aletes now usurped the kingdom of Mycenae, believing the malicious rumour [? spread by Oeax] that Orestes and Pylades had been sacrificed on the altar of Tauric Artemis. But Electra, doubting its truth, went to consult the Delphic Oracle. Iphigeneia had just arrived at Delphi, and [? Oeax] pointed her out to Electra as Orestes's murderess. Revengefully she seized a firebrand from the altar and, not recognizing Iphigeneia after the lapse of years, was about to blind her with it, when Orestes himself entered and explained all. The reunited children of Agamemnon then went joyfully back to Mycenae, where Orestes ended the feud between the House of Atreus and the House of Thyestes, by killing Aletes; whose sister Erigone, it is said, would also have perished by his hand, had not Artemis snatched her away to Attica. But afterwards Orestes relented towards her.[1]

b. Some say that Iphigeneia died either at Brauron, or at Megara, where she now has a sanctuary; others, that Artemis immortalized her as the Younger Hecate. Electra, married to Pylades, bore him Medon and Strophius the Second; she lies buried at Mycenae. Orestes married his cousin Hermione – having been present at the sacrificial murder of Achilles's son Neoptolemus, to whom she was betrothed.[2] By her he became the father of Tisamenus, his heir and successor; and by Erigone his second wife, of Penthilus.[3]

c. When Menelaus died, the Spartans invited Orestes to become their king, preferring him, as a grandson of Tyndareus, to Nicostratus and Megapenthes, begotten by Menelaus on a slave-girl. Orestes who, with the help of troops furnished by his Phocian allies, had already added a large part of Arcadia to his Mycenaean domains, now made himself master of Argos as well; for King Cylarabes, grandson of Capaneus, left no issue. He also subdued Achaea but, in obedience to the Delphic Oracle, finally emigrated from Mycenae to Arcadia where, at the age of seventy, he died of a snake bite at Oresteium, or Orestia, the town which he had founded during his exile.[4]

d. Orestes was buried at Tegea, but in the reign of Anaxandrides, co-king with Aristo, and the only Laconian who ever had two wives and occupied two houses at the same time, the Spartans, in despair because they had hitherto lost every battle fought with the Tegeans, sent to Delphi for advice, and were instructed to possess themselves of Orestes's bones. Since the whereabouts of these were unknown, they sent Lichas, one of Sparta's benefactors, to ask for further enlightenment. He was given the following response in hexameters:

> *Level and smooth the plain of Arcadian Tegea. Go thou*
> *Where two winds are ever, by strong necessity, blowing;*
> *Where stroke rings upon stroke, where evil lies upon evil;*
> *There all-teeming earth doth enclose the prince whom thou seekest.*
> *Bring thou him to thy house, and thus be Tegea's master!*

Because of a temporary truce between the two states, Lichas had no difficulty in visiting Tegea; where he came upon a smith forging a sword of iron, instead of bronze, and gazed open-mouthed at the novel sight. 'Does this work surprise you?' cried the jovial smith. 'Well, I have something here to surprise you even more! It is a coffin, seven cubits long, containing a corpse of the same length, which I found beneath the smithy floor while I was digging yonder well.'

e. Lichas guessed that the winds mentioned in the verses must be those raised by the smith's bellows; the strokes those of his hammer; and the evil lying upon evil, his hammer-head beating out the iron sword – for the Iron Age brought in cruel days. He at once returned with the news to Sparta, where the judges, at his own suggestion, pretended to condemn him for a crime of violence; then, fleeing to Tegea as if from execution, he persuaded the smith to hide him in the smithy. At midnight, he stole the bones out of the coffin and hurried back to Sparta, where he re-interred them near the sanctuary of the Fates; the tomb is still shown. Spartan armies have ever since been consistently victorious over the Tegeans.[5]

f. Pelops's spear-sceptre, which his grandson Orestes also wielded, was discovered in Phocis about this time: lying buried with a hoard of gold on the frontier between Chaeronea and Phanoteus, where it had probably been hidden by Electra. When an inquest was held on this treasure-trove, the Phanotians were content with the gold; but the Chaeroneans took the sceptre, and now worship it as their supreme deity. Each priest of the spear, appointed for one year, keeps it in his own house, offering daily victims to its divinity, beside tables lavishly spread with every kind of food.[6]

g. Yet some deny that Orestes died in Arcadia. They say that after his term of exile there, he was ordered by an oracle to visit Lesbos and

Tenedos and found colonies, with settlers gathered from various cities, including Amyclae. He did so, calling his new people Aeolians because Aeolis was their nearest common ancestor, but died soon after building a city in Lesbos. This migration took place, they say, four generations before the Ionian. Others, however, declare that Orestes's son Penthilus, not Orestes himself, conquered Lesbos; that his grandson Gras, aided by the Spartans, occupied the country between Ionia and Mysia, now called Aeolis; and that another grandson, Archelaus, took Aeolian settlers to the present city of Cyzicene, near Dascylium, on the southern shores of the Sea of Marmara.⁷

h. Tisamenus meanwhile succeeded to his father's dominions, but was driven from the capital cities of Sparta, Mycenae, and Argos by the sons of Heracles, and took refuge with his army in Achaea. His son Cometes emigrated to Asia.⁸

1. Hyginus: *Fabula* 122.
2. Euripides: *Iphigeneia Among the Taurians* 1464 and 915; Pausanias: i. 43. 1 and x. 24. 4–5; Hellanicus, quoted by Pausanias: ii. 16. 5; Hyginus: *Fabula* 123; Strabo: ix. 3. 9.
3. Apollodorus: *Epitome* vi. 28; Cinaethon, quoted by Pausanias: ii. 18. 5; Tzetzes: *On Lycophron* 1374.
4. Pausanias: ii. 18. 5 and viii. 5. 1–3; Asclepiades, quoted by scholiast on Euripides's *Orestes* 1647; Apollodorus: *loc. cit.*; Tzetzes: *loc. cit.*
5. Pausanias: iii. 3. 7; iii. 11. 8; iii. 3. 5–7 and viii. 54. 3; Herodotus: i. 67–8.
6. Pausanias: ix. 40. 6.
7. Pindar: *Nemean Odes* xi. 33–5; Hellanicus, quoted by Tzetzes: *On Lycophron* 1374; Pausanias: iii. 2. 1; Strabo: xiii. 1. 3.
8. Pausanias: ii. 8. 6–7 and vii. 6. 21.

*

1. Iphigeneia seems to have been a title of the earlier Artemis, who was not merely maiden, but also nymph – 'Iphigeneia' means 'mothering a strong race' – and 'crone', namely the Solemn Ones or Triple Hecate. Orestes is said to have reigned in so many places that his name must also be regarded as a title. His death by snake bite at Arcadian Oresteia links him with other primitive kings: such as Apesantus son of Acrisius (see 123. *e*), identifiable with Opheltes of Nemea (see 106. *g*); Munitus son of Athamas (see 168. *e*); Mopsus the Lapith (see 154. *f*), bitten by a Libyan snake; and Egyptian Ra, an aspect of Osiris, also bitten by a Libyan snake. These bites are always in the heel; in some cases, among them those of Cheiron and Pholus the Centaurs, Talus the Cretan, Achilles the Myrmidon, and Philoctetes the Euboean, the venom seems to have been conveyed on an arrow-point (see 92. *10*). The Arcadian Orestes was, in fact, a Pelasgian with Libyan connexions.

2. Artemis's rescue of Erigone from Orestes's vengeance is one more incident in the feud between the House of Thyestes, assisted by Artemis, and the House of Atreus, assisted by Zeus. Tisamenus's name ('avenging strength') suggests that the feud was bequeathed to the succeeding generation: because, according to one of Apollodorus's accounts (*Epitome* vi. 28), he was Erigone's son, not Hermione's. Throughout the story of this feud it must be remembered that the Artemis who here measures her strength with Zeus is the earlier matriarchal Artemis, rather than Apollo's loving twin, the maiden huntress; the mythographers have done their best to obscure Apollo's active participation, on Zeus's side, in this divine quarrel.

3. Giants' bones, usually identified with those of a tribal ancestor, were regarded as a magical means of protecting a city; thus the Athenians, by oracular inspiration, recovered what they claimed to be Theseus's bones from Scyros and brought them back to Athens (see 104. *i*). These may well have been unusually large, because a race of giants – of which the Hamitic Watusi who live in Equatorial Africa are an offshoot – flourished in neolithic Europe, and their seven-foot skeletons have occasionally been found even in Britain. The Anakim of Palestine and Caria (see 88. *3*) belonged to this race. However, if Orestes was an Achaean of the Trojan War period, the Athenians could not have found and measured his skeleton, since the Homeric nobles practised cremation, not inhumation in the neolithic style.

4. 'Evil lying upon evil' is usually interpreted as the iron sword that was being forged on an iron anvil; but stone anvils were the rule until a comparatively late epoch, and the hammer-head as it rests upon the sword is the more likely explanation – though, indeed, iron hammers were also rare until Roman times. Iron was too holy and infrequent a metal for common use by the Mycenaeans – not being extracted from ore, but collected in the form of divinely-sent meteorites – and when eventually iron weapons were imported into Greece from Tibarene on the Black Sea, the smelting process and manufacture remained secret for some time. Blacksmiths continued to be called 'bronze workers' even in the Hellenistic period. But as soon as anyone might possess an iron weapon or tool, the age of myth came to an end; if only because iron was not included among the five metals sacred to the goddess and linked with her calendar rites: namely, silver, gold, copper, tin, and lead (see 53. *2*).

5. Pelops's spear-sceptre, token of sovereignty, evidently belonged to the ruling priestess; thus, according to Euripides, the spear with which Oenomaus was killed – presumably the same instrument – was hidden

in Iphigeneia's bedroom; Clytaemnestra then claims to possess it (Sophocles: *Electra* 651); and Electra is said by Pausanias to have brought it to Phocis. The Greeks of Asia Minor were pleased to think that Orestes had founded the first Aeolian colony there: his name being one of their royal titles. They may have been relying on a tradition that concerned a new stage in the history of kingship: when the king's reign came to an end, he was now spared death and allowed to sacrifice a surrogate – an act of homicide that would account for Orestes's second exile – after which he might lead a colony overseas. The mythographers who explained that the Spartans preferred Orestes to Menelaus's sons because these were born of a slave-woman, did not realize that descent was still matrilinear. Orestes, as a Mycenaean, could reign by marriage to the Spartan heiress Hermione; her brothers must seek kingdoms elsewhere. In Argolis a princess could have free-born children by a slave; and there was nothing to prevent Electra's peasant husband at Mycenae from raising claimants for the throne.

6. The psalmist's tradition that 'the days of a man are three score and ten,' is founded not on observation, but on religious theory: seven was the number of holiness, and ten of perfection. Orestes similarly attained seventy years.

7. Anaxandrides's breach of the monogamic tradition may have been due to dynastic necessity; perhaps Aristo, his co-king, died too soon before the end of his reign to warrant a new coronation and, since he had ruled by virtue of his marriage to an heiress, Anaxandrides substituted for him both as king and husband.

8. Hittite records show that there was already an Achaean kingdom in Lesbos during the late fourteenth century B.C.

118

THE BIRTH OF HERACLES

ELECTRYON, son of Perseus, High King of Mycenae and husband of Anaxo, marched vengefully against the Taphians and Teleboans. They had joined in a successful raid on his cattle, planned by one Pterelaus, a claimant to the Mycenaean throne; which had resulted in the death of Electryon's eight sons. While he was away, his nephew King Amphitryon of Troezen acted as regent. 'Rule well, and when I return victorious, you shall marry my daughter Alcmene,' Electryon cried in farewell. Amphitryon, informed by the King of Elis that the stolen cattle were now in his possession, paid the large ransom demanded, and recalled Electryon to identify them. Electryon, by no means pleased to learn that Amphitryon expected him to repay this ransom, asked harshly what right had the Eleans to sell stolen property, and why did Amphitryon condone in a fraud? Disdaining to reply, Amphitryon vented his annoyance by throwing a club at one of the cows which had strayed from the herd; it struck her horns, rebounded, and killed Electryon. Thereupon Amphitryon was banished from Argolis by his uncle Sthenelus; who seized Mycenae and Tiryns and entrusted the remainder of the country, with Midea for its capital, to Atreus and Thyestes, the sons of Pelops.[1]

b. Amphitryon, accompanied by Alcmene, fled to Thebes, where King Creon purified him and gave his sister Perimede in marriage to Electryon's only surviving son, Licymnius, a bastard borne by a Phrygian woman named Midea.[2] But the pious Alcmene would not lie with Amphitryon until he had avenged the death of her eight brothers. Creon therefore gave him permission to raise a Boeotian army for this purpose, on condition that he freed Thebes of the Teumessian vixen; which he did by borrowing the celebrated hound Laelaps from Cephalus the Athenian. Then, aided by Athenian, Phocian, Argive, and Locrian contingents, Amphitryon overcame the Teleboans and Taphians, and bestowed their islands on his allies, among them his uncle Heleius.

c. Meanwhile, Zeus, taking advantage of Amphitryon's absence, impersonated him and, assuring Alcmene that her brothers were now avenged – since Amphitryon had indeed gained the required victory that very morning – lay with her all one night, to which he gave the length of three.[3] For Hermes, at Zeus's command, had ordered Helius to quench the solar fires, have the Hours unyoke his team, and spend the following day at home; because the procreation of so great a champion as Zeus had in mind could not be accomplished in haste. Helius obeyed, grumbling about the good old times, when day was day, and night was night; and when Cronus, the then Almighty God, did not leave his lawful wife and go off to Thebes on love adventures. Hermes next ordered the Moon to go slowly, and Sleep to make mankind so drowsy that no one would notice what was happening.[4] Alcmene, wholly deceived, listened delightedly to Zeus's account of the crushing defeat inflicted on Pterelaus at Oechalia, and sported innocently with her supposed husband for the whole thirty-six hours. On the next day, when Amphitryon returned, eloquent of victory and of his passion for her, Alcmene did not welcome him to the marriage couch so rapturously as he had hoped. 'We never slept a wink last night,' she complained. 'And surely you do not expect me to listen twice to the story of your exploits?' Amphitryon, unable to understand these remarks, consulted the seer Teiresias, who told him that he had been cuckolded by Zeus; and thereafter he never dared sleep with Alcmene again, for fear of incurring divine jealousy.[5]

d. Nine months later, on Olympus, Zeus happened to boast that he had fathered a son, now at the point of birth, who would be called Heracles, which means 'Glory of Hera', and rule the noble House of Perseus. Hera thereupon made him promise that any prince born before nightfall to the House of Perseus should be High King. When Zeus swore an unbreakable oath to this effect, Hera went at once to Mycenae, where she hastened the pangs of Nicippe, wife of King Sthenelus. She then hurried to Thebes, and squatted cross-legged at Alcmene's door, with her clothing tied into knots, and her fingers locked together; by which means she delayed the birth of Heracles, until Eurystheus, son of Sthenelus, a seven-months child, already lay in his cradle. When Heracles appeared, one hour too late, he was found to have a twin named Iphicles, Amphitryon's son and the younger by a night. But some say that Heracles, not Iphicles, was the younger by a night; and others, that the twins were begotten on the same night, and born together, and that Father Zeus divinely illumined the birth chamber. At first, Heracles was called Alcaeus, or Palaemon.[6]

e. When Hera returned to Olympus, and calmly boasted of her success in keeping Eileithyia, goddess of childbirth, from Alcmene's door, Zeus fell into a towering rage; seizing his eldest daughter Ate, who had blinded him to Hera's deceit, he took a mighty oath that she should never visit Olympus again. Whirled around his head by her golden hair, Ate was sent hurtling down to earth. Though Zeus could not go back on his word and allow Heracles to rule the House of Perseus, he persuaded Hera to agree that, after performing whatever twelve labours Eurystheus might set him, his son should become a god.[7]

f. Now, unlike Zeus's former human loves, from Niobe onwards, Alcmene had been selected not so much for his pleasure – though she surpassed all other women of her day in beauty, stateliness, and wisdom – as with a view to begetting a son powerful enough to protect both gods and men against destruction. Alcmene, sixteenth in descent from the same Niobe, was the last mortal woman with whom Zeus lay, for he saw no prospect of begetting a hero to equal Heracles by any other; and he honoured Alcmene so highly that, instead of roughly violating her, he took pains to disguise himself as Amphitryon and woo her with affectionate words and caresses. He knew Alcmene to be incorruptible and when, at dawn, he presented her with a Carchesian goblet, she accepted it without question as spoil won in the victory: Telebus's legacy from his father Poseidon.[8]

g. Some say that Hera did not herself hinder Alcmene's travail, but sent witches to do so, and that Historis, daughter of Teiresias, deceived them by raising a cry of joy from the birth chamber – which is still shown at Thebes – so that they went away and allowed the child to be born. According to others, it was Eileithyia who hindered the travail on Hera's behalf, and a faithful handmaiden of Alcmene's, the yellow-haired Galanthis, or Galen, who left the birth chamber to announce, untruly, that Alcmene had been delivered. When Eileithyia sprang up in surprise, unclasping her fingers and uncrossing her knees, Heracles was born, and Galanthis laughed at the successful deception – which provoked Eileithyia to seize her by the hair and turn her into a weasel. Galanthis continued to frequent Alcmene's house, but was punished by Hera for having lied: she was condemned in perpetuity to bring forth her young through the mouth. When the Thebans pay Heracles divine honours, they still offer preliminary sacrifices to Galanthis, who is also called Galinthias and described as Proetus's daughter; saying that she was Heracles's nurse and that he built her a sanctuary.[9]

h. This Theban account is derided by the Athenians. They hold that Galanthis was a harlot, turned weasel by Hecate in punishment for practising unnatural lust, who when Hera unduly prolonged Alcmene's labour, happened to run past and frighten her into delivery.[10]

i. Heracles's birthday is celebrated on the fourth day of every month; but some hold that he was born as the Sun entered the Tenth Sign; others that the Great Bear, swinging westward at midnight over Orion – which it does as the Sun quits the Twelfth Sign – looked down on him in his tenth month.[11]

1. Apollodorus: ii. 4. 5–6; Tzetzes: *On Lycophron* 932; Hesiod: *Shield of Heracles* 11 ff.
2. Apollodorus: *loc. cit.*
3. Hesiod: *Shield of Heracles* 1–56; Apollodorus: ii. 4. 7–8; Hyginus: *Fabula* 28; Tzetzes: *On Lycophron* 33 and 932; Pindar: *Isthmian Odes* vii. 5.

4. Lucian: *Dialogues of the Gods* x.
5. Hesiod: *Shield of Heracles* 1–56; Apollodorus: ii. 4. 7–8; Hyginus: *Fabula* 29; Tzetzes: *On Lycophron* 33 and 932; Pindar: *Isthmian Odes* vii. 5.
6. Hesiod: *Shield of Heracles* i. 35, 56, and 80; Homer: *Iliad* xix. 95; Apollodorus: ii. 4–5; Theocritus, quoted by scholiast on Pindar's *Nemean Odes* i. 36; Plautus: *Amphitryo* 1096; Diodorus Siculus: iv. 10; Tzetzes: *On Lycophron* 662.
7. Homer: *Iliad* xix. 119 ff. and 91; Diodorus Siculus: iv. 9 and 14.
8. Hesiod: *Shield of Heracles* 4 ff. and 26 ff.; Pherecydes, quoted by Athenaeus: xi. 7; Athenaeus: xi. 99; Plautus: *Amphitryo* 256 ff.
9. Pausanias: ix. 11. 1–2; Ovid: *Metamorphoses* ix. 285 ff.; Aelian: *Nature of Animals* xii. 5; Antoninus Liberalis: *Transformations* 29.
10. Aelian: *Nature of Animals* xv. 11; Antoninus Liberalis: *loc. cit.*
11. Philochorus: *Fragment* 177; Ovid: *Metamorphoses* ix. 285 ff.; Theocritus: *Idylls* xxiv. 11–12.

*

1. Alcmene ('strong in wrath') will have originally been a Mycenaean title of Hera, whose divine sovereignty Heracles ('glory of Hera') protected against the encroachments of her Achaean enemy Perseus ('destroyer'). The Achaeans eventually triumphed, and their descendants claimed Heracles as a member of the usurping House of Perseus. Hera's detestation of Heracles is likely to be a later invention; he was worshipped by the Dorians who overran Elis and there humbled the power of Hera.

2. Diodorus Siculus (iii. 73) writes of three heroes named Heracles: an Egyptian; a Cretan Dactyl; and the son of Alcmene. Cicero raises this number to six (*On the Nature of the Gods* iii. 16); Varro to forty-four (Servius on Virgil's *Aeneid* viii. 564). Herodotus (ii. 42) says that when he asked for Heracles's original home, the Egyptians referred him to Phoenicia. According to Diodorus Siculus (i. 17 and 24; iii. 73), the Egyptian Heracles, called Som, or Chon, lived ten thousand years before the Trojan War, and his Greek namesake inherited his exploits. The story of Heracles is, indeed, a peg on which a great number of related, unrelated, and contradictory myths have been hung. In the main, however, he represents the typical sacred king of early Hellenic Greece, consort of a tribal nymph, the Moon-goddess incarnate; his twin Iphicles acted as his tanist. This Moon-goddess has scores of names: Hera, Athene, Auge, Iole, Hebe, and so forth. On an early Roman bronze mirror Jupiter is shown celebrating a sacred marriage between 'Hercele' and 'Juno'; moreover, at Roman weddings the knot in the bride's girdle consecrated to Juno was called the 'Herculean knot', and the bridegroom had to untie it (Festus: 63). The Romans derived this tradition from the Etruscans, whose Juno was named 'Unial'. It may be assumed that the central

story of Heracles was an early variant of the Babylonian Gilgamesh epic – which reached Greece by way of Phoenicia. Gilgamesh has Enkidu for his beloved comrade, Heracles has Iolaus. Gilgamesh is undone by his love for the goddess Ishtar, Heracles by his love for Deianeira. Both are of divine parentage. Both harrow Hell. Both kill lions and overcome divine bulls; and when sailing to the Western Isle Heracles, like Gilgamesh, uses his garment for a sail (see 132. *c*). Heracles finds the magic herb of immortality (see 35. *b*) as Gilgamesh does, and is similarly connected with the progress of the sun around the Zodiac.

3. Zeus is made to impersonate Amphitryon because when the sacred king underwent a rebirth at his coronation, he became titularly a son of Zeus, and disclaimed his mortal parentage (see 74. 1). Yet custom required the mortal tanist – rather than the divinely born king, the elder of the twins – to lead military expeditions; and the reversal of this rule in Heracles's case suggests that he was once the tanist, and Iphicles the sacred king. Theocritus certainly makes Heracles the younger of the twins, and Herodotus (ii. 43), who calls him a son of Amphitryon, surnames him 'Alcides' – after his grandfather Alcaeus, not 'Cronides' after his grandfather Cronus. Moreover, when Iphicles married Creon's youngest daughter, Heracles married an elder one; although in matrilinear society the youngest was commonly the heiress, as appears in all European folktales. According to Hesiod's *Shield of Heracles* (89 ff.), Iphicles humbled himself shamefully before Eurystheus; but the circumstances, which might throw light on this change of roles between the twins, are not explained. No such comradeship as existed between Castor and Polydeuces, or Idas and Lynceus, is recorded between Heracles and Iphicles. Heracles usurps his twin's functions and prerogatives, leaving him an ineffective and spiritless shadow who soon fades away, unmourned. Perhaps at Tiryns, the tanist usurped all the royal power, as sometimes happens in Asiatic states where a religious king rules jointly with a war-king, or Shogun.

4. Hera's method of delaying childbirth is still used by Nigerian witches; the more enlightened now reinforce the charm by concealing imported padlocks beneath their clothes.

5. The observation that weasels, if disturbed, carry their young from place to place in their mouths, like cats, gave rise to the legend of their viviparous birth. Apuleius's account of the horrid performance of Thessalian witches disguised as weasels, Hecate's attendants, and Pausanias's mention of human sacrifices offered to the Teumessian Vixen (see 89. *h*), recall Cerdo ('weasel' or 'vixen'), wife of Phoroneus, who is said to have introduced Hera's worship into the Peloponnese (see 57. *a*). The Theban cult of Galinthias is a relic of primitive Hera-worship, and when the witches delayed Heracles's birth they will have been disguised as

weasels. This myth is more than usually confused; though it appears that
Zeus's Olympianism was resented by conservative religious opinion in
Thebes and Argolis, and that the witches made a concerted attack on the
House of Perseus.

6. To judge from Ovid's remark about the Tenth Sign, and from the
story of the Erymanthian Boar, which presents Heracles as the Child
Horus, he shared a midwinter birthday with Zeus, Apollo, and other
calendar gods. The Theban year began at midwinter. If, as Theocritus
says, Heracles was ten months old at the close of the twelfth, then
Alcmene bore him at the spring equinox, when the Italians, Babylonians,
and others, celebrated New Year. No wonder that Zeus is said to have
illumined the birth chamber. The fourth day of the month will have been
dedicated to Heracles because every fourth year was his, as founder of the
Olympic Games.

119

THE YOUTH OF HERACLES

ALCMENE, fearing Hera's jealousy, exposed her newly-born child in a
field outside the walls of Thebes; and here, at Zeus's instigation, Athene
took Hera for a casual stroll. 'Look, my dear! What a wonderfully
robust child!' said Athene, pretending surprise as she stopped to pick
him up. 'His mother must have been out of her mind to abandon him
in a stony field! Come, you have milk. Give the poor little creature
suck!' Thoughtlessly Hera took him and bared her breast, at which
Heracles drew with such force that she flung him down in pain, and a
spurt of milk flew across the sky and became the Milky Way. 'The
young monster!' Hera cried. But Heracles was now immortal, and
Athene returned him to Alcmene with a smile, telling her to guard and
rear him well. The Thebans still show the place where this trick was
played on Hera; it is called 'The Plain of Heracles'.[1]

b. Some, however, say that Hermes carried the infant Heracles to
Olympus; that Zeus himself laid him at Hera's breast while she slept;
and that the Milky Way was formed when she awoke and pushed him
away, or when he greedily sucked more milk than his mouth would
hold, and coughed it up. At all events, Hera was Heracles's foster-
mother, if only for a short while; and the Thebans therefore style him
her son, and say that he had been Alcaeus before she gave him suck, but
was renamed in her honour.[2]

c. One evening, when Heracles had reached the age of eight or ten months or, as others say, one year, and was still unweaned, Alcmene having washed and suckled her twins, laid them to rest under a lamb-fleece coverlet, on the broad brazen shield which Amphitryon had won from Pterelaus. At midnight, Hera sent two prodigious azure-scaled serpents to Amphitryon's house, with strict orders to destroy Heracles. The gates opened as they approached; they glided through, and over the marble floors to the nursery – their eyes shooting flames, and poison dripping from their fangs.³

d. The twins awoke, to see the serpents writhed above them, with darting, forked tongues; for Zeus again divinely illuminated the chamber. Iphicles screamed, kicked off the coverlet and, in an attempt to escape, rolled from the shield to the floor. His frightened cries, and the strange light shining under the nursery door, roused Alcmene. 'Up with you, Amphitryon!' she cried. Without waiting to put on his sandals, Amphitryon leaped from the cedar-wood bed, seized his sword which hung close by on the wall, and drew it from its polished sheath. At that moment the light in the nursery went out. Shouting to his drowsy slaves for lamps and torches, Amphitryon rushed in; and Heracles, who had not uttered so much as a whimper, proudly displayed the serpents, which he was in the act of strangling, one in either hand. As they died, he laughed, bounced joyfully up and down, and threw them at Amphitryon's feet.

e. While Alcmene comforted the terror-stricken Iphicles, Amphitryon spread the coverlet over Heracles again, and returned to bed. At dawn, when the cock had crowed three times, Alcmene summoned the aged Teiresias and told him of the prodigy. Teiresias, after foretelling Heracles's future glories, advised her to strew a broad hearth with dry faggots of gorse, thorn and brambles, and burn the serpents upon them at midnight. In the morning, a maid-servant must collect their ashes, take them to the rock where the Sphinx had perched, scatter them to the winds, and run away without looking back. On her return, the palace must be purged with fumes of sulphur and salted spring water; and its roof crowned with wild olive. Finally, a boar must be sacrificed at Zeus's high altar. All this Alcmene did. But some hold that the serpents were harmless, and placed in the cradle by Amphitryon himself; he had wished to discover which of the twins was his son, and now he knew well.⁴

f. When Heracles ceased to be a child, Amphitryon taught him how to drive a chariot, and how to turn corners without grazing the goal. Castor gave him fencing lessons, instructed him in weapon drill, in cavalry and infantry tactics, and in the rudiments of strategy. One of Hermes's sons became his boxing teacher – it was either Autolycus, or else Harpalycus, who had so grim a look when fighting that none dared face him. Eurytus taught him archery; or it may have been the Scythian Teutarus, one of Amphitryon's herdsmen, or even Apollo.[5] But Heracles surpassed all archers ever born, even his companion Alcon, father of Phalerus the Argonaut, who could shoot through a succession of rings set on the helmets of soldiers standing in file, and could cleave arrows held up on the points of swords or lances. Once, when Alcon's son was attacked by a serpent, which wound its coils about him, Alcon shot with such skill as to wound it mortally without hurting the boy.[6]

g. Eumolpus taught Heracles how to sing and play the lyre; while Linus, son of the River-god Ismenius, introduced him to the study of literature. Once, when Eumolpus was absent, Linus gave the lyre lessons as well; but Heracles, refusing to change the principles in which he had been grounded by Eumolpus, and being beaten for his stubbornness, killed Linus with a blow of the lyre.[7] At his trial for murder, Heracles quoted a law of Rhadamanthys, which justified forcible resistance to an aggressor, and thus secured his own acquittal. Nevertheless Amphitryon, fearing that the boy might commit further crimes of violence, sent him away to a cattle ranch, where he remained until his eighteenth year, outstripping his contemporaries in height, strength, and courage. Here he was chosen to be a laurel-bearer of Ismenian Apollo; and the Thebans still preserve the tripod which Amphitryon dedicated for him on this occasion. It is not known who taught Heracles astronomy and philosophy, yet he was learned in both these subjects.[8]

h. His height is usually given as four cubits. Since, however, he stepped out the Olympian stadium, making it six hundred feet long, and since later Greek stadia are also nominally six hundred feet long, but considerably shorter than the Olympic, the sage Pythagoras decided that the length of Heracles's stride, and consequently his stature, must have been in the same ratio to the stride and stature of other men, as the length of the Olympic stadium is to that of other stadia. This calculation made him four cubits and one foot high – yet some hold that he was not above average stature.[9]

i. Heracles's eyes flashed fire, and he had an unerring aim, both with javelin and arrow. He ate sparingly at noon; for supper his favourite food was roast meat and Doric barley-cakes, of which he ate sufficient (if that is credible) to have made a hired labourer grunt 'enough!' His tunic was short-skirted and neat; and he preferred a night under the stars to one spent indoors.[10] A profound knowledge of augury led him especially to welcome the appearance of vultures, whenever he was about to undertake a new Labour. 'Vultures', he would say, 'are the most righteous of birds: they do not attack even the smallest living creature.'[11]

j. Heracles claimed never to have picked a quarrel, but always to have given aggressors the same treatment as they intended for him. One Termerus used to kill travellers by challenging them to a butting match; Heracles's skull proved the stronger, and he crushed Termerus's head as though it had been an egg. Heracles was, however, naturally courteous, and the first mortal who freely yielded the enemy their dead for burial.[12]

1. Diodorus Siculus: iv. 9; Tzetzes: *On Lycophron* 1327; Pausanias: ix. 25. 2.
2. Eratosthenes: *Catasterismoi* 44; Hyginus: *Poetic Astronomy* ii. 43; Ptolemy Hephaestionos, quoted by Photius p. 477; Diodorus Siculus: iv. 10.
3. Apollodorus: ii. 4. 8; Theocritus: *Idylls* xxiv; Scholiast on Pindar's *Nemean Odes* i. 43.
4. Servius on Virgil's *Aeneid* viii. 288; Theocritus: *loc. cit.*; Pindar: *Nemean Odes* i. 35 ff.; Pherecydes, quoted by Apollodorus: ii. 4. 8.
5. Theocritus: *loc. cit.*; Apollodorus: ii. 4. 9; Tzetzes: *On Lycophron* 56; Diodorus Siculus: iv. 14.
6. Servius on Virgil's *Eclogues* v. 11; Valerius Flaccus: i. 399 ff.; Apollonius Rhodius: i. 97; Hyginus: *Fabula* 14.
7. Pausanias: ix. 29. 3; Theocritus: *loc. cit.*; Apollodorus: ii. 4. 9; Diodorus Siculus: iii. 67.
8. Apollodorus: *loc. cit.*; Diodorus Siculus: iv. 10; Pausanias: ix. 10. 4; Scholiast on Apollonius Rhodius: i. 865; Servius on Virgil's *Aeneid* i. 745.
9. Apollodorus: ii. 4. 9; Plutarch, quoted by Aulus Gellius: i. 1; Herodotus, quoted by Tzetzes: *On Lycophron* 662; Pindar: *Isthmian Odes* iv. 53.
10. Apollodorus: *loc. cit.*; Theocritus: *Idyll* xxiv; Plutarch: *Roman Questions* 28.
11. Plutarch: *Roman Questions* 93.

12. Plutarch: *Theseus* 11 and 29.

*

1. According to another account, the Milky Way was formed when Rhea forcibly weaned Zeus (see 7. *b*). Hera's suckling of Heracles is a myth apparently based on the sacred king's ritual rebirth from the queen-mother (see 145. *3*).

2. An ancient icon on which the post-Homeric story of the strangled serpents is based, will have shown Heracles caressing them while they cleansed his ears with their tongues, as happened to Melampus (see 72. *c*), Teiresias (see 105. *g*), Cassandra (see 158. *p*), and probably the sons of Laocoön (see 167. *3*). Without this kindly attention he would have been unable to understand the language of vultures; and Hera, had she really wanted to kill Heracles, would have sent a Harpy to carry him off. The icon has been misread by Pindar, or his informant, as an allegory of the New Year Solar Child, who destroys the power of Winter, symbolized by the serpents. Alcmene's sacrifice of a boar to Zeus is the ancient mid-winter one, surviving in the Christmas boar's head of Old England. Wild olive in Greece, like birch in Italy and North-western Europe, was the New Year tree, symbol of inception, and used as a besom to expel evil spirits (see 53. *7*); Heracles had a wild-olive tree for his club, and brought a sapling to Olympia from the land of the Hyperboreans (see 138. *j*). What Teiresias told Alcmene to light was the Candlemas bonfire, still lighted on 2 February in many parts of Europe: its object being to burn away the old scrub and encourage young shoots to grow.

3. The cake-eating Dorian Heracles, as opposed to his cultured Aeolian and Achaean predecessors, was a simple cattle-king, endowed with the limited virtues of his condition, but making no pretensions to music, philosophy, or astronomy. In Classical times, the mythographers, re-membering the principle of *mens sana in corpore sano*, forced a higher education upon him, and interpreted his murder of Linus as a protest against tyranny, rather than against effeminacy. Yet he remained an em-bodiment of physical, not mental, health; except among the Celts (see 132. *3*), who honoured him as the patron of letters and all the bardic arts. They followed the tradition that Heracles, the Idaean Dactyl whom they called Ogmius, represented the first consonant of the Hyperborean tree-alphabet, Birch or Wild Olive (see 52. *3* and 125. *1*), and that 'on a switch of birch was cut the first message ever sent, namely Birch seven times repeated' (*White Goddess* p. 121).

4. Alcon's feat of shooting the serpent suggests an archery trial like that described in the fifteenth-century *Malleus Maleficarum*: when the candidate for initiation into the archers' guild was required to shoot at an object placed on his own son's cap – either an apple or a silver penny. The

brothers of Laodemeia, competing for the sacred kingship (see 163. n), were asked to shoot through a ring placed on a child's breast; but this myth must be misreported, since child-murder was not their object. It seems that the original task of a candidate for kingship had been to shoot through the coil of a golden serpent, symbolizing immortality, set on a head-dress worn by a royal child; and that in some tribes this custom was changed to the cleaving of an apple, and in others to the shooting between the recurved blades of a double axe, or through the crest-ring of a helmet; but later, as marksmanship improved, through either a row of helmet-rings, the test set Alcon; or a row of axe-blades, the test set Odysseus (see 171. h). Robin Hood's merry men, like the German archers, shot at silver pennies, because these were marked with a cross; the archer-guilds being defiantly anti-Christian.

5. Greek and Roman archers drew the bow-string back to the chest, as children shoot, and their effective range was so short that the javelin remained the chief missile weapon of the Roman armies until the sixth century A.D., when Belisarius armed his cataphracts with heavy bows, and taught them to draw the string back to the ear, in Scythian fashion. Heracles's accurate marksmanship is therefore accounted for by the legend that his tutor was Teutarus the Scythian – the name is apparently formed from *teutaein*, 'to practise assiduously', which the ordinary Greek archer does not seem to have done. It may be because of the Scythians' outstanding skill with the bow that they were described as Heracles's descendants: and he was said to have bequeathed a bow to Scythes, the only one of his sons who could bend it as he did (see 132. v).

120

THE DAUGHTERS OF THESPIUS

In his eighteenth year, Heracles left the cattle ranch and set out to destroy the lion of Cithaeron, which was havocking the herds of Amphitryon and his neighbour, King Thespius, also called Thestius, the Athenian Erechtheid. The lion had another lair on Mount Helicon, at the foot of which stands the city of Thespiae. Helicon has always been a gay mountain: the Thespians celebrate an ancient festival on its summit in honour of the Muses, and play amorous games at its foot around the statue of Eros, their patron.[1]

b. King Thespius had fifty daughters by his wife Megamede, daughter of Arneus, as gay as any in Thespiae. Fearing that they might make unsuitable matches, he determined that every one of them should have a child by Heracles, who was now engaged all day in hunting the lion; for Heracles lodged at Thespiae for fifty nights running. 'You may have my eldest daughter Procris as your bed-fellow,' Thespius told him hospitably. But each night another of his daughters visited Heracles, until he had laid with every one. Some say, however, that he enjoyed them all in a single night, except one, who declined his embraces and remained a virgin until her death, serving as his priestess in the shrine at Thespiae: for to this day the Thespian priestess is required to be chaste. But he had begotten fifty-one sons on her sisters: Procris, the eldest, bearing him the twins Antileon and Hippeus; and the youngest sister, another pair.[2]

c. Having at last tracked down the lion, and dispatched it with an untrimmed club cut from a wild-olive tree which he uprooted on Helicon, Heracles dressed himself in its pelt and wore the gaping jaws for a helmet. Some, however, say that he wore the pelt of the Nemean Lion; or of yet another beast, which he killed at Teumessus near Thebes; and that it was Alcathous who accounted for the lion of Cithaeron.[3]

1. Apollodorus: ii. 4. 8–9; Pausanias: ix. 26. 4; 27. 1 and 31. 1; Scholiast on Theocritus's *Idyll* xiii. 6.
2. Apollodorus: ii. 4. 10 and 7. 8; Pausanias: ix. 27. 5; Diodorus Siculus: iv. 29; Scholiast on Hesiod's *Theogony* 56.
3. Theocritus: *Idyll* xxv; Apollodorus: ii. 4. 10; Diodorus Siculus: iv. 11; Lactantius on Statius's *Thebaid* i. 355–485; Pausanias: i. 41. 4.

*

1. Thespius's fifty daughters – like the fifty Danaids, Pallantids, and Nereids, or the fifty maidens with whom the Celtic god Bran (Phoroneus) lay in a single night – must have been a college of priestesses serving the Moon-goddess, to whom the lion-pelted sacred king had access once a year during their erotic orgies around the stone phallus called Eros ('erotic desire'). Their number corresponded with the lunations which fell between one Olympic Festival and the next. 'Thesius' is perhaps a masculinization of *thea hestia*, 'the goddess Hestia'; but Thespius ('divinely sounding') is not an impossible name, the Chief-priestess having an oracular function.

2. Hyginus (*Fabula* 162) mentions only twelve Thespiads, perhaps because this was the number of Latin Vestals who guarded the phallic Palladium and who seem to have celebrated a similar annual orgy on the Alban Hill, under the early Roman monarchy.

3. Both the youngest and the eldest of Thespius's daughters bore Heracles twins: namely, a sacred king and his tanist. The mythographers are confused here, trying to reconcile the earlier tradition that Heracles married the youngest daughter – matrilineal ultimogeniture – with the patrilineal rights of primogeniture. Heracles, in Classical legend, is a patrilineal figure; with the doubtful exception of Macaria (see 146. *b*), he begets no daughters at all. His virgin-priestess at Thespiae, like Apollo's Pythoness at Delphi, theoretically became his bride when the prophetic power overcame her, and could therefore be enjoyed by no mortal husband.

4. Pausanias, dissatisfied with the myth, writes that Heracles could neither have disgraced his host by this wholesale seduction of the Thespiads, nor dedicated a temple to himself – as though he were a god – so early in his career; and consequently refuses to identify the King of Thespiae with the Thespiads' father.

The killing of a lion was one of the marriage tasks imposed on the candidate for kingship (see 123. *1*).

5. Heracles cut his club from the wild-olive, the tree of the first month, traditionally used for the expulsion of evil spirits (see 52. *3*; 89. *7*; 119. *2*, etc.).

121

ERGINUS

SOME years before these events, during Poseidon's festival at Onchestus, a trifling incident vexed the Thebans, whereupon Menoeceus's charioteer flung a stone which mortally wounded the Minyan King Clymenus. Clymenus was carried back, dying, to Orchomenus where, with his last breath, he charged his sons to avenge him. The eldest of these, Erginus, whose mother was the Boeotian princess Budeia, or Buzyge, mustered an army, marched against the Thebans, and utterly defeated them. By the terms of a treaty then confirmed with oaths, the Thebans would pay Erginus an annual tribute of one hundred cattle for twenty years in requital for Clymenus's death.[1]

b. Heracles, on his return from Helicon, fell in with the Minyan heralds as they went to collect the Theban tribute. When he inquired their business, they replied scornfully that they had come once more to remind the Thebans of Erginus's clemency in not lopping off the ears, nose, and hands of every man in the city. 'Does Erginus indeed hanker for such tribute?' Heracles asked angrily. Then he maimed the heralds in the very manner that they had described, and sent them back to Orchomenus, with their bloody extremities tied on cords about their necks.[2]

c. When Erginus instructed King Creon at Thebes to surrender the author of this outrage, he was willing enough to obey, because the Minyans had disarmed Thebes; nor could he hope for the friendly intervention of any neighbour, in so bad a cause. Yet Heracles persuaded his youthful comrades to strike a blow for freedom. Making a round of the city temples, he tore down all the shields, helmets, breastplates, greaves, swords, and spears, which had been dedicated there as spoils; and Athene, greatly admiring such resolution, girded these on him and on his friends. Thus Heracles armed every Theban of fighting age, taught them the use of their weapons, and himself assumed command. An oracle promised him victory if the noblest-born person in Thebes would take his own life. All eyes turned expectantly towards Antipoenus, a descendant of the Sown Men; but, when he grudged dying for the common good, his daughters Androcleia and Alcis gladly did so in his stead, and were afterwards honoured as heroines in the Temple of Famous Artemis.[3]

d. Presently, the Minyans marched against Thebes, but Heracles ambushed them in a narrow pass, killing Erginus and the greater number of his captains. This victory, won almost single-handed, he exploited by making a sudden descent on Orchomenus, where he battered down the gates, sacked the palace, and compelled the Minyans to pay a double tribute to Thebes. Heracles had also blocked up the two large tunnels built by the Minyans of old, through which the river Cephissus emptied into the sea; thus flooding the rich cornlands of the Copaic Plain.[4] His object was to immobilize the cavalry of the Minyans, their most formidable arm, and carry war into the hills, where he could meet them on equal terms; but, being a friend of all mankind, he later unblocked these tunnels. The shrine of Heracles the Horsebinder at Thebes commemorates an incident in this campaign: Heracles came by night into the Minyan camp and, after stealing the chariot horses, which he bound to trees a long way off, put the sleeping men to the sword. Unfortunately, Amphitryon, his foster-father, was killed in the fighting.[5]

e. On his return to Thebes, Heracles dedicated an altar to Zeus the

Preserver; a stone lion to Famous Artemis; and two stone images to Athene the Girder-on-of-Arms. Since the gods had not punished Heracles for his ill-treatment of Erginus's heralds, the Thebans dared to honour him with a statue, called Heracles the Nose-docker.⁶

f. According to another account, Erginus survived the Minyan defeat and was one of the Argonauts who brought back the Golden Fleece from Colchis. After many years spent in recovering his former prosperity, he found himself rich indeed, but old and childless. An oracle advising him to put a new shoe on the battered plough coulter, he married a young wife, who bore him Trophonius and Agamedes, the renowned architects, and Azeus too.⁷

1. Apollodorus: ii. 4. 11; Pausanias: ix. 37. 1–2; Eustathius on Homer p. 1076; Scholiast on Apollonius Rhodius: i. 185.
2. Diodorus Siculus: iv. 10.
3. Diodorus Siculus: *loc. cit.*; Apollodorus: ii. 4. 11; Pausanias: ix. 17. 1.
4. Euripides: *Heracles* 220; Diodorus Siculus: *loc. cit.*; Pausanias: ix. 38. 5; Strabo: ix. 11. 40.
5. Polyaenus: i. 3. 5; Diodorus Siculus: iv. 18. 7; Pausanias: ix. 26. 1; Apollodorus: ii. 4. 11.
6. Euripides: *Heracles* 48–59; Pausanias: ix. 17. 1–2 and 25. 4.
7. Pausanias: ix. 37. 2–3 and 25. 4; Eustathius on Homer p. 272.

*

1. Heracles's treatment of the Minyan heralds is so vile – a herald's person being universally held sacrosanct, with whatever insolence he might behave – that he must here represent the Dorian conquerors of 1050 B.C., who disregarded all civilized conventions.

2. According to Strabo (ix. 2. 18), certain natural limestone channels which drained the waters of the Cephissus were sometimes blocked and at other times freed by earthquakes; but eventually the whole Copaic Plain became a marsh, despite the two huge tunnels which had been cut by the Bronze Age Minyans – Minoanized Pelasgians – to make the natural channels more effective. Sir James Frazer, who visited the Plain about fifty years ago, found that three of the channels had been artificially blocked with stones in ancient times, perhaps by the Thebans who destroyed Orchomenus in 368 B.C., put all the male inhabitants to the sword, and sold the women into slavery (Pausanias: ix. 15. 3). Recently a British company has drained the marshland and restored the plain to agriculture.

3. When the city of Thebes was in danger (see 105. *i* and 106. *j*), the Theban Oracle frequently demanded a royal *pharmacos*; but only in a fully patriarchal society would Androcleia and Alcis have leaped to death.

Their names, like those of Erechtheus's daughters, said to have been sacrificed in the same way (see 47. *d*), seem to be titles of Demeter and Persephone, who demanded male sacrifices. It looks as if two priestesses 'paid the penalty instead of' the sacred king – thereafter renamed Antipoenus – who refused to follow Menoeceus's example. In this sense the Sphinx leaped from the cliff and dashed herself to pieces (see 105. 6).

4. 'Heracles the Horse-binder' may refer to his capture of Diomedes's wild mares, and all that this feat implied (see 130. 1).

5. Athene Girder-on-of-Arms was the earlier Athene, who distributed arms to her chosen sons; in Celtic and German myths, the giving of arms is a matriarchal prerogative, properly exercised at a sacred marriage (see 95. 5).

122

THE MADNESS OF HERACLES

HERACLES's defeat of the Minyans made him the most famous of heroes; and his reward was to marry King Creon's eldest daughter Megara, or Megera, and be appointed protector of the city; while Iphicles married the youngest daughter. Some say that Heracles had two sons by Megara; others that he had three, four, or even eight. They are known as the Alcaids.[1]

b. Heracles next vanquished Pyraechmus, King of the Euboeans, an ally of the Minyans, when he marched against Thebes; and created terror throughout Greece by ordering his body to be torn in two by colts and exposed unburied beside the river Heracleius, at a place called the Colts of Pyraechmus, which gives out a neighing echo whenever horses drink there.[2]

c. Hera, vexed by Heracles's excesses, drove him mad. He first attacked his beloved nephew Iolaus, Iphicles's eldest son, who managed to escape his wild lunges; and then, mistaking six of his own children for enemies, shot them down, and flung their bodies into a fire, together with two other sons of Iphicles, by whose side they were performing martial exercises. The Thebans celebrate an annual festival in honour of these eight mail-clad victims. On the first day, sacrifices are offered and fires burn all night; on the second, funeral games are held and the winner is crowned with white myrtle. The celebrants grieve in memory of the brilliant futures that had been planned for Heracles's sons. One was to have ruled Argos, occupying Eurystheus's palace, and Heracles had thrown his lion pelt over his shoulders; another was to have been king of Thebes, and in his right hand Heracles had set the mace of defence, Daedalus's deceitful gift; a third was promised Oechalia, which Heracles afterwards laid waste; and the choicest brides had been chosen for them all – alliances with Athens, Thebes, and Sparta. So dearly did Heracles love these sons that many deny now his guilt, preferring to believe that they were treacherously slain by his guests: by Lycus, perhaps, or as Socrates has suggested, by Augeias.[3]

d. When Heracles recovered his sanity, he shut himself up in a dark chamber for some days, avoiding all human intercourse and then, after purification by King Thespius, went to Delphi, to inquire what he should do. The Pythoness, addressing him for the first time as Heracles, rather than Palaemon, advised him to reside at Tiryns; to serve Eurystheus for twelve years; and to perform whatever Labours might be set him, in payment for which he would be rewarded with immortality. At this, Heracles fell into deep despair, loathing to serve a man whom he knew to be far inferior to himself, yet afraid to oppose his father Zeus. Many friends came to solace him in his distress; and, finally, when the passage of time had somewhat alleviated his pain, he placed himself at Eurystheus's disposal.[4]

e. Some, however, hold that it was not until his return from Tartarus that Heracles went mad and killed the children; that he killed Megara too; and that the Pythoness then told him: 'You shall no longer be called Palaemon! Phoebus Apollo names you Heracles, since from Hera you shall have undying fame among men!' – as though he had done Hera a great service. Others say that Heracles was Eurystheus's lover, and performed the Twelve Labours for his gratification; others again, that he undertook to perform them only if Eurystheus would annul the sentence of banishment passed on Amphitryon.[5]

f. It has been said that when Heracles set forth on his Labours, Hermes gave him a sword, Apollo a bow and smooth-shafted arrows, feathered with eagle feathers; Hephaestus a golden breast-plate; and Athene a robe. Or that Athene gave him the breast-plate, but Hephaestus bronze greaves and an adamantine helmet. Athene and Hephaestus, it is added, vied with one another throughout in benefiting Heracles: she gave him enjoyment of peaceful pleasures; he, protection from the dangers of war. The gift of Poseidon was a team of horses; that of Zeus a magnificent and unbreakable shield. Many were the stories worked on this shield in enamel, ivory, electrum, gold, and lapis lazuli; moreover, twelve serpents' heads carved about the boss clashed their jaws whenever Heracles went into battle, and terrified his opponents.[6] The truth, however, is that Heracles scorned armour and, after his first Labour, seldom carried even a spear, relying rather on his club, bow and arrows. He had little use for the bronze-tipped club which Hephaestus gave him, preferring to cut his own from wild-olive: first on Helicon, next at Nemea. This second club he later replaced with a third, also cut from wild-olive, by the shores of the Saronic Sea: the club which, on his visit to Troezen, he leaned against the image of Hermes. It struck root, sprouted, and is now a stately tree.[7]

g. His nephew Iolaus shared in the Labours as his charioteer, or shield-bearer.[8]

1. Scholiast on Pindar's *Isthmian Odes* iv. 114 and 61; Apollodorus: ii. 4. 11; Diodorus Siculus: iv. 10; Hyginus: *Fabula* 31; Tzetzes: *On Lycophron* 38.
2. Plutarch: *Parallel Stories* 7.
3. Diodorus Siculus: iv. 11; Apollodorus: ii. 4. 12; Pindar: *loc. cit.*; Euripides: *Heracles* 462 ff.; Lysimachus, quoted by scholiast on Pindar's *Isthmian Odes* iv. 114.
4. Diodorus Siculus: iv. 10–11; Apollodorus: *loc. cit.*
5. Euripides: *Heracles* 1 ff. and 1000 ff.; Tzetzes: *On Lycophron* 38 and 662–3; Diotimus: *Heraclea*, quoted by Athenaeus xiii. 8.
6. Apollodorus: ii. 4. 11; Hesiod: *Shield of Heracles* 122 ff., 141 ff., 161 ff., and 318–19; Pausanias: v. 8. 1.
7. Euripides: *Heracles* 159 ff.; Apollonius Rhodius: i. 1196; Diodorus Siculus: iv. 14; Theocritus: *Idyll* xxv; Apollodorus: ii. 4. 11; Pausanias: ii. 31. 13.
8. Plutarch: *On Love* 17; Pausanias: v. 8. 1 and 17. 4; Euripides: *Children of Heracles* 216.

*

1. Madness was the Classical Greek excuse for child-sacrifice (see 27. *e* and 70. *g*); the truth being that the sacred king's boy-surrogates (see 42. 2; 81. *8*; and 156. 2) were burned alive after he had lain hidden for twenty-four hours in a tomb, shamming death, and then reappeared to claim the throne once more.

2. The death of Pyraechmus, torn in two by wild horses, is a familiar one (see 71. 1). Heracles's title Palaemon identifies him with Melicertes of Corinth, who was deified under that name; Melicertes is Melkarth, the Lord of the City, the Tyrian Heracles. The eight Alcaids seem to have been members of a sword-dancing team whose performance, like that of the eight morris-dancers in the English Christmas Play, ended in the victim's resurrection. Myrtle was the tree of the thirteenth twenty-eight-day month, and symbolized departure; wild-olive, the tree of the first month, symbolized inception (see 119. 2). Electryon's eight sons (see 118. a), may have formed a similar team at Mycenae.

3. Heracles's homosexual relations with Hylas, Iolaus, and Eurystheus, and the accounts of his luxurious armour, are meant to justify Theban military custom. In the original myth, he will have loved Eurystheus's daughter, not Eurystheus himself. His twelve Labours, Servius points out, were eventually equated with the Twelve Signs of the Zodiac; although Homer and Hesiod do not say that there were twelve of them, nor does the sequence of Labours correspond with that of the Signs. Like the Celtic God of the Year, celebrated in the Irish *Song of Amergin*, the Pelasgian Heracles seems to have made a progress through a thirteen-month year. In Irish and Welsh myth the successive emblems were: stag, or bull; flood; wind; dewdrop; hawk; flower; bonfire; spear; salmon; hill; boar; breaker; sea-serpent. But Gilgamesh's adventures in the Babylonian Gilgamesh epic are related to the signs of the Zodiac, and the Tyrian Heracles had much in common with him. Despite Homer and Hesiod, the scenes pictured on ancient shields seem not to have been dazzling works of art, but rough pictograms, indicative of the owner's origin and rank, scratched on the spiral band which plated each shield.

4. The occasion on which the twelve Olympians heaped gifts on Heracles was doubtless his sacred marriage, and they will have all been presented to him by his priestess-bride – Athene, Auge, Iole, or whatever her name happened to be – either directly, or by the hands of attendants (see 81. l). Here Heracles was being armed for his Labours, that is to say, for his ritual combats and magical feats.

123

THE FIRST LABOUR: THE NEMEAN LION

THE First Labour which Eurystheus imposed on Heracles, when he came to reside at Tiryns, was to kill and flay the Nemaen, or Cleonaean lion, an enormous beast with a pelt proof against iron, bronze, and stone.[1]

b. Although some call this lion the offspring of Typhon, or of the Chimaera and the Dog Orthrus, others say that Selene bore it with a fearful shudder and dropped it to earth on Mount Tretus near Nemea, beside a two-mouthed cave; and that, in punishment for an unfulfilled sacrifice, she set it to prey upon her own people, the chief sufferers being the Bambinaeans.²

c. Still others say that, at Hera's desire, Selene created the lion from sea foam enclosed in a large ark; and that Iris, binding it with her girdle, carried it to the Nemean mountains. These were named after a daughter of Asopus, or of Zeus and Selene; and the lion's cave is still shown about two miles from the city of Nemea.³

d. Arriving at Cleonae, between Corinth and Argos, Heracles lodged in the house of a day-labourer, or shepherd, named Molorchus, whose son the lion had killed. When Molorchus was about to offer a ram in propitiation of Hera, Heracles restrained him. 'Wait thirty days,' he said. 'If I return safely, sacrifice to Saviour Zeus; if I do not, sacrifice to me as a hero!'

e. Heracles reached Nemea at midday, but since the lion had depopulated the neighbourhood, he found no one to direct him; nor were any tracks to be seen. Having first searched Mount Apesas – so called after Apesantus, a shepherd whom the lion had killed; though some say that Apesantus was a son of Acrisius, who died of a snake-bite in his heel – Heracles visited Mount Tretus, and presently descried the lion coming back to its lair, bespattered with blood from the day's slaughter.⁴ He shot a flight of arrows at it, but they rebounded harmlessly from the thick pelt, and the lion licked its chops, yawning. Next, he used his sword, which bent as though made of lead; finally he heaved up his club and dealt the lion such a blow on the muzzle that it entered its double-mouthed cave, shaking its head – not for pain, however, but because of the singing in its ears. Heracles, with a rueful glance at his shattered club, then netted one entrance of the cave, and went in by the other. Aware now that the monster was proof against all weapons, he began to wrestle with it. The lion bit off one of his fingers; but, holding its head in chancery, Heracles squeezed hard until it choked to death.⁵

f. Carrying the carcass on his shoulders, Heracles returned to Cleonae, where he arrived on the thirtieth day, and found Molorchus on the point of offering him a heroic sacrifice; instead, they sacrificed together to Saviour Zeus. When this had been done, Heracles cut himself a new club and, after making several alterations in the Nemean Games hitherto celebrated in honour of Opheltes, and rededicating them to Zeus, took the lion's carcass to Mycenae. Eurystheus, amazed and terrified, forbade him ever again to enter the city; in future he was to display the fruits of his Labours outside the gates.[6]

g. For a while, Heracles was at a loss how to flay the lion, until, by divine inspiration, he thought of employing its own razor-sharp claws, and soon could wear the invulnerable pelt as armour, and the head as a helmet. Meanwhile, Eurystheus ordered his smiths to forge him a brazen urn, which he buried beneath the earth. Henceforth, whenever the approach of Heracles was signalled, he took refuge in it and sent his orders by a herald – a son of Pelops, named Copreus, whom he had purified for murder.[7]

h. The honours received by Heracles from the city of Nemea in recognition of this feat, he later ceded to his devoted allies of Cleonae, who fought at his side in the Elean War, and fell to the number of three hundred and sixty. As for Molorchus, he founded the near-by city of Molorchia, and planted the Nemean Wood, where the Nemean Games are now held.[8]

i. Heracles was not the only man to strangle a lion in those days. The same feat was accomplished by his friend Phylius as the first of three love-tasks imposed on him by Cycnus, a son of Apollo by Hyria. Phylius had also to catch alive several monstrous man-eating birds, not unlike vultures, and after wrestling with a fierce bull, lead it to the altar of Zeus. When all three tasks had been accomplished, Cycnus further demanded an ox which Phylius had won as a prize at certain funeral games. Heracles advised Phylius to refuse this and press for a settlement of his claim with Cycnus who, in desperation, leaped into a lake; thereafter called the Cycnean lake. His mother Hyria followed him to his death, and both were transformed into swans.[9]

1. Apollodorus: ii. 5. 1; Valerius Flaccus: i. 34; Diodorus Siculus: iv. 11.
2. Apollodorus: *loc. cit.*; Hesiod: *Theogony* 326 ff.; Epimenides: *Fragment* 5, quoted by Aelian: *Nature of Animals* xii. 7; Plutarch: *On the Face Appearing in the Orb of the Moon* 24; Servius on Virgil's *Aeneid* viii. 295; Hyginus: *Fabula* 30; Theocritus: *Idyll* xxv. 200 ff.
3. Demodocus: *History of Heracles* i, quoted by Plutarch: *On Rivers* 18; Pausanias: ii. 15. 2–3; Scholiast on the *Hypothesis* of Pindar's *Nemean Odes*.
4. Strabo: viii. 6. 19; Apollodorus: ii. 5. 1; Servius on Virgil's *Georgics* iii. 19; Lactantius on Statius's *Thebaid* iv. 161; Plutarch: *loc. cit.*; Theocritus: *Idyll* xxv. 211 ff.
5. Bacchylides: xiii. 53; Theocritus: *loc. cit.*; Ptolemy Hephaes-

tionos: ii., quoted by Photius p. 474; Apollodorus: *loc. cit.*; Diodorus Siculus: iv. 11; Euripides: *Heracles* 153.

6. Apollodorus: *loc. cit.* and ii. 4. 11; Scholiast on the *Hypothesis* of Pindar's *Nemean Odes*.

7. Theocritus: *Idyll* xxv. 272 ff.; Diodorus Siculus: iv. 11; Euripides: *Heracles* 359 ff.; Apollodorus: *loc. cit.*

8. Aelian: *Varia Historia* iv. 5; Stephanus of Byzantium *sub* Molorchia; Virgil: *Georgics* iii. 19; Servius: *ad loc.*

9. Antoninus Liberalis: *Transformations* 12; Ovid: *Metamorphoses* vii. 371 ff.

*

1. The sacred king's ritual combat with wild beasts formed a regular part of the coronation ritual in Greece, Asia Minor, Babylonia, and Syria; each beast representing one season of the year. Their number varied with the calendar: in a three-seasoned year, they consisted, like the Chimaera, of lion, goat, and serpent (see 75. *2*) – hence the statement that the lion of Cithaeron was the Chimaera's child by Orthrus the Dog-star (see 34. *3*); or of bull, lion, and serpent, which were Dionysus's seasonal changes (see 27. *4*), according to Euripides's *Bacchae*; or of lion, horse, and dog, like Hecate's heads (see 31. *7*). But in a four-seasoned year, they will have been bull, ram, lion, and serpent, like the heads of Phanes (see 2. *b*) described in *Orphic Fragment* 63; or bull, lion, eagle, and seraph, as in Ezekiel's vision (*Ezekiel* i); or, more simply, bull, lion, scorpion, and water-snake, the four Signs of the Zodiac which fell at the equinoxes and solstices. These last four appear, from the First, Fourth, Seventh, and Eleventh Labours, to be the beasts which Heracles fought; though the boar has displaced the scorpion – the scorpion being retained only in the story of Orion, another Heracles, who was offered a princess in marriage if he killed certain wild beasts (see 41. *a–d*). The same situation recurs in the story of Cycnus and Phylius – with its unusual substitution of vultures for the serpent – though Ovid and Antoninus Liberalis have given it a homosexual twist. Theoretically, by taming these beasts, the king obtained dominion over the seasons of the year ruled by them. At Thebes, Heracles's native city, the Sphinx-goddess ruled a two-seasoned year; she was a winged lioness with a serpent's tail (see 105. *3*); hence, he wore a lion pelt and mask, rather than a bull mask like Minos (see 98. *2*). The lion was shown with the other calendar beasts in the new-moon ark, an icon which, it seems, gave rise both to the story of Noah and the Flood, and to that of Dionysus and the pirates (see 27. *5*); hence Selene ('the Moon') is said to have created it.

2. Photius denies that Heracles lost his finger in fighting the lion; Ptolemy Hephaestionos says (*Nova Historia* ii), that he was poisoned by a

sting-ray (see 171. 3). But it is more probable that he bit it off to placate
the ghosts of his children – as Orestes did when pursued by his mother's
Erinnyes. Another two-mouthed cave is mentioned incidentally in
Odyssey xiii. 103 ff., as one near which Odysseus first slept on his return
to Ithaca at the head of the Bay of Phorcys. Its northern entrance was for
men, the southern for gods; and it contained two-handled jars used as
hives, stone basins, and plentiful spring-water. There were also stone
looms – stalactites? – on which the Naiads wove purple garments. If
Porphyry (*On the Cave of the Nymphs*) was right in making this a cave
where rites of death and divine rebirth were practised, the basins served
for blood and the springs for lustration. The jars would then be burial urns
over which souls hovered like bees (see 90. 3), and the Naiads (daughters
of the Death-god Phorcys, or Orcus) would be Fates weaving garments
with royal clan-marks for the reborn to wear (see 10. 1). The Nemean
Lion's cave is two-mouthed because this First Labour initiated Heracles's
passage towards his ritual death, after which he becomes immortal and
marries the goddess Hebe.

3. The death of three hundred and sixty Cleonaeans suggests a calendar
mystery – this being the number of days in the sacred Egyptian year,
exclusive of the five set apart in honour of Osiris, Isis, Nephthys, Set, and
Horus. Heracles's modifications of the Nemean Games may have involved a change in the local calendar.

4. If the King of Mycenae, like Orion's enemy Oenopion of Hyria
(see 41. c), took refuge in a bronze urn underground and emerged only
after the danger had passed, he will have made an annual pretence at
dying, while his surrogate reigned for a day, and then reappeared.
Heracles's children were among such surrogates (see 122. 1).

5. Apesantus was one of several early heroes bitten in the heel by a
viper (see 177. 1). He may be identified with Opheltes (see 106. g) of
Nemea, though what part of Opheltes's body the serpent bit is not related.

124

THE SECOND LABOUR: THE LERNAEAN HYDRA

THE Second Labour ordered by Eurystheus was the destruction of the
Lernaean Hydra, a monster born to Typhon and Echidne, and reared
by Hera as a menace to Heracles.[1]

b. Lerna stands beside the sea, some five miles from the city of Argos.
To the west rises Mount Pontinus, with its sacred grove of plane-trees

stretching down to the sea. In this grove, bounded on one flank by the river Pontinus – beside which Danaus dedicated a shrine to Athene – and on the other by the river Amymone, stand images of Demeter, Dionysus the Saviour, and Prosymne, one of Hera's nurses; and, on the shore, a stone image of Aphrodite, dedicated by the Danaids. Every year, secret nocturnal rites are held at Lerna in honour of Dionysus, who descended to Tartarus at this point when he went to fetch Semele; and, not far off, the Mysteries of Lernaean Demeter are celebrated in an enclosure which marks the place where Hades and Persephone also descended to Tartarus.[2]

c. This fertile and holy district was once terrorized by the Hydra, which had its lair beneath a plane-tree at the sevenfold source of the river Amymone and haunted the unfathomable Lernaean swamp near by – the Emperor Nero recently tried to sound it, and failed – the grave of many an incautious traveller.[3] The Hydra had a prodigious dog-like body, and eight or nine snaky heads, one of them immortal; but some credit it with fifty, or one hundred, or even ten thousand heads. At all events, it was so venomous that its very breath, or the smell of its tracks, could destroy life.[4]

d. Athene had pondered how Heracles might best kill this monster and, when he reached Lerna, driven there in his chariot by Iolaus, she pointed out the Hydra's lair to him. On her advice, he forced the Hydra to emerge by pelting it with burning arrows, and then held his breath while he caught hold of it. But the monster twined around his feet, in an endeavour to trip him up. In vain did he batter at its heads with his club: no sooner was one crushed, than two or three more grew in its place.[5]

e. An enormous crab scuttered from the swamp to aid the Hydra, and nipped Heracles's foot; furiously crushing its shell, he shouted to Iolaus for assistance. Iolaus set one corner of the grove alight and then, to prevent the Hydra from sprouting new heads, seared their roots with blazing branches; thus the flow of blood was checked.[6]

f. Now using a sword, or a golden falchion, Heracles severed the immortal head, part of which was of gold, and buried it, still hissing, under a heavy rock beside the road to Elaeus. The carcass he disembowelled, and dipped his arrows in the gall. Henceforth, the least wound from one of them was invariably fatal.

g. In reward for the crab's services, Hera set its image among the twelve signs of the Zodiac; and Eurystheus would not count this

Labour as duly accomplished, because Iolaus had supplied the fire-brands.[7]

1. Hesiod: *Theogony* 313 ff.
2. Pausanias: ii. 37. 1–3 and 5; ii. 36. 6–8.
3. Pausanias: ii. 37. 4; Apollodorus: ii. 5. 2; Strabo: viii. 6. 8.
4. Euripides: *Heracles* 419–20; Zenobius: *Proverbs* vi. 26; Apollodorus: *loc. cit.*; Simonides, quoted by scholiast on Hesiod's *Theogony* p. 257, ed. Heinsius; Diodorus Siculus: iv. 11; Hyginus: *Fabula* 30.
5. Hesiod: *Theogony* 313 ff.; Apollodorus: *loc. cit.*; Hyginus: *loc. cit.*; Servius on Virgil's *Aeneid* vi. 287.
6. Apollodorus: *loc. cit.*; Hyginus: *loc. cit.* and *Poetic Astronomy* ii. 23; Diodorus Siculus: iv. 11.
7. Euripides: *Ion* 192; Hesiod: *Theogony* 313 ff.; Apollodorus: *loc. cit.*; Alexander Myndius, quoted by Photius p. 475.

*

1. The Lernaean Hydra puzzled the Classical mythographers. Pausanias held that it might well have been a huge and venomous water-snake; but that 'Pisander had first called it many-headed, wishing to make it seem more terrifying and, at the same time, add to the dignity of his own verses' (Pausanias: ii. 37. 4). According to the euhemeristic Servius (on Virgil's *Aeneid* vi. 287), the Hydra was a source of underground rivers which used to burst out and inundate the land: if one of its numerous channels were blocked, the water broke through elsewhere, therefore Heracles first used fire to dry the ground, and then closed the channels.

2. In the earliest version of this myth, Heracles, as the aspirant for kingship, is likely to have wrestled in turn with a bull, a lion, a boar, or scorpion, and then dived into a lake to win gold from the water-monster living in its depth. Jason was set much the same tasks, and the helpful part played by Medea is here given to Athene – as Heracles's bride-to-be. Though the Hydra recalls the sea-serpent which Perseus killed with a golden falchion, or new-moon sickle, it was a fresh-water monster, like most of those mentioned by Irish and Welsh mythographers – *piastres* or *avancs* (see 148. 5) – and like the one recorded in the Homeric epithet for Lacedaemon, namely *cetoessa*, 'of the water-monster', doubtless haunting some deep pool of the Eurotas (see 125. 3). The dog-like body is a reminiscence of the sea-monster Scylla (see 16. 2), and of a seven-headed monster (on a late Babylonian cylinder-seal) which the hero Gilgamesh kills. Astrologers have brought the crab into the story so as to make Heracles's Twelve Labours correspond with the Signs of the Zodiac; but it should properly have figured in his struggle with the Nemean lion, the next Sign.

3. This ritual myth has become attached to that of the Danaids, who

were the ancient water-priestesses of Lerna. The number of heads given the Hydra varies intelligibly: as a college of priestesses it had fifty heads; as the sacred cuttle-fish, a disguise adopted by Thetis – who also had a college of fifty priestesses (see 81. *1*) – it had eight snaky arms ending in heads, and one head on its trunk, together making nine in honour of the Moon-goddess; one hundred heads suggest the *centuriae*, or war bands, which raided Argos from Lerna; and ten thousand is a typical embellishment by Euripides, who had little conscience as a mythographer. On Greek coins, the Hydra usually has seven heads: doubtless a reference to the seven outlets of the river Amymone.

4. Heracles's destruction of the Hydra seems to record a historical event: the attempted suppression of the Lernaean fertility rites. But new priestesses always appeared in the plane-tree grove – the plane-tree suggests Cretan religious influence, as does the cuttle-fish – until the Achaeans, or perhaps the Dorians, burned it down. Originally, it is clear, Demeter formed a triad with Hecate as Crone, here called Prosymne, 'addressed with hymns', and Persephone the Maiden; but Dionysus's Semele (see 27. *k*) ousted Persephone. There was a separate cult of Aphrodite – Thetis by the seaside.

125

THE THIRD LABOUR: THE CERYNEIAN HIND

HERACLES's Third Labour was to capture the Ceryneian Hind, and bring her alive from Oenoe to Mycenae. The swift, dappled creature had brazen hooves and golden horns like a stag, so that some call her a stag.[1] She was sacred to Artemis who, when only a child, saw five hinds, larger than bulls, grazing on the banks of the dark-pebbled Thessalian river Anaurus at the foot of the Parrhasian Mountains; the sun twinkled on their horns. Running in pursuit, she caught four of them, one after the other, with her own hands, and harnessed them to her chariot; the fifth fled across the river Celadon to the Ceryneian Hill – as Hera intended, already having Heracles's Labours in mind. According to another account, this hind was a masterless monster which used to ravage the fields, and which Heracles, after a severe struggle, sacrificed to Artemis on the summit of Mount Artemisium.[2]

b. Loth either to kill or wound the hind, Heracles performed this Labour without exerting the least force. He hunted her tirelessly for one whole year, his chase taking him as far as Istria and the Land of the

Hyperboreans. When, exhausted at last, she took refuge on Mount Artemisium, and thence descended to the river Ladon, Heracles let fly and pinned her forelegs together with an arrow, which passed between bone and sinew, drawing no blood. He then caught her, laid her across his shoulders, and hastened through Arcadia to Mycenae. Some, however, say that he used nets; or followed the hind's track until he found her asleep underneath a tree. Artemis came to meet Heracles, rebuking him for having ill-used her holy beast, but he pleaded necessity, and put the blame on Eurystheus. Her anger was thus appeased, and she let him carry the hind alive to Mycenae.³

c. Another version of the story is that this hind was one which Taygete the Pleiad, Alcyone's sister, had dedicated to Artemis in gratitude for being temporarily disguised as a hind and thus enabled to elude Zeus's embraces. Nevertheless, Zeus could not long be deceived, and begot Lacedaemon on her; whereupon she hanged herself on the summit of Mount Amyclaeus, thereafter called Mount Taygetus.⁴ Taygete's niece and namesake married Lacedaemon and bore him Himerus, whom Aphrodite caused to deflower his sister Cleodice unwittingly, on a night of promiscuous revel. Next day, learning what he had done, Himerus leaped into the river, now sometimes known by his name, and was seen no more; but oftener it is called the Eurotas, because Lacedaemon's predecessor, King Eurotas, having suffered an ignominious defeat at the hands of the Athenians – he would not wait for the full moon before giving battle – drowned himself in its waters. Eurotas, son of Myles, the inventor of water mills, was Amyclas's father, and grandfather both of Hyacinthus and of Eurydice, who married Acrisius.⁵

<ol>
<li>Apollodorus: ii. 5. 3; Diodorus Siculus: iv. 13; Euripides: Heracles 375 ff.; Virgil: Aeneid vi. 802; Hyginus: Fabula 30.</li>
<li>Apollodorus: loc. cit.; Callimachus: Hymn to Delos 103 and Hymn to Artemis 100 ff.; Euripides: loc. cit.; Pausanias: ii. 25. 3.</li>
<li>Apollodorus: loc. cit.; Diodorus Siculus: iv. 13; Pindar: Olympian Odes iii. 26–7; Hyginus: Fabula 30.</li>
<li>Pindar: Olympian Odes iii. 29 ff.; Apollodorus: ii. 10. 1; Plutarch: On Rivers 17.</li>
<li>Pausanias: iii. 1. 2–3 and 20.2; Plutarch: loc. cit.; Apollodorus: iii. 10. 3.</li>
</ol>

*

1. This Third Labour is of a different order from most of the others. Historically it may record the Achaean capture of a shrine where Artemis was worshipped as Elaphios ('hind-like'); her four chariot-stags represent the years of the Olympiad, and at the close of each a victim dressed in deer-skins was hunted to death (see 22. 1). Elaphios, at any rate, is said to have been Artemis's nurse, which means Artemis herself (Pausanias: vi. 22. 11). Mythically, however, the Labour seems to concern Heracles the Dactyl (see 52. 3), identified by the Gauls with Ogmius (Lucian: Heracles i), who invented the Ogham alphabet and all bardic lore (see 132. 3). The chase of the hind, or roe, symbolized the pursuit of Wisdom, and she is found, according to the Irish mystical tradition, harboured under a wild-apple tree (White Goddess p. 217). This would explain why Heracles is not said by anyone, except the ill-informed Euripides, to have done the roe any harm: instead he pursued her indefatigably without cease, for an entire year, to the Land of the Hyperboreans, experts in these very mysteries. According to Pollux, Heracles was called Melon ('of apples'), because apples were offered to him, presumably in recognition of his wisdom; but such wisdom came only with death, and his pursuit of the hind, like his visit to the Garden of the Hesperides, was really a journey to the Celtic Paradise. Zeus had similarly chased Taygete, who was a daughter of Atlas and therefore a non-Hellenic character.

2. In Europe, only reindeer does have horns, and reports of these may have come down from the Baltic by the Amber Route; reindeer, unlike other deer, can of course be harnessed.

3. The drowning of Taygete's son Himerus, and of her father-in-law Eurotas, suggests that early kings of Sparta were habitually sacrificed to the Eurotas water-monster, by being thrown, wrapped in branches, into a deep pool. So, it seems, was Tantalus (see 108. 3), another son of Taygete (Hyginus: Fabula 82). Lacedaemon means 'lake demon' (see 124. 2), and Laconia is the domain of Lacone ('lady of the lake'), whose image was rescued from the Dorian invaders by one Preugenes and brought to Patrae in Achaea (Pausanias: vii. 20. 4). The story behind Taygete's metamorphosis seems to be that the Achaean conquerors of Sparta called themselves Zeus, and their wives Hera. When Hera came to be worshipped as a cow, the Lelegian cult of Artemis the Hind was suppressed. A ritual marriage between Zeus as bull and Hera as cow may have been celebrated, as in Crete (see 90. 7).

4. Nights of promiscuous revel were held in various Greek states (see 44. a), and during the Alban Holiday at Rome: a concession to archaic sexual customs which preceded monogamy.

THE FOURTH LABOUR: THE ERYMANTHIAN BOAR

THE Fourth Labour imposed on Heracles was to capture alive the Erymanthian Boar: a fierce, enormous beast which haunted the cypress-covered slopes of Mount Erymanthus, and the thickets of Arcadian Mount Lampeia; and ravaged the country around Psophis.[1] Mount Erymanthus takes its name from a son of Apollo, whom Aphrodite blinded because he had seen her bathing; Apollo in revenge turned himself into a boar and killed her lover Adonis. Yet the mountain is sacred to Artemis.[2]

b. Heracles, passing through Pholoë on his way to Erymanthus – where he killed one Saurus, a cruel bandit – was entertained by the Centaur Pholus, whom one of the ash-nymphs bore to Silenus. Pholus set roast meat before Heracles, but himself preferred the raw, and dared not open the Centaurs' communal wine jar until Heracles reminded him that it was the very jar which, four generations earlier, Dionysus had left in the cave against this very occasion.[3] The Centaurs grew angry when they smelt the strong wine. Armed with great rocks, up-rooted fir-trees, firebrands, and butchers' axes, they made a rush at Pholus's cave. While Pholus hid in terror, Heracles boldly repelled Ancius and Agrius, his first two assailants, with a volley of firebrands.[4] Nephele, the Centaurs' cloudy grandmother, then poured down a smart shower of rain, which loosened Heracles's bow-string and made the ground slippery. However, he showed himself worthy of his former achievements, and killed several Centaurs, among them Oreus and Hylaeus. The rest fled as far as Malea, where they took refuge with Cheiron, their king, who had been driven from Mount Pelion by the Lapiths.[5]

c. A parting arrow from Heracles's bow passed through Elatus's arm, and stuck quivering in Cheiron's knee. Distressed at the accident to his old friend, Heracles drew out the arrow and though Cheiron himself supplied the vulneraries for dressing the wound, they were of no avail and he retired howling in agony to his cave; yet could not die, because he was immortal. Prometheus later offered to accept immortality in his stead, and Zeus approved this arrangement; but some say that Cheiron chose death not so much because of the pain he suffered as because he had grown weary of his long life.[6]

d. The Centaurs now fled in various directions: some with Eurytion to Pholoë; some with Nessus to the river Evenus; some to Mount Malea; others to Sicily, where the Sirens destroyed them. Poseidon received the remainder at Eleusis, and hid them in a mountain. Among those whom Heracles later killed was Homadus the Arcadian, who had tried to rape Eurystheus's sister Alcyone; by thus nobly avenging an insult offered to an enemy, Heracles won great fame.[7]

e. Pholus, in the meantime, while burying his dead kinsmen, drew out one of Heracles's arrows and examined it. 'How can so robust a creature have succumbed to a mere scratch?' he wondered. But the arrow slipped from his fingers and, piercing his foot, killed him there and then. Heracles broke off the pursuit and returned to Pholoë, where he buried Pholus with unusual honours at the foot of the mountain which has taken his name. It was on this occasion that the river Anigrus acquired the foul smell which now clings to it from its very source on Mount Lapithus: because a Centaur named Pylenor, whom Heracles had winged with an arrow, fled and washed his wound there. Some, however, hold that Melampus had caused the stench some years before, by throwing into the Anigrus the foul objects used for purifying the daughters of Proetus.[8]

f. Heracles now set off to chase the boar by the river Erymanthus. To take so savage a beast alive was a task of unusual difficulty; but he dislodged it from a thicket with loud halloos, drove it into a deep snow drift, and sprang upon its back. He bound it with chains, and carried it alive on his shoulders to Mycenae; but when he heard that the Argonauts were gathering for their voyage to Colchis, dropped the boar outside the market place and, instead of waiting for further orders from Eurystheus, who was hiding in his bronze jar, went off with Hylas to join the expedition. It is not known who dispatched the captured boar, but its tusks are preserved in the temple of Apollo at Cumae.[9]

g. According to some accounts, Cheiron was accidentally wounded by an arrow that pierced his left foot, while he and Pholus and the young Achilles were entertaining Heracles on Mount Pelion. After nine days, Zeus set Cheiron's image among the stars as the Centaur. But others hold that the Centaur is Pholus, who was honoured by Zeus in this way because he excelled all men in the art of prophesying from entrails. The Bowman in the Zodiac is likewise a Centaur: one Crotus, who lived on Mount Helicon, greatly beloved by his foster-sisters, the Muses.[10]

1. Ovid: *Heroides* ix. 87; Apollonius Rhodius: i. 127; Apollodorus: ii. 5. 4; Diodorus Siculus: iv. 12.

2. Ptolemy Hephaestionos: i. 306; Homer: *Odyssey* vi. 105.

3. Pausanias: vi. 21. 5; Apollodorus: *loc. cit.*; Diodorus Siculus: *loc. cit.*

4. Tzetzes: *On Lycophron* 670; Diodorus Siculus: *loc. cit.*; Apollodorus: *loc. cit.*

5. Pausanias: iii. 18. 9; Virgil: *Aeneid* viii. 293–4; Diodorus Siculus: *loc. cit.*; Apollodorus: *loc. cit.*

6. Apollodorus: *loc. cit.*; Lucian: *Dialogues of the Dead* 26.

7. Tzetzes: *On Lycophron* 670; Apollodorus: *loc. cit.*; Diodorus Siculus: *loc. cit.*

8. Apollodorus: *loc. cit.*; Diodorus Siculus: *loc. cit.*; Pausanias: v. 5. 6.

9. Apollodorus: *loc. cit.*; Pausanias: viii. 24. 2; Diodorus Siculus: *loc. cit.*; Apollonius Rhodius: i. 122 ff.

10. Theocritus: *Idyll* vii; Ovid: *Fasti* v. 380 ff.; Hyginus: *Poetic Astronomy* ii. 38 and 27; *Fabula* 224.

*

1. Boars were sacred to the Moon because of their crescent-shaped tusks, and it seems that the tanist who killed and emasculated his twin, the sacred king, wore boar-disguise when he did so (see 18. *7* and 151. *2*). The snowdrift in which the Erymanthian Boar was overcome indicates that this Labour took place at midwinter. Here Heracles is the Child Horus and avenges the death of his father Osiris on his uncle Set who comes disguised as a boar; the Egyptian taboo on boar's flesh was lifted only at midwinter. The boar's head Yuletide ceremony has its origin in this same triumph of the new sacred king over his rival. Adonis is murdered to avenge the death of Erymanthus, the previous year's tanist, whose name, 'divining by lots', suggests that he was chosen by lot to kill the sacred king. Mount Erymanthus being sacred to Artemis, not Aphrodite, Artemis must have been the goddess who took her bath, and the sacred king, not his tanist, must have seen her doing so (see 22. *i*).

2. It is probable that Heracles's battle with the Centaurs, like the similar battle at Peirithous's wedding (see 102. *2*), originally represented the ritual combat between a newly installed king and opponents in beast-disguise. His traditional weapons were arrows, one of which, to establish his sovereignty, he shot to each of the four quarters of the sky, and a fifth straight up into the air. Frontier wars between the Hellenes and the pre-Hellenic mountaineers of Northern Greece are also perhaps recorded in this myth.

3. Poisoned arrows dropped upon, or shot into, a knee or foot, caused the death not only of Pholus and Cheiron, but also of Achilles, Cheiron's pupil (see 92. *10* and 164. *j*): all of them Magnesian sacred kings, whose

souls the Sirens naturally received. The presence of Centaurs at Malea derives from a local tradition that Pholus's father Silenus was born there (Pausanias: iii. 25. 2); Centaurs were often represented as half goat, rather than half horse. Their presence at Eleusis, where Poseidon hid them in a mountain, suggests that when the initiate into the Mysteries celebrated a sacred marriage with the goddess, hobby-horse dancers took part in the proceedings.

127

THE FIFTH LABOUR: THE STABLES OF AUGEIAS

HERACLES's Fifth Labour was to cleanse King Augeias's filthy cattle yard in one day. Eurystheus gleefully pictured Heracles's disgust at having to load the dung into baskets and carry these away on his shoulders. Augeias, King of Elis, was the son of Helius, or Eleius, by Naupiadame, a daughter of Amphidamas; or, some say, by Iphiboë. Others call him the son of Poseidon. In flocks and herds he was the wealthiest man on earth: for, by a divine dispensation, his were immune against disease and inimitably fertile, nor did they ever miscarry. Although in almost every case they produced female offspring, he nevertheless had three hundred white-legged black bulls and two hundred red stud-bulls; besides twelve outstanding silvery-white bulls, sacred to his father Helius. These twelve defended his herds against marauding wild beasts from the wooded hills.[1]

b. Now, the dung in Augeias's cattle yard and sheepfolds had not been cleared away for many years, and though its noisome stench did not affect the beasts themselves, it spread a pestilence across the whole Peloponnese. Moreover, the valley pastures were so deep in dung that they could no longer be ploughed for grain.[2]

c. Heracles hailed Augeias from afar, and undertook to cleanse the yard before nightfall in return for a tithe of the cattle. Augeias laughed incredulously, and called Phyleus, his eldest son, to witness Heracles's offer. 'Swear to accomplish the task before nightfall', Phyleus demanded. The oath which Heracles now took by his father's name was the first and last one he ever swore. Augeias likewise took an oath to keep his side of the bargain. At this point, Phaethon, the leader of the twelve white bulls, charged at Heracles, mistaking him for a lion; whereupon he seized the bull's left horn, forced its neck downwards, and floored it by main strength.[3]

d. On the advice of Menedemus the Elean, and aided by Iolaus, Heracles first breached the wall of the yard in two places, and next diverted the neighbouring rivers Alpheus and Peneius, or Menius, so that their streams rushed through the yard, swept it clean and then went on to cleanse the sheepfolds and the valley pastures. Thus Heracles accomplished this Labour in one day, restoring the land to health, and not soiling so much as his little finger. But Augeias, on being informed by Copreus that Heracles had already been under orders from Eurystheus to cleanse the cattle yards, refused to pay the reward and even dared deny that he and Heracles had struck a bargain.

e. Heracles suggested that the case be submitted to arbitration; yet when the judges were seated, and Phyleus, subpoenaed by Heracles, testified to the truth, Augeias sprang up in a rage and banished them both from Elis, asserting that he had been tricked by Heracles, since the River-gods, not he, had done the work. To make matters even worse, Eurystheus refused to count this Labour as one of the ten, because Heracles had been in Augeias's hire.

f. Phyleus then went to Dulichium; and Heracles to the court of Dexamenus, King of Olenus, whose daughter Mnesimache he later rescued from the Centaur Eurytion.[4]

1. Apollodorus: ii. 5. 5 and 7. 2; Diodorus Siculus: iv. 13; Pausanias: v. 1. 7; Tzetzes: *On Lycophron* 41; Hyginus: *Fabula* 14.
2. Apollodorus: ii. 5. 5; Servius on Virgil's *Aeneid* viii. 300; Diodorus Siculus: *loc. cit.*; Pausanias: *loc. cit.*
3. Pausanias: *loc. cit.*; Apollodorus: *loc. cit.*; Plutarch: *Roman Questions* 28; Theocritus: *Idyll* xxv. 115 ff.
4. Ptolemy Hephaestionos: v, quoted by Photius p. 486; Hyginus: *Fabula* 30; Pausanias: *loc. cit.*; Apollodorus: *loc. cit.*; Diodorus Siculus: *loc. cit.*; Servius: *loc. cit.*; Callimachus: *Hymn to Delos* 102.

*

1. This confused myth seems to be founded on the legend that Heracles, like Jason, was ordered to tame two bulls, yoke them, clean an overgrown hill, then plough, sow, and reap it in a single day – the usual tasks set a candidate for kingship (see 152. *3*). Here, the hill had to be cleared not of trees and stones, as in the Celtic versions of the myth, but of dung – probably because the name of Eurystheus's herald, who delivered the order, was Copreus ('dung man'). Sir James Frazer, commenting on Pausanias (v. 10. 9), quotes a Norse tale, 'The Mastermaid', in which a prince who wishes to win a giant's daughter must first clean three stables. For each pitch-fork of dung which he tosses out, ten return. The princess then advises him to turn the pitchfork upside-down and use the handle. He does so, and the stable is soon cleansed. Frazer suggests that, in the original version, Athene may have given Heracles the same advice; more likely, however, the Norse tale is a variant of this Labour. Augeias's cattle are irrelevant to the story, except to account for the great mass of dung to be removed. Cattle manure, as the myth shows, was not valued by Greek farmers. Hesiod, in his *Works and Days*, does not mention it; and H. Mitchell (*Economics of Ancient Greece*) shows that the grazing of cattle on fallow land is prohibited in several ancient leases. Odysseus's dog Argus did, indeed, lie on a midden used for dunging the estate (*Odyssey* xvii. 299), but wherever the *Odyssey* may have been written – and it certainly was not on the Greek mainland – the references to agriculture and arboriculture suggest a survival of Cretan practice. According to some mythographers, Augeias was the son of Eleius, which means no more than 'King of Elis'; according to others, a son of Poseidon, which suggests that he was an Aeolian. But Eleius has here been confused with Helius, the Corinthian Sun-god; and Augeias is therefore credited with a herd of sacred cattle, like that owned by Sisyphus (see 67. *1*). The number of heads in such herds was 350, representing twelve complete lunations less the sacred five-day holiday of the Egyptian year (see 42. *1*); that they were lunar cattle was proved by their red, white, and black colours (see 90. *3*); and the white bulls represent these twelve lunations. Such sacred cattle were often stolen – as by Heracles himself in his Tenth Labour – and the sequel to his quarrel with Augeias was that he won these twelve bulls as well.

2. The Fifth Labour, which properly concerns only ploughing, sowing, and reaping tasks has, in fact, been confused with two others: the Tenth, namely the lifting of Geryon's cattle; and the Seventh, namely the capture of Poseidon's white Cretan bull – which was not, however, used for ploughing. In the cult of Poseidon – who is also described as Augeias's father – young men wrestled with bulls, and Heracles's struggle against Phaethon, like Theseus's against the Minotaur, is best understood as a coronation rite: by magical contact with the bull's horn, he became capable of fertilizing the land, and earned the title of Potidan, or Poseidon, given to the Moon-goddess's chosen lover. Similarly, in a love-contest Heracles fought the river Achelous, represented as a bull-headed man, and broke off his cornucopia (see 141. *d*). The deflection of the Alpheius suggests that the icon from which this incident is deduced showed

Heracles twisting the Cretan Bull around by the horns, beside the banks of a river, where numerous cattle were grazing. This bull was mistaken for a river-god, and the scene read as meaning that he had deflected the river in order to cleanse the fields for ploughing.

128

THE SIXTH LABOUR: THE STYMPHALIAN BIRDS

HERACLES's Sixth Labour was to remove the countless brazen-beaked, brazen-clawed, brazen-winged, man-eating birds, sacred to Ares which, frightened by the wolves of Wolves' Ravine on the Orchomenan Road, had flocked to the Stymphalian Marsh.[1] Here they bred and waded beside the river of the same name, occasionally taking to the air in great flocks, to kill men and beasts by discharging a shower of brazen feathers and at the same time muting a poisonous excrement, which blighted the crops.

b. On arrival at the marsh, which lay surrounded by dense woods, Heracles found himself unable to drive away the birds with his arrows; they were too numerous. Moreover, the marsh seemed neither solid enough to support a man walking, nor liquid enough for the use of a boat. As Heracles paused irresolutely on the bank, Athene gave him a pair of brazen castanets, made by Hephaestus; or it may have been a rattle. Standing on a spur of Mount Cyllene, which overlooks the marsh, Heracles clacked the castanets, or shook the rattle, raising such a din that the birds soared up in one great flock, mad with terror. He shot down scores of them as they flew off to the Isle of Ares in the Black Sea, where they were afterwards found by the Argonauts; some say that Heracles was with the Argonauts at the time, and killed many more of the birds.[2]

c. Stymphalian birds are the size of cranes, and closely resemble ibises, except that their beaks can pierce a metal breast-plate, and are not hooked. They also breed in the Arabian Desert, and there cause more trouble even than lions or leopards by flying at travellers' breasts and transfixing them. Arabian hunters have learned to wear protective cuirasses of plaited bark, which entangle those deadly beaks and enable them to seize and wring the necks of their assailants. It may be that a flock of these birds migrated from Arabia to Stymphalus, and gave their name to the whole breed.[3]

d. According to some accounts, the so-called Stymphalian Birds were women: daughters of Stymphalus and Ornis, whom Heracles killed because they refused him hospitality. At Stymphalus, in the ancient temple of Stymphalian Artemis, images of these birds are hung from the roof, and behind the building stand statues of maidens with birds' legs. Here also Temenus, a son of Pelasgus, founded three shrines in Hera's honour: in the first she was worshipped as Child, because Temenus had reared her; in the second as Bride, because she had married Zeus; in the third as Widow, because she had repudiated Zeus and retired to Stymphalus.[4]

1. Pausanias: viii. 22. 4–6; Apollodorus: ii. 5. 6.
2. Apollonius Rhodius: ii. 1052 ff.; Pausanias: *loc. cit.*; Servius on Virgil's *Aeneid* viii. 300; Apollonius Rhodius: ii. 1037 and 1053, with scholiast; Diodorus Siculus: iv. 13; Apollodorus: *loc. cit.*; Hyginus: *Fabula* 30.
3. Pausanias: viii. 22. 4.
4. Mnaseas, quoted by scholiast on Apollonius Rhodius: ii. 1054; Pausanias: viii. 22. 2. and 5.

*

1. Though Athene continues to help Heracles, this Labour does not belong to the marriage-task sequence but glorifies him as the healer who expels fever demons, identified with marsh-birds. The helmeted birds shown on Stymphalian coins are spoon-bills, cousins to the cranes which appear in English medieval carvings as sucking the breath of sick men. They are, in fact, bird-legged Sirens, personifications of fever; and castanets, or rattles, were used in ancient times (and still are among primitive peoples) to drive away fever demons. Artemis was the goddess who had power to inflict or cure fever with her 'merciful shafts'.

2. The Stymphalian marsh used to increase in size considerably whenever the underground channel which carried away its waters became blocked, as happened in Pausanias's time (viii. 22. 6); and Iphicratus, when besieging the city, would have blocked it deliberately, had not a sign from heaven prevented him (Strabo: viii. 8. 5). It may well be that in one version of the story Heracles drained the marsh by freeing the channel; as he had previously drained the Plain of Tempe (Diodorus Siculus: iv. 18).

3. The myth, however, seems to have a historical, as well as a ritual, meaning. Apparently a college of Arcadian priestesses, who worshipped the Triple-goddess as Maiden, Bride, and Crone, took refuge at Stym-

phalus, after having been driven from Wolves' Ravine by invaders who worshipped Wolfish Zeus; and Mnaseas has plausibly explained the expulsion, or massacre, of the Stymphalian Birds as the suppression of this witch-college by Heracles – that is to say, by a tribe of Achaeans. The name Stymphalus suggests erotic practices.

4. Pausanias's 'strong-beaked Arabian birds' may have been sun-stroke demons, kept at bay by bark spine-protectors, and confused with the powerfully beaked ostriches, which the Arabs still hunt.

Leuc-erodes, 'white heron', is the Greek name for spoon-bill; an ancestor of Herod the Great is said to have been a temple slave to Tyrian Heracles (Africanus, quoted by Eusebius: *Ecclesiastical History* i. 6. 7), which accounts for the family name. The spoon-bill is closely related to the ibis, another marsh-bird, sacred to the god Thoth, inventor of writing; and Tyrian Heracles, like his Celtic counterpart, was a protector of learning, which made Tyre famous (*Ezekiel* xxviii. 12). In Hebrew tradition, his priest Hiram of Tyre exchanged riddles with Solomon.

129

THE SEVENTH LABOUR: THE CRETAN BULL

EURYSTHEUS ordered Heracles, as his Seventh Labour, to capture the Cretan Bull; but it is much disputed whether this was the bull sent by Zeus, which ferried Europe across to Crete, or the one, withheld by Minos from sacrifice to Poseidon, which sired the Minotaur on Pasiphaë. At this time it was ravaging Crete, especially the region watered by the river Tethris, rooting up crops and levelling orchard walls.[1]

b. When Heracles sailed to Crete, Minos offered him every assistance in his power, but he preferred to capture the bull single-handed, though it belched scorching flames. After a long struggle, he brought the monster across to Mycenae, where Eurystheus, dedicating it to Hera, set it free. Hera however, loathing a gift which redounded to Heracles's glory, drove the bull first to Sparta, and then back through Arcadia and across the Isthmus to Attic Marathon, whence Theseus later dragged it to Athens as a sacrifice to Athene.[2]

c. Nevertheless, many still deny the identity of the Cretan and Marathonian bulls.[3]

1. Apollodorus: ii. 5. 7; Diodorus Siculus: iv. 13; Pausanias: i. 27. 9; First Vatican Mythographer: 47.

2. Diodorus Siculus: *loc. cit.*; Servius on Virgil's *Aeneid* viii. 294;
Apollodorus: *loc. cit.*; First Vatican Mythographer: *loc. cit.*
3. Theon: *On Aratus* p. 24.

*

1. The combat with a bull, or a man in bull's disguise – one of the
ritual tasks imposed on the candidate for kingship (see 123. *1*) – also
appears in the story of Theseus and the Minotaur (see 98. *2*), and of
Jason and the fire-breathing bulls of Aeëtes (see 152. *3*). When the immortality implicit in the sacred kingship was eventually offered to every
initiate of the Dionysian Mysteries, the capture of a bull and its dedication to Dionysus Plusodotes ('giver of wealth') became a common rite
both in Arcadia (Pautanias: viii. 19. 2) and Lydia (Strabo: xiv. 1. 44),
where Dionysus held the title of Zeus. His principal theophany was as a
bull, but he also appeared in the form of a lion and a serpent (see 27. *4*).
Contact with the bull's horn (see 127. *2*) enabled the sacred king to fertilize the land in the name of the Moon-goddess by making rain – the
magical explanation being that a bull's bellow portended thunder-
storms, which *rhombi*, or bull-roarers, were accordingly swung to induce.
Torches were also flung to simulate lightning (see 68. *a*) and came to
suggest the bull's fiery breath.

2. Dionysus is called Plutodotes ('wealth-giver') because of his cornucopia, torn from a bull, which was primarily a water charm (see 142. *b*);
he developed from Cretan Zagreus, and among Zagreus's changes are
lion, a horned serpent, a bull, and 'Cronus making rain' (see 30. *3*).

130

THE EIGHTH LABOUR: THE MARES
OF DIOMEDES

EURYSTHEUS ordered Heracles, as his Eighth Labour, to capture the
four savage mares of Thracian King Diomedes – it is disputed whether
he was the son of Ares and Cyrene, or born of an incestuous relationship
between Asterië and her father Atlas – who ruled the warlike Bistones,
and whose stables, at the now vanished city of Tirida, were the terror of
Thrace. Diomedes kept the mares tethered with iron chains to bronze
mangers, and fed them on the flesh of his unsuspecting guests. One
version of the story makes them stallions, not mares, and names them
Podargus, Lampon, Xanthus, and Deinus.[1]

b. With a number of volunteers, Heracles set sail for Thrace, visiting his friend King Admetus of Pherae on the way. Arrived at Tirida, he overpowered Diomedes's grooms and drove the mares down to the sea, where he left them on a knoll in charge of his minion Abderus, and then turned to repel the Bistones as they rushed in pursuit. His party being outnumbered, he overcame them by ingeniously cutting a channel which caused the sea to flood the low-lying plain; when they turned to run, he pursued them, stunned Diomedes with his club, dragged his body around the lake that had now formed, and set it before his own mares, which tore at the still living flesh. Their hunger being now fully assuaged – for, while Heracles was away, they had also devoured Abderus – he mastered them without much trouble.[2]

c. According to another account Abderus, though a native of Opus in Locris, was employed by Diomedes. Some call him the son of Hermes; and others the son of Heracles's friend, Opian Menoetius, and thus brother to Patroclus who fell at Troy. After founding the city of Abdera beside Abderus's tomb, Heracles took Diomedes's chariot and harnessed the mares to it, though hitherto they had never known bit or bridle. He drove them speedily back across the mountains until he reached Mycenae, where Eurystheus dedicated them to Hera and set them free on Mount Olympus.[3] They were eventually destroyed by wild beasts; yet it is claimed that their descendants survived until the Trojan War and even until the time of Alexander the Great. The ruins of Diomedes's palace are shown at Cartera Come, and at Abdera athletic games are still celebrated in honour of Abderus – they include all the usual contests, except chariot-racing; which accounts for the story that Abderus was killed when the man-eating mares wrecked a chariot to which he had harnessed them.[4]

1. Apollodorus: ii. 5. 8; Hyginus: *Fabulae* 250 and 30; Pliny: *Natural History* iv. 18; Diodorus Siculus: iv. 15.
2. Apollodorus: *loc. cit.*; Euripides: *Alcestis* 483; Strabo: *Fragments* 44 and 47; Diodorus Siculus: *loc. cit.*
3. Hyginus: *Fabula* 30; Apollodorus: *loc. cit.*; Diodorus Siculus: iv. 39; Homer: *Iliad* xi. 608; Euripides: *Heracles* 380 ff.
4. Apollodorus: *loc. cit.*; Servius on Virgil's *Aeneid* i. 756; Diodorus Siculus: iv. 15; Strabo: *Fragment* 44; Philostratus: *Imagines* ii. 25; Hyginus: *Fabula* 250.

*

1. The bridling of a wild horse, intended for a sacrificial horse feast (see 75. *3*), seems to have been a coronation rite in some regions of Greece.

Heracles's mastery of Arion (see 138. *g*) − a feat also performed by Oncus and Adrastus (Pausanias: viii. 25. 5) − is paralleled by Bellerophon's capture of Pegasus. This ritual myth has here been combined with a legend of how Heracles, perhaps representing the Teans who seized Abdera from the Thracians (Herodotus: i. 168), annulled the custom by which wild women in horse-masks used to chase and eat the sacred king at the end of his reign (see 27. *d*); instead he was killed in an organized chariot crash (see 71. *1*; 101. *g* and 109. *j*). The omission of chariot-racing from the funeral games at Abdera points to a ban on this revised sacrifice. Podargus is called after Podarge the Harpy, mother of Xanthus, an immortal horse given by Poseidon to Peleus as a wedding present (see 81. *m*); Lampus recalls Lampon, one of Eos's team (see 40. *a*). Diodorus's statement that these mares were let loose on Olympus may mean that the cannibalistic horse cult survived there until Hellenistic times.

2. Canals, tunnels, or natural underground conduits were often described as the work of Heracles (see 127. *d*; 138. *d* and 142. *3*).

131

THE NINTH LABOUR: HIPPOLYTE'S GIRDLE

HERACLES'S Ninth Labour was to fetch for Eurystheus's daughter Admete the golden girdle of Ares worn by the Amazonian queen Hippolyte. Taking one ship or, some say, nine, and a company of volunteers, among whom were Iolaus, Telamon of Aegina, Peleus of Iolcus and, according to some accounts, Theseus of Athens, Heracles set sail for the river Thermodon.[1]

b. The Amazons were children of Ares by the Naiad Harmonia, born in the glens of Phrygian Acmonia; but some call their mother Aphrodite, or Otrere, daughter of Ares.[2] At first they lived beside the river Amazon, now named after Tanais, a son of the Amazon Lysippe, who offended Aphrodite by his scorn of marriage and his devotion to war. In revenge, Aphrodite caused Tanais to fall in love with his mother; but, rather than yield to an incestuous passion, he flung himself into the river and drowned. To escape the reproaches of his ghost, Lysippe then led her daughters around the Black Sea coast, to a plain by the river Thermodon, which rises in the lofty Amazonian mountains. There they formed three tribes, each of which founded a city.[3]

c. Then as now, the Amazons reckoned descent only through the mother, and Lysippe had laid it down that the men must perform all household tasks, while the women fought and governed. The arms and legs of infant boys were therefore broken to incapacitate them for war or travel. These unnatural women, whom the Scythians call Oeorpata, showed no regard for justice or decency, but were famous warriors, being the first to employ cavalry.[4] They carried brazen bows and short shields shaped like a half moon; their helmets, clothes, and girdles were made from the skins of wild beasts.[5] Lysippe, before she fell in battle, built the great city of Themiscyra, and defeated every tribe as far as the river Tanais. With the spoils of her campaigns she raised temples to Ares, and others to Artemis Tauropolus whose worship she established. Her descendants extended the Amazonian empire westward across the river Tanais, to Thrace; and again, on the southern coast, westward across the Thermodon to Phrygia. Three famous Amazonian queens, Marpesia, Lampado, and Hippo, seized a great part of Asia Minor and Syria, and founded the cities of Ephesus, Smyrna, Cyrene, and Myrine. Other Amazonian foundations are Thiba and Sinope.[6]

d. At Ephesus, they set up an image of Artemis under a beech-tree, where Hippo offered sacrifices; after which her followers performed first a shield dance, and then a round dance, with rattling quivers, beating the ground in unison, to the accompaniment of pipes – for Athene had not yet invented the flute. The temple of Ephesian Artemis, later built around this image and unrivalled in magnificence even by that of Delphic Apollo, is included among the seven wonders of the world; two streams, both called Selenus, and flowing in opposite directions, surround it. It was on this expedition that the Amazons captured Troy, Priam being then still a child. But while detachments of the Amazonian army went home laden with vast quantities of spoil, the rest, staying to consolidate their power in Asia Minor, were driven out by an alliance of barbarian tribes, and lost their queen Marpesia.[7]

e. By the time that Heracles came to visit the Amazons, they had all returned to the river Thermodon, and their three cities were ruled by Hippolyte, Antiope, and Melanippe. On his way, he put in at the island of Paros, famous for its marble, which King Rhadamanthys had bequeathed to one Alcaeus, a son of Androgeus; but four of Minos's sons, Eurymedon, Chryses, Nephalion, and Philolaus, had also settled there. When a couple of Heracles's crew, landing to fetch water, were murdered by Minos's sons, he indignantly killed all four of them, and pressed the Parians so hard that they sent envoys offering, in requital for the dead sailors, any two men whom he might choose to be his slaves. Satisfied by this proposal, Heracles raised the siege and chose King Alcaeus and his brother Sthenelus, whom he took aboard his ship. Next, he sailed through the Hellespont and Bosphorus to Mariandyne in Mysia, where he was entertained by King Lycus the Paphlagonian, son of Dascylus and grandson of Tantalus.[8] In return, he supported Lycus in a war with the Bebrycans, killing many, including their king Mygdon, brother of Amycus, and recovered much Paphlagonian land from the Bebrycans; this he restored to Lycus, who renamed it Heracleia in his honour. Later, Heracleia was colonized by Megarians and Tanagrans on the advice of the Pythoness at Delphi, who told them to plant a colony beside the Black Sea, in a region dedicated to Heracles.[9]

f. Arrived at the mouth of the river Thermodon, Heracles cast anchor in the harbour of Themiscyra, where Hippolyte paid him a visit and, attracted by his muscular body, offered him Ares's girdle as a love gift. But Hera had meanwhile gone about, disguised in Amazon dress, spreading a rumour that these strangers planned to abduct Hippolyte; whereupon the incensed warrior-women mounted their horses and charged down on the ship. Heracles, suspecting treachery, killed Hippolyte off hand, removed her girdle, seized her axe and other weapons, and prepared to defend himself. He killed each of the Amazon leaders in turn, putting their army to flight after great slaughter.[10]

g. Some, however, say that Melanippe was ambushed, and ransomed by Hippolyte at the price of the girdle; or contrariwise. Or that Theseus captured Hippolyte, and presented her girdle to Heracles who, in return, allowed him to make Antiope his slave. Or that Hippolyte refused to give Heracles the girdle and that they fought a pitched battle; she was thrown off her horse, and he stood over her, club in hand, offering quarter, but she chose to die rather than yield. It is even said that the girdle belonged to a daughter of Briareus the Hundred-handed One.[11]

h. On his return from Themiscyra, Heracles came again to Mariandyne, and competed in the funeral games of King Lycus's brother Priolas, who had been killed by the Mysians, and for whom dirges are still sung. Heracles boxed against the Mariandynian champion Titias, knocked out all his teeth and killed him with a blow to the temple. In proof of his regret for this accident, he subdued the Mysians and the Phrygians on Dascylus's behalf; but he also subdued the Bithynians, as far as the mouth of the river Rhebas and the summit of Mount Colone, and claimed their kingdom for himself. Pelops's Paphlagonians voluntarily surrendered to him. However, no sooner had Heracles departed, than the Bebrycans, under Amycus, son of Poseidon, once more robbed Lycus of his land, extending their frontier to the river Hypius.[12]

i. Sailing thence to Troy, Heracles rescued Hesione from a sea-monster; and continued his voyage to Thracian Aenus, where he was entertained by Poltys; and, just as he was putting to sea again, shot and killed on the Aenian beach Poltys's insolent brother Sarpedon, a son of Poseidon. Next, he subjugated the Thracians who had settled in Thasos, and bestowed the island on the sons of Androgeus, whom he had carried off from Paros; and at Torone was challenged to a wrestling match by Polygonus and Telegonus, sons of Proteus, both of whom he killed.[13]

j. Returning to Mycenae at last, Heracles handed the girdle to Eurystheus, who gave it to Admete. As for the other spoil taken from the Amazons: he presented their rich robes to the Temple of Apollo at Delphi, and Hippolyte's axe to Queen Omphale, who included it among the sacred regalia of the Lydian kings. Eventually it was taken to a Carian temple of Labradian Zeus, and placed in the hand of his divine image.[14]

k. Amazons are still to be found in Albania, near Colchis, having been driven there from Themiscyra at the same time as their neighbours, the Gargarensians. When they reached the safety of the Albanian mountains, the two peoples separated: the Amazons settling at the foot of the Caucasian Mountains, around the river Mermodas, and the Gargarensians immediately to the north. On an appointed day every spring, parties of young Amazons and young Gargarensians meet at the summit of the mountain which separates their territories and, after performing a joint sacrifice, spend two months together, enjoying promiscuous intercourse under the cover of night. As soon as an Amazon finds herself pregnant, she returns home. Whatever girl-children are born become Amazons, and the boys are sent to the Gargarensians who, because they have no means of ascertaining their paternity, distribute them by lot among their huts.[15] In recent times, the Amazon queen Minythyia set out from her Albanian court to meet Alexander the Great in tiger-haunted Hyrcania; and there enjoyed his company for thirteen days, hoping to have offspring by him – but died childless soon afterwards.[16]

l. These Amazons of the Black Sea must be distinguished from Dionysus's Libyan allies who once inhabited Hespera, an island in Lake Tritonis which was so rich in fruit-bearing trees, sheep and goats, that they found no need to grow corn. After capturing all the cities in the island, except holy Mene, the home of the Ethiopian fish-eaters (who mine emeralds, rubies, topazes, and sard) they defeated the neighbouring Libyans and nomads, and founded the great city of Chersonesus, so called because it was built on a peninsula.[17] From this base they attacked the Atlantians, the most civilized nation west of the Nile, whose capital is on the Atlantic island of Cerne. Myrine, the Amazonian queen, raised a force of thirty thousand cavalry and three thousand infantry. All of them carried bows with which, when retreating, they used to shoot accurately at their pursuers, and were armoured with the skins of the almost unbelievably large Libyan serpents.

m. Invading the land of the Atlantians, Myrine defeated them decisively and, crossing over to Cerne, captured the city; she then put every man to the sword, enslaved the women and children, and razed the city walls. When the remaining Atlantians agreed to surrender, she treated them fairly, made friends with them and, in compensation for their loss of Cerne, built the new city of Myrine, where she settled the captives and all others desirous of living there. Since the Atlantians now offered to pay her divine honours, Myrine protected them against the neighbouring tribe of Gorgons, of whom she killed a great many in a pitched battle, besides taking no less than three thousand prisoners.[18] That night, however, while the Amazons were holding a victory banquet, the prisoners stole their swords and, at a signal, the main body of Gorgons who had rallied and hidden in an oak-wood, poured down from all sides to massacre Myrine's followers.

n. Myrine contrived to escape – her dead lie buried under three huge mounds, still called the Mounds of the Amazons – and, after traversing most of Libya, entered Egypt with a new army, befriended King Horus, the son of Isis, and passed on to the invasion of Arabia. Some hold that it was these Libyan Amazons, not those from the Black Sea, who conquered Asia Minor; and that Myrine, after selecting the most suitable sites in her new empire, founded a number of coastal cities, including Myrine, Cyme, Pitane, Priene, and others farther inland. She also subdued several of the Aegean Islands, notably Lesbos, where she built the city of Mitylene, named after a sister who had shared in the campaign. While Myrine was still engaged in conquering the islands, a storm overtook her fleet; but the Mother of the Gods bore every ship safely to Samothrace, then uninhabited, which Myrine consecrated to her, founding altars and offering splendid sacrifices.

o. Myrine then crossed over to the Thracian mainland, where King Mopsus and his ally, the Scythian Sipylus, worsted her in fair fight, and she was killed. The Amazon army never recovered from this setback: defeated by the Thracians in frequent engagements, its remnants finally retired to Libya.[19]

1. Scholiast on Pindar's *Nemean Odes* iii. 64; Apollodorus: ii. 5. 9; Justin: ii. 4; Pindar: *Nemean Odes* iii. 38 and *Fragment* 172; Philochorus, quoted by Plutarch: *Theseus* 26.

2. Apollonius Rhodius: ii. 990–2; Cicero: *In Defence of Flaccus* 15; Scholiast on Homer's *Iliad* i. 189; Hyginus: *Fabula* 30; Scholiast on Apollonius Rhodius: ii. 1033.

3. Servius on Virgil's *Aeneid* xi. 659; Plutarch: *On Rivers* 14; Apollonius Rhodius: ii. 976–1000.

4. Arrian: *Fragment* 58; Diodorus Siculus: ii. 451; Herodotus: iv. 100; Apollonius Rhodius: ii. 987–9; Lysias, quoted by Tzetzes: *On Lycophron* 1332.

5. Pindar: *Nemean Odes* iii. 38; Servius on Virgil's *Aeneid* i. 494; Strabo: xi. 5. 1.

6. Diodorus Siculus: ii. 45–6; Strabo: xi. 5. 4; Justin: ii. 4; Hecataeus: *Fragment* 352.

7. Callimachus: *Hymn to Artemis* 237 ff.; Hyginus: *Fabulae* 223 and 225; Pliny: *Natural History* v. 31; Homer: *Iliad* iii. 189; Tzetzes: *On Lycophron* 69; Justin: ii. 4.

8. Diodorus Siculus: v. 79; Herodotus: vii. 72; Scholiast on Apollonius Rhodius: ii. 754.

9. Strabo: xii. 3. 4; Apollodorus: ii. 5. 9; Pausanias: v. 26. 6; Justin: xvi. 3.

10. Diodorus Siculus: iv. 16; Apollodorus: *loc. cit.*; Plutarch: *Greek Questions* 45.

11. Apollonius Rhodius: ii. 966–9, Diodorus Siculus: *loc. cit.*; Tzetzes: *On Lycophron* 1329; Ibycus, quoted by scholiast on Apollonius Rhodius: *loc. cit.*

12. Apollonius Rhodius: ii. 776 ff.

13. Apollodorus: ii. 5. 9.

14. Apollodorus: *loc. cit.*; Tzetzes: *On Lycophron* 1327; Euripides: *Heracles* 418 and *Ion* 1145; Plutarch: *Greek Questions* 45.

15. Strabo: xi. 5. 1–2 and 4; Servius on Virgil's *Aeneid* xi. 659.

16. Justin: ii. 4; Cleitarchus, quoted by Strabo: xi. 5. 4.

17. Diodorus Siculus: iii. 52–3.

18. Diodorus Siculus: iii. 54.

19. Diodorus Siculus: iii. 55.

*

1. If Admete was the name of the princess for whose sake Heracles performed all these marriage tasks, the removal of her girdle in the wedding chamber must have marked the end of his Labours. But first Admete will have struggled with him, as Hippolyte did, and as Penthesileia struggled with Achilles (see 164. *a* and *2*), or Thetis with Peleus (see 81. *k*) – whose introduction into the story is thus explained. In that case, she will have gone through her usual transformations, which suggests that the cuttlefish-like Hydra was Admete – the gold-guarding serpent which he overcame being Ladon (see 133. *a*) – and that she may also have turned into a crab (see 124. *e*), a hind (see 125. *c*), a wild mare (see 16. *f*), and a cloud (see 126. *b*) before he contrived to win her maidenhead.

2. A tradition of armed priestesses still lingered at Ephesus and other cities in Asia Minor; but the Greek mythographers, having forgotten the former existence of similar colleges at Athens and other cities in Greece itself, sent Heracles in search of Hippolyte's girdle to the Black Sea, where matriarchal tribes were still active (see 100. *1*). A three-tribe system is the general rule in matriarchal society. That the girdle belonged to a daughter of Briareus ('strong'), one of the Hundred-handed Ones, points to an early setting of the marriage-test story in Northern Greece.

3. Admete is another name for Athene, who must have appeared in the icons standing by, under arms, watching Heracles's feats and helping him when in difficulties. Athene was Neith, the Love-and-Battle goddess of the Libyans (see 8. *1*); her counterpart in Asia Minor was the great Moon-goddess Marian, Myrine, Ay-Mari, Mariamne or Marienna, who gave her name to Mariandyne – 'Marian's Dune' – and to Myrine, the city of the gynocratic Lemnians (see 149. *1*); and whom the Trojans worshipped as 'Leaping Myrine' (Homer: *Iliad* ii. 814). 'Smyrna' is 'Myrine' again, preceded by the definite article. Marienna, the Sumerian form, means 'High fruitful Mother', and the Ephesian Artemis was a fertility-goddess.

4. Myrine is said to have been caught in a storm and saved by the Mother of the Gods – in whose honour she founded altars at Samothrace – because she was herself the Mother of the Gods, and her rites saved sailors from shipwreck (see 149. *2*). Much the same mother-goddess was anciently worshipped in Thrace, the region of the river Tanais (Don), Armenia, and throughout Asia Minor and Syria. Theseus's expedition to Amazonia, a myth modelled on that of Heracles, confuses the issue, and has tempted mythographers to invent the fictitious invasion of Athens by Amazons and Scythians combined (see 100. *c*).

5. That the Amazons set up an image under an Ephesian beech is a mistake made by Callimachus who, being an Egyptian, was unaware that beeches did not grow so far south; it must have been a date-palm, symbol of fertility (see 14. *2*), and a reminder of the goddess's Libyan origin, since her statue was hung with large golden dates, generally mistaken for breasts. Mopsus's defeat of the Amazons is the story of the Hittites' defeat by the Moschians about 1200 B.C.; the Hittites had originally been wholly patriarchal, but under the influence of the matriarchal societies of Asia Minor and Babylonia had accepted goddess-worship. At Hattusas, their capital, a sculptural relief of a battle-goddess has recently been discovered by Garstang; who regards the Ephesian Artemis cult as of Hittite origin. The victories over the Amazons secured by Heracles, Theseus, Dionysus, Mopsus, and others, record, in fact, setbacks to the matriarchal system in Greece, Asia Minor, Thrace, and Syria.

6. Stephanus of Byzantium (*sub* Paros) records the tradition that Paros was a Cretan colony. Heracles's expedition there refers to a Hellenic occupation of the island. His bestowal of Thasos on the sons of Androgeus is a reference to its capture by a force of Parians mentioned in Thucydides iv. 104: this took place towards the close of the eighth century B.C. Euboeans colonized Torone at about the same time, representing Toronē ('shrill queen') as a daughter of Proteus (Stephanus of Byzantium *sub* Torone). Hippolyte's double axe (*labrys*) was not, however, placed in Labradean Zeus's hand instead of a thunderbolt; it was itself a thunderbolt, and Zeus carried it by permission of the Cretan goddess who ruled in Lydia.

7. The Gargarensians are the Gogarenians, whom Ezekiel calls Gog (*Ezekiel* xxxviii and xxxix).

8. In his account of Myrine, Diodorus Siculus quotes early Libyan traditions which had already acquired a fairy-tale lustre; it is established, however, that in the third millennium B.C. neolithic emigrants went out from Libya in all directions, probably expelled by an inundation of their fields (see 39. *3–6*). The Nile Delta was largely populated by Libyans.

9. According to Apollonius Rhodius (i. 1126–9), Titias was 'one of the only three Idaean Dactyls ("fingers") who dispense doom'. He names another Dactyl 'Cyllenius'. I have shown (*White Goddess* p. 281) that in finger-magic Titias, the Dactyl, represented the middle finger; that Cyllenius, *alias* Heracles, was the thumb; and that Dascylus, the third Dactyl, was the index-finger, as his name implies (see 53. *1*). These three raised, while the fourth and little finger are turned down, made the 'Phrygian blessing'. Originally given in Myrine's name, it is now used by Catholic priests in that of the Christian Trinity.

10. Tityus, whom Apollo killed (see 21. *d*), may be a doublet of Titias. Myrine's capture of the island of Cerne seems a late and unauthorized addition to the story. Cerne has been identified with Fedallah near Fez;

or with Santa Cruz near Cape Ghir, or (most plausibly) with Arguin, a little south of Cabo Blanco. It was discovered and colonized by the Carthaginian Hanno, who described it as lying as far from the Pillars of Heracles as these lay from Carthage, and it became the great emporium of West African trade.

*

11. So much for the mythical elements of the Ninth Labour. Yet Heracles's expedition to the Thermodon and his wars in Mysia and Phrygia must not be dismissed as wholly unhistorical. Like the voyage of the *Argo* (see 148. *10*), they record Greek trading ventures in the Black Sea perhaps as far back as the middle of the second millennium B.C.; and the intrusion of Minyans from Iolcus, Aeacans from Aegina, and Argives in these waters suggests that though Helen may have been beautiful, and may have eloped with Paris of Troy, it was not her face that launched a thousand ships, but mercantile interest. Achilles the son of Peleus, Ajax the son of Telamon, and Diomedes the Argive were among the Greek allies of Agamemnon who insisted that Priam should allow them the free passage through the Hellespont enjoyed by their fathers – unless he wished his city to be sacked as Laomedon's had been, and for the same reason (see 137. *1*). Hence the dubious Athenian claims to have been represented in Heracles's expedition by Theseus, in the voyage of the *Argo* by Phalerus, and at Troy by Menestheus, Demophon, and Acamas. These were intended to justify their eventual control of Black Sea trade which the destruction of Troy and the decline of Rhodes had allowed them to seize (see 159. *2*; 160. *2–3* and 162. *3*).

132

THE TENTH LABOUR: THE CATTLE OF GERYON

HERACLES's Tenth Labour was to fetch the famous cattle of Geryon from Erytheia, an island near the Ocean stream, without either demand or payment. Geryon, a son of Chrysaor and Callirrhoë, a daughter of the Titan Oceanus, was the King of Tartessus in Spain, and reputedly the strongest man alive.[1] He had been born with three heads, six hands, and three bodies joined together at the waist. Geryon's shambling red cattle, beasts of marvellous beauty, were guarded by the herdsman Eurytion, son of Ares, and by the two-headed watchdog Orthrus – formerly Atlas's property – born of Typhon and Echidne.[2]

b. During his passage through Europe, Heracles destroyed many wild beasts and, when at last he reached Tartessus, erected a pair of pillars facing each other across the straits, one in Europe, one in Africa. Some hold that the two continents were formerly joined together, and that he cut a channel between them, or thrust the cliffs apart; others say that, on the contrary, he narrowed the existing straits to discourage the entry of whales and other sea-monsters.³

c. Helius beamed down upon Heracles who, finding it impossible to work in such heat, strung his bow and let fly an arrow at the god. 'Enough of that!' cried Helius angrily. Heracles apologized for his ill-temper, and unstrung his bow at once. Not to be outdone in courtesy, Helius lent Heracles his golden goblet, shaped like a water-lily, in which he sailed to Erytheia; but the Titan Oceanus, to try him, made the goblet pitch violently upon the waves. Heracles again drew his bow, which frightened Oceanus into calming the sea. Another account is that Heracles sailed to Erytheia in a brazen urn, using his lion pelt as a sail.⁴

d. On his arrival, he ascended Mount Abas. The dog Orthrus rushed at him, barking, but Heracles's club struck him lifeless; and Eurytion, Geryon's herdsman, hurrying to Orthrus's aid, died in the same manner. Heracles then proceeded to drive away the cattle. Menoetes, who was pasturing the cattle of Hades near by – but Heracles had left these untouched – took the news to Geryon. Challenged to battle, Heracles ran to Geryon's flank and shot him sideways through all three bodies with a single arrow; but some say that he stood his ground and let loose a flight of three arrows. As Hera hastened to Geryon's assistance, Heracles wounded her with an arrow in the right breast, and she fled. Thus he won the cattle, without either demand or payment, and embarked in the golden goblet, which he then sailed across to Tartessus and gratefully returned to Helius. From Geryon's blood sprang a tree which, at the time of the Pleiades' rising, bears stoneless cherry-like fruit. Geryon did not, however, die without issue: his daughter Erytheia became by Hermes the mother of Norax, who led a colony to Sardinia, even before the time of Hyllus, and there founded Nora, the oldest city in the island.⁵

e. The whereabouts of Erytheia, also called Erythrea, or Erythria, is disputed. Though some describe it as an island beyond the Ocean stream, others place it off the coast of Lusitania.⁶ Still others identify it with the island of Leon, or with an islet hard by, on which the earliest city of Gades was built, and where the pasture is so rich that the milk yields no whey but only curds, and the cattle must be cupped every fifty days, lest they choke for excess of blood. This islet, sacred to Hera, is called either Erytheia, or Aphrodisias. Leon, the island on which the present city of Gades stands, used to be called Cotinusa, from its olives, but the Phoenicians renamed it Gadira, or 'Fenced City'. On the western cape stands a temple of Cronus, and the city of Gades; on the eastern, a temple of Heracles, remarkable for a spring which ebbs at flood tide, and flows at ebb tide; and Geryon lies buried in the city, equally famed for a secret tree that takes diverse forms.[7]

f. According to another account, however, Geryon's cattle were not pastured in any island, but on the mountain slopes of the farther part of Spain, confronting the Ocean; and 'Geryon' was a title of the renowned King Chrysaor, who ruled over the whole land, and whose three strong and courageous sons helped him in the defence of his kingdom, each leading an army recruited from warlike races. To combat these, Heracles assembled a large expedition in Crete, the birthplace of his father Zeus. Before setting out, he was splendidly honoured by the Cretans and, in return, rid their island of bears, wolves, serpents, and other noxious creatures, from which it is still immune. First, he sailed to Libya, where he killed Antaeus, slaughtered the wild beasts that infested the desert, and gave the country unsurpassed fertility. Next, he visited Egypt, where he killed Busiris; then he marched westward, across North Africa, annihilating the Gorgons and the Libyan Amazons as he went, founded the city of Hecatompylus, now Capsa, in southern Numidia, and reached the Ocean near Gades. There he set up pillars on either side of the straits and, ferrying his army across to Spain, found that the sons of Chrysaor, with their three armies, were encamped at some distance from one another. He conquered and killed them, each in turn, and finally drove off Geryon's famous herds, leaving the government of Spain to the most worthy of the surviving inhabitants.[8]

g. The Pillars of Heracles are usually identified with Mount Calpe in Europe, and Abyle, or Abilyx in Africa. Others make them the islets near Gades, of which the larger is sacred to Hera. All Spaniards and Libyans, however, take the word 'Pillars' literally, and place them at Gades, where brazen columns are consecrated to Heracles, eight cubits high and inscribed with the cost of their building; here sailors offer sacrifices whenever they return safely from a voyage. According to the people of Gades themselves, the King of Tyre was ordered by an oracle to found a colony near the Pillars of Heracles, and sent out three successive parties of exploration. The first party, thinking that the oracle had referred to Abyle and Calpe, landed inside the straits, where the city of Exitani now stands; the second sailed about two hundred miles beyond the straits, to an island sacred to Heracles, opposite the Spanish city of Onoba; but both were discouraged by unfavourable omens when they offered sacrifices, and returned home. The third party reached Gades, where they raised a temple to Heracles on the eastern cape and successfully founded the city of Gades on the western.[9]

h. Some, however, deny that it was Heracles who set up these pillars, and assert that Abyle and Calpe were first named 'The Pillars of Cronus', and afterwards 'The Pillars of Briareus', a giant whose power extended thus far; but that, the memory of Briareus (also called Aegaeon) having faded, they were renamed in honour of Heracles – perhaps because the city of Tartessus, which stands only five miles from Calpe, was founded by him, and used to be known as Heracleia. Vast ancient walls and ship-sheds are still shown there.[10] But it must be remembered that the earliest Heracles had also been called Briareus. The number of Heracles's Pillars is usually given as two; but some speak of three, or four.[11] So-called Pillars of Heracles are also reported from the northern coast of Germany; from the Black Sea; from the western extremity of Gaul; and from India.[12]

i. A temple of Heracles stands on the Sacred Promontory in Lusitania, the most westerly point of the world. Visitants are forbidden to enter the precinct by night, the time when the gods take up their abode in it. Perhaps when Heracles set up his pillars to mark the utmost limits of legitimate seafaring, this was the site he chose.[13]

j. How he then drove the cattle to Mycenae is much disputed. Some say that he forced Abyle and Calpe into temporary union and went across the resultant bridge into Libya; but according to a more probable account he passed through the territory of what is now Abdera, a Phoenician settlement, and then through Spain, leaving behind some of his followers as colonists.[14] In the Pyrenees, he courted and buried the Bebrycan princess Pyrene, from whom this mountain range takes its name; the river Danube is said to have its source there, near a city also named in her honour. He then visited Gaul, where he abolished a barbarous native custom of killing strangers, and won so many hearts by his generous deeds that he was able to found a large city, to which he gave the name Alesia, or 'Wandering', in commemoration of his travels. The Gauls to this day honour Alesia as the hearth and mother-city of their whole land – it was unconquered until Caligula's reign – and claim descent from Heracles's union with a tall princess named Galata, who chose him as her lover and bred that warlike people.[15]

k. When Heracles was driving Geryon's cattle through Liguria, two sons of Poseidon named Ialebion and Dercynus tried to steal them from him, and were both killed. At one stage of his battle with hostile Ligurian forces, Heracles ran out of arrows, and knelt down, in tears, wounded and exhausted. The ground being of soft mould, he could find no stones to throw at the enemy – Ligys, the brother of Ialebion, was their leader – until Zeus, pitying his tears, overshadowed the earth with a cloud, from which a shower of stones hailed down; and with these he put the Ligurians to flight. Zeus set among the stars an image of Heracles fighting the Ligurians, known as the constellation Engonasis. Another memorial of this battle survives on earth: namely the broad, circular plain lying between Marseilles and the mouths of the river Rhône, about fifteen miles from the sea, called 'The Stony Plain', because it is strewn with stones the size of a man's fist; brine springs are also found there.[16]

l. In his passage over the Ligurian Alps, Heracles carved a road fit for his armies and baggage trains; he also broke up all robber bands that infested the pass, before entering what is now Cis-alpine Gaul and Etruria. Only after wandering down the whole coast of Italy, and crossing into Sicily, did it occur to him: 'I have taken the wrong road!' The Romans say that, on reaching the Albula – afterwards called the Tiber – he was welcomed by King Evander, an exile from Arcadia. At evening, he swam across, driving the cattle before him, and lay down to rest on a grassy bed.[17] In a deep cave near by, lived a vast, hideous, three-headed shepherd named Cacus, a son of Hephaestus and Medusa, who was the dread and disgrace of the Aventine Forest, and puffed flames from each of his three mouths. Human skulls and arms hung nailed above the lintels of his cave, and the ground inside gleamed white with the bones of his victims. While Heracles slept, Cacus stole the two finest of his bulls; as well as four heifers, which he dragged backwards by their tails into his lair.[18]

m. At the first streak of dawn, Heracles awoke, and at once noticed that the cattle were missing. After searching for them in vain, he was about to drive the remainder onward, when one of the stolen heifers lowed hungrily. Heracles traced the sound to the cave, but found the entrance barred by a rock which ten yoke of oxen could hardly have moved; nevertheless, he heaved it aside as though it had been a pebble and, undaunted by the smoky flames which Cacus was now belching, grappled with him and battered his face to pulp.[19]

n. Aided by King Evander, Heracles then built an altar to Zeus, at which he sacrificed one of the recovered bulls, and afterwards made arrangements for his own worship. Yet the Romans tell this story in order to glorify themselves; the truth being that it was not Heracles who killed Cacus, and offered sacrifices to Zeus, but a gigantic herdsman named Garanus, or Recaranus, the ally of Heracles.[20]

o. King Evander ruled rather by personal ascendancy than by force: he was particularly reverenced for the knowledge of letters which he had imbibed from his prophetic mother, the Arcadian nymph Nicostrate, or Themis; she was a daughter of the river Ladon, and though already married to Echenus, bore Evander to Hermes. Nicostrate persuaded Evander to murder his supposed father; and, when the Arcadians banished them both, went with him to Italy, accompanied by a body of Pelasgians.[21] There, some sixty years before the Trojan War, they founded the small city of Pallantium, on the hill beside the river Tiber, later called Mount Palatine; the site having been Nicostrate's choice; and soon there was no more powerful king than Evander in all Italy. Nicostrate, now called Carmenta, adapted the thirteen-consonant Pelasgian alphabet, which Cadmus had brought back from Egypt, to form the fifteen-consonant Latin one. But some assert that it was Heracles who taught Evander's people the use of letters, which is why he shares an altar with the Muses.[22]

p. According to the Romans, Heracles freed King Evander from the tribute owed to the Etruscans; killed King Faunus, whose custom was to sacrifice strangers at the altar of his father Hermes; and begot Latinus, the ancestor of the Latins, on Faunus's widow, or daughter. But the Greeks hold that Latinus was a son of Circe by Odysseus. Heracles, at all events, suppressed the annual Cronian sacrifice of two men, who were flung into the river Tiber, and forced the Romans to use puppets instead; even now, in the month of May, when the moon is full, the chief Vestal Virgin, standing on the oaken-timbered Pons Sublicius, throws whitewashed images of old men, plaited from bulrushes, and called 'Argives', into the yellow stream.[23] Heracles is also believed to have founded Pompeii and Herculaneum; to have fought giants on the Phlegraean Plain of Cumae; and to have built a causeway one mile long across the Lucrine Gulf, now called the Heracleian Road, down which he drove Geryon's cattle.[24]

q. It is further said that he lay down to rest near the frontier of Rhegium and Epizephyrian Locris and, being much disturbed by cicadas, begged the gods to silence them. His prayer was immediately granted; and cicadas have never been heard since on the Rhegian side of the river Alece, although they sing lustily on the Locrian side. That day a bull broke away from the herd and, plunging into the sea, swam over to Sicily. Heracles, going in pursuit, found it concealed among the herds of Eryx, King of the Elymans, a son of Aphrodite by Butes.[25] Eryx, who was a wrestler and a boxer, challenged him to a fivefold contest. Heracles accepted the challenge, on condition that Eryx would stake his kingdom against the runaway bull, and won the first four events; finally, in the wrestling match, he lifted Eryx high into the air, dashed him to the ground and killed him – which taught the Sicilians that not everyone born of a goddess is necessarily immortal. In this manner, Heracles won Eryx's kingdom, which he left the inhabitants to enjoy until one of his own descendants should come to claim it.[26]

r. Some say that Eryx – whose wrestling-ground is still shown – had a daughter named Psophis, who bore Heracles two sons: Echephron and Promachus. Having been reared in Erymanthus, they renamed it Psophis after their mother; and there built a shrine to Erycinian Aphrodite, of which today only the ruins remain. The hero-shrines of Echephron and Promachus have long since lost their importance, and Psophis is usually regarded as a daughter of Xanthus, the grandson of Arcas.[27]

s. Continuing on his way through Sicily, Heracles came to the site where now stands the city of Syracuse; there he offered sacrifices, and instituted the annual festival beside the sacred chasm of Cyane, down which Hades snatched Core to the Underworld. To those who honoured Heracles in the Plain of Leontini, he left undying memorials of his visit. Close to the city of Agyrium, the hoof marks of his cattle were found imprinted on a stony road, as though in wax; and, regarding this as an intimation of his own immortality, Heracles accepted from the inhabitants those divine honours which he had hitherto consistently refused. Then, in acknowledgement of their favours, he dug a lake four furlongs in circumference outside the city walls, and established local sanctuaries of Iolaus and Geryon.[28]

t. Returning to Italy in search of another route to Greece, Heracles drove his cattle up the eastern coast, to the Lacinian Promontory, where the ruler, King Lacinius, was afterwards able to boast that he had put Heracles to flight; this he did merely by building a temple to Hera, at the sight of which Heracles departed in disgust. Six miles farther on, Heracles accidentally killed one Croton, buried him with every honour, and prophesied that, in time to come, a great city would rise, called by his name. This prophecy Heracles made good after his deification: he appeared in a dream to one of his descendants, the Argive Myscelus, threatening him with terrible punishments if he did not lead a party of colonists to Sicily and found the city; and when the Argives were about to condemn Myscelus to death for defying their embargo on emigration, he miraculously turned every black voting-pebble into a white one.[29]

u. Heracles then proposed to drive Geryon's cattle through Istria into Epirus, and thence to the Peloponnese by way of the Isthmus. At at the head of the Adriatic Gulf Hera sent a gadfly, which stampeded the cows, driving them across Thrace and into the Scythian desert. There Heracles pursued them, and one cold, stormy night drew the lion pelt about him and fell fast asleep on a rocky hillside. When he awoke, he found that his chariot-mares, which he had unharnessed and put out to graze, were likewise missing. He wandered far and wide in search of them until he reached the wooded district called Hylaea, where a strange being, half woman, half serpent, shouted at him from a cave. She had his mares, she said, but would give them back to him only if he became her lover. Heracles agreed, though with a certain reluctance, and kissed her thrice; whereupon the serpent-tailed woman embraced him passionately, and when, at last, he was free to go, asked him: 'What of the three sons whom I now carry in my womb? When they grow to manhood, shall I settle them here where I am mistress, or shall I send them to you?'

v. 'When they grow up, watch carefully!' Heracles replied. 'And if ever one of them bends this bow – thus, as I now bend it – and girds himself with this belt – thus, as I now gird myself – choose him as the ruler of your country.'

So saying, he gave her one of his two bows, and his girdle which had a golden goblet hanging from its clasp; then went on his way. She named her triplets Agathyrsus, Gelonus, and Scythes. The eldest two were unequal to the tasks that their father had set, and she drove them away; but Scythes succeeded in both and was allowed to remain, thus becoming the ancestor of all royal Scythian kings who, to this day, wear golden goblets on their girdles.[30] Others, however, say that it was Zeus, not Heracles, who lay with the serpent-tailed woman, and that, when his three sons by her were still ruling the land, there fell from the sky four golden implements: a plough, a yoke, a battle axe, and a cup. Agathyrsus first ran to recover them, but as he came close, the gold flamed up and burned his hands. Gelonus was similarly rejected. However, when Scythes, the youngest, approached, the fire died down at once; whereupon he carried home the four golden treasures and the elder brothers agreed to yield him the kingdom.[31]

w. Heracles, having recovered his mares and most of the strayed cattle, drove them back across the river Strymon, which he dammed with stones for the purpose, and encountered no further adventures until the giant herdsman Alcyoneus, having taken possession of the Corinthian Isthmus, hurled a rock at the army which once more followed Heracles, crushing no less than twelve chariots and double that number of horsemen. This was the same Alcyoneus who twice stole Helius's sacred cattle: from Erytheia, and from the citadel of Corinth. He now ran forward, picked up the rock again, and this time hurled it at Heracles, who bandied it back with his club and so killed the giant; the very rock is still shown on the Isthmus.[32]

1. Pausanias: iv. 36. 3; Apollodorus: ii. 5. 10; Servius on Virgil's *Aeneid* vi. 289; Hesiod: *Theogony* 981.

2. Hesiod: *Theogony* 287 ff.; Lucian: *Toxaris* 72; Apollodorus: *loc. cit.*; Livy: i. 7; Servius on Virgil's *Aeneid* viii. 300; Scholiast on Apollonius Rhodius: iv. 1399.

3. Apollodorus: ii. 5. 10; Diodorus Siculus: iv. 18; Pomponius Mela: i. 5. 3 and ii. 6. 6.

4. Apollodorus: *loc. cit.*; Pherecydes, quoted by Athenaeus: xi. 39; Servius on Virgil's *Aeneid* vii. 662 and viii. 300.

5. Apollodorus: *loc. cit.*; Hyginus: *Fabula* 30; Euripides: *Heracles* 423; Servius on Virgil's *Aeneid* vii. 662; Pausanias: x. 17. 4; Ptolemy Hephaestionos, quoted by Photius: p. 475; Pindar: *Fragment* 169.

6. Solinus: xxiii. 12; Pomponius Mela: iii. 47; Hesiod: *Theogony* 287 ff.; Pliny: *Natural History* iv. 36.

7. Pherecydes, quoted by Strabo: iii. 2. 11; Strabo: iii. 5. 3–4 and 7; Timaeus, quoted by Pliny: *loc. cit.*; Polybius, quoted by Strabo: iii. 5. 7; Pausanias: i. 35. 6.

8. Diodorus Siculus: iii. 55 and iv. 17–19.

9. Pliny: *Natural History* iii. *Proem*; Strabo: iii. 5. 5.

10. Eustathius on Dionysius's *Description of the Earth* 64 ff.; Scholiast on Pindar's *Nemean Odes* iii. 37; Aristotle, quoted by Aelian: *Varia Historia* v. 3; Pliny: *Natural History* iii. 3; Timotheus, quoted by Strabo: iii. 1. 7.

11. Erasmus: *Chiliades* i. 7; Zenobius: *Proverbs* v. 48; Aeschylus: *Prometheus Bound* 349 and 428; Hesychius *sub* stelas distomous.

12. Tacitus: *Germania* 34; Servius on Virgil's *Aeneid* xi. 262; Scymnius Chius: 188; Strabo: ii. 5. 6.

13. Strabo: iii. 1. 4; Pindar: *Nemean Odes* iii. 21 ff.

14. Avienus: *Ora Maritima* 326; Apollodorus: ii. 5. 10; Strabo: iii. 4. 3; Asclepiades of Myrtea, quoted by Strabo: *loc. cit.*

15. Silius Italicus: iii. 417; Herodotus: ii. 33; Diodorus Siculus: iv. 19 and 24.

16. Apollodorus: ii. 5. 10; Tzetzes: *Chiliades* ii. 340 ff. and *On Lycophron* 1312; Aeschylus: *Prometheus Unbound*, quoted by Hyginus: *Poetic Astronomy* ii. 6 and by Strabo: iv. 1. 7; Theon: *On Aratus* p. 12, ed. Morell.

17. Diodorus Siculus: iv. 21; Ovid: *Fasti* v. 545 ff.; Livy: i. 7.

18. Propertius: *Elegies* iv. 9. 10; Ovid: *Fasti* i. 545 ff.; Livy: *loc. cit.*; Virgil: *Aeneid* viii. 207–8.

19. Livy: *loc. cit.*; Virgil: *Aeneid* viii. 217 and 233 ff.; Ovid: *loc. cit.*

20. Plutarch: *Roman Questions* 18; Ovid: *loc. cit.*; Livy: *loc. cit.*; Verrius Flaccus, quoted by Servius on Virgil's *Aeneid* viii. 203; Aurelius Victor: *On the Origins of the Roman Race* 8.

21. Servius on Virgil's *Aeneid* viii. 51; 130 and 336; Livy: i. 7; Plutarch: *Roman Questions* 56; Pausanias: viii. 43. 2; Dionysius: *Roman Antiquities* i. 31.

22. Servius on Virgil's *Aeneid* viii. 130 and 336; Ovid: *Fasti* v. 94–5 and i. 542; Hyginus: *Fabula* 277; Juba, quoted by Plutarch: *Roman Questions* 59.

23. Plutarch: *Roman Questions* 18 and 32; Dercyllus: *Italian History* iii, quoted by Plutarch: *Parallel Stories* 38; Tzetzes: *On Lycophron* 1232; Justin: xliii. 1; Hesiod: *Theogony* 1013; Ovid: *Fasti* v. 621 ff.

24. Solinus: ii. 5; Dionysius: i. 44; Diodorus Siculus: iv. 21–2 and 24; Strabo: vi. 3. 5 and 4. 6.

25. Diodorus Siculus: iv. 22; Strabo: vi. 1. 19; Apollodorus: ii. 5. 10; Servius on Virgil's *Aeneid* i. 574.

26. Pausanias: iv. 36. 3; Diodorus Siculus: iv. 23; Apollodorus: *loc. cit.*; Tzetzes: *On Lycophron* 866; Servius on Virgil's *Aeneid* x. 551.

27. Tzetzes: *loc. cit.*; Pausanias: viii. 24. 1 and 3.

28. Diodorus Siculus: iv. 23–4 and v. 4.

29. Diodorus Siculus: iv. 24; Servius on Virgil's *Aeneid* iii. 552; Ovid: *Metamorphoses* xv. 12 ff.

30. Diodorus Siculus: iv. 25; Herodotus: iv. 8–10.

31. Diodorus Siculus: ii. 43; Herodotus: iv. 5.

32. Apollodorus: ii. 5. 10 and i. 6. 1; Pindar: *Nemean Odes* iv. 27 ff. and *Isthmian Odes* vi. 32 ff.; Scholiast on Pindar's *Nemean Odes loc. cit.* and *Isthmian Odes* vi. 32.

*

1. The main theme of Heracles's Labours is his performance of certain ritual feats before being accepted as consort to Admete, or Auge, or Athene, or Hippolyte, or whatever the Queen's name was. This wild Tenth Labour may originally have been relevant to the same theme, if it records the patriarchal Hellenic custom by which the husband bought his bride with the proceeds of a cattle raid. In Homeric Greece, women were valued at so many cattle, and still are in parts of East and Central Africa. But other irrelevant elements have become attached to the myth, including a visit to the Western Island of Death, and his successful return, laden with spoil; the ancient Irish parallel is the story of Cuchulain who harrowed Hell – Dun Scaith, 'shadow city' – and brought back three cows and a magic cauldron, despite storms which the gods of the dead sent against him. The bronze urn in which Heracles sailed to Erytheia was an appropriate vessel for a visit to the Island of Death, and has perhaps been confused with the bronze cauldron. In the Eleventh Tablet of the Babylonian Gilgamesh Epic, Gilgamesh makes a similar journey to a sepulchral island across a sea of death, using his garment for a sail. This incident calls attention to many points of resemblance between the Heracles and Gilgamesh myths; the common source is probably Sumerian. Like Heracles, Gilgamesh kills a monstrous lion and wears its pelt (see 123. *e*); seizes a sky-bull by the horns and overcomes it (see 129. *b*); discovers a secret herb of invulnerability (see 135. *b*); takes the same journey as the Sun (see 132. *d*); and visits a Garden of the Hesperides where, after killing a dragon coiled about a sacred tree, he is rewarded with two sacred objects from the Underworld (see 133. *e*). The relations of Gilgamesh and his comrade Enkidu closely resemble those of Theseus, the Athenian Heracles, and his comrade Peirithous who goes down to Tartarus and fails to return (see 103. *c* and *d*); and Gilgamesh's adventure with the Scorpions has been awarded to the Boeotian Orion (see 41. *3*).

2. Pre-Phoenician Greek colonies planted in Spain, Gaul, and Italy under Heracles's protection have contributed to the myth; and, in the geographical sense, the Pillars of Heracles – at which one band of settlers arrived about the year 1100 B.C. – are Ceuta and Gibraltar.

3. In a mystical Celto-Iberian sense, however, the Pillars are alphabetical abstractions. 'Marwnad Ercwlf', an ancient Welsh poem in the *Red Book of Hergest*, treats of the Celtic Heracles – whom the Irish called 'Ogma Sunface' and Lucian, 'Ogmius' (see 125. *1*) – and records how Ercwlf raised 'four columns of equal height capped with red gold', apparently the four columns of five letters each, which formed the twenty-lettered Bardic alphabet known as the Boibel-Loth (*White Goddess* pp. 133, 199, and 278). It seems that, about the year 400 B.C., this new alphabet, the Greek letter-names of which referred to Celestial Heracles's journey in the sun-goblet, his death on Mount Oeta, and his powers as city-founder and judge (*White Goddess* p. 136), displaced the Beth-Luis-Nion tree-alphabet, the letter-names of which referred to the murderous sacrifice of Cronus by the wild women (*White Goddess* p. 374). Since the Gorgons had a grove on Erytheia – 'Red Island', identified by Phere-cydes with the island of Gades – and since 'trees' in all Celtic languages means 'letters', I read 'the tree that takes diverse forms' as meaning the Beth-Luis-Nion alphabet, whose secret the Gorgons guarded in their sacred grove until Heracles 'annihilated' them. In this sense, Heracles's raid on Erytheia, where he killed Geryon and the dog Orthrus – the Dog-star Sirius – refers to the supersession of the Cronus-alphabet by the Heracles-alphabet.

4. Hesiod (*Theogony* 287) calls Geryon *tricephalon*, 'three-headed'; another reading of which is *tricarenon*, meaning the same thing. 'Tricare-non' recalls *Tarvos Trigaranus*, the Celtic god with two left hands, shown in the company of cranes and a bull on the Paris Altar, felling a willow-tree. *Geryon*, a meaningless word in Greek, seems to be a worn-down form of *Trigaranus*. Since alike in Greek and Irish tradition cranes are associated with alphabetical secrets (see 52. 6), and with poets, Geryon appears to be the Goddess's guardian of the earlier alphabet: in fact, Cronus accompanied by the Dactyls. At the sepulchral island of Erytheia, Cronus-Geryon, who was once a sun-hero of the Heracles-Briareus type, had become a god of the dead, with Orthrus as his Cerberus; and the Tenth Labour, therefore, has been confused with the Twelfth, Menoe-tes figuring in both. Though the 'stoneless cherry-like fruit' sprung from Geryon's blood may have been arbutus-berries, native to Spain, the story has been influenced by the sacredness to Cronus-Saturn of the early-fruiting cornel-cherry (*White Goddess* p. 171), which yields a red dye like the kerm-berry. Chrysaor's part in the story is important. His name means 'golden falchion', the weapon associated with the Cronus cult, and he was said to be the Gorgon Medusa's son (see 33. b; 73. h and 138. j).

5. Norax, Geryon's grandson by Erytheia and Hermes – Hermes is recorded to have brought the tree-alphabet from Greece to Egypt, and back again – seems to be a miswriting of *Norops*, the Greek word for 'Sun-face'. This genealogy has been turned inside-out by the Irish mythographers: they record that their own Geryon, whose three persons were known as Brian, Iuchar, and Iucharba – a form of Mitra, Varuna, and Indra – had Ogma for a grandfather, not a grandson, and that his son

was the Celt-Iberian Sun-god Lugh, Llew, or Lugos. They also insisted that the alphabet had come to them from Greece by way of Spain. Cronus's crow was sacred to Lugos, according to Plutarch who records (*On Rivers and Mountains* v) that 'Lugdunum' – Lyons, the fortress of Lugos – 'was so called because an auspice of crows suggested the choice of its site; *lug* meaning a crow in the Allobrigian dialect.'

6. Verrius Flaccus seems to have been misreported by Servius; he is more likely to have said that 'three-headed Garanus (Geryon), not Cacus, was the name of Heracles's victim, and Evander aided Heracles.' This would fit in with the account of how Evander's mother Carmenta suppressed the thirteen-consonant alphabet, Cronus's Beth-Luis-Nion, in favour of Heracles-Ogma's fifteen-consonant Boibel-Loth (*White Goddess* p. 272). King Juba, whom Plutarch quotes as saying that Heracles taught Evander's people the use of letters, was an honorary magistrate of Gades, and must have known a good deal of local alphabetic lore. In this Evander story, Heracles is plainly described as an enemy of the Cronus cult, since he abolishes human sacrifice. His circumambulation of Italy and Sicily has been invented to account for the many temples there raised to him; his fivefold contest with Eryx, to justify the sixth-century colonizing expeditions which Pentathlus of Cnidos, the Heraclid, and Dorieus the Spartan, led to the Eryx region. The Heracles honoured at Agyrium, a Sicel city, may have been an ancestor who led the Sicels across the straits from Italy about the year 1050 B.C. (Thucydides: vi. 2. 5). He was also made to visit Scythia; the Greek colonists on the western and northern shores of the Black Sea incorporated a Scythian Heracles, an archer hero (see 119. 5), in the omniumgatherum Tenth Labour. His bride, the serpent-tailed woman, was an Earth-goddess, mother of the three principal Scythian tribes mentioned by Herodotus; in another version of the myth, represented by the English ballad of *The Laidley Worm*, when he has kissed her three times, she turns into 'the fairest woman you ever did see'.

7. The Alcyoneus anecdote seems to have become detached from the myth of the Giants' assault on Olympus and their defeat at Heracles's hands (see 35. *a–e*). But Alcyoneus's theft of Helius's cattle from Erytheia, and again from the citadel of Corinth, is an older version of Heracles's theft of Geryon's cattle; their owner being an active solar consort of the Moon-goddess, not a banished and enfeebled god of the Dead.

8. The arrow which Heracles shot at the noon-day sun will have been one discharged at the zenith during his coronation ceremony (see 126. 2 and 135. 1).

THE ELEVENTH LABOUR: THE APPLES
OF THE HESPERIDES

HERACLES had performed these Ten Labours in the space of eight years and one month; but Eurystheus, discounting the Second and the Fifth, set him two more. The Eleventh Labour was to fetch fruit from the golden apple-tree, Mother Earth's wedding gift to Hera, with which she had been so delighted that she planted it in her own divine garden. This garden lay on the slopes of Mount Atlas, where the panting chariot-horses of the Sun complete their journey, and where Atlas's sheep and cattle, one thousand herds of each, wander over their undisputed pastures. When Hera found, one day, that Atlas's daughters, the Hesperides, to whom she had entrusted the tree, were pilfering the apples, she set the ever-watchful dragon Ladon to coil around the tree as its guardian.[1]

b. Some say that Ladon was the offspring of Typhon and Echidne; others, that he was the youngest-born of Ceto and Phorcys; others again, that he was a parthogenous son of Mother Earth. He had one hundred heads, and spoke with divers tongues.[2]

c. It is equally disputed whether the Hesperides lived on Mount Atlas in the Land of the Hyperboreans; or on Mount Atlas in Mauretania; or somewhere beyond the Ocean stream; or on two islands near the promontory called the Western Horn, which lies close to the Ethiopian Hesperiae, on the borders of Africa. Though the apples were Hera's, Atlas took a gardener's pride in them and, when Themis warned him: 'One day long hence, Titan, your tree shall be stripped of its gold by a son of Zeus,' Atlas, who had not then been punished with his terrible task of supporting the celestial globe upon his shoulders, built solid walls around the orchard, and expelled all strangers from his land; it may well have been he who set Ladon to guard the apples.[3]

d. Heracles, not knowing in what direction the Garden of the Hesperides lay, marched through Illyria to the river Po, the home of the oracular sea-god Nereus. On the way he crossed the Echedorus, a small Macedonian stream, where Cycnus, the son of Ares and Pyrene, challenged him to a duel. Ares acted as Cycnus's second, and marshalled the combatants, but Zeus hurled a thunderbolt between them and they broke off the fight. When at last Heracles came to the Po, the river-nymphs, daughters of Zeus and Themis, showed him Nereus asleep. He seized the hoary old sea-god and, clinging to him despite his many Protean changes, forced him to prophesy how the golden apples could be won. Some say, however, that Heracles went to Prometheus for this information.[4]

e. Nereus had advised Heracles not to pluck the apples himself, but to employ Atlas as his agent, meanwhile relieving him of his fantastic burden; therefore, on arriving at the Garden of the Hesperides, he asked Atlas to do him this favour. Atlas would have undertaken almost any task for the sake of an hour's respite, but he feared Ladon, whom Heracles thereupon killed with an arrow shot over the garden wall. Heracles now bent his back to receive the weight of the celestial globe, and Atlas walked away, returning presently with three apples plucked by his daughters. He found the sense of freedom delicious. 'I will take these apples to Eurystheus myself without fail,' he said, 'if you hold up the heavens for a few months longer.' Heracles pretended to agree but, having been warned by Nereus not to accept any such offer, begged Atlas to support the globe for only one moment more, while he put a pad on his head. Atlas, easily deceived, laid the apples on the ground and resumed his burden; whereupon Heracles picked them up and went away with an ironical farewell.

f. After some months Heracles brought the apples to Eurystheus, who handed them back to him; he then gave them to Athene, and she returned them to the nymphs, since it was unlawful that Hera's property should pass from their hands.[5] Feeling thirsty after this Labour, Heracles stamped his foot and made a stream of water gush out, which later saved the lives of the Argonauts when they were cast up high and dry on the Libyan desert. Meanwhile Hera, weeping for Ladon, set his image among the stars as the constellation of the Serpent.[6]

g. Heracles did not return to Mycenae by a direct route. He first traversed Libya, whose King Antaeus, son of Poseidon and Mother Earth, was in the habit of forcing strangers to wrestle with him until they were exhausted, whereupon he killed them; for not only was he a strong and skilful athlete, but whenever he touched the earth, his strength revived. He saved the skulls of his victims to roof a temple of Poseidon.[7] It is not known whether Heracles, who was determined to end this barbarous practice, challenged Antaeus, or was challenged by him. Antaeus, however, proved no easy victim, being a giant who lived in a cave beneath a towering cliff, where he feasted on the flesh of lions, and slept on the bare ground in order to conserve and increase his already colossal strength. Mother Earth, not yet sterile after her birth of the Giant, had conceived Antaeus in a Libyan cave, and found more reason to boast of him than even of her monstrous elder children, Typhon, Tityus, and Briareus. It would have gone ill with the Olympians if he had fought against them on the Plains of Phlegra.

h. In preparation for the wrestling match, both combatants cast off their lion pelts, but while Heracles rubbed himself with oil in the Olympian fashion, Antaeus poured hot sand over his limbs lest contact with the earth through the soles of his feet alone should prove insufficient. Heracles planned to preserve his strength and wear Antaeus down, but after tossing him full length on the ground, he was amazed to see the giant's muscles swell and a healthy flush suffuse his limbs as Mother Earth revived him. The combatants grappled again, and presently Antaeus flung himself down of his own accord, not waiting to be thrown; upon which, Heracles, realizing what he was at, lifted him high into the air, then cracked his ribs and, despite the hollow groans of Mother Earth, held him aloft until he died.[8]

i. Some say that this conflict took place at Lixus, a small Mauretanian city some fifty miles from Tangier, near the sea, where a hillock is shown as Antaeus's tomb. If a few basketsful of soil are taken from this hillock, the natives believe, rain will fall and continue to fall until they are replaced. It is also claimed that the Gardens of the Hesperides were the near-by island, on which stands an altar of Heracles; but, except for a few wild-olive trees, no trace of the orchard now remains. When Sertorius took Tangier, he opened the tomb to see whether Antaeus's skeleton were as large as tradition described it. To his astonishment, it measured sixty cubits, so he at once closed up the tomb and offered Antaeus heroic sacrifices. It is said locally either that Antaeus founded Tangier, formerly called Tingis; or that Sophax, whom Tinga, Antaeus's widow, bore to Heracles, reigned over that country, and gave his mother's name to the city. Sophax's son Diodorus subdued many African nations with a Greek army recruited from the Mycenaean colonists whom Heracles had settled there.[9] The Mauretanians are of eastern origin and, like the Pharusii, descended from certain Persians who accompanied Heracles to Africa; but some hold that they are descendants of those Canaanites whom Joshua the Israelite expelled from their country.[10]

j. Next, Heracles visited the Oracle at Ammon, where he asked for an interview with his father Zeus; but Zeus was loth to reveal himself and, when Heracles persisted, flayed a ram, put on the fleece, with the ram's head hiding his own, and issued certain instructions. Hence the Egyptians give their images of Zeus Ammon a ram's face. The Thebans sacrifice rams only once a year when, at the end of Zeus's festival, they slay a single ram and use its fleece to cover Zeus's image; after which the worshippers beat their breasts in mourning for the victim, and bury it in a sacred tomb.[11]

k. Heracles then struck south, and founded a hundred-gated city, named Thebes in honour of his birthplace; but some say that Osiris had already founded it. All this time, the King of Egypt was Antaeus's brother Busiris, a son of Poseidon by Lysianassa, the daughter of Epaphus or, as others say, by Anippe, a daughter of the river Nile.[12] Now, Busiris's kingdom had once been visited with drought and famine for eight or nine years, and he had sent for Greek augurs to give him advice. His nephew, a learned Cyprian seer, named Phrasius, Thrasius, or Thasius, son of Pygmalion, announced that the famine would cease if every year one stranger were sacrificed in honour of Zeus. Busiris began with Phrasius himself, and afterwards sacrificed other chance guests, until the arrival of Heracles, who let the priests hale him off to the altar. They bound his hair with a fillet, and Busiris, calling upon the gods, was about to raise the sacrificial axe, when Heracles burst his bonds and slew Busiris, Busiris's son Amphidamas, and all the priestly attendants.[13]

l. Next, Heracles traversed Asia and put in at Thermydrae, the harbour of Rhodian Lindus, where he unyoked one of the bullocks from a farmer's cart, sacrificed it, and feasted on its flesh, while the owner stood upon a certain mountain and cursed him from afar. Hence the Lindians still utter curses when they sacrifice to Heracles. Finally he reached the Caucasus Mountains, where Prometheus had been fettered for thirty years – or one thousand, or thirty thousand years – while every day a griffon-vulture, born of Typhon and Echidne, tore at his liver. Zeus had long repented of his punishment, because Prometheus had since sent him a kindly warning not to marry Thetis, lest he might beget one greater than himself; and now, when Heracles pleaded for Prometheus's pardon, granted this without demur.[14] Having once, however, condemned him to everlasting punishment, Zeus stipulated that, in order still to appear a prisoner, he must wear a ring made from his chains and set with Caucasian stone – and this was the first ring ever to contain a setting. But Prometheus's sufferings were destined to last until some immortal should voluntarily go to Tartarus in his stead; so Heracles reminded Zeus of Cheiron, who was longing to resign the gift of immortality ever since he had suffered his incurable wound. Thus no further impediment remained, and Heracles, invoking Hunter Apollo, shot the griffon-vulture through the heart and set Prometheus free.[15]

m. Mankind now began to wear rings in Prometheus's honour, and also wreaths; because when released, Prometheus was ordered to crown himself with a willow wreath, and Heracles, to keep him company, assumed one of wild-olive.[16]

n. Almighty Zeus set the arrow among the stars as the constellation Sagitta; and to this day the inhabitants of the Caucasus Mountains regard the griffon-vulture as the enemy of mankind. They burn out its nests with flaming darts, and set snares for it to avenge Prometheus's suffering.[17]

1. Apollodorus: ii. 5. 11; Euripides: *Heracles* 396; Pherecydes: *Marriage of Hera* ii, quoted by scholiast on Apollonius Rhodius: iv. 1396; Eratosthenes: *Catasterismoi* iii; Hyginus: *Poetic Astronomy* ii. 3; Germanicus Caesar: *On Aratus's Phenomena*; *sub* Draco.

2. Apollodorus: ii. 5. 11; Hesiod: *Theogony* 333–5; Scholiast on Apollonius Rhodius: iv. 1396.

3. Apollodorus: *loc. cit.*; Scholiast on Virgil's *Aeneid* iv. 483; Hesiod: *Theogony* 215; Pliny: *Natural History* vi. 35–6; Ovid: *Metamorphoses* iv. 637 ff.

4. Apollodorus: *loc. cit.*; Herodotus: vii. 124–7; Hyginus: *Poetic Astronomy* ii. 15.

5. Apollodorus: *loc. cit.*; Pherecydes, quoted by scholiast on Apollonius Rhodius: iv. 1396; Apollonius Rhodius: 1396–1484.

6. Hyginus: *Poetic Astronomy* ii. 3.

7. Apollodorus: *loc. cit.*; Hyginus: *Fabula* 31; Diodorus Siculus: iv. 17.

8. Diodorus Siculus: *loc. cit.*; Apollodorus: *loc. cit.*; Pindar: *Isthmian Odes* iv. 52–5; Lucan: iv. 589–655.

9. Pliny: *Natural History* v. 1; Strabo: xvii. 3. 2; Pomponius Mela: iii. 106; Plutarch: *Sertorius* 9.

10. Strabo: xvii. 3. 7; Pliny: *Natural History* v. 8; Procopius: *On the Vandal War* ii. 10.

11. Callisthenes, quoted by Strabo: xvii. 1. 43; Herodotus: ii. 42.

12. Diodorus Siculus: i. 15 and iv. 18; Ovid: *Ibis* 399; Apollodorus: ii. 5. 11; Agathon of Samos, quoted by Plutarch: *Parallel Stories* 38.

13. Philargyrius on Virgil's *Georgics* iii. 5; Apollodorus: *loc. cit.*; Hyginus: *Fabulae* 31 and 56; Ovid: *Art of Love* i. 649.

14. Apollodorus: *loc. cit.*; Hyginus: *Fabula* 54; Strabo: xi. 5. 5; Aeschylus, quoted by Hyginus: *Poetic Astronomy* ii. 15; Hesiod: *Theogony* 529 ff.

15. Servius on Virgil's *Eclogues* vi. 42; Hyginus: *loc. cit.*; Pliny: *Natural History* xxxiii. 4 and xxxvii. 1; Aeschylus: *Prometheus Bound* 1025 and *Prometheus Unbound*, Fragment 195, quoted by Plutarch: *On Love* 14; Apollodorus: *loc. cit.*

16. Athenaeus: xv. 11–13; Aeschylus: *Fragments* 202 and 235, quoted by Athenaeus p. 674d; Apollodorus: *loc. cit.*

17. Hyginus: *Poetic Astronomy* ii. 15; Philostratus: *Life of Apollonius of Tyana* ii. 3.

*

1. The different locations of the Hesperides represent different views of what constituted the Farthest West. One account placed the scene of this Labour at Berenice, formerly called the city of the Hesperides (Pliny: *Natural History* v. 5), Eusperides (Herodotus: iv. 171), or Euesperites (Herodotus: iv. 198), but renamed after the wife of Ptolemy Euergetes. It was built on Pseudopenias (Strabo: xvii. 3. 20), the western promontory of the Gulf of Sirte. This city, washed by the river Lathon, or Lethon, had a sacred grove, known as the 'Gardens of the Hesperides'. Moreover, the Lathon flowed into a Hesperian Lake: and near by lay another, Lake Tritonis, enclosing a small island with a temple of Aphrodite (Strabo: *loc. cit.*; Pliny: *loc. cit.*), to whom the apple-tree was sometimes said to belong (Servius on Virgil's *Aeneid* iv. 485). Herodotus (*loc. cit.*) describes this as one of the few fertile parts of Libya; in the best years, the land brought forth one hundredfold.

2. Besides these geographical disputes, there were various rationalizations of the myth. One view was that the apples had really been beautiful sheep (*melon* means both 'sheep' and 'apple'), or sheep with a peculiar red fleece resembling gold, which were guarded by a shepherd named Dragon to whom Hesperus's daughters, the Hesperides, used to bring food. Heracles carried off the sheep (Servius on Virgil's *Aeneid: loc. cit.*; Diodorus Siculus: iv. 26) and killed (Servius: *loc. cit.*) or abducted, the shepherd (Palaephatus: 19). Palaephatus (*loc. cit.*) makes Hesperus a native of Carian Miletus, which was still famous for its sheep, and says that though Hesperus had long been dead at the time of Heracles's raid, his two daughters survived him.

3. Another view was that Heracles rescued the daughters of Atlas, who had been abducted from their family orchard by Egyptian priests; and Atlas, in gratitude, not only gave him the object of his Labour, but taught him astronomy into the bargain. For Atlas, the first astronomer, knew so much that he carried the celestial globe upon his shoulders, as it were; hence Heracles is said to have taken the globe from him (Diodorus

Siculus: iii. 60 and iv. 27). Heracles did indeed become Lord of the Zodiac, but the Titan astronomer whom he superseded was Coeus (*alias* Thoth), not Atlas (see 1.*3*).

4. The true explanation of this Labour is, however, to be found in ritual, rather than allegory. It will be shown (see 148. *5*) that the candidate for the kingship had to overcome a serpent and take his gold; and this Heracles did both here and in his battle with the Hydra. But the gold which he took should not properly have been in the form of golden apples – those were given him at the close of his reign by the Triple-goddess, as his passport to Paradise. And, in this funerary context, the Serpent was not his enemy, but the form that his own oracular ghost would assume after he had been sacrificed. Ladon was hundred-headed and spoke with divers tongues because many oracular heroes could call themselves 'Heracles': that is to say, they had been representatives of Zeus, and dedicated to the service of Hera. The Garden of the three Hesperides – whose names identify them with the sunset (see 33. *7* and 39. *1*) – is placed in the Far West because the sunset was a symbol of the sacred king's death. Heracles received the apples at the close of his reign, correctly recorded as a Great Year of one hundred lunations. He had taken over the burden of the sacred kingship from his predecessor, and with it the title 'Atlas', 'the long-suffering one'. It is likely that the burden was originally not the globe, but the sun-disk (see 67. *2*).

5. Nereus's behaviour is modelled on that of Proteus (see 169. *a*), whom Menelaus consulted on Pharos (Homer: *Odyssey* iv. 581 ff.). Heracles is said to have ascended the Po, because it led to the Land of the Hyperboreans (see 125. *b*). We know that the straw-wrapped gifts from the Hyperboreans to Delos came by this route (Herodotus: iv. 33). But though their land was, in one sense, Britain – as the centre of the Boreas cult – it was Libya in another, and the Caucasus in another; and the Paradise lay either in the Far West, or at the back of the North Wind, the mysterious region to which the wild geese flew in summertime (see 161. *4*). Heracles's wanderings illustrate this dubiety. If he was in search of the Libyan Paradise, he would have consulted Proteus King of Pharos (see 169. *a*); if of the Caucasian Paradise, Prometheus (which is, indeed, Apollodorus's version); if of the Northern, Nereus, who lived near the sources of the Po, and whose behaviour resembled that of Proteus.

6. Antaeus's bones were probably those of a stranded whale, about which a legend grew at Tangier: 'This must have been a giant – only Heracles could have killed him. Heracles, who put up those enormous pillars at Ceuta and Gibraltar!' A wrestling match between the candidate for kingship and local champions was a widely observed custom: the fight with Antaeus for the possession of the kingdom, like Theseus's fight with Sciron (see 96. *3*), or Odysseus's with Philomeleides (see 161. *f*),

must be understood in this context. Praxiteles, the sculptor of the Par-
thenon, regarded the overthrow of Antaeus as a separate labour (Pausanias: iv. 11. 4).

7. An ancient religious association linked Dodona and Ammon; and
the Zeus worshipped in each was originally a shepherd-king, annually
sacrificed, as on Mounts Pelion and Laphystius. Heracles did right to visit
his father Zeus when passing through Libya; Perseus had done so on his
way to the East, and Alexander the Great followed suit centuries later.

8. The god Set had reddish hair, and the Busirians therefore needed
victims with hair of that colour to offer Osiris, whom Set murdered; red-
heads were rare in Egypt, but common among the Hellenes (Diodorus
Siculus: i. 88; Plutarch: *On Isis and Osiris* 30, 33 and 73). Heracles's killing
of Busiris may record some punitive action taken by the Hellenes, whose
nationals had been waylaid and killed; there is evidence for an early
Hellenic colony at Chemmis.

9. Curses uttered during sacrifices to Heracles (see 143. *a*) recall the
well-established custom of cursing and insulting the king from a near-by
hill while he is being crowned, in order to ward off divine jealousy –
Roman generals were similarly insulted at their triumphs while they
impersonated Mars. But sowers also cursed the seed as they scattered it in
the furrows.

10. The release of Prometheus seems to have been a moral fable invented by Aeschylus, not a genuine myth (see 39. *h*). His wearing of the
willow-wreath – corroborated on an Etruscan mirror – suggests that he
had been dedicated to the Moon-goddess Anatha, or Neith, or Athene
(see 9. *1*). Perhaps he was originally bound with willow thongs to the
sacrificial altar of her autumn festival (see 116. *4*).

11. According to one legend, Typhon killed Heracles in Libya, and
Iolaus restored him to life by holding a quail to his nostrils (Eudoxus of
Cnidus: *Circuit of the Earth* i, quoted by Athenaeus: ix. 11). But it was
the Tyrian Heracles Melkarth, whom the god Esmun ('he whom we
evoke'), or Asclepius, restored in this way; the meaning is that the year
begins in March with the arrival of the quails from Sinai, and that quail-
orgies were then celebrated in honour of the goddess (see 14. *3*).

134

THE TWELFTH LABOUR: THE CAPTURE
OF CERBERUS

HERACLES's last, and most difficult, Labour was to bring the dog
Cerberus up from Tartarus. As a preliminary, he went to Eleusis where

he asked to partake of the Mysteries and wear the myrtle wreath.[1] Nowadays, any Greek of good repute may be initiated at Eleusis, but since in Heracles's day Athenians alone were admitted, Theseus suggested that a certain Pylius should adopt him. This Pylius did, and when Heracles had been purified for his slaughter of the Centaurs, because no one with blood-stained hands could view the Mysteries, he was duly initiated by Orpheus's son Musaeus, Theseus acting as his sponsor.[2] However, Eumolpus, the founder of the Greater Mysteries, had decreed that no foreigners should be admitted, and therefore the Eleusinians, loth to refuse Heracles's request, yet doubtful whether his adoption by Pylius would qualify him as a true Athenian, established the Lesser Mysteries on his account; others say that Demeter herself honoured him by founding the Lesser Mysteries on this occasion.[3]

b. Every year, two sets of Eleusinian Mysteries are held: the Greater in honour of Demeter and Core, and the Lesser in honour of Core alone. These Lesser Mysteries, a preparation for the Greater, are a dramatic reminder of Dionysus's fate, performed by the Eleusinians at Agrae on the river Ilissus in the month Anthesterion. The principal rites are the sacrifice of a sow, which the initiates first wash in the river Cantharus, and their subsequent purification by a priest who bears the name Hydranus.[4] They must then wait at least one year until they may participate in the Greater Mysteries, which are held at Eleusis itself in the month Boedromion; and must also take an oath of secrecy, administered by the mystagogue, before being prepared for these. Meanwhile, they are refused admittance to the sanctuary of Demeter, and wait in the vestibule throughout the solemnities.[5]

c. Thus cleansed and prepared, Heracles descended to Tartarus from Laconian Taenarum; or, some say, from the Acherusian peninsula near Heracleia on the Black Sea, where marks of his descent are still shown at a great depth. He was guided by Athene and Hermes – for whenever, exhausted by his Labours, he cried out in despair to Zeus, Athene always came hastening down to comfort him.[6] Terrified by Heracles's scowl, Charon ferried him across the river Styx without demur; in punishment of which irregularity he was fettered by Hades for one entire year. As Heracles stepped ashore from the crazy boat, all the ghosts fled, except Meleager and the Gorgon Medusa. At sight of Medusa he drew his sword, but Hermes reassured him that she was only a phantom; and when he aimed an arrow at Meleager, who was wearing bright armour, Meleager laughed. 'You have nothing to fear from the dead,' he said, and they chatted amicably for awhile, Heracles offering in the end to marry Meleager's sister Deianeira.[6]

d. Near the gates of Tartarus, Heracles found his friends Theseus and Peirithous fastened to cruel chairs, and wrenched Theseus free, but was obliged to leave Peirithous behind; next, he rolled away the stone under which Demeter had imprisoned Ascalaphus; and then, wishing to gratify the ghosts with a gift of warm blood, slaughtered one of Hades's cattle. Their herdsman, Menoetes, or Menoetius, the son of Ceuthonymus, challenged him to a wrestling match, but was seized around the middle and had his ribs crushed. At this, Persephone, who came out from her palace and greeted Heracles like a brother, intervened and pleaded for Menoetes's life.[8]

e. When Heracles demanded Cerberus, Hades, standing by his wife's side, replied grimly: 'He is yours, if you can master him without using your club or your arrows.' Heracles found the dog chained to the gates of Acheron, and resolutely gripped him by the throat – from which rose three heads, each maned with serpents. The barbed tail flew up to strike, but Heracles, protected by the lion pelt, did not relax his grip until Cerberus choked and yielded.[9]

f. On his way back from Tartarus, Heracles wove himself a wreath from the tree which Hades had planted in the Elysian Fields as a memorial to his mistress, the beautiful nymph Leuce. The outer leaves of this wreath remained black, because that is the colour of the Underworld; but those next to Heracles's brow were bleached a silver-white by his glorious sweat. Hence the white poplar, or aspen, is sacred to him: its colour signifying that he has laboured in both worlds.[10]

g. With Athene's assistance, Heracles recrossed the river Styx in safety, and then half-dragged, half-carried Cerberus up the chasm near Troezen, through which Dionysus had conducted his mother Semele. In the temple of Saviour Artemis, built by Theseus over the mouth of this chasm, altars now stand sacred to the infernal deities. At Troezen, also, a fountain discovered by Heracles and called after him is shown in front of Hippolytus's former palace.[11]

h. According to another account, Heracles dragged Cerberus, bound with adamantine chains, up a subterrene path which leads to the gloomy cave of Acone, near Mariandyne on the Black Sea. As Cerberus resisted, averting his eyes from the sunlight, and barking furiously with all three mouths, his slaver flew across the green fields and gave birth to the poisonous plant aconite, also called hecateis, because Hecate was the first to use it. Still another account is that Heracles came back to the upper air through Taenarum, famous for its cave-like temple with an image of Poseidon standing before it; but if a road ever led thence to the Underworld, it has since been blocked up. Finally, some say that he emerged from the precinct of Laphystian Zeus, on Mount Laphystius, where stands an image of Bright-eyed Heracles.[12]

i. Yet all agree at least that, when Heracles brought Cerberus to Mycenae, Eurystheus, who was offering a sacrifice, handed him a slave's portion, reserving the best cuts for his own kinsmen; and that Heracles showed his just resentment by killing three of Eurystheus's sons: Perimedes, Eurybius, and Eurypilus.[13]

j. Besides the aconite, Heracles also discovered the following simples: the all-heal heracleon, or 'wild origanum'; the Siderian heracleon, with its thin stem, red flower, and leaves like the coriander's, which grows near lakes and rivers, and is an excellent remedy for all wounds inflicted by iron; and the hyoscyamos, or henbane, which causes vertigo and insanity. The Nymphaean heracleon, which has a club-like root, was named after a certain nymph deserted by Heracles, who died of jealousy; it makes men impotent for the space of twelve days.[14]

1. Homer: *Odyssey* xi. 624; Apollodorus: ii. 5. 12.
2. Herodotus: viii. 65; Apollodorus: *loc. cit.*; Plutarch: *Theseus* 30 and 33; Diodorus Siculus: iv. 25.
3. Tzetzes: *On Lycophron* 1328; Diodorus Siculus: iv. 14.
4. Scholiast on Aristophanes's *Plutus* 85 and *Peace* 368; Stephanus of Byzantium *sub* Agra; Plutarch: *Demetrius* 26 and *Phocion* 28; Aristophanes: *Acharnians* 703, with scholiast on 720; Varro: *On Country Matters* ii. 4; Hesychius *sub* Hydranus; Polyaenus: v. 17.
5. Plutarch: *Phocion* 28; Seneca: *Natural Questions* vii. 31.
6. Apollodorus: ii. 5. 12; Xenophon: *Anabasis* ci. 2. 2; Homer: *Odyssey* xi. 626 and *Iliad* viii. 362 ff.
7. Servius on Virgil's *Aeneid* vi. 392; Apollodorus: *loc. cit.*; Bacchylides: *Epincia* v. 71 ff. and 165 ff.
8. Apollodorus: *loc. cit.*; Tzetzes: *Chiliades*: ii. 396 ff.
9. Apollodorus: *loc. cit.*
10. Servius on Virgil's *Aeneid* viii. 276 and *Eclogues* vii. 61.
11. Homer: *Iliad* viii. 369; Apollodorus: *loc. cit.*; Pausanias: ii. 31. 12 and ii. 32. 3.
12. Ovid: *Metamorphoses* vii. 409 ff.; Germanicus Caesar on Virgil's *Georgics* ii. 152; Pausanias: iii. 25. 4 and ix. 34. 4.

13. Anticlides, quoted by Athenaeus: iv. 14; Scholiast on Thucydides: i. 9.

14. Pliny: *Natural History* xxv. 12, 15, 27, and 37.

*

1. This myth seems to have been deduced from an icon which showed Heracles descending to Tartarus, where Hecate the Goddess of the Dead welcomed him in the form of a three-headed monster – perhaps with one head for each of the seasons (see 31. *f* and 75. 2) – and, as a natural sequel to her gift of the golden apples, led him away to the Elysian Fields. Cerberus, in fact, was here carrying off Heracles; not contrariwise. The familiar version is a logical result of his elevation to godhead: a hero must remain in the Underworld, but a god will escape and take his gaoler with him. Moreover, deification of a hero in a society which formerly worshipped only the Goddess implies that the king has defied immemorial custom and refused to die for her sake. Thus the possession of a golden dog was proof of the Achaean High King's sovereignty and escape from matriarchal tutelage (see 24. 4). Menoetes's presence in Tartarus, and Heracles's theft of one of Hades's cattle, shows that the Tenth Labour is another version of the Twelfth: a harrowing of Hell (see 132. 1). To judge from the corresponding Welsh myth, Menoetes's father, though purposely 'nameless', was the alder-god Bran, or Phoroneus, or Cronus; which agrees with the context of the Tenth Labour (*White Goddess* p. 48).

2. The Greater Eleusinian Mysteries were of Cretan origin, and held in Boedromion ('running for help') which, in Crete, was the first month of the year, roughly September, and so named, according to Plutarch (*Theseus* 27), to commemorate Theseus's defeat of the Amazons, which means his suppression of the matriarchal system. Originally, the Mysteries seem to have been the sacred king's preparation, at the autumnal equinox, for his approaching death at midwinter – hence the premonitory myrtle wreath (see 109. 4) – in the form of a sacred drama, which advised him what to expect in the Underworld. After the abolition of royal male sacrifices, a feature of matriarchy, the Mysteries were open to all judged worthy of initiation; as in Egypt, where the *Book of the Dead* gave similar advice, any man of good repute could become an Osiris by being purified of all uncleanness and undergoing a mock death. In Eleusis, Osiris was identified with Dionysus. White poplar leaves were a Sumerian symbol of renascence and, in the tree-calendar, white poplar stood for the autumnal equinox (see 52. 3).

3. The Lesser Mysteries, which became a preparation for the Greater, seem to have been an independent Pelasgian festival, also based on the hope of rebirth, but taking place early in February at Candlemas, when the trees first leaf – which is the meaning of 'Anthesterion'.

4. Now, since Dionysus was identified with Osiris, Semele must be Isis; and we know that Osiris did not rescue Isis from the Underworld, but she, him. Thus the icon at Troezen will have shown Semele restoring Dionysus to the upper air. The goddess who similarly guides Heracles is Isis again; and his rescue of Alcestis was probably deduced from the same icon – he is led, not leading. His emergence in the precinct of Mount Laphystius makes an interesting variant. No cavern exists on the summit, and the myth must refer to the death and resurrection of the sacred king which was celebrated there – a rite that helped to form the legend of the Golden Fleece (see 70. 2 and 148. 10).

5. Aconite, a poison and paralysant, was used by the Thessalian witches in the manufacture of their flying ointment: it numbed the feet and hands and gave them a sensation of being off the ground. But since it was also a febrifuge, Heracles, who drove the fever-birds from Stymphalus, became credited with its discovery.

6. The sequence of Heracles's feats varies considerably. Diodorus Siculus and Hyginus arrange the Twelve Labours in the same order as Apollodorus, except that they both place the Fourth before the Third, and the Sixth before the Fifth; and that Diodorus places the Twelfth before the Eleventh. Nearly all mythographers agree that the killing of the Nemean Lion was the First Labour, but in Hyginus's sequence of 'the Twelve Labours of Heracles set by Eurystheus' (*Fabula* 30), it is preceded by the strangling of the serpents. In one place, Diodorus Siculus associates the killing of Anaeus and Busiris with the Tenth Labour (iv. 17–18); in another, with the Eleventh (iv. 27). And while some writers make Heracles sail with the Argonauts in his youth (Silius Italicus: i. 512); others place this adventure after the Fourth Labour (Apollonius Rhodius: i. 122); and others after the Eighth (Diodorus Siculus: iv. 15). But some make him perform the Ninth (Valerius Flaccus: *Argonautica* v. 91) and Twelfth (*ibid.*: ii. 382) Labours, and break the horns of 'both bulls' (*ibid.*: i. 36) before he sailed with the Argonauts; and others deny that he sailed at all, on the ground that he was then serving as Queen Omphale's slave (Herodotus, quoted by Apollodorus: i. 9. 19).

7. According to *Lycophron* 1328, Heracles was initiated into the Eleusinian Mysteries before setting out on the Ninth Labour; but Philochorus (quoted by Plutarch: *Theseus* 26) says that Theseus had him initiated in the course of its performance (*ibid.*: 30), and was rescued by him from Tartarus during the Twelfth Labour (Apollodorus: ii. 5. 12). According to Pausanias (i. 27. 7), Theseus was only seven years old when Heracles came to Troezen, wearing the lion pelt; and cleared the Isthmus of malefactors on his way to Athens, at the time when Heracles was serving Omphale (Apollodorus: ii. 6. 3). Euripides believed that Heracles had fought with Ares's son Cycnus before setting out on the Eighth Labour

(*Alcestis* 501 ff.); Propertius (iv. 19. 41), that he had already visited Tartarus when he killed Cacus; and Ovid (*Fasti* v. 388), that Cheiron died accidentally when Heracles had almost completed his Labours, not during the Fourth.

8. Albricus (22) lists the following Twelve Labours in this order, with allegorical explanations: defeating the Centaurs at a wedding; killing the lion; rescuing Alcestis from Tartarus and chaining Cerberus; winning the apples of the Hesperides; destroying the Hydra; wrestling with Achelous; killing Cacus; winning the mares of Diomedes; defeating Antaeus; capturing the boar; lifting the cattle of Geryon; holding up the heavens.

9. Various Labours and bye-works of Heracles were represented on Apollo's throne at Amyclae (Pausanias: iii. 18. 7–9); and in the bronze shrine of Athene on the Spartan acropolis (Pausanias: iii. 17. 3). Praxiteles's gable sculptures on the Theban shrine of Heracles showed most of the Twelve Labours, but the Stymphalian Birds were missing, and the wrestling match with Antaeus replaced the cleansing of Augeias's stables. The evident desire of so many cities to be associated with Heracles's Labours suggests that much the same ritual marriage-task drama, as a preliminary to coronation, was performed over a wide area.

135

THE MURDER OF IPHITUS

WHEN Heracles returned to Thebes after his Labours, he gave Megara, his wife, now thirty-three years old, in marriage to his nephew and charioteer Iolaus, who was only sixteen, remarking that his own union with her had been inauspicious.[1] He then looked about for a younger and more fortunate wife; and, hearing that his friend Eurytus, a son of Melanius, King of Oechalia, had offered to marry his daughter Iole to any archer who could outshoot him and his four sons, took the road there.[2] Eurytus had been given a fine bow and taught its use by Apollo himself, whom he now claimed to surpass in marksmanship, yet Heracles found no difficulty in winning the contest. The result displeased Eurytus excessively and, when he learned that Heracles had discarded Megara after murdering her children, he refused to give him Iole. Having drunk a great deal of wine to gain confidence, 'You could never compare with me and my sons as an archer,' he told Heracles, 'were it not that you unfairly use magic arrows, which cannot miss their mark. This contest is void, and I would not, in any case, entrust my beloved daughter to such a ruffian as yourself! Moreover, you are Eurystheus's slave and, like a slave, deserve only blows from a free man.' So saying, he drove Heracles out of the Palace. Heracles did not retaliate at once, as he might well have done; but swore to take vengeance.[3]

b. Three of Eurytus's sons, namely Didaeon, Clytius, and Toxeus, had supported their father in his dishonest pretensions. The eldest, however, whose name was Iphitus, declared that Iole should in all fairness have been given to Heracles; and when, soon afterwards, twelve strong-hooved brood-mares and twelve sturdy mule-foals disappeared from Euboea, he refused to believe that Heracles was the thief. As a matter of fact, they had been stolen by the well-known thief Autolycus, who magically changed their appearance and sold them to the unsuspecting Heracles as if they were his own.[4] Iphitus followed the tracks of the mares and foals and found that they led towards Tiryns, which made him suspect that Heracles was, after all, avenging the insult offered him by Eurytus. Coming suddenly face to face with Heracles, who had just returned from his rescue of Alcestis, he concealed his suspicions and merely asked for advice in the matter. Heracles did not recognize the beasts from Iphitus's description as those sold to him by Autolycus, and with his usual heartiness promised to search for them if Iphitus would consent to become his guest. Yet he now divined that he was suspected of theft, which galled his sensitive heart. After a grand banquet, he led Iphitus to the top of the highest tower in Tiryns. 'Look about you!' he demanded, 'and tell me whether your mares are grazing anywhere in sight.' 'I cannot see them', Iphitus admitted. 'Then you have falsely accused me in your heart of being a thief!' Heracles roared, distraught with anger, and hurled him to his death.[5]

c. Heracles presently went to Neleus, King of Pylus, and asked to be purified; but Neleus refused, because Eurytus was his ally. Nor would any of his sons, except the youngest, Nestor, consent to receive Heracles, who eventually persuaded Deiphobus, the son of Hippolytus, to purify him at Amyclae. However, he still suffered from evil dreams, and went to ask the Delphic Oracle how he might be rid of them.[6] The Pythoness Xenoclea refused to answer this question. 'You murdered your guest,' she said. 'I have no oracles for such as you!' 'Then I shall be obliged to institute an oracle of my own!' cried Heracles. With that, he plundered the shrine of its votive offerings and even pulled away the tripod on which Xenoclea sat. 'Heracles of Tiryns is a very different man from his Canopic namesake,' the Pythoness said severely as he carried the tripod from the shrine; she meant that the Egyptian Heracles had once come to Delphi and behaved with courtesy and reverence.[7]

d. Up rose the indignant Apollo, and fought Heracles until Zeus parted the combatants with a thunderbolt, making them clasp hands in friendship. Heracles restored the sacred tripod, and together they founded the city of Gythium, where images of Apollo, Heracles, and Dionysus now stand side by side in the market place. Xenoclea then gave Heracles the following oracle: 'To be rid of your affliction you must be sold into slavery for one whole year and the price you fetch must be offered to Iphitus's children.[8] Zeus is enraged that you have violated the laws of hospitality, whatever the provocation.' 'Whose slave am I to be?' asked Heracles humbly. 'Queen Omphale of Lydia will purchase you,' Xenoclea replied. 'I obey,' said Heracles, 'but one day I shall enslave the man who has brought this suffering upon me, and all his family too!'[9] Some, however, say that Heracles did not return the tripod and that, when one thousand years later, Apollo heard that it had been taken to the city of Pheneus, he punished the Pheneans by blocking the channel which Heracles had dug to carry off the heavy rains, and flooded their city.[10]

e. Another wholly different account of these events is current, according to which Lycus the Euboean, son of Poseidon and Dirce, attacked Thebes during a time of sedition, killed King Creon, and usurped the throne. Believing Copreus's report that Heracles had died, Lycus tried to seduce Megara and, when she resisted him, would have killed her and the children had Heracles not returned from Tartarus just in time to exact vengeance. Thereupon Hera, whose favourite Lycus was, drove Heracles mad: he killed Megara and his own sons, also his minion, the Aetolian Stichius.[11] The Thebans, who show the children's tomb, say that Heracles would have killed his foster-father Amphitryon as well, if Athene had not knocked him insensible with a huge stone; to which they point, saying: 'We nick-name it "The Chastener".' But Amphitryon had, in fact, died long before, in the Orchomenan campaign. The Athenians claim that Theseus, grateful to Heracles for his rescue from Tartarus, arrived at this juncture with an Athenian army, to help Heracles against Lycus. He stood aghast at the murder, yet promised Heracles every honour for the rest of his life, and after his death as well, and brought him to Athens, where Medea cured his madness with medicines. Sicalus then purified him once more.[12]

1. Plutarch: *On Love* 9; Apollodorus: ii. 6. 1; Pausanias: x. 29. 3.

2. Diodorus Siculus: iv. 31; Pausanias: iv. 33. 5; Sophocles: *Trachinian Women* 260 ff.

3. Hyginus: *Fabula* 14; Apollonius Rhodius: i. 88–9; Homer: *Odyssey* viii. 226–8; Apollodorus: *loc. cit.*; Diodorus Siculus: *loc. cit.*; Sophocles: *loc. cit.*

4. Hesiod, quoted by scholiast on Sophocles's *Trachinian Women* 266; Homer: *Odyssey* xxi. 15 ff.; Diodorus Siculus: *loc. cit.*; Apollodorus: ii. 6. 2; Scholiast on Homer's *Odyssey* xxi. 22.

5. Apollodorus: *loc. cit.*; Sophocles: *Trachinian Women* 271; Homer: *loc. cit.*, with scholiast quoting Pherecydes; Diodorus Siculus: *loc. cit.*

6. Apollodorus: *loc. cit.*; Diodorus Siculus: *loc. cit.*

7. Apollodorus: *loc. cit.*; Pausanias: x. 13. 4; Hyginus: *Fabula* 32.

8. Apollodorus: *loc. cit.*; Hyginus: *loc. cit.*; Pausanias: ii. 21. 7; Diodorus Siculus: *loc. cit.*

9. Sophocles: *Trachinian Women* 248 ff. and 275 ff.; Hyginus: *loc. cit.*; Servius on Virgil's *Aeneid* viii. 300.

10. Plutarch: *On the Slowness of Divine Vengeance* 12; Pausanias: viii. 14. 3.

11. Hyginus: *Fabula* 32; Euripides: *Heracles* 26 ff. and 553; Servius on Virgil's *Aeneid* viii. 300; Scholiast on Sophocles's *Trachinian Women* 355; Ptolemy Hephaestionos: vii, quoted by Photius p. 490.

12. Euripides: *Heracles* 26 ff., 1163 ff., and 1322; Pausanias: ix. 11. 2; Diodorus Siculus: iv. 55; Menocrates, quoted by scholiast on Pindar's *Isthmian Odes* iv. 104 ff.

*

1. In matrilineal society, divorce of a royal wife implies abandonment of the kingdom which has been her marriage portion; and it seems likely that, once the ancient conventions were relaxed in Greece, a sacred king could escape death at the end of his reign by abandoning his kingdom and marrying the heiress of another. If this is so, Eurytus's objection to Heracles as a son-in-law will not have been that he had killed his children – the annual victims sacrificed while he reigned at Thebes – but that he had evaded his royal duty of dying. The winning of a bride by a feat of archery was an Indo-European custom: in the *Mahabharata*, Arjuna wins Draupadi thus, and in the *Ramayana*, Rama bends Shiva's powerful bow and wins Sita. Moreover, the shooting of one arrow towards each cardinal point of the compass, and one towards the zenith (see 126. 2 and 132. 8), formed part of the royal marriage rites in India and Egypt. The mares may have figured sacrificially at the marriage of Heracles and Iole, when he became King of Oechalia (see 81. *4*). Iphitus, at any rate, is the king's surrogate flung from the Theban walls at the end of every year, or at any other time in placation of some angry deity (see 105. *6*; 106. *j*; and 121. *3*).

2. Heracles's seizure of the Delphic tripod apparently records a Dorian capture of the shrine; as the thunderbolt thrown between Apollo and Heracles records a decision that Apollo should be allowed to keep his Oracle, rather than yield it to Heracles – provided that he served the Dorian interests as patron of the Dymanes, a tribe belonging to the Doric League. It was notorious that the Spartans, who were Dorians, controlled the Delphic Oracle in Classical times. Euripides omits the tripod incident in his *Heracles* because, in 421 B.C., the Athenians had been worsted by the Treaty of Nicias in their attempt to maintain the Phocians' sovereignty over Delphi; the Spartans insisted on making it a separate puppet state which they themselves controlled. In the middle of the fourth century, when the dispute broke out again, the Phocians seized Delphi and appropriated some of its treasures to raise forces in their own defence; but were badly beaten, and all their cities destroyed.

3. The Pythoness's reproach seems to mean that the Dorians, who had conquered the Peloponnese, called themselves 'Sons of Heracles', and did not show her the same respect as their Achaean, Aeolian, and Ionian predecessors, whose religious ties were with the agricultural Libyans of the Egyptian Delta, rather than with the Hellenic cattle-kings; Xenoclea's predecessor Herophile ('dear to Hera'), had been Zeus's daughter by Lamia and called 'Sibyl' by the Libyans over whom she ruled (Pausanias: x. 12. 1; Euripides: *Prologue* to *Lamia*). Cicero confirms this view when he denies that Alcmene's son (i.e. the pre-Dorian Heracles) was the one who fought Apollo for the tripod (*On the Nature of the Gods* iii). Attempts were later made, in the name of religious decency, to patch up the quarrel between Apollo the Phocian and Heracles the Dorian. Thus Plutarch, a Delphic priest, suggests (*Dialogue on the E at Delphi* 6) that Heracles became an expert diviner and logician, and 'seemed to have seized the tripod in friendly rivalry with Apollo.' When describing Apollo's vengeance on the people of Pheneus, he tactfully suppresses the fact that it was Heracles who had dug them the channel (see 138. *d*).

136

OMPHALE

HERACLES was taken to Asia and offered for sale as a nameless slave by Hermes, patron of all important financial transactions, who afterwards handed the purchase money of three silver talents to Iphitus's orphans. Nevertheless, Eurytus stubbornly forbade his grandchildren to accept any monetary compensation, saying that only blood would pay for blood; and what happened to the silver, Hermes alone knows.[1] As the Pythoness had foretold, Heracles was bought by Omphale, Queen of Lydia, a woman with a good eye for a bargain; and he served her faithfully either for one year, or for three, ridding Asia Minor of the bandits who infested it.[2]

b. This Omphale, a daughter of Jordanes and, according to some authorities, the mother of Tantalus, had been bequeathed the kingdom by her unfortunate husband Tmolus, son of Ares and Theogone. While out hunting on Mount Carmanorium – so called in honour of Carmanor son of Dionysus and Alixirrhoë, who was killed there by a wild boar – he fell in love with a huntress named Arrhippe, a chaste attendant of Artemis. Arrhippe, deaf to Tmolus's threats and entreaties, fled to her mistress's temple where, disregarding its sanctity, he ravished her on the goddess's own couch. She hanged herself from a beam, after invoking Artemis, who thereupon let loose a mad bull; Tmolus was tossed into the air, fell on pointed stakes and sharp stones and died in torment. Theoclymenus, his son by Omphale, buried him where he lay, renaming the mountain 'Tmolus'; a city of the same name, built upon its slopes, was destroyed by a great earthquake in the reign of the Emperor Tiberius.[3]

c. Among the many bye-works which Heracles performed during this servitude was his capture of the two Ephesian Cercopes, who had constantly robbed him of his sleep. They were twin brothers named either Passalus and Acmon; or Olus and Eurybatus; or Sillus and Triballus – sons of Oceanus by Theia, and the most accomplished cheats and liars known to mankind, who roamed the world, continually practising new deceptions. Theia had warned them to keep clear of Heracles and her words 'My little White-bottoms, you have yet to meet the great Black-bottom!' becoming proverbial, 'white-bottom' now means 'cowardly, base, or lascivious'.[4] They would buzz around Heracles's bed in the guise of bluebottles, until one night he grabbed them, forced them to resume their proper shape, and bore them off, dangling head-downwards from a pole which he carried over his shoulder. Now, Heracles's bottom, which the lion's pelt did not cover, had been burned as black as an old leather shield by exposure to the sun, and by the fiery breaths of Cacus and of the Cretan bull; and the Cer-

copes burst into a fit of immoderate laughter to find themselves sus-
pended upside-down, staring at it. Their merriment surprised Heracles,
and when he learned its cause, he sat down upon a rock and laughed so
heartily himself that they persuaded him to release them. But though
we know of an Asian city named Cercopia, the haunts of the Cercopes
and a rock called 'Black Bottom' are shown at Thermopylae; this
incident therefore is likely to have taken place on another occasion.[5]

d. Some say that the Cercopes were eventually turned to stone for
trying to deceive Zeus; others, that he punished their fraudulence by
changing them into apes with long yellow hair, and sending them to
the Italian islands named Pithecusae.[6]

e. In a Lydian ravine lived one Syleus, who used to seize passing
strangers and force them to dig his vineyard; but Heracles tore up the
vines by their roots. Again, when Lydians from Itone began plundering
Omphale's country, Heracles recovered the spoil and razed their city.[7]
And at Celaenae lived Lityerses the farmer, a bastard son of King Minos,
who would offer hospitality to wayfarers but force them to compete
with him in reaping his harvest. If their strength flagged, he would
whip them and at evening, when he had won the contest, would behead
them and conceal their bodies in sheaves, chanting lugubriously as he
did so. Heracles visited Celaenae in order to rescue the shepherd Daphnis, a son of Hermes who, after searching throughout the world for
his beloved Pimplea, carried off by pirates, had at last found her among
the slave-girls of Lityerses. Daphnis was challenged to the reaping contest, but Heracles taking his place out-reaped Lityerses, whom he
decapitated with a sickle, throwing the trunk into the river Maeander.
Not only did Daphnis win back his Pimplea, but Heracles gave her
Lityerses's palace as a dowry. In honour of Lityerses, Phrygian reapers
still sing a harvest dirge closely resembling that raised in honour of
Maneros, son of the first Egyptian king, who also died in the harvest
field.[8]

f. Finally, beside the Lydian river Sagaris, Heracles shot dead a
gigantic serpent which was destroying men and crops; and the grateful
Omphale, having at last discovered his identity and parentage, released
him and sent him back to Tiryns, laden with gifts; while Zeus contrived
the constellation Ophiuchus to commemorate the victory. This river
Sagaris, by the way, was named after a son of Myndon and Alexirrhoë
who, driven mad by the Mother of the Gods for slighting her Mysteries
and insulting her eunuch priests, drowned himself in its waters.[9]

g. Omphale had bought Heracles as a lover rather than a fighter. He fathered on her three sons, namely Lamus; Agelaus, ancestor of a famous King Croesus who tried to immolate himself on a pyre when the Persians captured Sardis; and Laomedon.[10] Some add a fourth, Tyrrhenus, or Tyrsenus, who invented the trumpet and led Lydian emigrants to Eturia, where they took the name Tyrrhenians; but it is more probable that Tyrrhenus was the son of King Atys, and a remote descendant of Heracles and Omphale.[11] By one of Omphale's women, named Malis, Heracles was already the father of Cleodaeus, or Cleolaus; and of Alcaeus, founder of the Lydian dynasty which King Croesus ousted from the throne of Sardis.[12]

h. Reports reached Greece that Heracles had discarded his lion pelt and his aspen wreath, and instead wore jewelled necklaces, golden bracelets, a woman's turban, a purple shawl, and a Maeonian girdle. There he sat – the story went – surrounded by wanton Ionian girls, teasing wool from the polished wool-basket, or spinning the thread; trembling, as he did so, when his mistress scolded him. She would strike him with her golden slipper if ever his clumsy fingers crushed the spindle, and make him recount his past achievements for her amusement; yet apparently he felt no shame. Hence painters show Heracles wearing a yellow petticoat, and letting himself be combed and manicured by Omphale's maids, while she dresses up in his lion pelt, and wields his club and bow.[13]

i. What, however, had happened was no more than this. One day, when Heracles and Omphale were visiting the vineyards of Tmolus, she in a purple, gold-embroidered gown, with perfumed locks, he gallantly holding a golden parasol over her head, Pan caught sight of them from a high hill. Falling in love with Omphale, he bade farewell to the mountain-goddesses, crying: 'Henceforth she alone shall be my love!' Omphale and Heracles reached their destination, a secluded grotto, where it amused them to exchange clothes. She dressed him in a net-work girdle, absurdly small for his waist, and her purple gown. Though she unlaced this to the fullest extent, he split the sleeves; and the ties of her sandals were far too short to meet across his instep.

j. After dinner, they went to sleep on separate couches, having vowed a dawn sacrifice to Dionysus, who requires marital purity from his devotees on such occasions. At midnight, Pan crept into the grotto and, fumbling about in the darkness, found what he thought was Omphale's couch, because the sleeper was clad in silk. With trembling hands he untucked the bed-clothes from the bottom, and wormed his way in; but Heracles, waking and drawing up one foot, kicked him across the grotto. Hearing a loud crash and a howl, Omphale sprang up and called for lights, and when these came she and Heracles laughed until they cried to see Pan sprawling in a corner, nursing his bruises. Since that day, Pan has abhorred clothes, and summons his officials naked to his rites; it was he who revenged himself on Heracles by spreading the rumour that his whimsical exchange of garments with Omphale was habitual and perverse.[14]

1. Apollodorus: ii. 6. 3; Diodorus Siculus: iv. 31; Pherecydes, quoted by scholiast on Homer's *Odyssey* xxi. 22.
2. Sophocles: *Trachinian Women* 253; Apollodorus: ii. 6. 2; Diodorus Siculus: *loc. cit.*
3. Apollodorus: ii. 6. 3; Plutarch: *On Rivers* 7; Tacitus: *Annals* ii. 47.
4. Apollodorus: *loc. cit.*; Suidas *sub* Cercopes; Scholiast on Lucian's *Alexander* 4; Tzetzes: *On Lycophron* 91.
5. W. H. Roscher: *Lexikon der griechischen und römischen Mytologie* ii. 1166 ff.; K. O. Müller: *Dorians* i. 464; Ptolemy Claudius: v. 2; Herodotus: vii. 216.
6. Suidas *sub* Cercopes; Harpocration *sub* Cercopes, quoting Xenagoras; Eustathius on Homer's *Odyssey* xix. 247; Ovid: *Metamorphoses* xiv. 88 ff.
7. Tzetzes: *Chiliades* ii. 432 ff.; Diodorus Siculus: iv. 31; Dionysius: *Description of the Earth* 465; Stephanus of Byzantium *sub* Itone.
8. Scholiast on Theocritus's *Idylls* x. 41; Athenaeus: x. 615 and xiv. 619; Eustathius on Homer 1164; Hesychius, Photius, and Suidas *sub* Lityerses; Pollux: iv. 54.
9. Hyginus: *Poetic Astronomy* ii. 14; Plutarch: *On Rivers* 12.
10. Diodorus Siculus: iv. 31; Bacchylides: iii. 24–62; Apollodorus: ii. 6. 3; Palaephatus: 45.
11. Pausanias: ii. 21. 3; Herodotus: i. 94; Strabo: v. 2. 2; Dionysius of Halicarnassus: i. 28.
12. Hellanicus: *Fragment* 102, ed. Didot; Diodorus Siculus: *loc. cit.*; Eusebius: *Preparation for the Gospel* ii. 35; Herodotus: i. 7.
13. Ovid: *Heroides* ix. 54 ff.; Lucian: *Dialogues of the Gods* 13; Plutarch: *On Whether an Aged Man Ought to Meddle in State Affairs* 4.
14. Ovid: *Fasti* ii. 305.

*

1. Carmanor will have been a title of Adonis (see 18. 7), also killed by a boar. Tmolus's desecration of the temple of Artemis cannot be dated; neither can the order that Heracles should compensate Eurytus for his son's murder. Both events, however, seem to be historical in origin. It is

likely that Omphale stands for the Pythoness, guardian of the Delphic *omphalus*, who awarded the compensation, making Heracles a temple-slave until it should be paid, and that, 'Omphale' being also the name of a Lydian queen, the scene of his servitude was changed by the mythographers, to suit another set of traditions.

2. The Cercopes, as their various pairs of names show, were *ceres*, or Spites, coming in the shape of delusive and mischievous dreams, and could be foiled by an appeal to Heracles who, alone, had power over the Nightmare (see 35. *3–4*). Though represented at first as simple ghosts, like Cecrops (whose name is another form of *cercops*), in later works of art they figure as *cercopithecoi*, 'apes', perhaps because of Heracles's association with Gibraltar, one of his Pillars, from which Carthaginian merchants brought them as pets for rich Greek and Roman ladies. No apes seem to have frequented Ischia and Procida, two islands to the north of the Bay of Naples, which the Greeks called Pithecusae; their name really refers to the *pithoi*, or jars, manufactured there (Pliny: *Natural History* iii. 6. 12).

3. The vine-dressers' custom of seizing and killing a stranger at the vintage season, in honour of the Vine-spirit, was widespread in Syria and Asia Minor; and a similar harvest sacrifice took place both there and in Europe. Sir James Frazer has discussed this subject exhaustively in his *Golden Bough*. Heracles is here credited with the abolition of human sacrifice: a social reform on which the Greeks prided themselves, even when their wars grew more and more savage and destructive.

4. Classical writers made Heracles's servitude to Omphale an allegory of how easily a strong man becomes enslaved by a lecherous and ambitious woman; and that they regarded the navel as the seat of female passion sufficiently explains Omphale's name in this sense. But the fable refers, rather, to an early stage in the development of the sacred kingship from matriarchy to patriarchy, when the king, as the Queen's consort, was privileged to deputize for her in ceremonies and sacrifices – but only if he wore her robes. Reveillout has shown that this was the system at Lagash in early Sumerian times, and in several Cretan works of art men are shown wearing female garments for sacrificial purposes – not only the spotted trouser-skirt, as on the Hagia Triada sarcophagus, but even, as on a palace-fresco at Cnossus, the flounced skirt. Heracles's slavery is explained by West African matriarchal native customs: in Loango, Daura, and the Abrons, as Briffault has pointed out, the king is of servile birth and without power; in Agonna, Latuka, Ubemba, and elsewhere, there is only a queen, who does not marry but takes servile lovers. Moreover, a similar system survived until Classical times among the ancient Locrian nobility who had the privilege of sending priestesses to Trojan Athene (see 158. *8*); they were forced to emigrate in 683 B.C. from

Central Greece to Epizephyrian Locri, on the toe of Italy, 'because of the scandal caused by their noblewomen's indiscriminate love affairs with slaves' (see 18. 8). These Locrians, who were of non-Hellenic origin and made a virtue of pre-nuptial promiscuity in the Cretan, Carian, or Amorite style (Clearchus: 6), insisted on strictly matrilinear succession (Dionysius: *Description of the Earth* 365–7; Polybius: xii. 6b). The same customs must have been general in pre-Hellenic Greece and Italy, but it is only at Bagnara, near the ruins of Epizephyrian Locri, that the matri-archal tradition is recalled today. The Bagnarotte wear long, pleated skirts, and set off barefoot on their commercial rounds which last for several days, leaving the men to mind the children; they can carry as much as two *quintals* on their heads. The men take holidays in the spring swordfish season, when they show their skill with the harpoon; and in the summer, when they go to the hills and burn charcoal. Although the official patron of Bagnera is St Nicholas, no Bagnarotte will acknowledge his existence; and their parish priest complains that they pay far more attention to the Virgin than even to the Son – the Virgin having suc-ceeded Core, the Maid, for whose splendid temple Locri was famous in Classical times.

137

HESIONE

AFTER serving as a slave to Queen Omphale, Heracles returned to Tiryns, his sanity now fully restored, and at once planned an expedition against Troy.[1] His reasons were as follows. He and Telamon, either on their way back from the country of the Amazons, or when they landed with the Argonauts at Sigeium, had been astonished to find Laomedon's daughter Hesione, stark naked except for her jewels, chained to a rock on the Trojan shore.[2] It appeared that Poseidon had sent a sea-monster to punish Laomedon for having failed to pay him and Apollo their stipulated fee when they built the city walls and tended his flocks. Some say that he should have sacrificed to them all the cattle born in his kingdom that year; others, that he had promised them only a low wage as day-labourers, but even so cheated them of more than thirty Trojan drachmae. In revenge, Apollo sent a plague, and Poseidon ordered this monster to prey on the plainsfolk and ruin their fields by spewing sea water over them. According to another account, Laomedon fulfilled his obligations to Apollo, but not to Poseidon, who therefore sent the plague as well as the monster.[3]

b. Laomedon visited the Oracle of Zeus Ammon, and was advised by him to expose Hesione on the seashore for the monster to devour. Yet he obstinately refused to do so unless the Trojan nobles would first let him sacrifice their own daughters. In despair, they consulted Apollo who, being no less angry than Poseidon, gave them little satisfaction. Most parents at once sent their children abroad for safety, but Laomedon tried to force a certain Phoenodamas, who had kept his three daughters at home, to expose one of them; upon which Phoenodamas harangued the assembly, pleading that Laomedon was alone responsible for their present distress, and should be made to suffer for it by sacrificing his daughter. In the end, it was decided to cast lots, and the lot fell upon Hesione, who was accordingly bound to the rock, where Heracles found her.[4]

c. Heracles now broke her bonds, went up to the city, and offered to destroy the monster in return for the two matchless, immortal, snow-white horses, or mares, which could run over water and standing corn like the wind, and which Zeus had given Laomedon as compensation for the rape of Ganymedes. Laomedon readily agreed to the bargain.[5]

d. With Athene's help, the Trojans then built Heracles a high wall which served to protect him from the monster as it poked its head out of the sea and advanced across the plain. On reaching the wall, it opened its great jaws and Heracles leaped fully-armed down its throat. He spent three days in the monster's belly, and emerged victorious, although the struggle had cost him every hair on his head.[6]

e. What happened next is much disputed. Some say that Laomedon gave Hesione to Heracles as his bride – at the same time persuading him to leave her, and the mares, at Troy, while he went off with the Argonauts – but that, after the Fleece had been won, his cupidity got the better of him, and he refused to let Heracles have either Hesione or the mares. Others say that he had made this refusal a month or two previously, when Heracles came to Troy in search of Hylas.[7]

f. The most circumstantial version, however, is that Laomedon cheated Heracles by substituting mortal horses for the immortal ones; whereupon Heracles threatened to make war on Troy, and put to sea in a rage. First he visited the island of Paros, where he raised an altar to Zeus and Apollo; and then the Isthmus of Corinth, where he prophesied Laomedon's doom; finally he recruited soldiers in his own city of Tiryns.[8]

g. Laomedon, in the meantime, had killed Phoenodamas and sold his three daughters to Sicilian merchants come to buy victims for the wild-beast shows; but in Sicily they were rescued by Aphrodite, and the eldest, Aegesta, lay with the river Crimissus, who took the form of a dog – and bore him a son, Aegestes, called Acestes by the Latins.[9] This Aegestes, aided by Anchises's bastard son Elymus, whom he brought from Troy, founded the cities of Aegesta, later called Segesta; Entella, which he named after his wife; Eryx; and Asca. Aegesta is said to have eventually returned to Troy and there married one Capys, by whom she became the mother of Anchises.[10]

h. It is disputed whether Heracles embarked for Troy with eighteen long ships of fifty oars each; or with only six small craft and scanty forces.[11] But among his allies were Iolaus; Telamon son of Aeacus; Peleus; the Argive Oicles; and the Boeotian Deimachus.[12]

i. Heracles had found Telamon at Salamis feasting with his friends. He was at once offered the golden wine-bowl and invited to pour the first libation to Zeus; having done so, he stretched out his hands to heaven and prayed: 'O Father, send Telamon a fine son, with a skin as tough as this lion pelt, and courage to match!' For he saw that Periboea, Telamon's wife, was on the point of giving birth. Zeus sent down his eagle in answer, and Heracles assured Telamon that the prayer would be granted; and, indeed, as soon as the feast was over, Peribeoa gave birth to Great Ajax, around whom Heracles threw the lion pelt, thus making him invulnerable, except in his neck and arm-pit, where the quiver had interposed.[13]

j. On disembarking near Troy, Heracles left Oicles to guard the ships, while he himself led the other champions in an assault on the city. Laomedon, taken by surprise, had no time to marshal his army, but supplied the common folk with swords and torches and hurried them down to burn the fleet. Oicles resisted him to the death, fighting a noble rear-guard action, while his comrades launched the ships and escaped. Laomedon then hurried back to the city and, after a skirmish with Heracles's straggling forces, managed to re-enter and bar the gates behind him.

k. Having no patience for a long siege, Heracles ordered an immediate assault. The first to breach the wall and enter was Telamon, who chose the western curtain built by his father Aeacus as the weakest spot, but Heracles came hard at his heels, mad with jealousy. Telamon, suddenly aware that Heracles's drawn sword was intended for his own vitals, had the presence of mind to stoop and collect some large stones dislodged from the wall. 'What are you at?' roared Heracles. 'Building an altar to Heracles the Victor, Heracles the Averter of Ills!' answered the resourceful Telamon. 'I leave the sack of Troy to you.'[14] Heracles thanked him briefly, and raced on. He then shot down Laomedon and all his sons, except Podarces, who alone had maintained that Heracles should be given the immortal mares; and sacked the city. After glutting his vengeance, he rewarded Telamon with the hand of Hesione, whom he gave permission to ransom any one of her fellow captives. She chose Podarces. 'Very well,' said Heracles. 'But first he must be sold as a slave.' So Podarces was put up for sale, and Hesione redeemed him with the golden veil which bound her head: hence Podarces won the name of Priam, which means 'redeemed'. But some say that he was a mere infant at the time.[15]

l. Having burned Troy and left its highways desolate, Heracles set Priam on the throne, and put to sea. Hesione accompanied Telamon to Salamis, where she bore him Teucer; whether in wedlock or in bastardy is not agreed.[16] Later she deserted Telamon, escaped to Asia Minor, and swam across to Miletus, where King Arion found her hidden in a wood. There she bore Telamon a second son, Trambelus, whom Arion reared as his own, and appointed king of Telamon's Asiatic kinsmen the Lelegians or, some say, of the Lesbians. When, in the course of the Trojan War, Achilles raided Miletus, he killed Trambelus, learning too late that he was Telamon's son, which caused him great grief.[17]

m. Some say that Oicles did not fall at Troy, but was still alive when the Erinnyes drove his grandson Alcmaeon mad. His tomb is shown in Arcadia, near the Megalopolitan precinct of Boreas.[18]

n. Heracles now sailed from the Troad, taking with him Glaucia, a daughter of the river Scamander. During the siege, she had been Deimachus's mistress, and when he fell in battle, had applied to Heracles for protection. Heracles led her aboard his ship, overjoyed that the stock of so gallant a friend should survive: for Glaucia was pregnant, and later gave birth to a son named Scamander.[19]

o. Now, while Sleep lulled Zeus into drowsiness, Hera summoned Boreas to raise a storm, which drove Heracles off his course to the island of Cos. Zeus awoke in a rage and threatened to cast Sleep down from the upper air into the gulf of Erebus; but she fled as a suppliant to Night, whom even Zeus dared not displease. In his frustration he began tossing the gods about Olympus. Some say that it was on this occasion that he chained Hera by her wrists to the rafters, tying anvils to her ankles; and hurled Hephaestus down to earth. Having thus vented his ill-temper to the full, he rescued Heracles from Cos and led him back to Argos, where his adventures are variously described.[20]

p. Some say that the Coans mistook him for a pirate and tried to prevent his approach by pelting his ship with stones. But he forced a landing, took the city of Astypalaea in a night assault, and killed the king, Eurypylus, a son of Poseidon and Astypalaea. He was himself wounded by Chalcodon, but rescued by Zeus when on the point of being despatched.[21] Others say that he attacked Cos because he had fallen in love with Chalciope, Eurypylus's daughter.[22]

q. According to still another account, five of Heracles's six ships foundered in the storm. The surviving one ran aground at Laceta on the island of Cos, he and his shipmates saving only their weapons from the wreck. As they stood wringing the sea water out of their clothes, a flock of sheep passed by, and Heracles asked the Meropian shepherd, one Antagoras, for the gift of a ram; whereupon Antagoras, who was of powerful build, challenged Heracles to wrestle with him, offering the ram as a prize. Heracles accepted the challenge but, when the two champions came to grips, Antagoras's Meropian friends ran to his assistance, and the Greeks did the same for Heracles, so that a general rough-and-tumble ensued. Exhausted by the storm and by the number of his enemies, Heracles broke off the fight and fled to the house of a stout Thracian matron, in whose clothes he disguised himself, thus contriving to escape.

r. Later in the day, refreshed by food and sleep, he fought the Meropians again and worsted them; after which he was purified of their blood and, still dressed in women's clothes, married Chalciope, by whom he became the father of Thessalus.[23] Annual Sacrifices are now offered to Heracles on the field where this battle was fought; and Coan bridegrooms wear women's clothes when they welcome their brides home – as the priest of Heracles at Antimacheia also does before he begins a sacrifice.[24]

s. The women of Astypalaea were offended at Heracles, and abused him, whereupon Hera honoured them with horns like cows; but some say that this was a punishment inflicted on them by Aphrodite for daring to extol their beauty above hers.[25]

t. Having laid waste Cos, and all but annihilated the Meropians, Heracles was guided by Athene to Phlegra, where he helped the gods to win their battle against the giants.[26] Thence he came to Boeotia where, at his insistence, Scamander was elected king. Scamander renamed the river Inachus after himself, and a near-by stream after his mother Glaucia; he also named the spring Acidusa after his wife, by whom he had three daughters, still honoured locally under the name of 'Maidens'.[27]

1. Apollodorus: ii. 4. 6.

2. Apollodorus: ii. 5. 9; Hyginus: *Fabula* 89; Diodorus Siculus: iv. 42; Tzetzes: *On Lycophron* 34.

3. Apollodorus: *loc. cit.*; Hyginus: *loc. cit.*; Lucian: *On Sacrifices* 4; Tzetzes: *loc. cit.*; Diodorus Siculus: *loc. cit.*; Servius on Virgil's *Aeneid* iii. 3.

4. Servius on Virgil's *Aeneid* v. 30 and i. 554; Tzetzes: *On Lycophron* 472; Hyginus: *Fabula* 89.

5. Diodorus Siculus: iv. 42; Tzetzes: *On Lycophron* 34; Valerius Flaccus: ii. 487; Hyginus: *loc. cit.*; Apollodorus: ii. 5. 9; Hellanicus, quoted by scholiast on Homer's *Iliad* xx. 146.

6. Homer: *Iliad* xx. 145–8; Tzetzes: *loc. cit.*; Hellanicus: *loc. cit.*

7. Diodorus Siculus: iv. 42 and 49; Servius on Virgil's *Aeneid* i. 623.

8. Apollodorus: ii. 5. 9; Hellanicus: *loc. cit.*; Pindar: *Fragment* 140a, ed. Schroeder, and *Isthmian Odes* vi. 26 ff.

9. Tzetzes: *On Lycophron* 472 and 953; Servius on Virgil's *Aeneid* i. 554 and v. 30.

10. Tzetzes: *On Lycophron* 472, 953, and 965; Servius on Virgil's *Aeneid* i. 554; v. 30 and 73.

11. Diodorus Siculus: iv. 32; Apollodorus: ii. 6. 4; Homer: *Iliad* v. 638 ff.

12. Scholiast on Pindar's *Nemean Odes* iii. 61 and *Isthmian Odes* i. 21–3; Apollodorus: *loc. cit.* and i. 8. 2; Homer: *Odyssey* xv. 243; Plutarch: *Greek Questions* 41.

13. Apollodorus: iii. 12. 7; Pindar: *Isthmian Odes* vi. 35 ff.; Tzetzes: *On Lycophron* 455; Scholiast on Sophocles's *Ajax* 833; Scholiast On Homer's *Iliad* xxiii. 821.

14. Apollodorus: ii. 6. 4; Hellanicus, quoted by Tzetzes: *On Lycophron* 469.

15. Diodorus Siculus: iv. 32; Tzetzes: *On Lycophron* 337; Apollodorus: *loc. cit.*; Hyginus: *Fabula* 89; Homer: *Iliad* v. 638 ff.

16. Apollodorus: iii. 12. 7; Servius on Virgil's *Aeneid* iii. 3; Homer: *Iliad* viii. 283 ff., and scholiast on 284.

17. Tzetzes: *On Lycophron* 467; Athenaeus: ii. 43; Parthenius: *Love Stories* 26.

18. Apollodorus: iii. 7. 5; Pausanias: viii. 36. 4.

19. Plutarch: *Greek Questions* 41.

20. Homer: *Iliad* xiv. 250 ff. and xv. 18 ff.; Apollodorus: i. 3. 5 and ii. 7. 1.

21. Apollodorus: ii. 7. 1.

22. Scholiast on Pindar's *Nemean Odes* iv. 40.

23. Apollodorus: ii. 7. 8; Homer: *Iliad* ii. 678–9.

24. Plutarch: *Greek Questions* 58.

25. Ovid: *Metamorphoses* vii. 363–4; Lactantius: *Stories of Ovid's Metamorphoses* vii. 10.

26. Apollodorus: ii. 7. 1; Pindar: *Isthmian Odes* vi. 31 ff.

27. Plutarch: *Greek Questions* 41.

*

1. This legend concerns the sack of the fifth, or pre-Homeric, city of Troy: probably by Minyans, that is to say Aeolian Greeks, supported by Lelegians, when a timely earthquake overthrew its massive walls (see 158. *8*). From the legend of the Golden Fleece we gather that Laomedon had opposed Lelegian as well as Minyan mercantile ventures in the Black Sea (see 148. *10*), and that the only way to bring him to reason was to destroy his city, which commanded the Hellespont and the Scamander plain where the East-West fair was annually held. The Ninth Labour refers to Black Sea enterprises of the same sort (see 131. *11*). Heracles's task was assisted by an earthquake, dated about 1260 B.C.

2. Heracles's rescue of Hesione, paralleled by Perseus's rescue of Andromeda (see 73. *7*), is clearly derived from an icon common in Syria and Asia Minor: Marduk's conquest of the Sea-monster Tiamat, an emanation of the goddess Ishtar, whose power he annulled by chaining her to a rock. Heracles is swallowed by Tiamat, and disappears for three days before fighting his way out. So also, according to a Hebrew moral tale apparently based on the same icon, Jonah spent three days in the Whale's belly; and so Marduk's representative, the King of Babylon, spent a period in demise every year, during which he was supposedly fighting Tiamat (see 71. *1*; 73. *7* and 103. *1*). Marduk's or Perseus's white solar horse here becomes the reward for Hesione's rescue. Heracles's loss of hair emphasizes his solar character: a shearing of the sacred king's locks when the year came to an end, typified the reduction of his magical strength, as in the story of Samson (see 91. *1*). When he reappeared, he had no more hair than an infant. Hesione's ransom of Podarces may represent the Queen-mother of Seha's (Scamander?) intervention with the Hittite King Mursilis on behalf of her scapegrace son Manapadattas.

3. Phoenodamas's three daughters represent the Moon-goddess in triad, ruling the three-cornered island of Sicily. The dog was sacred to her

as Artemis, Aphrodite, and Hecate. Greek-speaking Sicilians were addicted to the Homeric epics, like the Romans, and equally anxious to claim Trojan ancestry on however insecure grounds. Scamander's three daughters represent the same goddess in Boeotia. Glaucia's bearing of a child to Scamander was not unusual. According to the pseudo-Aeschines (*Dialogues* 10. 3), Trojan brides used to bathe in the river, and cry: 'Scamander, take my virginity!'; which points to an archaic period when it was thought that river water would quicken their wombs (see 68. 2).

4. To what Hellenic conquest of the Helladic island of Cos Heracles's visit refers is uncertain, but the subsequent wearing of women's dress by the bridegroom, when he welcomed his bride home, seems to be a concession to the former matrilocal custom by which she welcomed him to her house, not contrariwise (see 160. 3). A cow-dance will have been performed on Cos, similar to the Argive rite honouring the Moon-goddess Io (see 56. 1). At Antimacheia, the sacred king was still at the primitive stage of being the Queen's deputy, and obliged therefore to wear female dress (see 18. 8 and 136. 4).

5. Laomedon's mares were of the same breed as those sired at Troy by Boreas (see 29. *e*).

6. The Inachus was an Argive river; Plutarch seems to be the sole authority for a Boeotian Inachus, or Scamander.

138

THE CONQUEST OF ELIS

NOT long after his return, Heracles collected a force of Tirynthians and Arcadians and, joined by volunteers from the noblest Greek families, marched against Augeias, King of Elis, whom he owed a grudge on account of the Fifth Labour.[1] Augeias, however, foreseeing this attack, had prepared to resist it by appointing as his generals Eurytus and Cteatus, the sons of his brother Actor and Molione, or Moline, a daughter of Molus; and by giving a share in the Elean government to the valiant Amarynceus, who is usually described as a son of the Thessalian immigrant Pyttius.[2]

b. The sons of Actor are called Moliones, or Molionides, after their mother, to distinguish them from those of the other Actor, who married Aegina. They were twins, born from a silver egg, and surpassed all their contemporaries in strength; but, unlike the Dioscuri, had been joined together at the waist from birth.[3] The Moliones married the twin daughters of Dexamenus the Centaur and, one generation later, their sons reigned in Elis jointly with Augeias's grandson and Amarynceus's son. Each of these four commanded ten ships in the expedition to Troy. Actor already possessed a share of the kingdom through his mother Hyrmine, a daughter of Neleus, whose name he gave to the now vanished city of Hyrmine.[4]

c. Heracles did not cover himself with glory in this Elean War. He fell sick, and when the Moliones routed his army, which was encamped in the heart of Elis, the Corinthians intervened by proclaiming the Isthmian Truce. Among those wounded by the Moliones was Heracles's twin brother Iphicles; his friends carried him fainting to Pheneus in Arcadia, where he eventually died and became a hero. Three hundred and sixty Cleonensians also died bravely, fighting at Heracles's side; to them he ceded the honours awarded him by the Nemeans after he had killed the lion.[5] He now retired to Olenus, the home of his friend Dexamenus, father-in-law of the Moliones, whose youngest daughter Deianeira he deflowered, after promising to marry her. When Heracles had passed on, the Centaur Eurytion asked for her hand, which Dexamenus feared to refuse him; but on the wedding day Heracles reappeared without warning, shot down Eurytion and his brothers, and took Deianeira away with him. Some say, however, that Heracles's bride was named Mnesimache, or Hippolyte; on the ground that Deianeira is more usually described as the daughter of Oeneus. Dexamenus had been born at Bura, famous for its dice-oracle of Heracles.[6]

d. When Heracles returned to Tiryns, Eurystheus accused him of designs on the high kingship in which he had himself been confirmed by Zeus, and banished him from Argolis. With his mother Alcmene, and his nephew Iolaus, Heracles then rejoined Iphicles at Pheneus, where he took Laonome, daughter of Guneus, as his mistress. Through the middle of the Pheneatian Plain, he dug a channel for the river Aroanius, some fifty furlongs long and as much as thirty feet deep; but the river soon deserted this channel, which has caved in here and there, and returned to its former course. He also dug deep chasms at the foot of the Phenean Mountains to carry off flood water; these have served their purpose well, except that on one occasion, after a cloud-burst, the Aroanius rose and inundated the ancient city of Pheneus – the high-water marks of this flood are still shown on the mountainside.[7]

e. Afterwards, hearing that the Eleans were sending a procession to honour Poseidon at the Third Isthmian Festival, and that the Moliones would witness the games and take part in the sacrifices, Heracles ambushed them from a roadside thicket below Cleonae, and shot both dead; and killed their cousin, the other Eurytus, as well, a son of King Augeias.[8]

f. Molione soon learned who had murdered her sons, and made the Eleans demand satisfaction from Eurystheus, on the ground that Heracles was a native of Tiryns. When Eurystheus disclaimed responsibility for the misdeeds of Heracles, whom he had banished, Molione asked the Corinthians to exclude all Argives from the Isthmian Games until satisfaction had been given for the murder. This they declined to do, whereupon Molione laid a curse on every Elean who might take part in the festival. Her curse is still respected: no Elean athlete will ever enter for the Isthmian Games.[9]

g. Heracles now borrowed the black-maned horse Arion from Oncus, mastered him, raised a new army in Argos, Thebes, and Arcadia, and sacked the city of Elis. Some say that he killed Augeias and his sons, restored Phyleus, the rightful king, and set him on the Elean throne; others, that he spared Augeias's life at least. When Heracles decided to repeople Elis by ordering the widows of the dead Eleans to lie with his soldiers, the widows offered a common prayer to Athene that they might conceive at the first embrace. This prayer was heard and, in gratitude, they founded a sanctuary of Athene the Mother. So widespread was the joy at this fortunate event that the place where they had met their new husbands, and the stream flowing by it, was called *Bady*, which is the Elean word for 'sweet'. Heracles then gave the horse Arion to Adrastus, saying that, after all, he preferred to fight on foot.[10]

h. About this time, Heracles won his title of Buphagus, or 'Ox-eater'. It happened as follows. Lepreus, the son of Caucon and Astydameia, who founded the city of Lepreus in Arcadia (the district derived its name from the leprosy which had attacked the earliest settlers), had foolishly advised King Augeias to fetter Heracles when he asked to be paid for having cleansed the cattle-yards. Hearing that Heracles was on his way to the city, Astydameia persuaded Lepreus to receive him courteously and plead for forgiveness. This Heracles granted, but challenged Lepreus to a triple contest: of throwing the discus, drinking bucket after bucket of water, and eating an ox. Then, though Heracles won the discus-throw and the drinking-match, Lepreus ate the ox in less time than he. Flushed with success, he challenged Heracles to a duel, and was at once clubbed to death; his tomb is shown at Phigalia. The Lepreans, who worship Demeter and Zeus of the White Poplar, have always been subjects of Elis; and if one of them ever wins a prize at Olympia, the herald proclaims him an Elean from Lepreus. King Augeias is still honoured as a hero by the Eleans, and it was only during the reign of Lycurgus the Spartan that they were persuaded to forget their enmity of Heracles and sacrifice to him also; by which means they averted a pestilence.[11]

i. After the conquest of Elis, Heracles assembled his army at Pisa, and used the spoil to establish the famous four-yearly Olympic Festival and Games in honour of his father Zeus, which some claim was only the eighth athletic contest ever held.[12] Having measured a precinct for Zeus, and fenced off the Sacred Grove, he stepped out the stadium, named a neighbouring hillock 'The Hill of Cronus', and raised six altars to the Olympian gods: one for every pair of them. In sacrificing to Zeus, he burnt the victims' thighs upon a fire of white poplar wood cut from trees growing by the Thesprotian river Acheron; he also founded a sacrificial hearth in honour of his great-grandfather Pelops, and assigned him a shrine. Being much plagued by flies on this occasion, he offered a second sacrifice to Zeus the Averter of Flies: who sent them buzzing across the river Alpheius. The Eleans still sacrifice to this Zeus, when they expel the flies from Olympia.[13]

j. Now, at the first full moon after the summer solstice all was ready for the Festival, except that the valley lacked trees to shade it from the sun. Heracles therefore returned to the Land of the Hyperboreans, where he had admired the wild olives growing at the source of the Danube, and persuaded Apollo's priests to give him one for planting in Zeus's precinct. Returning to Olympia, he ordained that the Aetolian umpire should crown the victors with its leaves: which were to be their only reward, because he himself had performed his Labours without payment from Eurystheus. This tree, called 'The Olive of the Fair Crown', still grows in the Sacred Grove behind Zeus's temple. The branches for the wreaths are lopped with a golden sickle by a nobly-born boy, both of whose parents must be alive.[14]

k. Some say that Heracles won all the events by default, because none dared compete against him; but the truth is that every one was hotly disputed. No other entrants could, however, be found for the wrestling match, until Zeus, in disguise, condescended to enter the ring.

The match was drawn, Zeus revealed himself to his son Heracles, all the spectators cheered, and the full moon shone as bright as day.[15]

l. But the more ancient legend is that the Olympic Games were founded by Heracles the Dactyl, and that it was he who brought the wild olive from the land of the Hyperboreans. Charms and amulets in honour of Heracles the Dactyl are much used by sorceresses, who have little regard for Heracles son of Alcmene. Zeus's altar, which stands at an equal distance between the shrine of Pelops and the sanctuary of Hera, but in front of both, is said to have been built by this earlier Heracles, like the altar at Pergamus, from the ashes of the thigh-bones he sacrificed to Zeus. Once a year, on the nineteenth day of the Elean month Elaphius, soothsayers fetch the ashes from the Council Hall, and after moistening them with water from the river Alpheius – no other will serve – apply a fresh coat of this plaster to the altar.[16]

m. This is not, however, to deny that Heracles the son of Alcmene refounded the Games: for an ancient walled gymnasium is shown at Elis, where athletes train. Tall plane-trees grow between the running-tracks, and the enclosure is called Xystus because Heracles exercised himself there by *scraping* up thistles. But Clymenus the Cretan, son of Cardis a descendant of the Dactyl, had celebrated the Festival, only fifty years after the Deucalionian Flood; and subsequently Endymion had done the same, and Pelops, and Amythaon son of Cretheus, also Pelias and Neleus, and some say Augeias.[17]

n. The Olympic Festival is held at an interval alternately of forty-nine and fifty months, according to the calendar, and now lasts for five days: from the eleventh to the fifteenth of the month in which it happens to fall. Heralds proclaim an absolute armistice throughout Greece for the whole of this month, and no athlete is permitted to attend who has been guilty of any felony or offence against the gods. Originally, the Festival was managed by the Pisans; but, after the final return of the Heraclids, their Aetolian allies settled in Elis and were charged with the task.[18]

o. On the northern side of the Hill of Cronus, a serpent called Sosipolis is housed in Eileithyia's shrine; a white-veiled virgin-priestess feeds it with honey-cakes and water. This custom commemorates a miracle which drove away the Arcadians when they fought against the holy land of Elis: an unknown woman came to the Elean generals with a suckling child and gave it to them as their champion. They believed her, and when she sat the child down between the two armies, it changed into a serpent; the Arcadians fled, pursued by the Eleans, and suffered fearful losses. Eileithyia's shrine marks the place where the serpent disappeared into the Hill of Cronus. On the summit, sacrifices are offered to Cronus at the spring equinox in the month of Elaphius, by priestesses known as 'Queens'.[19]

1. Apollodorus: ii. 7. 2; Pindar: *Olympian Odes* x. 31–3.
2. Pausanias: v. 1. 8 and v. 2. 2; Eustathius on Homer's *Iliad* ix. 834 and xxiii. 1442.
3. Homer: *Iliad* xi. 709; Apollodorus: *loc. cit.*; Ibycus, quoted by Athenaeus: ii. 50; Porphyry: *Questions Relevant to Homer's Iliad* 265; Plutarch: *On Brotherly Love* i.
4. Pausanias: v. 1. 8 and v. 3. 4; Homer: *Iliad* ii. 615–24; Scholiast on Apollonius Rhodius i. 172.
5. Apollodorus: *loc. cit.*; Pindar: *Olympian Odes* x. 31–3; Pausanias: v. 2. 1 and viii. 14. 6; Aelian: *Varia Historia* iv. 5.
6. Hyginus: *Fabula* 33; Apollodorus: ii. 5. 5 and 7. 5; Diodorus Siculus: iv. 33; Pausanias: vii. 25. 5–6.
7. Diodorus Siculus: *loc. cit.*; Pausanias: viii. 14. 1–3.
8. Apollodorus: ii. 7. 2; Diodorus Siculus: *loc. cit.*; Pausanias: ii. 15. 1; Pindar: *Olympian Odes* x. 26 ff.
9. Pausanias: v. 2. 2–3.
10. Pausanias: viii. 25. 5 and v. 3. 1; Apollodorus: ii. 7. 2; Homeric scholiast, quoted by Meursius: *On Lycophron* 40; Servius on Virgil's *Aeneid* vii. 666.
11. Athenaeus: x. 412; Pausanias: v. 4. 1; 4. 4 and 5. 3–4.
12. Pindar: *Olympian Odes* x. 43 ff.; Tzetzes: *On Lycophron* 41; Hyginus: *Fabula* 273.
13. Pindar: *loc. cit.*; Apollodorus: *loc. cit.*; Pausanias: v. 13. 1 and 14. 2–3.
14. Pindar: *Olympian Odes* iii. 11 ff.; Diodorus Siculus: iv. 14; Pausanias: v. 15. 3.
15. Diodorus Siculus: *loc. cit.*; Pindar: *Olympian Odes* x. 60 ff.; Pausanias: v. 8. 1; Tzetzes: *On Lycophron* 41.
16. Pausanias: v. 7. 4 and 13. 5; Diodorus Siculus: v. 64.
17. Pausanias: vi. 23. 1 and v. 8. 1.
18. Scholiast on Pindar's *Olympian Odes* iii. 35 and v. 6; Demosthenes: *Against Aristocrates* pp. 631–2; Strabo: viii. 3. 33.
19. Pausanias: vi. 20. 1–3.

*

1. This myth apparently records an unsuccessful Achaean invasion of the Western Peloponnese followed, at the close of the thirteenth century B.C., by a second, successful, invasion which has, however, been confused with the Dorian invasion of the eleventh century B.C. – Heracles having

also been a Dorian hero. The murder of Eurytion may be deduced from the same wedding-icon that showed the killing of Pholus. Heracles's digging of the Aroanian channel is paralleled by similar feats in Elis (see 121. *d*), Boeotia (see 142. *3*), and Thrace (see 130. *b*); and the honours paid to the three hundred and sixty Cleonensians probably refer to a calendar mystery, since three hundred and sixty are the number of days in the Egyptian year, exclusive of the five sacred to Osiris, Horus, Set, Isis, and Nephthys.

2. The leprosy associated with Lepreus was *vitiligo*, a skin disease caused by foul food, which the Moon-goddess of the white poplar could cure (*White Goddess*, p. 432); true leprosy did not reach Europe until the first century B.C.

3. Heracles's title of Buphagus originally referred to the eating of an ox by his worshippers.

4. Sosopolis must have been the ghost of Cronus after whom the hillock was called, and whose head was buried on its northern slopes, to protect the stadium which lay behind it, near the junction of the Cladeus and Alpheius. His British counterpart Bran similarly guarded Tower Hill, commanding London (see 146. *2*). The spring equinox, when fawns are dropped, occurs during the alder-month of the tree-calendar, also called Elaphius ('of the fawn'), and peculiarly sacred to Cronus-Bran (*White Goddess*, pp. 168–72 and 206–7). This suggests that, originally, the Elean New Year began at the spring solstice, as in parts of Italy, when the King of the old year, wearing horns like Actaeon (see 22. *1*), was put to death by the wild women, or 'Queens'; Heracles the Dactyl belongs to this cult (see 53. *b*). The Pelopians seem to have changed the calendar when they arrived with their solar chariot and porpoise, making the funeral games celebrate the midsummer murder and supersession of Zeus, the sacred king, by his tanist – as the king revenged himself on the tanist at midwinter. In Classical times, therefore, the Elean New Year was celebrated in the summer. The mention of Pelops suggests that the king was sacrificially eaten and the ashes of his bones mixed with water to plaster the Goddess's altar. He was called the Green Zeus, or Achilles (see 164. *5*), as well as Heracles.

5. Wild olive, used in Greece to expel old-year demons and spites, who took the form of flies, was introduced from Libya, where the cult of the North Wind originated (see 48. *1* and 133. *5*), rather than the North. At Olympia, it will have been mistletoe (or Ioranthus), not wild-olive, which the boy lopped with a golden sickle (see 7. *1* and 50. *2*); wild-olive figured in the Hyperborean tree-calendar (see 119. *3*). The girls' foot-race for the position of priestess to Hera was the earliest event; but when the single year of the king's reign was prolonged to a Great Year of nominally a hundred months – to permit a more exact synchronization

of solar and lunar time – the king reigned for one half of this period, his tanist for the other. Later, both ruled concurrently under the title of Moliones, and were no less closely united than the kings of Sparta (see 74. 1). It may be that a case of Siamese twins had occurred in Greece to reinforce the metaphor. But Augeias's division of Elis, reported by Homer, shows that at a still later stage, the sacred king retained a third part of his kingdom when he was due to retire; as Proetus did at Argos. Amarynceus's share was evidently gained by conquest.

6. Molione is perhaps a title of the Elean Moon-goddess, the patroness of the Games, meaning 'Queen of the Moly'; the *moly* being a herb which elsewhere defied moon-magic (see 170. 5). She was also known as Agamede ('very cunning'); and this is the name of Augeias's sorceress daughter, who 'knew all the drugs that grow on earth' (Homer: *Iliad* xi. 739–41). In Classical Greece, 'Athene the Mother' was a strange and indecent concept and had to be explained away (see 25. 2 and 141. 1), but the Elean tradition suggests that erotic orgies had been celebrated in her honour beside the river Bady.

7. The mastery of Arion, it seems, formed part of the coronation rite at Arcadian Oncus (see 130. 1).

139

THE CAPTURE OF PYLUS

HERACLES next sacked and burned the city of Pylus, because the Pylians had gone to the aid of Elis. He killed all Neleus's sons, except the youngest, Nestor, who was away at Gerania, but Neleus himself escaped with his life.[1]

b. Athene, champion of justice, fought for Heracles; and Pylus was defended by Hera, Poseidon, Hades, and Ares. While Athene engaged Ares, Heracles made for Poseidon, club against trident, and forced him to give way. Next, he ran to assist Athene, spear in hand, and his third lunge pierced Ares's shield, dashing him headlong to the ground; then, with a powerful thrust at Ares's thigh, he drove deep into the divine flesh. Ares fled in anguish to Olympus, where Apollo spread soothing unguents on the wound and healed it within the hour; so he renewed the fight, until one of Heracles's arrows pierced his shoulder, and forced him off the field for good. Meanwhile, Heracles had also wounded Hera in the right breast with a three-barbed arrow.[2]

c. Neleus's eldest son, Periclymenus the Argonaut, was gifted by

Poseidon with boundless strength and the power of assuming whatever shape he pleased, whether of bird, beast, or tree. On this occasion he turned himself first into a lion, then into a serpent and after a while, to escape scrutiny, perched on the yoke-boss of Heracles's horses in the form of an ant, or fly, or bee.[3] Heracles, nudged by Athene, recognized Periclymenus and reached for his club, whereupon Periclymenus became an eagle, and tried to peck out his eyes, but a sudden arrow from Heracles's bow pierced him underneath his wing. He tumbled to earth, and the arrow was driven through his neck by the fall, killing him. Some say, however, that he flew away in safety; and that Heracles had attacked Poseidon on an earlier occasion, after the murder of Iphitus, when Neleus refused to purify him; and that the fight with Hades took place at the other Pylus, in Elis, when Heracles was challenged for carrying off Cerberus without permission.[4]

d. Heracles gave the city of Messene to Nestor, in trust for his own descendants, remembering that Nestor had taken no part in robbing him of Geryon's cattle; and soon came to love him more even than Hylas and Iolaus. It was Nestor who first swore an oath by Heracles.[5]

e. The Eleans, though they themselves rebuilt Pylus, took advantage of the Pylians' weakness to oppress them in petty ways. Neleus kept his patience until one day, having sent a chariot and a prize-winning team of four horses to contest for a tripod in the Olympic Games, he learned that Augeias had appropriated them and sent the charioteer home on foot. At this, he ordered Nestor to make a retaliatory raid on the Elean Plain; and Nestor managed to drive away fifty herds of cattle, fifty flocks of sheep, fifty droves of swine, fifty flocks of goats, and one hundred and fifty chestnut mares, many with foal, beating off the Eleans who opposed him and blooding his spear in this, his first fight. Neleus's heralds then convoked all in Pylus who were owed a debt by the Eleans, and when he had divided the booty among the claimants, keeping back the lion's share for Nestor, sacrificed lavishly to the gods. Three days later, the Eleans advanced on Pylus in full array – among them the two orphaned sons of the Moliones, who had inherited their title – and crossed the Plain from Thryoessa. But Athene came by night to warn and marshal the Pylians; and when battle had been joined, Nestor, who was on foot, struck down Amarynceus, the Elean commander and, seizing his chariot, rushed like a black tempest through the Elean ranks, capturing fifty other chariots and killing a hundred men. The Moliones would also have fallen to his busy spear, had not Poseidon wrapped them in an impenetrable mist and spirited them away. The Eleans, hotly pursued by Nestor's army, fled as far as the Olenian Rock, where Athene called a halt.[6]

f. A truce being then agreed upon, Amarynceus was buried at Buprasium, and awarded funeral games, in which numerous Pylians took part. The Moliones won the chariot race by crowding Nestor at the turn, but he is said to have won all the other events: the boxing and the wrestling match, the foot-race and the javelin-throw. Of these feats, it is only right to add, Nestor himself, in garrulous old age, was the principal witness; since by the grace of Apollo, who granted him the years of which his maternal uncles had been deprived, he lived for three centuries, and no contemporary survived to gainsay him.[7]

1. Pausanias: ii. 2. 2; iii. 26. 6 and v. 3. 1; Apollodorus: ii. 7. 3, Diodorus Siculus: iv. 68.
2. Pausanias: vi. 25. 3; Scholiast on Homer's *Iliad* xi. 689; Hesiod: *Shield of Heracles* 359 ff.; Pindar: *Olympian Odes* x. 30–1; Homer: *Iliad* v. 392 ff.; Tzetzes: *On Lycophron* 39.
3. Apollonius Rhodius: i. 156–60; Eustathius on Homer's *Odyssey* xi. 285; Scholiast on Homer's *Iliad* ii. 336 and xi. 286.
4. Apollodorus: i. 9. 9; Hesiod, quoted by scholiast on Apollonius Rhodius i. 156; Ovid: *Metamorphoses* xii. 548 ff.; Hyginus: *Fabula* 10; Scholiast on Pindar's *Olympian Odes* ix. 30 ff.
5. Pausanias: ii. 18. 6; Philostratus: *Heroica* 2.
6. Pausanias: vi. 22. 3; Homer: *Iliad* xi. 671 and 761.
7. Homer: *Iliad* xxiii. 630–42; Hyginus: *Fabula* 10.

*

1. The capture of Pylus seems to be another incident in the thirteenth-century Achaean invasion of the Peloponnese. Hera, Poseidon, Hades, and Ares, the elder deities, are aiding Elis; the younger ones, Athene reborn from Zeus's head, and Heracles as Zeus's son, oppose them. Heracles's defeat of Periclymenus, the shape-shifter, may mark the suppression of a New Year child-sacrifice; and Periclymenus's power to take the shape of any tree refers, apparently, to the succession of thirteen months through which the *interrex* passed in his ritual ballet, each month having an emblematic tree, from wild-olive to myrtle (see 52. *3* and 169. *6*). The wounding of Hades presents Heracles as the champion destined to cheat the grave and become immortal (see 145. *h*); moreover, according to Homer (*Iliad* v. 319 ff.), he wounded Hades 'at Pylus, among the corpses' – which could equally mean: 'at the gate, among the dead'; the gate being that of the Underworld, perhaps in the Far North (see 170. *4*). If so, Hades is a substitute for Cronus, whom Heracles defeated in the sepulchral island of Erytheia (see 132. *d*), and the encounter is a doublet of the Twelfth Labour, when he harrowed Hell. Heracles's Pylian allies, significantly aided by Athene, are described by Homer (*Iliad* xi. 617 and 761) as Achaeans, though Neleus's dynasty was, in fact, Aeolian.

2. Heracles's wounding of Hera in the right breast with a three-barbed arrow seems to allegorize the Dorian invasion of the Western Peloponnese when the three tribes, who called themselves Sons of Heracles, humbled the power of the Elean Goddess (see 146. *1*).

140

THE SONS OF HIPPOCOÖN

HERACLES decided to attack Sparta and punish the sons of Hippocoön. They had not only refused to purify him after the death of Iphitus, and fought against him under Neleus's command, but also murdered his friend, Oeonus. It happened that Oeonus son of Licymnius, who had accompanied Heracles to Sparta, was strolling about the city when, just outside Hippocoön's palace, a huge Molossian hound ran at him; in self-defence, he threw a stone which struck it on the muzzle. Out darted the sons of Hippocoön and beat him with cudgels. Heracles ran to Oeonus's rescue from the other end of the street, but arrived too late. Oeonus was cudgelled to death, and Heracles, wounded in the hollow of his hand and in the thigh, fled to the shrine of Eleusinian Demeter, near Mount Taygetus; where Asclepius hid him and healed his wounds.[1]

b. Having mustered a small army, Heracles now marched to Tegea in Arcadia and there begged Cepheus the son of Aleus to join him with his twenty sons. At first, Cepheus refused, fearing for the safety of Tegea if he left home. But Heracles, whom Athene had given a lock of the Gorgon's hair in a brazen jar, presented it to Cepheus's daughter Aerope: should the city be attacked, he said, she was to display the lock thrice from its walls, turning her back to the enemy, who would immediately flee. As events proved, however, Aerope had no need of the charm.[2]

c. Thus Cepheus joined the expedition against Sparta, in which, by ill fortune, he and seventeen of his sons fell. Some say that Iphicles was also killed, but this is likely to have been the Aetolian Argonaut of that name, not Amphitryon's son. Heracles's army suffered few other casualties, whereas the Spartans lost Hippocoön and all his twelve sons, with numerous other men of high rank; and their city was taken by storm. Heracles then restored Tyndareus, leaving him the kingdom in trust for his own descendants.[3]

d. Since Hera, inexplicably, had not thwarted him in this campaign, Heracles built her a shrine at Sparta, and sacrificed goats, having no other victims at his disposal. The Spartans are thus the only Greeks who surname Hera 'Goat-eating', and offer goats to her. Heracles also raised a temple to Athene of the Just Deserts; and, on the road to Therapne, a shrine to Cotylaean Asclepius which commemorates the wound in the hollow of his hand. A shrine at Tegea, called 'The Common Hearth of the Arcadians', is remarkable for its statue of Heracles with the wound in his thigh.[4]

1. Apollodorus: ii. 7. 3; Pausanias: iii. 15. 3; iii. 19. 7; iii. 20. 5 and viii. 53. 3.
2. Apollodorus: *loc. cit.*; Pausanias: viii. 47. 4.
3. Apollodorus: *loc. cit.* and iii. 10. 5; Diodorus Siculus: iv. 33.
4. Pausanias: iii. 15. 7, iii. 19. 7 and viii. 53. 3.

*

1. Here the Heracles myth is lost in saga; and pseudo-myth is introduced to explain such anomalies as Goat-eating Hera, Hollow-of-the-Hand Asclepius, Heracles of the Wounded Thigh, and Tegea's long immunity from capture. But Hera's wild women had once eaten Zagreus, Zeus, and Dionysus in wild-goat form; Asclepius's statue probably held medicines in the hollow of the hand; the wound in Heracles's thigh will have been made by a boar (see 157. *e*); and the Tegeans may have displayed a Gorgon's head on their gates as a prophylactic charm. To assault a city thus protected was, as it were, to violate the maiden-goddess Athene: a superstition also fostered by the Athenians.

2. Whenever Heracles leaves an Achaean, Aetolian, Sicilian, or Pelasgian city in trust for his descendants, this is an attempted justification of its later seizure by the Dorians (see 132. *q* and *6*; 143. *d*; and 146. *e*).

141

AUGE

ALEUS, king of Tegea, the son of Apheidas, married Neaera, a daughter of Pereus, who bore him Auge, Cepheus, Lycurgus, and Aphidamas. An ancient shrine of Athene Alea, founded at Tegea by Aleus, still contains a sacred couch of the goddess.[1]

b. When, on a visit to Delphi, Aleus was warned by the Oracle that Neaera's two brothers would die by the hand of her daughter's son, he hurried home and appointed Auge a priestess of Athene, threatening to kill her if she were unchaste. Whether Heracles came to Tegea on his way to fight King Augeias, or on his return from Sparta, is disputed; at all events, Aleus entertained him hospitably in Athene's temple. There, flushed with wine, Heracles violated the virgin-priestess beside a fountain which is still shown to the north of the shrine; since, however, Auge made no outcry, it is often suggested that she came there by assignation.[2]

c. Heracles continued on his way, and at Stymphalus begot Eures on Parthenope, the daughter of Stymphalus; but meanwhile pestilence and famine came upon Tegea, and Aleus, informed by the Pythoness that a crime had been committed in Athene's sacred precinct, visited it and found Auge far gone with child. Though she wept and declared that Heracles had violated her in a fit of drunkenness, Aleus would not believe this. He dragged her to the Tegean market place, where she fell upon her knees at the site of the present temple of Eileithyia, famed for its image of 'Auge on her Knees'.[3] Ashamed to kill his daughter in public, Aleus engaged King Nauplius to drown her. Nauplius accordingly set out with Auge for Nauplia; but on Mount Parthenius she was overtaken by labour-pangs, and made some excuse to turn aside into a wood. There she gave birth to a son and, hiding him in a thicket, returned to where Nauplius was patiently waiting for her by the roadside. However, having no intention of drowning a princess when he could dispose of her at a high price in the slave-market, he sold Auge to some Carian merchants who had just arrived at Nauplia and who, in turn, sold her to Teuthras, king of Mysian Teuthrania.[4]

d. Auge's son was suckled by a doe on Mount Parthenius (where he now has a sacred precinct) and some cattle-men found him, named him Telephus, and took him to their master, King Corythus. At the same time, by a coincidence, Corythus's shepherds discovered Atalanta's infant son, whom she had borne to Meleager, exposed on the same hillside: they named him Parthenopaeus, which is 'son of a pierced maidenhead', because Atalanta was pretending to be still a virgin.[5]

e. When Telephus grew to manhood, he approached the Delphic Oracle for news of his parents. He was told: 'Sail and seek King

Teuthras the Mysian'. In Mysia he found Auge, now married to Teuthras, from whom he learned that she was his mother and Heracles his father; and this he could well believe, for no woman had ever borne Heracles a son so like himself. Teuthras thereupon gave Telephus his daughter Argiope in marriage, and appointed him heir to the kingdom.

f. Others say that Telephus, after having killed Hippothous and Nereus, his maternal uncles, went silent and speechless to Mysia in search of his mother. 'The silence of Telephus' became proverbial; but Parthenopaeus came with him as spokesman.⁷ It happened that the renowned Argonaut Idas, son of Aphareus, was about to seize the Mysian throne, and Teuthras in desperation promised to resign it to Telephus and give him his adopted daughter in marriage, if only Idas were driven away. Thereupon Telephus, with Parthenopaeus's help, routed Idas in a single battle. Now, Teuthras's adopted daughter happened to be Auge, who did not recognize Telephus, nor did he know that she was his mother. Faithful to Heracles's memory, she took a sword into her bedroom on the wedding night, and would have killed Telephus when he entered, had not the gods sent a large serpent between them. Auge threw down the sword in alarm and confessed her murderous intentions. She then apostrophized Heracles; and Telephus, who had been on the point of matricide, was inspired to cry out: 'O mother, mother!' They fell weeping into each other's arms, and the next day, returned with Teuthras's blessing to their native land. Auge's tomb is shown at Pergamus beside the river Caicus. The Pergamenians claim to be Arcadian emigrants who crossed to Asia with Telephus, and offer him heroic sacrifices.⁸

g. Others say that Telephus married Astyoche, or Laodice, a daughter of Trojan Priam. Others, again, that Heracles had lain with Auge at Troy when he went there to fetch Laomedon's immortal horses. Still others, that Aleus locked Auge and her infant in an ark, which he committed to the waves; and that, under Athene's watchful care, the chest drifted towards Asia Minor and was cast ashore at the mouth of the river Caicus, where King Teuthras married Auge and adopted Telephus.⁹

h. This Teuthras, hunting on Mount Teuthras, once pursued a monstrous boar, which fled to the temple of Orthosian Artemis. He was about to force his way in, when the boar cried out: 'Spare me, my lord! I am the Goddess's nursling!' Teuthras paid no attention, and killed it, thereby offending Artemis so deeply that she restored the boar to life, punished Teuthras with leprous scabs and sent him raving away to the mountain peaks. However, his mother, Leucippe, hastened to the forest, taking with her the seer Polyeidus, and appeased Artemis with bountiful sacrifices. Teuthras was cured of his leprous scabs by means of the stone Antipathes, which is still found in quantities on the summit of Mount Teuthras; whereupon Leucippe built an altar to Orthosian Artemis, and had a man-headed mechanical boar made, entirely from gold, which when pursued, takes refuge in the temple, and utters the words 'Spare me!'[10]

i. While Heracles was in Arcadia he visited Mount Ostracina, where he seduced Phialo, a daughter of the hero Alcimedon. When she bore a son named Aechmagoras, Alcimedon turned them both out of his cave to die of hunger on the mountain. Aechmagoras cried piteously, and a well-intentioned jay flew off to find Heracles, mimicking the sound, and thus drew him to the tree where Phialo sat, gagged and bound by her cruel father. Heracles rescued them, and the child grew to manhood. The neighbouring spring has been called Cissa, after the jay, ever since.[11]

1. Apollodorus: iii. 9. 1; Pausanias: viii. 4. 5–6 and 47. 2.
2. Alcidamas: *Odysseus* 14–16; Diodorus Siculus: iv. 33; Apollodorus: ii. 7. 4; Pausanias: viii. 4. 6 and 47. 3.
3. Diodorus Siculus: *loc. cit.*; Apollodorus: ii. 7. 8; Pausanias: viii. 48. 5.
4. Callimachus: *Hymn to Delos* 70; Diodorus Siculus: *loc. cit.*; Apollodorus: i. 7. 4 and iii. 9. 1.
5. Pausanias: viii. 54. 5; Apollodorus: iii. 9. 1; Diodorus Siculus: iv. 33; Hyginus: *Fabula* 99.
6. Pausanias: x. 28. 4; Alcidamas: *Odysseus* 14–16; Apollodorus: *loc. cit.*; Diodorus Siculus: *loc. cit.*
7. Hyginus: *Fabula* 244; Aristotle: *Poetics* 24. 1460a; Alexis, quoted by Athenaeus: x. 18. 421d; Amphis, quoted by Athenaeus: vi. 5. 224d.
8. Pausanias: i. 4. 6; v. 13. 2 and viii. 4. 6.
9. Hyginus: *Fabula* 101; Dictys Cretensis: ii. 5; Hesiod: *Oxyrhynchus Papyrus* 1359, *Fragment* 1; Hecataeus, quoted by Pausanias: viii. 4. 6; Euripides, quoted by Strabo: xiii. 1. 69.
10. Plutarch: *On Rivers* 21.
11. Pausanias: viii. 12. 2.

*

1. Athene's couch at Tegea, and Heracles's alleged violation of her priestess Auge, identify this Athene with Neith, or Anatha, an orgiastic Moon-goddess, whose priestess performed an annual marriage with the sacred king to ensure good crops. Relics of this custom were found in

Heracles's temple at Rome, where his bride was called Acca – counterpart of the Peloponnesian White Goddess Acco – and at Jerusalem where, before the religious reforms of the Exile, a sacred marriage seems to have been celebrated every September between the High-priest, a representative of Jehovah, and the goddess Anatha. Professor Raphael Patai summarizes the evidence for the Jerusalem marriage in his *Man and Temple* (pp. 88–94, London, 1947). The divine children supposedly born of such unions became the Corn-spirits of the coming year; thus Athene Alea was a corn-goddess, patroness of corn-mills. The numerous sons whom Heracles fathered on nymphs witness to the prevalence of this religious theory. He is credited with only one anomalous daughter, Macaria ('blessed').

The Auge myth has been told to account for an Arcadian emigration to Mysia, probably under pressure from the Achaeans; also for Tegean festivities in honour of the New Year god as fawn which, to judge from the Hesiod fragment, had their counterpart in the Troad.

2. That Auge and her child drifted in an ark to the river Caicus – a scene illustrated on the altar of Pergamus, and on Pergamene coins – means merely that the cult of Auge and Telephus had been imported into Mysia by Tegean colonists, and that Auge, as the Moon-goddess, was supposed to ride in her crescent boat to the New Year celebrations. Athene's subsequent change from orgiastic bride to chaste warrior-maiden has confused the story: in some versions Teuthras becomes Auge's bridegroom, but in others he piously adopts her. Hyginus's version is based on some late and artificial drama.

3. The myth of the golden boar refers partly to the curative properties of the *antipathes* stone on Mount Teuthras; partly, perhaps, to a Mysian custom of avenging the death of Adonis, who had been killed by Apollo in the form of a boar. It looks as if Adonis's representative, a man wearing a boar's hide with golden tusks, was now spared if he could take refuge from his pursuers in the sanctuary of Apollo's sister Artemis. The kings of Tegea, Auge's birthplace, were, it seems, habitually killed by boars (see 140. *1* and 157. *e*).

4. Phialo's adventure with the jay is an anecdotal fancy, supposed to account for the name of the spring, which may originally have been sacred to a jay totem-clan.

142

DEIANEIRA

AFTER spending four years in Pheneus, Heracles decided to leave the Peloponnese. At the head of a large Arcadian force, he sailed across to

Calydon in Aetolia, where he took up his residence. Having now no legitimate sons, and no wife, he courted Deianeira, the supposed daughter of Oeneus, thus keeping his promise to the ghost of her brother Meleager. But Deianeira was really the daughter of the god Dionysus, by Oeneus's wife Althaea, as had become apparent when Meleager died and Artemis turned his lamenting sisters into guinea-fowl; for Dionysus then persuaded Artemis to let Deianeira and her sister Gorge retain their human shapes.[1]

b. Many suitors came to Oeneus's palace in Pleuron, demanding the hand of lovely Deianeira, who drove a chariot and practised the art of war; but all abandoned their claims when they found themselves in rivalry with Heracles and the River-god Achelous. It is common knowledge that immortal Achelous appears in three forms: as a bull, as a speckled serpent, and as a bull-headed man. Streams of water flow continually from his shaggy beard, and Deianeira would rather have died than marry him.[2]

c. Heracles, when summoned by Oeneus to plead his suit, boasted that if he married Deianeira, she would not only have Zeus for a father-in-law, but enjoy the reflected glory of his own Twelve Labours.

Achelous (now in bull-headed form) scoffed at this, remarking that he was a well-known personage, the father of all Greek waters, not a footloose stranger like Heracles, and that the Oracle of Dodona had instructed all visitants to offer him sacrifices. Then he taunted Heracles: 'Either you are not Zeus's son, or your mother is an adulteress!'

Heracles scowled. 'I am better at fighting than debating,' he said, 'and I will not hear my mother insulted!'

d. Achelous cast aside his green garment, and wrestled with Heracles until he was thrown on his back, whereupon he deftly turned into a speckled serpent and wriggled away.

'I strangled serpents in my cradle!' laughed Heracles, stooping to grip his throat. Next, Achelous became a bull and charged; Heracles nimbly stepped aside and, catching hold of both his horns, hurled him to the ground with such force that the right horn snapped clean off. Achelous retired, miserably ashamed, and hid his injury under a chaplet of willow-branches.[3] Some say that Heracles returned the broken horn to Achelous in exchange for the horn of Goat Amaltheia; and some, that it was changed into Amaltheia's by the Naiads, and that Heracles presented it to Oeneus as a bridal gift.[4] Others say that in the course of his Twelfth Labour, he took the horn down to Tartarus, filled by the

Hesperides with golden fruit and now called the Cornucopia, as a gift for Plutus, Tyche's assistant.[5]

e. After marrying Deianeira, Heracles marched with the Calydonians against the Thesprotian city of Ephyra – later Cichyrus – where he overcame and killed King Phyleus. Among the captives was Phyleus's daughter Astyoche, by whom Heracles became the father of Tlepolemus; though some say that Tlepolemus's mother was Astydameia, daughter of Amyntor, whom Heracles abducted from Elean Ephyra, a city famous for its poisons.[6]

f. On the advice of an Oracle, Heracles now sent word to his friend Thespius: 'Keep seven of your sons in Thespiae, send three to Thebes, and order the remaining forty to colonize the island of Sardinia!' Thespius obeyed. Descendants of those who went to Thebes are still honoured there; and descendants of those who stayed behind in Thespiae, the so-called Demuchi, governed the city until recent times. The forces led to Sardinia by Iolaus included Thespian and Athenian contingents, this being the first Greek colonial expedition in which the kings came of different stock from the common people. Having defeated the Sardinians in battle, Iolaus divided the island into provinces, planted olive-trees, and made it so fertile that the Carthaginians have since been prepared to undergo immense troubles and danger for its possession. He founded the city of Olbia, and encouraged the Athenians to found that of Ogryle. With the consent of the sons of Thespius, who regarded Iolaus as their second father, he called the colonists after himself, Iolarians; and they still sacrifice to Father Iolaus, just as the Persians do to Father Cyrus. It has been said that Iolaus eventually returned to Greece, by way of Sicily, where some of his followers settled and awarded him hero rites; but according to the Thebans, who should know, none of the colonists ever came back.[7]

g. At a feast three years later, Heracles grew enraged with a young kinsman of Oeneus, variously named Eunomus, Eurynomus, Ennomus, Archias, or Chaerias, the son of Architeles, who was told to pour water on Heracles's hands, and clumsily splashed his legs. Heracles boxed the boy's ears harder than he intended, and killed him. Though forgiven by Architeles for this accident, Heracles decided to pay the due penalty of exile, and went away with Deianeira, and their son Hyllus, to Trachis, the home of Amphitryon's nephew Ceyx.[8]

h. A similar accident had occurred at Phlius, a city which lies to the east of Arcadia, when Heracles returned from the Garden of the Hesperides. Disliking the drink set before him, he struck Cyathus, the cup-bearer, with one finger only, but killed him none the less. A chapel to Cyathus's memory has been built against Apollo's Phlian temple.[9]

i. Some say that Heracles wrestled against Achelous before the murder of Iphitus, which was the cause of his removal to Trachis; others, that he went there when first exiled from Tiryns.[10] At all events, he came with Deianeira to the river Evenus, then in full flood, where the Centaur Nessus, claiming that he was the gods' authorized ferry-man and chosen because of his righteousness, offered, for a small fee, to carry Deianeira dry-shod across the water while Heracles swam. He agreed, paid Nessus the fare, threw his club and bow over the river, and plunged in. Nessus, however, instead of keeping to his bargain, gal-loped off in the opposite direction with Deianeira in his arms; then threw her to the ground and tried to violate her. She screamed for help, and Heracles, quickly recovering his bow, took careful aim and pierced Nessus through the breast from half a mile away.

j. Wrenching out the arrow, Nessus told Deianeira: 'If you mix the seed which I have spilt on the ground with blood from my wound, add olive oil, and secretly anoint Heracles's shirt with the mixture, you will never again have cause to complain of his unfaithfulness.' Deianeira hurriedly collected the ingredients in a jar, which she sealed and kept by her without saying a word to Heracles on the subject.[11]

k. Another version of the story is that Nessus offered Deianeira wool soaked in his own blood, and told her to weave it into a shirt for Heracles. A third version is that he gave her his own blood-stained shirt as a love-charm, and then fled to a neighbouring tribe of Locrians, where he died of the wound; but his body rotted unburied, at the foot of Mount Taphiassus, tainting the country with its noisome smell – hence these Locrians are called Ozolian. The spring beside which he died still smells foetid and contains clots of blood.[12]

l. By Deianeira, Heracles had already become the father of Hyllus, Ctesippus, Glenus, and Hodites; also of Macaria, his only daughter.[13]

1. Diodorus Siculus: iv. 34; Apollodorus: i. 8. 1 and ii. 7. 5; Bacchy-lides: *Epinicia* v. 165 ff.; Antoninus Liberalis: *Transformations* 2.
2. Ovid: *Metamorphoses* ix. 1–100; Apollodorus: i. 8. 1; Sophocles: *Trachinian Women* 1 ff.
3. Ovid: *loc. cit.*; Ephorus, quoted by Macrobius: v. 18; Tzetzes: *On Lycophron* 50.

4. Apollodorus: *loc. cit.* and ii. 7. 5; Ovid: *loc. cit.*; Diodorus Siculus: iv. 35; Strabo: x. 2. 19.

5. Hyginus: *Fabula* 31; Lactantius on Statius's *Thebaid* iv. 106.

6. Strabo: vii. 7. 5 and 11; Apollodorus: ii. 7. 6; Diodorus Siculus: iv. 36; Pindar: *Olympian Odes* vii. 23 ff., with scholiast; Homer: *Iliad* ii. 658–60 and *Odyssey* i. 259–61.

7. Apollodorus: *loc. cit.*; Diodorus Siculus: iv. 29–30; Pausanias: vii. 2. 2; x. 17. 4 and ix. 23. 1.

8. Diodorus Siculus: iv. 36; Apollodorus: *loc. cit.*; Tzetzes: *On Lycophron* 50; Eustathius on Homer's *Iliad* p. 1900; Scholiast on Sophocles's *Trachinian Women* 39.

9. Pausanias: ii. 13. 8.

10. Sophocles: *Trachinian Women* 1–40; Pausanias: i. 32. 5.

11. Apollodorus: ii. 7. 6; Sophocles: *Trachinian Women* 555–61; Ovid: *Metamorphoses* ix. 101 ff.; Diodorus Siculus: iv. 46.

12. Scholiast on Horace's *Epodes* iii; Ovid: *loc. cit.*; Pausanias: x. 38. 1; Strabo: ix. 4. 8.

13. Apollodorus: ii. 7. 8; Diodorus Siculus: iv. 37; Pausanias: i. 32. 5.

*

1. The story of Meleager's sisters is told to account for a guinea-fowl cult of Artemis on Leros (see 80.3).

2. Deianeira's love of war reveals her as a representative of the pre-Olympian Battle-goddess Athene, with whose sacred marriages in different localities this part of the Heracles legend is chiefly concerned (see 141. 1).

3. Heracles's contest with Achelous, like that of Theseus with the Minotaur, should be read as part of the royal marriage ritual. Bull and Serpent stood for the waxing and the waning year – 'the bull who is the serpent's father, and the serpent whose son is the bull' – over both of which the sacred king won domination. A bull's horn, regarded from earliest times as the seat of fertility, enroyalled the candidate for kingship who laid hold of it when he wrestled either with an actual bull, or with a bull-masked opponent. The Babylonian hero Enkidu, Gilgamesh's mortal twin, and devotee of the Queen of Heaven, seized the Bull of Heaven by the horns and killed it with his sword; and the winning of a cornucopia was a marriage-task imposed on the Welsh hero Peredur in the *Mabinogion* (see 148. 5). In Crete, the bull cult had succeeded that of the wild-goat, whose horn was equally potent. But it seems that the icon which showed this ritual contest was interpreted by the Greeks as illustrating Heracles's struggle with the River Achelous: namely the dyking and draining of the Paracheloitis, a tract of land, formed of the silt brought down by the Achelous, which had slowly been joining the Echinadian Isles to the mainland; and the consequent recovery of a large

area of farmland. Heracles was often credited with engineering feats such as these (Strabo: x. 2. 19; Diodorus Siculus: iv. 35). The sacrifice ordered by the Dodonian Oracle will hardly have been to the river Achelous; more likely it was prescribed for Achelois, the Moon-goddess 'who drives away pain'.

4. Eunomus and Cyathus will have been boy-victims: surrogates for the sacred king at the close of his reign.

5. Nessus's attempted rape of Deianeira recalls the disorderly scenes at the wedding of Peirithous, when Theseus (the Athenian Heracles) intervened to save Hippodameia from assault by the Centaur Eurytion (see 102. *d*). Since the Centaurs were originally depicted as goat-men, the icon on which the incident is based probably showed the Queen riding on the goat-king's back, as she did at the May Eve celebrations of Northern Europe, before her sacred marriage; Eurytion is the 'interloper', a stock-character made familiar by the comedies of Aristophanes, who still appears at Northern Greek marriage festivities. The earliest mythical example of the interloper is the same Enkidu: he interrupted Gilgamesh's sacred marriage with the Goddess of Erech, and challenged him to battle. Another interloper is Agenor, who tried to take Andromeda from Perseus at his wedding feast (see 73. *l*).

6. The first settlers in Sardinia, neolithic Libyans, managed to survive in the mountainous parts; subsequent immigrants – Cretans, Greeks, Carthaginians, Romans, and Jews – attempted to hold the coastal districts, but malaria always defeated them. Only during the last few years has the mortality been checked by spraying the pools where the malarial mosquito breeds.

7. 'Ozolian' ('smelly'), a nickname given to the Locrians settled near Phocis, to distinguish them from their Opuntian and Epizephyrian kinsfolk, probably referred to their habit of wearing undressed goat-skins which had a foetid smell in damp weather. The Locrians themselves preferred to derive it from *ozoi*, 'vine shoots' (Pausanias: x. 38. 1), because of the first vinestock planted in their country (see 38. 7).

143

HERACLES IN TRACHIS

STILL accompanied by his Arcadian allies, Heracles came to Trachis where he settled down for awhile, under the protection of Ceyx. On his way, he had passed through the country of the Dryopians, which is overshadowed by Mount Parnassus, and found their king Theiodamas, the son of Dryops, ploughing with a yoke of oxen.[1] Being hungry and also eager for a pretext to make war on the Dryopians – who, as everyone knew, had no right to the country – Heracles demanded one of the oxen; and, when Theiodamas refused, killed him. After slaughtering the ox, and feasting on its flesh, he bore off Theiodamas's infant son Hylas, whose mother was the nymph Menodice, Orion's daughter.[2] But some call Hylas's father Ceyx, or Euphemus, or Theiomenes; and insist that Theiodamas was the Rhodian ploughman who cursed from afar while Heracles sacrificed one of his oxen.[3]

b. It seems that Phylas, Theiodamas's successor, violated Apollo's temple at Delphi. Outraged on Apollo's behalf, Heracles killed Phylas and carried off his daughter Meda; she bore him Antiochus, founder of the Athenian deme which bears his name.[4] He then expelled the Dryopians from their city on Mount Parnassus, and gave it to the Malians who had helped in its conquest. The leading Dryopians he took to Delphi and dedicated them at the shrine as slaves; but, Apollo having no use for them, they were sent away to the Peloponnese, where they sought the favour of Eurystheus the High King. Under his orders, and with the assistance of other fugitive compatriots, they built three cities, Asine, Hermione, and Eion. Of the remaining Dryopians, some fled to Euboea, others to Cyprus and to the island of Cynthos. But only the men of Asine still pride themselves on being Dryopians; they have built a shrine to their ancestor Dryops, with an ancient image, and celebrate mysteries in his honour every second year.[5]

c. Dryops was Apollo's son by Dia, a daughter of King Lycaon, for fear of whom she hid the infant in a hollow oak; hence his name. Some say that Dryops himself brought his people from the Thessalian river Spercheius to Asine, and that he was a son of Spercheius by the nymph Polydora.[6]

d. A boundary dispute had arisen between the Dorians of Hestiaeotis, ruled by King Aegimius, and the Lapiths of Mount Olympus, former allies of the Dryopians, whose king was Coronus, a son of Caeneus. The Dorians, greatly outnumbered by the Lapiths, fled to Heracles and appealed for help, offering him in return a third share of their kingdom; whereupon Heracles and his Arcadian allies defeated the Lapiths, slew Coronus and most of his subjects, and forced them to quit the disputed land. Some of them settled at Corinth. Aegimius then held Heracles's third share in trust for his descendants.[7]

e. Heracles now came to Itonus, a city of Phthiotis, where the ancient temple of Athene stands. Here he met Cycnus, a son of Ares and Pelopia, who was constantly offering valuable prizes to guests who dared fight a chariot duel with him. The ever-victorious Cycnus would cut off their heads and use the skulls to decorate the temple of his father Ares. This, by the way, was not the Cycnus whom Ares had begotten on Pyrene and transformed into a swan when he died.[8]

f. Apollo, growing vexed with Cycnus, because he waylaid and carried off herds of cattle which were being sent for sacrifice to Delphi, incited Heracles to accept Cycnus's challenge. It was agreed that Heracles should be supported by his charioteer Iolaus, and Cycnus by his father Ares. Heracles, though this was not his usual style of fighting, put on the polished bronze greaves which Hephaestus had made for him, the curiously wrought golden breast-plate given him by Athene, and a pair of iron shoulder-guards. Armed with bow and arrows, spear, helmet, and a stout shield which Zeus had ordered Hephaestus to supply, he lightly mounted his chariot.

g. Athene, descending from Olympus, now warned Heracles that, although empowered by Zeus to kill and despoil Cycnus, he must do no more than defend himself against Ares and, even if victorious, not deprive him of either his horses or his splendid armour. She then mounted beside Heracles and Iolaus, shaking her aegis, and Mother Earth groaned as the chariot whirled forward. Cycnus drove to meet them at full speed, and both he and Heracles were thrown to the ground by the shock of their encounter, spear against shield. Yet they sprang to their feet and, after a short combat, Heracles thrust Cycnus through the neck. He then boldly faced Ares, who hurled a spear at him; and Athene, with an angry frown, turned it aside. Ares ran at Heracles sword in hand, only to be wounded in the thigh for his pains, and Heracles would have dealt him a further blow as he lay on the ground, had not Zeus parted the combatants with a thunderbolt. Heracles and Iolaus then despoiled Cycnus's corpse and resumed their interrupted journey; while Athene led the fainting Ares back to Olympus. Cycnus was buried by Ceyx in the valley of the Anaurus but, at Apollo's command, the swollen river washed away his headstone.[9]

h. Some, however, say that Cycnus lived at Amphanae, and that Heracles transfixed him with an arrow beside the river Peneius, or at Pegasae.[10]

i. Passing through Pelasgiotis, Heracles now came to Ormenium, a small city at the foot of Mount Pelion, where King Amyntor refused to give him his daughter Astydameia. 'You are married already,' he said, 'and have betrayed far too many princesses for me to trust you with another.' Heracles attacked the city and, after killing Amyntor, carried off Astydameia, who bore him Ctesippus or, some say, Tlepolemus.[11]

1. Diodorus Siculus: iv. 36; Probus, on Virgil's *Georgics* iii. 6; Scholiast on Apollonius Rhodius: i. 131.

2. Apollodorus: ii. 7. 7; Apollonius Rhodius: i. 1212 ff.; Hyginus: *Fabula* 14.

3. Nicander, quoted by Antoninus Liberalis: 26; Hellanicus, quoted by scholiast on Apollonius Rhodius: i. 131 and 1207; Philostratus: *Imagines* ii. 24.

4. Diodorus Siculus: iv. 37; Pausanias: i. 5. 2.

5. Diodorus Siculus: *loc. cit.*; Herodotus: viii. 46; Pausanias: iv. 34. 6 and viii. 34. 6.

6. Tzetzes: *On Lycophron* 480; Aristotle, quoted by Strabo: viii. 6. 13; Antoninus Liberalis: *Transformations* 32.

7. Apollodorus: ii. 7. 7; Diodorus Siculus: iv. 37.

8. Euripides: *Heracles* 389–93; Pausanias: i. 27. 7; Scholiast on Pindar's *Olympian Odes* ii. 82 and x. 15; Eustathius on Homer's *Iliad* p. 254.

9. Hesiod: *Shield of Heracles* 57–138 and 318–480; Hyginus: *Fabula* 31; Apollodorus: ii. 7. 7; Diodorus Siculus: iv. 37; Euripides: *loc. cit.*

10. Pausanias: i. 27. 7; Hesiod: *Shield of Heracles* 318–480.

11. Diodorus Siculus: iv. 37; Strabo: ix. 5. 18; Apollodorus: iii. 13. 8 and ii. 7. 7–8; Pindar: *Olympian Odes* vii. 23 ff., with scholiast.

*

1. Heracles's sacrifice of a plough ox, Theiodamas's cursing, and the appearance of the infant Hylas from a furrow, are all parts of the pre-Hellenic sowing ritual. Ox blood propitiates the Earth-goddess, curses avert divine anger from the sprouting seeds, the child represents the coming crop – namely Plutus, whom Demeter bore to Iasius after they had embraced in the thrice-ploughed field (see 24. *a*). Theiodamas is the spirit of the old year, now destroyed. The annual mourning for the doomed tree-spirit Hylas (see 150. *d–e*) has here been confused with mourning for the doomed corn-spirit.

2. Heracles's expulsion of the Dryopians from Parnassus with Dorian assistance, and the Dryopian emigration to Southern Greece, are likely to have taken place in the twelfth century B.C., before the Dorian invasion

of the Peloponnese (see 146. 1). His combat with Cycnus recalls Pelops's race with Oenomaus (see 109. d–j), another son of Ares, and equally notorious as a head-hunter. In both cases one of the chariots contained a woman: namely Oenomaus's daughter Hippodameia (the subject of his contention with Pelops) and Athene, who is, apparently, the same character – namely the new king's destined bride. Cycnus, like Spartan Polydeuces, is a king of the swan cult whose soul flies off to the far northern otherworld (see 161. 4).

3. Aegimius's name – if it means 'acting the part of a goat' – suggests that he performed a May Eve goat-marriage with the tribal queen, and that in his war against the Lapiths of Northern Thessaly his Dorians fought beside the Centaurs, the Lapiths' hereditary enemies who, like the Satyrs, are depicted in early works of art as goat-men (see 142. 5).

4. Cypselus the tyrant of Corinth, famous for his carved chest, claimed descent from the Lapith royal house of Caeneus (see 78. 1).

144

IOLE

AT Trachis Heracles mustered an army of Arcadians, Melians, and Epicnemidian Locrians, and marched against Oechalia to revenge himself on King Eurytus, who refused to surrender the princess Iole, fairly won in an archery contest; but he told his allies no more than that Eurytus had been unjustly exacting tribute from the Euboeans. He stormed the city, riddled Eurytus and his son with arrows and, after burying certain of his comrades who had fallen in the battle, namely Ceyx's son Hippasus, and Argeius and Melas, sons of Licymnius, pillaged Oechalia and took Iole captive.[1] Rather than yield to Heracles, Iole had allowed him to murder her entire family before her very eyes, and then leaped from the city wall; yet she survived, because her skirts were billowed out by the wind and broke the fall. Now Heracles sent her, with other Oechalian women, to Deianeira at Trachis, while he visited the Euboean headland of Cenaeum.[2] It should be noted here that when taking leave of Deianeira, Heracles had divulged a prophecy: at the end of fifteen months, he was fated either to die, or to spend the remainder of his life in perfect tranquillity. The news had been conveyed to him by the twin doves of the ancient oak oracle at Dodona.[3]

b. It is disputed which of several towns named Oechalia was sacked on this occasion: whether the Messenian; the Thessalian; the Euboean; the Trachinian; or the Aetolian.[4] Messenian Oechalia is the most likely of these, since Eurytus's father Melaneus, King of the Dryopians – a skilled archer, and hence called a son of Apollo – came to Messenia in the reign of Perieres, son of Aeolus, who gave him Oechalia as his home. Oechalia was called after Melaneus's wife. Here, in a sacred cypress-grove, heroic sacrifices to Eurytus, whose bones are preserved in a brazen urn, initiate the Great Goddess's Mysteries. Others identify Oechalia with Andania, a mile from the cypress-grove, where these Mysteries were formerly held. Eurytus was one of the heroes whom the Messenians invited to dwell among them when Epaminondas restored their Peloponnesian patrimony.[5]

1. Athenaeus: xi. 461; Apollodorus: ii. 7. 7.
2. Nicias of Mallus, quoted by Plutarch: *Parallel Stories* 13; Hyginus: *Fabula* 35; Sophocles: *Trachinian Women* 283 ff.; Apollodorus: *loc. cit.*
3. Sophocles: *Trachinian Women* 44–5.
4. Homer: *Iliad* ii. 596 and 730; *Odyssey* xxi. 13–14; Servius on Virgil's Aeneid viii. 291; Strabo: ix. 5. 17 and x. 1. 10.
5. Antoninus Liberalis: *Transformations* 4; Pausanias: iv. 2. 2; 3. 6; 33. 5–6 and 27. 4; Strabo: x. 1. 18.

*

1. Eurytus had refused to yield Iole on the ground that Heracles was a slave (see 135. *a*). Though Iole's suicidal leap makes a plausible story – Mycenaean skirts were bell-shaped, and my father once saw a mid-Victorian suicide saved by her vast crinoline – it has most likely been deduced from a Mycenaean picture of the goddess hovering above an army as it assaulted her city. The name Oechalia, 'house of flour', shows that the goddess in whose honour the mysteries were performed was Demeter.

145

THE APOTHEOSIS OF HERACLES

HAVING consecrated marble altars and a sacred grove to his father Zeus on the Cenaean headland, Heracles prepared a thanksgiving sacrifice for the capture of Oechalia. He had already sent Lichas back to ask Deianeira for a fine shirt and a cloak of the sort which he regularly wore on such occasions.[1]

b. Deianeira, comfortably installed at Trachis, was by now resigned to Heracles's habit of taking mistresses; and, when she recognized Iole as the latest of these, felt pity rather than resentment for the fatal beauty which had been Oechalia's ruin. Yet was it not intolerable that Heracles expected Iole and herself to live together under the same roof? Since she was no longer young, Deianeira decided to use Nessus's supposed love-charm as a means of holding her husband's affection. Having woven him a new sacrificial shirt against his safe return, she covertly unsealed the jar, soaked a piece of wool in the mixture, and rubbed the shirt with it. When Lichas arrived she locked the shirt in a chest which she gave to him, saying: 'On no account expose the shirt to light or heat until Heracles is about to wear it at the sacrifice.' Lichas had already driven off at full speed in his chariot when Deianeira, glancing at the piece of wool which she had thrown down into the sunlit courtyard, was horrified to see it burning away like saw-dust, while red foam bubbled up from the flag-stones. Realizing that Nessus had deceived her, she sent a courier post-haste to recall Lichas and, cursing her folly, swore that if Heracles died she would not survive him.[2]

c. The courier arrived too late at the Cenaean headland. Heracles had by now put on the shirt and sacrificed twelve immaculate bulls as the first-fruits of his spoils: in all, he had brought to the altar a mixed herd of one hundred cattle. He was pouring wine from a bowl on the altars and throwing frankincense on the flames when he let out a sudden yell as if he had been bitten by a serpent. The heat had melted the Hydra's poison in Nessus's blood, which coursed all over Heracles's limbs, corroding his flesh. Soon the pain was beyond endurance and, bellowing in anguish, he overturned the altars. He tried to rip off the shirt, but it clung to him so fast that his flesh came away with it, laying bare the bones. His blood hissed and bubbled like spring water when red-hot metal is being tempered. He plunged headlong into the nearest stream, but the poison burned only the fiercer; these waters have been scalding hot ever since and are called Thermopylae, or 'hot passage'.[3]

d. Ranging over the mountain, tearing up trees as he went, Heracles came upon the terrified Lichas crouched in the hollow of a rock, his knees clasped with his hands. In vain did Lichas try to exculpate himself:

Heracles seized him, whirled him thrice about his head and flung him into the Euboean Sea. There he was transformed: he became a rock of human appearance, projecting a short distance above the waves, which sailors still call Lichas and on which they are afraid to tread, believing it to be sentient. The army, watching from afar, raised a great shout of lamentation, but none dared approach until, writhing in agony, Heracles summoned Hyllus, and asked to be carried away to die in solitude. Hyllus conveyed him to the foot of Mount Oeta in Trachis (a region famous for its white hellebore), the Delphic Oracle having already pointed this out to Licymnius and Iolaus as the destined scene of their friend's death.[4]

e. Aghast at the news, Deianeira hanged herself or, some say, stabbed herself with a sword in their marriage bed. Heracles's one thought had been to punish her before he died, but when Hyllus assured him that she was innocent, as her suicide proved, he sighed forgivingly and expressed a wish that Alcmene and all his sons should assemble to hear his last words. Alcmene, however, was at Tiryns with some of his children, and most of the others had settled at Thebes. Thus he could reveal Zeus's prophecy, now fulfilled, only to Hyllus: 'No man alive may ever kill Heracles; a dead enemy shall be his downfall.' Hyllus then asked for instructions, and was told: 'Swear by the head of Zeus that you will convey me to the highest peak of this mountain, and there burn me, without lamentation, on a pyre of oak-branches and trunks of the male wild-olive. Likewise swear to marry Iole as soon as you come of age.' Though scandalized by these requests, Hyllus promised to observe them.[5]

f. When all had been prepared, Iolaus and his companions retired a short distance, while Heracles mounted the pyre and gave orders for its kindling. But none dared obey, until a passing Aeolian shepherd named Poeas ordered Philoctetes, his son by Demonassa, to do as Heracles asked. In gratitude, Heracles bequeathed his quiver, bow, and arrows to Philoctetes and, when the flames began to lick at the pyre, spread his lion-pelt over the platform at the summit and lay down, with his club for pillow, looking as blissful as a garlanded guest surrounded by wine-cups. Thunderbolts then fell from the sky and at once reduced the pyre to ashes.[6]

g. In Olympus, Zeus congratulated himself that his favourite son had behaved so nobly. 'Heracles's immortal part', he announced, 'is safe from death, and I shall soon welcome him to this blessed region.

But if anyone here grieves at his deification, so richly merited, that god or goddess must nevertheless approve it willy-nilly!'

All the Olympians assented, and Hera decided to swallow the insult, which was clearly aimed at her, because she had already arranged to punish Philoctetes, for his kindly act, by the bite of a Lemnian viper.

h. The thunderbolts had consumed Heracles's mortal part. He no longer bore any resemblance to Alcmene but, like a snake that has cast its slough, appeared in all the majesty of his divine father. A cloud received him from his companions' sight as, amid peals of thunder, Zeus bore him up to heaven in his four-horse chariot; where Athene took him by the hand and solemnly introduced him to her fellow deities.[7]

i. Now, Zeus had destined Heracles as one of the Twelve Olympians, yet was loth to expel any of the existing company of gods in order to make room for him. He therefore persuaded Hera to adopt Heracles by a ceremony of rebirth: namely, going to bed, pretending to be in labour, and then producing him from beneath her skirts – which is the adoption ritual still in use among many barbarian tribes. Henceforth, Hera regarded Heracles as her son and loved him next only to Zeus. All the immortals welcomed his arrival; and Hera married him to her pretty daughter Hebe, who bore him Alexiares and Anicetus. And, indeed, Heracles had earned Hera's true gratitude in the revolt of the Giants by killing Pronomus, when he tried to violate her.[8]

j. Heracles became the porter of heaven, and never tires of standing at the Olympian gates, towards nightfall, waiting for Artemis's return from the chase. He greets her merrily, and hauls the heaps of prey out of her chariot, frowning and wagging a finger in disapproval if he finds only harmless goats and hares. 'Shoot wild boars,' he says, 'that trample down crops and gash orchard-trees; shoot man-killing bulls, and lions, and wolves! But what harm have goats and hares done us?' Then he flays the carcasses, and voraciously eats any titbits that take his fancy.[9] Yet while the immortal Heracles banquets at the divine table, his mortal phantom stalks about Tartarus, among the twittering dead; bow drawn, arrow fitted to the string. Across his shoulder is slung a golden baldric, terrifyingly wrought with lions, bears, wild boars, and scenes of battle and slaughter.[10]

k. When Iolaus and his companions returned to Trachis, Menoetius, the son of Actor, sacrificed a ram, a bull, and a boar to Heracels, and instituted his hero-worship at Locrian Opus; the Thebans soon followed suit; but the Athenians, led by the people of Marathon, were the first to worship him as a god, and all mankind now follows their glorious example.[11] Heracles's son Phaestus found that the Sicyonians were offering his father hero-rites, but himself insisted on sacrificing to him as a god. To this day, therefore, the people of Sicyon, after killing a lamb and burning its thighs on the altar to Heracles the god, devote part of its flesh to Heracles the hero. At Oeta, he is worshipped under the name of Cornopion because he scared away the locusts which were about to settle on the city; but the Ionians of Erythrae worship him as Heracles Ipoctonus, because he destroyed the *ipes*, which are worms that attack vines in almost every other region.

l. A Tyrian image of Heracles, now in his shrine at Erythrae, is said to represent Heracles the Dactyl. It was found floating on a raft in the Ionian Sea off Cape Mesate, exactly half way between the harbour of Erythrae and the island of Chios. The Erythraeans on one side and the Chians on the other, strained every nerve to tow the raft to their own shore – but without success. At last an Erythraean fisherman named Phormio, who had lost his sight, dreamed that the women of Erythrae must plait a rope from their shorn tresses; with this, the men would be able to tow the raft home. The women of a Thracian clan that had settled in Erythrae complied, and the raft was towed ashore; and only their descendants are now permitted to enter the shrine where the rope is laid up. Phormio recovered his sight, and kept it until he died.[12]

1. Sophocles: *Trachinian Women* 298 and 752–4; Apollodorus: ii. 7. 7; Diodorus Siculus: iv. 38.
2. Sophocles: *Trachinian Women* 460–751; Hyginus: *Fabula* 36.
3. Sophocles: *Trachinian Women* 756 ff.; Nonnus – Westermann's *Mythographi Graeci: Appendix Narrationum* xxviii. 8; Tzetzes: *On Lycophron* 50–51.
4. Ovid: *Metamorphoses* ix. 155 ff.; Hyginus: *Fabula* 36; Sophocles: *Trachinian Women* 783 ff.; Apollodorus: ii. 7. 7; Pliny: *Natural History* xxv. 21; Diodorus Siculus: iv. 38.
5. Apollodorus: *loc. cit.*; Sophocles: *Trachinian Women* 912 to end.
6. Diodorus Siculus: *loc. cit.*; Hyginus: *Fabula* 102; Ovid: *Metamorphoses* ix. 299 ff.
7. Ovid: *Metamorphoses* ix. 241–73; Apollodorus: *loc. cit.*; Hyginus: *loc. cit.*; Pausanias: iii. 18. 7.
8. Diodorus Siculus: iv. 39; Hesiod on Onomacritus: *Fragment*, ed. Evelyn-White pp. 615–16, Loeb; Pindar: *Isthmian Odes* iv. 59 and

Nemean Odes x. 18; Apollodorus: *loc. cit.*; Sotas of Byzantium, quoted by Tzetzes: *On Lycophron* 1349–50.

9. Callimachus: *Hymn to Artemis* 145 ff.
10. Homer: *Odyssey* xi. 601 ff.
11. Diodorus Siculus: iv. 39; Pausanias: i. 15. 4.
12. Pausanias: ii. 10. 1; ix. 27. 5 and vii. 5. 3; Strabo: xiii. 1. 64.

*

1. Before sacrificing and thus immortalizing the sacred king – as Calypso promised to immortalize Odysseus (see 170. *w*) – the Queen will have stripped him of his clothes and regalia. What floggings and mutilations he suffered until he was laid on the pyre for immortalization is not suggested here, but the icons from which the account seems to be deduced probably showed him bleeding and in agony, as he struggled into the white linen shirt which consecrated him to the Death-goddess.

2. A tradition that Heracles died on the Cenaean headland has been reconciled with another that had him die on Mount Oeta, where early inscriptions and statuettes show that the sacred king continued to be burned in effigy for centuries after he ceased to be burned in the flesh. Oak is the correct wood for the midsummer bonfire; wild-olive is the wood of the New Year, when the king began his reign by expelling the spirits of the old year. Poeas, or Philoctetes, who lighted the pyre, is the king's tanist and successor; he inherits his arms and bed – Iole's marriage to Hyllus must be read in this light – and dies by snake-bite at the end of the year.

3. Formerly, Heracles's soul had gone to the Western Paradise of the Hesperides; or to the silver castle, the Corona Borealis, at the back of the North Wind – a legend which Pindar has uncomprehendingly included in a brief account of the Third Labour (see 125. *k*). His admission to the Olympian Heaven – where, however, he never secured a seat among the twelve, as Dionysus did (see 27. 5) – is a late conception. It may be based on the misreading of the same sacred icon which accounts for the marriage of Peleus and Thetis (see 81. *1–5*), for the so-called rape of Ganymedes (see 29. *1*), and for the arming of Heracles (see 123. *1*). This icon will have shown Athene, or Hebe, the youthful queen and bride, introducing the king to twelve witnesses of the sacred marriage, each representing a clan of a religious confederacy or a month of the sacred year; he has been ritually reborn either from a mare, or (as here) from a woman. Heracles figures as a heavenly porter because he died at midsummer – the year being likened to an oaken door which turned on a hinge, opened to its widest extent at the midsummer solstice, then gradually closed, as the days began to shorten (*White Goddess* pp. 175–7). What kept him from becoming a full Olympian seems to have been the authority of Homer: the *Odyssey* had recorded the presence of his shade in Tartarus.

4. If the Erythraean statue of Heracles was of Tyrian provenience, the rope in the temple will have been woven not of women's hair but of hair shorn from the sacred king before his death at the winter solstice – as Delilah shore that of Samson, a Tyrian sun-hero. A similar sun-hero had been sacrificed by the Thracian women who adopted his cult (see 28. 2). The statue was probably towed on a raft to avoid the hallowing of a merchant vessel and its consequent withdrawal from trade. 'Ipoctonus' may have been a local variant of Heracles's more usual title Ophioctonus, 'serpent-killing'. His renovation by death 'like a snake that casts its slough', was a figure borrowed from the Egyptian *Book of the Dead*; snakes were held to put off old age by casting their slough, 'slough' and 'old age' both being *geros* in Greek (see 160. 11). He rides to Heaven in a four-horse chariot as a solar hero and patron of the Olympic Games; each horse representing one of the four years between the Games, or one season of a year divided by equinoxes and solstices. A square image of the sun, worshipped as Heracles the Saviour, stood in the Great Goddess's precinct at Megalopolis (Pausanias: viii. 31. 4); it was probably an ancient altar, like several square blocks found in the palace at Cnossus, and another found in the West Court of the palace at Phaestus.

5. Hebe, Heracles's bride, may not, perhaps, be the goddess as Youth, but a deity mentioned in the 48th and 49th *Orphic Hymns* as Hipta the Earth-mother, to whom Dionysus was delivered for safe-keeping. Proclus says (*Against Timaeus* ii. 124c) that she carried him on her head in a winnowing basket. Hipta is associated with Zeus Sabazius (see 27. 3) in two early inscriptions from Maeonia, then inhabited by a Lydo-Phrygian tribe; and Professor Kretschmer has identified her with the Mitannian goddess Hepa, Hepit, or Hebe, mentioned in the texts from Boghaz-Keui and apparently brought to Maeonia from Thrace. If Heracles married this Hebe, the myth concerns the Heracles who did great deeds in Phrygia (see 131. *h*), Mysia (see 131. *e*), and Lydia (see 136. *a–f*); he can be identified with Zeus Sabazius. Hipta was well known throughout the Middle East. A rock-carving at Hattusas in Lycaonia (see 13. 2) shows her mounted on a lion, about to celebrate a sacred marriage with the Hittite Storm-god. She is there called Hepatu, said to be a Hurrian word, and Professor B. Hrozný (*Civilization of the Hittites and Subareans*, ch. xv) equates her with Hawwa, 'the Mother of All Living', who appears in *Genesis* ii as Eve. Hrozný mentions the Canaanite prince of Jerusalem Abdihepa; and Adam, who married Eve, was a tutelary hero of Jerusalem (Jerome: *Commentary on Ephesians* v. 15).

THE CHILDREN OF HERACLES

ALCMENE, the mother of Heracles, had gone to Tiryns, taking some of his sons with her; others were still at Thebes and Trachis. Eurystheus now decided to expel them all from Greece, before they could reach manhood and depose him. He therefore sent a message to Ceyx, demanding the extradition not only of the Heraclids, but also of Iolaus, the whole house of Licymnius, and Heracles's Arcadian allies. Too weak to oppose Eurystheus, they left Trachis in a body – Ceyx pleading that he was powerless to help them – and visited most of the great Greek cities as suppliants, begging for hospitality. The Athenians under Theseus alone dared defy Eurystheus: their innate sense of justice prevailed when they saw the Heraclids seated at the Altar of Mercy.[1]

b. Theseus settled the Heraclids and their companions at Tricorythus – a city of the Attic tetrapolis – and would not surrender them to Eurystheus, which was the cause of the first war between Athens and the Peloponnese. For, when all the Heraclids had grown to manhood, Eurystheus assembled an army and marched against Athens; Iolaus, Theseus, and Hyllus being appointed to command the combined Athenians and Heraclids. But some say that Theseus had now been succeeded by his son Demophon. Since an oracle announced that the Athenians must be defeated unless one of Heracles's children would die for the common good, Macaria, Heracles's only daughter, killed herself at Marathon, and thus gave her name to the Macarian spring.[2]

c. The Athenians, whose protection of the Heraclids is even today a source of civic pride, then defeated Eurystheus in a pitched battle and killed his sons Alexander, Iphimedon, Eurybius, Mentor, and Perimedes, besides many of his allies. Eurystheus fled in his chariot, pursued by Hyllus, who overtook him at the Scironian Rocks and there cut off his head, from which Alcmene gouged the eyes with weaving-pins; his tomb is shown near by.[3] But some say that he was captured by Iolaus at the Scironian Rocks, and taken to Alcmene, who ordered his execution. The Athenians interceded for him, though in vain, and before the sentence was carried out, Eurystheus shed tears of gratitude and declared that he would reveal himself, even in death, as their firm friend, and a sworn enemy to the Heraclids. 'Theseus,' he cried, 'you need not pour libations or blood on my tomb: even without such offerings I undertake to drive all enemies from the land of Attica!' Then he was executed and buried in front of Athene's sanctuary at Pellene, midway between Athens and Marathon. A very different account is that the Athenians assisted Eurystheus in a battle which he fought against the Heraclids at Marathon; and that Iolaus, having cut off his head beside the Macarian spring, close to the chariot road, buried it at Tricorythus, and sent the trunk to Gargettus for burial.[4]

d. Meanwhile, Hyllus and the Heraclids who had settled by the Electrian Gate at Thebes invaded the Peloponnese, capturing all its cities in a sudden onset; but when, next year, a plague broke out and an oracle announced: 'The Heraclids have returned before the due time!' Hyllus withdrew to Marathon. Obeying his father's last wish, he had married Iole and been adopted by Aegimius the Dorian; he now went to ask the Delphic Oracle when 'the due time' would come, and was warned to 'wait for the third crop'. Taking this to mean three years, he rested until these had passed and then marched again. On the Isthmus he was met by Atreus, who had meanwhile succeeded to the Mycenaean throne and rode at the head of an Achaean army.[5]

e. To avoid needless slaughter Hyllus challenged any opponent of rank to single combat. 'If I win,' he said, 'let the throne and kingdom be mine. If I lose, we sons of Heracles will not return along this road for another fifty years.' Echemus, King of Tegea, accepted the challenge, and the duel took place on the Corintho–Megarid frontier. Hyllus fell, and was buried in the city of Megara; whereupon the Heraclids honoured his undertaking and once more retired to Tricorythus, and thence to Doris, where they claimed from Aegimius that share of the kingdom which their father had entrusted to him. Only Licymnius and his sons, and Heracles's son Tlepolemus, who was invited to settle at Argos, remained in the Peloponnese. Delphic Apollo, whose seemingly unsound advice had earned him many reproaches, explained that by the 'third crop' he meant the third generation.[6]

f. Alcmene went back to Thebes and, when she died there at a great age, Zeus ordered Hermes to plunder the coffin which the Heraclids were carrying to the grave; and this he did, adroitly substituting a stone for the body, which he carried off to the Islands of the Blessed. There, revived and rejuvenated, Alcmene became the wife of Rhadamanthys. Meanwhile, finding the coffin too heavy for their shoulder, the Heraclids opened it, and discovered the fraud. They set up the stone in a sacred grove at Thebes, where Alcmene is now worshipped as a goddess. But some say that she married Rhadamanthys at Ocaleae, before her death; and others, that she died in Megara, where her tomb is still shown, on a journey from Argos to Thebes – they add, that when a dispute arose among the Heraclids, some wishing to convey her corpse back to Argos, others to continue the journey, the Delphic Oracle advised them to bury her in Megara. Another so-called tomb of Alcmene is shown at Haliartus.[7]

g. The Thebans awarded Iolaus a hero-shrine, close to Amphitryon's, where lovers plight their troths for Heracles's sake; although it is generally admitted that Iolaus died in Sardinia.[8]

h. At Argos, Tlepolemus accidentally killed his beloved grand-uncle Licymnius. He was chastising a servant with an olive-wood club when Licymnius, now old and blind, stumbled between them and caught a blow on his skull. Threatened with death by the other Heraclids, Tlepolemus built a fleet, gathered a large number of companions and, on Apollo's advice, fled to Rhodes, where he settled after long wandering and many hardships.[9] In those days Rhodes was inhabited by Greek settlers under Triops, a son of Phorbas, with whose consent Tlepolemus divided the island into three parts and is said to have founded the cities of Lindus, Ialysus, and Cameirus. His people were favoured and enriched by Zeus. Later, Tlepolemus sailed to Troy with a fleet of nine Rhodian ships.[10]

i. Heracles begot another Hyllus on the water-nymph Melite, daughter of the River-god Aegaeus, in the land of the Phaeacians. He had gone there after the murder of his children, in the hope of being purified by King Nausithous and by Macris, the nurse of Dionysus. This was the Hyllus who emigrated to the Cronian Sea with a number of Phaecian settlers, and gave his name to the Hyllaeans.[11]

j. The latest-born of all the Heraclids is said to have been the Thasian athelte Theagenes, whose mother was visited one night in the temple of Heracles by someone whom she took for his priest, her husband Timosthenes, but who proved to be the god himself.[12]

k. The Heraclids eventually reconquered the Peloponnese in the fourth generation under Temenus, Cresphontes, and the twins Procles and Eurysthenes, after killing the High King Tisamenes of Mycenae, a son of Orestes. They would have succeeded earlier, had not one of their princes murdered Carnus, an Acarnanian poet, as he came towards them chanting prophetic verses; mistaking him for a magician sent against them by Tisamenes. In punishment of this sacrilege the Heraclid fleet was sunk and famine caused their army to disband. The Delphic Oracle now advised them 'to banish the slayer for ten years and take Triops as a guide in his place.' They were about to fetch Triops son of Phorbas from Rhodes, when Temenus noticed an Aetolian chieftain named Oxylus, who had just expiated some murder or other with a year's exile in Elis, riding by on a one-eyed horse. Now, Triops means 'three-eyed', and Temenus therefore engaged him as guide and, landing on the coast of Elis with his Heraclid kinsmen, soon conquered the whole Peloponnese, and divided it by lot. The lot marked with a toad meant Argos and went to Temenus; that marked with a serpent meant Sparta and went to the twins Procles and Eurysthenes; that marked with a fox meant Messene and went to Cresphontes.[13]

1. Sophocles: *Trachinian Women* 1151–5; Hecataeus, quoted by Longinus: *De Sublimitate* 27; Diodorus Siculus: iv. 57; Apollodorus: ii. 8. 1 and iii. 7. 1; Pausanias: i. 32. 5.

2. Diodorus Siculus: *loc. cit.*; Apollodorus: ii. 8. 1; Pausanias: *loc. cit*; Pherecydes, quoted by Antoninus Liberalis: *Transformations* 33; Zenobius: *Proverbs* ii. 61.

3. Lysias: ii. 11–16; Isocratas: *Panegyric* 15–16; Apollodorus: ii. 8. 1 Diodorus Siculus: *loc. cit.*; Pausanias: i. 44. 14.

4. Euripides: *Children of Heracles* 843 ff., 928 ff. and 1026 ff.; Strabo: viii. 6. 19.

5. Pherecydes, quoted by Antoninus Liberalis: *Transformations* 33; Strabo: ix. 40. 10.

6. Pausanias: i. 44. 14 and 41. 3; Diodorus Siculus: iv. 58; Apollodorus: ii. 81. 2.

7. Diodorus Siculus: *loc. cit.*; Apollodorus: ii. 4. 11 and iii. 1. 2; Pausanias: i. 41. 1; Plutarch: *Lysander* 28.

8. Pindar: *Pythian Odes* ix. 79 ff.; Plutarch: *On Love* 17; Pausanias: ix. 23. 1.

9. Homer: *Iliad* ii. 653–70; Apollodorus: ii. 8. 2; Pindar: *Olympian Odes* vii. 27 ff.

10. Diodorus Siculus: iv. 58; Homer: *loc. cit.*; Apollodorus: *Epitome* iii. 13.

11. Apollonius Rhodius: iv. 538 ff.

12. Pausanias: vi. 11. 12.

13. Apollodorus: ii 8. 2–5; Pausanias: ii. 18. 7, iii. 13. 4, v. 3. 5–7 and viii. 5. 6; Strabo: viii. 3. 33; Herodotus: vi. 52.

*

1. The disastrous invasion of the Mycenaean Peloponnese by uncultured patriarchal mountaineers from Central Greece which, according to

Pausanias (iv. 3. 3) and Thucydides (i. 12. 3), took place about 1100 B.C., was called the Dorian because its leaders came from the small state of Doris. Three tribes composed this Dorian League: the Hylleids, who worshipped Heracles; the Dymanes ('enterers'), who worshipped Apollo; and the Pamphylloi ('men from every tribe'), who worshipped Demeter. After overrunning Southern Thessaly, the Dorians seem to have allied themselves with the Athenians before they ventured to attack the Peloponnese. The first attempt failed, though Mycenae was burned about 1100 B.C., but a century later they conquered the eastern and southern regions, having by now destroyed the entire ancient culture of Argolis. This invasion, which caused emigrations from Argolis to Rhodes, from Attica to the Ionian coast of Asia Minor, and apparently also from Thebes to Sardinia, brought the Dark Ages into Greece.

2. Strategic burial of a hero's head is commonplace in myth: thus, according to the *Mabinogion*, Bran's head was buried on Tower Hill to guard London from invasion by way of the Thames: and according to Ambrose (*Epistle* vii. 2), Adam's head was buried at Golgotha, to protect Jerusalem from the north. Moreover, Euripides (*Rhesus* 413–15) makes Hector declare that the ghosts even of strangers could serve as Troy's guardian spirits (see 28. 6). Both Tricorythus and Gargettus lie at narrow defiles commanding the approaches to Attica. Iolaus's pursuit of Eurystheus past the Scironian Rocks seems to have been borrowed from the same icon that suggested the myth of Hippolytus (see 101. g).

3. The land of the Phaeacians (see 170. y) was Corcyra, or Drepane, now Corfu, off which lay the sacred islet of Macris (see 154. a); the Cronian Sea was the Gulf of Finland, whence amber seems to have been fetched by Corcyrian enterprise – Corcyra is associated with the Argonaut amber-expedition to the head of the Adriatic (see 148. 9).

4. Triops, the Greek colonist of Rhodes, is a masculinization of the ancient Triple-goddess Danaë, or Damkina, after whose three persons Lindus, Ialysus, and Cameirus were named. According to other accounts, these cities were founded by the Telchines (see 54. a), or by Danaus (see 60. d).

5. Alcmene being merely a title of Hera's, there was nothing remarkable in the dedication of a temple to her.

6. Polygnotus, in his famous painting at Delphi, showed Menelaus with a serpent badge on his shield (Pausanias: x. 26. 3) – presumably the water-serpent of Sparta (see 125. 3). A fox helped the Messenian hero Aristomenes to escape from a pit into which the Spartans had thrown him (Pausanias: iv. 18. 6); and the goddess as vixen was well known in Greece (see 49. 2 and 89. 8). The toad seems to have become the Argive emblem, not only because it had a reputation of being dangerous to handle, and of causing a hush of awe among all who saw it (Pliny:

Natural History xxxii. 18), but because Argos was first called Phoronicum (see 57. *a*); in the syllabary which preceded the alphabet at Argos, the radicals PHRN could be expressed by a toad, *phryne*.

147

LINUS

THE child Linus of Argos must be distinguished from Linus, the son of Ismenius, whom Heracles killed with a lyre. According to the Argives, Psamathe, the daughter of Crotopus, bore the child Linus to Apollo and, fearing her father's wrath, exposed him on a mountain. He was found and reared by shepherds, but afterwards torn in pieces by Crotopus's mastiffs. Since Psamathe could not disguise her grief, Crotopus soon guessed that she was Linus's mother, and condemned her to death. Apollo punished the city of Argos for this double crime by sending a sort of Harpy named Poene, who snatched young children from their parents until one Coroebus took it upon himself to destroy her. A plague then descended on the city and, when it showed no sign of abating, the Argives consulted the Delphic Oracle, which advised them to propitiate Psamathe and Linus. Accordingly they offered sacrifices to their ghosts, the women and maidens chanting dirges, still called *linoi*; and since Linus had been reared among lambs, named the festival *arnis*, and the month in which it was held *arneios*. The plague still raging, at last Coroebus went to Delphi and confessed to Poene's murder. The Pythoness would not let him return to Argos, but said: 'Carry my tripod hence, and build a temple to Apollo wherever it falls from your hands!' This happened to him on Mount Geraneia, where he founded first the temple and then the city of Tripodisci, and took up residence there. His tomb is shown in the market place at Megara; surmounted by a group of statuary, which depicts Poene's murder – the most ancient sculptures of that kind still surviving in Greece.[1] This second Linus is sometimes called Oetolinus, and harpists mourn him at banquets.[2]

b. A third Linus likewise lies buried at Argos: he was the poet whom some describe as a son of Oeagrus and the Muse Calliope – thus making him Orpheus's brother. Others call him the son of Apollo and the Muse

Urania, or Arethusa, a daughter of Poseidon; or of Hermes and Urania; others, again, of Amphimarus, Poseidon's son, and Urania; still others, of Magnes and the Muse Clio.[3] Linus was the greatest musician who ever appeared among mankind, and jealous Apollo killed him. He had composed ballads in honour of Dionysus and other ancient heroes, afterwards recording them in Pelasgian letters; also an epic of the Creation. Linus, in fact, invented rhythm and melody, was universally wise, and taught both Thamyris and Orpheus.[4]

c. The lament for Linus spread all over the world and is the theme, for instance, of the Egyptian *Song of Maneros*. On Mount Helicon, as one approached the Muses' grove, Linus's portrait is carved in the wall of a small grotto, where annual sacrifices to him precede those offered to the Muses. It is claimed that he lies buried at Thebes, and that Philip, father of Alexander the Great, after defeating the Greeks at Chaeronea, removed his bones to Macedonia, in accordance with a dream; but afterwards dreamed again, and sent them back.[5]

1. Pausanias: i. 43. 7 and ii. 19. 7; Conon: *Narrations* 19; Athenaeus: iii. 99.
2. Sappho, quoted by Pausanias: ix. 29. 3; Homer: *Iliad* xviii. 569–70; Hesiod, quoted by Diogenes Laertius: viii. 1. 25.
3. Apollodorus: i. 3. 2; Hyginus: *Fabula* 161; *Contest of Homer and Hesiod* 314; Diogenes Laertius: *Prooemium* 3; Pausanias: ix. 29. 3; Tzetzes: *On Lycophron* 831.
4. Diodorus Siculus: iii. 67; Diogenes Laertius: *loc. cit.*; Hesiod, quoted by Clement of Alexandria: *Stromateis* i. p. 121.
5. Pausanias: *loc. cit.*

*

1. Pausanias connects the myth of the Child Linus with that of Maneros, the Egyptian Corn-spirit, for whom dirges were chanted at harvest time; but Linus seems to have been the spirit of the flax-plant (*linos*), sown in spring and harvested in summer. He had Psamathe for mother because, according to Pliny (*Natural History* xix. 2), 'they sowed flax in *sandy* soil.' His grandfather, and murderer, was Crotopus because – again according to Pliny – the yellowing flax-stalks, after having been plucked out by the roots, and hung up in the open air, were bruised with the 'pounding feet' of tow-mallets. And Apollo, whose priests wore linen, and who was patron of all Greek music, fathered him. Linus's destruction by dogs evidently refers to the maceration of the flax-stems with iron hatchets, a process which Pliny describes in the same passage. Frazer suggests, although without supporting evidence, that Linus is a

Greek mishearing of the Phoenician *ai lanu*, 'woe upon us'. Oetolinus means 'doomed Linus'.

2. The myth has, however, been reduced to the familiar pattern of the child exposed for fear of a jealous grandfather and reared by shepherds; which suggests that the linen industry in Argolis died out, owing to the Dorian invasion or Egyptian underselling, or both, and was replaced by a woollen industry; yet the annual dirges for the child Linus continued to be chanted. The flax industry is likely to have been established by the Cretans who civilized Argolis; the Greek word for flax-rope is *merinthos*, and all -*inthos* words are of Cretan origin.

3. Coroebus, when he killed Poene ('punishment'), probably forbade child sacrifices at the Linus festival, and substituted lambs, renaming the month 'Lamb Month'; he has been identified with an Elean of the same name who won the foot-race at the First Olympiad (776 B.C.). Tripodiscus seems to have no connexion with tripods, but to be derived from *tripodizein*, 'to fetter thrice'.

4. Since the flax-harvest was the occasion of plaintive dirges and rhythmic pounding, and since at midsummer – to judge from the Swiss and Suabian examples quoted in Frazer's *Golden Bough* – young people leaped around a bonfire to make the flax grow high, another mystical Linus was presumed: one who attained manhood and became a famous musician, the inventor of rhythm and melody. This Linus had a Muse mother, and for his father Arcadian Hermes, or Thracian Oeagrius, or Magnes, the eponymous ancestor of the Magnesians; he was, in fact, not a Hellene, but guardian of the pre-Hellenic Pelasgian culture, which included the tree-calendar and Creation lore. Apollo, who tolerated no rivals in music – as he had shown in the case of Marsyas (see 21.*f*) – is said to have killed him off-hand; but this was an incorrect account, since Apollo adopted, rather than murdered, Linus. Later, his death was more appropriately laid at the door of Heracles, patron of the uncivilized Dorian invaders (see 146. 1).

5. Linus is called Orpheus's brother because of a similarity in their fate (see 28. 2). In the Austrian Alps (I am informed by Margarita Schön-Wels) men are not admitted to the flax-harvest, or to the process of drying, beating, and macerating, or to the spinning-rooms. The ruling spirit is the *Harpatsch*: a terrifying hag, whose hands and face are rubbed with soot. Any man who meets her accidentally, is embraced, forced to dance, sexually assaulted, and smeared with soot. Moreover, the women who beat the flax, called *Bechlerinnen*, chase and surround any stranger who blunders into their midst. They make him lie down, step over him, tie his hands and feet, wrap him in tow, scour his face and hands with prickly flax-waste, rub him against the rough bark of a felled tree, and finally roll him downhill. Near Feldkirch, they only make the trespasser

lie down and step over him; but elsewhere they open his trouser-flies and stuff them with flax-waste, which is so painful that he has to escape bare-legged. Near Salzburg, the Bechlerinnen untrouser the trespasser themselves, and threaten to castrate him; after his flight, they purify the place by burning twigs and clashing sickles together.

6. Little is known of what goes on in the spinning-rooms, the women being so secretive; except that they chant a dirge called the *Flachses Qual* ('Flax's Torment'), or *Leinen Klage* ('Linen Lament'). It seems likely, then, that at the flax-harvest women used to catch, sexually assault, and dismember a man who represented the flax-spirit; but since this was also the fate of Orpheus, who protested against human sacrifice and sexual orgies (see 28. *d*), Linus has been described as his brother. The *Harpatsch* is familiar: she is the carline-wife of the corn harvest, representative of the Earth-goddess. Sickles are clashed solely in honour of the moon; they are not used in the flax harvest. Linus is credited with the invention of music because these dirges are put into the mouth of the Flax-spirit himself, and because some lyre-strings were made from flaxen thread.

148

THE ARGONAUTS ASSEMBLE

AFTER the death of King Cretheus the Aeolian, Pelias, son of Poseidon, already an old man, seized the Iolcan throne from his half-brother Aeson, the rightful heir. An oracle presently warning him that he would be killed by a descendant of Aeolus, Pelias put to death every prominent Aeolian he dared lay hands upon, except Aeson, whom he spared for his mother Tyro's sake, but kept a prisoner in the palace; forcing him to renounce his inheritance.

b. Now, Aeson had married Polymele, also known as Amphinome, Perimede, Alcimede, Polymede, Polypheme, Scarphe, or Arne, who bore him one son, by name Diomedes.[1] Pelias would have destroyed the child without mercy, had not Polymele summoned her kinswomen to weep over him, as though he were still-born, and then smuggled him out of the city to Mount Pelion; where Cheiron the Centaur reared him, as he did before, or afterwards, with Asclepius, Achilles, Aeneas, and other famous heroes.[2]

c. A second oracle warned Pelias to beware a one-sandalled man and when, one day on the seashore, a group of his princely allies joined him in a solemn sacrifice to Poseidon, his eye fell upon a tall, long-haired Magnesian youth, dressed in a close-fitting leather tunic and a leopard-skin. He was armed with two broad-bladed spears, and wore only one sandal.³

d. The other sandal he had lost in the muddy river Anaurus – which some miscall the Evenus, or Enipeus – by the contrivance of a crone who, standing on the farther bank, begged passers-by to carry her across. None took pity on her, until this young stranger courteously offered her his broad back; but he found himself staggering under the weight, since she was none other than the goddess Hera in disguise. For Pelias had vexed Hera by withholding her customary sacrifices, and she was determined to punish him for this neglect.⁴

e. When, therefore, Pelias asked the stranger roughly: 'Who are you, and what is your father's name?', he replied that Cheiron, his foster-father, called him Jason, though he had formerly been known as Diomedes, son of Aeson.

Pelias glared at him balefully. 'What would you do,' he inquired suddenly, 'if an oracle announced that one of your fellow-citizens were destined to kill you?'

'I should send him to fetch the golden ram's fleece from Colchis,' Jason replied, not knowing that Hera had placed those words in his mouth. 'And, pray, whom have I the honour of addressing?'

f. When Pelias revealed his identity, Jason was unabashed. He boldly claimed the throne usurped by Pelias, though not the flocks and herds which had gone with it; and since he was strongly supported by his uncle Pheres, king of Pherae, and Amathaon, king of Pylus, who had come to take part in the sacrifice, Pelias feared to deny him his birth-right. 'But first,' he insisted, 'I require you to free our beloved country from a curse!'

g. Jason then learned that Pelias was being haunted by the ghost of Phrixus, who had fled from Orchomenus a generation before, riding on the back of a divine ram, to avoid being sacrificed. He took refuge in Colchis where, on his death, he was denied proper burial; and, according to the Delphic Oracle, the land of Iolcus, where many of Jason's Minyan relatives were settled, would never prosper unless his ghost were brought home in a ship, together with the golden ram's fleece. The fleece now hung from a tree in the grove of Colchian Ares, guarded night and day by an unsleeping dragon. Once this pious feat had been accomplished, Pelias declared, he would gladly resign the kingship, which was becoming burdensome for a man of his advanced years.⁵

h. Jason could not deny Pelias this service, and therefore sent heralds to every court of Greece, calling for volunteers who would sail with him. He also prevailed upon Argus the Thespian to build him a fifty-oared ship; and this was done at Pagasae, with seasoned timber from Mount Pelion; after which Athene herself fitted an oracular beam into the *Argo*'s prow, cut from her father Zeus's oak at Dodona.⁶

i. Many different muster-rolls of the Argonauts – as Jason's companions are called – have been compiled at various times; but the following names are those given by the most trustworthy authorities:

Acastus, son of King Pelias
Actor, son of Deion the Phocian
Admetus, prince of Pherae
Amphiaraus, the Argive seer
Great Ancaeus of Tegea, son of Poseidon
Little Ancaeus, the Lelegian of Samos
Argus the Thespian, builder of the *Argo*
Ascalaphus the Orchomenan, son of Ares
Asterius, son of Cometes, a Pelopian
Atalanta of Calydon, the virgin huntress
Augeias, son of King Phorbas of Elis
Butes of Athens, the bee-master
Caeneus the Lapith, who had once been a woman
Calais, the winged son of Boreas
Canthus the Euboean
Castor, the Spartan wrestler, one of the Dioscuri
Cepheus, son of Aleus the Arcadian
Coronus the Lapith, of Gyrton in Thessaly
Echion, son of Hermes, the herald
Erginus of Miletus
Euphemus of Taenarum, the swimmer
Euryalus, son of Mecisteus, one of the Epigoni
Eurydamas the Dolopian, from Lake Xynias
Heracles of Tiryns, the strongest man who ever lived, now a god
Hylas the Dryopian, squire to Heracles
Idas, son of Aphareus of Messene
Idmon the Argive, Apollo's son
Iphicles, son of Thestius the Aetolian

Iphitus, brother of King Eurystheus of Mycenae

Jason, the captain of the expedition

Laertes, son of Acrisius the Argive

Lynceus, the look-out man, brother to Idas

Melampus of Pylus, son of Poseidon

Meleager of Calydon

Mopsus the Lapith

Nauplius the Argive, son of Poseidon, a noted navigator

Oïleus the Locrian, father of Ajax

Orpheus, the Thracian poet

Palaemon, son of Hephaestus, an Aetolian

Peleus the Myrmidon

Peneleos, son of Hippalcimus, the Boeotian

Periclymenus of Pylus, the shape-shifting son of Poseidon

Phalerus, the Athenian archer

Phanus, the Cretan son of Dionysus

Poeas, son of Thaumacus the Magnesian

Polydeuces, the Spartan boxer, one of the Dioscuri

Polyphemus, son of Elatus, the Arcadian

Staphylus, brother of Phanus

Tiphys, the helmsman, of Boeotian Siphae

Zetes, brother of Calais

– and never before or since was so gallant a ship's company gathered together.[7]

j. The Argonauts are often known as Minyans, because they brought back the ghost of Phrixus, grandson of Minyas, and the fleece of his ram; and because many of them, including Jason himself, sprang from the blood of Minyas's daughters. This Minyas, a son of Chryses, had migrated from Thessaly to Orchomenus in Boeotia, where he founded a kingdom, and was the first king ever to build a treasury.[8]

1. Scholiast on Homer's *Odyssey* xii. 70; Diodorus Siculus: iv. 50. 1; Apollonius Rhodius: i. 232; Apollodorus: i. 9. 16; Scholiast on Apollonius Rhodius: i. 45; Tzetzes: *On Lycophron* 872.
2. Pindar: *Pythian Odes* iv. 198 ff. and *Nemean Odes* iii. 94 ff.; Homer: *Iliad* xvi. 143.
3. Apollonius Rhodius: i. 7; Apollodorus: *loc. cit.*; Pindar: *Pythian Odes* iv. 128 ff.
4. Apollonius Rhodius: i. 8–17; Apollodorus: *loc. cit.*; Pindar: *loc. cit.*; Hyginus: *Fabula* 13; Valerius Flaccus: i. 84.

5. Apollodorus: *loc. cit.*; Pindar: *loc. cit.*; Diodorus Siculus: iv. 40; Scholiast on Homer's *Odyssey* xii. 70; Hesiod: *Theogony* 992 ff.

6. Pindar: *loc. cit.*; Valerius Flaccus: i. 39; Apollodorus: *loc. cit.*

7. Apollodorus: *loc. cit.*; Pindar: *loc. cit.*; Hyginus: *Fabulae* 12 and 14–23; Apollonius Rhodius: i. 20; Diodorus Siculus: iv. 40–9; Tzetzes: *On Lycophron* 175; Ovid: *Metamorphoses* vii. 1 ff.; Valerius Flaccus: *Argonautica* i. *passim*.

8. Apollonius Rhodius: i. 229; Pausanias: ix. 36. 3.

*

1. In Homer's day, a ballad cycle about the *Argo*'s voyage to the land of Aeëtes ('mighty') was 'on everyone's lips' (*Odyssey* xii. 40), and he places the Planctae – through which she had passed even before Odysseus did – near the Islands of the Sirens, and not far from Scylla and Charybdis. All these perils occur in the fuller accounts of the *Argo*'s return from Colchis.

2. According to Hesiod, Jason, son of Aeson, after accomplishing many grievous tasks imposed by Pelias, married Aeëtes's daughter who came with him to Iolcus, where 'she was subject to him' and bore his son Medeius, whom Cheiron educated. But Hesiod seems to have been misinformed: in heroic times no princess was brought to her husband's home – he came to hers (see *137. 4* and *160. 3*). Thus Jason either married Aeëtes's daughter and settled at his court, or else he married Pelias's daughter and settled at Iolcus. Eumelus (eighth century) reports that, when Corinthus died without issue, Medea successfully claimed the vacant throne of Corinth, being a daughter of Aeëtes who, not content with his heritage, had emigrated thence to Colchis; and that Jason, her husband, thereupon became king.

3. Neither Colchis, nor its capital of Aea, are mentioned in these early accounts, which describe Aeëtes as the son of Helius, and the brother of Aeaean Circe. Nor must it be supposed that the story known to Homer had much in common with the one told by Apollodorus and Apollonius Rhodius; the course, even, of the *Argo*'s outward voyage, let alone her homeward one, was not yet fixed by Herodotus's time – for Pindar, in his *Fourth Pythian Ode* (462 B.C.), had presented a version very different from his.

4. The myth of Pelias and Diomedes – Jason's original name – seems to have been about a prince exposed on a mountain, reared by horseherds, and set seemingly impossible tasks by the king of a neighbouring city, not necessarily a usurper: such as the yoking of fire-breathing bulls, and the winning of a treasure guarded by a sea-monster – Jason, half-dead in the sea-monster's maw, is the subject of Etruscan works of art. His reward will have been to marry the royal heiress. Similar myths are common in Celtic mythology – witness the labours imposed upon Kil-hwych, the *Mabinogion* hero, when he wished to marry the sorceress Olwen – and apparently refer to ritual tests of a king's courage before his coronation.

5. It is indeed from the *Tale of Kilhwych and Olwen*, and from the similar *Tale of Peredur Son of Evrawc*, also in the *Mabinogion*, that the most plausible guesses can be made at the nature of Diomedes's tasks. Kil-hwych, falling in love with Olwen, was ordered by her father to yoke a yellow and a brindled bull, to clear a hill of thorns and scrub, sow this with corn, and then harvest the grain in a single day (see 127. 1 and 152. 3); also to win a horn of plenty, and a magic Irish cauldron. Peredur, falling in love with an unknown maiden, had to kill a water-monster, called the *Avanc*, in a lake near the Mound of Mourning – Aeaea means 'mourn-ing'. On condition that he swore faith with her, she gave him a magic stone, which enabled him to defeat the Avanc, and win 'all the gold a man might desire'. The maiden proved to be the Empress of Cristinobyl, a sorceress, who lived in great style 'towards India'; and Peredur re-mained her lover for fourteen years. Since the only other Welsh hero to defeat an *Avanc* was Hu Gadarn the Mighty, ancestor of the Cymry, who by yoking two bulls to the monster, dragged it out of the Conwy River (*Welsh Triads* iii. 97), it seems likely that Jason also hauled his monster from the water, with the help of his fire-breathing team.

6. The Irish cauldron fetched by Kilhwych was apparently the one mentioned in the *Tale of Peredur*: a cauldron of regeneration, like that subsequently used by Medea – a giant had found it at the bottom of an Irish lake. Diomedes may have been required to fetch a similar one for Pelias. The scene of his labours will have been some ungeographical country 'towards the rising sun'. No cornucopia is mentioned in the Argonaut legend, but Medea, for no clear reason, rejuvenates the nymph Macris and her sisters, formerly the nurses of Dionysus, when she meets them on Drepane, or Corcyra. Since Dionysus had much in common with the infant Zeus, whose nurse, the goat Amaltheia, provided the original cornucopia (see 7. *b*), Medea may have helped Diomedes to win another cornucopia from the nymphs by lending them her services. Heracles's Labours (like those of Theseus and Orion) are best understood as marriage tasks and included 'the breaking of the horns of both bulls' (the Cretan and the Acheloan – see 134. *6*).

7. This marriage-task myth, one version of which seems to have been current at Iolcus, with Pelias as villain, and another at Corinth, with Corinthus as villain, evidently became linked to the semi-historical legend of a Minyan sea expedition sent out from Iolcus by the Orchomenans. Orchomenus belonged to the ancient amphictyony, or league, of Cal-aureia (Strabo: viii. 6. 14), presided over by the Aeolian god Poseidon

which included six seaside states of Argos and Attica; it was the only inland city of the seven and strategically placed between the Gulf of Corinth and the Thessalian Gulf. Its people, like Hesiod's Boeotians, may have been farmers in the winter and sailors in the summer.

8. The supposed object of the expedition was to recover a sacred fleece, which had been carried away 'to the land of Aeëtes' by King Phrixus, a grandson of Minyas, when about to be sacrificed on Mount Laphystium (see 70. *d*), and to escort Phrixus's ghost home to Orchomenus. Its leader will have been a Minyan – which Diomedes son of Aeson was not – perhaps Cytisorus (Herodotus: vii. 197), son of Phrixus, whom Apollonius Rhodius brings prominently into the story (see 151. *f* and 152. *b*), and who won the surname Jason ('healer') at Orchomenus when he checked the drought and plague caused by Phrixus's escape. Nevertheless, Diomedes was a Minyan on his mother's side; and descent is likely to have been matrilinear both at Orchomenus and Pelasgian Iolcus.

9. In this Minyan legend, the land of Aeëtes cannot have lain at the other end of the Black Sea; all the early evidence points to the head of the Adriatic. The Argonauts are believed to have navigated the river Po, near the mouth of which, across the Gulf, lay Circe's Island of Aeaea, now called Lussin; and to have been trapped by Aeëtes's Colchians at the mouth of the Ister – not the Danube but, as Diodorus Siculus suggests, the small river Istrus, which gives Istria its name. Medea then killed her brother Apsyrtus, who was buried in the neighbouring Apsyrtides; and when she and Jason took refuge with Alcinous, King of Drepane (Corcyra), a few days' sail to the southward, the Colchians, cheated of their vengeance, feared to incur Aeëtes's anger by returning empty-handed and therefore built the city of Pola on the Istrian mainland. Moreover, Siren-land, the Clashing Rocks, Scylla and Charybdis, all lie close to Sicily, past which the *Argo* was then blown by the violent north-easter.

'Colchis' may, in fact, be an error for 'Colicaria' on the Lower Po, not far from Mantua, apparently a station on the Amber Route; since Helius's daughters, who wept amber tears, are brought into the story as soon as the *Argo* enters the Po (see 42. *d*). Amber was sacred to the Sun, and Electra ('amber'), the island at which the *Argo* is said to have touched, will hardly have been Samothrace, as the scholiasts believe; but 'the land of Aeëtes', a trading post at the terminus of the Amber Route – perhaps Corinthian, because Aeëtes had brought his Sun cult from Corinth, but perhaps Pelasgian, because according to Dionysius's *Description of the Earth* (i. 18) a Pelasgian colony, originating from Dodona, once maintained a powerful fleet at one of the mouths of the Po.

10. To the ungeographical myth of Diomedes, now combined with the legend of a Minyan voyage to the land of Aeëtes, a third element was added: the tradition of an early piratical raid along the southern coast of the Black Sea, made at the orders of another Minyan king. The sixth city of Troy, by its command of the Hellespont, enjoyed a monopoly of the Black Sea trade, which this raid will have been planned to challenge (see 137. 1). Now, the Minyans' supposed objective on their Adriatic voyage was not a golden, but, according to Simonides (quoted by scholiast on Apollonius Rhodius: iv. 77) a purple, fleece which the First Vatican Mythographer describes as that 'in which Zeus used to ascend to Heaven'. In other words, it was a black fleece worn in a royal rain-making rite, like the one still performed every May Day on the summit of Mount Pelion: where an old man in a black sheepskin mask is killed and brought to life again by his companions, who are dressed in white fleeces (*Annals of the British School at Athens* xvi. 244-9, 1909-16). According to Dicearchus (ii. 8), this rite was performed in Classical times under the auspices of Zeus Actaeus, or Acraeus ('of the summit'). Originally the man in the black sheepskin mask will have been the king, Zeus's representative, who was sacrificed at the close of his reign. The use of the same ceremony on Mount Pelion as on Mount Laphystium will account for the combining of the two Iolcan traditions, namely the myth of Diomedes and the legend of the Black Sea raid, with the tradition of a Minyan voyage to undo the mischief caused by Phrixus.

11. Yet the Minyans' commission will hardly have been to bring back the lost Laphystian fleece, which was easily replaced: they are far more likely to have gone in search of amber, with which to propitiate the injured deity, the Mountain-goddess. It should be remembered that the Minyans held 'Sandy Pylus' on the western coast of the Peloponnese – captured from the Lelegians by Neleus with the help of Iolcan Pelasgians (see 94. *c*) – and that, according to Aristotle (*Mirabilia* 82), the Pylians brought amber from the mouth of the Po. On the site of this Pylus (now the village of Kakovatos) huge quantities of amber have recently been unearthed.

12. On the easterly voyage this fleece became 'golden', because Diomedes's feat of winning the sea-monster treasure had to be included; and because, as Strabo points out, the Argonauts who broke into the Black Sea went in search of alluvial gold from the Colchian Phasis (now the Rion), collected by the natives in fleeces laid on the river bed. Nor was it only the confusion of Colchis with Colicaria, of Aea ('earth') with Aeaea ('wailing'), and of the Pelionian black fleece with the Laphystian, that made these different traditions coalesce. The dawn palace of Aeëtes's father Helius lay in Colchis (see 42. *a*), the most easterly country known to Homer; and *Jasonica*, shrines of Heracles the Healer, were reported from the Eastern Gulf of the Black Sea, where the Aeolians had established trading posts. According to some authorities, Heracles led the

Black Sea expedition. Moreover, since Homer had mentioned Jason only
as the father of Euneus, who provided the Greeks with wine during the
siege of Troy (see 162. i), and since Lemnos lay east of Thessaly, the *Argo*
was also thought to have headed east. The Wandering, or Clashing,
Rocks, which Homer placed in Sicilian waters, have thus been transferred
to the Bosphorus.

13. Every city needed a representative Argonaut to justify its trading
rights in the Black Sea, and travelling minstrels were willing enough to
introduce another name or two into this composite ballad cycle. Several
nominal rolls of Argonauts therefore survive, all irreconcilable, but for
the most part based on the theory that they used a fifty-oared vessel – not,
indeed, an impossibility in Mycenaean times; Tzetzes alone gives a
hundred names. Yet not even the most hardened sceptic seems to have
doubted that the legend was in the main historical, or that the voyage took
place before the Trojan War, sometime in the thirteenth century B.C.

14. Jason's single sandal proved him to be a fighting man. Aetolian
warriors were famous for their habit of campaigning with only the left
foot shod (Macrobius: v. 18–21; Scholiast on Pindar's *Pythian Odes* iv.
133), a device also adopted during the Peloponnesian War by the Plat-
aeans, to gain better purchase in the mud (Thucydides: iii. 22). Why the
foot on the shield side, rather than the weapon side, remained shod, may
have been because it was advanced in a hand-to-hand struggle, and could
be used for kicking an opponent in the groin. Thus the left was the hostile
foot, and never set on the threshold of a friend's house; the tradition
survives in modern Europe, where soldiers invariably march off to war
with the left foot foremost.

15. Hera's quarrel with Pelias, over the withholding of her sacrifice,
suggests tension between a Poseidon-worshipping Achaean dynasty at
Iolcus and the goddess-worshipping Aeolo-Magnesians, their subjects.

149

THE LEMNIAN WOMEN AND KING CYZICUS

HERACLES, after capturing the Erymanthian Boar, appeared suddenly
at Pagasae, and was invited by a unanimous vote to captain the *Argo*;
but generously agreed to serve under Jason who, though a novice, had
planned and proclaimed the expedition. Accordingly, when the ship
had been launched, and lots drawn for the benches, two oarsmen to
each bench, it was Jason who sacrificed a yoke of oxen to Apollo of
Embarkations. As the smoke of his sacrifice rose propitiously to heaven

in dark, swirling columns, the Argonauts sat down to their farewell banquet, at which Orpheus with his lyre appeased certain drunken brawls. Sailing thence by the first light of dawn, they shaped a course for Lemnos.[1]

b. About a year before this, the Lemnian men had quarrelled with their wives, complaining that they stank, and made concubines of Thracian girls captured on raids. In revenge, the Lemnian women murdered them all without pity, old and young alike, except King Thoas, whose life his daughter Hypsipyle secretly spared, setting him adrift in an oarless boat. Now, when the *Argo* hove in sight and the Lemnian women mistook her for an enemy ship from Thrace, they donned their dead husbands' armour and ran boldly shoreward, to repel the threatened attack. The eloquent Echion, however, landing staff in hand as Jason's herald, soon set their minds at rest; and Hysipyle called a council at which she proposed to send a gift of food and wine to the Argonauts, but not to admit them into her city of Myrine, for fear of being charged with the massacre. Polyxo, Hypsipyle's aged nurse, then rose to plead that, without men, the Lemnian race must presently become extinct. 'The wisest course', she said, 'would be to offer yourselves in love to those well-born adventurers, and thus not only place our island under strong protection, but breed a new and stalwart stock.'

c. This disinterested advice was loudly acclaimed, and the Argonauts were welcomed to Myrine. Hypsipyle did not, of course, tell Jason the whole truth but, stammering and blushing, explained that after much ill-treatment at the hands of their husbands, her companions had risen in arms and forced them to emigrate. The vacant throne of Lemnos, she said, was now his for the asking. Jason, although gratefully accepting her offer, declared that before settling in fertile Lemnos he must complete his quest of the Golden Fleece. Nevertheless, Hypsipyle soon persuaded the Argonauts to postpone their departure; for each adventurer was surrounded by numerous young women, all itching to bed with him.[2] Hypsipyle claimed Jason for herself, and royally she entertained him; it was then that he begot Euneus, and his twin Nebrophonus, whom some call Deiphilus, or Thoas the Younger. Euneus eventually became king of Lemnos and supplied the Greeks with wine during the Trojan War.

d. Many children were begotten on this occasion by the other Argonauts too and, had it not been for Heracles, who was guarding the *Argo* and at last strode angrily into Myrine, beating upon the house doors with his club and summoning his comrades back to duty, it is unlikely that the golden fleece would ever have left Colchis. He soon forced them down to the shore; and that same night they sailed for Samothrace, where they were duly initiated into the mysteries of Persephone and her servants, the Cabeiri, who save sailors from shipwreck.[3]

e. Afterwards, when the Lemnian women discovered that Hypsipyle, in breach of her oath, had spared Thoas – he was cast ashore on the island of Sicinos, and later reigned over the Taurians – they sold her into slavery to King Lycurgus of Nemea. But some say that Thracian pirates raided Myrine and captured her. On attaining manhood, Euneus purified the island of blood guilt, and the rites he used are still repeated at the annual festival of the Cabeiri: for the space of nine days, all Lemnian hearth-fires are extinguished, and offerings made to the dead, after which new fire is brought by ship from Apollo's altar at Delos.[4]

f. The Argonauts sailed on, leaving Imbros to starboard and, since it was well known that King Laomedon of Troy guarded the entrance to the Hellespont and let no Greek ship enter, they slipped through the Straits by night, hugging the Thracian coast, and reached the Sea of Marmara in safety. Approaching Dolionian territory, they landed at the neck of a rugged peninsula, named Arcton, which is crowned by Mount Dindymum. Here they were welcomed by King Cyzicus, the son of Aeneus, Heracles's former ally, who had just married Cleite of Phrygian Percote and warmly invited them to share his wedding banquet. While the revelry was still in progress, the *Argo*'s guards were attacked with rocks and clubs by certain six-handed Earth-born giants from the interior of the peninsula, but beat them off.

g. Afterwards, the Argonauts dedicated their anchor-stone to Athene, in whose temple it is shown to this day, and, taking aboard a heavier one, rowed away with cordial farewells, shaping a course for the Bosphorus. But a north-easterly wind suddenly whirled down upon them, and soon they were making so little way that Tiphys decided to about ship, and ran back to the lee of the peninsula. He was driven off his course; and the Argonauts, beaching their ship at random in the pitch-dark, were at once assailed by well-armed warriors. Only when they had overcome these in a fierce battle, killing some and putting the remainder to flight, did Jason discover that he had made the eastern shore of Arcton, and that noble King Cyzicus, who had mistaken the Argonauts for pirates, lay dead at his feet. Cleite, driven mad by

the news, hanged herself; and the nymphs of the grove wept so piteously that their tears formed the fountain which now bears her name.

h. The Argonauts held funeral games in Cyzicus's honour, but
remained weather-bound for many days more. At last a halcyon flut-
tered above Jason's head, and perched twittering on the prow of the
Argo; whereupon Mopsus, who understood the language of birds, explained that all would be well if they placated the goddess Rhea. She
had exacted Cyzicus's death in requital for that of her sacred lion's,
killed by him on Mount Dindymum, and was now vexed with the
Argonauts for having caused such carnage among her six-armed
Earth-born brothers. They therefore raised an image to the goddess,
carved by Argus from an ancient vine-stock, and danced in full armour
on the mountain top. Rhea acknowledged their devotion: she made a
spring – now called the Spring of Jason – gush from the neighbouring
rocks. A fair breeze then arose, and they continued the voyage. The
Dolionians, however, prolonged their mourning to a full month,
lighting no fires, and subsisting on uncooked foods, a custom which is
still observed during the annual Cyzican Games.[5]

1. Apollonius Rhodius: i. 317 ff.
2. Apollonius Rhodius: i. 1–607; Herodotus: vi. 138; Apollodorus:
   i. 9. 17; *Argonautica Orphica* 473 ff.; Valerius Flaccus: *Argonautica*
   ii. 77; Hyginus: *Fabula* 15.
3. Homer: *Iliad* vii. 468, with scholiast; Statius: *Thebaid* vi. 34;
   Apollonius Rhodius: *loc. cit.*; Apollodorus: *loc. cit.*; Valerius
   Flaccus: *loc. cit.*; Hyginus: *loc. cit.*; *Fragments of Sophocles* ii. 51 ff.,
   ed. Pearson.
4. Apollodorus: iii. 6. 4; Hyginus: *loc. cit.*; Philostratus: *Heroica* xx.
   24.
5. First Vatican Mythographer: 49; Apollonius Rhodius: i. 922 ff.
   and 935–1077; *Argonautica Orphica* 486 ff.; Valerius Flaccus:
   Argonautica ii. 634; Hyginus: *Fabula* 16.

*

1. Jason is made to call at Lemnos because, according to Homer,
Euneus, who reigned there during the Trojan War, was his son; and
because Euphemus, another Argonaut, begot Leucophanes ('white appearance') on a Lemnian woman (Tzetzes: *On Lycophron* 886; Scholiast
on Pindar's *Pythian Odes* iv. 455), thus becoming the ancestor of a long-
lived Cyrenean dynasty. The Lemnian massacre suggests that the islanders
retained the gynocratic form of society, supported by armed priestesses,
which was noted among certain Libyan tribes in Herodotus's time (see

8. *1*), and that visiting Hellenes could understand this anomaly only in terms of a female revolution. Myrine was the name of their goddess (see 131. *3*). Perhaps the Lemnian women were said to have stunk because they worked in woad – used by their Thracian neighbours for tattooing – which has so nauseous and lingering a smell that Norfolk woad-making families have always been obliged to intermarry.

2. Samothrace was a centre of the Helladic religion, and initiates into its Moon-goddess Mysteries – the secret of which has been well kept – were entitled to wear a purple amulet (Apollonius Rhodius: i. 197; Diodorus Siculus: v. 49), valued as a protection against dangers of all kinds, but especially shipwreck. Philip of Macedon and his wife Olympias became initiates (Aristophanes: *Peace* 277, with scholiast); Germanicus Caesar was prevented from taking part in the Mysteries only by an omen and died soon after (Tacitus: *Annals* ii. 54). Certain ancient bronze vessels laid up in Samothrace were said to have been dedicated by the Argonauts.

3. Rhea's brothers, the six-armed Earth-born of Bear Island, are perhaps deduced from pictures of shaggy men, wearing bear-skins with the paws extended. The account of Cyzicus's death is circumstantial enough to suggest a genuine tradition of the Black Sea raid, though one as little connected with the annual extinction of fires at Cyzicus, as was the supposed Lemnian massacre with a similar ceremony at Myrine, during the nine-day festival of the Cabeiri. At the close of the year, when the sacred king was sacrificed, fires were habitually extinguished in many kingdoms, to be renewed afterwards as one of the rites in the new king's installation.

4. The killing of Rhea's lion probably refers to the suppression of her worship at Cyzicus in favour of Olympianism.

5. Halcyons were messengers of the Sea-goddess Alcyone ('the queen who wards off [storms]' – see 45. *1–2*).

150

HYLAS, AMYCUS AND PHINEUS

AT Heracles's challenge the Argonauts now engaged in a contest to see who could row the longest. After many laborious hours, relieved only by Orpheus's lyre, Jason, the Dioscuri, and Heracles alone held out; their comrades having each in turn confessed themselves beaten. Castor's strength began to ebb, and Polydeuces, who could not otherwise induce him to desist, shipped his own oar. Jason and Heracles, however, continued to urge the *Argo* forward, seated on opposite sides of the ship, until presently, as they reached the mouth of the river Chius in Mysia, Jason fainted. Almost at once Heracles's oar snapped. He glared about him, in anger and disgust; and his weary companions, thrusting their oars through the oar-holes again, beached the *Argo* by the riverside.

b. While they prepared the evening meal, Heracles went in search of a tree which would serve to make him a new oar. He uprooted an enormous fir, but when he dragged it back for trimming beside the camp fire, found that his squire Hylas had set out, an hour or two previously, to fetch water from the near-by pool of Pegae, and not yet returned; Polyphemus was away, searching for him. Hylas had been Heracles's minion and darling ever since the death of his father, Theiodamas, king of the Dryopians, whom Heracles had killed when refused the gift of a plough-ox.

Crying 'Hylas! Hylas!', Heracles plunged frantically into the woods and soon met Polyphemus, who reported: 'Alas, I heard Hylas shouting for help; and ran towards his voice. But when I reached Pegae I found no signs of a struggle either with wild beasts or with other enemies. There was only his water-pitcher lying abandoned by the pool side.' Heracles and Polyphemus continued their search all night, and forced every Mysian whom they met to join in it, but to no avail; the fact being that Dryope and her sister-nymphs of Pegae had fallen in love with Hylas, and enticed him to come and live with them in an underwater grotto.

c. At dawn, a favourable breeze sprang up and, since neither Heracles nor Polyphemus appeared, though everyone shouted their names until the hillsides echoed, Jason gave orders for the voyage to be resumed. This decision was loudly contested and, as the *Argo* drew farther away from the shore, several of the Argonauts accused him of having marooned Heracles to avenge his defeat at rowing. They even tried to make Tiphys turn the ship about; but Calais and Zetes interposed, which is why Heracles later killed them in the island of Tenos, where he set a tottering logan-stone upon their tomb.

d. After threatening to lay Mysia waste unless the inhabitants continued their search for Hylas, dead or alive, and then leading a successful raid on Troy, Heracles resumed his Labours; but Polyphemus settled near Pegae and built the city of Crius, where he reigned until the

Chalybians killed him in battle.[1] For Heracles's sake, the Mysians still sacrifice once a year to Hylas at Prusa, near Pegae; their priest thrice calls his name aloud, and the devotees pretend to search for him in the woods.[2]

e. Hylas, indeed, suffered the same fate as Bormus, or Borimus, son of Upius, a Mariandynian youth of extraordinary beauty who once, at harvest time, went to a well to fetch water for the reapers. He too was drawn into the well by the nymphs and never seen again. The country people of Bithynia celebrate his memory every year at harvest time with plaintive songs to the accompaniment of flutes.[3]

f. Some therefore deride the story of Hylas, saying that he was really Bormus, and that Heracles had been abandoned at Magnesian Aphetae, close to Pagasae, when he went ashore to draw water, soon after the voyage began; the oracular beam of the *Argo* having announced that he would be too heavy for her to carry. Others, on the contrary, say that he not only reached Colchis, but commanded the expedition throughout.[4]

g. Next, the *Argo* touched at the island of Bebrycos, also in the Sea of Marmara, ruled by the arrogant King Amycus, a son of Poseidon. This Amycus fancied himself as a boxer, and used to challenge strangers to a match, which invariably proved their undoing; but if they declined, he flung them without ceremony over a cliff into the sea. He now approached the Argonauts, and refused them food or water unless one of their champions would meet him in the ring. Polydeuces, who had won the boxing contest at the Olympic Games, stepped forward willingly, and drew on the raw-hide gloves which Amycus offered him.

h. Amycus and Polydeuces went at it, hammer and tongs, in a flowery dell, not far from the beach. Amycus's gloves were studded with brazen spikes, and the muscles on his shaggy arms stood out like boulders covered with seaweed. He was by far the heavier man, and the younger by several years; but Polydeuces, fighting cautiously at first, and avoiding his bull-like rushes, soon discovered the weak points in his defence and, before long, had him spitting blood from a swollen mouth. After a prolonged bout, in which neither showed the least sign of flagging, Polydeuces broke through Amycus's guard, flattened his nose with a straight left-handed punch, and dealt further merciless punishment on either side of it, using hooks and jolts. In pain and desperation, Amycus grasped Polydeuces's left fist and tugged at it with his left hand, while he brought up a powerful right swing; but Polydeuces threw himself in the direction of the tug. The swing went wide, and he countered with a stunning right-handed hook to the ear, followed by so irresistible an upper cut that it broke the bones of Amycus's temple and killed him instantly.

i. When they saw their king lying dead, the Bebrycans sprang to arms, but Polydeuces's cheering companions routed them easily and sacked the royal palace. To placate Poseidon, Amycus's father, Jason then offered a holocaust of twenty red bulls, which were found among the spoils.[5]

j. The Argonauts put to sea again on the next day, and came to Salmydessus in Eastern Thrace, where Phineus, the son of Agenor, reigned. He had been blinded by the gods for prophesying the future too accurately, and was also plagued by a pair of Harpies; loathsome, winged, female creatures who, at every meal, flew into the palace and snatched victuals from his table, befouling the rest, so that it stank and was inedible. One Harpy was called Aellopus, and the other Ocypete.[6] When Jason asked Phineus for advice on how to win the golden fleece, he was told: 'First rid me of the Harpies!' Phineus's servants spread the Argonauts a banquet, upon which the Harpies immediately descended, playing their usual tricks. Calais and Zetes, however, the winged sons of Boreas, arose sword in hand, and chased them into the air and far across the sea. Some say that they caught up with the Harpies at the Strophades islands, but spared their lives when they turned back and implored mercy; for Iris, Hera's messenger, intervened, promising that they would return to their cave in Cretan Dicte and never again molest Phineus. Others say that Ocypete made terms at these islands, but that Aellopus flew on, only to be drowned in the Peloponnesian river Tigris, now called Harpys after her.

k. Phineus instructed Jason how to navigate the Bosphorus, and gave him a detailed account of what weather, hospitality, and fortune to expect on his way to Colchis, a country first colonized by the Egyptians, which lies at the easternmost end of the Black Sea, under the shadow of the Caucasus Mountains. He added: 'And once you have reached Colchis, trust in Aphrodite!'[7]

l. Now, Phineus had married first Cleopatra, sister to Calais and Zetes and then, on her death, Idaea, a Scythian princess. Idaea was jealous of Cleopatra's two sons, and suborned false witnesses to accuse them of all manner of wickedness. Calais and Zetes, however, detecting the conspiracy, freed their nephews from prison, where they were being daily flogged by Scythian guards, and Phineus not only restored them to favour, but sent Idaea back to her father.[8]

m. And some say that Phineus was blinded by the gods after the Argonauts' visit, because he had given them prophetic advice.[9]

1. Apollonius Rhodius: i. 1207 ff.; Theocritus: *Idylls* xiii; *Argonautica Orphica* 646 ff.; Valerius Flaccus: *Argonautica* iii. 521 ff.; Hyginus: *Fabula* 14; Apollodorus: i. 9. 19.
2. Theocritus: *Idylls* xiii. 73 ff.; Strabo: xii. 4. 3; Antoninus Liberalis: *Transformations* 26.
3. Athenaeus: xiv. 620; Aeschylus: *Persian Women* 941; Scholiast on Dionysius's *Description of the Earth* 791; Pollux: iv. 54.
4. Herodotus: i. 193; Apollodorus: i. 9. 19; Theocritus: *Idylls* xiii. 73 ff.
5. Apollodorus: i. 9. 20; Apollonius Rhodius: ii. 1 ff.; Theocritus: *Idylls* xxii. 27 ff.; *Argonautica Orphica* 661 ff.; Valerius Flaccus: *Argonautica* iv. 99 ff.; Hyginus: *Fabula* 17; Lactantius on Statius's *Thebaid* iii. 353.
6. Apollodorus: i. 9. 21; Hesiod: *Theogony* 265–9.
7. Herodotus: ii. 147; Apollodorus: *loc. cit.*; Apollonius Rhodius ii. 176 ff.; Valerius Flaccus: *Argonautica* iv. 22 ff.; Hyginus: *Fabula* 19; First Vatican Mythographer: 27; Servius on Virgil's *Aeneid* iii. 209.
8. Diodorus Siculus: iv. 44.
9. Apollodorus: *loc. cit.*

*

1. In the legend of the Iolcans' easterly voyage to the Black Sea – though not in that of the Minyans' westerly voyage to Istria – Heracles may have led the expedition. The story of Hylas's disappearance was invented to explain the Mysian rites, still practised at Prusa, near Pegae, in Roman times, of mourning for Adonis of the Woods. Hylas's fate at the hands of Dryope and her nymphs will have been that of Leucippus (see 21. 6), Actaeon (see 22. *i*), Orpheus (see 28. *d*), or any other sacred kings of the oak cult: namely, to be dismembered and eaten by wild women, who then purified themselves in a spring and announced that he had unaccountably vanished. 'Dryope' means 'woodpecker' (literally: 'oakface'), a bird whose tapping on the oak-trunk suggested the search for Hylas, a Dryopian by birth, and was held to portend wet weather (see 56. 1); the main object of this sacrifice being to bring on the autumn rains. Heracles, as the new king, will have pretended to join in the search for his predecessor. Bormus, or Borimus, is possibly a variant of Brimos's son Brimus (see 24. 6).

2. The story of Amycus may be derived from an icon which showed the funeral games celebrated after the old king had been flung over a cliff (see 96. 3 and 6). Boxing, a Cretan sport, mentioned in the *Iliad* and *Odyssey*, seems to have been clean enough until the civic rivalry of the Olympic Games introduced professionalism. Roman amphitheatre pugilists used spiked gloves and knuckledusters, not the traditional rawhide thongs; Theocritus, in his expert account of the Polydeuces-Amycus fight, is lamenting the lost glories of the ring.

Harpies were originally personifications of the Cretan Death-goddess as a whirlwind (Homer: *Odyssey* i. 241 and xx. 66 and 77) but, in this context, appear to have been sacred birds, kites or sea-eagles, for which the Thracians regularly set out food. Diodorus Siculus, when describing the Argonauts' visit to Phineus's court, studiously avoids any mention of the Harpies – for fear perhaps of incurring their wrath – yet contrives to hint that blind Phineus's second wife, a Scythian, tricked him by pretending that Harpies were snatching away his food, and befouling what they left, whereas his own servants were doing this at her orders. Phineus was slowly starving to death when Calais and Zetes – the brothers of his first wife – detected her guilt and released their nephews from the prison into which she had persuaded Phineus to cast them.

3. The Strophades ('turning') islands were so called because ships could expect the wind to turn as they approached.

4. Logan-stones, enormous boulders so carefully balanced that they will rock from side to side at the least impulse, are funerary monuments, apparently set up by avenue-building emigrants from Libya, towards the end of the third millennium. A few are still working in Cornwall and Devon, others have been displaced by the concerted efforts of idle soldiers or tourists. The dedication of a Tenian logan-stone to Calais and Zetes, the winged sons of Boreas, suggests that spirits of heroes were invoked to rock the boulder in the form of winds, and thus crush a live victim laid underneath.

151

FROM THE SYMPLEGADES TO COLCHIS

PHINEUS had warned the Argonauts of the terrifying rocks, called Symplegades, or Planctae, or Cyaneae which, perpetually shrouded in sea mist, guarded the entrance to the Bosphorus. When a ship attempted to pass between them, they drove together and crushed her; but, at

Phineus's advice, Euphemus let loose a dove or, some say, a heron, to fly ahead of the *Argo*. As soon as the rocks had nipped off her tail feathers, and recoiled again, the Argonauts rowed through with all speed, aided by Athene and by Orpheus's lyre, and lost only their stern ornament. Thereafter, in accordance with a prophecy, the rocks remained rooted, one on either side of the straits, and though the force of the current made the ship all but unmanageable, the Argonauts pulled at their oars until they bent like bows, and gained the Black Sea without disaster.[1]

b. Coasting along the southern shore, they presently touched at the islet of Thynias, where Apollo deigned to appear before them in a blaze of divine glory. Orpheus at once raised an altar and sacrificed a wild goat to him as Apollo of the Dawn. At his instance, the Argonauts now swore never to desert one another in time of danger, an oath commemorated in the Temple of Harmonia since built on this island.

c. Thence they sailed to the city of Mariandyne – famous for the near-by chasm up which Heracles dragged the dog Cerberus from the Underworld – and were warmly welcomed by King Lycus. News that his enemy, King Amycus, was dead had already reached Lycus by runner, and he gratefully offered the Argonauts his son Dascylus to guide them on their journey along the coast. The following day, as they were about to embark, Idmon the seer was attacked by a ferocious boar lurking in the reed-beds of the river Lycus, which gashed his thigh deeply with its great tusks. Idas sprang to Idmon's assistance and, when the boar charged again, impaled it on his spear; however, Idmon bled to death despite their care, and the Argonauts mourned him for three days. Then Tiphys sickened and died, and his comrades were plunged in grief as they raised a barrow over his ashes, beside the one that they had raised for Idmon. Great Ancaeus first, and after him Erginus, Nauplius and Euphemus, all offered to take Tiphys's place as navigator; but Ancaeus was chosen, and served them well.[2]

d. From Mariandyne they continued eastward under sail for many days, until they reached Sinope in Paphlagonia, a city named after the river Asopus's daughter, to whom Zeus, falling in love with her, had promised whatever gift she wished. Sinope craftily chose virginity, made her home here, and spent the remainder of her life in happy solitude. At Sinope, Jason found recruits to fill three of the vacant seats on his benches: namely the brothers Deileon, Autolycus, and Phlogius, of Tricca, who had accompanied Heracles on his expedition to the

Amazons but, being parted from him by accident, were now stranded in this outlandish region.

e. The *Argo* then sailed past the country of the Amazons; and that of the iron-working Chalybians, who neither till the soil, nor tend flocks, but live wholly on the gains of their forges; and the country of the Tibarenians, where it is the custom for husbands to groan, as if in child-bed, while their wives are in labour; and the country of the Moesy-noechians, who live in wooden castles, couple promiscuously, and carry immensely long spears and white shields in the shape of ivy-leaves.³

f. Near the islet of Ares, great flocks of birds flew over the *Argo*, dropping brazen plumes, one of which wounded Oileus in the shoulder. At this, the Argonauts, recalling Phineus's injunctions, donned their helmets and shouted at the top of their voices; half of them rowing, while the remainder protected them with shields, against which they clashed their swords. Phineus had also counselled them to land on the islet, and this they now did, driving away myriads of birds, until not one was left. That night they praised his wisdom, when a huge storm arose and four Aeolians clinging to a baulk of timber were cast ashore, close to their camp; these castaways proved to be Cytisorus, Argeus, Phrontis, and Melanion, sons of Phrixus by Chalciope, daughter to King Aeëtes of Colchis, and thus closely related to many of those present. They had been shipwrecked on a journey to Greece, where they were intending to claim the Orchomenan kingdom of their grand-father Athamas. Jason greeted them warmly, and all together offered sober sacrifices on a black stone in the temple of Ares, where its foundress, the Amazon Antiope, had once sacrificed horses. When Jason explained that his mission was to bring back the soul of Phrixus to Greece, and also recover the fleece of the golden ram on which he had ridden, Cytisorus and his brothers found themselves in a quandary: though owing devotion to their father's memory, they feared to offend their grandfather by demanding the fleece. However, what choice had they but to make common cause with these cousins who had saved their lives?⁴

g. The *Argo* then coasted past the island of Philyra, where Cronus once lay with Philyra, daughter of Oceanus, and was surprised by Rhea in the act; whereupon he had turned himself into a stallion, and gall-oped off, leaving Philyra to bear her child, half man, half horse – which proved to be Cheiron the learned Centaur. Loathing the monster she now had to suckle, Philyra prayed to become other than she was; and was metamorphosed into a linden-tree. But some say that this took place in Thessaly, or Thrace; not on the island of Philyra.[5]

h. Soon the Caucasus Range towered above the Argonauts, and they entered the mouth of the broad Phasis river, which waters Colchis. First pouring a libation of wine mixed with honey to the gods of the land, Jason concealed the *Argo* in a sheltered backwater, where he called a council of war.[6]

1. Apollonius Rhodius: ii. 329; *Argonautica Orphica* 688; Homer: *Odyssey* xii. 61; Herodotus: iv. 85; Pliny: *Natural History* vi. 32; Valerius Flaccus: iv. 561 ff.; Apollodorus: i. 9. 22.
2. Apollonius Rhodius: ii. 851–98; *Argonautica Orphica* 729 ff.; Tzetzes: *On Lycophron* 890; Valerius Flaccus: v. 13 ff.; Hyginus: *Fabulae* 14 and 18; Apollodorus: i. 9. 23.
3. Apollonius Rhodius: ii. 946–1028; Valerius Flaccus: v. 108; *Argonautica Orphica* 738–46; Xenophon: *Anabasis* v. 4. 1–32 and 5. 1–3.
4. Apollonius Rhodius: ii. 1030–1230.
5. Apollonius Rhodius: ii. 1231–41; Hyginus: *Fabula* 138; Philargurius on Virgil's *Georgics* iii. 93; Valerius Flaccus: v. 153; *Argonautica Orphica* 747.
6. Apollonius Rhodius: ii. 1030–1285; *Argonautica Orphica* 747–55; Valerius Flaccus: v. 153–83.

*

1. The Clashing, Wandering, or Blue Rocks, shrouded in sea mist, seem to have been ice-floes from the Russian rivers adrift in the Black Sea; reports of these were combined with discouraging accounts of the Bosphorus, down which the current, swollen by the thawing of the great Russian rivers, often runs at five knots. Other Wandering Islands in the Baltic Sea seem to have been known to the amber-merchants (see 170. 4).

2. Cenotaphs later raised by Greek colonists to honour the heroes Idmon and Tiphys may account for the story of their deaths during the voyage. Idmon is said to have been killed by a boar, like Cretan Zeus, Ancaeus, and Adonis – all early sacred kings (see 18. 7). The name Idmon ('knowing') suggests that his was an oracular shrine and, indeed, Apollonius Rhodius describes him as a seer.

3. Mariandyne is named after Ma-ri-enna (Sumerian for 'high fruitful mother of heaven'), *alias* Myrine, Ay-mari, of Mariamne, a well-known goddess of the Eastern Mediterranean. *Chalybs* was the Greek for 'iron', and 'Chalybians' seems to have been another name for the Tibarenians, the first iron workers of antiquity. In *Genesis* x. 2, their land is called Tubal (*Tubal = Tibar*), and Tubal Cain stands for the Tibarenians who

had come down from Armenia into Canaan with the Hyksos hordes. Modified forms of the *couvade* practised by the Tibarenians survive in many parts of Europe. The customs of the Moesynoechians, described by Xenophon – whose *Anabasis* Apollonius Rhodius had studied – are remarkably similar to those of the Scottish Picts and the Irish Sidhe, tribes which came to Britain in the early Bronze Age from the Black Sea region.

4. Jason's encounter with the birds on the islet of Ares, now Puga Islet, near the Kessab river, suggests that the *Argo* arrived there at the beginning of May; she will have navigated the Bosphorus before the current grew too powerful to stem, and reached Puga at the time of the great spring migration of birds from the Sinai peninsula. It appears that a number of exhausted birds, having flown across the mountains of Asia Minor, on their way to the Volga, found their usual sanctuary of Puga islet overcrowded and alighted on the *Argo*, frightening the superstitious crew nearly out of their wits. According to Nicoll's *Birds of Egypt*, these migrants include 'kestrels, larks, harriers, ducks and waders', but since the islet was dedicated to Ares, they are credited by the mythographers with brazen feathers and hostile intentions. Heracles's expulsion of the Stymphalian birds to an island in the Eastern Black Sea is likely to have been deduced from the Argonauts' adventure, rather than contrariwise as is usually supposed.

5. Cheiron's fame as a doctor, scholar, and prophet won him the title Son of Philyra ('linden'); he is also called a descendant of Ixion (see 63. *d*). Linden flowers were much used in Classical times as a restorative, and still are; moreover, the bast, or inner bark, of the linden provided handy writing tablets, and when torn into strips was used in divination (Herodotus: iv. 67; Aelian: *Varia Historia* xiv. 12). But Philyra island will have derived its name from a clump of linden-trees which grew there, rather than from any historical ties with Thessaly or Thrace. None of these coastal islands is more than a hundred yards long.

6. Colchis is now known as Georgia, and the Phasis river as the Rion.

152

THE SEIZURE OF THE FLEECE

IN Olympus, Hera and Athene were anxiously debating how their favourite, Jason, might win the golden fleece. At last they decided to approach Aphrodite, who undertook that her naughty little son Eros would make Medea, King Aeëtes's daughter, conceive a sudden passion for him. Aphrodite found Eros rolling dice with Ganymedes, but cheating at every throw, and begged him to let fly one of his arrows at Medea's heart. The payment she offered was a golden ball enamelled with blue rings, formerly the infant Zeus's plaything; when tossed into the air, it left a track like a falling star. Eros eagerly accepted this bribe, and Aphrodite promised her fellow-goddesses to keep Medea's passion glowing by means of a novel charm: a live wryneck, spread-eagled to a firewheel.

b. Meanwhile, at the council of war held in the backwater, Jason proposed going with Phrixus's sons to the near-by city of Colchian Aea, where Aeëtes ruled, and demanding the fleece as a favour; only if this were denied would they resort to guile or force. All welcomed his suggestion, and Augeias, Aeëtes's half-brother, joined the party. They approached Aea by way of Circe's riverside cemetery, where male corpses wrapped in untanned ox-hides were exposed on the tops of willow-trees for birds to eat – the Colchians bury only female corpses. Aea shone splendidly down on them from a hill, sacred to Helius, Aeëtes's father, who stabled his white horses there. Hephaestus had built the royal palace in gratitude for Helius's rescue of him when over-whelmed by the Giants during their assault on Olympus.

c. King Aeëtes's first wife, the Caucasian nymph Asterodeia, mother of Chalciope, Phrixus's widow, and of Medea, Hecate's witch-priestess, was dead some years before this; and his second wife, Eidyia, had now borne him a son, Apsyrtus.

d. As Jason and his companions approached the palace, they were met first by Chalciope, who was surprised to see Cytisorus and her other three sons returning so soon and, when she heard their story, showered thanks on Jason for his rescue of them. Next came Aeëtes, accompanied by Eidyia and showing great displeasure – for Laomedon had undertaken to prevent all Greeks from entering the Black Sea – and asked Aegeus, his favourite grandson, to explain the intrusion. Aegeus replied that Jason, to whom he and his brothers owed their lives, had come to fetch away the golden fleece in accordance with an oracle. Seeing that Aeëtes's face wore a look of fury, he added at once: 'In return for which favour, these noble Greeks will gladly subject the Sauromatians to your Majesty's rule.' Aeëtes gave a contemptuous laugh, then ordered Jason – and Augeias, whom he would not deign to acknowledge as his brother – to return whence they came, before he had their tongues cut out and their hands lopped off.

e. At this point, the princess Medea emerged from the palace, and when Jason answered gently and courteously, Aeëtes, somewhat ashamed of himself, undertook to yield the fleece, though on what seemed impossible terms. Jason must yoke two fire-breathing brazen-footed bulls, creations of Hephaestus; plough the Field of Ares to the extent of four ploughgates; and then sow it with the serpent's teeth given him by Athene, a few left over from Cadmus's sowing at Thebes. Jason stood stupefied, wondering how to perform these unheard-of feats, but Eros aimed one of his arrows at Medea, and drove it into her heart, up to the feathers.

f. Chalciope, visiting Medea's bedroom that evening, to enlist her help on behalf of Cytisorus and his brothers, found that she had fallen head over heels in love with Jason. When Chalcipoe offered herself as a go-between, Medea eagerly undertook to help him yoke the fire-breathing bulls and win the fleece; making it her sole condition that she should sail back in the *Argo* as his wife.

g. Jason was summoned, and swore by all the gods of Olympus to keep faith with Medea for ever. She offered him a flask of lotion, blood-red juice of the two-stalked, saffron-coloured Caucasian crocus, which would protect him against the bulls' fiery breath; this potent flower first sprang from the blood of the tortured Prometheus. Jason gratefully accepted the flask and, after a libation of honey, unstoppered it and bathed his body, spear and shield in the contents. He was thus able to subdue the bulls and harness them to a plough with an adamantine yoke. All day he ploughed, and at nightfall sowed the teeth, from which armed men immediately sprouted. He provoked these to fight one against another, as Cadmus had done on a similar occasion, by throwing a stone quoit into their midst; then dispatched the wounded survivors.

h. King Aeëtes, however, had no intention of parting with the fleece, and shamelessly repudiated his bargain. He threatened to burn the *Argo*, which was now moored off Aea, and massacre her crew; but Medea, in whom he had unwisely confided, led Jason and a party of Argonauts to the precinct of Ares, some six miles away. There the fleece hung, guarded by a loathsome and immortal dragon of a thousand coils, larger than the *Argo* herself, and born from the blood of the monster Typhon, destroyed by Zeus. She soothed the hissing dragon with incantations and then, using freshly-cut sprigs of juniper, sprinkled soporific drops on his eyelids. Jason stealthily unfastened the fleece from the oak-tree, and together they hurried down to the beach where the *Argo* lay.

i. An alarm had already been raised by the priests of Ares, and in a running fight, the Colchians wounded Iphitus, Meleager, Argus, Atalanta, and Jason. Yet all of them contrived to scramble aboard the waiting *Argo*, which was rowed off in great haste, pursued by Aeëtes's galleys. Iphitus alone succumbed to his wounds; Medea soon healed the others with vulneraries of her own invention.[1]

j. Now, the Sauromatians whom Jason had undertaken to conquer were descendants of three shiploads of Amazons captured by Heracles during his Ninth Labour; they broke their fetters and killed the sailors set as guards over them, but knowing nothing of seamanship, drifted across to the Cimmerian Bosphorus, where they landed at Cremni in the country of the free Scythians. There they captured a herd of wild horses, mounted them and began to ravage the land. Presently the Scythians, discovering from some corpses which fell into their hands that the invaders were women, sent out a band of young men to offer the Amazons love rather than battle. This did not prove difficult, but the Amazons consented to marry them only if they would move to the eastern bank of the river Tanais; where their descendants, the Sauromatians, still live and preserve certain Amazon customs, such as that every girl must have killed a man in battle before she can find a husband.[2]

1. Apollodorus: i. 9. 23; Apollonius Rhodius: ii. 1260–iv. 246; Diodorus Siculus: iv. 48. 1–5; Valerius Flaccus: v. 177–viii. 139; Hyginus: *Fabula* 22; Pindar: *Pythian Odes* iv. 221 ff.; Ovid: *Metamorphoses* vii. 1. 138–9; Plutarch: *On Rivers* v. 4; *Argonautica Orphica* 755–1012.
2. Herodotus: iv. 110–17.

*

1. This part of the legend embodies the primitive myth of the tasks imposed on Diomedes by the king whose daughter he wished to marry.

2. Aphrodite's love charm, carefully described by Theocritus (*Idylls* ii. 17), was used throughout Greece, including Socrates's circle (Xenophon: *Memorabilia* iii. 11. 17). Because the wryneck builds in willows, hisses like a snake and lays white eggs, it has always been sacred to the moon; Io ('moon') sent it as her messenger to amorous Zeus (see 56. *a*). One of its popular names in Europe is 'cuckoo's mate', and the cuckoo appears in the story of how Zeus courted the Moon-goddess Hera (see

12. *a*). Fire-kindling by friction was sympathetic magic to cause love – as the English word *punk* means both tinder and a harlot. Eros with torch and arrows is post-Homeric but, by the time of Apollonius Rhodius, his naughty behaviour and Aphrodite's despair had become a literary joke (see 18. *a*) which Apuleius took one stage further in *Cupid and Psyche*.

3. The Colchian custom of wrapping corpses in hides and exposing them on the tops of willow-trees recalls the Parsee custom of leaving them on platforms for the vultures to eat, in order not to defile the sacred principle of fire, the Sun's holy gift, by the act of cremation. Apollonius Rhodius mentions it, apparently to emphasize Pelias's concern for Phrixus's ghost: being a Greek, he could not consider it an adequate funeral rite. Aeëtes's fire-breathing bulls, again, recall those brazen ones in which prisoners were roasted alive by Phalaris of Agrigentum – a Rhodian colony – presumably in honour of their god Helius, whose symbol was a brazen bull (Pindar: *Pythian Odes* i. 185, with scholiast); but the sown men with whom Jason contended are inappropriate to the story. Though it was reasonable for Cadmus, a Canaanite stranger, to fight the Pelasgian autochthons when he invaded Boeotia (see 58. *g*), Jason as a native-born candidate for the kingship will rather have been set Kilhwych's task of ploughing, sowing, and reaping a harvest in one day (see 148. *5*) – a ritual act easily mimed at midsummer – then wrestled with a bull and fought the customary mock battle against men in beast-disguise. His winning of the golden fleece is paralleled by Heracles's winning of the golden apples, which another unsleeping dragon guarded (see 133. *a*). At least four of Heracles's Labours seem to have been imposed on him as a candidate for the kingship (see 123. *1*; 124. *2*; 127. *1* and 129. *1*).

4. Jason and Heracles are, in fact, the same character so far as the marriage-task myth is concerned; and the First and Seventh Labours survive vestigially here in the killing of the Mariandynian Boar and the Cyzican Lion, with both of which Jason should have been credited. 'Jason' was, of course, a title of Heracles.

5. Medea's Colchian crocus is the poisonous *colchicum*, or meadow-saffron, used by the ancients as the most reliable specific against gout, as it still remains. Its dangerous reputation contributed to Medea's.

6. The Sauromatians were the mounted Scythian bowmen of the steppes (see 132. *6*); no wonder Aeëtes laughed at the notion that Jason and his heavily armed infantry could subdue them.

THE MURDER OF APSYRTUS

MANY different accounts survive of the *Argo*'s return to Thessaly, though it is generally agreed that, following Phineus's advice, the Argonauts sailed counter-sunwise around the Black Sea. Some say that when Aeëtes overtook them, near the mouth of the Danube, Medea killed her young half-brother Apsyrtus, whom she had brought aboard, and cut him into pieces, which she consigned one by one to the swift current. This cruel stratagem delayed the pursuit, because obliging Aeëtes to retrieve each piece in turn for subsequent burial at Tomi.[1] The true name of Medea's half-brother is said to have been Aegialeus; for 'Apsyrtus', meaning 'swept down', merely records what happened to his mangled limbs after he had died.[2] Others place the crime at Aea itself, and say that Jason also killed Aeëtes.[3]

b. The most circumstantial and coherent account, however, is that Apsyrtus, sent by Aeëtes in pursuit of Jason, trapped the *Argo* at the mouth of the Danube, where the Argonauts agreed to set Medea ashore on a near-by island sacred to Artemis, leaving her in charge of a priestess for a few days; meanwhile a king of the Brygians would judge the case and decide whether she was to return home or follow Jason to Greece, and in whose possession the fleece should remain. But Medea sent a private message to Apsyrtus, pretending that she had been forcibly abducted, and begging him to rescue her. That night, when he visited the island and thereby broke the truce, Jason followed, lay in wait and struck him down from behind. He then cut off Apsyrtus's extremities, and thrice licked up some of the fallen blood, which he spat out again each time, to prevent the ghost from pursuing him. As soon as Medea was once more aboard the *Argo*, the Argonauts attacked the leaderless Colchians, scattered their flotilla, and escaped.[4]

c. Some would have it that, after Apsyrtus's murder, the *Argo* turned back and sailed up the Phasis into the Caspian Sea, and thence into the Indian Ocean, regaining the Mediterranean by way of Lake Tritonis.[5] Others, that she sailed up the Danube and Save, and then down the Po, which joins the Save, into the Adriatic Sea;[6] but was pursued by storms and driven around the whole coast of Italy, until she reached Circe's island of Aeaea. Others again, that she sailed up the Danube, and then reached Circe's island by way of the Po and the eddying pools where it is joined by the mighty Rhône.⁷

d. Still others hold that the Argonauts rowed up the Don until they reached its source; then dragged the *Argo* to the headwaters of another river which runs north into the Gulf of Finland. Or that from the Danube they dragged her to the source of the river Elbe and, borne on its waters, reached Jutland. And that they then shaped a westerly course towards the Ocean, passing by Britain and Ireland, and reached Circe's island after sailing between the Pillars of Heracles and along the coasts of Spain and Gaul.⁸

e. These are not, however, feasible routes. The truth is that the *Argo* returned by the Bosphorus, the way she had come, and passed through the Hellespont in safety, because the Trojans could no longer oppose her passage. For Heracles, on his return from Mysia, had collected a fleet of six ships [supplied by the Dolionians and their Percotean allies] and, sailing up the river Scamander under cover of darkness, surprised and destroyed the Trojan fleet. He then battered his way into Troy with his club, and demanded from King Laomedon the man-eating mares of King Diomedes, which he had left in his charge some years previously. When Laomedon denied any knowledge of these, Heracles killed him and all his sons, except the infant Podarces, or Priam, whom he appointed king in his stead.⁹

f. Jason and Medea were no longer aboard the *Argo*. Her oracular beam had spoken once more, refusing to carry either of them until they had been purified of murder, and from the mouth of the Danbue they had set out overland for Aeaea, the island home of Medea's aunt Circe. This was not the Campanian Aeaea where Circe later went to live, but her former Istrian seat; and Medea led Jason there by the route down which the straw-wrapped gifts of the Hyperboreans are yearly brought to Delos. Circe, to whom they came as suppliants, grudgingly purified them with the blood of a young sow.¹⁰

g. Now, their Colchian pursuers had been warned not to come back without Medea and the fleece and, guessing that she had gone to Circe for purification, followed the *Argo* across the Aegean Sea, around the Peloponnese, and up the Illyrian coast, rightly concluding that Medea and Jason had arranged to be fetched from Aeaea.¹¹

h. Some, however, say that Apsyrtus was still commanding the Colchian flotilla at this time, and that Medea trapped and murdered him in one of the Illyrian islands now called the Apsyrtides.¹²

1. Apollodorus: i. 9. 24; Pherecydes, quoted by scholiast on Apollonius Rhodius: iv. 223 and 228; Ovid: *Tristia* iii. 9; Stephanus of Byzantium *sub* Tomeus.
2. Cicero: *On the Nature of the Gods* iii. 19; Justin: xlii. 3; Diodorus Siculus: iv. 45.
3. Sophocles, quoted by scholiast on Apollonius Rhodius: iv. 228; Euripides: *Medea* 1334; Diodorus Siculus: iv. 48.
4. Apollonius Rhodius: iv. 212–502.
5. Pindar: *Pythian Odes* iv. 250 ff.; Mimnermus, quoted by Strabo: i. 2. 40.
6. Apollodorus: i. 9. 24; Diodorus Siculus: iv. 56. 7–8.
7. Apollonius Rhodius: iv. 608–560.
8. Timaeus, quoted by Diodorus Siculus: iv. 56. 3; *Argonautica Orphica* 1030–1204.
9. Diodorus Siculus: iv. 48; Homer: *Odyssey* xii. 69 ff. and *Iliad* v. 638 ff.
10. Apollodorus: *loc. cit.*; Herodotus: iv. 33; Apollonius Rhodius: iv. 659–717.
11. Hyginus: *Fabula* 23; Apollodorus: *loc. cit.*
12. Strabo: vii. 5. 5.

*

1. The combination of the westerly with the easterly voyage passed muster until Greek geographical knowledge increased and it became impossible to reconcile the principal elements in the story: namely, the winning of the fleece from the Phasis, and the purification of Medea and Jason by Circe, who lived either in Istria or off the western coast of Italy. Yet, since no historian could afford to offend his public by rejecting the voyage as fabulous, the Argonauts were supposed, at first, to have returned from the Black Sea by way of the Danube, the Save, and the Adriatic; then, when explorers found that the Save does not enter the Adriatic, a junction was presumed between the Danube and the Po, down which the *Argo* could have sailed; and when, later, the Danube proved to be navigable only up to the Iron Gates, and not to join the Po, she was held to have passed up the Phasis into the Caspian Sea, and thus into the Indian Ocean (where another Colchis stretched along the Malabar coast – Ptolemy Hephaestionos: viii. 1. 10), and back by way of the 'Ocean Stream' and Lake Tritonis.

2. The feasibility of this third route, too, being presently denied, mythographers suggested that the *Argo* had sailed up the Don, presumed to have its source in the Gulf of Finland, from which she could circumnavigate Europe, and return to Greece through the Straits of Gibraltar. Or somehow to have reached the Elbe by way of the Danube and a long *portage*, then sailed down to its mouth and so home, coasting past Ireland

and Spain. Diodorus Siculus, who had the sense to see that the *Argo* could have returned only through the Bosphorus, as she came, discussed this problem most realistically, and made the illuminating point that the Ister (now the Danube) was often confused with the Istrus, a trifling stream which entered the Adriatic near Trieste. Indeed, even in the time of Augustus, the geographer Pomponius Mela could report (ii. 3. 13 and 4. 4) that the western branch of the Danube 'flows into the Adriatic with a turbulence and violence equal to that of the Po'. The seizure of the fleece, the Colchians' pursuit, and the death of Apsyrtus, will all have originally taken place in the northern Adriatic. Ovid preferred to believe that Apsyrtus had been murdered at the mouth of the Danube and buried at Tomi: because that was his own destined death-place.

3. Aeaea (see 170. *i–l* and 5) is said to have belonged to Chryses, father of Minyas, and great-grandfather of Phrixus; and *Chryses* means 'golden'. It may well have been his spirit, rather than that of Phrixus, which the Minyans were ordered to appease when they fetched the fleece. According to Strabo, Phrixus enjoyed a hero-shrine in Moschia on the Black Sea, 'where a ram is never sacrificed'; this will, however, have been a late foundation, prompted by the fame of the *Argo*'s voyage – thus the Romans also built temples to Greek heroes and heroines ficti- tiously introduced into their national history.

4. The name 'Apsyrtus', which commemorates the sweeping of his remains downstream, was perhaps a local title of Orpheus after his dis- memberment by the Maenads (see 28. *d*).

5. Valerius Flaccus and Diodorus Siculus both record that Heracles sacked Troy on the outward, not the homeward, voyage; but this seems to be a mistake.

154

THE *ARGO* RETURNS TO GREECE

ARRIVED at Corcyra, which was then named Drepane, the Colchians found the *Argo* beached opposite the islet of Macris; her crew were joyfully celebrating the successful outcome of their expedition. The Colchian leader now visited King Alcinous and Queen Arete, demand- ing on Aeëtes's behalf the surrender of Medea and the fleece. Arete, to whom Medea had appealed for protection, kept Alcinous awake that night by complaining of the ill-treatment to which fathers too often subject their errant daughters: for instance, of Nycteus's cruelty to

Antiope, and of Acrisius's to Danaë. 'Even now,' she said, 'that poor princess Metope languishes in an Epeirot dungeon, at the orders of her ogreish father, King Echetus! She has been blinded with brazen spikes, and set to grind iron barley-corns in a heavy quern: "When they are flour, I will restore your sight," he taunts the poor girl. Aeëtes is capable of treating this charming Medea with equal barbarity, if you give him the chance.'[1]

b. Arete finally prevailed upon Alcinous to tell her what judgement he would deliver next morning, namely: 'If Medea is still a virgin, she shall return to Colchis; if not, she is at liberty to stay with Jason.' Leaving him sound asleep, Arete sent her herald to warn Jason what he must expect; and he married Medea without delay in the Cave of Macris, the daughter of Aristaeus and sometime Dionysus's nurse. The Argonauts celebrated the wedding with a sumptuous banquet and spread the golden fleece over the bridal couch. Judgement was duly delivered in the morning, Jason claimed Medea as his wife, and the Colchians could neither implement Aeëtes's orders nor, for fear of his wrath, return home. Some therefore settled in Corcyra, and others occupied those Illyrian islands, not far from Circe's Aeaea, which are now called the Apsyrtides; and afterwards built the city of Pola on the Istrian mainland.[2]

c. When, a year or two later, Aeëtes heard of these happenings, he nearly died of rage and sent a herald to Greece demanding the person of Medea and requital for the injuries done him; but was informed that no requital had yet been made for Io's abduction by men of Aeëtes's race (though the truth was that she fled because a gadfly pursued her) and none should therefore be given for the voluntary departure of Medea.[3]

d. Jason now needed only to double Cape Malea, and return with the fleece to Iolcus. He cruised in safety past the Islands of the Sirens, where the ravishing strains of these bird-women were countered by the even lovelier strains of Orpheus's lyre. Butes alone sprang overboard in an attempt to swim ashore, but Aphrodite rescued him; she took him to Mount Eryx by way of Lilybaeum, and there made him her lover. Some say that the Sirens, who had already lost their wings as a result of an unsuccessful singing contest with the Muses, sponsored by Hera, committed suicide because of their failure to outcharm Orpheus; yet they were still on their island when Odysseus came by a generation later.[4]

e. The Argonauts then sailed in fine weather along the coast of

Eastern Sicily, where they watched the matchless white herds of Helius grazing on the shore, but refrained from stealing any of them.[5] Suddenly they were struck by a frightful North Wind which, in nine days' time, drove them to the uttermost parts of Libya; there, an enormous wave swept the *Argo* over the perilous rocks which line the coast and retreated, leaving her high and dry a mile or more inland. A lifeless desert stretched as far as the eye could see, and the Argonauts had already prepared themselves for death, when the Triple-goddess Libya, clad in goat skins, appeared to Jason in a dream and gave him reassurance. At this, they took heart, and [setting the *Argo* on rollers] moved her by the force of their shoulders to the salt Lake Tritonis, which lay several miles off, a task that occupied twelve days. All would have died of thirst, but for a spring which Heracles, on his way to fetch the golden apples of the Hesperides, had recently caused to gush from the ground.[6]

f. Canthus was now killed by Caphaurus, a Garamantian shepherd whose flocks he was driving off, but his comrades avenged him.[7] And hardly had the two corpses been buried than Mopsus trod upon a Libyan serpent which bit him in the heel; a thick mist spread over his eyes, his hair fell out, and he died in agony. The Argonauts, after giving him a hero's burial, once more began to despair, being unable to find any outlet to the Lake.[8]

g. Jason, however, before he embarked on this voyage, had consulted the Pythoness at Delphi who gave him two massive brazen tripods, with one of which Orpheus now advised him to propitiate the deities of the land. When he did so, the god Triton appeared and took up the tripod without so much as a word of thanks; but Euphemus barred his way and asked him politely: 'Pray, my lord, will you kindly direct us to the Mediterranean Sea?' For answer, Triton merely pointed towards the Tacapae river but, as an afterthought, handed him a clod of earth, which gave his descendants sovereignty over Libya to this day. Euphemus acknowledged the gift with the sacrifice of a sheep, and Triton consented to draw the *Argo* along by her keel, until once more she entered the Mediterranean Sea, predicting, as he went, that when the descendant of a certain Argonaut should seize and carry off the brazen tripod from his temple, a hundred Greek cities would rise around Lake Tritonis. The Libyan troglodytes, overhearing these words, at once hid the tripod in the sand; and the prophecy has not yet been fulfilled.[9]

h. Heading northward, the Argonauts reached Crete, where they were prevented from landing by Talos the bronze sentinel, a creation of Hephaestus, who pelted the *Argo* with rocks, as was his custom. Medea called sweetly to this monster, promising to make him immortal if he drank a certain magic potion; but it was a sleeping draught and, while he slept, she removed the bronze nail which stoppered the single vein running from his neck to his ankles. Out rushed the divine ichor, a colourless liquid serving him for blood, and he died. Some, however, say that, bewitched by Medea's eyes, Talos staggered about, grazed his heel against a rock, and bled to death. Others, that Poeas shot him in the heel with an arrow.[10]

i. On the following night, the *Argo* was caught in a storm from the south, but Jason invoked Apollo, who sent a flash of light, revealing to starboard the island of Anaphe, one of the Sporades, where Ancaeus managed to beach the ship. In gratitude, Jason raised an altar to Apollo; and Medea's twelve Phaeacian bond-maidens, given her by Queen Arete, laughed merrily when, for lack of a victim, he and his comrades poured water libations upon the burning brands of the sacrifice. The Argonauts taunted them in reply, and tussled amorously with them – a custom which survives to this day at the Autumn Festival of Anaphe.

j. Sailing to Aegina, they held a contest: as to who could first draw a pitcher of water and carry it back to the ship; a race still run by the Aeginetans. From Aegina it was a simple voyage to Iolcus, such as scores of ships make every year, and they made it in fair weather without danger.[11]

k. Some minstrels arrange these events in a different order: they say that the Argonauts repopulated Lemnos on the homeward journey, not as they were sailing for Colchis;[12] others, that their visit to Libya took place before the voyage to Aea began, when Jason went in the *Argo* to consult the Delphic Oracle and was driven off his course by a sudden storm.[13] Others again hold that they cruised down the western coast of Italy and named a harbour in the island of Elba, where they landed, 'Argous' after the *Argo*, and that when they scraped off their sweat on the beach, it turned into pebbles of variegated forms. Further, that they founded the temple of Argive Hera at Leucania; that, like Odysseus, they sailed between Scylla and Charybdis; and that Thetis with her Nereids guided them past the flame-spouting Planctae, or Wandering Rocks, which are now firmly anchored to the sea-bed.[14]

l. Still others maintain that Jason and his companions explored the country about Colchian Aea, advancing as far as Media; that one of them, Armenus, a Thessalian from Lake Boebe, settled in Armenia, and gave his name to the entire country. This view they justify by pointing out that the heroic monuments in honour of Jason, which Armenus erected at the Caspian Gates, are much revered by the barbarians; and that the Armenians still wear the ancient Thessalian dress.[15]

1. Apollonius Rhodius: iv. 1090–95; Homer: *Odyssey* xviii. 83 and xxi. 307, with scholiast.
2. Strabo: i. 2. 39 and vii. 5. 5; Apollonius Rhodius: iv. 511 –21; Hyginus: *Fabula* 23; Apollodorus: i. 9. 25; Callimachus, quoted by Strabo: i. 2. 39.
3. Herodotus: i. 1.
4. Pausanias: ix. 34. 2; Strabo: vi. 1. 1; *Argonautica Orphica* 1284; Homer: *Odyssey* xii. 1–200.
5. Apollonius Rhodius: iv. 922–79; *Argonautica Orphica* 1270–97; Hyginus: *Fabula* 14.
6. Apollonius Rhodius: iv. 1228–1460.
7. Hyginus: *loc. cit.*; Apollonius Rhodius: iv. 1461–95; Valerius Flaccus: vi. 317 and vii. 422.
8. Tzetzes: *On Lycophron* 881; Apollonius Rhodius: iv. 1518–36.
9. Pindar: *Pythian Odes* iv. 17–39 and 255–61; Apollonius Rhodius: iv. 1537–1628; Diodorus Siculus: iv. 56. 6; *Argonautica Orphica* 1335–6; Herodotus: iv. 179.
10. Apollodorus: i. 9. 26; Apollonius Rhodius: iv. 1639–93; *Argonautica Orphica* 1337–40; Lucian: *On the Dance* 49; Sophocles, quoted by scholiast on Apollonius Rhodius: iv. 1638.
11. Apollonius Rhodius: iv. 1765–72; Apollodorus: *loc. cit.*; *Argonautica Orphica* 1344–8.
12. Pindar: *Pythian Odes* iv. 252.
13. Herodotus: iii. 127.
14. Strabo: v. 2. 6 and vi. 1. 1; Apollodorus: i. 9. 24; Apollonius Rhodius: iv. 922 ff.
15. Strabo: xi. 14. 12 and 13. 10.

*

1. The myth of Metope, given in full neither by Homer nor by Apollonius Rhodius, recalls those of Arne (see 43. *2*) and Antiope (see 76. *b*). She has, it seems, been deduced from an icon showing the Fate-goddess seated in a tomb; her quern being the world-mill around which, according to Varro's *Treatise on Rustic Affairs*, the celestial system turns, and which appears both in the Norse *Edda*, worked by the giantesses Fenja and Menja, and in *Judges*, worked by the blinded Tyrian Sun-hero Samson. Demeter, goddess of corn-mills, was an underground deity.

2. Herodotus's account of Aeëtes's embassy to Greece makes little sense, unless he held that the Argive princess Io did not flee to Colchis in

a fit of madness, disguised as a heifer, and eventually become deified by the Egyptians as Isis (see 56. *b*), but was taken in a raid by the Colchians (whom he describes as relics of Pharaoh Sesostris's army that invaded Asia) and sold into Egypt.

3. The three Sirens – Homer makes them only two – were singing daughters of Earth, who beguiled sailors to the meadows of their island, where the bones of former victims lay mouldering in heaps (*Odyssey* xii. 39 ff. and 184 ff.). They were pictured as bird-women, and have much in common with the Birds of Rhiannon in Welsh myth, who mourned for Bran and other heroes; Rhiannon was a mare-headed Demeter. Siren-land is best understood as the sepulchral island which receives the dead king's ghost, like Arthur's Avalon (see 31. 2); the Sirens were both the priestesses who mourned for him, and the birds that haunted the island – servants of the Death-goddess. As such, they belonged to a pre-Olympian cult – which is why they are said to have been worsted in a contest with Zeus's daughters, the Muses. Their home is variously given as the Siren-usian Islands off Paestum; Capri; and 'close to Sicilian Cape Pelorus' (Strabo: i. 2. 12). Pairs of Sirens were still carved on tombs in the time of Euripides (*Helen* 167), and their name is usually derived from *seirazein*, 'to bind with a cord'; but if, as is more likely, it comes from the other *seirazein* which means 'to dry up', the two Sirens will have represented twin aspects of the goddess at midsummer when the Greek pastures dry up: Ante-vorta and Post-vorta – she who looks prophetically forward to the new king's reign and she who mourns the old (see 170. 7). The mermaid type of Siren is post-Classical.

4. Helius's herd consisted of three hundred and fifty head, the gift of his mother, the Moon-goddess (see 42. 1 and 170. 10). Several colonies from Corinth and Rhodes, where his sky-bull was worshipped, had been planted in Sicily. Odysseus knew Helius as 'Hyperion' (see 170. *u*).

5. Lake Tritonis, once an enormous inland sea that had overwhelmed the lands of the neolithic Atlantians, has been slowly shrinking ever since, and though still of respectable size in Classical times – the geographer Scylax reckoned it at some nine hundred square miles – is now reduced to a line of salt marshes (see 39. 6). Neith, the skin-clad Triple-goddess of Libya, anticipated Athene with her aegis (see 8. 1).

6. Mopsus, whose death by snake-bite in the heel was a common one (see 106. *g*; 117. *c* and 168. *e*) appears also in the myth of Derceto (see 89. 2), the Philistine Dictynna. Another Mopsus, Teiresias's grandson, survived the Trojan War (see 169. *c*).

7. Caphaurus is an odd name for a Libyan – *caphaura* being the Arabic for 'camphor', which does not grow in Libya – but the mythographers had a poor sense of geography.

8. Talos the bronze man is a composite character: partly sky-bull,

partly sacred king with a vulnerable heel, partly a demonstration of the *cire-perdue* method of bronze casting (see 92. 8).

9. The water-sacrifice at Anaphe recalls that offered by the Jews on the Day of Willows, the climax of their festival of Tabernacles, when water was brought up in solemn procession from the Pool of Siloam; the Aeginetan water-race will have been part of a similar ceremony. Tabernacles began as an autumn fertility feast and, according to the Talmud, the Pharisees found it difficult to curb the traditional 'lightheadedness' of the women.

10. 'Pebbles of variegated form', iron crystals, are still found on the shores of Elba.

11. Thetis guided the *Argo* through the Planctae at the entrance to the Straits of Messina, as Athene guided her through the Planctae at the entrance to the Bosphorus. Odysseus avoided them by choosing the passage between Scylla and Charybdis (see 170. *t*). The western Planctae are the volcanic Lipari Islands.

12. Armenia, meaning Ar-Minni, 'the high land of Minni' – Minni is summoned by Jeremiah (li. 27) to war against Babylon – has no historical connexion with Armenus of Lake Boebe. But *Minni* is apparently the Minyas whom Josephus mentions (*Antiquities* i. 1. 6) when describing Noah's Flood: and the name of the Thessalian Minyas, ancestor of the Minyans, offered a plausible link between Armenia and Thessaly.

155

THE DEATH OF PELIAS

ONE autumn evening, the Argonauts regained the well-remembered beach of Pagasae, but found no one there to greet them. Indeed, it was rumoured in Thessaly that all were dead; Pelias had therefore been emboldened to kill Jason's parents, Aeson and Polymele, and an infant son, Promachus, born to them since the departure of the *Argo*. Aeson, however, asked permission to take his own life and, his plea being granted, drank bull's blood and thus expired; whereupon Polymele killed herself with a dagger or, some say, a rope, after cursing Pelias, who mercilessly dashed out Promachus's brains on the palace floor.[1]

b. Jason, hearing this doleful story from a solitary boatman, forbade him to spread the news of the *Argo*'s homecoming, and summoned a council of war. All his comrades were of the opinion that Pelias deserved death, but when Jason demanded an immediate assault on Iolcus, Acastus remarked that he could hardly be expected to oppose his father; and the others thought it wiser to disperse, each to his own home and there, if necessary, raise contingents for a war on Jason's behalf. Iolcus, indeed, seemed too strongly garrisoned to be stormed by a company so small as theirs.

c. Medea, however, spoke up and undertook to reduce the city singlehanded. She instructed the Argonauts to conceal their ship, and themselves, on some wooded and secluded beach within sight of Iolcus. When they saw a torch waved from the palace roof, this would mean that Pelias was dead, the gates open, and the city theirs for the taking.

d. During her visit to Anaphe, Medea had found a hollow image of Artemis and brought it aboard the *Argo*. She now dressed her twelve Phaeacian bond-maidens in strange disguises and led them, each in turn carrying the image, towards Iolcus. On reaching the city gates Medea, who had given herself the appearance of a wrinkled crone, ordered the sentinels to let her pass. She cried in a shrill voice that the goddess Artemis had come from the foggy land of the Hyperboteans, in a chariot drawn by flying serpents, to bring good fortune to Iolcus. The startled sentinels dared not disobey, and Medea with her bond-maidens, raging through the streets like maenads, roused the inhabitants to a religious frenzy.

e. Awakened from sleep, Pelias inquired in terror what the goddess required of him. Medea answered that Artemis was about to acknowledge his piety by rejuvenating him, and thus allowing him to beget heirs in place of the unfilial Acastus, who had lately died in a shipwreck off the Libyan coast. Pelias doubted this promise, until Medea, by removing the illusion of old age that she had cast about herself, turned young again before his very eyes. 'Such is the power of Artemis!' she cried. He then watched while she cut a bleary-eyed old ram into thirteen pieces and boiled them in a cauldron. Using Colchian spells, which he mistook for Hyperborean ones, and solemnly conjuring Artemis to assist her, Medea then pretended to rejuvenate the dead ram – for a frisky lamb was hidden, with other magical gear, inside the goddess's hollow image. Pelias, now wholly deceived, consented to lie on a couch, where Medea soon charmed him to sleep. She then commanded his daughters, Alcestis, Evadne, and Amphinome, to cut him up, just as they had seen her do with the ram, and boil the pieces in the same cauldron.

f. Alcestis piously refused to shed her father's blood in however good a cause; but Medea, by giving further proof of her magic powers, persuaded Evadne and Amphinome to wield their knives with resolution. When the deed was done, she led them up to the roof, each carrying a torch, and explained that they must invoke the Moon while the cauldron was coming to a boil. From their ambush, the Argonauts saw the distant gleam of torches and, welcoming the signal, rushed into Iolcus, where they met with no opposition.

g. Jason, however, fearing Acastus's vengeance, resigned the kingdom to him, neither did he dispute the sentence of banishment passed on him by the Iolcan Council: for he hoped to sit upon a richer throne elsewhere.[2]

h. Some deny that Aeson was forced to take his own life, and declare that, on the contrary, Medea, after first draining the effete blood from his body, restored his youth by a magic elixir, as she had also restored Macris and her sister-nymphs on Corcyra; and presented him, stalwart and vigorous, to Pelias at the palace gates. Having thus persuaded Pelias to undergo the same treatment, she deceived him by omitting the appropriate spells, so that he died miserably.[3]

i. At Pelias's funeral games, celebrated the following day, Euphemus won the two-horse chariot race; Polydeuces, the boxing contest; Meleager, the javelin throw; Peleus, the wrestling match; Zetes, the shorter foot race, and his brother Calais (or, some say, Iphiclus) the longer one; and Heracles, now returned from his visit to the Hesperides, the all-in fighting. But during the four-horse chariot race, which Heracles's charioteer Iolaus won, Glaucus, son of Sisyphus, was devoured by his horses which the goddess Aphrodite had maddened with hippomanes.[4]

j. As for Pelias's daughters: Alcestis married Admetus of Pherae, to whom she had long been affianced; Evadne and Amphinome were banished by Acastus to Mantinea in Arcadia where, after purification, they succeeded in making honourable marriages.[5]

1. Diodorus Siculus: iv. 50. 1; Apollodorus: i. 9. 16 and 27; Valerius Flaccus: i. 777 ff.
2. Apollodorus: i. 9. 27; Diodorus Siculus: iv. 51. 1–53. 1; Pausanias: viii. 11. 2; Plautus: *Pseudolus* iii. 868 ff.; Cicero: *On Old Age* xxiii. 83; Ovid: *Metamorphoses* vii. 297–349; Hyginus: *Fabula* 24.

3. *Hypothesis* to Euripides's *Medea*; Scholiast on Euripides's *Knights* 1321; Ovid: *Metamorphoses* vii. 251–94.
4. Pausanias: v. 17. 9; Hyginus: *Fabula* 278.
5. Diodorus Siculus: iv. 53. 2; Hyginus: *Fabula* 24; Pausanias: viii. 11. 2.

*

1. The Cretans and Mycenaeans used bull's blood, plentifully diluted with water, as a magic to fertilize crops and trees; only the priestess of Mother Earth could drink it pure without being poisoned (see 51. 4).

2. Classical mythographers find it hard to decide how far Medea was an illusionist or cheat, and how far her magic was genuine. Cauldrons of regeneration are common in Celtic myth (see 148. 5–6); hence Medea pretends to be a Hyperborean, that may mean a British, goddess. The underlying religious theory seems to have been that at midsummer the sacred king, wearing a black ram's mask, was slaughtered on a mountain top and his pieces stewed into a soup, for the priestesses to eat; his spirit would then pass into one of them, to be born again as a child in the next lambing season. Phrixus's avoidance of this fate had been the original cause of the Argonauts' expedition (see 70. 2 and 148. g).

3. Medea's serpent-drawn chariot – serpents are underworld creatures – had wings because she was both earth-goddess and moon-goddess. She appears in triad here as Persephone-Demeter-Hecate: the three daughters of Pelias dismembering their father. The theory that the Sun-king marries the Moon-queen, who then graciously invites him to mount her chariot (see 24. m), changed as the patriarchal system hardened: by Classical times, the serpent-chariot was Helius's undisputed property, and in the later myth of Medea and Theseus (see 154. d) he lent it to his grand-daughter Medea only because she stood in peril of death (see 156. d). The Indian Earth-goddess of the *Ramayana* also rides in a serpent-chariot.

4. Callimachus seems to credit the huntress Cyrene with winning the foot race at Pelias's funeral games (see 82. a).

156

MEDEA AT EPHYRA

JASON first visited Boeotian Orchomenus, where he hung up the golden fleece in the temple of Laphystian Zeus; next, he beached the *Argo* on the Isthmus of Corinth, and there dedicated her to Poseidon.

b. Now, Medea was the only surviving child of Aeëtes, the rightful king of Corinth, who when he emigrated to Colchis had left behind as his regent a certain Bunus. The throne having fallen vacant, by the death without issue of the usurper Corinthus, son of Marathon (who styled himself 'Son of Zeus'), Medea claimed it, and the Corinthians accepted Jason as their king. But, after reigning for ten prosperous and happy years, he came to suspect that Medea had secured his succession by poisoning Corinthus; and proposed to divorce her in favour of Glauce the Theban, daughter of King Creon.

c. Medea, while not denying her crime, held Jason to the oath which he had sworn at Aea in the name of all the gods, and when he protested that a forced oath was invalid, pointed out that he also owed the throne of Corinth to her. He answered: 'True, but the Corinthians have learned to have more respect for me than for you.' Since he continued obdurate Medea, feigning submission, sent Glauce a wedding gift by the hands of the royal princes – for she had borne Jason seven sons and seven daughters – namely, a golden crown and a long white robe. No sooner had Glauce put them on, than unquenchable flames shot up, and consumed not only her – although she plunged headlong into the palace fountain – but King Creon, a crowd of other distinguished Theban guests, and everyone else assembled in the palace, except Jason; who escaped by leaping from an upper window.

d. At this point Zeus, greatly admiring Medea's spirit, fell in love with her, but she repulsed all his advances. Hera was grateful: 'I will make your children immortal,' said she, 'if you lay them on the sacrificial altar in my temple.' Medea did so; and then fled in a chariot drawn by winged serpents, a loan from her grandfather Helius, after bequeathing the kingdom to Sisyphus.[1]

e. The name of only one of Medea's daughters by Jason is remembered: Eriopis. Her eldest son, Medeius, or Polyxenus, who was being educated by Cheiron on Mount Pelion, afterwards ruled the country of Media; but Medeius's father is sometimes called Aegeus.[2] The other sons were Mermerus, Pheres, or Thessalus, Alcimedes, Tisander, and Argus; all of whom the Corinthians, enraged by the murder of Glauce and Creon, seized and stoned to death. For this crime they have ever since made expiation: seven girls and seven boys, wearing black garments and with their heads shaven, spend a whole year in the temple of Hera on the Heights, where the murder was committed.[3] By order of the Delphic Oracle, the dead children's corpses were buried in the

Temple, their souls, however, became immortal, as Hera had promised. There are those who charge Jason with condoning this murder, but explain that he was vexed beyond endurance by Medea's ambition on behalf of his children.[4]

f. Others again, misled by the dramatist Euripides, whom the Corinthians bribed with fifteen talents of silver to absolve them of guilt, pretend that Medea killed two of her own children;[5] and that the remainder perished in the palace which she had set on fire – except Thessalus, who escaped and later reigned over Iolcus, giving his name to all Thessaly; and Pheres, whose son Mermerus inherited Medea's skill as a poisoner.[6]

1. Eumelus: *Fragments* 2–4; Diodorus Siculus: iv. 54; Apollodorus: i. 9. 16; Ovid: *Metamorphoses* vii. 391–401; Ptolemy Hephaestionos ii.; Apuleius: *Golden Ass* i. 10; Tzetzes: *On Lycophron* 175; Euripides: *Medea*.

2. Hesiod: *Theogony* 981 ff.; Pausanias: ii. 3. 7 and iii. 3. 7; Hyginus: *Fabulae* 24 and 27.

3. Apollodorus: i. 9. 28; Pausanias: ii. 3. 6; Aelian: *Varia Historia* v. 21; Scholiast on Euripides's *Medea* 9 and 264; Philostratus: *Heroica* xx. 24.

4. Diodorus Siculus: v. 55; Scholiast on Euripides's *Medea* 1387.

5. Scholiast on Euripides: *loc. cit.*; Hyginus: *Fabula* 25; Euripides: *Medea* 1271; Servius on Virgil's *Eclogue* viii. 47.

6. Diodorus Siculus: iv. 54; Homer: *Odyssey* i. 260, with scholiast.

*

1. The number of Medea's children recalls that of the Titans and Titanesses (see 1. 3 and 43. 4), but the fourteen boys and girls who were annually confined in Hera's Temple may have stood for the odd and even days of the first half of the sacred month.

2. Glauce's death was perhaps deduced from an icon showing the annual holocaust in the Temple of Hera, like that described by Lucian at Hierapolis (*On the Syrian Goddess* 49). But Glauce will have been the diademed priestess who directed the conflagration, not its victim; and the well, her ritual bath. Lucian explains that the Syrian goddess was, on the whole, Hera; though she also had some attributes of Athene and the other goddesses (*ibid.* 32). Here Eriopis ('large-eyed') points to cow-eyed Hera, and Glauce ('owl') to owl-eyed Athene. In Lucian's time, domestic animals were hung from the branches of trees piled in the temple court of Hierapolis, and burned alive; but the death of Medea's fourteen children, and the expiation made for them suggest that human victims were originally offered. Melicertes, the Cretan god who presided

over the Isthmian Games at Corinth (see 70. *h* and 96. *6*), was Melkarth, 'protector of the city', the Phoenician Heracles, in whose name children were certainly burned alive at Jerusalem (*Leviticus* xviii. 21 and xx. 2; 1 *Kings* xi. 7; 2 *Kings* xxiii. 10; *Jeremiah* xxxii. 35). Fire, being a sacred element, immortalized the victims, as it did Heracles himself when he ascended his pyre on Mount Oeta, lay down and was consumed (see 145. *f*).

3. Whether Medea, Jason, or the Corinthians sacrificed the children became an important question only later, when Medea had ceased to be identified with Ino, Melicertes's mother, and human sacrifice denoted barbarism. Since any drama which won a prize at the Athenian festival in honour of Dionysus at once acquired religious authority, it is very probable that the Corinthians recompensed Euripides well for his generous manipulation of the now discreditable myth.

4. Zeus's love for Medea, like Hera's for Jason (Homer: *Odyssey* xii. 72; Apollonius Rhodius: iii. 66), suggests that 'Zeus' and 'Hera' were titles of the Corinthian king and queen (see 43. *2* and 68. *1*). Corinthus, though the son of Marathon, was also styled 'son of Zeus', and Marathon's father Epopeus ('he who sees all') had the same wife as Zeus (Pausanias: ii. 1. 1; Asius: *Fragment* 1).

157

MEDEA IN EXILE

MEDEA fled first to Heracles at Thebes, where he had promised to shelter her should Jason ever prove unfaithful, and cured him of the madness that had made him kill his children; nevertheless, the Thebans would not permit her to take up residence among them because Creon, whom she had murdered, was their King. So she went to Athens, and King Aegeus was glad to marry her. Next, banished from Athens for her attempted poisoning of Theseus, she sailed to Italy and taught the Marrubians the art of snake-charming; they still worship her as the goddess Angitia.[1] After a brief visit to Thessaly, where she unsuccessfully competed with Thetis in a beauty contest judged by Idomeneus the Cretan, she married an Asian king whose name has not survived but who is said to have been Medeius's true father.

b. Hearing, finally, that Aeëtes's Colchian throne had been usurped by her uncle Perses, Medea went to Colchis with Medeius, who killed

Perses, set Aeëtes on his throne again, and enlarged the kingdom of Colchis to include Media. Some pretend that she was by that time reconciled to Jason, and took him with her to Colchis; but the history of Medea has, of course, been embellished and distorted by the extravagant fancies of many tragic dramatists.[2] The truth is that Jason, having forfeited the favour of the gods, whose names he had taken in vain when he broke faith with Medea, wandered homeless from city to city, hated of men. In old age he came once more to Corinth, and sat down in the shadow of the *Argo*, remembering his past glories, and grieving for the disasters that had overwhelmed him. He was about to hang himself from the prow, when it suddenly toppled forward and killed him. Poseidon then placed the image of the *Argo*'s stern, which was innocent of homicide, among the stars.[3]

c. Medea never died, but became an immortal and reigned in the Elysian Fields where some say that she, rather than Helen, married Achilles.[4]

d. As for Athamas, whose failure to sacrifice Phrixus had been the cause of the Argonauts' expedition, he was on the point of being himself sacrificed at Orchomenus, as the sin-offering demanded by the Oracle of Laphystian Zeus, when his grandson Cytisorus returned from Aeaea and rescued him. This vexed Zeus, who decreed that, henceforth, the eldest son of the Athamantids must avoid the Council Hall in perpetuity, on pain of death; a decree which has been observed ever since.[5]

e. The homecomings of the Argonauts yield many tales; but that of Great Ancaeus, the helmsman, is the most instructive. Having survived so many hardships and perils, he returned to his palace at Tegea, where a seer had once warned him that he would never taste the wine of a vineyard which he had planted some years previously. On the day of his arrival, Ancaeus was informed that his steward had harvested the first grapes, and that the wine awaited him. He therefore filled a winecup, set it to his lips and, calling the seer, reproached him for prophesying falsely. The seer answered: 'Sire, there is many a slip 'twixt the cup and the lip!', and at that instant Ancaeus's servants ran up, shouting: 'My lord, a wild boar! It is ravaging your vineyard!' He set down the untasted cup, grasped his boar-spear, and hurried out; but the boar lay concealed behind a bush and, charging, killed him.[6]

1. Diodorus Siculus: iv. 54; Apollodorus: i. 9. 28; Plutarch: *Theseus* 12; Servius on Virgil's *Aeneid* vii. 750.

2. Ptolemy Hephaestionos: v.; Diodorus Siculus: iv. 55–66. 2; Hyginus: *Fabula* 26; Justin: xlii. 2; Tacitus: *Annals* vi. 34.
3. Diodorus Siculus: iv. 55; Scholiast on the *Hypothesis* of Euripides's *Medea*; Hyginus: *Poetic Astronomy* xxxvi.
4. Scholiast on Euripides's *Medea* 10; and on Apollonius Rhodius: iv. 814.
5. Herodotus: vii. 197.
6. Scholiast on Apollonius Rhodius: i. 185.

*

1. An Attic cult of Demeter as Earth-goddess has given rise to the story of Medea's stay at Athens (see 97. *b*). Similar cults account for her visits to Thebes, Thessaly, and Asia Minor; but the Marrubians may have emigrated to Italy from Libya, where the Psyllians were adept in the art of snake-charming (Pliny: *Natural History* vii. 2). Medea's reign in the Elysian fields is understandable: as the goddess who presided over the cauldron of regeneration, she could offer heroes the chance of another life on earth (see 31. *c*). Helen ('moon') will have been one of her titles (see 159. *1*).

2. In the heroic age, it seems, the king of Orchomenus, when his reign ended, was led for sacrifice to the top of Mount Laphystium. This king was also a priest of Laphystian Zeus, an office hereditary in the matrilinear Minyan clan; and at the time of the Persian Wars, according to Herodotus, the clan chief was still expected to attend the Council Hall when summoned for sacrifice. No one, however, forced him to obey this summons, and he seems from Herodotus's account to have been represented by a surrogate except on occasions of national disaster, such as a plague or drought, when he would feel obliged to attend in person.

The deaths of Jason and Ancaeus are moral tales, emphasizing the dangers of excessive fame, prosperity, or pride. But Ancaeus dies royally in his own city, from the gash of a boar's tusk (see 18. *7*); whereas Jason, like Bellerophon (see 75. *f*) and Oedipus (see 105. *k*), wanders from city to city, hated of men, and is eventually killed by accident. In the Isthmus where Jason had reigned, the custom was for the royal *pharmacos* to be thrown over the cliff, but rescued from the sea by a waiting boat and banished to the life of an anonymous beggar, taking his ill-luck with him (see 89. *6* and 98. *7*).

3. Sir Isaac Newton was the first, so far as I know, to point out the connexion between the Zodiac and the *Argo*'s voyage; and the legend may well have been influenced at Alexandria by the Zodiacal Signs: the Ram of Phrixus, the Bulls of Aeëtes, the Dioscuri as the Heavenly Twins, Rhea's Lion, the Scales of Alcinous, the Water-carriers of Aegina, Heracles as Bowman, Medea as Virgin, and the Goat, symbol of lechery, to record the love-making on Lemnos. When the Egyptian Zodiacal Signs are used, the missing elements appear: Serpent for Scorpion; and Scarab, symbol of regeneration, for Crab.

158

THE FOUNDATION OF TROY

ONE story told about the foundation of Troy is that, in time of famine, a third of the Cretan people, commanded by Prince Scamander, set out to found a colony. On reaching Phrygia, they pitched their camp beside the sea, not far from the city of Hamaxitus,[1] below a high mountain which they named Ida in honour of Zeus's Cretan home. Now, Apollo had advised them to settle wherever they should be attacked by earth-born enemies under cover of darkness; and that same night a horde of famished field mice invaded the tents and nibbled at bow-strings, leather shield-straps, and all other edible parts of the Cretans' war-gear. Scamander accordingly called a halt, dedicated a temple to Sminthian Apollo (around which the city of Sminthium soon grew) and married the nymph Idaea, who bore him a son, Teucer. With Apollo's help, the Cretans defeated their new neighbours, the Bebrycians, but in the course of the fighting Scamander had leaped into the river Xanthus, which thereupon took his name. Teucer, after whom the settlers were called Teucrians, succeeded him. Yet some say that Teucer himself led the Cretan immigrants, and was welcomed to Phrygia by Dardanus, who gave him his daughter in marriage and called his own subjects Teucrians.[2]

b. The Athenians tell a wholly different story. They deny that the Teucrians came from Crete, and record that a certain Teucer, belonging to the deme of Troes, emigrated from Athens to Phrygia; and that Dardanus, Zeus's son by the Pleiad Electra, and a native of Arcadian Pheneus, was welcomed to Phrygia by this Teucer, not contrariwise. In support of this tradition it is urged that Erichthonius appears in the genealogy both of the Athenian and the Teucrian royal houses.[3] Dardanus, the Athenians go on to say, married Chryse, the daughter of Pallas, who bore him two sons, Idaeus and Deimas. These reigned for a while over the Arcadian kingdom founded by Atlas, but were parted by the calamities of the Deucalionian Flood. Deimas remained in Arcadia, but Idaeus went with his father Dardanus to Samothrace, which they colonized together, the island being thereafter called Dardania. Chryse had brought Dardanus as her dowry the sacred images of the Great Deities whose priestess she was, and he now introduced their cult into Samothrace, though keeping their true names a secret. Dardanus also founded a college of Salian priests to perform the necessary rites; which were the same as those performed by the Cretan Curetes.[4]

c. Grief at the death of his brother Iasion drove Dardanus across the sea to the Troad. He arrived alone, paddling a raft made of an inflated skin which he had ballasted with four stones. Teucer received him hospitably and, on condition that he helped to subdue certain neighbouring tribes, gave him a share of the kingdom and married him to the princess Bateia. Some say that this Bateia was Teucer's aunt; others, that she was his daughter.[5]

d. Dardanus proposed to found a city on the small hill of Ate, which rises from the plain where Troy, or Ilium, now stands; but when an oracle of Phrygian Apollo warned him that misfortune would always attend its inhabitants, he chose a site on the lower slopes of Mount Ida, and named his city Dardania.[6] After Teucer's death, Dardanus succeeded to the remainder of the kingdom, giving it his own name, and extended his rule over many Asiatic nations; he also sent out colonies to Thrace and beyond.[7]

e. Meanwhile, Dardanus's youngest son Idaeus had followed him to the Troad, bringing the sacred images; which enabled Dardanus to teach his people the Samothracian Mysteries. An oracle then assured him that the city which he was about to found would remain invincible only so long as his wife's dowry continued under Athene's protection.[8] His tomb is still shown in that part of Troy which was called Dardania before it merged with the villages of Ilium and Tros into a single city. Idaeus settled on the Idaean Mountains which, some say, are called after him; and there instituted the worship and Mysteries of the Phrygian Mother of the Gods.[9]

f. According to the Latin tradition, Iasion's father was the Tyrrhenian prince Corythus; and his twin, Dardanus, the son of Zeus by Corythus's wife Electra. Both emigrated from Etruria, after dividing these sacred images between them: Iasion went to Samothrace, and Dardanus to the Troad. While battling with the Bebrycians, who tried to throw the Tyrrhenians back into the sea, Dardanus lost his helmet and, although his troops were in retreat, led them back to recover it. This time he was victorious, and founded a city named Corythus on the battle-field: as much in memory of his helmet (*corys*), as of his father.¹⁰

g. Idaeus had two elder brothers, Erichthonius and Ilus, or Zacyn-thus; and a daughter, Idaea, who became Phineus's second wife. When Erichthonius succeeded to the kingdom of Dardanus, he married Asty-oche, the daughter of Simoeis, who bore him Tros.¹¹ Erichthonius, described also as a king of Crete, was the most prosperous of men, owner of the three thousand mares with which Boreas fell in love. Tros succeeded his father Erichthonius, and not only Troy but the whole Troad took his name. By his wife Callirrhoë, a daughter of Scamander, he became the father of Cleopatra the Younger, Ilus the Younger, Assaracus, and Ganymedes.¹²

h. Meanwhile, Ilus the brother of Erichthonius had gone to Phrygia where, entering for the games which he found in progress, he was vic-torious in the wrestling match and won fifty youths and fifty maidens as his prize. The Phrygian king (whose name is now forgotten) also gave him a dappled cow, and advised him to found a city wherever she should first lie down. Ilus followed her; she lay down on reaching the hill of Ate; and there he built the city of Ilium though, because of the warning oracle delivered to his father Dardanus, he raised no fortifica-tions. Some, however, say that it was one of Ilus's own Mysian cows which he followed, and that his instructions came from Apollo. But others hold that Ilium was founded by Locrian immigrants, and that they gave the name of their mountain Phriconis to the Trojan moun-tain of Cyme.¹³

i. When the circuit of the city boundaries had been marked out, Ilus prayed to Almighty Zeus for a sign, and next morning noticed a wooden object lying in front of his tent, half buried in the earth, and overgrown with weeds. This was the Palladium, a legless image three cubits high, made by Athene in memory of her dead Libyan playmate Pallas. Pallas, whose name Athene added to her own, held a spear aloft in the right hand, and a distaff and spindle in the left; around her breast was wrapped the aegis. Athene had first set up the image on Olympus, beside Zeus's throne, where it received great honour; but, when Ilus's great-grandmother, the Pleiad Electra, was violated by Zeus and de-filed it with her touch, Athene angrily cast her, with the image, down to earth.¹⁴

j. Apollo Smintheus now advised Ilus: 'Preserve the Goddess who fell from the skies, and you will preserve your city: for wherever she goes, she carries empire!' Accordingly he raised a temple on the citadel to house the image.[15]

k. Some say that the temple was already rising when the image descended from heaven as the goddess's gift. It dropped through a part of the roof which had not yet been completed, and was found standing exactly in its proper place.[16] Others say that Electra gave the Palladium to Dardanus, her son by Zeus, and that it was carried from Dardania to Ilium after his death.[17] Others, again, say that it fell from heaven at Athens, and that the Athenian Teucer brought it to the Troad. Still others believe that there were two Palladia, an Athenian and a Trojan, the latter carved from the bones of Pelops, just as the image of Zeus at Olympia was carved from Indian ivory; or, that there were many Palladia, all similarly cast from heaven, including the Samothracian images brought to the Troad by Idaeus.[18] The College of Vestals at Rome now guard what is reputed to be the genuine Palladium. No man may look at it with impunity. Once, while it was still in Trojan hands, Ilus rushed to its rescue at an alarm of fire, and was blinded for his pains; later, however, he contrived to placate Athene and regained his sight.[19]

l. Eurydice, daughter of Adrastus, bore to Ilus Laomedon, and Themiste who married the Phrygian Capys and, some say, became the mother of Anchises.[20] By Strymo, a daughter of Scamander and Leucippe, or Zeuxippe, or Thoösa, Laomedon had five sons: namely, Tithonus, Lampus, Clytius, Hicetaon, and Podarces; as well as three daughters: Hesione, Cilla, and Astyoche. He also begot bastard twins on the nymph-shepherdess Calybe. It was he who decided to build the famous walls of Troy and was lucky enough to secure the services of the gods Apollo and Poseidon, then under Zeus's displeasure for a revolt they made against him and forced to serve as day-labourers. Poseidon did the building, while Apollo played the lyre and fed Laomedon's flocks; and Aeacus the Lelegian lent Poseidon a hand. But Laomedon cheated the gods of their pay and earned their bitter resentment. This was the reason why he and all his sons – except Podarces, now renamed Priam – perished in Heracles's sack of Troy.[21]

m. Priam, to whom Heracles generously awarded the Trojan throne, surmised that the calamity which had befallen Troy was due to its luckless site, rather than to the anger of the gods. He therefore sent one of his nephews to ask the Pythoness at Delphi whether a curse still lay on the hill of Ate. But the priest of Apollo, Panthous the son of Othrias, was so beautiful that Priam's nephew, forgetting his commission, fell in love with him and carried him back to Troy. Though vexed, Priam had not the heart to punish his nephew. In compensation for the injury done he appointed Panthous priest of Apollo and, ashamed to consult the Pythoness again, rebuilt Troy on the same foundations. Priam's first wife was Arisbe, a daughter of Merops, the seer. When she had borne him Aesacus, he married her to Hyrtacus, by whom she became the mother of the Hyrtacides: Asius and Nisus.[22]

n. This Aesacus, who learned the art of interpreting dreams from his grandfather Merops, is famous for the great love he showed Asterope, a daughter of the river Cebren: when she died, he tried repeatedly to kill himself by leaping from a sea-cliff until, at last, the gods took pity on his plight. They turned Aesacus into a diving bird, thus allowing him to indulge his obsession with greater decency.[23]

o. Hecabe, Priam's second wife – whom the Latins call Hecuba – was a daughter of Dymas and the nymph Eunoë; or, some say, of Cisseus and Telecleia; or of the river Sangarius and Metope; or of Glaucippe, the daughter of Xanthus.[24] She bore Priam nineteen of his fifty sons, the remainder being the children of concubines; all fifty occupied adjacent bed-chambers of polished stone. Priam's twelve daughters slept with their husbands on the farther side of the same courtyard.[25] Hecabe's eldest son was Hector, whom some call the son of Apollo; next, she bore Paris; then Creusa, Laodice, and Polyxena; then Deiphobus, Helenus, Cassandra, Pammon, Polites, Antiphus, Hipponous, and Polydorus. But Troilus was certainly begotten on her by Apollo.[26]

p. Among Hecabe's younger children were the twins Cassandra and Helenus. At their birthday feast, celebrated in the sanctuary of Thymbraean Apollo, they grew tired of play and fell asleep in a corner, while their forgetful parents, who had drunk too much wine, staggered home without them. When Hecabe returned to the temple, she found the sacred serpents licking the children's ears, and screamed for terror. The serpents at once disappeared into a pile of laurel boughs, but from that hour both Cassandra and Helenus possessed the gift of prophecy.[27]

q. Another account of the matter is that one day Cassandra fell asleep in the temple, Apollo appeared and promised to teach her the art of prophecy if she would lie with him. Cassandra, after accepting his gift, went back on the bargain; but Apollo begged her to give him one kiss and, as she did so, spat into her mouth, thus ensuring that none would ever believe what she prophesied.[28]

r. When, after several years of prudent government, Priam had restored Troy to its former wealth and power, he summoned a Council to discuss the case of his sister Hesione, whom Telamon the Aeacid had taken away to Greece. Though he himself was in favour of force, the Council recommended that persuasion should first be tried. His brother-in-law Antenor and his cousin Anchises therefore went to Greece and delivered the Trojan demands to the assembled Greeks at Telamon's court; but were scornfully sent about their business. This incident was a main cause of the Trojan War,[29] the gloomy end of which Cassandra was now already predicting. To avoid scandal, Priam locked her up in a pyramidal building on the citadel; the wardress who cared for her had orders to keep him informed of all her prophetic utterances.[30]

1. Strabo: xiii. 1. 48.
2. Servius on Virgil's *Aeneid* iii. 108; Strabo: *loc. cit.*; Tzetzes: *On Lycophron* 1302.
3. Apollodorus: iii. 12. 1; Servius on Virgil's *Aeneid* iii. 167; Strabo: *loc. cit.*
4. Dionysius of Halicarnassus: *Roman Antiquities* i. 61 and ii. 70–1; Eustathius on Homer's *Iliad* p. 1204; Conon: *Narrations* 21; Servius on Virgil's *Aeneid* viii. 285.
5. Apollodorus: iii. 12. 1; Lycophron: 72 ff., with Tzetzes's comments; Scholiast on Homer's *Iliad* xx. 215; Servius on Virgil's *Aeneid* iii. 167; Tzetzes: *On Lycophron* 29.
6. Tzetzes: *loc. cit.*; Diodorus Siculus: v. 48; Strabo: *Fragment* 50; Homer: *Iliad* xx. 215 ff.
7. Apollodorus: *loc. cit.*; Servius: *loc. cit.*; Diodorus Siculus: *loc. cit.*
8. Strabo: *loc. cit.*; Dionysius of Halicarnassus: i. 61; Eustathius on Homer's *Iliad* p. 1204; Conon: *Narrations* 21; Servius on Virgil's *Aeneid* ii. 166.
9. Tzetzes: *On Lycophron* 72; Dionysius of Halicarnassus: *loc. cit.*
10. Servius: *loc. cit.*; vii. 207 and iii. 15.
11. Apollodorus: iii. 12. 2 and iii. 15. 3; Dionysius of Halicarnassus: i. 50. 3.
12. Homer: *Iliad* xx. 220 ff.; Dionysius of Halicarnassus: i. 62; Apollodorus: iii. 12. 2.
13. Apollodorus: iii. 12. 3; Tzetzes: *On Lycophron* 29: Lesses of Lampsacus, quoted by Tzetzes: *loc. cit.*; Pindar: *Olympian Odes* viii. 30 ff., with scholiast; Strabo: xiii. 1. 3 and 3. 3.
14. Ovid: *Fasti* vi. 420 ff.; Apollodorus: *loc. cit.*

15. Ovid: *loc cit.*; Apollodorus: *loc. cit.*

16. Dictys Cretensis: v. 5.

17. Scholiast on Euripides's *Phoenician Women* 1136; Dionysius of Halicarnassus: i. 61; Servius on Virgil's *Aeneid* ii. 166.

18. Clement of Alexandria: *Protrepticon* iv. 47; Servius: *loc. cit.*; Pherecydes, quoted by Tzetzes: *On Lycophron* 355; *Etymologicum Magnum*: *sub* Palladium pp. 649–50.

19. Dercyllus: *Foundations of Cities* i, quoted by Plutarch: *Parallel Stories* 17.

20. Apollodorus: iii. 12. 2 and 3.

21. Apollodorus: ii. 59; ii. 6. 4 and iii. 12. 3; Scholiast on Homer's *Iliad* iii. 250; Homer: *Iliad* vi. 23–6; xxi. 446 and vii. 542; Horace: *Odes* iii. 3. 21; Pindar: *Olympic Odes* viii. 41, with scholiast; Diodorus Siculus: iv. 32.

22. Servius on Virgil's *Aeneid* ii. 319; Apollodorus: iii. 12. 5; Homer: *Iliad* ii. 831 and 837; Virgil: *Aeneid* ix. 176–7.

23. Servius on Virgil's *Aeneid* v. 128; Apollodorus: *loc. cit.*; Ovid: *Metamorphoses* xi. 755–95.

24. Perecydes, quoted by scholiast on Homer's *Iliad* xvi. 718; and on Euripides's *Hecabe* 32; Athenion, quoted by scholiast on Homer: *loc. cit.*; Apollodorus: *loc. cit.*

25. Homer: *Iliad* xxiv. 495–7 and vi. 242–50.

26. Stesichorus, quoted by Tzetzes: *On Lycophron* 266; Apollodorus: *loc. cit.*

27. Anticlides, quoted by scholiast on Homer's *Iliad* vii. 44.

28. Hyginus: *Fabula* 93; Apollodorus: iii. 12. 5; Servius on Virgil's *Aeneid* ii. 247.

29. Benoit: *Roman de Troie* 385 and 3187 ff.; *The Seege or Batayle of Troye* 349 ff. and 385; Tzetzes: *On Lycophron* 340; Dares: 5; Servius on Virgil's *Aeneid* iii. 80.

30. Aeschylus: *Agamemnon* 1210; Tzetzes: *Hypothesis of Lycophron's Alexandra*; *On Lycophron* 29 and 350.

*

1. The situation of Troy on a well-watered plain at the entrance to the Hellespont, though establishing it as the main centre of Bronze Age trade between East and West, provoked frequent attacks from all quarters. Greek, Cretan, and Phrygian claims to have founded the city were not irreconcilable, since by Classical times it had been destroyed and rebuilt often enough: there were ten Troys in all, the seventh being the Homeric city. The Troy with which Homer is concerned seems to have been peopled by a federation of three tribes – Trojans, Ilians, and Dardanians – a usual arrangement in the Bronze Age.

2. 'Sminthian Apollo' points to Crete, *Sminthos* being the Cretan word for 'mouse', a sacred animal not only at Cnossus (see 90. *3*), but in

Philistia (1 *Samuel* vi. 4) and Phocis (Pausanias: x. 12. 5); and Erich-thonius, the fertilizing North Wind, was worshipped alike by the Pelasgians of Athens and the Thracians (see 48. *3*). But the Athenian claim to have founded Troy may be dismissed as political propaganda. The white mice kept in Apollo's temples were prophylactic both against plague and against sudden invasions of mice such as Aelian (*History of Animals* xii. 5. and 41) and Aristotle (*History of Animals* vi. 370) mention. Dardanus may have been a Tyrrhenian from Lydia (see 136. *g*) or Samothrace; but Servius errs in recording that he came from Etruria, where the Tyrrhenians settled long after the Trojan War. 'Zacinthus', a Cretan word, figuring in the Trojan royal pedigree, was the name of an island belonging to Odysseus's kingdom; and this suggests that he claimed hereditary rights at Troy.

3. The Palladium, which the Vestal Virgins guarded at Rome, as the luck of the city, held immense importance for Italian mythographers; they claimed that it had been rescued from Troy by Aeneas (Pausanias: ii. 23. 5) and brought to Italy. It was perhaps made of porpoise-ivory (see 108. 5). 'Palladium' means a stone or other cult-object around which the girls of a particular clan danced, as at Thespiae (see 120. *a*), or young men leaped, *pallas* being used indiscriminately for both sexes. The Roman College of Salii was a society of leaping priests. When such cult-objects became identified with tribal prosperity and were carefully guarded against theft or mutilation, *palladia* was read as meaning *palta*, 'or things hurled from heaven'. *Palta* might not be hidden from the sky; thus the sacred thunder-stone of Terminus at Rome stood under a hole in the roof of Juppiter's temple – which accounts for the similar opening at Troy.

4. Worship of meteorites was easily extended to ancient monoliths, the funerary origin of which had been forgotten; then from monolith to stone image, and from stone image to wooden or ivory image is a short step. But the falling of a shield from heaven – Mars's *ancile* (Ovid: *Fasti* iii. 259–73) is the best-known instance – needs more explanation. At first, meteorites, as the only genuine *palta*, were taken to be the origin of lightning, which splits forest trees. Next, neolithic stone axes, such as the one recently found in the Mycenaean sanctuary of Asine, and early Bronze Age celts or pestles, such as Cybele's pestle at Ephesus (*Acts* xix. 35), were mistaken for thunderbolts. But the shield was also a thunder instrument. Pre-Hellenic rain-makers summoned storms by whirling bull-roarers to imitate the sound of rising wind and, for thunder, beat on huge, tightly-stretched ox-hide shields, with double-headed drum-sticks like those carried by the Salian priests in the Anagni relief. The only way to keep a bull-roarer sounding continuously is to whirl it in a figure-of-eight, as boys do with toy windmills, and since torches, used to imitate lightning, were, it seems, whirled in the same pattern, the rain-making shield was cut to form a figure-of-eight, and the double drum-stick beat continuously on both sides. This is why surviving Cretan icons show the Thunder-spirit descending as a figure-of-eight shield; and why therefore ancient shields were eventually worshipped as *palta*. A painted limestone tablet from the Acropolis at Mycenae proves, by the colour of the flesh, that the Thunder-spirit was a goddess, rather than a god; on a gold ring found near by, the sex of the descending shield is not indicated.

5. Cassandra and the serpents recall the myth of Melampus (see 122. *c*), and Apollo's spitting into her mouth that of Glaucus (see 90. *f*). Her prison was probably a bee-hive tomb from which she uttered prophecies in the name of the hero who lay buried there (see 43. 2 and 154. 1).

6. Aesacus, the name of Priam's prophetic son, meant the myrtle-branch which was passed around at Greek banquets as a challenge to sing or compose. Myrtle being a death-tree (see 101. 1 and 109. 4), such poems may originally have been prophecies made at a hero-feast. The diving bird was sacred to Athene in Attica and associated with the drowning of the royal *pharmacos* (see 94. 1). Scamander's leaping into the river Xanthus must refer to a similar Trojan custom of drowning the old king (see 108. 3); his ghost supposedly impregnated girls when they came there to bathe (see 137. 3). Tantalus, who appears to have suffered the same fate, married Xanthus's daughter (see 108. *b*).

7. Priam had fifty sons, nineteen of whom were legitimate; this suggests that at Troy the length of the king's reign was governed by the nineteen-year metonic cycle, not the cycle of one hundred lunations shared between king and tanist, as in Crete (see 138. 5) and Arcadia (see 38. 2). His twelve daughters were perhaps guardians of the months.

8. The importance of Aeacus's share in building the walls of Troy should not be overlooked: Apollo had prophesied that his descendants should be present at its capture both in the first and the fourth generation (see 66. *i*), and only the part built by Aeacus could be breached (Pindar: *Pythian Odes* viii. 39–46). Andromache reminded Hector that this part was the curtain on the west side of the wall 'near the fig tree', where the city might be most easily assailed (Homer: *Iliad* vi. 431–9), and 'where the most valiant men who follow the two Ajax's have thrice attempted to force an entry – whether some soothsayer has revealed the secret to them, or whether their own spirit urges them on.' Dörpfeld's excavations of Troy proved that the wall was, unaccountably, weakest at this point; but the Ajax's or 'Aeacans' needed no soothsayer to inform them of this if, as Polybius suggests, 'Aeacus' came from Little Ajax's city of Opuntian Locris. Locris, which seems to have provided the Ilian element in Homeric Troy, and enjoyed the privilege of nominating Trojan priestesses (see 168. 2), was a pre-Hellenic Lelegian district with matri-linear and even matriarchal institutions (see 136. 4); another tribe of

Lelegians, perhaps of Locrian descent, lived at Pedasus in the Troad. One of their princesses, Laothoë, came to Troy and had a child by Priam (Homer: *Iliad* xxi. 86). It seems to have been the Locrian priestesses' readiness to smuggle away the Palladium to safety in Locris that facilitated the Greeks' capture of the city (see 168. 4).

9. Since one Teucer was Scamander's son, and another was Aeacus's grandson and son of Priam's sister Hesione (see 137. 2), the Teucrian element at Troy may be identified with the Lelegian, or Aeacan, or Ilian; the other two elements being the Lydian, or Dardanian, or Tyrrhenian; and the Trojan, or Phrygian.

159

PARIS AND HELEN

WHEN Helen, Leda's beautiful daughter, grew to womanhood at Sparta in the palace of her foster-father Tyndareus, all the princes of Greece came with rich gifts as her suitors, or sent their kinsmen to represent them. Diomedes, fresh from his victory at Thebes, was there with Ajax, Teucer, Philoctetes, Idomeneus, Patroclus, Menestheus, and many others. Odysseus came too, but empty-handed, because he had not the least chance of success – for, even though the Dioscuri, Helen's brothers, wanted her to marry Menestheus of Athens, she would, Odysseus knew, be given to Prince Menelaus, the richest of the Achaeans, represented by Tyndareus's powerful son-in-law Agamemnon.[1]

b. Tyndareus sent no suitor away, but would, on the other hand, accept none of the proffered gifts; fearing that his partiality for any one prince might set the others quarrelling. Odysseus asked him one day: 'If I tell you how to avoid a quarrel will you, in return, help me to marry Icarius's daughter Penelope?' 'It is a bargain,' cried Tyndareus. 'Then,' continued Odysseus, 'my advice to you is: insist that all Helen's suitors swear to defend her chosen husband against whoever resents his good fortune.' Tyndareus agreed that this was a prudent course. After sacrificing a horse, and jointing it, he made the suitors stand on its bloody pieces, and repeat the oath which Odysseus had formulated; the joints were then buried at a place still called 'The Horse's Tomb'.

c. It is not known whether Tyndareus himself chose Helen's husband, or whether she declared her own preference by crowning him with a wreath.[2] At all events, she married Menelaus, who became King of Sparta after the death of Tyndareus and the deification of the Dioscuri. Yet their marriage was doomed to failure: years before, while sacrificing to the gods, Tyndareus had stupidly overlooked Aphrodite, who took her revenge by swearing to make all three of his daughters – Clytaemnestra, Timandra, and Helen – notorious for their adulteries.[3]

d. Menelaus had one daughter by Helen, whom she named Hermione; their sons were Aethiolas, Maraphius – from whom the Persian family of the Maraphions claim descent – and Pleisthenes. An Aetolian slave-girl named Pieris later bore Menelaus twin bastards: Nicostratus and Megapenthes.[4]

e. Why, it is asked, had Zeus and Themis planned the Trojan War? Was it to make Helen famous for having embroiled Europe and Asia? Or to exalt the race of the demi-gods, and at the same time to thin out the populous tribes that were oppressing the surface of Mother Earth? Their reason must remain obscure, but the decision had already been taken when Eris threw down a golden apple inscribed 'For the Fairest' at the wedding of Peleus and Thetis. Almighty Zeus refused to decide the ensuing dispute between Hera, Athene, and Aphrodite, and let Hermes lead the goddesses to Mount Ida, where Priam's lost son Paris would act as arbiter.[5]

f. Now, just before the birth of Paris, Hecabe had dreamed that she brought forth a faggot from which wriggled countless fiery serpents. She awoke screaming that the city of Troy and the forests of Mount Ida were ablaze. Priam at once consulted his son Aesacus, the seer, who announced: 'The child about to be born will be the ruin of our country! I beg you to do away with him.'[6]

g. A few days later, Aesacus made a further announcement: 'The royal Trojan who brings forth a child today must be destroyed, and so must her offspring!' Priam thereupon killed his sister Cilla, and her infant son Munippus, born that morning from a secret union with Thymoetes, and buried them in the sacred precinct of Tros. But Hecabe was delivered of a son before nightfall, and Priam spared both their lives, although Herophile, priestess of Apollo, and other seers, urged Hecabe at least to kill the child. She could not bring herself to do so; and in the end Priam was prevailed upon to send for his chief herdsman, one Agelaus, and entrust him with the task. Agelaus, being too soft-hearted to use a rope or a sword, exposed the infant on Mount Ida, where he was suckled by a she-bear. Returning after five days, Agelaus was amazed at the portent, and brought the waif home in a wallet – hence the name 'Paris' – to rear with his own new-born son;[7] and took a dog's tongue to Priam as evidence that his command had been obeyed. But some say that Hecabe bribed Agelaus to spare Paris and keep the secret from Priam.[8]

h. Paris's noble birth was soon disclosed by his outstanding beauty, intelligence, and strength: when little more than a child, he routed a band of cattle-thieves and recovered the cows they had stolen, thus winning the surname Alexander.[9] Though ranking no higher than a slave at this time, Paris became the chosen lover of Oenone, daughter of the river Oeneus, a fountain-nymph. She had been taught the art of prophecy by Rhea, and that of medicine by Apollo while he was acting as Laomedon's herdsman. Paris and Oenone used to herd their flocks and hunt together; he carved her name in the bark of beech-trees and poplars.[10] His chief amusement was setting Agelaus's bulls to fight one another; he would crown the victor with flowers, and the loser with straw. When one bull began to win consistently, Paris pitted it against the champions of his neighbours' herds, all of which were defeated. At last he offered to set a golden crown upon the horns of any bull that could overcome his own; so, for a jest, Ares turned himself into a bull, and won the prize. Paris's unhesitating award of this crown to Ares surprised and pleased the gods as they watched from Olympus; which is why Zeus chose him to arbitrate between the three goddesses.[11]

i. He was herding his cattle on Mount Gargarus, the highest peak of Ida, when Hermes, accompanied by Hera, Athene, and Aphrodite, delivered the golden apple and Zeus's message: 'Paris, since you are as handsome as you are wise in affairs of the heart, Zeus commands you to judge which of these goddesses is the fairest.'

Paris accepted the apple doubtfully. 'How can a simple cattle-man like myself become an arbiter of divine beauty?' he cried. 'I shall divide this apple between all three.'

'No, no, you cannot disobey Almighty Zeus!' Hermes replied hurriedly. 'Nor am I authorized to give you advice. Use your native intelligence!'

'So be it,' sighed Paris. 'But first I beg the losers not to be vexed with me. I am only a human being, liable to make the stupidest mistakes.'

The goddesses all agreed to abide by his decision.

'Will it be enough to judge them as they are?' Paris asked Hermes, 'or should they be naked?'

'The rules of the contest are for you to decide,' Hermes answered with a discreet smile.

'In that case, will they kindly disrobe?'

Hermes told the goddesses to do so, and politely turned his back.

j. Aphrodite was soon ready, but Athene insisted that she should remove the famous magic girdle, which gave her an unfair advantage by making everyone fall in love with the wearer. 'Very well,' said Aphrodite spitefully. 'I will, on condition that you remove your helmet – you look hideous without it.'

'Now, if you please, I must judge you one at a time,' announced Paris, 'to avoid distractive arguments. Come here, Divine Hera! Will you other two goddesses be good enough to leave us for a while?'

'Examine me conscientiously,' said Hera, turning slowly around, and displaying her magnificent figure, 'and remember that if you judge me the fairest, I will make you lord of all Asia, and the richest man alive.'[12]

'I am not to be bribed, my Lady. . . . Very well, thank you. Now I have seen all that I need to see. Come, Divine Athene!'

k. 'Here I am,' said Athene, striding purposefully forward. 'Listen, Paris, if you have enough common sense to award me the prize, I will make you victorious in all your battles, as well as the handsomest and wisest man in the world.'

'I am a humble herdsman, not a soldier,' said Paris. 'You can see for yourself that peace reigns throughout Lydia and Phrygia, and that King Priam's sovereignty is uncontested. But I promise to consider fairly your claim to the apple. Now you are at liberty to put on your clothes and helmet again. Is Aphrodite ready?'

l. Aphrodite sidled up to him, and Paris blushed because she came so close that they were almost touching.

'Look carefully, please, pass nothing over. . . . By the way, as soon as I saw you, I said to myself: "Upon my word, there goes the handsomest young man in Phrygia! Why does he waste himself here in the wilderness herding stupid cattle?" Well, why do you, Paris? Why not move into a city and lead a civilized life? What have you to lose by marrying someone like Helen of Sparta, who is as beautiful as I am, and no less passionate? I am convinced that, once you two have met, she will abandon her home, her family, everything, to become your mistress. Surely you have heard of Helen?'

'Never until now, my Lady. I should be most grateful if you would describe her.'

m. 'Helen is of fair and delicate complexion, having been hatched from a swan's egg. She can claim Zeus for a father, loves hunting and wrestling, caused one war while she was still a child – and, when she came of age, all the princes of Greece were her suitors. At present she is married to Menelaus, brother of the High King Agamemnon; but that makes no odds – you can have her if you like.'

'How is that possible, if she is already married?'

'Heavens! How innocent you are! Have you never heard that it is my divine duty to arrange affairs of this sort? I suggest now that you tour Greece with my son Eros as your guide. Once you reach Sparta, he and I will see that Helen falls head over heels in love with you.'

'Would you swear to that?' Paris asked excitedly.

Aphrodite uttered a solemn oath, and Paris, without a second thought, awarded her the golden apple.

By this judgement he incurred the smothered hatred of both Hera and Athene, who went off arm-in-arm to plot the destruction of Troy; while Aphrodite, with a naughty smile, stood wondering how best to keep her promise.[13]

n. Soon afterwards, Priam sent his servants to fetch a bull from Agelaus's herd. It was to be a prize at the funeral games now annually celebrated in honour of his dead son. When the servants chose the champion bull, Paris was seized by a sudden desire to attend the games, and ran after them. Agelaus tried to restrain him: 'You have your own private bull fights, what more do you want?' But Paris persisted and in the end, Agelaus accompanied him to Troy.

o. It was a Trojan custom that, at the close of the sixth lap of the chariot race, those who had entered for the boxing match should begin fighting in front of the throne. Paris decided to compete and, despite Agelaus's entreaties, sprang into the arena and won the crown, by sheer courage rather than by skill. He also came home first in the foot-race, which so exasperated Priam's sons that they challenged him to another; thus he won his third crown. Ashamed at this public defeat, they decided to kill him and set an armed guard at every exit of the stadium, while Hector and Deiphobus attacked him with their swords.

Paris leaped for the protection of Zeus's altar, and Agelaus ran towards Priam, crying: 'Your Majesty, this youth is your long-lost son!' Priam at once summoned Hecabe who, when Agelaus displayed a rattle which had been found in Paris's hands, confirmed his identity. He was taken triumphantly to the palace, where Priam celebrated his return with a huge banquet and sacrifices to the gods. Yet, as soon as the priests of Apollo heard the news, they announced that Paris must be put to death immediately, else Troy would perish. This was reported to Priam, who answered: 'Better that Troy should fall, than that my wonderful son should die!'[14]

p. Paris's married brothers presently urged him to take a wife; but he told them that he trusted Aphrodite to choose one for him, and used to offer her prayers every day. When another Council was called to discuss the rescue of Hesione, peaceful overtures having failed, Paris volunteered to lead the expedition, if Priam would provide him with a large, well-manned fleet. He cunningly added that, should he fail to bring Hesione back, he might perhaps carry off a Greek princess of equal rank to hold in ransom for her. His heart was, of course, secretly set on going to Sparta to fetch back Helen.[15]

q. That very day, Menelaus arrived unexpectedly at Troy and inquired for the tombs of Lycus and Chimaerus, Prometheus's sons by Celaeno the Atlantid: he explained that the remedy which the Delphic Oracle had prescribed him for a plague now ravaging Sparta was to offer them heroic sacrifices. Paris entertained Menelaus and begged, as a favour, to be purified by him at Sparta, since he had accidentally killed Antenor's young son Antheus with a toy sword. When Menelaus agreed, Paris, on Aphrodite's advice, commissioned Phereclus, the son of Tecton, to build the fleet which Priam had promised him; the figurehead of his flag-ship was to be an Aphrodite holding a miniature Eros. Paris's cousin Aeneas, Anchises's son, agreed to accompany him.[16] Cassandra, her hair streaming loose, foretold the conflagration that the voyage would cause, and Helenus concurred; but Priam took no notice of either of his prophetic children. Even Oenone failed to dissuade Paris from the fatal journey, although he wept when kissing her good-bye. 'Come back to me if ever you are wounded,' she said, 'because I alone can heal you.'[17]

r. The fleet put out to sea, Aphrodite sent a favouring breeze, and Paris soon reached Sparta, where Menelaus feasted him for nine days. At the banquet, Paris presented Helen with the gifts that he had brought from Troy; and his shameless glances, loud sighs and bold signals caused her considerable embarrassment. Picking up her goblet he would set his lips to that part of the rim from which she had drunk; and once she found the words 'I love you, Helen!' traced in wine on the table top. She grew terrified that Menelaus might suspect her of encouraging Paris's passion; but, being an unobservant man, he cheerfully sailed off to Crete, where he had to attend the obsequies of his grandfather Catreus, leaving her to entertain the guests and rule the kingdom during his absence.[18]

s. Helen eloped with Paris that very night, and gave herself to him in love at the first port of call, which was the island of Cranaë. On the mainland, opposite Cranaë, stands a shrine of Aphrodite the Uniter, founded by Paris to celebrate this occasion.[19] Some record untruthfully that Helen rejected his advances, and that he carried her off by force while she was out hunting; or by a sudden raid on the city of Sparta; or by disguising himself, with Aphrodite's aid, as Menelaus. She abandoned her daughter Hermione, then nine years of age, but took away her son Pleisthenes, the greater part of the palace treasures, and gold to the value of three talents stolen from Apollo's temple; as well as five serving women, among whom were the two former queens, Aethra the mother of Theseus, and Theisadië, Peirithous's sister.[20]

t. As they steered towards Troy, a great storm sent by Hera forced Paris to touch at Cyprus. Thence he sailed to Sidon, and was entertained by the king whom, being now instructed in the ways of the Greek world, he treacherously murdered and robbed in his own banqueting hall. While the rich booty was being embarked, a company of Sidonians attacked him; these he beat off, after a bloody fight and the loss of two ships, and came safely away. Fearing pursuit by Menelaus, Paris delayed for several months in Phoenicia, Cyprus, and Egypt; but, reaching Troy at last, he celebrated his wedding with Helen.[21] The Trojans welcomed her, entranced by such divine beauty; and one day, finding a stone on the Trojan citadel, which dripped blood when rubbed against another, she recognized this as a powerful aphrodisiac and used it to keep Paris's passion ablaze. What was more, all Troy, not Paris only, fell in love with her; and Priam took an oath never to let her go.[22]

u. An altogether different account of the matter is that Hermes stole Helen at Zeus's command, and entrusted her to King Proteus of Egypt; meanwhile, a phantom Helen, fashioned from clouds by Hera (or, some say, by Proteus) was sent to Troy at Paris's side: with the sole purpose of provoking strife.[23]

v. Egyptian priests record, no less improbably, that the Trojan fleet was blown off its course, and that Paris landed at the Salt Pans in the Canopic mouth of the Nile. There stands Heracles's temple, a sanctuary for runaway slaves who, on arrival, dedicate themselves to the god and receive certain sacred marks on their bodies. Paris's servants fled here and, after securing the priests' protection, accused him of having abducted Helen. The Canopic warden took cognizance of the matter and reported it to King Proteus at Memphis, who had Paris arrested and brought before him, together with Helen and the stolen treasure. After a close interrogation, Proteus banished Paris but detained Helen and the treasure in Egypt, until Menelaus should come to recover them. In Memphis stands a temple of Aphrodite the Stranger, said to have been dedicated by Helen herself.

Helen bore Paris three sons, Bunomus, Aganus, and Idaeus, all of them killed at Troy while still infants by the collapse of a roof; and one daughter, also called Helen.[24] Paris had an elder son by Oenone, named Corythus, whom, in jealousy of Helen, she sent to guide the avenging Greeks to Troy.[25]

1. Apollodorus: iii. 10. 8; Hyginus: *Fabula* 81; Ovid: *Heroides* xvii. 104; Hesiod: *The Catalogues of Women, Fragment* 68, pp. 192 ff., ed. Evelyn-White.
2. Hesiod: *loc. cit.*; Apollodorus: iii. 10. 9; Pausanias: iii. 20. 9; Hyginus: *Fabula* 78.
3. Stesichorus, quoted by scholiast on Euripides's *Orestes* 249; Hyginus: *loc. cit.*; Apollodorus: iii. 11. 2.
4. Homer: *Odyssey* iv. 12–14; Scholiast on Homer's *Iliad* iii. 175; *Cypria*, quoted by scholiast on Euripides's *Andromache* 898; Pausanias: ii. 18. 5.
5. *Cypria*, quoted by Proclus: *Chrestomathy* 1; Apollodorus: *Epitome* iii. 1–2; *Cypria*, quoted by scholiast on Homer's *Iliad* i. 5.
6. Apollodorus: iii. 12. 5; Hyginus: *Fabula* 91; Tzetzes: *On Lycophron* 86; Pindar: *Fragment of Paean* 8, pp. 544–6, ed. Sandys.
7. Tzetzes: *On Lycophron* 224 and 314; Servius on Virgil's *Aeneid* ii. 32; Pausanias: x. 12. 3; Scholiast on Euripides's *Andromache* 294; and on *Iphigeneia in Aulis* 1285; Apollodorus: *loc. cit.*; Hyginus: *Fabula* 91; Konrad von Würzburg: *Der trojanische Krieg* 442 ff. and 546 ff.
8. Dictys Cretensis: iii. Rawlinson: *Excidium Troiae*.
9. Apollodorus: *loc. cit.*; Ovid: *Heroides* xvi. 51–2 and 359–60.
10. Ovid: *Heroides* v. 12–30 and 139; Tzetzes: *On Lycophron* 57; Apollodorus: iii. 12. 6.

11. *Trojanska Priča* p. 159; Rawlinson: *Excidium Troiae*.

12. Ovid: *Heroides* xvi. 71–3 and v. 35–6; Lucian: *Dialogues of the Gods* 20; Hyginus: *Fabula* 92.

13. Hyginus: *loc. cit.*; Ovid: *Heroides* xvi. 149–52; Lucian: *loc. cit.*

14. Rawlinson: *Excidium Troiae*; Hyginus: *Fabula* 91; Servius on Virgil's *Aeneid* v. 370; Ovid: *Heroides* xvi. 92 and 361–2.

15. Dares: 4–8; Rawlinson: *loc. cit.*

16. Tzetzes: *On Lycophron* 132; *Cypria*, quoted by Proclus: *Chresto-mathy* 1; Homer: *Iliad* v. 59 ff.; Apollodorus: *Epitome* iii. 2; Ovid: *Heroides* xvi. 115–16.

17. *Cypria*, quoted by Proclus: *loc. cit.*; Ovid: *Heorides* xvi. 119 ff. and 45 ff.; Apollodorus: iii. 12. 6.

18. Ovid: *Heroides* xvi. 21–3; xvii. 74 ff.; 83 and 155 ff.; Apollo-dorus: *Epitome* iii. 3; *Cypria*, quoted by Proclus: *loc. cit.*

19. Ovid: *Heroides* xvi. 259–62; *Cypria*, quoted by Proclus: *loc. cit.*; Pausanias: iii. 22. 2; Apollodorus: *loc. cit.*; Homer: *Iliad* iii. 445.

20. Servius on Virgil's *Aeneid* i. 655; Eustathius on Homer, p. 1946; Apollodorus: *loc. cit.*; *Cypria*, quoted by Proclus: *loc. cit.*; Dares: 10; Tzetzes: *On Lycophron* 132 ff.; Hyginus: *Fabula* 92.

21. Homer: *Odyssey* iv. 227–30; Proclus: *Chrestomathy* 1; Dictys Cretensis: i. 5; Apollodorus: *Epitome* iii. 4; Tzetzes: *On Lycophron* 132 ff.

22. Servius on Virgil's *Aeneid* ii. 33.

23. Apollodorus: *Epitome* iii. 5; Euripides: *Electra* 128 and *Helen* 31 ff.; Servius on Virgil's *Aeneid* i. 655 and ii. 595; Stesichorus, quoted by Tzetzes: *On Lycophron* 113.

24. Herodotus: ii. 112–15; Dictys Cretensis: v. 5; Tzetzes: *On Lyco-phron* 851; Ptolemy Hephaestionos: iv.

25. Conon: *Narrations* 22; Tzetzes: *On Lycophron* 57 ff.

*

1. Stesichorus, the sixth-century Sicilian poet, is credited with the story that Helen never went to Troy and that the war was fought for 'only a phantom'. After writing a poem which presented her in a most unfavourable light, he went blind, and afterwards learned that he lay under her posthumous displeasure (see 164. *m*). Hence his palinode begin-ning: 'This tale is true, thou didst not go aboard The well-benched ships, nor reach the towers of Troy,' a public declamation of which restored his sight (Plato: *Phaedrus* 44; Pausanias: iii. 19. 11). And, indeed, it is not clear in what sense Paris, or Theseus before him, had abducted Helen. 'Helen' was the name of the Spartan Moon-goddess, marriage to whom, after a horse-sacrifice (see 81. *4*), made Menelaus king; yet Paris did not usurp the throne. It is of course possible that the Trojans raided Sparta, carrying off the heiress and the palace treasures in retaliation for a Greek

sack of Troy, which Hesione's story implies. Yet though Theseus's Helen was, perhaps, flesh and blood (see 103. 4), the Trojan Helen is far more likely to have been 'only a phantom', as Stesichorus claimed.

2. This is to suggest that the *mnēstēres tēs Helenēs*, 'suitors of Helen', were really *mnēstēres tou hellēspontou*, 'those who were mindful of the Hellespont', and that the solemn oath which these kings took on the bloody joints of the horse sacred to Poseidon, the chief patron of the expedition, was to support the rights of any member of the confederacy to navigate the Hellespont, despite the Trojans and their Asiatic allies (see 148. 10; 160. 1 and 162. 3). After all, the Hellespont bore the name of their own goddess Helle. The Helen story comes, in fact, from the Ugarit epic *Keret*, in which Keret's lawful wife Huray is abducted to Udm.

3. Paris's birth follows the mythical pattern of Aeolus (see 43. c), Pelias (see 68. d), Oedipus (see 105. a), Jason (see 148. b), and the rest; he is the familiar New Year child, with Agelaus's son for twin. His defeat of the fifty sons of Priam in a foot-race is no less familiar (see 53. 3 and 60. m). 'Oenone' seems to have been a title of the princess whom he won on this occasion (see 53. 3; 60. 4; 98. 7 and 160. d).

He did not, in fact, award the apple to the fairest of the three goddesses. This tale is mistakenly deduced from the icon which showed Heracles being given an apple-bough by the Hesperides (see 133. 4) – the naked Nymph-goddess in triad – Adanus of Hebron being immortalized by the Canaanite Mother of All Living, or the victor of the foot-race at Olympia receiving his prize (see 53. 7); as is proved by the presence of Hermes, Conductor of Souls, his guide to the Elysian Fields.

4. During the fourteenth century B.C., Egypt and Phoenicia suffered from frequent raids by the Keftiu, or 'peoples of the sea', in which the Trojans seem to have taken a leading part. Among the tribes that gained a foothold in Palestine were the Girgashites (*Genesis* x. 16), namely Teucrians from Gergis, or Gergithium, in the Troad (Homer: *Iliad* viii. 304; Herodotus: v. 122 and vii. 43; Livy: xxxviii. 39). Priam and Anchises figure in the Old Testament as Piram and Achish (*Joshua* x. 3 and 1 *Samuel* xxvii. 2); and Pharez, an ancestor of the racially mixed tribe of Judah, who fought with his twin inside their mother's womb (*Genesis* xxxviii. 29), seems to be Paris. Helen's 'bleeding stone', found on the Trojan citadel, is explained by the execution there of Priam's nephew Munippus: Paris remained the queen's consort at the price of annual child sacrifice. Antheus ('flowery'), is a similar victim: his name, a title of the Spring Dionysus (see 85. 2), was given to other unfortunate princes, cut down in the flower of their lives; among them the son of Poseidon, killed and flayed by Cleomenes (Philostephanus: *Fragment* 8); and Antheus of Halicarnassus, drowned in a well by Cleobis (Parthenius: *Narrations* 14).

5. Cilla, whose name means 'the divinatory dice made from ass's

bone' (Hesychius *sub* Cillae) must be Athene, the goddess of the Trojan citadel, who invented this art of prognostication (see 17. 3) and presided over the death of Munippus.

160

THE FIRST GATHERING AT AULIS

WHEN Paris decided to make Helen his wife, he did not expect to pay for his outrage of Menelaus's hospitality. Had the Cretans been called to account when, in the name of Zeus, they stole Europe from the Phoenicians? Had the Argonauts been asked to pay for their abduction of Medea from Colchis? Or the Athenians for their abduction of Cretan Ariadne? Or the Thracians for that of Athenian Oreithyia?[1] This case, however, proved to be different. Hera sent Iris flying to Crete with news of the elopement; and Menelaus hurried to Mycenae, where he begged his brother Agamemnon to raise levies at once and lead an army against Troy.

b. Agamemnon consented to take this course only if the envoys whom he now sent to Troy, demanding Helen's return and compensation for the injury done to Menelaus, came back empty-handed. When Priam denied all knowledge of the matter – Paris being still in Southern waters – and asked what satisfaction his own envoys had been offered for the rape of Hesione, heralds were sent by Menelaus to every prince who had taken his oath on the bloody joints of the horse, reminding him that Paris's act was an affront to the whole of Greece. Unless the crime were punished in an exemplary fashion, nobody could henceforth be sure of his wife's safety. Menelaus now fetched old Nestor from Pylus, and together they travelled over the Greek mainland, summoning the leaders of the expedition.[2]

c. Next, accompanied by Menelaus and Palamedes, the son of Nauplius, Agamemnon visited Ithaca, where he had the greatest difficulty in persuading Odysseus to join the expedition. This Odysseus, though he passed as the son of Laertes, had been secretly begotten by Sisyphus on Anticleia, daughter of the famous thief Autolycus. Just after the birth, Autolycus came to Ithaca and on the first night of his stay, when supper ended, took the infant on his knee. 'Name him, father,' said Anticleia. Autolycus answered: 'In the course of my life I have antagonized many princes, and I shall therefore name this grandson Odysseus, meaning The Angry One, because he will be the victim of my enmities. Yet if he ever comes to Mount Parnassus to reproach me, I shall give him a share of my possessions, and assuage his anger.' As soon as Odysseus came of age, he duly visited Autolycus but, while out hunting with his uncles, was gashed in the thigh by a boar, and carried the scar to his grave. However, Autolycus looked after him well enough, and he returned to Ithaca laden with the promised gifts.[3]

d. Odysseus married Penelope, daughter of Icarius and the Naiad Periboea; some say, at the request of Icarius's brother Tyndareus, who arranged for him to win a suitors' race down the Spartan street called 'Apheta'. Penelope, formerly named Arnaea, or Arnacia, had been flung into the sea by Nauplius at her father's order; but a flock of purple-striped ducks buoyed her up, fed her, and towed her ashore. Impressed by this prodigy, Icarius and Periboea relented, and Arnaea won the new name of Penelope, which means 'duck'.[4]

e. After marrying Penelope to Odysseus, Icarius begged him to remain at Sparta and, when he refused, followed the chariot in which the bridal pair were driving away, entreating her to stay behind. Odysseus, who had hitherto kept his patience, turned and told Penelope: 'Either come to Ithaca of your own free will; or, if you prefer your father, stay here without me!' Penelope's only reply was to draw down her veil. Icarius, realizing that Odysseus was within his rights, let her go, and raised an image to Modesty, which is still shown some four miles from the city of Sparta, at the place where this incident happened.[5]

f. Now, Odysseus had been warned by an oracle: 'If you go to Troy, you will not return until the twentieth year, and then alone and destitute.' He therefore feigned madness, and Agamemnon, Menelaus, and Palamedes found him wearing a peasant's felt cap shaped like a half-egg, ploughing with an ass and an ox yoked together, and flinging salt over his shoulder as he went. When he pretended not to recognize his distinguished guests, Palamedes snatched the infant Telemachus from Penelope's arms and set him on the ground before the advancing team. Odysseus hastily reined them in to avoid killing his only son and, his sanity having thus been established, was obliged to join the expedition.[6]

g. Menelaus and Odysseus then travelled with Agamemnon's herald

Talthybius to Cyprus, where King Cinyras, another of Helen's former suitors, handed them a breastplate as a gift for Agamemnon, and swore to contribute fifty ships. He kept his promise, but sent only one real ship and forty-nine small earthenware ones, with dolls for crews, which the captain launched as he approached the coast of Greece. Invoked by Agamemnon to avenge this fraud, Apollo is said to have killed Cinyras, whereupon his fifty daughters leapt into the sea and became halcyons; the truth is, however, that Cinyras killed himself when he discovered that he had committed incest with his daughter Smyrne.[7]

h. Calchas the priest of Apollo, a Trojan renegade, had foretold that Troy could not be taken without the aid of young Achilles, the seventh son of Peleus. Achilles's mother Thetis had destroyed his other brothers by burning away their mortal parts, and he would have perished in the same way, had not Peleus snatched him from the fire, replacing his charred ankle-bone with one borrowed from the disinterred skeleton of the giant Damysus. But some say that Thetis dipped him in the river Styx, so that only the heel by which she held him was not immortalized.[8]

i. When Thetis deserted Peleus, he took the child to Cheiron the Centaur, who reared him on Mount Pelion, feeding him on the umbles of lions and wild boars, and the marrow of bears, to give him courage; or, according to another account, on honey-comb, and fawns' marrow to make him run swiftly. Cheiron instructed him in the arts of riding, hunting, pipe-playing, and healing; the Muse Calliope, also, taught him how to sing at banquets. When only six years of age he killed his first boar, and thenceforth was constantly dragging the panting bodies of boars and lions back to Cheiron's cave. Athene and Artemis gazed in wonder at this golden-haired child, who was so swift of foot that he could overtake and kill stags without the help of hounds.[9]

j. Now, Thetis knew that her son would never return from Troy if he joined the expedition, since he was fated either to gain glory there and die early, or to live a long but inglorious life at home. She disguised him as a girl, and entrusted him to Lycomedes, king of Scyros, in whose palace he lived under the name of Cercysera, Aissa, or Pyrrha; and had an intrigue with Lycomedes's daughter Deidameia, by whom he became the father of Pyrrhus, later called Neoptolemus. But some say that Neoptolemus was the son of Achilles and Iphigeneia.[10]

k. Odysseus, Nestor, and Ajax were sent to fetch Achilles from Scyros, where he was rumoured to be hidden. Lycomedes let them search the palace, and they might never have detected Achilles, had not Odysseus laid a pile of gifts – for the most part jewels, girdles, embroidered dresses and such – in the hall, and asked the court-ladies to take their choice. Then Odysseus ordered a sudden trumpet-blast and clash of arms to sound outside the palace and, sure enough, one of the girls stripped herself to the waist and seized the shield and spear which he had included among the gifts. It was Achilles, who now promised to lead his Myrmidons to Troy.[11]

l. Some authorities disdain this as a fanciful tale and say that Nestor and Odysseus came on a recruiting tour to Phthia, where they were entertained by Peleus, who readily allowed Achilles, now fifteen years of age, to go off under the tutorship of Phoenix, the son of Amyntor and Cleobule; and that Thetis gave him a beautiful inlaid chest, packed with tunics, wind-proof cloaks, and thick rugs for the journey.[12] This Phoenix had been accused by Phthia, his father's concubine, of having violated her. Amyntor blinded Phoenix, at the same time setting a curse of childlessness on him; and whether the accusation was true or false, childless he remained. However, he fled to Phthia, where Peleus not only persuaded Cheiron to restore his sight, but appointed him king of the neighbouring Dolopians. Phoenix then volunteered to become the guardian of Achilles who, in return, became deeply attached to him. Some, therefore, hold that Phoenix's blindness was not true loss of sight, but metaphorical of impotence – a curse which Peleus lifted by making him a second father to Achilles.[13]

m. Achilles had an inseparable companion: his cousin Patroclus, who was older than he, though neither so strong, nor so swift, nor so well-born. The name of Patroclus's father is sometimes given as Menoetius of Opus, and sometimes as Aeacus; and his mother is variously called Sthenele, daughter of Acastus; Periopis, daughter of Pheres; Polymele, daughter of Peleus; or Philomele, daughter of Actor.[14] He had fled to Peleus's court after killing Amphidamas's son Cleiteonymus, or Aeanes, in a quarrel over a game of dice.[15]

n. When the Greek fleet was already drawn up at Aulis, a protected beach in the Euboean straits, Cretan envoys came to announce that their King Idomeneus, son of Deucalion, would bring a hundred ships to Troy, if Agamemnon agreed to share the supreme command with him; and this condition was accepted. Idomeneus, a former suitor of Helen's, and famous for his good looks, brought as his lieutenant Meriones, son of Molus, reputedly one of Minos's bastards. He bore the figure of a cock on his shield, because he was descended from Helius, and wore a helmet garnished with boars' tusks.[16] Thus the expedition became a Creto-Hellene enterprise. The Hellenic land forces were commanded by Agamemnon, with Odysseus, Palamedes and Diomedes as his lieutenants; and the Hellenic fleet by Achilles, with the support of Great Ajax and Phoenix.[17]

o. Of all his counsellors, Agamemnon set most store by Nestor King of Pylus, whose wisdom was unrivalled, and whose eloquence sweeter than honey. He ruled over three generations of men, but remained, despite his great age, a bold fighter, and the one commander who surpassed the Athenian king Menestheus in cavalry and infantry tactics. His sound judgement was shared by Odysseus, and these two always advised the same course for the successful conduct of the war.[18]

p. Great Ajax, son of Telamon and Periboea, came from Salamis. He was second only to Achilles in courage, strength, and beauty, and stood head and shoulders taller than his nearest rival, carrying a shield of proof made from seven bulls' hides. His body was invulnerable, except in the armpit, and some say, at the neck, because of the charm Heracles had laid upon him.[19] As he went aboard his vessel, Telamon gave him this parting advice: 'Set your mind on conquest, but always with the help of the gods.' Ajax boasted: 'With the help of the gods, any coward or fool can win glory; I trust to do so even without them!' By this boast, and others like it, he incurred divine anger. On one occasion, when Athene came to urge him on in battle, he shouted back: 'Be off, Goddess, and encourage my fellow-Greeks: for, where I am, no enemy will ever break through!'[20] Ajax's half-brother Teucer, a bastard son of Telamon and Hesione, and the best archer in Greece, used to fight from behind Ajax's shield, returning to its shelter as a child runs to his mother.[21]

q. Little Ajax the Locrian, son of Oïleus and Eriopis, though small, outdid all the Greeks in spear-throwing and, next to Achilles, ran the swiftest. He was the third member of Great Ajax's team of fighters, and could easily be recognized by his linen corslet and the tame serpent, longer than a man, which followed him everywhere like a dog.[22] His half-brother Medon, a bastard son of Oïleus and the nymph Rhene, came from Phylace, where he had been banished for having slain Eriopis's brother.[23]

r. Diomedes, the son of Tydeus and Deipyle, came from Argos, accompanied by two fellow-Epigoni, namely Sthenelus, son of Capaneus, and Euryalus the Argonaut, son of Mecisteus. He had been deeply in love with Helen, and took her abduction by Paris as a personal affront.[24]

s. Tlepolemus the Argive, a son of Heracles, brought nine ships from Rhodes.[25]

t. Before leaving Aulis, the Greek fleet received supplies of corn, wine, and other provisions from Anius, king of Delos, whom Apollo had secretly begotten on Rhoeo, daughter of Staphylus and Chrysothemis. Rhoeo was locked in a chest and set adrift by her father when he found her with child; but, being washed ashore on the coast of Euboea, gave birth to a boy whom she named Anius, because of the *trouble* she had suffered on his account; and Apollo made him his own prophetic priest-king at Delos. Some say, however, that Rhoeo's chest drifted directly to Delos.[26]

u. By his wife Dorippe, Anius was the father of three daughters: Elais, Spermo, and Oeno, who are called the Winegrowers; and of a son, Andron, king of Andros, to whom Apollo taught the art of augury. Being himself a priest of Apollo, Anius dedicated the Winegrowers to Dionysus, wishing his family to be under the protection of more than one god. In return, Dionysus granted that whatever Elais touched, after invoking his help, should be turned into oil; whatever Spermo touched, into corn; and whatever Oeno touched, into wine.[27] Thus Anius found it easy enough to provision the Greek fleet. Yet Agamemnon was not satisfied: he sent Menelaus and Odysseus to Delos, where they asked Anius whether they might take the Winegrowers on the expedition. Anius refused this request, telling Menelaus that it was the will of the gods that Troy should be taken only in the tenth year. 'Why not all remain here on Delos for the intervening period?' he suggested hospitably. 'My daughters will keep you supplied with food and drink until the tenth year, and they shall then accompany you to Troy, if necessary.' But, because Agamemnon had strictly ordered: 'Bring them to me, whether Anius consents or not!', Odysseus bound the Winegrowers, and forced them to embark in his vessel.[28] When they escaped, two of them fleeing to Euboea and the other to Andros, Agamemnon sent ships in pursuit, and threatened war if they were not given up. All three surrendered, but called upon Dionysus, who turned them into doves; and to this day doves are closely protected on Delos.[29]

v. At Aulis, while Agamemnon was sacrificing to Zeus and Apollo, a blue serpent with blood-red markings on its back darted from beneath the altar, and made straight for a fine plane-tree which grew near by. On the highest branch lay a sparrow's nest, containing eight young birds and their mother: the serpent devoured them all and then, still coiled around the branch, was turned to stone by Zeus. Calchas explained this portent as strengthening Anius's prophecy: nine years must pass before Troy could be taken, but taken it would be. Zeus further heartened them all with a flash of lightning on their right, as the fleet set sail.[30]

w. Some say that the Greeks left Aulis a month after Agamemnon had persuaded Odysseus to join them, and Calchas piloted them to Troy by his second-sight. Others, that Oenone sent her son Corythus to guide them.[31] But, according to a third, more generally accepted account, they had no pilot, and sailed in error to Mysia, where they disembarked and began to ravage the country, mistaking it for the Troad. King Telephus drove them back to their ships and killed the brave Thersander, son of Theban Polyneices, who alone had stood his ground. Then up ran Achilles and Patroclus, at sight of whom Telephus turned and fled along the banks of the river Caicus. Now, the Greeks had sacrificed to Dionysus at Aulis, whereas the Mysians had neglected him; as a punishment, therefore, Telephus was tripped up by a vine that sprang unexpectedly from the soil, and Achilles wounded him in the thigh with the famous spear which only he could wield, Cheiron's gift to his father Peleus.[32]

x. Thersander was buried at Mysian Elaea, where he now has a hero-shrine; the command of his Boeotians passed first to Peneleos and next, when he was killed by Telephus's son Eurypylus, to Thersander's son Tisamenus, who had not been of age at the time of his father's death. But some pretend that Thersander survived, and was one of those who hid in the Wooden Horse.[33]

y. Having bathed their wounded in the hot Ionian springs near Smyrna, called 'The Baths of Agamemnon', the Greeks put to sea once more but, their ships being scattered by a violent storm which Hera had raised, each captain steered for his own country. It was on this occasion that Achilles landed at Scyros, and formally married Deidameia.[34] Some believe that Troy fell twenty years after the abduction of Helen: that the Greeks made this false start in the second year; and that eight years elapsed before they embarked again. But it is far more probable that their council of war at Spartan Hellenium was held in the same year as their retirement from Mysia; they were still, it is said, in great perplexity because they had no competent pilot to steer them to Troy.[35]

z. Meanwhile, Telephus's wound still festered, and Apollo announced that it could be healed only by its cause. So he visited Agamemnon at Mycenae, clad in rags like a suppliant, and on Clytaemnestra's advice snatched the infant Orestes from his cradle. 'I will kill your son,' he cried, 'unless you cure me!' But Agamemnon, having been warned by an oracle that the Greeks could not take Troy without Telephus's advice, gladly undertook to aid him, if he would guide the fleet to Troy. When Telephus agreed, Achilles, at Agamemnon's request, scraped some rust off his spear into the wound and thus healed it; with the further help of the herb *achilleos*, a vulnerary which he had himself discovered.[36] Telephus later refused to join the expedition, on the ground that his wife, Laodice, also called Hiera, or Astyoche, was Priam's daughter; but he showed the Greeks what course to shape, and Calchas confirmed the accuracy of his advice by divination.[37]

1. Herodotus: i. 1–4; Ovid: *Heroides* xvi. 341–50.
2. Herodotus: i. 3; *Cypria*, quoted by Proclus: *Chrestomathy* 1; Apollodorus: *Epitome* iii. 6.
3. Hyginus: *Fabula* 95; Homer: *Odyssey* xxiv. 115–19 and xix. 399–466; Apollodorus: *Epitome* iii. 12; Servius on Virgil's *Aeneid* vi. 529.
4. Apollodorus: iii. 10. 6 and 9; Pausanias: iii. 12. 2; Tzetzes: *On Lycophron* 792; Didymus, quoted by Eustathius on Homer, p. 1422.
5. Pausanias: iii. 20. 2.
6. Hyginus: *loc. cit.*; Servius on Virgil's *Aeneid* ii. 81; Tzetzes: *On Lycophron* 818; Apollodorus: *Epitome* iii. 7.
7. Apollodorus: *Epitome* iii. 9; Eustathius on Homer's *Iliad* xi. 20; Nonnus: *Dionysiaca* xiii. 451; Hyginus: *Fabula* 242.
8. Apollodorus: iii. 13. 8; Ptolemy Hephaestionos: vi.; Lycophron: *Alexandra* 178 ff., with scholiast; Scholiast on Homer's *Iliad* xvi. 37; Scholiast on Aristophanes's *Clouds* 1068; Scholiast on Apollonius Rhodius: iv. 816.
9. Servius on Virgil's *Aeneid* vi. 57; Fulgentius: *Mythologicon* iii. 7; Apollodorus: iii. 13. 6; Philostratus: *Heroica* xx. 2 and xix. 2; *Argonautica Orphica* 392 ff.; Statius: *Achilleid* i. 269 ff.; Homer: *Iliad* xi. 831–2; Pindar: *Nemean Odes* iii. 43 ff.
10. Apollodorus: iii. 13. 8; Homer: *Iliad* ix. 410 ff.; Ptolemy Hephaestionos: i; Tzetzes: *On Lycophron* 183.
11. Apollodorus: *loc. cit.*; Scholiast on Homer's *Iliad* xix. 332; Ovid: *Metamorphoses* xiii. 162 ff.; Hyginus: *Fabula* 96.

12. Homer: *Iliad* ix. 769 ff.; 438 ff. and xvi. 298.
13. Apollodorus: *loc. cit.*; Tzetzes: *On Lycophron* 421; Homer: *Iliad* ix. 447 ff. and 485.
14. Homer: *Iliad* xi. 786–7; Pindar: *Olympian Odes* ix. 69–70; Hesiod, quoted by Eustathius on Homer's *Iliad* i. 337; Apollodorus: *loc. cit.*; Hyginus: *Fabula* 97; Scholiast on Apollonius Rhodius: iv. 816.
15. Apollodorus: *loc. cit.*; Strabo: ix. 4. 2.
16. Apollodorus: iii. 3. 1; Philostratus: *Heroica* 7; Diodorus Siculus: v. 79; Hyginus: *Fabula* 81; Pausanias: v. 23. 5; Homer: *Iliad* x. 61 ff.
17. Dictys Cretensis: i. 16; Apollodorus: *Epitome* iii. 6.
18. Homer: *Iliad* ii. 21 and i. 247–52; iv. 310 ff.; ii. 553–5; *Odyssey* iii. 244 and 126–9.
19. Homer: *Iliad* xvii. 279–80 and iii. 226–7; Sophocles: *Ajax* 576 and 833, with scholiast; Scholiast on Homer's *Iliad* xxiii. 821; Tzetzes: *On Lycophron* 455 ff.
20. Sophocles: *Ajax* 762–77.
21. Homer: *Iliad* viii. 266–72.
22. Homer: *Iliad* xiii. 697; ii. 527–30; xiv. 520 and xiii. 701 ff.; Hyginus: *Fabula* 97; Philostratus: *Heroica* viii. 1.
23. Homer: *Iliad* ii. 728 and xiii. 694–7.
24. Apollodorus: i. 8. 5; Hyginus: *loc. cit.*; Homer: *Iliad* ii. 564–6.
25. Homer: *Iliad* ii. 653–4; Hyginus: *loc. cit.*
26. Dictys Cretensis: i. 23; Servius on Virgil's *Aeneid* iii. 80; Diodorus Siculus: v. 62; Tzetzes: *On Lycophron* 570.
27. Tzetzes: *loc. cit.*; Apollodorus: *Epitome* iii. 10; Ovid: *Metamorphoses* xiii. 650 ff.; Servius: *loc. cit.*
28. Stesichorus, quoted by scholiast on Homer's *Odyssey* vi. 164; Tzetzes: *On Lycophron* 583; Servius: *loc. cit.*; Pherecydes, quoted by Tzetzes: *On Lycophron* 570.
29. Ovid: *Metamorphoses* 643–74; Servius: *loc. cit.*
30. Apollodorus: *Epitome* iii. 15; Homer: *Iliad* ii. 303–53; Ovid: *Metamorphoses* xii. 13–23.
31. Homer: *Odyssey* xxiv. 118–19 and *Iliad* i. 71; Tzetzes: *On Lycophron* 57 ff.
32. Apollodorus: *Epitome* iii. 17; Pindar: *Olympian Odes* ix. 70 ff.; Tzetzes: *On Lycophron* 206 and 209; Scholiast on Homer's *Iliad*, i. 59; Homer: *Iliad* xvi. 140–4.
33. Pausanias: ix. 5. 7–8; Virgil: *Aeneid* ii. 261.
34. Philostratus: *Heroica* iii. 35; Apollodorus: *Epitome* iii. 18; *Cypria* quoted by Proclus: *Chrestomathy* 1.
35. Homer: *Iliad* xxiv. 765; Apollodorus: *loc. cit.*; Pausanias: iii. 12. 5.
36. Apollodorus: *Epitome* iii. 19–20; Hyginus: *Fabula* 101; Pliny: *Natural History* xxv. 19.
37. Hyginus: *loc. cit.*; Philostratus: *Heroica* ii. 18; Scholiast on Homer's *Odyssey* i. 520; Apollodorus: *Epitome* iii. 20.

*

1. After the fall of Cnossus, about the year 1400 B.C., a contest for sea-power arose between the peoples of the Eastern Mediterranean. This is reflected in Herodotus's account, which John Malalas supports (see 58. *4*), of the raids preceding Helen's abduction, and in Apollodorus's record of how Paris raided Sidon (see 159. *t*), and Agamemnon's people, Mysia. A Trojan confederacy offered the chief obstacle to Greek mercantile ambitions, until the High King of Mycenae gathered his allies, including the Greek overlords of Crete, for a concerted attack on Troy. The naval war, as opposed to the siege of Troy, may well have lasted for nine or ten years.

2. Among Agamemnon's independent allies were the islanders of Ithaca, Same, Dulichium, and Zacynthus led by Odysseus; the Southern Thessalians led by Achilles; and their Aeacan cousins from Locris and Salamis, led by the two Ajaxes. These chieftains proved an awkward team to handle and Agamemnon could keep them from each other's throats only by intrigue, with the loyal support of his Peloponnesian henchmen Menelaus of Sparta, Diomedes of Argos, and Nestor of Pylus. Ajax's rejection of the Olympian gods and his affront to the Zeus-born Athene have been misrepresented as evidence of atheism; they record, rather, his religious conservatism. The Aeacids were of Lelegian stock and worshipped the pre-Hellenic goddess (see 158. *8* and 168. *2*).

3. The Thebans and Athenians seem to have kept out of the war; though Athenian forces are mentioned in the *Catalogue of Ships*, they play no memorable part before Troy. But the presence of King Menestheus has been emphasized to justify later Athenian expansion along the Black Sea coast (see 162. *3*). Odysseus is a key-figure in Greek mythology. Despite his birth from a daughter of the Corinthian Sun-god and his old-fashioned foot-race winning of Penelope, he breaks the ancient matrilocal rule by insisting that Penelope shall come to his kingdom, rather than he to hers (see 137. *4*). Also, like his father Sisyphus (see 67. *2*), and Cretan Cinyras (see 18. *5*), he refuses to die at the end of his proper term – which is the central allegory of the *Odyssey* (see 170. *1* and 171. *3*). Odysseus, moreover, is the first mythical character credited with an irrelevant physical peculiarity: legs short in proportion to his body, so that he 'looks nobler sitting than standing.' The scarred thigh, however, should be read as a sign that he escaped the death incumbent on boar-cult kings (see 18. *3* and 151. *2*).

4. Odysseus's pretended madness, though consistent with his novel reluctance to act as behoved a king, seems to be misreported. What he did was to demonstrate prophetically the uselessness of the war to which he had been summoned. Wearing a conical hat which marked the mystagogue or seer, he ploughed a field up and down. Ox and ass stood for Zeus and Cronus, or summer and winter; and each furrow, sown with salt, for a wasted year. Palamedes, who also had prophetic powers (see 52.

6), then seized Telemachus and halted the plough, doubtless at the tenth furrow, by setting him in front of the team: he thereby showed that the *decisive battle*, which is the meaning of 'Telemachus', would take place then.

5. Achilles, a more conservative character, hides among women, as befits a solar hero (*White Goddess* p. 212), and takes arms in the fourth month, when the Sun has passed the equinox and so from the tutelage of his mother, Night. Cretan boys were called *scotioi*, 'children of darkness' (see 27. 2), while confined to the women's quarters, not having yet been given arms and liberty by the priestess-mother (see 121. 5). In the *Mabinogion*, Odysseus's ruse for arming Achilles is used by Gwydion (the god Odin, or Woden) on a similar occasion: wishing to release Llew Llaw Gyffes, another solar hero, from the power of his mother Arianrhod, he creates a noise of battle outside the castle and frightens her into giving Llew Llaw sword and shield. The Welsh is probably the elder version of the myth, which the Argives dramatized on the first day of the fourth month by a fight between boys dressed in girls' clothes and women dressed in men's – the festival being called the Hybristica ('shameful behaviour'). Its historical excuse was that, early in the fifth century, the poetess Telesilla, with a company of women, had contrived to hold Argos against King Cleomenes of Sparta, after the total defeat of the Argive army (Plutarch: *On the Virtues of Women* 4). Since Patroclus bears an inappropriately patriarchal name ('glory to the father'), he may have once been Phoenix ('blood red'), Achilles's twin and tanist under the matrilinear system.

6. All the Greek leaders before Troy are sacred kings. Little Ajax's tame serpent cannot have accompanied him into battle: he did not have one until he became an oracular hero. Idomeneus's boar's tusk helmet, attested by finds in Crete and Mycenaean Greece, was originally perhaps worn by the tanist (see 18. 7); his cock, sacred to the sun, and representing Zeus Velchanos, must be a late addition to Homer because the domestic hen did not reach Greece until the sixth century B.C. The original device is likely to have been a cock partridge (see 92. 1). These cumbrous shields consisted of bull's hides sewn together, the extremities being rounded off, and the waist nipped, in figure-of-eight shape, for ritual use. They covered the entire body from chin to ankle. Achilles ('lipless') seems to have been a common title of oracular heroes, since there were Achilles cults at Scyros, Phthia, and Elis (Pausanias: vi. 23. 3).

7. Rhoeo, daughter of Staphylus and Chrysothemis ('Pomegranate, daughter of Bunch of Grapes and Golden Order') came to Delos in a chest and is the familiar fertility-goddess with her new-moon boat. She also appears in triad as her grand-daughters the Winegrowers, whose names mean 'olive oil', 'grain' and 'wine'. Their mother is Dorippe, or 'gift mare', which suggests that Rhoeo was the mare-headed Demeter

(see 16. 5). Her cult survives vestigially today in the three-cupped *kernos*, a vessel used by Greek Orthodox priests to hold the gifts of oil, grain, and wine brought to church for sanctification. A *kernos* of the same type has been found in an early Minoan tomb at Koumasa; and the Winegrowers, being great-grandchildren of Ariadne, must have come to Delos from Crete (see 27. 8).

8. The Greeks' difficulty in finding their way to Troy is contradicted by the ease with which Menelaus had sailed there; perhaps in the original legend Trojan Aphrodite cast a spell which fogged their memory, as she afterwards dispersed the fleets on the return voyage (see 169. 2).

9. Achilles's treatment of the spear wound, based on the ancient homoeopathic principle that 'like cures like', recalls Melampus's use of rust from a gelding-knife to restore Iphiclus (see 72. e).

10. Maenads, in vase-paintings, sometimes have their limbs tattooed with a woof-and-warp pattern formalized as a ladder. If their faces were once similarly tattooed as a camouflage for woodland revelling, this might explain the name Penelope ('with a web over her face'), as a title of the orgiastic mountain-goddess; alternatively, she may have worn a net in her orgies, like Dictynna and the British goddess Goda (see 89. 2 and 3). Pan's alleged birth from Penelope, after she had slept promiscuously with all her suitors in Odysseus's absence (see 161. l), records a tradition of pre-Hellenic sexual orgies; the penelope duck, like the swan, was probably a totem-bird of Sparta (see 62. 3–4).

11. No commentator has hitherto troubled to explain precisely why Calchas's nest of birds should have been set on a plane-tree and devoured by a serpent; but the fact is that serpents cast their slough each year and renew themselves, and so do plane-trees – which makes them both symbols of regeneration. Calchas therefore knew that the birds which were devoured stood for years, not months. Though later appropriated by Apollo, the plane was the Goddess's sacred tree in Crete and Sparta (see 58. 3), because its leaf resembled a green hand with the fingers stretched out to bless – a gesture frequently found in her archaic statuettes. The blue spots on the serpent showed that it was sent by Zeus, who wore a blue nimbus as god of the sky. Cinyras's toy ships perhaps reflect a Cyprian custom borrowed from Egypt, of burying terracotta ships beside dead princes for their voyage to the Otherworld.

12. The fifty daughters of Cinyras's who turned into halcyons will have been a college of Aphrodite's priestesses. One of her titles was 'Alcyone', 'the queen who wards off [storms]', and the halcyons, or kingfishers, which were sacred to her, portended calms (see 45. 2).

THE SECOND GATHERING AT AULIS

CALCHAS, the brother of Leucippe and Theonoë, had learned the art of prophecy from his father Thestor. One day, Theonoë was walking on the seashore near Troy, when Carian pirates bore her off, and she became mistress to King Icarus. Thestor at once set out in pursuit, but was shipwrecked on the Carian coast and imprisoned by Icarus. Several years later, Leucippe, who had been a mere child when these sad events took place, went to Delphi for news of her father and sister. Advised by the Pythoness to disguise herself as a priest of Apollo and go to Caria in search of them, Leucippe obediently shaved her head and visited the court of King Icarus; but Theonoë, not seeing through the disguise, fell in love with her, and told one of the guards: 'Bring that young priest to my bedroom!' Leucippe, failing to recognize Theonoë, and fearing to be put to death as an imposter, rebuffed her; whereupon Theonoë, since she could not ask the palace servants to commit sacrilege by killing a priest, gave orders that one of the foreign prisoners must do so, and sent a sword for his use.

b. Now, the prisoner chosen was Thestor, who went to the bedroom in which Leucippe had been locked, displayed his sword, and despairingly told her his story. 'I will not kill you, sir,' he said, 'because I too worship Apollo, and prefer to kill myself! But let me first reveal my name: I am Thestor, son of Idmon the Agonaut, a Trojan priest.' He was about to plunge the sword into his own breast, when Leucippe snatched it away. 'Father, father!' she exclaimed, 'I am Leucippe, your daughter! Do not turn this weapon against yourself; use it to kill King Icarus's abominable concubine. Come, follow me!' They hurried to Theonoë's embroidery-chamber. 'Ah, lustful one,' cried Leucippe, bursting in and dragging Thestor after her. 'Prepare to die by the hand of my father, Thestor son of Idmon!' Then it was Theonoë's turn to exclaim: 'Father, father!'; and when the three had wept tears of joy, and given thanks to Apollo, King Icarus generously sent them all home, laden with gifts.[1]

c. Now Priam, after rejecting Agamemnon's demand for the return of Helen, sent Thestor's son Calchas, a priest of Apollo, to consult the Delphic Pythoness. Having foretold the fall of Troy and the total ruin of Priam's house, she ordered Calchas to join the Greeks and prevent them from raising the siege until they were victorious. Calchas then swore an oath of friendship with Achilles, who lodged him in his own house, and presently brought him to Agamemnon.[2]

d. When the Greek fleet assembled for the second time at Aulis, but was windbound there for many days, Calchas prophesied that they would be unable to sail unless Agamemnon sacrificed the most beautiful of his daughters to Artemis. Why Artemis should have been vexed is disputed. Some say that, on shooting a stag at long range, Agamemnon had boasted: 'Artemis herself could not have done better!'; or had killed her sacred goat; or had vowed to offer her the most beautiful creature born that year in his kingdom, which happened to be Iphigeneia; or that his father Atreus had withheld a golden lamb which was her due.[3] At any rate, Agamemnon refused to do as he was expected, saying that Clytaemnestra would never let Iphigeneia go. But when the Greeks swore: 'We shall transfer our allegiance to Palamedes if he continues obdurate,' and when Odysseus, feigning anger, prepared to sail home, Menelaus came forward as peace-maker. He suggested that Odysseus and Talthybius should fetch Iphigeneia to Aulis, on the pretext of marrying her to Achilles as a reward for his daring feats in Mysia. To this ruse Agamemnon agreed, and though he at once sent a secret message, warning Clytaemnestra not to believe Odysseus, Menelaus intercepted this, and she was tricked into bringing Iphigeneia to Aulis.[4]

e. When Achilles found that his name had been misused, he undertook to protect Iphigeneia from injury; but she nobly consented to die for the glory of Greece, and offered her neck to the sacrificial axe without a word of complaint. Some say that, in the nick of time, Artemis carried her off to the land of the Taurians, substituting a hind at the altar; or a she-bear; or an old woman. Others, that a peal of thunder was heard and that, at Artemis's order and Clytaemnestra's plea, Achilles intervened, saved Iphigeneia, and sent her to Scythia; or that he married her, and that she, not Deidameia, bore him Neoptolemus.[5]

f. But whether Iphigeneia died or was spared, the north-easterly gale dropped, and the fleet set sail at last. They first touched at Lesbos, where Odysseus entered the ring against King Philomeleides, who always compelled his guests to wrestle with him; and, amid the loud cheers of every Greek present, threw him ignominiously. Next, they landed on Tenedos, which is visible from Troy, and was then ruled by

Tenes who, though reputedly the son of Cycnus and Procleia, daughter of Laomedon, could call Apollo his father.

g. This Cycnus, a son of Poseidon and Calyce, or Harpale, ruled Colonae. He had been born in secret, and exposed on the seashore, but was found by some fishermen who saw a swan flying down to comfort him.[6] After the death of Procleia, he married Phylonome, daughter of Tragasus: she fell in love with her step-son Tenes, failed to seduce him, and vengefully accused him of having tried to violate her. She called the flautist Molpus as a witness; and Cycnus, believing them, locked Tenes and his sister Hemithea in a chest and set them adrift on the sea. They were washed ashore on the island of Tenedos, hitherto called Leucophrys, which means 'white brow'.[7] Later, when Cycnus learned the truth, he had Molpus stoned to death, buried Phylonome alive and, hearing that Tenes survived and was living on Tenedos, hastened there to admit his error. But Tenes, in an unforgiving mood, cut the cables of Cycnus's ship with an axe: hence the proverbial expression for an angry refusal – 'He cut him with an axe from Tenedos.' Finally, however, Tenes softened, and Cycnus settled near him on Tenedos.[8]

h. Now, Thetis had warned Achilles that if ever he killed a son of Apollo, he must himself die by Apollo's hand; and a servant named Mnemon accompanied him for the sole purpose of reminding him of this. But Achilles, when he saw Tenes hurling a huge rock from a cliff at the Greek ships, swam ashore, and thoughtlessly thrust him through the heart. The Greeks then landed and ravaged Tenedos; and realizing too late what he had done, Achilles put Mnemon to death because he had failed to remind him of Thetis's words. He buried Tenes where his shrine now stands: no flautist may enter there, nor may Achilles's name be mentioned.[9] Achilles also killed Cycnus with a blow on the head, his only vulnerable part; and pursued Hemithea, who fled from him like a hind, but would have been overtaken and violated, had not the earth swallowed her up. It was in Tenedos, too, that Achilles first quarrelled with Agamemnon, whom he accused of having invited him to join the expedition only as an afterthought.[10]

i. Palamedes offered a hecatomb to Apollo Smintheus in gratitude for the Tenedan victory but, as he did so, a water-snake approached the altar and bit Philoctetes, the famous archer, in the foot. Neither unguents nor fomentations availed, and the wound grew so noisome, and Philoctetes's groans so loud, that the army could no longer tolerate his company. Agamemnon therefore ordered Odysseus to put him ashore in a deserted district of Lemnos, where he sustained life for several years by shooting birds; and Medon assumed the command of his troops.[11]

j. According to another account, the accident happened on Chryse, an islet off Lemnos, which has since vanished beneath the sea. There either the nymph Chryse fell in love with Philoctetes and, when he rejected her advances, provoked a viper to bite him while he was clearing away the earth from a buried altar of Athene Chryse; or else a serpent that guarded Athene's temple bit him when he came too close.[12]

k. According to a third account, Philoctetes was bitten in Lemnos itself by a serpent which Hera sent as a punishment for his having dared to kindle Heracles's funeral pyre. He was, at the time, raptly gazing at the altar raised to Athene by Jason, and planning to raise another to Heracles.[13]

l. A fourth account is that Philoctetes was bitten while admiring Troilus's tomb in the temple of Thymbraean Apollo.[14] A fifth, that he was wounded by one of Heracles's envenomed arrows. Heracles, it is said, had made him swear never to divulge the whereabouts of his buried ashes; but when the Greeks learned that Troy could not be sacked without the use of Heracles's arrows, they went in search of Philoctetes. Though at first denying all knowledge of Heracles, he ended by telling them exactly what had happened on Mount Oeta; so they eagerly asked him where they might find the grave. This question he refused to answer, but they became so insistent that he went to the place, and there wordlessly stamped on the ground. Later, as he passed the grave on his way to the Trojan War, one of Heracles's arrows leaped from the quiver and pierced his foot: a warning that one must not reveal divine secrets even by a sign or hint.[15]

1. Hyginus: *Fabula* 190.
2. Benoit: *Le Roman de Troie.*
3. Ptolemy Hephaestionos: vi, quoted by Photius p. 483; Euripides: *Iphigeneia Among the Taurians;* Apollodorus: *Epitome* iii. 21.
4. Ptolemy Hephaestionos: *loc. cit.;* Euripides: *loc. cit.;* Apollodorus: *Epitome* iii. 22; Dictys Cretensis: i. 20.
5. Euripides: *Iphigeneia in Aulis;* Sophocles: *Electra* 574; Apollodorus: *loc. cit.;* Dictys Cretensis: i. 19; Tzetzes: *On Lycophron* 183.
6. Homer: *Odyssey* iv. 342–4; Apollodorus: *Epitome* iii. 23–4; Pausanias: x. 14. 2; Hyginus: *Fabula* 157; Scholiast on Pindar's *Olympian Odes* ii. 147; Tzetzes: *On Lycophron* 232–3.
7. Apollodorus: *Epitome* iii. 24; Pausanias: *loc. cit.;* Tzetzes: *loc. cit.*
8. Apollodorus: *Epitome* iii. 25; Pausanias: x. 14. 2; Tzetzes: *loc. cit.*

9. Tzetzes: *loc. cit.*; Plutarch: *Greek Questions* 28.

10. Tzetzes: *loc. cit.*; Apollodorus: *Epitome* iii. 31; *Cypria*, quoted by Proclus: *Chrestomathy* 1.

11. Dictys Cretensis: ii. 14; *Cypria*, quoted by Proclus: *loc. cit.*; Apollodorus: *Epitome* iii. 27; Homer: *Iliad* ii. 727.

12. Pausanias: viii. 33. 2; Tzetzes: *On Lycophron* 911; Sophocles: *Philoctetes* 1327; Philostratus: *Imagines* 17; Eustathius on Homer p. 330.

13. Hyginus: *Fabula* 102; Scholiast on Sophocles's *Philoctetes*, verses 2, 193 and 266.

14. Philostratus: *loc. cit.*

15. Servius on Virgil's *Aeneid* iii. 402.

*

1. The lost play from which Hyginus has taken the story of Thestor and his daughters shows the Greek dramatists at their most theatrical; it has no mythological value.

2. A version of the 'Jephthah's daughter' myth (see 169. 5) seems to have been confused with Agamemnon's sacrifice of a priestess at Aulis, on a charge of raising contrary winds by witchcraft; Sir Francis Drake once hanged one of his sailors, a spy in Cecil's pay, on the same charge. Agamemnon's high-handed action, it seems, offended conservative opinion at home, women being traditionally exempt from sacrifice. The Taurians, to whom Iphigeneia was said to have been sent by Artemis, lived in the Crimea and worshipped Artemis as a man-slayer; Agamemnon's son Orestes fell into their clutches (see 116. *e*).

3. Odysseus's wrestling match with King Philomeleides, whose name means 'dear to the apple-nymphs', is probably taken from a familiar icon, showing the ritual contest in which the old king is defeated by the new and given an apple-bough (see 53. *b*).

4. Achilles killed a second Cycnus (see 162. *f*); Heracles killed a third (see 143. *g*), and was prevented by Zeus from killing a fourth (see 133. *d*). The name implied that swans conveyed these royal souls to the Northern Paradise. When Apollo appears in ancient works of art riding on swan-back, or in a chariot drawn by swans (Overbeck: *Griechische Kunstmythologie*) on a visit to the Hyperboreans, this is a polite way of depicting his representative's annual death at midsummer. Singing swans then fly north to their breeding grounds in the Arctic circle, and utter two trumpet-like notes as they go; which is why Pausanias (i. 30. 3) says that swans are versed in the Muses' craft. 'Swans sing before they die': the sacred king's soul departs to the sound of music.

5. Philoctetes's wound has been associated with many different localities because the icon from which his story derives was widely current. He is the sacred king of Tenedos, Lemnos, Euboea, or any other

Halladic state, receiving the prick of an envenomed arrow in his foot (see 126. 3; 154. h; 164. j and 166. e) beside the goddess's altar.

6. Heracles was not the only sacred king whose grave remained a secret; this seems to have been common practice on the Isthmus of Corinth (see 67. j), and among the primitive Hebrews (*Deuteronomy* xxxiv. 6).

7. Tenes hurling rocks may be a misinterpretation of the familiar icon which shows a sun-hero pushing the sun-boulder up to the zenith (see 67. 2), since Talos, a Cretan sun-hero, also hurled rocks at approaching ships (see 154. h). The ships in this icon would merely indicate that Crete, or Tenedos, was a naval power.

162

NINE YEARS OF WAR

A T what point the Greeks sent Priam envoys to demand the return of Helen and of Menelaus's property is disputed. Some say, soon after the expedition had landed in the Troad; others, before the ships assembled at Aulis; but it is commonly held that the embassy, consisting of Menelaus, Odysseus, and Palamedes, went ahead from Tenedos.[1] The Trojans, however, being determined to keep Helen, would have murdered them all had not Antenor, in whose house they were lodging, forbidden the shameful deed.[2]

b. Vexed by this obduracy, the Greeks sailed from Tenedos and beached their ships within sight of Troy. The Trojans at once flocked down to the sea and tried to repel the invaders with showers of stones. Then, while all the others hesitated – even Achilles, whom Thetis had warned that the first to land would be the first to die – Protesilaus leaped ashore, killed a number of Trojans, and was struck dead by Hector; or it may have been Euphorbus; or Aeneas's friend Achates.[3]

c. This Protesilaus, an uncle of Philoctetes, and son of that Iphiclus whom Melampus cured of impotence, had been called Iolaus, but was renamed from the circumstance of his death.[4] He lies buried in the Thracian Chersonese, near the city of Elaeus, where he is now given divine honours. Tall elm-trees, planted by nymphs, stand within his precinct and overshadow the tomb. The boughs which face Troy across the sea burst early into leaf, but presently go bare; while those on the other side are still green in winter-time. When the elms grow so high that the walls of Troy can be clearly discerned by a man posted in their upper branches, they wither; saplings, however, spring again from the roots.[5]

d. Protesilaus's wife Laodameia, daughter of Acastus (whom some call Polydora daughter of Meleager) missed him so sadly that as soon as he sailed for Troy she made a brazen, or wax, statue of him and laid it in her bed. But this was poor comfort, and when news came of his death, she begged the gods to take pity and let him revisit her, if only for three hours. Almighty Zeus granted Laodameia's request, and Hermes brought up Protesilaus's ghost from Tartarus to animate the statue. Speaking with its mouth, Protesilaus then adjured her not to delay in following him, and the three hours had no sooner ended than she stabbed herself to death in his embrace.[6] Others say that Laodameia's father Acastus forced her to remarry, but that she spent her nights with Protesilaus's statue until one day a servant, bringing apples for a dawn sacrifice, looked through a crack in the bedroom-door and saw her embracing what he took to be a lover. He ran and told Acastus who, bursting into the room, discovered the truth. Rather than that she should torture herself by fruitless longing, Acastus ordered the statue to be burned; but Laodameia threw herself into the flames and perished with it.[7]

e. According to another tradition, Protesilaus survived the Trojan War and set sail for home. He took back, as his prisoner, Priam's sister Aethylla. On the way he landed at the Macedonian peninsula of Pellene but, while he went ashore in search of water, Aethylla persuaded the other captive women to burn the ships; and Protesilaus, thus obliged to remain on Pellene, founded the city of Scione. This, however, is an error: Aethylla, with Astyoche and her fellow-captives, set fire to the vessels beside the Italian river Navaethus, which means 'burning of ships'; and Protesilaus did not figure among their captors.[8]

f. Achilles was the second Greek to land on the Trojan shore, closely followed by his Myrmidons, and killed Cycnus son of Poseidon with a well-flung stone. Thereupon the Trojans broke and fled back to their city, while the remainder of the Greeks disembarked and pressed murderously on the rout. According to another account, Achilles, mindful of Protesilaus's fate, was the very last to land, and then took such a prodigious leap from his ship that a spring gushed out where his feet struck the shore. In the ensuing battle, it is said, Cycnus, who was invulnerable, killed Greeks by the hundred; but Achilles, after trying sword and spear against him in vain, battered furiously at his face with the hilt of his sword, forced him backwards until he tripped over a stone, then knelt on his breast and strangled him with the straps of his helmet; however, Poseidon turned his spirit into a swan, which flew away. The Greeks then laid siege to Troy and drew up their ships behind a stockade.⁹

g. Now, the city was fated not to fall if Troilus could attain the age of twenty. Some say that Achilles fell in love with him as they fought together, and 'I will kill you,' he said, 'unless you yield to my caresses!' Troilus fled and took sanctuary in the temple of Thymbraean Apollo; but Achilles cared nothing for the god's wrath and since Troilus remained coy, beheaded him at the altar, the very place where he himself later perished.¹⁰ Others say that Achilles speared Troilus while he was exercising his horses in the temple precinct; or that he lured him out by offering a gift of doves, and that Troilus died with crushed ribs and livid face, in such bear-like fashion did Achilles make love. Others, again, say that Troilus sallied vengefully from Troy after the death of Memnon and encountered Achilles, who killed him – or else he was taken prisoner and then publicly slaughtered in cold blood at Achilles's orders – and that, being then middle-aged, with a swarthy complexion and a flowing beard, he can hardly have excited Achilles's passion. But whatever the manner of his death, Achilles caused it, and the Trojans mourned for him as grievously as for Hector.¹¹

h. Troilus is said to have loved Briseis, Calchas's beautiful daughter, who had been left behind in Troy by her father and, since she had played no part in his defection, continued to be treated there with courtesy. Calchas, knowing that Troy must fall, persuaded Agamemnon to ask Priam for her on his behalf, lest she should be made a prisoner of war. Priam generously gave his assent and several of his sons escorted Briseis to the Greek camp. Although she had sworn undying fidelity to Troilus, Briseis soon transferred her affections to Diomedes the Argive, who fell passionately in love with her and did his best to kill Troilus whenever he appeared on the battlefield.¹²

i. On a night expedition, Achilles captured Lycaon, surprising him in his father Priam's orchard, where he was cutting fig-tree shoots for use as chariot-rails. Patroclus took Lycaon to Lemnos, and sold him to Jason's son, King Euneus, who supplied the Greek forces with wine; the price being a silver Phoenician mixing-bowl. But Eëtion of Imbros ransomed him, and he returned to Troy, only to perish at the hand of Achilles twelve days later.[13]

j. Achilles now set out with a band of volunteers to ravage the Trojan countryside. On Mount Ida he cut off Aeneas the Dardanian from his cattle, chased him down the wooded slopes and, after killing the cattlemen and Priam's son Mestor, captured the herd and sacked the city of Lyrnessus, where Aeneas had taken refuge. Mynes and Epistrophus, sons of King Evenus, died in the fighting; but Zeus helped Aeneas to escape. Mynes's wife, another Briseis, daughter of Briseus, was made captive, and her father hanged himself.[14]

k. Though Aeneas had connived at Paris's abduction of Helen, he remained neutral for the first few years of the war; being born of the goddess Aphrodite by Anchises, the grandson of Tros, he resented the disdain shown him by his cousin Priam.[15] Yet Achilles's provocative raid obliged the Dardanians to join forces with the Trojans at last. Aeneas proved a skilled fighter and even Achilles did not disparage him: for if Hector was the hand of the Trojans, Aeneas was their soul. His divine mother frequently helped him in battle; and once, when Diomedes had broken his hip with the cast of a stone, rescued him from death; and when Diomedes had wounded her too, with a spear-thrust in the wrist, Apollo carried Aeneas off the field for Leto and Artemis to cure. On another occasion his life was saved by Poseidon who, though hostile to the Trojans, respected the decrees of fate and knew that the royal line of Aeneas must eventually rule Troy.[16]

l. Many cities allied to Troy were now taken by Achilles: Lesbos, Phocaea, Colophon, Smyrna, Clazomenae, Cyme, Aegialus, Tenos, Adramyttium, Dide, Endium, Linnaeum, Colone, Lyrnessus, Antandrus, and several others, including Hypoplacian Thebes, where another Eëtion, father of Hector's wife Andromache, and his comrade Podes, ruled over the Cilicians. Achilles killed Eëtion, and seven of his sons besides, but did not despoil his corpse: he burned it fully armoured and around the barrow which he heaped, mountain-nymphs planted a grove of elm-trees.[17] The captives included Astynome, or Chryseis, daughter of Chryses, priest of Apollo in the island of Sminthos. Some call Astynome Eëtion's wife; others say that Chryses had sent her to Lyrnessus for protection, or to attend a festival of Artemis. When the spoils were distributed, she fell to Agamemnon, as did Briseis to Achilles. From Hypoplacian Thebes, Achilles also brought away the swift horse Pedasus, whom he yoked to his immortal team.[18]

m. Great Ajax sailed to the Thracian Chersonese, where he captured Lycaon's blood-brother Polydorus – their mother was Laothoë – and in Teuthrania killed King Teuthras, and carried off great spoils, among them the princess Tecmessa, whom he made his concubine.[19]

n. As the tenth year of the war approached, the Greeks refrained from raiding the coast of Asia Minor, and concentrated their forces before Troy. The Trojans marshalled their allies against them – Dardanians, led by Aeneas and the two sons of Antenor; Thracian Ciconians; Paeonians; Paphlagonians; Mysians; Phrygians; Maeonians; Carians; Lycians; and so forth. Sarpedon, whom Bellerophon's daughter Laodemeia had borne to Zeus, led the Lycians. This is his story. When Laodameia's brother Isander and Hippolochus were contending for the kingdom, it was proposed that whichever of them might shoot an arrow through a gold ring hung upon a child's breast should be king. Each hotly demanded the other's child as the victim, but Laodameia prevented them from murdering each other by offering to tie the ring around the neck of her own son, Sarpedon. Astounded at such noble unselfishness, they both agreed to resign their claims to the kingdom in favour of Sarpedon; with whom Glaucus, the son of Hippolochus, was now reigning as co-king.[20]

o. Agamemnon had sent Odysseus on a foraging expedition to Thrace, and when he came back empty-handed, Palamedes son of Nauplius upbraided him for his sloth and cowardice. 'It was not my fault,' cried Odysseus, 'that no corn could be found. If Agamemnon had sent you in my stead, you would have had no greater success.' Thus challenged Palamedes set sail at once and presently reappeared with a ship-load of grain.[21]

p. After days of tortuous thought, Odysseus at last hit upon a plan by which he might be revenged on Palamedes; for his honour was wounded. He sent word to Agamemnon: 'The gods have warned me in a dream that treachery is afoot: the camp must be moved for a day and a night.' When Agamemnon gave immediate orders to have this done, Odysseus secretly buried a sackful of gold at the place where Palamedes's tent had been pitched. He then forced a Phrygian prisoner to write a letter, as if from Priam to Palamedes, which read: 'The gold that I have sent is the price you asked for betraying the Greek camp.' Having then ordered the prisoner to hand Palamedes this letter, Odysseus had him killed just outside the camp, before he could deliver it. Next day, when the army returned to the old site, someone found the prisoner's corpse and took the letter to Agamemnon. Palamedes was court-martialled and, when he hotly denied having received gold from Priam or anyone else, Odysseus suggested that his tent should be searched. The gold was discovered, and the whole army stoned Palamedes to death as a traitor.[22]

q. Some say that Agamemnon, Odysseus, and Diomedes were all implicated in this plot, and that they jointly dictated the false letter to the Phrygian and afterwards bribed a servant to hide it with the gold under Palamedes's bed. When Palamedes was led off to the place of stoning he cried aloud: 'Truth, I mourn for you, who have predeceased me!'[23]

r. Others, again, say that Odysseus and Diomedes, pretending to have discovered a treasure in a deep well, let Palamedes down into it by a rope, and then tumbled large stones on his head; or that they drowned him on a fishing excursion. Still others say that Paris killed him with an arrow. It is not even agreed whether his death took place at Trojan Colonae, at Geraestus, or on Tenedos; but he has a hero-shrine near Lesbian Methymna.[24]

s. Palamedes had deserved the gratitude of his comrades by the invention of dice, with which they whiled away their time before Troy; and the first set of which he dedicated in the temple of Tyche at Argos. But all envied him his superior wisdom, because he had also invented lighthouses, scales, measures, the discus, the alphabet, and the art of posting sentinels.[25]

t. When Nauplius heard of the murder, he sailed to Troy and claimed satisfaction; yet this was denied him by Agamemnon, who had been Odysseus's accomplice and enjoyed the confidence of all the Greek leaders. So Nauplius returned to Greece with his surviving son Oeax, and brought false news to the wives of Palamedes's murderers, saying to each: 'Your husband is bringing back a Trojan concubine as his new queen.' Some of these unhappy wives thereupon killed themselves. Others committed adultery: as did Agamemnon's wife Clytaemnestra, with Aegisthus; Diomedes's wife Aegialeia, with Cometes son of Sthenelus; and Idomeneus's wife Meda, with one Leucus.[26]

1. *Cypria*, quoted by Proclus: *Chrestomathy* 1; Tzetzes: *Antehomerica* 154 ff.; Scholiast on Homer's *Iliad* iii. 206.
2. Dictys Cretensis: i. 4; Apollodorus: *Epitome* iii. 28–9; Homer: *Iliad* iii. 207.
3. Apollodorus: *Epitome* iii. 29–30; Hyginus: *Fabula* 103; Eustathius on Homer pp. 325 and 326.

4. Hyginus: *loc. cit.*; Eustathius on Homer p. 245.

5. Pausanias: i. 34. 2; Tzetzes: *On Lycophron* 532–3; Philostratus: *Heroica* iii. 1; Quintus Smyrnaeus: *Posthomerica* vii. 408 ff.; Pliny: *Natural History* xvi. 88.

6. Hyginus: *Fabulae* 103 and 104; *Cypria*, quoted by Pausanias: iv. 2. 5; Ovid: *Heroides* xiii. 152; Eustathius on Homer p. 325; Apollodorus: *Epitome* iii. 30; Servius on Virgil's *Aeneid* vi. 447.

7. Eustathius on Homer, *loc. cit.*; Hyginus: *Fabula* 104.

8. Conon: *Narrations* 13; Apollodorus: *Epitome*, quoted by Tzetzes: *On Lycophron* 941; Strabo: vi. 1. 12.

9. Apollodorus: *Epitome* iii. 31; Tzetzes: *On Lycophron* 245; Ovid: *Metamorphoses* xii. 70–145.

10. First Vatican Mythographer: 210; Tzetzes: *On Lycophron* 307.

11. Eustathius on Homer's *Iliad* xxiv. 251, p. 1348; Servius on Virgil's *Aeneid* i. 478; Dictys Cretensis: iv. 9; Tzetzes: *loc. cit.*

12. Benoit: *Le Roman de Troie*.

13. Apollodorus: *Epitome* iii. 32; Homer: *Iliad* xxi. 34 ff. and 85–6; xxiii. 740–7 and vii. 467–8.

14. Apollodorus: *Epitome* iii. 32; Homer: *Iliad* ii. 690–3; xx. 89 ff. and 188 ff.; Eustathius on Homer's *Iliad* iii. 58; Scholiast on Homer's *Iliad* i. 184; *Cypria*, quoted by Proclus: *Chrestomathy* i; Dictys Cretensis: ii. 17.

15. Hyginus: *Fabula* 115; Homer: *Iliad* xiii. 460 ff. and xx. 181 ff.; Hesiod: *Theogony* 1007.

16. Homer: *Iliad* v. 305 ff.; xx. 178 ff. and 585 ff.; Philostratus: *Heroica* 13.

17. Homer: *Iliad* ix. 328–9; vi. 395–7; xvii. 575–7 and vi. 413–28; Apollodorus: *Epitome* iii. 33.

18. Dictys Cretensis: ii. 17; Homer: *Iliad* i. 366 ff. and xvi. 149–54; Eustathius on Homer pp. 77, 118 and 119.

19. Dictys Cretensis: ii. 18; Sophocles: *Ajax* 210; Horace: *Odes* ii. 4. 5.

20. Heracleides Ponticus: *Homeric Allegories* pp. 424–5; Homer: *Iliad* vi. 196 ff.; Apollodorus: *Epitome* iii. 34–5; Eustathius on Homer p. 894.

21. *Cypria*, quoted by Proclus: *loc. cit.*; Servius on Virgil's *Aeneid* ii. 81.

22. Apollodorus: *Epitome* iii. 8; Hyginus: *Fabula* 105.

23. Scholiast on Euripides's *Orestes* 432; Philostratus: *Heroica* 10.

24. Dictys Cretensis: ii. 15; *Cypria*, quoted by Pausanias: x. 31. 1; Tzetzes: *On Lycophron* 384 ff. and 1097; Dares: 28.

25. Pausanias: x. 31. 1 and ii. 20. 3; Philostratus: *loc. cit.*; Scholiast on Euripides's *Orestes* 432; Servius on Virgil's *Aeneid* ii. 81; Tzetzes: *On Lycophron* 384.

26. Apollodorus: *Epitome* vi. 8–9; Tzetzes: *On Lycophron* 384 ff.; Eustathius on Homer p. 24; Dictys Cretensis: vi. 2.

*

1. The *Iliad* deals in sequence only with the tenth year of the siege, and each mythographer has arranged the events of the preceding years in a different order. According to Apollodorus (*Epitome* iii. 32–3), Achilles kills Troilus; captures Lycaon; raids Aeneas's cattle; and takes many cities. According to the *Cypria* (quoted by Proclus: *Chrestomathy* i), the Greeks, failing to take Troy by assault, lay waste the country and cities round about; Aphrodite and Thetis contrive a meeting between Achilles and Helen; the Greeks decide to go home but are restrained by Achilles, who then drives off Aeneas's cattle, sacks many cities, and kills Troilus; Patroclus sells Lycaon on Lemnos; the spoils are divided; Palamedes is stoned to death.

2. According to Tzetzes (*On Lycophron* 307), Troilus outlives Memnon and Hector. Similarly, according to Dares the Phrygian, Troilus succeeds Hector as commander of the Trojan forces (Dares: 30), until one of his chariot horses is wounded and Achilles, driving up, runs him through; Achilles tries to drag away the body, but is wounded by Memnon, whom he kills; the Trojans take refuge within the city and Priam gives both Troilus and Memnon a magnificent funeral (Dares: 33).

3. The Trojan War is historical, and whatever the immediate cause may have been, it was a trade war. Troy controlled the valuable Black Sea trade in gold, silver, iron, cinnabar, ship's timber, linen, hemp, dried fish, oil, and Chinese jade. When once Troy had fallen, the Greeks were able to plant colonies all along the eastern trade route, which grew as rich as those of Asia Minor and Sicily. In the end, Athens, as the leading maritime power, profited most from the Black Sea trade, especially from its cheap grain; and it was the loss of a fleet guarding the entrance to the Hellespont that ruined her at Aegospotami in 405 B.C., and ended the long Peloponnesian Wars. Perhaps, therefore, the constant negotiations between Agamemnon and Priam did not concern the return of Helen so much as the restoration of the Greek rights to enter the Hellespont.

4. It is probable that the Greeks prepared for their final assault by a series of raids on the coasts of Thrace and Asia Minor, to cripple the naval power of the Trojan alliance; and that they maintained a camp at the mouth of the Scamander to prevent Mediterranean trade from reaching Troy, or the annual East-West Fair from being celebrated on the Plain. But the *Iliad* makes it clear that Troy was not besieged in the sense that her lines of communication with the interior were cut, and though, while Achilles was about, the Trojans did not venture by day through the Dardanian Gate, the one which led inland (*Iliad* v. 789); and the Greek laundresses feared to wash their clothes at the spring a bow's shot from the walls (*Iliad* xxii. 256); yet supplies and reinforcements entered freely, and the Trojans held Sestos and Abydos, which kept them in close touch with Thrace. That the Greeks boasted so loudly of a raid on the cattle of Mount Ida, and another on Priam's fig-orchard, suggests that they seldom went far inland. The fig-shoots used for the rail of Lycaon's chariot were apparently designed to place it under the protection of Aphrodite. In the pre-Trojan-War tablets found at Cnossus, a number of 'red-painted Cydonian chariots' are mentioned, 'with joinery work complete', but only the wood of the rails is specified: it is always fig. Yet fig was not nearly so suitable a wood for the purpose as many others available to the Cretans and Trojans.

5. Agamemnon had engaged in a war of attrition, the success of which Hector confesses (*Iliad* xvii. 225 and xviii. 287–92) when he speaks of the drain on Trojan resources caused by the drying up of trade, and the need to subsidize allies. The Paphlagonians, Thracians, and Mysians were producers, not merchants, and ready to have direct dealings with the Greeks. Only the mercantile Lycians, who imported goods from the South-east, seem to have been much concerned about the fate of Troy, which secured their northern trade routes; indeed, when Troy fell, the trade of Asia Minor was monopolized by Agamemnon's allies the Rhodians, and the Lycians were ruined.

6. The coldblooded treatment of women, suppliants, and allies serves as a reminder that the *Iliad* is not Bronze Age myth. With the fall of Cnossus (see 39. 7 and 89. 1) and the consequent disappearance of the *pax Cretensis*, imposed by the Cretan Sea-goddess upon all countries within her sphere of influence, a new Iron Age morality emerges: that of the conquering tyrant, a petty Zeus, who acknowledges no divine restraint. Iphigeneia's sacrifice, Odysseus's hateful revenge on Palamedes, the selling of Lycaon for a silver cup, Achilles's shameless pursuit of Troilus and the forced concubinage of Briseis and Chryseis are typical of barbarous saga. It is proper that Palamedes should have been the innocent victim of an unholy alliance between Agamemnon, Odysseus, and Diomedes, since he represents the Cretan culture planted in Argolis – the inventions with which he is credited being all of Cretan origin. His murder in a well may have been suggested by 'Truth, I mourn you, who have predeceased me!' and by the familiar connexion of truth with wells. *Palamedes* means 'ancient wisdom' and, like Hephaestus, his Lemnian counterpart, he was an oracular hero. His inventions reveal him at Thoth or Hermes (see 17. g). Dice have the some history as cards: they were oracular instruments before being used for games of chance (see 17. 3).

7. The elm-tree, which does not form part of the tree-calendar (see 53. 3), is mainly associated with the Dionysus cult, since the Greeks trained vines on elm-saplings; but elms were planted by nymphs around the tombs of Protesilaus and Eëtion, presumably because the leaves and bark served as vulneraries (Pliny: *Natural History* xxiv. 33), and promised

to be even more efficacious if taken from the graves of princes who had succumbed to many wounds.

8. Laodameia's perverse attachment to Protesilaus's statue may have been deduced from a sacred-wedding icon: in some Hittite marriage-seals, the procumbent king is carved so stiffly that he looks like a statue. The apple brought by a servant, and Acastus's sudden entry, suggest that the scene represented a queen's betrayal of a king to her lover the tanist, who cuts the fatal apple containing his soul – as in the Irish legend of Cuchulain, Dechtire, and Curoi.

Briseis (accusative case: *Briseida*) became confused with Chryses, or Chryseis, daughter of Chryses, who had borne a bastard to Agamemnon (see 116. *h*); and the medieval Latin legend of Criseis (accusative case: *Criseida*) developed vigorously until Henrysoun's *Testament of Cresseid* and Shakespeare's *Troilus and Cressida*.

9. Teuthrania may have been so called after the *teuthis*, or octopus, sacred to the Cretan Goddess (see 81. *1*), whose chief priestess was Tecmessa ('she who ordains').

Though the Sarpedon myth is confused, its elements are all familiar. Apparently the kingdom of Lycia, founded by another Sarpedon, uncle of another Glaucus – Greek-speaking Cretans of Aeolian or Pelasgian stock, who were driven overseas by the Achaeans – was a double one, with matrilinear succession, the title of the Moon-priestess being Laodemeia ('tamer of the people'). Its sacred king seems to have been ritually 'born from a mare' (see 81. *4* and 167. *2*) – hence his name, Hippolochus – and Isander ('impartial man') acted as his tanist. Sarpedon's name ('rejoicing in a wooden ark') refers apparently to the annual arrival of the New Year Child in a boat. Here the Child is the *interrex*, to whom Hippolochus resigns his kingship for a single day; he must then be suffocated in honey, like Cretan Glaucus (see 71. *d*), or killed in a chariot crash, like the Isthmian Glaucus (see 90. *1*), or transfixed with an arrow by the revived Hippolochus, like Learchus son of Athamas (see 70. *5*).

10. To shoot an apple poised upon the head, or at a penny set in the cap, of one's own son was a test of marksmanship prescribed to medieval archers, whose guild (as appears in the *Malleus Maleficarum* and in the *Little Geste of Robin Hood*) belonged to the pagan witch cult both in England and Celtic Germany. In England this test was, it seems, designed to choose a 'gudeman' for Maid Marian, by marriage to whom he became Robin Hood, Lord of the Greenwood. Since the northern witch cult had much in common with neolithic religion of the Aegean, it may be that the Lycians did not place the ring on a boy's breast, but on his head, and that it represented a golden serpent (see 119. *4*); or that it was the ring of an axe which he held in his hand, like those through which Odysseus shot when he recovered Penelope from the suitors (see 171.

h). The mythographer has perhaps confused the shooting test demanded of a new candidate for the kingship with the sacrifice of an *interrex*.

11. Aethylla means 'kindling timber', and the annual burning of a boat may have originated the Scione legend.

Protesilaus ('first of the people') must have been so common a royal title that several cities claimed his tomb.

163

THE WRATH OF ACHILLES

WINTER now drew on, and since this has never been a battle season among civilized nations, the Greeks spent it enlarging their camp and practising archery. Sometimes they came across Trojan notables in the temple of Thymbraean Apollo, which was neutral territory; and once, while Hecabe happened to be sacrificing there, Achilles arrived on the same errand and fell desperately in love with her daughter Polyxena. He made no declaration at the time but, returning to his hut in torment, sent the kindly Automedon to ask Hector on what terms he might marry Polyxena. Hector replied: 'She shall be his on the day that he betrays the Greek camp to my father Priam.' Achilles seemed willing enough to accept Hector's conditions, but drew back sullenly when informed that if he failed to betray the camp, he must swear instead to murder his cousin Great Ajax and the sons of Athenian Pleisthenes.[1]

b. Spring came and fighting was resumed. In the first engagement of the season Achilles sought out Hector, but the watchful Helenus pierced his hand with an arrow shot from an ivory bow, Apollo's love gift, and forced him to give ground. Zeus himself guided the arrowhead; and as he did so decided to relieve the Trojans, whom the raids and the consequent desertion of certain Asiatic allies had greatly discouraged, by plaguing the Greeks and detaching Achilles from his fellow-chieftains.[2] When, therefore, Chryses came to ransom Chryseis, Zeus persuaded Agamemnon to drive him away with opprobrious words; and Apollo, invoked by Chryses, posted himself vengefully near the ships, shooting deadly arrows among the Greeks day after day. Hundreds perished, though (as it happened) no kings or princes suffered, and on the tenth day Calchas made known the presence of

the god. At his instance, Agamemnon grudgingly sent Chryseis back
to her father, with propitiatory gifts, but recouped his loss by seizing
Briseis from Achilles, to whom she had been allotted; whereupon
Achilles, in a rage, announced that he would take no further part in the
War; and his mother Thetis indignantly approached Zeus, who promised her satisfaction on his behalf. But some say that Achilles kept out
of the fighting in order to show his goodwill towards Priam as Polyxena's father.[3]

c. When the Trojans became aware that Achilles and his Myrmidons
had withdrawn from the field, they took heart and made a vigorous
sortie. Agamemnon, in alarm, granted them a truce, during which
Paris and Menelaus were to fight a duel for the possession of Helen and
the stolen treasure. The duel, however, proved indecisive, because
when Aphrodite saw that Paris was getting the worst of it, she wrapped
him in a magic mist and carried him back to Troy. Hera then sent
Athene down to break the truce by making Pandarus son of Lycaon
shoot an arrow at Menelaus, which she did; at the same time she
inspired Diomedes to kill Pandarus and wound Aeneas and his mother
Aphrodite. Glaucus son of Hippolochus now opposed Diomedes, but
both recalled the close friendship that had bound their fathers, and
courteously exchanged arms.[4]

d. Hector challenged Achilles to single combat; and when Achilles
sent back word that he had retired from the war, the Greeks chose
Great Ajax as his substitute. These two champions fought without
pause until nightfall, when heralds parted them and each gaspingly
praised the other's skill and courage. Ajax gave Hector the brilliant
purple baldric by which he was later dragged to his death; and Hector
gave Ajax the silver-studded sword with which he was later to commit
suicide.[5]

e. An armistice being agreed upon, the Greeks raised a long barrow
over their dead, and crowned it with a wall beyond which they dug a
deep, palisaded trench. But they had omitted to appease the deities
who supported the Trojans and, when fighting was resumed, were
driven across the trench and behind the wall. That night the Trojans
encamped close to the Greek ships.[6]

f. In despair, Agamemnon sent Phoenix, Ajax, Odysseus and two
heralds to placate Achilles, offering him countless gifts and the return
of Briseis (they were to swear that she was still a virgin) if only he
would fight again. It should be explained that Chryses had meanwhile

brought back his daughter, who protested that she had been very well treated by Agamemnon and wished to remain with him; she was pregnant at the time and later gave birth to Chryses the Second, a child of doubtful paternity. Achilles greeted the deputation with a pleasant smile, but refused their offers, and announced that he must sail home next morning.[7]

g. That same night about the third watch when the moon was high, Odysseus and Diomedes, encouraged by a lucky auspice from Athene – a heron on their right hand – decided to raid the Trojan lines. They happened to stumble over Dolon, son of Eumelus, who had been sent out on patrol by the enemy and, after forcibly extracting information from him, cut his throat. Odysseus then hid Dolon's ferret-skin cap, wolf-skin cloak, bow and spear in a tamarisk bush and hurried with Diomedes to the right flank of the Trojan line where, they now knew, Rhesus the Thracian was encamped. He is variously described as the son of the Muse Euterpe, or Calliope, by Eioneus, or Ares, or Strymon. Having stealthily assassinated Rhesus and twelve of his companions in their sleep, they drove off his magnificent horses, white as snow and swifter than the wind, and recovered the spoils from the tamarisk bush on their way back.[8] The capture of Rhesus's horses was of the highest importance, since an oracle had foretold that Troy would become impregnable once they had eaten Trojan fodder and drunken from the river Scamander, and this they had not yet done. When the surviving Thracians awoke, to find King Rhesus dead and his horses gone, they fled in despair; the Greeks killed nearly every one of them.[9]

h. On the following day, however, after a fierce struggle, in which Agamemnon, Diomedes, Odysseus, Euryplus, and Machaon the surgeon were all wounded, the Greeks took to flight and Hector breached their wall.[10] Encouraged by Apollo, he pushed on towards the ships and, despite assistance lent by Poseidon to the two Ajaxes and Idomeneus, broke through the Greek line. At this point Hera, who hated the Trojans, borrowed Aphrodite's girdle and persuaded Zeus to come and sleep with her; a ruse which allowed Poseidon to turn the battle in the Greeks' favour. But Zeus, soon discovering that he had been duped, revived Hector (nearly killed by Ajax with a huge stone), ordered Poseidon off the field, and restored the Trojans' courage. Forward they went again: Medon killing Periphetes son of Copreus, and many other champions.[11]

i. Even Great Ajax was forced to yield ground; and Achilles, when he saw flames swirling from the stern of Protesilaus's ship, set on fire by the Trojans, so far forgot his grudge as to marshal the Myrmidons and hurry them to Patroclus's assistance. Patroclus had flung a spear into the mass of Trojans gathered around Protesilaus's ship and transfixed Puraechmes, king of the Paeonians. At this the Trojans, mistaking him for Achilles, fled; and Patroclus extinguished the fire, saving the bows of the ship at least, and cut down Sarpedon. Though Glaucus tried to rally his Lycians and so protect Sarpedon's body from despoilment, Zeus let Patroclus chase the whole Trojan army towards the city; Hector being the first to retire, wounded severely by Ajax.

j. The Greeks stripped Sarpedon of his armour, but at Zeus's orders Apollo rescued the body, which he prepared for burial, whereupon Sleep and Death bore it away to Lycia. Patroclus meanwhile pressed on the rout, and would have taken Troy single-handed, had not Apollo hastily mounted the wall, and thrice thrust him back with a shield as he attempted to scale it. Fighting continued until nightfall, when Apollo, wrapped in a thick mist, came up behind Patroclus and buffeted him smartly between the shoulderblades. Patroclus's eyes started from his head; his helmet flew off; his spear was shattered into splinters; his shield fell to the ground; and Apollo grimly unlaced his corslet. Euphorbus son of Panthous, observing Patroclus's plight, wounded him without fear of retaliation, and as he staggered away, Hector, who had returned to the battle, despatched him with a single blow.[12]

k. Up ran Menelaus and killed Euphorbus – who is said, by the way, to have been reincarnate centuries later in the philosopher Pythagoras – and strutted off to his hut with the spoils; leaving Hector to strip Patroclus of his borrowed armour. Menelaus and Great Ajax then reappeared and together defended Patroclus's body until dusk, when they contrived to carry it back to the ships. But Achilles, on hearing the news, rolled in the dust, and yielded to an ecstasy of grief.[13]

l. Thetis entered her son's hut carrying a new suit of armour, which included a pair of valuable tin greaves, hurriedly forged by Hephaestus. Achilles put the suit on, made peace with Agamemnon (who delivered Briseis to him inviolate, swearing that he had taken her in anger, not lust) and set out to avenge Patroclus.[14] None could stand against his wrath. The Trojans broke and fled to the Scamander, where he split them into two bodies, driving one across the plain towards the city, and penning the other in a bend of the river. Furiously, the River-god rushed at him, but Hephaestus took Achilles's part and dried up the waters with a scorching flame. The Trojan survivors regained the city, like a herd of frightened deer.[15]

m. When Achilles at last met Hector and engaged him in single combat, both sides drew back and stood watching amazed. Hector turned and began to run around the city walls. He hoped by this manoeuvre to weary Achilles, who had long been inactive and should therefore have been short of breath. But he was mistaken. Achilles chased him thrice around the walls, and whenever he made for the shelter of a gate, counting on the help of his brothers, always headed him off. Finally Hector halted and stood his ground, but Achilles ran him through the breast, and refused his dying plea that his body might be ransomed for burial. After possessing himself of the armour, Achilles slit the flesh behind the tendons of Hector's heels. He then passed leather thongs through the slits, secured them to his chariot and, whipping up Balius, Xanthus, and Pedasus, dragged the body towards the ships at an easy canter. Hector's head, its black locks streaming on either side, churned up a cloud of dust behind him. But some say that Achilles dragged the corpse three times around the city walls, by the baldric which Ajax had given him.[16]

n. Achilles now buried Patroclus. Five Greek princes were sent to Mount Ida in search of timber for the funeral pyre, upon which Achilles sacrificed not only horses, and two of Patroclus's own pack of nine hounds, but twelve noble Trojan captives, several sons of Priam among them, by cutting their throats. He even threatened to throw Hector's corpse to the remaining hounds; Aphrodite, however, restrained him. At Patroclus's funeral games Diomedes won the chariot race, and Epeius, despite his cowardice, the boxing-match; Ajax and Odysseus tied in the wrestling match.[17]

o. Still consumed by grief, Achilles rose every day at dawn to drag Hector's body three times around Patroclus's tomb. Yet Apollo protected it from corruption and laceration and, eventually, at the command of Zeus, Hermes led Priam to the Greek camp under cover of night, and persuaded Achilles to accept a ransom.[18] On this occasion Priam showed great magnanimity towards Achilles whom he had found asleep in his hut and might easily have murdered. The ransom agreed upon was Hector's weight in gold. Accordingly, the Greeks set up a pair of scales outside the city walls, laid the corpse on one pan, and invited the Trojans to heap gold in the other. When Priam's treasury had been ransacked of ingots and jewels, and Hector's huge bulk still depressed the pan, Polyxena, watching from the wall, threw down her bracelets to supply the missing weight. Overcome by admiration, Achilles told Priam: 'I will cheerfully barter Hector against Polyxena. Keep your gold; marry her to me; and if you then restore Helen to Menelaus, I undertake to make peace between your people and ours.' Priam, for the moment, was content to ransom Hector at the agreed price in gold; but promised to give Polyxena to Achilles freely if he persuaded the Greeks to depart without Helen. Achilles replied that he would do what he could, and Priam then took away the corpse for burial. So great an uproar arose at Hector's funeral – the Trojans lamenting, the Greeks trying to drown their dirges with boos and cat-calls – that birds flying overhead fell down stunned by the noise.[19]

p. At the command of an oracle, Hector's bones were eventually taken to Boeotian Thebes, where his grave is still shown beside the fountain of Oedipus. Some quote the Oracle as follows:

'Hearken, ye men of Thebes, who dwell in the city of Cadmus,
    Should you desire your land to be prosperous, wealthy and blameless,
Carry the bones of Hector, Priam's son, to your city.
Asia holds them now; there Zeus will attend to his worship.'

Others say that when a plague ravaged Greece, Apollo ordered the reburial of Hector's bones in a famous Greek city which had taken no part in the Trojan War.[20]

q. A wholly different tradition makes Hector a son of Apollo, whom Penthesileia the Amazon killed.[21]

1. Dictys Cretensis: iii. 1–3.
2. Ptolemy Hephaestionos: vi.; Dictys Cretensis: iii. 6; *Cypria*, quoted by Proclus: *Chrestomathy* 1.
3. Homer: *Iliad* i; Dictys Cretensis: ii. 30; First Vatican Mythographer: 211.
4. Homer: *Iliad* iii.; iv. 1–129; v. 1–417 and vi. 119–236.
5. Athenaeus: i. 8; Rawlinson: *Excidum Troiae*; Homer: *Iliad* vii. 66–132; Hyginus: *Fabula* 112.
6. Homer: *Iliad* vii. 436–50 and viii.
7. Dictys Cretensis: ii. 47; Hyginus: *Fabula* 121; Homer: *Iliad* ix.
8. Servius on Virgil's *Aeneid* i. 473; Apollodorus: i. 3. 4; Homer: *Iliad* x.
9. Servius: *loc. cit.*; Dictys Cretensis: ii. 45–6.
10. Homer: *Iliad* xi and xii.
11. Homer: *Iliad* xii–xiv.

12. Dictys Cretensis: ii. 43; Homer: *Iliad* xvi.
13. Hyginus: *Fabula* 112; Philostratus: *Life of Apollonius of Tyana* i. 1 and *Heroica* 19. 4; Pausanias: ii. 17. 3; Homer: *Iliad* xvii.
14. Dictys Cretensis: ii. 48–52; Homer: *Iliad* xviii–xix.
15. Homer: *Iliad* xxi.
16. Homer: *Iliad* xxii.
17. Hyginus: *loc. cit.*; Virgil: *Aeneid* i. 487; Dictys Cretensis: iii. 12–14; Homer: *Iliad* xxiii.
18. Homer: *Iliad* xxiv.
19. Servius on Virgil's *Aeneid* i. 491; Rawlinson: *Excidium Troiae*; Dares: 27; Dictys Cretensis: iii. 16 and 27.
20. Pausanias: ix. 18. 4; Tzetzes: *On Lycophron* 1194.
21. Stesichorus, quoted by Tzetzes: *On Lycophron* 266; Ptolemy Hephaestionos: vi., quoted by Photius p. 487.

*

1. According to Proclus (*Chrestomathy* xcix. 19–20), *Homerus* means 'blind' rather than 'hostage', which is the usual translation; minstrelsy was a natural vocation for the blind, since blindness and inspiration often went together (see 105. *h*). The identity of the original Homer has been debated for some two thousand five hundred years. In the earliest tradition he is plausibly called an Ionian from Chios. A clan of Homeridae, or 'Sons of the Blind Man', who recited the traditional Homeric poems and eventually became a guild (Scholiast on Pindar's *Nemean Odes* ii. 1), had their headquarters at Delos, the centre of the Ionian world, where Homer himself was said to have recited (*Homeric Hymn* iii. 165–73). Parts of the *Iliad* date from the tenth century B.C.; the subject matter is three centuries older. By the sixth century unauthorized recitals of the *Iliad* were slowly corrupting the text; Peisistratus, tyrant of Athens, therefore ordered an official recension, which he entrusted to four leading scholars. They seem to have done the task well but, since Homer had come to be regarded as a prime authority in disputes between cities, Peisistratus's enemies accused him of interpolating verses for political ends (Strabo: ix. 1. 10).

2. The twenty-four books of the *Iliad* have grown out of a poem called 'The Wrath of Achilles' – which could perhaps have been recited in a single night, and which dealt with the quarrel between Achilles and Agamemnon over the possession of a captured princess. It is unlikely that the text of the central events has been radically edited since the first *Iliad* of about 750 B.C. Yet the quarrels are so unedifying, and all the Greek leaders behave so murderously, deceitfully, and shamelessly, while the Trojans by contrast behave so well, that it is obvious on whose side the author's sympathy lay. As a legatee of the Minoan court bards he found his spiritual home among the departed glories of Cnossus and Mycenae, not beside the camp fires of the barbarous invaders from the North.

Homer faithfully describes the lives of his new overlords, who have usurped ancient religious titles by marrying tribal heiresses and, though calling them godlike, wise, and noble, holds them in deep disgust. They live by the sword and perish by the sword, disdaining love, friendship, faith, or the arts of peace. They care so little for the divine names by which they swear that he dares jest in their presence about the greedy, sly, quarrelsome, lecherous, cowardly Olympians who have turned the world upside down. One would dismiss him as an irreligious wretch, were he not clearly a secret worshipper of the Great Goddess of Asia (whom the Greeks had humiliated in this war); and did not glints of his warm and honourable nature appear whenever he is describing family life in Priam's palace. Homer has drawn on the Babylonian *Gilgamesh* epic for the Achilles story; with Achilles as Gilgamesh, Thetis as Ninsun, Patroclus as Enkidu.

3. Achilles's hysterical behaviour when he heard that Patroclus was dead must have shocked Homer, but he has clothed the barbarities of the funeral in mock-heroic language, confident that his overlords will not recognize the sharpness of the satire – Homer may be said, in a sense, to have anticipated Goya, whose caricature-portraits of the Spanish royal family were so splendidly painted that they could be accepted by the victims as honest likenesses. But the point of the *Iliad* as satire has been somewhat blunted by the Homeridae's need to placate their divine hosts at Delos; Apollo and Artemis must support the Trojans and display dignity and discretion, in contrast at least with the vicious deities of the Hellenic camp. One result of the *Iliad's* acceptance by Greek city authorities as a national epic was that no one ever again took the Olympian religion seriously, and Greek morals always remained barbarous – except in places where Cretan mystery cults survived and the mystagogues required a good-conduct certificate from their initiates. The Great Goddess, though now officially subordinate to Zeus, continued to exert a strong spiritual influence at Eleusis, Corinth and Samothrace, until the suppression of her mysteries by early Byzantine emperors. Lucian, who loved his Homer and succeeded him as the prime satirist of the Olympians, also worshipped the Goddess, to whom he had sacrificed his first hair-clippings at Hierapolis.

4. Hector's bones were said to have been brought to Thebes from Troy, yet 'Hector' was a title of the Theban sacred king before the Trojan War took place; and he suffered the same fate when his reign ended – which was to be dragged in the wreck of a circling chariot, like Glaucus (see 71. *a*), Hippolytus (see 101. *g*), Oenomaus (see 109. *g*), and Abderus (see 130. *b*). Since 'Achilles' was also a title rather than a name, the combat may have been borrowed from the lost Theban saga of 'Oedipus's Sheep', in which co-kings fought for the throne (see 106. 2).

THE DEATH OF ACHILLES

THE Amazon Queen Penthesileia, daughter of Otrere and Ares, had sought refuge in Troy from the Erinnyes of her sister Hippolyte (also called Glauce, or Melanippe), whom she had accidentally shot, either while out hunting or, according to the Athenians, in the fight which followed Theseus's wedding with Phaedra. Purified by Priam, she greatly distinguished herself in battle, accounting for many Greeks, among them (it is said) Machaon, though the commoner account makes him fall by the hand of Eurypylus, son of Telephus.[1] She drove Achilles from the field on several occasions – some even claim that she killed him and that Zeus, at the plea of Thetis, restored him to life but at last he ran her through, fell in love with her dead body, and committed necrophily upon it there and then.[2] When he later called for volunteers to bury Penthesileia, Thersites, a son of Aetolian Agrius, and the ugliest Greek at Troy, who had gouged out her eyes with his spear as she lay dying, jeeringly accused Achilles of filthy and unnatural lust. Achilles turned and struck Thersites so hard that he broke every tooth in his head and sent his ghost scurrying down to Tartarus.[3]

b. This caused high indignation among the Greeks, and Diomedes, who was a cousin of Thersites and wished to show his disdain for Achilles, dragged Penthesileia's body along by the foot and threw it into the Scamander; whence, however, it was rescued and buried on the bank with great honour – some say by Achilles; others, by the Trojans. Achilles then set sail for Lesbos, where he sacrificed to Apollo, Artemis, and Leto; and Odysseus, a sworn enemy to Thersites, purified him of the murder. The dying Penthesileia, supported by Achilles, is carved on the throne of Zeus at Olympia.[4] Her nurse, the Amazon Clete, hearing that she had fled to Troy after the death of Hippolyte, set out to search for her, but was driven by contrary winds to Italy, where she settled and founded the city of Clete.[5]

c. Priam had by now persuaded his half-brother, Tithonus of Assyria, to send his son Memnon the Ethiopian to Troy; the bribe he offered was a golden vine.[6] A so-called palace of Memnon is shown in Ethiopia, although when Tithonus emigrated to Assyria and founded Susa, Memnon, then only a child, had gone with him. Susa is now commonly known as the City of Memnon; and its inhabitants as Cissians, after Memnon's mother Cissia. His palace on the Acropolis was standing until the time of the Persians.[7]

d. Tithonus governed the province of Persia for the Assyrian king Teutamus, Priam's overlord, who put Memnon in command of a thousand Ethiopians, a thousand Susians, and two hundred chariots. The Phrygians still show the rough, straight road, with camp-sites every fifteen miles or so, by which Memnon, after he had subjugated all the intervening nations, marched to Troy. He was black as ebony, but the handsomest man alive, and like Achilles wore armour forged by Hephaestus.[8] Some say that he led a large army of Ethiopians and Indians to Troy by way of Armenia, and that another expedition sailed from Phoenicia at his orders under a Sidonian named Phalas. Landing on Rhodes, the inhabitants of which favoured the Greek cause, Phalas was asked in public: 'Are you not ashamed, sir, to assist Paris the Trojan and other declared enemies of your native city?' The Phoenician sailors, who now heard for the first time where they were bound, stoned Phalas to death as a traitor and settled in Ialysus and Cameirus, after dividing among themselves the treasure and munitions of war which Phalas had brought with him.[9]

e. Meanwhile, at Troy, Memnon killed several leading Greeks, including Antilochus, son of Nestor, when he came to his father's rescue: for Paris had shot one of Nestor's chariot horses and terror made its team-mate unmanageable.[10] This Antilochus had been exposed as a child on Mount Ida by his mother Anaxibia, or Eurydice, and there suckled by a bitch. Though too young to sail from Aulis at the beginning of the war, he followed some years later and begged Achilles to soothe Nestor's anger at his unexpected arrival. Achilles, delighted with Antilochus's warlike spirit, undertook to mediate between them and, at his desire, Nestor introduced him to Agamemnon.[11] Antilochus was one of the youngest, handsomest, swiftest and most courageous Greeks who fought at Troy and Nestor, having been warned by an oracle to protect him against an Ethiopian, appointed Chalion as his guardian; but in vain.[12] The bones of Antilochus were laid beside those of his friends, Achilles and Patroclus, whose ghosts he accompanied to the Asphodel Fields.[13]

f. That day, with the help of Memnon's Ethiopians, the Trojans nearly succeeded in burning the Greek ships, but darkness fell and they retired. After burying their dead, the Greeks chose Great Ajax to engage Memnon; and next morning the single combat had already begun, when Thetis sought out Achilles, who was absent from the camp, and broke the news of Antilochus's death. Achilles hastened back to take vengeance, and while Zeus, calling for a pair of scales, weighed his fate against that of Memnon,[14] he brushed Ajax aside and made the combat his own. The pan containing Memnon's fate sank in Jove's hand, Achilles dealt the death-blow, and presently black head and bright armour crowned the flaming pyre of Antilochus.[15]

g. Some, however, report that Memnon was ambushed by Thessalians; and that his Ethiopians, having burned his body, carried the ashes to Tithonus; and that they now lie buried on a hill overlooking the mouth of the river Aesepus, where a village bears his name.[16] Eos, who is described as Memnon's mother, implored Zeus to confer immortality upon him and some further honour as well. A number of phantom hen-birds, called Memnonides, were consequently formed from the embers and smoke of his pyre, and rising into the air, flew three times around it. At the fourth circuit they divided into two flocks, fought with claws and beaks, and fell down upon his ashes as a funeral sacrifice. Memnonides still fight and fall at his tomb when the Sun has run through all the signs of the Zodiac.[17]

h. According to another tradition, these birds are Memnon's girl companions, who lamented for him so excessively that the gods, in pity, metamorphosed them into birds. They make an annual visit to his tomb, where they weep and lacerate themselves until some of them fall dead. The Hellespontines say that when the Memnonides visit Memnon's grave beside the Hellespont, they use their wings to sprinkle it with water from the river Aesepus; and that Eos still weeps tears of dew for him every morning. Polygnotus has pictured Memnon facing his rival Sarpedon and dressed in a cloak embroidered with these birds. The gods are said to observe the anniversaries of both their deaths as days of mourning.[18]

i. Others believe that Memnon's bones were taken to Cyprian Paphus, and thence to Rhodes, where his sister Himera, or Hemera, came to fetch them away. The Phoenicians who had rebelled against Phalas allowed her to do so on condition that she did not press for the return of their stolen treasure. To this she agreed, and brought the urn to Phoenicia; she buried it there at Palliochis and then disappeared.[19] Others, again, say that Memnon's tomb is to be seen near Palton in Syria, beside the river Badas. His bronze sword hangs on the wall of

Asclepius's temple at Nicomedeia; and Egyptian Thebes is famous for a colossal black statue – a seated stone figure – which utters a sound like the breaking of a lyre-string every day at sunrise. All Greek-speaking people call it Memnon; not so the Egyptians.[20]

j. Achilles now routed the Trojans and pursued them towards the city, but his course, too, was run. Poseidon and Apollo, pledged to avenge the deaths of Cycnus and Troilus, and to punish certain insolent boasts that Achilles had uttered over Hector's corpse, took counsel together. Veiled with cloud and standing by the Scaean Gate, Apollo sought out Paris in the thick of battle, turned his bow and guided the fatal shaft. It struck the one vulnerable part of Achilles's body, the right heel, and he died in agony.[21] But some say that Apollo, assuming the likeness of Paris, himself shot Achilles; and that this was the account which Neoptolemus, Achilles's son, accepted. A fierce battle raged all day over the corpse. Great Ajax struck down Glaucus, despoiled him of his armour, sent it back to the camp and, despite a shower of darts, carried dead Achilles through the midst of the enemy, Odysseus bringing up the rear. A tempest sent by Zeus then put an end to the struggle.[22]

k. According to another tradition, Achilles was the victim of a plot. Priam had offered him Polyxena in marriage on condition that the siege of Troy was raised. But Polyxena, who could not forgive Achilles for murdering her brother Troilus, made him disclose the vulnerability of his heel, since there is no secret that women cannot extract from men in proof of love. At her request he came, barefoot and unarmed, to ratify the agreement by sacrificing to Thymbraean Apollo; then, while Deiphobus clasped him to his breast in pretended friendship, Paris, hiding behind the god's image, pierced his heel with a poisoned arrow or, some say, a sword. Before dying, however, Achilles seized firebrands from the altar and laid about him vigorously, felling many Trojans and temple servants.[23] Meanwhile, Odysseus, Ajax, and Diomedes, suspecting Achilles of treachery, had followed him to the temple. Paris and Deiphobus rushed past them through the doorway, they entered, and Achilles, expiring in their arms, begged them, after Troy fell, to sacrifice Polyxena at his tomb. Ajax carried the body out of the shrine on his shoulders; the Trojans tried to capture it, but the Greeks drove them off and conveyed it to the ships. Some say, on the other hand, that the Trojans won the tussle and did not surrender Achilles's body until the ransom which Priam paid for Hector had been returned.[24]

l. The Greeks were dismayed by their loss. Poseidon, however, promised Thetis to bestow on Achilles an island in the Black Sea, where the coastal tribes would offer him divine sacrifices for all eternity. A company of Nereids came to Troy to mourn with her and stood desolately around his corpse, while the nine Muses chanted the dirge. Their mourning lasted seventeen days and nights, but though Agamemnon and his fellow-leaders shed many tears, none of the common soldiers greatly regretted the death of so notorious a traitor. On the eighteenth day, Achilles's body was burned upon a pyre and his ashes, mixed with those of Patroclus, were laid in a golden urn made by Hephaestus, Thetis's wedding gift from Dionysus; this was buried on the headland of Sigaeum, which dominates the Hellespont, and over it the Greeks raised a lofty cairn as a landmark.[25] In a neighbouring village called Achilleum stands a temple sacred to Achilles, and his statue wearing a woman's ear-ring.[26]

m. While the Achaeans were holding funeral games in his honour – Eumelus winning the chariot race, Diomedes the foot-race, Ajax the discus-throw, and Teucer the archery contest – Thetis snatched Achilles's soul from the pyre and conveyed it to Leuce, an island about twenty furlongs in circumference, wooded and full of beasts, both wild and tame, which lies opposite the mouths of the Danube, and is now sacred to him. Once, when a certain Crotonian named Leonymus, who had been severely wounded in the breast while fighting his neighbours, the Epizephyrian Locrians, visited Delphi to inquire how he might be cured, the Pythoness told him: 'Sail to Leuce. There Little Ajax, whose ghost your enemies invoked to fight for them, will appear and heal your wound.' He returned some months later, safe and well, reporting that he had seen Achilles, Patroclus, Antilochus, Great Ajax, and finally Little Ajax, who had healed him. Helen, now married to Achilles, had said: 'Pray, Leonymus, sail to Himera, and tell the libeller of Helen that the loss of his sight is due to her displeasure.' Sailors on the northward run from the Bosphorus to Olbia frequently hear Achilles chanting Homer's verses across the water, the sound being accompanied by the clatter of horses' hooves, shouts of warriors, and clash of arms.[27]

n. Achilles first lay with Helen, not long before his death, in a dream arranged by his mother Thetis. This experience afforded him such pleasure that he asked Helen to display herself to him in waking life on the wall of Troy. She did so, and he fell desperately in love. Since he was her fifth husband, they call him Pemptus, meaning 'fifth', in Crete; Theseus, Menelaus, Paris, and finally Deiphobus, having been his predecessors.[28]

o. But others hold that Achilles remains under the power of Hades, and complains bitterly of his lot as he strides about the Asphodel Meadows; others, again, that he married Medea and lives royally in the Elysian Fields, or the Islands of the Blessed.[29]

p. By order of an oracle, a cenotaph was set up for Achilles in the ancient gymnasium at Olympia; there, at the opening of the festival, as the sun is sinking, the Elean women honour him with funeral rites. The Thessalians, at the command of the Dodonian Oracle, also sacrifice annually to Achilles; and on the road which leads northwards from Sparta stands a sanctuary built for him by Prax, his great-grandson, which is closed to the general public; but the boys who are required to fight in a near-by plane-tree grove enter and sacrifice to him beforehand.[30]

1. Quintus Smyrnaeus: *Posthomerica* i. 18 ff.; Apollodorus: *Epitome* v. 1–2; Lesches: *Little Iliad*, quoted by Pausanias: iii. 26. 7.
2. Eustathius on Homer p. 1696; Apollodorus: *loc. cit.*; Rawlinson: *Excidium Troiae*.
3. Apollodorus: i. 8. 6; Homer: *Iliad* ii. 212 ff., with scholiast on 219; Tzetzes: *On Lycophron* 999.
4. Tzetzes: *loc. cit.*; Servius on Virgil's *Aeneid* i. 495; Tryphiodorus: 37; Arctinus of Miletus: *Aethiopis*, quoted by Proclus: *Chrestomathy* 2; Pausanias: x. 31. 1 and v. 11. 2.
5. Tzetzes: *On Lycophron* 995.
6. Servius on Virgil's *Aeneid* i. 493; Apollodorus: iii. 12. 4 and *Epitome* v. 3.
7. Diodorus Siculus: ii. 22; Pausanias: i. 42. 2; Herodotus: v. 54; Strabo: xv. 3. 2; Aeschylus, quoted by Strabo: *loc. cit.*
8. Diodorus Siculus: *loc. cit.*; Pausanias: x. 31. 2; Ovid: *Amores* i. 8. 3–4; Homer: *Odyssey* xi. 522; Arctinus, quoted by Proclus: *Chrestomathy* 2.
9. Dictys Cretensis: iv. 4.
10. Apollodorus: *Epitome* v. 3; Pindar: *Pythian Odes* vi. 28 ff.
11. Apollodorus: i. 9. 9. and iii. 10. 8; Homer: *Odyssey* iii. 452; Hyginus: *Fabula* 252; Philostratus: *Heroica* iii. 2.
12. Homer: *Odyssey* iii. 112; xxiv. 17 and *Iliad* xxxiii. 556; Eustathius on Homer p. 1697.
13. Homer: *Odyssey* xxiv. 16 and 78; Pausanias: iii. 19. 11.
14. Dictys Cretensis: iv. 5; Quintus Smyrnaeus: *Posthomerica* ii. 224 ff.; Philostratus: *Imagines* ii. 7; Aeschylus: *Psychostasia*, quoted by Plutarch: *How a Young Man Should Listen to Poetry* 2.

15. Dictys Cretensis: iv. 6; Philostratus: *Heroica* iii. 4.
16. Diodorus Siculus: ii. 22; Strabo: xiii. 1. 11.
17. Apollodorus: iii. 12. 4; Arctinus of Miletus: *Aethiopis*, quoted by Proclus: *Chrestomathy* 2; Ovid: *Metamorphoses* xiii. 578 ff.
18. Servius on Virgil's *Aeneid* i. 755 and 493; Pausanias: x. 31. 2; Scholiast on Aristophanes's *Clouds* 622.
19. Dictys Cretensis: vi. 10.
20. Simonides, quoted by Strabo: xv. 3. 2; Pausanias: iii. 3. 6 and i. 42. 2.
21. Arctinus of Miletus: *Aethiopis*, quoted by Proclus: *Chestomathy* 2; Ovid: *Metamorphoses* xii. 580 ff.; Hyginus: *Fabula* 107; Apollodorus: *Epitome* v. 3.
22. Hyginus: *loc. cit.*; Apollodorus: *Epitome* v. 4; Homer: *Odyssey* xxiv. 42.
23. Rawlinson: *Excidium Troiae*; Dares: 34; Dictys Cretensis: iv. 11; Servius on Virgil's *Aeneid* vi. 57; Second Vatican Mythographer: 205.
24. Dictys Cretensis: iv. 10–13; Servius on Virgil's *Aeneid* iii. 322; Tzetzes: *On Lycophron* 269.
25. Quintus Smyrnaeus: iii. 766–80; Apollodorus: *Epitome* v. 5; Dictys Cretensis: iv. 13–14; Tzetzes: *Posthomerica* 431–67; Homer: *Odyssey* xxiv. 43–84.
26. Strabo: xi. 2.6; Arctinus of Miletus: *Aethiopis*, quoted by Proclus: *Crestomathy* 2; Apollodorus: *loc. cit.*
27. Pausanias: iii. 19. 11; Philostratus: *Heroica* xx. 32–40.
28. Tzetzes: *On Lycophron* 143 and 174; Servius on Virgil's *Aeneid* i. 34.
29. Homer: *Odyssey* xi. 471–540; Ibycus, quoted by scholiast on Apollonius Rhodius: iv. 815; Apollodorus: *loc. cit.*
30. Philostratus: *Heroica* xix. 14; Pausanias: vi. 23. 2 and iii. 20. 8.

*

1. Penthesileia was one of the Amazons defeated by Theseus and Heracles: that is to say, one of Athene's fighting priestesses, defeated by the Aeolian invaders of Greece (see 100. 1 and 131. 2). The incident has been staged at Troy because Priam's confederacy is said to have comprised all the tribes of Asia Minor. Penthesileia does not appear in the *Iliad*, but Achilles's outrage of her corpse is characteristically Homeric, and since she is mentioned in so many other Classical texts, a passage about her may well have been suppressed by Peisistratus's editors. Dictys Cretensis (iv. 2–3) modernizes the story: he says that she rode up at the head of a large army and, finding Hector dead, would have gone away again, had not Paris bribed her to stay with gold and silver. Achilles speared

Penthesileia in their first encounter, and dragged her from the saddle by the hair. As she lay dying on the ground, the Greek soldiers cried: 'Throw this virago to the dogs as a punishment for exceeding the nature of womankind!' Though Achilles demanded an honourable funeral, Diomedes took the corpse by its feet and dragged it into the Scamander.

Old Nurses in Greek legend usually stand for the Goddess as Crone (see 24. 9); and Penthesileia's nurse Clete ('invoked') is no exception.

2. Cissia ('ivy') seems to be an early title of the variously named goddess who presided over the ivy and vine revels in Greece, Thrace, Asia Minor, and Syria (see 168. 3); Memnon's 'Cissians', however, are a variant of 'Susians' ('lily-men'), so called in honour of the Lily-goddess Susannah, or Astarte. Priam probably applied for help not to the Assyrians but to the Hittites, who may well have sent reinforcements by land, and also by sea, from Syria. 'Memnon' ('resolute'), a common title of Greek kings – intensified in 'Agamemnon' ('very resolute') – has here been confused with Mnemon, a title of Artaxerxes the Assyrian, and with Amenophis, the name of the Pharoah in whose honour the famous black singing statue was constructed at Thebes. The first rays of the sun warmed the hollow stone, making the air inside expand and rush through the narrow throat.

3. Achilles in his birth, youth, and death is mythologically acceptable as the ancient Pelasgian sacred king, destined to become the 'lipless' oracular hero. His mythic opponent bore various names, such as 'Hector' and 'Paris' and 'Apollo'. Here it is Memnon son of Cissia. Achilles's duel with Memnon, each supported by his mother, was carved on the Chest of Cypselus (Pausanias: v. 19. 1), and on the throne of Apollo at Amyclae (Pausanias: iii. 18. 7); besides figuring in a large group by the painter Lycius, which the inhabitants of Apollonia dedicated at Olympia (Pausanias: v. 22. 2). These two represent sacred king and tanist – Achilles, son of the Sea-goddess, bright Spirit of the Waxing Year: Memnon, son of the Ivy-goddess, dark Spirit of the Waning Year, to whom the golden vine is sacred. They kill each other alternately, at the winter and summer solstices; the king always succumbs to a heel-wound, his tanist is beheaded with a sword. Achilles, in this ancient sense, untainted by the scandalous behaviour of the Achaean and Dorian chieftains who usurped the name, was widely worshipped as a hero; and the non-Homeric story of his betrayal by Polyxena, who wormed from him the secret of his vulnerable heel, places him beside Llew Llaw, Cuchulain, Samson, and other Bronze Age heroes of honest repute. His struggle with Penthesileia is therefore likely to have been of the same sort as his father Peleus's struggle with Thetis (see 81. k). The recipient of Helen's message from Leuce – which is now a treeless Rumanian prison island – was the poet Stesichorus (see 31. 9 and 159. 1).

4. Because Memnon came from the East to help Priam, he was styled 'the son of Eos' ('dawn'); and because he needed a father, Eos's lover Tithonus seemed the natural choice (see 40. *c*). A fight at the winter solstice between girls in bird-disguise, which Ovid records, is a more likely explanation of the Memnonides than that they are fanciful embodiments of sparks flying up from a corpse on the pyre; the fight will originally have been for the high-priestess-ship, in Libyan style (see 8. *1*).

5. Achilles as the sacred king of Olympia was mourned after the summer solstice, when the Olympic funeral games were held in his honour; his tanist, locally called 'Cronus', was mourned after the winter solstice (see 138. *4*). In the British Isles these feasts fell on Lammas and St Stephen's Day respectively; but though the corpse of the golden-crested wren, the bird of Cronus, is still carried in procession through country districts on St Stephen's Day, the British Memnonides 'fell a-sighing and a-sobbing' only for the robin, not for his victim, the wren: the tanist, not the sacred king.

6. Achilles's hero-shrine in Crete must have been built by Pelasgian immigrants; but the plane is a Cretan tree. Since the plane-leaf represented Rhea's green hand, Achilles may have been called Pemptus ('fifth') to identify him with Acesidas, the fifth of her Dactyls, namely the oracular little finger, as Heracles was identified with the first, the virile thumb (see 53. *1*).

7. Priam's golden vine, his bribe to Tithonus for sending Memnon, seems to have been the one given Tros by Zeus in compensation for the rape of Ganymedes (see 29. *b*).

165

THE MADNESS OF AJAX

WHEN Thetis decided to award the arms of Achilles to the most courageous Greek left alive before Troy, only Ajax and Odysseus, who had boldly defended the corpse together,[1] dared come forward to claim them. Some say that Agamemnon, from a dislike of the whole House of Aeacus, rejected Ajax's pretensions and divided the arms between Menelaus and Odysseus, whose goodwill he valued far more highly;[2] others, that he avoided the odium of a decision by referring the case to the assembled Greek leaders, who settled it by a secret ballot; or that he referred it to the Cretans and other allies; or that he forced his Trojan prisoners to declare which of the two claimants had done them most harm.[3] But the truth is that, while Ajax and Odysseus were still competitively boasting of their achievements, Nestor advised Agamemnon to send spies by night to listen under the Trojan walls for the enemy's unbiased opinion on the matter. The spies overheard a party of young girls chattering together; and when one praised Ajax for bearing dead Achilles from the battlefield through a storm of missiles, another, at Athene's instigation, replied: 'Nonsense! Even a slave-woman will do as much, once someone has set a corpse on her shoulders; but thrust weapons into her hand, and she will be too frightened to use them. Odysseus, not Ajax, bore the brunt of our attack.'[4]

b. Agamemnon therefore awarded the arms to Odysseus. He and Menelaus would never, of course, have dared to insult Ajax in this manner had Achilles still been alive: for Achilles thought the world of his gallant cousin. It was Zeus himself who provoked the quarrel.[5]

c. In a dumb rage, Ajax planned to revenge himself on his fellow-Greeks that very night; Athene, however, struck him with madness and turned him loose, sword in hand, among the cattle and sheep which had been lifted from Trojan farms to form part of the common spoil. After immense slaughter, he chained the surviving beasts together, hauled them back to the camp, and there continued his butcher's work. Choosing two white-footed rams, he lopped off the head and tongue of one, which he mistook for Agamemnon, or Menelaus; and tied the other upright to a pillar, where he flogged it with a horse's halter, screaming abuse and calling it perfidious Odysseus.[6]

d. At last coming to his senses in utter despair, he summoned Eurysaces, his son by Tecmessa, and gave him the huge, sevenfold shield after which he had been named. 'The rest of my arms will be buried with me when I die,' he said. Ajax's half-brother Teucer, son of Priam's captive sister Hesione, happened to be away in Mysia, but Ajax left a message appointing him guardian of Eurysaces, who was to be taken home to his grandparents Telamon and Eriboea of Salamis. Then, with a word to Tecmessa that he would escape Athene's anger by bathing in a sea pool and finding some untrodden patch of ground where the sword might be securely buried, he set out, determined on death.

e. He fixed the sword – the very one which Hector had exchanged for the purple baldric – upright in the earth, and after calling on Zeus to tell Teucer where his corpse might be found; on Hermes, to conduct his soul to the Asphodel Fields; and on the Erinnyes, for vengeance, threw himself upon it. The sword, loathing its task, doubled back in the shape of a bow, and dawn had broken before he contrived to commit suicide by driving the point underneath his vulnerable arm-pit.[7]

f. Meanwhile Teucer, returning from Mysia, narrowly escaped murder by the Greeks, who were indignant at the slaughter of their livestock. Calchas, having been granted no prophetic warning of the suicide, took Teucer aside and advised him to confine Ajax to his hut, as one maddened by the wrath of Athene. Podaleirius son of Asclepius agreed; he was as expert a physician as his brother Machaon was a surgeon, and had been the first to diagnose Ajax's madness from his flashing eyes.[8] But Teucer merely shook his head, having already been informed by Zeus of his brother's death, and went sadly out with Tecmessa to find the corpse.

g. There Ajax lay in a pool of blood, and dismay overcame Teucer. How could he return to Salamis, and face his father Telamon? As he stood, tearing his hair, Menelaus strode up and forbade him to bury Ajax, who must be left for the greedy kites and pious vultures. Teucer sent him about his business, and leaving Eurysaces in suppliant's dress to display locks of his own, Teucer's, and Tecmessa's hair, and so guard Ajax's corpse – over which Tecmessa had spread her robe – he came raging before Agamemnon. Odysseus intervened in the ensuing dispute, and not only urged Agamemnon to permit the funeral rites, but offered to help Teucer carry them out. This service Teucer declined, while acknowledging Odysseus's courtesy. Finally Agamemnon, on Calchas's advice, allowed Ajax to be buried in a suicide's coffin at Cape Rhoeteum, rather than burned on a pyre as if he had fallen honourably in battle.[9]

h. Some hold that the cause of the quarrel between Ajax and Odysseus was the possession of Palladium, and that it took place after Troy had fallen.[10] Others deny that Ajax committed suicide, and say that, since he was proof against steel, the Trojans killed him with lumps of clay, having been advised to do so by an oracle. But this may have been another Ajax[11].

i. Afterwards, when Odysseus visited the Asphodel Fields, Ajax was the only ghost who stood aloof from him, rejecting his excuses that Zeus had been responsible for this unfortunate affair. Odysseus had by that time wisely presented the arms to Achilles's son Neoptolemus; though the Aeolians who later settled at Troy say that he lost them in a shipwreck as he sailed home, whereupon by Thetis's contrivance the waves deposited them beside Ajax's tomb at Rhoeteum. During the reign of the Emperor Hadrian, high seas washed open the tomb and his bones were seen to be of gigantic size, the knee-caps alone being as large as a discus used by boys practising for the pentathlon; at the Emperor's orders, they were at once reinterred.[12]

j. The Salaminians report that a new flower appeared in their island when Ajax died: white, tinged with red, smaller than a lily and, like the hyacinth, bearing letters which spell *Ai! Ai!* ('*woe, woe!*'). But it is generally believed that the new flower sprang from Ajax's blood where he fell, since the letters also stand for *Aias Aiacides* – 'Ajax the Aeacid'. In the Salaminian market place stands a temple of Ajax, with an ebony image; and not far from the harbour a boulder is shown on which Telamon sat gazing at the ship which bore his sons away to Aulis.[13]

k. Teucer eventually returned to Salamis, but Telamon accused him of fractricide in the second degree, since he had not pressed Ajax's claim to the disputed arms. Forbidden to land, he pleaded his case from the sea while the judges listened on the shore; Telamon himself had been forced to do the same by his own father Aeacus, when accused of murdering his brother Phocus. But as Telamon had been found guilty and banished, so also was Teucer, on the ground that he had brought back neither Ajax's bones, nor Tecmessa, nor Eurysaces; which proved neglect. He set sail for Cyprus, where with Apollo's favour and the permission of King Belus the Sidonian he founded the other Salamis.[14]

l. The Athenians honour Ajax as one of their eponymous heroes, and insist that Philaeus, the son of Eurysaces, became an Athenian citizen and surrendered the sovereignty of Salamis to them.[15]

1. Homer: *Odyssey* xi. 543 ff.; *Argument* of Sophocles's *Ajax*.
2. Hyginus: *Fabula* 107.
3. Pindar: *Nemean Odes* viii. 26 ff.; Ovid: *Metamorphoses* xii. 620 ff.; Apollodorus: *Epitome* v. 6; Scholiast on Homer's *Odyssey* xi. 547.
4. Lesches: *Little Iliad*, quoted by scholiast on Aristophanes's *Knights* 1056.
5. Homer: *Odyssey* xi. 559–60.
6. Sophocles: *Ajax*, with *Argument*; Zenobius: *Proverbs* i. 43.
7. Sophocles: *Ajax*; Aeschylus, quoted by scholiast on *Ajax* 833 and on *Iliad* xxiii. 821; Arctinus of Miletus: *Aethiopis*, quoted by scholiast on Pindar's *Isthmian Odes* iii. 53.
8. Arctinus: *Sack of Ilium*, quoted by Eustathius on Homer's *Iliad* xiii. 515.
9. Apollodorus: *Epitome* v. 7; Philostratus: *Heroica* xiii. 7.
10. Dictys Cretensis: v. 14–15.

11. *Argument* of Sophocles's *Ajax*.

12. Homer: *Odyssey* xi. 543 ff.; Pausanias: i. 35. 3; Philostratus: *Heroica* i. 2.

13. Pausanias: i. 35. 2–3; Ovid: *Metamorphoses* xiii. 382 ff.

14. Pausanias: i. 28. 12 and viii. 15. 3; Servius on Virgil's *Aeneid* i. 619; Pindar: *Nemean Odes* iv. 60; Aeschylus: *Persians* i. 35. 2 and 5. 2.

15. Herodotus: vi. 35; Pausanias: i. 35. 2; Plutarch: *Solon* xi.

*

1. Here the mythological element is small. Ajax was perhaps shown on some Cyprian icon tying the ram to a pillar; not because he had gone mad, but because this was a form of sacrifice introduced into Cyprus from Crete (see 39. 2).

2. Homer's hyacinth is the blue larkspur – *hyacinthos grapta* – which has markings on the base of its petals resembling the early Greek letters *AI*; it had also been sacred to Cretan Hyacinthus (see 21. 8).

3. The bones of Ajax reinterred by Hadrian, like those of Theseus (see 104. i), probably belonged to some far more ancient hero. Peisistratus made use of Ajax's alleged connexion with Attica to claim sovereignty over the island of Salamis, previously held by Megara, and is said to have supported his claim by the insertion of forged verses (see 163. 1) into the Homeric canon (*Iliad* ii. 458–559; Aristotle: *Rhetoric* i. 15; Plutarch: *Solon* 10). *Aia* is an old form of *gaia* ('earth'), and *aias* ('Ajax') will have meant 'countryman'.

4. To kill a man with lumps of clay, rather than swords, was a primitive means of avoiding blood guilt; and this other Ajax's murder must therefore have been the work of his kinsmen, not the Trojan enemy.

5. That Odysseus and Ajax quarrelled for the possession of the Palladium is historically important; but Sophocles has carelessly confused Great Ajax with Little Ajax (see 166. 2).

166

THE ORACLES OF TROY

ACHILLES was dead, and the Greeks had begun to despair. Calchas now prophesied that Troy could not be taken except with the help of Heracles's bow and arrows. Odysseus and Diomedes were therefore deputed to sail for Lemnos and fetch them from Philoctetes, their present owner.[1]

b. Some say that King Actor's shepherd Phimachus, son of Dolophion, had sheltered Philoctetes and dressed his noisome wound for the past ten years. Others record that some of Philoctetes's Meliboean troops settled beside him in Lemnos, and that the Asclepiads had already cured him, with Lemnian earth, before the deputation arrived; or that Pylius, or Pelius, a son of Hephaestus, did so. Philoctetes is said to have then conquered certain small islands off the Trojan coast for King Eeneus, dispossessing the Carian population – a kindness which Euneus acknowledged by giving him the Lemnian district of Acesa.[2] Thus, it is explained, Odysseus and Diomedes had no need to tempt Philoctetes with offers of medical treatment; he came willingly enough, carrying his bow and arrows, to win the war for them and glory for himself. According to still another account, the deputation found him long dead of the wound and persuaded his heirs to let them borrow the bow.[3]

c. The truth is, however, that Philoctetes stayed in Lemnos, suffering painfully, until Odysseus tricked him into handing over the bow and arrows; but Diomedes (not, as some mistakenly say, Neoptolemus) declined to be implicated in the theft and advised Philoctetes to demand the return of his property. At this, the god Heracles intervened. 'Go with them to Troy, Philoctetes,' he said, 'and I will send an Asclepiad there to cure you; for Troy must fall a second time to my arrows. You shall be chosen from among the Greeks as the boldest fighter of all. You shall kill Paris, take part in the sack of Troy, and send home the spoils, reserving the noblest prize for your father Poeas. But remember: you cannot take Troy without Neoptolemus son of Achilles, nor can he do so without you!'[4]

d. Philoctetes obeyed, and on his arrival at the Greek camp was bathed with fresh water and put to sleep in Apollo's temple; as he slept, Machaon the surgeon cut away the decaying flesh from the wound, poured in wine, and applied healing herbs and the serpentine stone. But some say that Machaon's brother Podaleirius, the physician, took charge of the case.[5]

e. No sooner was Philoctetes about again, than he challenged Paris to a combat in archery. The first arrow he shot went wide, the second pierced Paris's bow-hand, the third blinded his right eye, and the fourth struck his ankle, wounding him mortally. Despite Menelaus's attempt to despatch Paris, he contrived to hobble from the field and take refuge in Troy. That night the Trojans carried him to Mount Ida, where he begged his former mistress, the nymph Oenone, to heal him; from an inveterate hatred of Helen, however, she cruelly shook her head and he was brought back to die. Presently Oenone relented, and ran to Troy with a basketful of healing drugs, but found him already dead. In a frenzy of grief she leaped from the walls, or hanged herself, or burned herself to death on his pyre – no one remembers which. Some excuse Oenone by saying that she would have healed Paris at once, had not her father prevented her; she was obliged to wait until he had left the house before bringing the simples, and then it proved too late.[6]

f. Helenus and Deiphobus now quarrelled for Helen's hand, and Priam supported Deiphobus's claim on the ground that he had shown the greater valour; but, though her marriage to Paris had been divinely arranged, Helen could not forget that she was still Queen of Sparta and wife to Menelaus. One night, a sentry caught her tying a rope to the battlements in an attempt to escape. She was led before Deiphobus, who married her by force – much to the disgust of the other Trojans. Helenus immediately left the city and went to live with Arisbe on the slopes of Mount Ida.[7]

g. Upon hearing from Calchas that Helenus alone knew the secret oracles which protected Troy, Agamemnon sent Odysseus to waylay and drag him to the Greek camp. Helenus happened to be staying as Chryses's guest in the temple of Thymbraean Apollo, when Odysseus came in search of him, and proved ready enough to disclose the oracles, on condition that he would be given a secure home in some distant land. He had deserted Troy, he explained, not because he feared death, but because neither he not Aeneas could overlook Paris's sacrilegious murder of Achilles in this very temple, for which no amends had yet been made to Apollo.[8]

h. 'So be it. Hold nothing back, and I will guarantee your life and safety,' said Odysseus.

'The oracles are brief and clear,' Helenus answered. 'Troy falls this summer, if a certain bone of Pelops is brought to your camp; if Neoptolemus takes the field; and if Athene's Palladium is stolen from the citadel – because the walls cannot be breached while it remains there.'[9]

Agamemnon at once sent to Pisa for Pelops's shoulder-blade. Meanwhile, Odysseus, Phoenix, and Diomedes sailed to Scyros, where they persuaded Lycomedes to let Neoptolemus come to Troy – some say that he was then only twelve years old. The ghost of Achilles appeared before him on his arrival, and he forthwith distinguished himself both in council and in war, Odysseus gladly resigning Achilles's arms to him.¹⁰

i. Eurypylus son of Telephus now reinforced the Trojans with an army of Mysians, and Priam, who had offered his mother Astyoche a golden vine if he came, betrothed him to Cassandra. Eurypylus proved a resolute fighter, and killed Machaon the surgeon; which is why, in Asclepius's sanctuary at Pergamus, where every service begins with a hymn celebrating Telephus, the name of his son Eurypylus may not be spoken on any occasion. Machaon's bones were taken back to Pylus by Nestor, and sick people are healed in the sanctuary at Geraneia; his garlanded bronze statue dominates the sacred place called 'The Rose'. Eurypylus himself was killed by Neoptolemus.¹¹

j. Shortly before the fall of Troy, the dissensions between Priam's sons grew so fierce that he authorized Antenor to negotiate peace with Agamemnon. On his arrival at the Greek camp Antenor, out of hatred for Deiphobus, agreed to betray the Palladium and the city into Odysseus's hands; his price was the kingship and half of Priam's treasure. Aeneas, he told Agamemnon, could also be counted upon to help.¹²

k. Together they concocted a plan, in pursuance of which Odysseus asked Diomedes to flog him mercilessly; then, bloodstained, filthy, and dressed in rags, he gained admittance into Troy as a runaway slave. Helen alone saw through his disguise, but when she privately questioned him, was fobbed off with evasive answers. Nevertheless, he could not decline an invitation to her house, where she bathed, anointed and clothed him in fine robes; and his identity being thus established beyond question, swore a solemn oath that she would not betray him to the Trojans – so far she had confided only in Hecabe – if he revealed all the details of his plan to her. Helen explained that she was now kept a prisoner in Troy, and longed to go home. At this juncture, Hecabe entered. Odysseus at once threw himself at her feet, weeping for terror, and implored her not to denounce him. Surprisingly enough, she agreed. He then hurried back, guided by Hecabe, and reached his friends in safety with a harvest of information; claiming to have killed a number of Trojans who would not open the gates for him.¹³

l. Some say that Odysseus stole the Palladium on this occasion, single-handed. Others say that he and Diomedes, as favourites of Athene, were chosen to do so, and that they climbed up to the citadel by way of a narrow and muddy conduit, killed the sleeping guards, and together took possession of the image, which priestess Theano, Antenor's wife, willingly surrendered.[14] The common account, however, is that Diomedes scaled the wall by climbing upon Odysseus's shoulders, because the ladder was short, and entered Troy alone. When he re-appeared, carrying the Palladium in his arms, the two of them set out for the camp, side by side, under a full moon; but Odysseus wanted all the glory. He dropped behind Diomedes, to whose shoulders the image was now strapped, and would have murdered him, had not the shadow of his sword caught Diomedes's eye, the moon being still low in the heavens. He spun about, drew his own sword and, disarming Odysseus, pinioned his hands and drove him back to the ships with repeated kicks and blows. Hence the phrase 'Diomedes's compulsion', often applied to those whose actions are coerced.[15]

m. The Romans pretend that Odysseus and Diomedes carried off a mere replica of the Palladium which was on public display, and that Aeneas, at the fall of Troy, rescued the authentic image, smuggled it out with the remainder of his sacred luggage, and brought it safe to Italy.[16]

1. Apollodorus: *Epitome* v. 8; Tzetzes: *On Lycophron* 911; Sophocles: *Philoctetes* i. ff.
2. Hyginus: *Fabula* 102; Eustathius on Homer p. 330; Ptolemy Hephaestionos: vi., quoted by Photius p.490; Philostratus: *Heroica* 5.
3. Ptolemy Hephaestionos: v., quoted by Photius p. 486; Pausanias: i. 22. 6.
4. Apollodorus: *loc. cit.*; Philostratus: *loc. cit.* and *Philoctetes* 915 ff. and 1409 ff.
5. Orpheus and Dionysius, quoted by Tzetzes: *On Lycophron* 911; Apollodorus: *loc. cit.*
6. Tzetzes: *On Lycophron* 61–2; 64 and 911; Lesches: *Little Iliad*; Apollodorus: iii. 12. 6.
7. Apollodorus: *Epitome* v.9; Tzetzes: *On Lycophron* 143 and 168; Euripides: *Trojan Women* 955–60; Servius on Virgil's *Aeneid* ii. 166.
8. Apollodorus: *Epitome* v. 9–10; Sophocles: *Philoctetes* 606; Orpheus, quoted by Tzetzes: *On Lycophron* 911; Dictys Cretensis: iv. 18.
9. Sophocles: *Philoctetes* 1337–42; Apollodorus: *loc. cit.*; Tzetzes: *loc. cit.*
10. Apollodorus: *Epitome* v. 11; Pausanias: v. 13. 3; Homer: *Odyssey* xi. 506 ff.; Philostratus: *Imagines* 2; Quintus Smyrnaeus: *Posthomerica* vi. 57–113 and vii. 169–430; Rawlinson: *Excidium Troiae*; Lesches: *loc. cit.*
11. Scholiast on Homer's *Odyssey* xi. 520; Dictys Cretensis: iv. 14;

Little Iliad, quoted by Pausanias: iii. 26. 7; Apollodorus: Epitome v. 12.

12. Dictys Cretensis: vi. 22 and v. 8.
13. Euripides: Hecabe 239–50; Homer: Odyssey iv. 242 ff.; Lesches: loc. cit.
14. Apollodorus: Epitome v. 13; Sophocles: Fragment 367; Servius on Virgil's Aeneid ii. 166; Scholiast on Homer's Iliad vi. 311; Suidas sub Palladium; Johannes Malalas: Chronographica v. p. 109, ed. Dindorf: Dictys Cretensis: v. 5 and 8.
15. Conon: Narrations 34; Servius: loc. cit.
16. Dionysius of Halicarnassus: i. 68 ff.; Ovid: Fasti vi. 434.

*

1. All this is idle romance, or drama, except for the stealing of the Palladium, Hecabe's mysterious refusal to betray Odysseus (see 168. 5), and the death of Paris from a wound in his ankle (see 92. 10; 126. 3 and 164. j). Pelops's shoulder-blade was probably of porpoise-ivory (see 109. 5). The account which makes Philoctetes succumb to poison – of Heracles's arrows dipped in the Hydra's blood – seems to be the earliest one (see 162. l).

2. Pausanias reports (v. 13. 3): 'When the Greeks returned from Troy, the ship that carried the shoulder-blade of Pelops was sunk off Euboea in a storm. Many years later an Eretrian fisherman named Damarmenus ("subduer of sails") drew up a bone in his net, which was of such astonishing size that he hid it in the sand while he went to ask the Delphic Oracle whose bone it was, and what ought to be done with it. Apollo had arranged that an Elean embassy should arrive that same day requiring a remedy for a plague. The Pythoness answered the Eleans: "Recover the shoulder-blade of Pelops." To Damarmenus she said: "Give your bone to those ambassadors." The Eleans rewarded him well, making the custodianship of the bone hereditary in his house. It was no longer to be seen when I visited Elis: doubtless age and the action of the sea-water in which it had lain so long had mouldered it away.'

167

THE WOODEN HORSE

ATHENE now inspired Prylis, son of Hermes, to suggest that entry should be gained into Troy by means of a wooden horse; and Epeius, son of Panopeus, a Phocian from Parnassus, volunteered to build one under Athene's supervision. Afterwards, of course, Odysseus claimed all the credit for this stratagem.[1]

b. Epeius had brought thirty ships from the Cyclades to Troy. He held the office of water-bearer to the House of Atreus; as appears in the frieze of Apollo's temple at Carthea, and though a skilled boxer and a consummate craftsman, was born a coward, in divine punishment for his father's breach of faith – Panopeus had falsely sworn in Athene's name not to embezzle any part of the Taphian booty won by Amphitryon. Epeius's cowardice has since become proverbial.[2]

c. He built an enormous hollow horse of fir planks, with a trap-door fitted into one flank, and large letters cut on the other which consecrated it to Athene: 'In thankful anticipation of a safe return to their homes, the Greeks dedicate this offering to the Goddess.'[3] Odysseus persuaded the bravest of the Greeks to climb fully armed up a rope-ladder and through the trap-door into the belly of the horse. Their number is variously given as twenty-three, thirty or more, fifty, and, absurdly enough, three thousand. Among them were Menelaus, Odysseus, Diomedes, Sthenelus, Acamas, Thoas, and Neoptolemus. Coaxed, threatened, and bribed, Epeius himself joined the party. He climbed up last, drew the ladder in after him and, since he alone knew how to work the trap-door, took his seat beside the lock.[4]

d. At nightfall, the remaining Greeks under Agamemnon followed Odysseus's instructions, which were to burn their camp, put out to sea, and wait off Tenedos and the Calydnian Islands until the following evening. Only Odysseus's first cousin Sinon, a grandson of Autolycus, stayed behind to light a signal beacon for their return.[5]

e. At break of day, Trojan scouts reported that the camp lay in ashes and that the Greeks had departed, leaving a huge horse on the seashore. Priam and several of his sons went out to view it and, as they stood staring in wonder, Thymoetes was the first to break the silence. 'Since this is a gift to Athene,' he said, 'I propose that we take it into Troy and haul it up to her citadel.' 'No, no!' cried Capys. 'Athene favoured the Greeks too long; we must either burn it at once or break it open to see what the belly contains.' But Priam declared: 'Thymoetes is right. We will fetch it in on rollers. Let nobody desecrate Athene's property.' The horse proved too broad to be squeezed through the gates. Even when the wall had been breached, it stuck four times. With enormous efforts the Trojans then hauled it up to the citadel; but at least took the precaution of repairing the breach behind them. Another heated argument followed when Cassandra announced that the horse contained armed men, and was supported in her view by the seer Laocoön, son of Antenor, whom some mistakenly call the brother of Anchises. Crying: 'You fools, never trust a Greek even if he brings you gifts!', he hurled his spear, which stuck quivering in the horse's flank and caused the weapons inside to clash together. Cheers and shouts arose: 'Burn it!' 'Hurl it over the walls!' But, 'Let it stay,' pleaded Priam's supporters.[6]

f. This argument was interrupted by the arrival of Sinon, whom a couple of Trojan soldiers were marching up in chains. Under interrogation, he said that Odysseus had long been trying to destroy him because he knew the secret of Palamedes's murder. The Greeks, he went on, were heartily sick of the war, and would have sailed home months before this, but that the uninterrupted bad weather prevented them. Apollo had advised them to placate the Winds with blood, as when they were delayed at Aulis. Whereupon,' Sinon continued, 'Odysseus dragged Calchas forward, and asked him to name the victim. Calchas would not give an immediate answer and went into retirement for ten days, at the end of which time, doubtless bribed by Odysseus, he entered the Council hut and pointed at me. All present welcomed this verdict, every man relieved at not being chosen as the scapegoat, and I was put in fetters; but a favourable wind sprang up, my companions hurriedly launched their vessels, and in the confusion I made my escape.'

g. Thus Priam was tricked into accepting Sinon as a suppliant, and had his fetters broken. 'Now tell us about this horse,' he said kindly. Sinon explained that the Greeks had forfeited Athene's support, on which they depended, when Odysseus and Diomedes stole the Palladium from her temple. No sooner had they brought it to their camp than the image was three times enveloped by flames, and its limbs sweated in proof of the goddess's wrath. Calchas thereupon advised Agamemnon to sail for home and assemble a fresh expedition in Greece, under better auspices, leaving the horse as a placatory gift to Athene. 'Why was it built so big?' asked Priam. Sinon, well coached by Odysseus, replied: 'To prevent you from bringing it into the city. Calchas foretells that if you despise this sacred image, Athene will ruin you; but once it enters Troy, you shall be empowered to marshal all the forces of Asia, invade Greece, and conquer Mycenae.'[7]

h. 'These are lies,' cried Laocoön, 'and sound as if they were invented by Odysseus. Do not believe him, Priam!' He added: 'Pray, my lord, give me leave to sacrifice a bull to Poseidon. When I come back I hope to see this wooden horse reduced to ashes.' It should be explained that the Trojans, having stoned their priest of Poseidon to death nine years before, had decided not to replace him until the war seemed to have ended. Now they chose Laocoön by lot to propitiate Poseidon. He was already the priest of Thymbraean Apollo, whom he had angered by marrying and begetting children, despite a vow of celibacy and, worse, by lying with his wife Antiope in sight of the god's image.[8]

i. Laocoön retired to select a victim and prepare the altar but, in warning of Troy's approaching doom, Apollo sent two great sea-serpents, named Porces and Chariboea, or Curissia, or Periboea, rushing towards Troy from Tenedos and the Calydnian Islands.[9]

They darted ashore and, coiling around the limbs of Laocoön's twin sons Antiphas and Thymbraeus, whom some call Melanthus, crushed them to death. Laocoön ran to their rescue, but he too died miserably. The serpents then glided up to the citadel and while one wound about Athene's feet, the other took refuge behind her aegis. Some, however, say that only one of Laocoön's sons was killed and that he died in the temple of Thymbraean Apollo, not beside Poseidon's altar; and others that Laocoön himself escaped death.[10]

j. This terrible portent served to convince the Trojans that Sinon had spoken the truth. Priam mistakenly assumed that Laocoön was being punished for hurling his spear at the horse, rather than for having insulted Apollo. He at once dedicated the horse to Athene and although Aeneas's followers retired in alarm to their huts on Mount Ida, nearly all Priam's Trojans began to celebrate the victory with banquets and merrymaking. The women gathered flowers from the river banks, garlanded the horse's mane, and spread a carpet of roses around its hooves.[11]

k. Meanwhile, inside the horse's belly, the Greeks had been trembling for terror, and Epeius wept silently, in an ecstasy of fear. Only Neoptolemus showed no emotion, even when the point of Laocoön's spear broke through the timbers close to his head. Time after time he nudged Odysseus to order the assault – for Odysseus was in command – and clutched his lance and sword-hilt menacingly. But Odysseus would not consent. In the evening Helen strolled from the palace and went around the horse three times, patting its flanks and, as if to amuse Deiphobus who was with her, teased the hidden Greeks by imitating the voice of each of their wives in turn. Menelaus and Diomedes, squatting in the middle of the horse next to Odysseus, were tempted to leap out when they heard themselves called by name; but he restrained them and, seeing that Antielus was on the point of answering, clapped a hand over his mouth and, some say, strangled him.[12]

l. That night, exhausted with feasting and revelry, the Trojans slept soundly, and not even the bark of a dog broke the stillness. But Helen lay awake, and a bright round light blazed above her chamber as a signal to the Greeks. At midnight, just before the full moon rose – the seventh of the year – Sinon crept from the city to kindle a beacon on Achilles's tomb, and Antenor waved a torch.[13]

Agamemnon answered these signals by lighting pine-wood chips in a cresset on the deck of his ship, which was now heaved-to a few bow-shots from the coast; and the whole fleet drove shoreward. Antenor, cautiously approaching the horse, reported in a low voice that all was well, and Odysseus ordered Epeius to unlock the trap-door.[14]

m. Echion, son of Portheus, leaping out first, fell and broke his neck; the rest descended by Epeius's rope-ladder. Some ran to open the gates for the landing party, others cut down drowsy sentries guarding the citadel and palace; but Menelaus could think only of Helen, and ran straight towards her house.[15]

1. Hyginus: *Fabula* 108; Tzetzes: *On Lycophron* 219 ff.; Apollodorus: *Epitome* v. 14.
2. Euripides: *Trojan Women* 10; Dictys Cretensis: i. 17; Stesichorus, quoted by Eustathius on Homer p. 1323; Athenaeus: x. p. 457; Homer: *Iliad* xxiii. 665; Tzetzes: *On Lycophron* 930; Hesychius *sub* Epeius.
3. Homer: *Odyssey* viii. 493; Apollodorus: *Epitome* v. 14–15.
4. Tzetzes: *loc. cit.* and *Posthomerica* 641–50; Quintus Smyrnaeus: *Posthomerica* xii. 314–35; Apollodorus: *Epitome* v. 14; *Little Iliad*, quoted by Apollodorus: *loc. cit.*; Hyginus: *loc. cit.*
5. Apollodorus: *Epitome* v. 14–15; Tzetzes: *On Lycophron* 344.
6. Virgil: *Aeneid* ii. 13–249; Lesches: *Little Iliad*; Tzetzes: *On Lycophron* 347; Apollodorus: *Epitome* v. 16–17; Hyginus: *Fabula* 135.
7. Virgil: *loc. cit.*
8. Euphorion, quoted by Servius on Virgil's *Aeneid* ii. 201; Hyginus: *loc. cit.*; Virgil: *loc. cit.*
9. Apollodorus: *Epitome* v. 18; Hyginus: *loc. cit.*; Tzetzes: *loc. cit.*; Lysimachus, quoted by Serv on Virgil's *Aeneid* ii. 211.

10. Thessandrus, quoted by Servius on Virgil's *Aeneid*: *loc. cit.*;
    Hyginus: *loc. cit.*; Quintus Smyrnaeus: *Posthomerica* xii. 444–97;
    Arctinus of Miletus: *Sack of Ilium*; Tzetzes: *loc. cit.*; Virgil: *loc. cit.*

11. Homer: *Odyssey* viii. 504 ff.; Apollodorus: *Epitome* v. 16–17;
    Arctinus of Miletus: *ibid.*; Lesches: *loc. cit.*; Tryphiodorus: *Sack of
    Troy* 316 ff. and 340–4.

12. Homer: *Odyssey* xi. 523–32 and iv. 271–89; Tryphiodorus: *Sack
    of Troy* 463–90.

13. Tryphiodorus: *Sack of Troy* 487–521; Servius on Virgil's *Aeneid*
    ii. 255; Lesches: *loc. cit.*, quoted by Tzetzes: *On Lycophron* 344;
    Apollodorus: *Epitome* v. 19.

14. Virgil: *Aeneid* ii. 256 ff.; Hyginus: *Fabula* 108; Apollodorus:
    Epitome v. 20; Tzetzes: *On Lycophron* 340.

15. Apollodorus: *loc. cit.*

*

1. Classical commentators on Homer were dissatisfied with the story
of the wooden horse. They suggested, variously, that the Greeks used a
horse-like engine for breaking down the wall (Pausanias: i. 23. 10); that
Antenor admitted the Greeks into Troy by a postern which had a horse
painted on it; or that the sign of a horse was used to distinguish the Greeks
from their enemies in the darkness and confusion; or that when Troy had
been betrayed, the oracles forbade the plundering of any house marked
with the sign of a horse – hence those of Antenor and others were spared;
or that Troy fell as the result of a cavalry action; or that the Greeks, after
burning their camp, concealed themselves behind Mount Hippius ('of
the horse').

2. Troy is quite likely to have been stormed by means of a wheeled
wooden tower, faced with wet horse hides as a protection against incen-
diary darts, and pushed towards the notoriously weak part of the defences
– the western curtain which Aeacus had built (see 158. *8*). But this would
hardly account for the legend that the Trojan leaders were concealed in
the horse's 'belly'. Perhaps the Homeridae invented this to explain a no
longer intelligible icon showing a walled city, a queen, a solemn assembly,
and the sacred king in the act of rebirth, head first, from a mare, which
was the sacred animal both of the Trojans (see 48. *3*) and of the Aeacids
(see 81. *4*). A wooden mare built of fir, the birth-tree (see 51. *5*), may have
been used in this ceremony, as a wooden cow facilitated the sacred marriage of Minos and Pasiphaë (see 88. *e*). Was the struggle between Odysseus and Antielus deduced perhaps from an icon that showed twins
quarrelling in the womb (see 73. *2*)?

3. The story of Laocoön's son, or sons, recalls that of the two serpents
strangled by Heracles (see 119. *2*). According to some versions, their
death occurred in Apollo's shrine, and Laocoön himself, like Amphi-

tryon, escaped unharmed. The serpents will, in fact, have merely been cleansing the boys' ears to give them prophetic powers. 'Antiphas' apparently means 'prophet' – 'one who speaks instead of' the god.

4. On the divine level this war was fought between Aphrodite, the Trojan Sea-goddess, and the Greek Sea-god Poseidon (see 169. 1) – hence Priam's suppression of Poseidon's priesthood.

5. Sweating images have been a recurrent phenomenon ever since the Fall of Troy; Roman gods later adopted this warning signal, and so did the Catholic saints who took their places.

6. In early saga Epeius's reputation for courage was such that his name became ironically applied to a braggart; and from braggart to coward is only a short step (see 88. 10).

168

THE SACK OF TROY

ODYSSEUS, it seems, had promised Hecabe and Helen that all who offered no resistance should be spared. Yet now the Greeks poured silently through the moonlit streets, broke into the unguarded houses, and cut the throats of the Trojans as they slept. Hecabe took refuge with her daughters beneath an ancient laurel-tree at the altar raised to Zeus of the Courtyard, where she restrained Priam from rushing into the thick of the fight. 'Remain among us, my lord,' she pleaded, 'in this safe place. You are too old and feeble for battle.' Priam, grumbling, did as she asked until their son Polites ran by, closely pursued by the Greeks, and fell transfixed before their eyes.[1] Cursing Neoptolemus, who had delivered the death blow, Priam hurled an ineffectual spear at him; whereupon he was hustled away from the altar steps, now red with Polites's blood, and butchered at the threshold of his own palace. But Neoptolemus, remembering his filial duty, dragged the body to Achilles's tomb on the Sigaean promontory, where he left it to rot, headless and unburied.[2]

b. Meanwhile Odysseus and Menelaus had made for Deiphobus's house, and there engaged in the bloodiest of all their combats, emerging victorious only with Athene's aid. Which of the two killed Deiphobus is disputed. Some even say that Helen herself plunged a dagger into his back; and that this action, and the sight of her naked breasts, so weakened the resolution of Menelaus, who had sworn 'She must die!', that he threw away his sword and led her in safety to the ships. Deiphobus's corpse was atrociously mangled, but Aeneas later raised a monument to him on Cape Rhoeteum.[3]

Odysseus saw Glaucus, one of Antenor's sons, fleeing down a street with a company of Greeks in hot pursuit. He intervened, and at the same time rescued Glaucus's brother Helicaon, who had been seriously wounded. Menelaus then hung a leopard's skin over the door of Antenor's house, as a sign that it should be spared.[4] Antenor, his wife Theano, and his four sons, were allowed to go free, taking all their goods with them; some days later they sailed away in Menelaus's ship, and settled first at Cyrene, next in Thrace, and finally at Henetica on the Adriatic.[5] Henetica was so called because Antenor took command of certain refugees from Paphlagonian Enete, whose King Pylaemenes had fallen at Troy, and led them in a successful war against the Euganei of the Northern Italian plain. The port and district where they disembarked was renamed 'New Troy', and they themselves are now known as Venetians. Antenor is also said to have founded the city of Padua.[6]

c. According to the Romans, the only other Trojan family spared by the Greeks was that of Aeneas who, like Antenor, had lately urged the surrender of Helen and the conclusion of a just peace; Agamemnon, seeing him lift the venerable Anchises upon his shoulders and carry him towards the Dardanian Gate without a sideways glance, gave orders that so pious a son should not be molested. Some, however, say that Aeneas was absent in Phrygia when the city fell.[7] Others, that he defended Troy to the last, then retired to the citadel of Pergamus and, after a second bold stand, sent his people forward under cover of darkness to Mount Ida, where he followed them as soon as he might with his family, his treasure, and the sacred images; and that, being offered honourable terms by the Greeks, he passed over into Thracian Pellene, and died either there or at Arcadian Orchomenus. But the Romans say that he wandered at last to Latium, founded the city of Lavinium and, falling in battle, was carried up to Heaven. All these are fables: the truth is that Neoptolemus led him away captive on board his ship, the most honourable prize won by any of the Greeks, and held him for ransom, which in due course the Dardanians paid.[8]

d. Helicaon's wife Laodice (whom some call the wife of Telephus) had lain with Acamas the Athenian, when he came to Troy in Dio-

medes's embassy ten years before, and secretly borne him a son named
Munitus, whom Helen's slave-woman Aethra – mother to Theseus,
and thus the infant's great-grandmother – had reared for her. At the
fall of Troy, as Laodice stood in the sanctuary of Tros, beside the tombs
of Cilla and Munippus, the earth gaped and swallowed her before the
eyes of all.[9]

e. In the confusion, Aethra fled with Munitus to the Greek camp,
where Acamas and Demophon recognized her as their long-lost grandmother, whom they had sworn either to rescue or to ransom. Demophon at once approached Agamemnon and demanded her repatriation,
with that of her fellow-captive, the sister of Peirithous. Menestheus of
Athens supported their plea, and since Helen had often shown her dislike of Aethra by setting a foot on her head and tugging at her hair,
Agamemnon gave his assent; but obliged Demophon and Acamas to
waive their claims to any other Trojan spoil. Unfortunately, when
Acamas landed in Thrace on his homeward voyage, Munitus, who was
accompanying him, died of a serpent's bite.[10]

f. No sooner had the massacre begun in Troy than Cassandra fled to
the temple of Athene and clutched the wooden image which had
replaced the stolen Palladium. There Little Ajax found her and tried to
drag her away, but she embraced the image so tightly that he had to
take it with him when he carried her off into concubinage; which
was the common fate of all Trojan women. Agamemnon, however,
claimed Cassandra as the particular award of his own valour, and
Odysseus obligingly put it about that Ajax had violated Cassandra in
the shrine; which was why the image kept its eyes upturned to Heaven,
as if horror-stricken.[11] Thus Cassandra became Agamemnon's prize,
while Ajax earned the hatred of the whole army; and, when the Greeks
were about to sail, Calchas warned the Council that Athene must be
placated for the insult offered to her priestess. To gratify Agamemnon,
Odysseus then proposed the stoning of Ajax; but he escaped by taking
sanctuary at Athene's altar, where he swore a solemn oath that Odysseus was lying as usual; nor did Cassandra herself support the charge of
rape. Nevertheless, Calchas's prophecy could hardly be disregarded;
Ajax therefore expressed sorrow for having forcibly removed the
image, and offered to expiate his crime. This he was prevented from
doing by death: the ship in which he sailed home to Greece being
wrecked on the Gyraean Rocks. When he scrambled ashore, Poseidon
split the rocks with his trident and drowned him; or, some say, Athene

borrowed Zeus's thunderbolt and struck him dead. But Thetis buried his body on the island of Myconos; and his fellow-countrymen wore black for a whole year, and now annually launch a black-sailed ship, heaped with gifts, and burn it in his honour.[12]

g. Athene's wrath then fell on the land of Opuntian Locris, and the Delphic Oracle warned Ajax's former subjects that they would have no relief from famine and pestilence unless they sent two girls to Troy every year for a thousand years. Accordingly, the Hundred Houses of Locris have ever since shouldered this burden in proof of their nobility. They choose the girls by lot, and land them at dead of night on the Rhoetean headland, each time varying the season; with them go kinsmen who know the country and can smuggle them into the sanctuary of Athene. If the Trojans catch these girls, they are stoned to death, burned as a defilement to the land, and their ashes scattered on the sea; but once inside the shrine, they are safe. Their hair is then shorn, they are given the single garment of a slave, and spend their days in menial temple duties until relieved by another pair. It happened many years ago that when the Trarians captured Troy and killed a Locrian priestess in the temple itself, the Locrians decided that their long penance must be over and therefore sent no more girls; but, famine and pestilence supervening, they hastened to resume their ancient custom, the term of which is only now drawing to an end. These girls gain Athene's sanctuary by way of an underground passage, the secret entrance to which is at some distance from the walls, and which leads to the muddy culvert used by Odysseus and Diomedes when they stole the Palladium. The Trojans have no notion how the girls contrive to enter, and never know on what night the relief is due to arrive, so that they seldom catch them, and then only by accident.[13]

h. After the massacre, Agamemnon's people plundered and burned Troy, divided the spoils, razed the walls, and sacrificed holocausts to their gods. The Council had debated for a while what should be done with Hector's infant son Astyanax, otherwise called Scamandrius; and when Odysseus recommended the systematic extirpation of Priam's descendants, Calchas settled the boy's fate by prophesying that, if allowed to survive, he would avenge his parents and his city. Though all other princes shrank from infanticide, Odysseus willingly hurled Astyanax from the battlements.[14] But some say that Neoptolemus, to whom Hector's widow Andromache had fallen as a prize in the division of spoil, snatched Astyanax from her, in anticipation of the Council's decree, whirled him around his head by one foot and flung him upon the rocks far below.[15] And others say that Astyanax leaped to his death from the wall, while Odysseus was reciting Calchas's prophecy and invoking the gods to approve the cruel rite.[16]

i. The Council also debated Polyxena's fate. As he lay dying, Achilles had begged that she should be sacrificed upon his tomb, and more recently had appeared in dreams to Neoptolemus and other chieftains, threatening to keep the fleet windbound at Troy until they fulfilled his demand. A voice was also heard complaining from the tomb: 'It is unjust that none of the spoil has been awarded to me!' And a ghost appeared on the Rhoetean headland, clad in golden armour, crying: 'Whither away, Greeks? Would you leave my tomb unhonoured?'[17]

j. Calchas now declared that Polyxena must not be denied to Achilles, who loved her. Agamemnon dissented, arguing that enough blood was already shed, of old men and infants as well as of warriors, to glut Achilles's vengeance, and that dead men, however famous, enjoyed no rights over live women. But Demophon and Acamas, who had been defrauded of their fair share in the spoils, clamoured that Agamemnon was expressing this view only to please Polyxena's sister Cassandra and make her submit more readily to his embraces. They asked: 'Which deserves the greater respect, Achilles's sword or Cassandra's bed?' Feeling ran high and Odysseus, intervening, persuaded Agamemnon to give way.[18]

k. The Council then instructed Odysseus to fetch Polyxena, and invited Neoptolemus to officiate as priest. She was sacrificed on Achilles's tomb, in the sight of the whole army, who hastened to give her honourable burial; whereupon favouring winds sprang up at once.[19] But some say that the Greek fleet had already reached Thrace when the ghost of Achilles appeared, threatening them with contrary winds, and that Polyxena was sacrificed there.[20] Others record that she went of her own free will to Achilles's tomb, before Troy fell, and threw herself on the point of a sword, thus expiating the wrong she had done him.[21]

l. Though Achilles had killed Polydorus, Priam's son by Laothoë, the youngest and best-loved of his children, yet another prince of the same name survived. He was Priam's son by Hecabe and had been sent for safety to the Thracian Chersonese, where his aunt Iliona, wife of King Polymnestor, reared him. Iliona treated Polydorus as though he were a true brother to Deiphilus, whom she had borne to Polymnestor.

Agamemnon, pursuing Odysseus's policy of extirpation, now sent messengers to Polymnestor promising him Electra for a wife and a dowry of gold if he would do away with Polydorus. Polymnestor accepted the bribe, yet could not bring himself to harm a child whom he had sworn to protect, and instead killed his own son Deiphilus in the presence of the messengers, who went back deceived. Polydorus, not knowing the secret of his birth, but realizing that he was the cause of Iliona's estrangement from Polymnestor, went to Delphi and asked the Pythoness: 'What ails my parents?' She answered: 'Is it a small thing that your city is reduced to ashes, your father butchered and your mother enslaved, that you should come to me with such a question?' He returned to Thrace in great anxiety, but found nothing changed since his departure. 'Can Apollo have been mistaken?' he wondered. Iliona told him the truth and, indignant that Polymnestor should have murdered his only child for gold and the promise of another queen, he first blinded and then stabbed him.[22]

m. Others say that Polymnestor was threatened by the Greeks with relentless war unless he would give up Polydorus and that, when he yielded, they brought the boy to their camp and offered to exchange him for Helen. Since Priam declined to discuss the proposal, Agamemnon had Polydorus stoned to death beneath the walls of Troy, afterwards sending his body to Helen with the message: 'Show Priam this, and ask him whether he regrets his decision.' It was an act of wanton spite, because Priam had pledged his word never to surrender Helen while she remained under Aphrodite's protection, and was ready to ransom Polydorus with the rich city of Antandrus.[23]

n. Odysseus won Hecabe as his prize, and took her to the Thracian Chersonese, where she uttered such hideous invectives against him and the other Greeks, for their barbarity and breaches of faith, that they found no alternative but to put her to death. Her spirit took the shape of one of those fearful black bitches that follow Hecate, leaped into the sea and swam away towards the Hellespont; they called the place of her burial 'The Bitch's Tomb'.[24] Another version of the story is that after the sacrifice of Polyxena, Hecabe found the dead body of Polydorus washed up on the shore, her son-in-law Polymnestor having murdered him for the gold with which Priam was defraying the expenses of his education. She summoned Polymnestor, promising to let him into the secret of a treasure concealed among the ruins of Troy, and when he approached with his two sons, drew a dagger from her bosom, stabbed the boys to death and tore out Polymnestor's eyes; a display of ill-temper which Agamemnon pardoned because of her age and misfortunes. The Thracian nobles would have taken vengeance on Hecabe with darts and stones, but she transformed herself into a bitch named Maera, and ran around howling dismally, so that they retired in confusion.[25]

o. Some say that Antenor founded a new Trojan kingdom upon the ruins of the old one. Others, that Astyanax survived and became King of Troy after the departure of the Greeks; and that, when he was expelled by Antenor and his allies, Aeneas put him back on the throne – to which, however, Aeneas's son Ascanius eventually succeeded, as had been prophesied. Be that as it may, Troy has never since been more than a shadow of its former self.[26]

1. Apollodorus: *Epitome* v. 21; Euripides: *Hecabe* 23; Virgil: *Aeneid* ii. 506–57.

2. Lesches: *Little Iliad*, quoted by Pausanias: x. 27. 1; Virgil: *loc. cit.*; Apollodorus: *loc. cit.*; Euripides: *Trojan Women* 16–17.

3. Homer: *Odyssey* viii. 517–20; Apollodorus: *Epitome* v. 22; Hyginus: *Fabula* 240; Pausanias: v 18. 1; Lesches: *Little Iliad*, quoted by scholiast on Aristophanes's *Lysistrata* 155; Virgil: *Aeneid* vi. 494 ff.; Dictys Cretensis: v. 12.

4. Apollodorus: *Epitome* v. 21; Homer: *Iliad* iii. 123; Lesches: *Little Iliad*, quoted by Pausanias: x. 26. 3; Servius on Virgil's *Aeneid* i. 246; Sophocles: *Capture of Troy*, quoted by Strabo: xiii. 1. 53.

5. Pausanias: x. 27. 2; Pindar: *Pythian Odes* v. 82 ff.; Servius on Virgil's *Aeneid* i. 246; Strabo: xiii. 1. 53.

6. Livy: i. 1; Servius on Virgil's *Aeneid* i. 246.

7. Livy: *loc. cit.*; Apollodorus: *Epitome* v. 21; Dionysius of Halicarnassus: i. 48.

8. Dionysius of Halicarnassus: i. 48, 49, and 64; Aelian: *Varia Historia* iii. 22; Hyginus: *Fabula* 254; Strabo: xiii. 608; Pausanias: viii. 12. 5; Virgil: *Aeneid*, passim; Plutarch: *Romulus* 3; Livy: i. 2; Lesches: *Little Iliad*, quoted by Tzetzes: *On Lycophron* 1268.

9. Hyginus: *Fabula* 101; Homer: *Iliad* iii. 123–4; Tzetzes: *On Lycophron* 495 ff. and 314; Apollodorus: *Epitome* v. 23.

10. Scholiast on Euripides's *Trojan Women* 31; Apollodorus: *Epitome* v. 22; Lesches: *Little Iliad*, quoted by Pausanias: x. 25. 3; Hyginus *Fabula* 243; Pausanias: v. 19. 1; Dio Chrysostom: *Orations* xi. i. p. 179, ed. Dindorff; Tzetzes: *On Lycophron* 495; Parthenius: *Love Stories* 16.

11. Arctinus of Miletus: *Sack of Ilium*; Virgil: *Aeneid* ii. 406; Apollodorus: *loc. cit.*; Scholiast on Homer's *Iliad* xiii. 66.

12. Tzetzes: *On Lycophron* 365; Apollodorus: *Epitome* v. 23; Pausanias: x. 31. 1; i. 15. 3 and x. 26. 1; Homer: *Odyssey* iv. 99.

13. Hyginus: *Fabula* 116; Scholiast on Homer's *Iliad* xiii. 66; Lycophron: 1141–73, with Tzetzes's *scholia*; Polybius: xii. 5; Plutarch: *On the Slowness of Divine Justice* xii; Strabo: xiii. 1. 40; Aelian: *Varia Historia, Fragment* 47; Aeneas Tacticus: xxxi. 24.

14. Homer: *Iliad* vi. 402; Apollodorus: *loc. cit.*; Euripides: *Trojan Women* 719 ff.; Hyginus: *Fabula* 109; Servius on Virgil's *Aeneid* ii. 457; Tryphiodorus: *Sack of Troy* 644–6.

15. Apollodorus: *loc. cit.*; Lesches: *Little Iliad*, quoted by Tzetzes: *On Lycophron* 1268; Pausanias: x. 25. 4.

16. Seneca: *Troades* 524 ff. and 1063 ff.

17. Servius on Virgil's *Aeneid* iii. 322; Tzetzes: *On Lycophron* 323; Quintus Smyrnaeus: *Posthomerica* xiv. 210–328; Euripides: *Hecabe* 107 ff.

18. Servius on Virgil's *Aeneid*: *loc. cit.*; Euripides: *loc. cit.*

19. Euripides: *Hecabe* 218 ff. and 521–82.

20. Ovid: *Metamorphoses* xiii. 439 ff.; Pausanias: x. 25. 4.

21. Philostratus: *Herioca* xix. 11.

22. Homer: *Iliad* xxii. 48 and xx. 407 ff.; Hyginus: *loc. cit.* and 240.

23. Dictys Cretensis: ii. 18, 22, and 27; Servius on Virgil's *Aeneid* iii. 6.

24. Apollodorus: *loc. cit.*; Hyginus: *Fabula* 111; Dictys Cretensis: v. 16; Tzetzes: *On Lycophron* 1176.

25. Euripides: *Hecabe*; Ovid: *Metamorphoses* xiii. 536 ff.

26. Dictys Cretensis: v. 17; Abas, quoted by Servius on Virgil's *Aeneid* ix. 264; Livy: i. 1.

*

1. Odysseus's considerate treatment of such renegades as Antenor and Calchas is contrasted here with the treachery he showed to his honest comrades Palamedes, Great Ajax, Little Ajax, and Diomedes, and with his savage handling of Astyanax, Polydorus, and Polyxena; but because Julius Caesar and Augustus claimed descent from Aeneas – another traitor spared by Odysseus, and regarded at Rome as a model of piety – the satiric implications are lost on modern readers. It is a pity that the exact terms of Hecabe's invectives against Odysseus and his comrades in dishonour, which must have expressed Homer's true feelings, have not survived; but her conversion into the Cretan Hecate, Maera, or Scylla, the sea-bitch (see 16. 2; 91. 2; and 170. *t*), suggests that he regarded the curses as valid – kingdoms founded on barbarity and ill-faith could never prosper. Maera was Scylla's emblem in heaven, the Lesser Dog-star, and when it rose, human sacrifices were offered at Marathon in Attica: the most famous victim being King Icarius (see 79. *1*), whose daughter

Odysseus had married and whose fate he will therefore have shared in the original myth (see 159. *b*).

2. The well-authenticated case of the Locrian girls is one of the strangest in Greek history, since Little Ajax's alleged violation of Cassandra was dismissed by reputable mythographers as an Odyssean lie, and it is clear that the Locrian girls gained entry into Troy as a matter of civic pride, not of penance. A genuine attempt was made by the Trojans to keep them out, if we can trust Aeneas Tacticus's account – he is discussing the danger of building cities with secret entrances – and that they were treated 'as a defilement of the land' if caught, and as slaves if they managed to gain entry, is consistent with this view. Little Ajax was the son of Locrian Oïleus; whose name, also borne by a Trojan warrior whom Agamemnon killed (*Iliad* xi. 9. 3), is an early form of 'Ilus'; and Priam's Ilium had, it seems, been partly colonized by Locrians, a pre-Hellenic tribe of Leleges (Aristotle: *Fragment* 560; Dionysius of Halicarnassus: i. 17; Strabo: xiii. 1. 3 and 3. 3). They gave the name of the Locrian mountain Phricones to what was hitherto called Cyme; and enjoyed a hereditary right to supply Athene with a quota of priestesses (see 158. *8*). This right they continued to exercise long after the Trojan War – when the city had lost its political power and became merely a place of sentimental pilgrimage – much to the disgust of the Trojans, who regarded the girls as their natural enemies.

3. The curse, effective for a thousand years, ended about 264 B.C. – which would correspond with the Delian (and thus the Homeric) dating of the Trojan War, though Eratosthenes reckoned it a hundred years later. Odysseus's secret conduit has been discovered in the ruins of Troy and is described by Walter Leaf in his *Troy: A Study in Homeric Geography* (London, 1912, pp. 126–44). But why did Theano turn traitress and surrender the Palladium? Probably because being a Locrian – Theano was also the name of the famous poetess of Epizephyrian Locri – she either disagreed with Priam's anti-Locrian trade policy, or knew that Troy must fall and wanted the image removed to safety, rather than captured by Agamemnon. Homer makes her a daughter of Thracian Cisseus, and there was at least one Locrian colony in Thrace, namely Abdera (see 130. *c*). As a Locrian, however, Theano will have reckoned descent matrilineally (Polybius: xii. 5. 6); and was probably surnamed Cisseis, 'ivy-woman', in honour of Athene whose chief festival fell during the ivy-month (see 52. *3*).

4. Sophocles, in the *Argument* to his *Ajax*, mentions a quarrel between Odysseus and Ajax over the Palladium after the fall of Troy; but this must have been Little Ajax, since Great Ajax had already killed himself. We may therefore suppose that Little Ajax, rather than Diomedes, led Odysseus up the conduit to fetch away the Palladium with the connivance of his compatriot Theano; that Odysseus accused Little Ajax of

laying violent hands on a non-Locrian priestess who clung to the image which Theano was helping him to remove; and that afterwards Ajax, while admitting his error, explained that he had been as gentle as possible in the circumstances. Such an event would have justified the Trojans of later centuries in trying to restrain the Locrian girls from exercising their rights as Trojan priestesses; in representing their continued arrival as a penance due for Ajax's crime, even though Athene had summarily punished him with a thunderbolt; and in treating them as menials. Odysseus may have insisted upon accompanying Little Ajax into the citadel, on the ground that Zacynthus, eponymous ancestor of his subjects the Zacynthians, figured in a list of early Trojan kings.

5. This, again, would explain Hecabe's failure to denounce Odysseus to the Trojans when he entered the city as a spy. She too is described as a 'daughter of Cisseus'; was she another Locrian from Thrace who connived at Ajax's removal of the Palladium? Hecabe had no cause to love Odysseus, and her reason for facilitating his escape can only have been to prevent him from denouncing her to the Trojans. Odysseus doubtless slipped out quietly by the culvert and not, as he boasted, by the gate 'after killing many Trojans'. Presumably he demanded old Hecabe as his share of the spoil because she had been a material witness of the Palladium incident and he wanted to stop her mouth. She seems, however, to have revealed everything before she died.

6. One of the principal causes of the Trojan War (see 158. r and 160. b) was Telamon's abduction of Priam's sister Hesione, the mother of Great Ajax and thus a kinswoman of Little Ajax; this points to long-standing friction between Priam and the Locrians of Greece. Patroclus, who caused the Trojans such heavy losses, was yet another Locrian, described as Abderus's brother.

The name Astyanax ('king of the city'), and the solemnity of the debate about his death, suggests that the icon on which the story is based represented the ritual sacrifice of a child at the dedication of a new city – an ancient custom in the Eastern Mediterranean (I Kings xvi. 34).

7. Agamemnon's allies did not long enjoy the fruits of their triumph over Troy. Between 1100 and 1050 B.C., the Dorian invasion overwhelmed Mycenaean culture in the Peloponnese and the Dark Ages supervened; it was a century or two before the Ionians, forced by the Dorians to emigrate to Asia Minor, began their cultural renascence; which was based solidly on Homer.

8. Aeneas's wanderings belong to Roman, not Greek, mythology; and have therefore been omitted here.

THE RETURNS

'LET us sail at once,' said Menelaus, 'while the breeze holds.' 'No, no,' replied Agamemnon, 'let us first sacrifice to Athene.' 'We Greeks owe Athene nothing!' Menelaus told him. 'She defended the Trojan citadel too long.' The brothers parted on ill terms and never saw each other again, for whereas Agamemnon, Diomedes, and Nestor enjoyed a prosperous homeward voyage, Menelaus was caught in a storm sent by Athene; and lost all but five vessels. These were blown to Crete, whence he crossed the sea to Egypt, and spent eight years in southern waters, unable to return. He visited Cyprus, Phoenicia, Ethiopia, and Libya, the princes of which received him hospitably and gave him many rich gifts. At last he came to Pharos, where the nymph Eidothea advised him to capture her prophetic father, Proteus the sea-god, who alone could tell him how to break the adverse spell and secure a southerly breeze.

Menelaus and three companions accordingly disguised themselves in stinking seal-skins and lay waiting on the shore, until they were joined at midday by hundreds of seals, Proteus's flock. Proteus himself then appeared and went to sleep among the seals: whereupon Menelaus and his party seized him, and though he turned successively into lion, serpent, panther, boar, running water, and leafy tree, held him fast and forced him to prophesy. He announced that Agamemnon had been murdered, and that Menelaus must visit Egypt once more and propitiate the gods with hecatombs. This he duly did, and no sooner had he raised a cenotaph to Agamemnon, beside the River of Egypt, than the winds blew fair at last. He arrived at Sparta, accompanied by Helen, on the very day that Orestes avenged Agamemnon's murder.[1]

b. A great many ships, though containing no leaders of note, were wrecked on the Euboean coast, because Nauplius had kindled a beacon on Mount Caphareus to lure his enemies to their death, as if guiding them into the shelter of the Pagasaean Gulf; but this crime became known to Zeus, and it was by a false beacon that Nauplius himself met his end many years later.[2]

c. Amphilochus, Calchas, Podaleirius and a few others travelled by land to Colophon, where Calchas died, as had been prophesied, on meeting a wiser seer than himself – none other than Mopsus, the son of Apollo and Teiresias's daughter Manto. A wild fig-tree covered with fruit grew at Colophon, and Calchas, wishing to abash Mopsus, challenged him as follows: 'Can you perhaps tell me, dear colleague, exactly how many figs will be harvested from that tree?' Mopsus, closing his eyes, as one who trusts to inner sight rather than vulgar computation, answered: 'Certainly: first ten thousand figs, then an Aeginetan bushel of figs, carefully weighed – yes, and a single fig left over.' Calchas laughed scornfully at the single fig, but when the tree had been stripped, Mopsus's intuition proved unerring. 'To descend from thousands to lesser quantities, dear colleague,' Mopsus now said, with an unpleasant smile, 'how many piglings, would you say, repose in the paunch of that pregnant sow; and how many of each sex will she farrow; and when?'

'Eight piglings, all male, and she will farrow them within nine days,' Calchas answered at random, hoping to be gone before his guess could be disproved. 'I am of a different opinion,' said Mopsus, again closing his eyes. 'My estimate is three piglings, only one of them a boar; and the time of their birth will be midday tomorrow, not a minute earlier or later.' Mopsus was right once more, and Calchas died of a broken heart. His comrades buried him at Nothium.[3]

d. The timorous Podaleirius, instead of asking his prophetic friends where he should settle, preferred to consult the Delphic Pythoness, who advised him irritably to go wherever he would suffer no harm, even if the skies were to fall. After much thought, he chose a place in Caria called Syrnos, ringed around with mountains; their summits would, he hoped, catch and support the blue firmament should Atlas ever let it slip from his shoulders. The Italians built Podaleirius a hero-shrine on Mount Drium in Daunia, at the summit of which the ghost of Calchas now maintains a dream oracle.[4]

e. A dispute arose between Mopsus and Amphilochus. They had jointly founded the city of Mallus in Cilicia, and when Amphilochus retired to his own city of Amphilochian Argos, Mopsus became sole sovereign. Amphilochus, dissatisfied with affairs at Argos, came back after twelve months to Mallus, expecting to resume his former powers, but Mopsus gruffly told him to begone. When the embarrassed Mallians suggested that this dispute should be decided by single combat, the rivals fought and each killed the other. The funeral pyres were so placed that Mopsus and Amphilochus could not exchange unseemly scowls during their cremation, yet the ghosts somehow became so tenderly linked in friendship that they set up a common oracle; which has now earned a higher reputation for truth even than Delphic Apollo's. All questions are written on wax tablets, and the responses given in dreams, at the remarkably low price of two coppers apiece.⁵

f. Neoptolemus sailed homeward as soon as he had offered sacrifices to the gods and to his father's ghost; and escaped the great tempest which caught Menelaus and Idomeneus, by taking the prophetic advice of his friend Helenus and running for Molossia. After killing King Phoenix and marrying his own mother to Helenus, who became king of the Molossians and founded a new capital city, Neoptolemus regained Ioclus at last.⁶ There he succeeded to the kingdom of his grandfather Peleus, whom the sons of Acastus had expelled;⁷ but on Helenus's advice did not stay to enjoy it. He burned his ships and marched inland to Lake Pambrotis in Epirus, near the Oracle of Dodona, where he was welcomed by a company of his distant kinsmen. They were bivouacking under blankets supported by spear-butts stuck into the ground. Neoptolemus remembered the words of Helenus: 'When you find a house with foundations of iron, wooden walls, and a woollen roof, halt, sacrifice to the gods, build a city!' Here he begot two more sons on Andromache, namely Pielus and Pergamus.

g. His end was inglorious. Going to Delphi, he demanded satisfaction for the death of his father Achilles whom Apollo, disguised as Paris, was said to have shot in his temple at Troy. When the Pythoness coldly denied him this, he plundered and burned the shrine. Next he went to Sparta, and claimed that Menelaus had betrothed Hermione to him before Troy; but that her grandfather Tyndareus had instead given her to Agamemnon's son Orestes. Orestes now being pursued by the Erinnyes, and under a divine curse, it was only just, he argued, that Hermione should become his wife. Despite Orestes's protests, the Spartans granted his plea, and the marriage took place at Sparta. Hermione, however, proving barren, Neoptolemus returned to Delphi and, entering the smoke-blackened sanctuary, which Apollo had decided to rebuild, asked why this should be.

h. He was ordered to offer placatory sacrifices to the god and, while doing so, met Orestes at the altar. Orestes would have killed him then and there, had not Apollo, foreseeing that Neoptolemus must die by another hand that very day, prevented it. Now, the flesh of the sacrifices offered to the god at Delphi has always been a perquisite of the temple servants; but Neoptolemus, in his ignorance, could not bear to see the fat carcasses of the oxen which he had slaughtered being hauled away before his eyes, and tried to prevent it by force. 'Let us be rid of this troublesome son of Achilles!' said the Pythoness shortly; whereupon one Machaereus, a Phocian, cut down Neoptolemus with his sacrificial knife.

'Bury him beneath the threshold of our new sanctuary,' she commanded. 'He was a famous warrior, and his ghost will guard it against all attacks. And if he has truly repented of his insult to Apollo, let him preside over processions and sacrifices in honour of heroes like himself.'

But some say that Orestes instigated the murder.[8]

i. Demophon the Athenian touched at Thrace on his return to Athens, and there Phyllis, a Bisaltian princess, fell in love with him. He married her and became king. When he tired of Thrace, and decided to resume his travels, Phyllis could do nothing to hold him. 'I must visit Athens and greet my mother, whom I last saw eleven years ago,' said Demophon. 'You should have thought of that before you accepted the throne,' Phyllis answered, in tears. 'It is not lawful to absent yourself for more than a few months at most.' Demophon swore by every god in Olympus that he would be back within the year; but Phyllis knew that he was lying. She accompanied him as far as the port called Enneodos, and there gave him a casket. 'This contains a charm,' Phyllis said. 'Open it only when you have abandoned all hope of returning to me.'

j. Demophon had no intention of going to Athens. He steered a south-easterly course for Cyprus, where he settled; and when the year was done, Phyllis cursed him in Mother Rhea's name, took poison, and died. At that very hour, curiosity prompted Demophon to open the casket, and the sight of its contents – who knows what they were? – made a lunatic of him. He leaped on his horse and galloped off in panic, belabouring its head with the flat of his sword until it stumbled and fell. The sword flew from his hand, stuck point upwards in the ground, and transfixed him as he was flung over the horse's head.

A story is told of another Thracian princess named Phyllis, who had fallen in love with Demophon's brother Acamas and, when storms delayed his return from Troy, died of sorrow and was metamorphosed into an almond-tree. These two princesses have often been confused.[9]

k. Diomedes, like Agamemnon and others, experienced Aphrodite's bitter enmity. He was first wrecked on the Lycian coast, where King Lycus would have sacrificed him to Ares, had not the princess Callirrhoë helped him to escape; and, on reaching Argos, found that his wife Aegialeia had been persuaded by Nauplius to live in adultery with Cometes or, some say, with Hippolytus. Retiring to Corinth, he learned there that his grandfather Oeneus needed assistance against certain rebels; so he sailed for Aetolia and set him firmly on his throne again. But some say that Diomedes had been forced to leave Argos long before the Trojan War, on his return from the Epigoni's successful Theban campaign; and that Agamemnon had since assisted him to win back his kingdom.[10] He spent the remainder of his life in Italian Daunia, where he married Euippe, daughter of King Daunus; and built many famous cities, including Brundisium, which may have been why Daunus jealously murdered him when he was an old man, and buried him in one of the islands now called the Diomedans. According to another account, however, he suddenly disappeared by an act of divine magic, and his comrades turned into gentle and virtuous birds, which still nest on those islands. Diomedes's golden armour has been preserved by the priests of Athene at Apulian Luceria, and he is worshipped as a god in Venetia, and throughout Southern Italy.[11]

l. Nauplius had also persuaded Idomeneus's wife Meda to be faithless. She took one Leucus for her lover, but he soon drove her and Idomeneus's daughter Cleisithyra from the palace and murdered them both in the temple where they had taken sanctuary. Leucus then seduced ten cities from allegiance to their rightful king, and usurped the throne. Caught in a storm as he sailed for Crete, Idomeneus vowed to dedicate to Poseidon the first person whom he met; and this happened to be his own son or, some say, another of his daughters. He was on the point of fulfilling his vow when a pestilence visited the country and interrupted the sacrifice. Leucus now had a good excuse for banishing Idomeneus, who emigrated to the Sallentine region of Calabria, and lived there until his death.[12]

m. Few of the other Greeks reached home again, and those who did found only trouble awaiting them. Philoctetes was expelled by rebels from his city of Meliboea in Thessaly, and fled to Southern Italy, where he founded Petelia, and Crimissa near Croton, and sent some of his followers to help Aegestes fortify Sicilian Aegesta. He dedicated his famous bow at Crimissa, in the sanctuary of Distraught Apollo, and when he died was buried beside the river Sybaris.[13]

n. Contrary winds forced Guneus to the Cynips river in Libya, and he made his home there. Pheidippus with his Coans went first to Andros and thence to Cyprus, where Agapenor had also settled. Menestheus did not resume his reign at Athens, but accepted the vacant kingship of Melos; some say, however, that he died at Troy. Elpenor's followers were wrecked on the shores of Epirus, and occupied Apollonia; those of Protesilaus, near Pellene in the Thracian Chersonese; and Tlepolemus's Rhodians, on one of the Iberian islands, whence a party of them sailed westward again to Italy and were helped by Philoctetes in their war against the barbarous Lucanians.[14] The tale of Odysseus's wanderings is now Homeric entertainment for twenty-four nights.

o. Only Nestor, who had always shown himself just, prudent, generous, courteous, and respectful to the gods, returned safe and sound to Pylus, where he enjoyed a happy old age, untroubled by wars, and surrounded by bold, intelligent sons. For so Almighty Zeus decreed.[15]

1. Apollodorus: *Epitome* vi. 1; Homer: *Odyssey* iii. 130 ff. and iv. 77–592; Hagias, quoted by Proclus (*Greek Epic Fragments* p. 53. ed. Kinkel).

2. Apollodorus: ii. 1. 5 and *Epitome* vi. 11; Euripides: *Helen* 766 ff. and 1126 ff.; Hyginus: *Fabula* 116; Servius on Virgil's *Aeneid* xi. 260.

3. Apollodorus: *Epitome* vi. 2–4; Strabo: xiv. 1. 27, quoting Hesiod, Sophocles, and Pherecydes; Tzetzes: *On Lycophron* 427 and 980.

4. Apollodorus: *Epitome* vi. 18; Pausanias: iii. 26. 7; Stephanus of Byzantium *sub* Syrna; Strabo: vi. 3. 9; Tzetzes: *On Lycophron* 1047.

5. Apollodorus: iii. 7. 7 and *Epitome* vi. 19; Tzetzes: *On Lycophron* 440–42; Strabo: xiv. 5. 16; Pausanias: i. 34. 3; Lucian: *Alexander* 19; Plutarch: *Why the Oracles Are Silent* 45; Cicero: *On Divination* i. 40. 88; Dio Cassius: lxxii. 7.

6. Apollodorus: *Epitome* vi. 12 and 13; Hagias: *loc. cit.*; Servius on Virgil's *Aeneid* ii. 166; Scholiast on Homer's *Odyssey* iii. 188.

7. Dictys Cretensis: vi. 7–9.

8. Homer: *Odyssey* iv. 1–9; Apollodorus: *Epitome* vi. 13–14; Euripides: *Andromache* 891–1085 and *Orestes* 1649, with scholiast; Hyginus: *Fabula* 123; Eustathius on Homer's *Odyssey* iv. 3; Scholiast on Euripides's *Andromache* 32 and 51; Ovid: *Heroides* viii. 31 ff.; *Fragments of Sophocles* ii. 441 ff., ed. Pearson; Pausanias: x. 7. 1 and x. 24. 4–5; Pindar: *Nemean Odes* vii. 50–70, with scholiast; Virgil: *Aeneid* iii. 330; Strabo: ix. 3. 9.

9. Apollodorus: *Epitome* v. 16; Tzetzes: *On Lycophron* 495; Lucian:

On the Dance 40; Hyginus: *Fabula* 59; Servius on Virgil's *Eclogues* v. 10.

10. Plutarch: *Parallel Stories* 23; Dictys Cretensis: vi. 2; Tzetzes: *On Lycophron* 609; Servius on Virgil's *Aeneid* viii. 9; Hyginus: *Fabula* 175; Apollodorus: i. 8. 6; Pausanias: iii 25. 2.

11. Pausanias: i. 11; Servius on Virgil's *Aeneid* viii. 9 and xi. 246; Tzetzes: *On Lycophron* 602 and 618; Strabo: vi. 3. 8–9; Scholiast on Pindar's *Nemean Odes* x. 12; Scylax: p. 6.

12. Apollodorus: *Epitome* vi. 10; Tzetzes: *On Lycophron* 384–6; Servius on Virgil's *Aeneid* iii. 121 and xi. 264; First Vatican Mythographer: 195; Second Vatican Mythographer: 210; Virgil: *Aeneid* 121 ff. and 400 ff.

13. Tzetzes: *On Lycophron* 911, quoting Apollodorus's *Epitome*; Homer: *Iliad* ii. 717 ff.; Strabo: vi. 1. 3; Aristotle: *Mirabilia* 107.

14. Tzetzes: *On Lycophron* 911; Pausanias: i. 17. 6.

15. Homer: *Odyssey* iv. 209; Pausanias: iv. 3. 4; Hyginus: *Fabula* 10.

*

1. The mythographers make Aphrodite fight against the Greeks because, as Love-goddess, she had backed Paris's abduction of Helen. But she was also the Sea-goddess whom the Trojans invoked to destroy the commercial confederacy patronized by Poseidon – and the storms allegedly raised by Athene or Poseidon to deny the victors a safe return must first have been ascribed to her. This principle of vengeance enabled a great many cities in Italy, Libya, Cyprus, and elsewhere to claim foundation by heroes shipwrecked on their way back from Troy; rather than by refugees from the Dorian invasion of Greece.

2. To bury a young warrior under a temple threshold was common practice, and since Neoptolemus had burned the old shrine at Delphi, the Pythoness naturally chose him as her victim when the a new building was planted on its ruins. The previous guardians of the threshold had been Agamedes and Trophonius (see 84. *b*).

3. Rhea, who sanctified the mysterious object in Demophon's casket, was also called Pandora, and this myth may therefore be an earlier version of how Epimetheus's wife Pandora opened the box of spites (see 39. *j*): a warning to men who pry into women's mysteries, rather than contrariwise. 'Mopsus' was an eighth century B.C. royal title in Cilicia.

4. The birds into which Diomedes's followers were transformed are described as 'virtuous' evidently to distinguish them from their cruel bird-neighbours, the Sirens (see 154. *d* and 3; 170. 7).

5. A vow like Idomeneus's was made by Maeander ('searching for a man'), when he vowed to the Queen of Heaven the first person who should congratulate him on his storm of Pessinus; and this proved to be his son Archelaus ('ruler of the people'). Maeander killed him and then

remorsefully leaped into the river (Plutarch: *On Rivers* ix. 1). A more
familiar version of the same myth is found in *Judges* xi. 30 ff., where
Jephthah vows his daughter as a burnt offering to Jehovah if he is
successful in war. These variants suggest that Idomeneus vowed a male
sacrifice to Aphrodite, rather than to Poseidon; as Maeander did to the
Queen of Heaven, and as Jephthah doubtless did to Anatha, who required
such burnt offerings on her holy Judaean mountains. It looks, indeed, as
if sacrifice of a royal prince in gratitude for a successful campaign was
once common practice – Jonathan would have been slaughtered by his
father, King Saul, after the victory near Michmash, had not the people
protested – and that the interruption of Idomeneus's sacrifice, like
Abraham's on Mount Moriah, or Athamas's on Mount Laphystium
(see 70. *d*) was a warning that this custom no longer pleased Heaven. The
substitution of a princess for a prince, as in the story of Jephthah, or in the
First Vatican Mythographer's account of Idomeneus's vow, marks the
anti-matriarchal reaction characteristic of heroic saga.

6. Menelaus's wanderings in the Southern Mediterranean refer to
Achaean piracies and attempts at colonization. According to Xanthus, an
early Lydian historian, the Phoenician city of Ascalon was founded by
Ascalus ('untilled'), brother of Pelops, and therefore a collateral ancestor
of Menelaus. Again, when Joshua conquered Canaan in the thirteenth
century B.C., the men of Gibeon (*Agabon* in one Septuagint text, meaning
Astu Achaivon, 'the city of the Achaeans') came as suppliants to Joshua in
Greek fashion, pleading that they were not native Canaanites, but Hiv-
ites, i.e. Achaeans, from overseas. Joshua recognized their rights as
foresters of the sacred groves and drawers of sacred water (*Joshua* ix).
It seems from verse 9 that they reminded Joshua of the ancient maritime
league of Keftiu presided over by Minos of Cnossus, to which the
Achaeans and Abraham's people both once belonged. Abraham, who
came into the Delta with the Hyksos kings, had married his sister Sarah
to 'Pharaoh', meaning the Cnossian ruler of Pharos – then the chief
trading depôt of the confederacy. But by the time of Menelaus, Cnossus
lay in ruins, the confederates had turned pirates and been defeated by
the Egyptians at the Battle of Piari (1229 B.C.) – 'I trapped them like
wildfowl, they were dragged, hemmed in, laid low on the beach, their
ships and goods were fallen into the sea' – and Pharos, no longer the
largest port in the ancient world, became a mere breeding place for seals.
A submarine disaster had overwhelmed its harbour works (see 39. *2*),
and in early Classical times foreign trade passed through Naucratis, the
Milesian *entrepôt* (see 25. *6*).

7. Menelaus's struggle with Proteus is a degenerate version of a familiar
myth: the Seal-goddess Thetis has been masculinized into Proteus, and
Menelaus, instead of waiting for the seal-skin to be discarded, and then

amorously grappling with the deity, as Peleus did (see 81. 1–3), uses a seal-skin as a disguise, calls upon three men to help him, and requires no more from his captive than an oracular answer. Proteus rapidly transforms himself, as Thetis did with Peleus, or as Dionysus-Zagreus, who is associated with Pharos (see 27. 7), did when threatened by the Titans. The Homeric list of his transformations is a muddled one: two or three seasonal sequences have been telescoped. Lion and boar are intelligible emblems of a two-season year (see 69. 1); so are bull, lion, and water-serpent, of a three-season year (see 27. 4 and 123. 1); the panther is sacred to Dionysus (see 27. 4); and the 'leafy tree', paralleled in the story of Periclymenus, refers perhaps to the sacred trees of the months (see 53. 3 and 139. 1). Proteus's changes make amusing fiction, but are wholly inappropriate to the oracular context, unless the real story is that after a reign of eight years, and the annual killing of an *interrex* in Cretan style, Menelaus became the oracular hero of a settlement founded beside the River of Egypt (see 112. 3).

170

ODYSSEUS'S WANDERINGS

ODYSSEUS, setting sail from Troy in the sure knowledge that he must wander for another ten years before he could hope to regain Ithaca, touched first at Ciconian Ismarus and took it by storm. In the pillage he spared only Maro, Apollo's priest, who gratefully presented him with several jars of sweet wine; but the Ciconians of the interior saw the pall of smoke spread high above the burned city, and charging down on the Greeks as they drank by the seashore, scattered them in all directions. When Odysseus had rallied and re-embarked his men with heavy losses, a fierce north-easterly gale drove him across the Aegean Sea towards Cythera.[1] On the fourth day, during a tempting lull, he tried to double Cape Malea and work up northward to Ithaca, but the wind rose again more violently than before. After nine days of danger and misery, the Libyan promontory where the Lotus-eaters live hove in sight. Now, the lotus is a stoneless, saffron-coloured fruit about the size of a bean, growing in sweet and wholesome clusters, though with the property of making those who have tasted it lose all memory of their own land; some travellers, however, describe it as a kind of apple from which a heavy cider is brewed. Odysseus landed to draw water, and sent out a patrol of three men, who ate the lotus offered them by the natives and so forgot their mission. After a while he went in search of them at the head of a rescue party, and though himself tempted to taste the lotus, refrained. He brought the deserters back by force, clapped them in irons, and sailed away without more ado.[2]

b. Next he came to a fertile, well-wooded island, inhabited only by countless wild goats, and shot some of these for food. There he beached the whole fleet, except a single ship in which he set out to explore the opposite coast. It proved to be the land of the fierce and barbarous Cyclopes, so called because of the large, round eye that glared from the centre of each forehead. They have lost the art of smithcraft known to their ancestors who worked for Zeus, and are now shepherds without laws, assemblies, ships, markets, or knowledge of agriculture; living sullenly apart from one another, in caverns hollowed from the rocky hills. Seeing the high, laurel-hung entrance of such a cavern, beyond a stock-yard walled with huge stones, Odysseus and his companions entered, unaware that the property belonged to a Cyclops named Polyphemus, a gigantic son of Poseidon and the nymph Thoösa, who loved to dine off human flesh. The Greeks made themselves at home by lighting a large fire; then slaughtered and roasted some kids that they found penned at the back of the cavern, helped themselves to cheese from baskets hung on the walls, and feasted cheerfully. Towards evening Polyphemus appeared. He drove his flock into the cavern and closed the entrance behind him with a slab of stone so huge that twenty teams of oxen could scarcely have stirred it; then, not observing that he had guests, sat down to milk his ewes and goats. Finally he glanced up from the pail and saw Odysseus and his comrades reclined around the hearth. He asked gruffly what business they had in his cavern. Odysseus replied: 'Gentle monster, we are Greeks on our way home after the sack of Troy; pray remember your duty to the gods and entertain us hospitably.' For answer Polyphemus snorted, seized two sailors by the feet, dashed out their brains on the floor, and devoured the carcasses raw, growling over the bones like any mountain lion.

c. Odysseus would have taken bloody vengeance before dawn, but dared not, because Polyphemus alone was strong enough to shift the stone from the entrance. He passed the night, head clasped between hands, elaborating a plan of escape, while Polyphemus snored dreadfully. For breakfast, the monster brained and killed another two sailors, after which he silently drove out his flock before him and closed the cavern with the same slab of stone; but Odysseus took a stake of green olive-wood, sharpened and hardened one end in the fire, then concealed it under a heap of dung. That evening the Cyclops returned and ate two more of the twelve sailors, whereupon Odysseus politely offered him an ivy-wood bowl of the heady wine given him by Maro in Ciconian Ismarus; fortunately, he had brought a full wine-skin ashore. Polyphemus drank greedily, called for a second bowlful, never in his life having tasted any drink stronger than buttermilk, and condescended to ask Odysseus his name. 'My name is Oudeis,' Odysseus replied, 'or that is what everyone calls me, for short.' Now, Oudeis means 'Nobody'. 'I will eat you last, friend Oudeis,' Polyphemus promised.

d. As soon as the Cyclops had fallen into a drunken sleep, the wine having been untempered with water, Odysseus and his remaining companions heated the stake in the embers of the fire, then drove it into the single eye and twisted it about, Odysseus bearing down heavily from above, as one drills a bolt hole in ship's timber. The eye hissed, and Polyphemus raised a horrible yell, which set all his neighbours hurrying from near and far to learn what was amiss.

'I am blinded and in frightful agony! It is the fault of Oudeis,' he bellowed.

'Poor wretch!' they replied. 'If, as you say, nobody is to blame, you must be in a delirious fever. Pray to our Father Poseidon for recovery, and stop making so much noise!'

They went off grumbling, and Polyphemus felt his way to the cavern mouth, removed the slab of stone and, groping expectantly with his hands, waited to catch the surviving Greeks as they tried to escape. But Odysseus took withies and tied each of his comrades in turn under the belly of a ram, the middle one of three, distributing the weight evenly. He himself chose an enormous tup, the leader of the flock, and prepared to curl up underneath it, gripping the fleece with his fingers and toes.

e. At dawn, Polyphemus let his flock out to pasture, gently stroking their backs to make sure that no one was astride of them. He lingered awhile talking sorrowfully to the beast under which Odysseus lay concealed, asking it: 'Why, dear ram, are you not to the fore, as usual? Do you pity me in my misfortune?' But at last he allowed it to pass.

f. Thus Odysseus contrived both to free his companions and to drive a flock of fat rams down to the ship. Quickly she was launched, and as the men seized their oars and began to row off, Odysseus could not refrain from shouting an ironical goodbye. For answer, Polyphemus hurled a large rock, which fell half a length ahead of the ship; its backwash nearly fetched her ashore again. Odysseus laughed, and cried: 'Should anyone ask who blinded you, answer that it was not Oudeis, but Odysseus of Ithaca!' The enraged Cyclops prayed aloud to Poseidon: 'Grant, father, that if my enemy Odysseus ever returns home, he may arrive late, in evil plight, from a foreign ship, having lost all his comrades; may he also find a heap of troubles massed on the threshold!' He hurled another, even larger, rock and this time it fell half a length astern of the ship; so that the wave which it raised carried her swiftly to the island where Odysseus's other followers were anxiously awaiting him. But Poseidon listened to Polyphemus, and promised the required vengeance.[3]

g. Odysseus now steered to the north, and presently reached the Isle of Aeolus, Warden of the Winds, who entertained him nobly for an entire month and, on the last day, handed him a bag of winds, explaining that while its neck was secured with silver wire, all would be well. He had not, he said, imprisoned the gentle West Wind, which would waft the fleet steadily over the Ionian Sea towards Ithaca, but Odysseus might release the others one by one, if for any reason he needed to alter his course. Smoke could already be descried rising from the chimneys of Odysseus's palace, when he fell asleep, overcome by exhaustion. His men, who had been watching for this moment, untied the bag, which promised to contain wine. At once the Winds roared homeward in a body, driving the ship before them; and Odysseus soon found himself on Aeolus's island again. With profuse apologies he asked for further help, but was told to begone and use oars this time; not a breath of West Wind should he be given. 'I cannot assist a man whom the gods oppose,' cried Aeolus, slamming the door in his face.[4]

h. After a seven days' voyage, Odysseus came to the land of the Laestrygones, ruled over by King Lamus, which is said by some to have lain in the north-western part of Sicily. Others place it near Formiae in Italy, where the noble House of Lamia claims descent from King Lamus; and this seems credible, because who would admit descent from cannibals, unless it were a matter of common tradition?[5] In the land of the Laestrygones, night and morning come so close together that shepherds leading home their flocks at sunset hail those who drive theirs out at dawn. Odysseus's captains boldly entered the harbour of Telepylus which, except for a narrow entrance, is ringed by abrupt cliffs, and beached their ships near a cart track that wound up a valley. Odysseus himself, being more cautious, made his ship fast to a rock outside the harbour, after sending three scouts inland to reconnoitre. They followed the track until they found a girl drawing water from a spring. She proved to be a daughter of Antiphates, a Laestrygonian chieftain, to whose house she led them. There, however, they were mercilessly set upon by a horde of savages who seized one of them and killed him for the pot; the other two ran off at full speed, but the savages, instead of pursuing them, made for the cliff tops and stove in the ships with a cascade of boulders before they could be launched. Then, descending to the beach, they massacred and devoured the crews at their leisure. Odysseus escaped by cutting the hawser of his ships with a sword, and calling on his comrades to row for dear life.[6]

i. He steered his sole remaining vessel due east and, after a long voyage, reached Aeaea, the Island of Dawn, ruled over by the goddess Circe, daughter of Helius and Perse, and thus sister to Aeëtes, the baleful king of Colchis. Circe was skilled in all enchantments, but had little love for human-kind. When lots were cast to decide who should stay to guard the ships and who should reconnoitre the island, Odysseus's mate Eurylochus was chosen to go ashore with twenty-two others. He found Aeaea rich in oaks and other forest trees, and at last came upon Circe's palace, built in a wide clearing towards the centre of the island. Wolves and lions prowled around but, instead of attacking Eurylochus and his party, stood upright on their hind legs and caressed them. One might have taken these beasts for human beings, and so indeed they were, though thus transformed by Circe's spells.

j. Circe sat in her hall, singing to her loom and, when Eurylochus's party raised a halloo, stepped out with a smile and invited them to dine at her table. All entered gladly, except Eurylochus himself who, suspecting a trap, stayed behind and peered anxiously in at the windows. The goddess set a mess of cheese, barley, honey, and wine before the hungry sailors; but it was drugged, and no sooner had they begun to eat than she struck their shoulders with her wand and transformed them into hogs. Grimly then she opened the wicket of a sty, scattered a few handfuls of acorns and cornel-cherries on the miry floor, and left them there to wallow.

k. Eurylochus came back, weeping, and reported this misfortune to

Odysseus, who seized his sword and went off, bent on rescue, though without any settled plan in his head. To his surprise he encountered the god Hermes, who greeted him politely and offered him a charm against Circe's magic: a scented white flower with a black root, called *moly*, which only the gods can recognize and cull. Odysseus accepted the gift gratefully and, continuing on his way, was in due course entertained by Circe. When he had eaten his drugged meal, she raised her wand and struck him on the shoulder. 'Go join your comrades in the sty,' she commanded. But having surreptitiously smelt the moly flower, he remained unenchanted, and leaped up, sword in hand. Circe fell weeping at his feet. 'Spare me,' she cried, 'and you shall share my couch and reign in Aeaea with me!' Well aware that witches have power to enervate and destroy their lovers, by secretly drawing off their blood in little bladders, Odysseus exacted a solemn oath from Circe not to plot any further mischief against him. This oath she swore by the blessed gods and, after giving him a deliciously warm bath, wine in golden cups, and a tasty supper served by a staid housekeeper, prepared to pass the night with him in a purple coverleted bed. Yet Odysseus would not respond to her amorous advances until she consented to free not only his comrades but all the other sailors enchanted by her. Once this was done, he gladly stayed in Aeaea until she had borne him three sons, Agrius, Latinus, and Telegonus.[7]

l. Odysseus longed to be on his way again, and Circe consented to let him go. But he must first visit Tartarus, and there seek out Teiresias the seer, who would prophesy the fate prepared for him in Ithaca, should he ever reach it, and afterwards. 'Run before the North Wind,' Circe said, 'until you come to the Ocean Stream and the Grove of Persephone, remarkable for its black poplars and aged willows. At the point where the rivers Phlegethon and Cocytus flow into the Acheron, dig a trench, and sacrifice a young ram and a black ewe – which I myself will provide – to Hades and Persephone. Let the blood enter the trench, and as you wait for Teiresias to arrive drive off all other ghosts with your sword. Allow him to drink as much as he pleases and then listen carefully to his advice.'

m. Odysseus forced his men aboard, unwilling though they were to sail from pleasant Aeaea to the land of Hades. Circe supplied a favourable breeze, which wafted them swiftly to the Ocean Stream and those lost frontiers of the world where the fog-bound Cimmerians, citizens of Perpetual Dusk, are denied all view of the Sun. When they sighted

Persephone's Grove, Odysseus landed, and did exactly as Circe had advised him. The first ghost to appear at the trench was that of Elpenor, one of his own crew who, only a few days previously, had drunken himself to sleep on the roof of Circe's palace, awoken in a daze, toppled over the edge, and killed himself. Odysseus, having left Aeaea so hurriedly that Elpenor's absence had escaped his notice until too late, now promised him decent burial. 'To think that you came here on foot quicker than I have come by ship!' he exclaimed. But he denied Elpenor the least sip of the blood, however piteously he might plead.

n. A mixed crowd of ghosts swarmed about the trench, men and women of all dates and every age, including Odysseus's mother Anticleia; but he would not let even her drink before Teiresias had done so. At last Teiresias appeared, lapped the blood gratefully, and warned Odysseus to keep his men under strict control once they had sighted Sicily, their next landfall, lest they be tempted to steal the cattle of the Sun-Titan Hyperion. He must expect great trouble in Ithaca, and though he could hope to avenge himself on the scoundrels who were devouring his substance there, his travels would not yet have finished. He must take an oar and carry it on his shoulder until he came to an inland region where no man salted his meat, and where the oar would be mistaken for a winnowing-bat. If he then sacrificed to Poseidon, he might regain Ithaca and enjoy a prosperous old age; but in the end death would come to him from the sea.

o. Having thanked Teiresias and promised him the blood of another black ewe on his return to Ithaca, Odysseus at last permitted his mother to quench her thirst. She gave him further news from home, but kept a discreet silence about her daughter-in-law's suitors. When she had said goodbye, the ghosts of numerous queens and princesses trooped up to lap the blood. Odysseus was delighted to meet such well-known personages as Antiope, Iocaste, Chloris, Pero, Leda, Iphimedeia, Phaedra, Procris, Ariadne, Maera, Clymene, and Eriphyle.

p. He next entertained a troop of former comrades: Agamemnon, who advised him to land on Ithaca in secret; Achilles, whom he cheered by reporting Neoptolemus's mighty feats; and Great Ajax, who had by no means yet forgiven him and strode sulkily away. Odysseus also saw Minos judging, Orion hunting, Tantalus and Sisyphus suffering, and Heracles – or rather his wraith, for Heracles himself banquets at ease among the immortal gods – who commiserated with him on his long labours.[8]

q. Odysseus sailed back safely to Aeaea, where he buried the body of Elpenor and planted his oar on the barrow as a memorial. Circe greeted him merrily. 'What hardihood to have visited the land of Hades!' she cried. 'One death is enough for most men; but now you will have had two!' She warned him that he must next pass the Island of the Sirens, whose beautiful voices enchanted all who sailed near. These children of Achelous or, some say, Phorcys, by either the Muse Terpsichore, or by Sterope, Porthaön's daughter, had girls' faces but birds' feet and feathers, and many different stories are told to account for this peculiarity: such as that they had been playing with Core when Hades abducted her, and that Demeter, vexed because they had not come to her aid, gave them wings, saying: 'Begone, and search for my daughter all over the world!' Or that Aphrodite turned them into birds because, for pride, they would not yield their maidenheads either to gods or men. They no longer had the power of flight, however, since the Muses had defeated them in a musical contest and pulled out their wing feathers to make themselves crowns. Now they sat and sang in a meadows among the heaped bones of sailors whom they had drawn to their death. 'Plug your men's ears with bees-wax,' advised Circe, 'and if you are eager to hear their music, have your crew bind you hand and foot to the mast, and make them swear not to let you escape, however harshly you may threaten them.' Circe warned Odysseus of other perils in store for him, when he came to say goodbye; and he sailed off, once more conveyed by a fair breeze.

r. As the ship approached Siren Land, Odysseus took Circe's advice, and the Sirens sang so sweetly, promising him foreknowledge of all future happenings on earth, that he shouted to his companions, threatening them with death if they would not release him; but, obeying his earlier orders, they only lashed him tighter to the mast. Thus the ship sailed by in safety, and the Sirens committed suicide for vexation.[9]

s. Some believe that there were only two Sirens; others, that there were three, namely Parthenope, Leucosia, and Ligeia; or Peisinoë, Aglaope, and Thelxepeia; or Aglaophonos, Thelxiope, and Molpe. Still others name four: Teles, Raidne, Thelxiope, and Molpe.[10]

t. Odysseus's next danger lay in passing between two cliffs, one of which harboured Scylla, and the other Charybdis, her fellow-monster. Charybdis, daughter of Mother Earth and Poseidon, was a voracious woman, who had been hurled by Zeus's thunderbolt into the sea and now, thrice daily, sucked in a huge volume of water and presently spewed it out again. Scylla, the once beautiful daughter of Hecate Crataeis by Phorcys, or Phorbas – or of Echidne by Typhon, Triton, or Tyrrhenius – had been changed into a dog-like monster with six fearful heads and twelve feet. This was done either by Circe when jealous of the sea-god Glaucus's love for her, or by Amphitrite, similarly jealous of Poseidon's love. She would seize sailors, crack their bones, and slowly swallow them. Almost the strangest thing about Scylla was her yelp: no louder than the whimper of a newly-born puppy. Trying to escape from Charybdis, Odysseus steered a trifle too near Scylla who, leaning over the gunwales, snatched six of his ablest sailors off the deck, one in each mouth, and whisked them away to the rocks, where she devoured them at leisure. They screamed and stretched out their hands to Odysseus, but he dared not attempt a rescue, and sailed on.[11]

u. Odysseus took this course in order to avoid the Wandering, or Clashing, Rocks, between which only the *Argo* had ever succeeded in passing; he was unaware that they were now rooted to the sea-bed. Soon he sighted Sicily, where Hyperion the Sun-Titan, whom some call Helius, had seven herds of splendid cattle at pasture, fifty to a herd, and large flocks of sturdy sheep as well. Odysseus made his men swear a solemn oath to be content with the provisions which Circe had supplied, and not steal a single cow. They then landed and beached the ship, but the South Wind blew for thirty days, food grew scarce, and though the sailors hunted or fished every day, they had little success. At last Eurylochus, desperate with hunger, drew his comrades aside and persuaded them to slaughter some of the cattle – in compensation for which, he hastened to add, they would build Hyperion a splendid temple on their return to Ithaca. They waited until Odysseus had fallen asleep, caught several cows, slaughtered them, sacrificed the thigh-bones and fat to the gods, and roasted enough good beef for a six days' feast.

v. Odysseus was horrified when he awoke to find what had happened; and so was Hyperion on hearing the story from Lampetia, his daughter and chief herdswoman. Hyperion complained to Zeus who, seeing that Odysseus's ship had been launched again, sent a sudden westerly storm to bring the mast crashing down on the helmsman's skull; and then flung a thunderbolt on deck. The ship foundered, and all aboard were drowned, except Odysseus. He contrived to lash the floating mast and keel together with the raw-hide back-stay, and clamber astride this makeshift vessel. But a southerly gale sprang up, and he found himself sucked towards Charybdis's whirlpool. Clutching at the bole of a wild fig-tree which grew from the cliff above, he hung on grimly until the mast and keel had been swallowed and regurgitated; then mounted them once more and paddled away with his hands. After nine days he drifted ashore on the island of Ogygia, where lived Calypso, the daughter of Thetis by Oceanus, or it may have been Nereus, or Atlas.[12]

w. Thickets of alder, black poplar, and cypress, with horned owls, falcons, and garrulous sea-crows roosting in their branches, sheltered Calypso's great cavern. A grape-vine twisted across the entrance. Parsley and irises grew thick in an adjoining meadow, which was fed by four clear streams. Here lovely Calypso welcomed Odysseus as he stumbled ashore, and offered him plentiful food, heady drink and a share of her soft bed. 'If you stay with me,' she pleaded, 'you shall enjoy immortality and ageless youth.' Some say that it was Calypso, not Circe, who bore him Latinus, besides the twins Nausithous and Nausinous.

x. Calypso detained Odysseus on Ogygia for seven years – or perhaps only for five – and tried to make him forget Ithaca; but he had soon tired of her embraces, and used to sit despondently on the shore, staring out to sea. At last, taking advantage of Poseidon's absence, Zeus sent Hermes to Calypso with an order for Odysseus's release. She had no option but to obey, and therefore told him to build a raft, which she would victual sufficiently: providing a sack of corn, skins of wine and water, and dried meat. Though Odysseus suspected a trap, Calypso swore by the Styx that she would not deceive him, and lent him axe, adze, augers, and all other necessary gear. He needed no urging, but improvised a raft from a score of tree-trunks lashed together; launched it on rollers; kissed Calypso goodbye, and set sail with a gentle breeze.

y. Poseidon had been visiting his blameless friends the Ethiopians, and as he drove home across the sea in his winged chariot, suddenly saw the raft. At once Odysseus was swept overboard by a huge wave, and the rich robes which he wore dragged him down to the sea-depths until his lungs seemed about to burst. Yet being a powerful swimmer, he managed to divest himself of the robes, regain the surface, and scramble back on the raft. The pitiful goddess Leucothea, formerly Ino, wife of Athamas, alighted beside him there, disguised as a seamew. In her beak she carried a veil, which she told Odysseus to wind around his middle before plunging into the sea again. This veil would save him, she promised. He hesitated to obey but, when another wave shattered the raft, wound the veil around him and swam off. Since Poseidon had now returned to his underwater palace near Euboea, Athene dared send a wind to flatten the waves in Odysseus's path, and two days later he was cast ashore, utterly exhausted, on the island of Drepane then occupied by the Phaeacians. He lay down in the shelter of a copse beside a stream, heaped dry leaves over himself, and fell fast asleep.[13]

z. Next morning the lovely Nausicaa, daughter of King Alcinous and Queen Arete, the royal pair who had once shown such kindness to Jason and Medea, came to wash her linen in the stream. When the work was done she played at ball with her women. Their ball happened to bounce into the water, a shout of dismay rang out, and Odysseus awoke in alarm. He had no clothes, but used a leafy olive-branch to conceal his nakedness and, creeping forward, addressed such honeyed words to Nausicaa that she discreetly took him under her protection and had him brought to the palace. There Alcinous heaped gifts on Odysseus and, after listening to his adventures, sent him off to Ithaca in a fine ship. His escort knew the island well. They cast anchor in the haven of Phorcys, but decided not to disturb his sound sleep, carried him ashore and laid him gently on the sand, stacking Alcinous's gifts beneath a tree not far off. Poseidon, however, was so vexed by the Phaeacians' kindness to Odysseus that he struck the ship with the flat of his hand as she sailed home, and turned her into stone, crew and all. Alcinous at once sacrificed twelve choice bulls to Poseidon, who was now threatening to deprive the city of its two harbours by dropping a great mountain between; and some say that he was as good as his word. 'This will teach us not to be hospitable in future!' Alcinous told Arete in bitter tones.[14]

1. Homer: *Odyssey* ix. 39–66.

2. Apollodorus: *Epitome* vii. 2–3; Homer: *Odyssey* ix. 82–104; Herodotus: iv. 177; Pliny: *Natural History* xiii. 32; Hyginus: *Fabula* 125.

3. Homer: *Odyssey* ix. 105–542; Hyginus: *loc. cit.*; Euripides: *Cyclops*; Apollodorus: *Epitome* vii. 4–9.

4. Homer: *Odyssey* x. 1–76; Hyginus: *loc. cit.*; Ovid: *Metamorphoses* xiv. 223–32.

5. Thucydides: i. 2; Pliny: *Natural History* iii. 5. 9 and 8. 14; Tzetzes: *On Lycophron* 662 and 956; Silius Italicus: vii. 410 and xiv. 126; Cicero: *Against Atticus* ii. 13; Horace: *Odes* iii. 17.

6. Homer: *Odyssey* x. 30–132; Hyginus: *loc. cit.*; Apollodorus: *Epitome* vii. 12; Ovid: *Metamorphoses* xiv. 233–44.

7. Homer: *Odyssey* x. 133–574 and xii. 1–2; Hyginus: *loc. cit.*; Ovid: *Metamorphoses* xiv. 246–404; Hesiod: *Theogony* 1011–14; Eustathius on Homer's *Odyssey* xvi. 118.

8. Homer: *Odyssey* xi; Hyginus: *loc. cit.*; Apollodorus: *Epitome* vii. 17.

9. Homer: *Odyssey* xii; Apollodorus: *Epitome* vii. 19; Apollonius Rhodius: iv. 898; Aelian: *On the Nature of Animals* xvii. 23; Ovid: *Metamorphoses* v. 552–62; Pausanias: ix. 34. 3; Hyginus: *Fabulae* 125 and 141; Sophocles: *Odysseus, Fragment* 861, ed. Pearson.

10. Plutarch: *Convivial Questions* ix. 14. 6; Scholiast on Homer's *Odyssey* xii. 39; Hyginus: *Fabulae loc. cit.* and *Preface*; Tzetzes: *On Lycophron* 712; Eustathius on Homer's *Odyssey* xii. 167.

11. Servius on Virgil's *Aeneid* iii. 420; Apollodorus: *Epitome* vii. 21; Homer: *Odyssey* xii. 73–126 and 222–59; Hyginus: *Fabulae* 125, 199 and *Preface*; Apollonius Rhodius: iv. 828, with scholiast; Eustathius on Homer p. 1714; Tzetzes: *On Lycophron* 45 and 650; Ovid: *Metamorphoses* xiii. 732 ff. and 906 ff.

12. Homer: *Odyssey* xii. 127–453; Apollodorus: i. 2. 7 and *Epitome* vii. 22–3; Hesiod: *Theogony* 359.

13. Homer: *Odyssey* v. 13–493 and vii. 243–66; Hyginus: *Fabula* 125; Hesiod: *Theogony* 1111 ff.; Scholiast on Apollonius Rhodius: iii. 200; Eustathius on Homer's *Odyssey* xvi. 118; Apollodorus: *Epitome* vii. 24.

14. Homer: *Odyssey* xiii. 1–187; Apollodorus: *Epitome* vii. 25; Hyginus: *loc. cit.*

*

1. Apollodorus records (*Epitome* vii. 29) that 'some have taken the *Odyssey* to be an account of a voyage around Sicily.' Samuel Butler came independently to the same view and read Nausicaa as a self-portrait of the authoress – a young and talented Sicilian noblewoman of the Eryx district. In his *Authoress of the Odyssey*, he adduces the intimate knowledge here shown of domestic life at court, contrasted with the sketchy knowledge of seafaring or pastoral economy, and emphasizes the 'preponderance of female interest'. He points out that only a woman could have made Odysseus interview the famous women of the past before the famous men and, in his farewell speech to the Phaeacians, hope that 'they will continue to please their wives and children,' rather than the other way about (*Odyssey* xiii. 44–5); or made Helen pat the Wooden Horse and tease the men inside (see 167. *k*). It is difficult to disagree with Butler. The light, humorous, naïve, spirited touch of the *Odyssey* is almost certainly a woman's. But Nausicaa has combined, and localized in her native Sicily, two different legends, neither of them invented by herself: Odysseus's semi-historical return from Troy, and the allegorical adventures of

another hero – let us call him Ulysses – who, like Odysseus's grandfather
Sisyphus (see 67. 2), would not die when his term of sovereignty ended.
The Odysseus legend will have included the raid on Ismarus; the tempest
which drove him far to the south-west; the return by way of Sicily and
Italy; the shipwreck on Drepane (Corfu); and his eventual vengeance on
the suitors. All, or nearly all, the other incidents belong to the Ulysses
story. Lotus-land, the cavern of the Cyclops, the harbour of Telepylus,
Aeaea, Persephone's Grove, Siren Land, Ogygia, Scylla and Charybdis,
the Depths of the Sea, even the Bay of Phorcys – all are different meta-
phors for the death which he evaded. To these evasions may be added his
execution of old Hecabe, otherwise known as Maera the Lesser Dog Star,
to whom Icarius's successor should have been sacrificed (see 168. 1).

2. Both Scylax (*Periplus* 10) and Herodotus (iv. 77) knew the Lotus-
eaters as a nation living in Western Libya near the matriarchal Gindanes.
Their staple was the palatable and nourishing *cordia myxa*, a sweet, sticky
fruit growing in grape-like clusters which, pressed and mixed with grain
(Pliny: *Natural History* xiii. 32; Theophrastus: *History of Plants* iv. 3. 1),
once fed an army marching against Carthage. *Cordia myxa* has been confused with *rhamnus zizyphus*, a sort of crab-apple which yields a rough
cider and has a stone instead of pips. The forgetfulness induced by lotus-
eating is sometimes explained as due to the potency of this drink; but
lotus-eating is not the same as lotus-drinking. Since, therefore, the sacred
king's tasting of an apple given him by the Belle Dame Sans Merci was
tantamount to accepting death at her hands (see 33. 7 and 133. 4), the
cautious Ulysses, well aware that pale kings and warriors languished in
the Underworld because of an apple, will have refused to taste the *rhamnus*. In a Scottish witch-cult ballad, Thomas the Rhymer is warned not to
touch the apples of Paradise shown him by the Queen of Elphame.

3. The cavern of the Cyclops is plainly a place of death, and Odysseus's
party consisted of thirteen men: the number of months for which the
primitive king reigned. One-eyed Polyphemus, who sometimes has a
witch-mother, occurs in folk-tale throughout Europe, and can be traced
back to the Caucasus; but the twelve companions figure only in the *Odyssey*. Whatever the meaning of the Caucasian tale may have been, A. B.
Cook in his *Zeus* (pp. 302–23) shows that the Cyclops's eye was a Greek
solar emblem. Yet when Odysseus blinded Polyphemus, to avoid being
devoured like his companions, the Sun itself continued to shine. Only
the eye of the god Baal, or Moloch, or Tesup, or Polyphemus ('famous'), who demanded human sacrifice, had been put out, and the king
triumphantly drove off his stolen rams. Since the pastoral setting of the
Caucasian tale was retained in the *Odyssey*, and its ogre had a single eye, he
could be mistaken for one of the pre-Hellenic Cyclopes, famous metal-
workers, whose culture had spread to Sicily, and who perhaps had an

eye tattooed in the centre of their foreheads as a clan mark (see 3. 2).

4. Telepylus, which means 'the far-off gate [of Hell]', lies in the extreme north of Europe, the Land of the Midnight Sun, where the incoming shepherd hails the outgoing shepherd. To this cold region, 'at the back of the North Wind', belong the Wandering, or Clashing, Rocks, namely ice-floes (see 151. 1), and also the Cimmerians, whose darkness at noon complemented their midnight sun in June. It was perhaps at Telepylus that Heracles fought Hades (see 139. 1); if so, the battle will have taken place during his visit to the Hyperboreans (see 125. 1). The Laestrygonians ('of a very harsh race') were perhaps Norwegian fiord-dwellers of whose barbarous behaviour the amber merchants were warned on their visits to Bornholm and the Southern Baltic coast.

5. Aeaea ('wailing') is a typical death island where the familiar Death-goddess sings as she spins. The Argonautic legend places it at the head of the Adriatic Gulf; it may well be Lussin near Pola (see 148. 9). Circe means 'falcon', and she had a cemetery in Colchis, planted with willows, sacred to Hecate. The men transformed into beasts suggest the doctrine of metempsychosis, but the pig is particularly sacred to the Death-goddess, and she feeds them on Cronus's cornel-cherries, the red food of the dead, so they are perhaps simply ghosts (see 24. 11 and 33. 7). What Hermes's *moly* was, the grammarians could not decide. Tzetzes (*On Lycophron* 679) says that the druggists call it 'wild rue'; but the description in the *Odyssey* suggests the wild cyclamen, which is difficult to find, besides being white-petalled, dark-bulbed and very sweet-scented. Late Classical writers attached the name 'moly' to a sort of garlic with a yellow flower which was believed to grow (as the onion, squill, and true garlic did) when the moon waned, rather than when it waxed, and hence to serve as a counter-charm against Hecate's moon magic. Marduk, the Babylonian hero, sniffed at a divine herb as an antidote to the noxious smell of the Sea-goddess Tiamat, but its species is not particularized in the epic (see 35. 5).

6. Persephone's black-poplar grove lay in the far-western Tartarus, and Odysseus did not 'descend' into it – like Heracles (see 134. c), Aeneas, and Dante – though Circe assumed that he had done so (see 31. a). Phlegethon, Cocytus, and Acheron belong properly to the Underground Hell. However, the authoress of the *Odyssey* had little geographical knowledge, and called upon West, South or North winds at random. Odysseus should have been taken by east winds to Ogygia and Persephone's Grove, and by south winds to Telepylus and Aeaea: yet she had some justification for making Odysseus steer due East to Aeaea, as the Land of Dawn, where the heroes Orion and Tithonus had met their deaths. The entrances of Mycenaean bee-hive tombs face east; and Circe, being Helius's daughter, had Eos ('dawn') for an aunt.

7. Sirens (see 154. 3) were carved on funeral monuments as death angels chanting dirges to lyre music, but also credited with erotic designs on the heroes whom they mourned; and, since the soul was believed to fly off in the form of a bird, were pictured, like the Harpies, as birds of prey waiting to catch and secure it. Though daughters of Phorcys, or Hell, and therefore first cousins of the Harpies, they did not live underground, or in caverns, but on a green sepulchral island resembling Aeaea or Ogygia; and proved particularly dangerous in windless weather at mid-day, the time of sunstroke and siesta-nightmares. Since they are also called daughters of Achelous, their island may originally have been one of the Echinades, at the mouth of the river Achelous (see 142. 3). The Sicilians placed them near Cape Pelorus (now Faro) in Sicily; the Latins, on the Sirenusian Islands near Naples, or on Capri (Strabo: i. 12 – see 154. d and 3).

8. 'Ogygia', the name of yet another sepulchral island, seems to be the same word as 'Oceanus', Ogen being an intermediate form; and Calypso ('hidden' or 'hider') is one more Death-goddess, as is shown by her cavern surrounded with alders – sacred to the Death-god Cronus, or Bran – in the branches of which perch his sea-crows, or choughs (see 98. 3), and her own horned owls and falcons. Parsley was an emblem of mourning (see 106. 3), and the iris a death flower (see 85. 1). She promised Odysseus ageless youth, but he wanted life, not heroic immortality.

9. Scylla ('she who rends'), daughter of Phorcys, or Hecate, and Charybdis ('the sucker-down'), are titles of the destructive Sea-goddess. These names became attached to rocks and currents on either side of the Straits of Messina, but must be understood in a larger sense (see 16. 2 and 91. 2). Leucothea (see 70. 4) as a seamew was the Sea-goddess mourning over a shipwreck (see 45. 2). Since the Cretan Sea-goddess was also represented as an octopus (see 81. 1), and Scylla dragged the sailors from Odysseus's ship, it may be that Cretans who traded with India knew of large tropical varieties, unknown in the Mediterranean, which are credited with this dangerous habit. The description of Scylla's yelp is of greater mythological importance than first appears: it identifies her with the white, red-eared death-hounds, the Spectral Pack, or Gabriel Ratches, of British legend, which pursue the souls of the damned. They were the ancient Egyptian hunting dogs, sacred to Anubis and still bred in the island of Iviza, which when in pursuit of their quarry make a 'questing' noise like the whimper of puppies or the music of the migrating barnacle-goose (see White Goddess p. 411).

10. Only two incidents falling between Odysseus's skirmish with the Ciconians and his arrival at Phaeacia seem not to concern the ninefold rejection of death: namely his visit to the Island of Aeolus, and the theft of Hyperion's cattle. But the winds under Aeolus's charge were spirits of

the dead (see 43. 5); and Hyperion's cattle are the herd stolen by Heracles on his Tenth Labour – essentially a harrowing of Hell (see 132. 1). That Odysseus claimed to have taken no part in the raid means little; neither did his maternal grandfather Autolycus (see 160. c) own up to his lifting of sun-cattle (see 67. c).

11. Odysseus, whose name, meaning 'angry', stands for the red-faced sacred king (see 27. *12*), is called 'Ulysses' or 'Ulixes' in Latin – a word probably formed from *oulos*, 'wound' and *ischea*, 'thigh' – in reference to the boar's-tusk wound which his old nurse recognized when he came back to Ithaca (see 160. c and 171. g). It was a common form of royal death to have one's thigh gored by a boar, yet Odysseus had somehow survived the wound (see 18. 7 and 151. 2).

171

ODYSSEUS'S HOMECOMING

WHEN Odysseus awoke he did not at first recognize his native island, over which Athene had cast a distortive glamour. Presently she came by, disguised as a shepherd boy, and listened to his long, lying tale of how he was a Cretan who, after killing Idomeneus's son, had fled northward in a Sidonian ship, and been put ashore here against his will. 'What island is this?' he asked. Athene laughed and caressed Odysseus's cheek: 'A wonderful liar you are, indeed!' she said. 'But for knowing the truth I might easily have been deceived. What surprises me, though, is that you did not penetrate my disguise. I am Athene; the Phaeacians landed you here at my instructions. I regret having taken so many years to fetch you home; but I did not dare offend my uncle Poseidon by supporting you too openly.' She helped him to stow away his Phaeacian cauldrons, tripods, purple cloaks and golden cups in the shelter of a cave, and then transformed him beyond recognition – withered his skin, thinned and whitened his red locks, clothed him in filthy rags, and directed him to the hut of Eumaeus, the faithful old palace-swineherd. Athene was just back from Sparta, where Telemachus had gone to ask Menelaus, recently returned from Egypt, whether he could supply any news of Odysseus.

Now, it should be explained that, presuming Odysseus's death, no less than one hundred and twelve insolent young princes of the islands which formed the kingdom – Dulichium, Same, Zacynthus, and Ithaca itself – were courting his wife Penelope, each hoping to marry her and take the throne; and had agreed among themselves to murder Telemachus on his return from Sparta.[1]

b. When they first asked Penelope to decide between them, she declared that Odysseus must certainly still be alive, because his eventual home-coming had been foretold by a reliable oracle; and later, being hard-pressed, promised a decision as soon as she completed the shroud which she must weave against the death of old Laertes, her father-in-law. But she took three years over the task, weaving by day and un-ravelling it by night, until at last the suitors detected the ruse. All this time they were disporting themselves in Odysseus's palace, drinking his wine, slaughtering his pigs, sheep, and cattle, and seducing his maid-servants.[2]

c. To Eumaeus, who received Odysseus kindly, he gave another false account of himself, though declaring on oath that Odysseus was alive and on the way home. Telemachus now landed unexpectedly, evading the suitors' plots to murder him, and came straight to Eumaeus's hut; Athene had sent him back in haste from Sparta. Odysseus, however, did not disclose his identity until Athene gave the word and magically restored him to his true appearance. A touching scene of recognition between father and son followed. But Eumaeus had not yet been taken into the secret, nor was Telemachus allowed to enlighten Penelope.

d. Once more disguised as a beggar, Odysseus went to spy upon the suitors. On the way he encountered his goat-herd Melantheus, who railed indecently at him and kicked him on the hip; yet Odysseus refrained from immediate vengeance. When he reached the palace court, he found old Argus, once a famous hunting hound, stretched on a dunghill, mangy, decrepit, and tormented by fleas. Argus wagged his raw stump of a tail and drooped his tattered ears in recognition of Odysseus, who covertly brushed away a tear as Argus expired.[3]

e. Eumaeus led Odysseus into the banqueting hall, where Telemachus, pretending not to know who he was, offered him hospitality. Athene then appeared, though inaudible and invisible to all but Odysseus, and suggested that he should make a round of the hall begging scraps from the suitors, and thus learn what sort of men they were. This he did, and found them no less niggardly than rapacious. The most shameless of the entire company, Antinous of Ithaca (to whom he told a wholly different tale of his adventures) angrily threw a footstool at him. Odysseus, nursing a bruised shoulder, appealed to the other suitors, who agreed that Antinous should have shown more courtesy; and Penelope, when her maids reported the incident, was scandalized. She sent for the supposed beggar, hoping to have news from him of her lost husband. Odysseus promised to visit the royal parlour that evening, and tell her whatever she wished to know.⁴

f. Meanwhile, a sturdy Ithacan beggar, nicknamed 'Irus' because, like the goddess Iris, he was at everyone's beck and call, tried to chase Odysseus from the porch. When he would not stir, Irus challenged him to a boxing match, and Antinous, laughing heartily, offered the winner a goat's haggis and a seat at the suitors' mess. Odysseus hoisted his rags, tucked them under the frayed belt which he was wearing, and squared up to Irus. The ruffian shrank away at sight of his bulging muscles, but was kept from precipitate flight by the taunts of the suitors; then Odysseus felled him with a single blow, taking care not to attract too much notice by making it a mortal one. The suitors applauded, sneered, quarrelled, settled to their afternoon's feasting, toasted Penelope, who now came to extract bridal gifts from them all (though with no intention of making a definite choice), and at nightfall dispersed to their various lodgings.⁵

g. Odysseus instructed Telemachus to take down the spears which hung on the walls of the banqueting hall and store them in the armoury, while he went to visit Penelope.

She did not know him, and he spun her a long, circumstantial yarn, describing a recent encounter with Odysseus; who had, he said, gone to consult Zeus's Oracle at Dodona, but should soon be back in Ithaca. Penelope listened attentively, and ordered Eurycleia, Odysseus's aged nurse, to give him a foot-bath. Eurycleia presently recognized the scar on his thigh, and cried out in joy and surprise; so he gripped her withered throat and hissed for silence. Penelope missed the incident; Athene had distracted her attention.⁶

h. On the following day, at another banquet, Agelaus of Same, one of the suitors, asked Telemachus whether he could not persuade his mother to make up her mind. Penelope thereupon announced that she was ready to accept any suitor who would emulate Odysseus's feat of shooting an arrow through twelve axe-rings; the axes to be set in a straight row with their butts planted in a trench. She showed them the bow which they must use: one given to Odysseus by Iphitus, twenty-five years ago, when he went to protest at Messene against the theft from Ithaca of three hundred sheep and their shepherds. It once belonged to Eurytus, the father of Iphitus, whom Apollo himself had instructed in archery, but whom Heracles outshot and killed. Some of the suitors now tried to string the powerful weapon, and were unable to bend it, even after softening the wood with tallow; it was therefore decided to postpone the trial until the next day. Telemachus, who came nearest to accomplishing the feat, laid down the bow again at a warning sign from Odysseus. Then Odysseus, despite protests and vulgar insults – in the course of which Telemachus was forced to order Penelope back to her room – seized the bow, strung it easily, and twanged the string melodiously for all to hear. Taking careful aim he shot an arrow through every one of the twelve axe-rings. Meanwhile Telemachus, who had hurriedly slipped out, re-entered with sword and spear, and Odysseus declared himself at last by shooting Antinous in the throat.

i. The suitors sprang up and rushed to the walls, only to find that the spears were no longer in their usual places. Eurymachus begged for mercy, and when Odysseus refused it, drew sword and lunged at him, whereupon an arrow transfixed his liver and he fell dying. A fierce fight ensued between the desperate suitors armed with swords, and Odysseus, unarmed except for the bow but posted before the main entrance to the hall. Telemachus ran back to the armoury, and brought shields, spears and helmets to arm his father and Eumaeus and Philoetius, the two faithful servants who were standing by him; for though Odysseus had shot down the suitors in heaps, his stock of arrows was nearly expended. Melantheus, stealing off by a side door to fetch weapons for the suitors, was caught and trussed up on his second visit to the armoury, before he had succeeded in arming more than a few of them. The slaughter then continued, and Athene in the guise of a swallow flew twittering around the hall until every one of the suitors and their supporters lay dead, except only Medon the herald, and Phemius the bard; these Odysseus spared, because they had not actively wronged him, and because their persons were sacrosanct. He now paused to ask Eurycleia, who had locked the palace women in their quarters, how many of these had remained true to his cause. She answered: 'Only twelve have disgraced themselves, my lord.' The guilty maid-servants were summoned and set to cleanse the hall of blood with sponges and water; when they had done, Odysseus hanged them in a row. They kicked a little, but soon all was over. Afterwards, Eumaeus and

Philoetius docked Melantheus of his extremities – nose, ears, hands, feet, and genitals, which were cast to the dogs.[7]

j. Odysseus, at last reunited with Penelope, and with his father Laertes, told them his various adventures, this time keeping to the truth. A force of Ithacan rebels approached, the kinsmen of Antinous and other dead suitors, and seeing that Odysseus was outnumbered, the aged Laertes joined vigorously in the fight, which was going well enough for them until Athene intervened and imposed a truce.[8] The rebels then brought a combined legal action against Odysseus, appointing as their judge Neoptolemus, King of the Epirot Islands. Odysseus agreed to accept his verdict, and Neoptolemus ruled that he should leave his kingdom and not return until ten years had passed, during which time the heirs of the suitors were ordered to compensate him for their depredations, with payments made to Telemachus, now king.[9]

k. Poseidon, however, still remained to be placated; and Odysseus set out on foot, as Teiresias had instructed, across the mountains of Epirus, carrying an oar over his shoulder. When he reached Thesprotis, the countryfolk cried: 'Stranger, why a winnowing-bat in Springtime?' He accordingly sacrificed a ram, bull, and boar to Poseidon, and was forgiven.[10] Since he could not return to Ithaca even yet, he married Callidice, Queen of the Thesprotians, and commanded her army in a war against the Brygians, under the leadership of Ares; but Apollo called for a truce. Nine years later, Polypoetes, Odysseus's son by Callidice, succeeded to the Thesprotian kingdom, and Odysseus went home to Ithaca, which Penelope was now ruling in the name of their young son Poliporthis; Telemachus had been banished to Cephallenia, because an oracle announced: 'Odysseus, your own son shall kill you!' At Ithaca, death came to Odysseus from the sea, as Teiresias had foretold. His son by Circe, Telegonus, sailing in search of him, raided Ithaca (which he mistook for Corcyra) and Odysseus sallied out to repel the attack. Telegonus killed him on the seashore, and the fatal weapon was a spear armed with the spine of a sting-ray. Having spent the required year in exile, Telegonus married Penelope. Telemachus then married Circe; thus both branches of the family became closely united.[11]

l. Some deny that Penelope remained faithful to Odysseus. They accuse her of companying with Amphinomus of Dulichium, or with all the suitors in turn, and say that the fruit of this union was the monstrous god Pan – at sight of whom Odysseus fled for shame to Aetolia, after sending Penelope away in disgrace to her father Icarius at Mantinea, where her tomb is still shown. Others record that she bore Pan to Hermes, and that Odysseus married an Aetolian princess, the daughter of King Thoas, begot on her his youngest son Leontophonus, and died in prosperous old age.[12]

1. Homer: *Odyssey* xiii. 187 ff. and xvi. 245–53; Apollodorus: *Epitome* vii. 26–30.
2. Homer: *Odyssey* xix. 136–58 and xiv. 80–109; Hyginus: *Fabula* 126; Apollodorus: *Epitome* vii. 31.
3. Homer: *Odyssey* xiv–xvi; Apollodorus: *Epitome* vii. 32.
4. Homer: *Odyssey* xvii; Apollodorus: *loc. cit.*
5. Homer: *Odyssey* xviii.
6. Homer: *Odyssey* xix.
7. Homer: *Odyssey* xx–xxii; Hyginus: *loc. cit.*; Apollodorus: *Epitome* vii. 33.
8. Homer: *Odyssey* xxii–xxiv.
9. Plutarch: *Greek Questions* 14.
10. Homer: *Odyssey* xi. 119–31; Apollodorus: *Epitome* vii. 34.
11. Apollodorus: *loc. cit.*; Eugammon of Cyrene, quoted by Proclus: *Epicorum Graecorum Fragmenta* 57 ff., ed. Kinkel; Hyginus: *Fabula* 127; Pausanias: viii. 12. 6; Scholiast on *Odyssey* xi. 134; Eustathius on *Odyssey* xi. 133; Parthenius: *Love Stories* 3; Tzetzes: *On Lycophron* 794; Dictys Cretensis: vi. 4 ff.; Servius on Virgil's *Aeneid* ii. 44; *Fragments of Sophocles* ii. 105 ff., ed. Pearson.
12. Servius: *loc. cit.*; Pausanias: viii. 12. 5 ff.; Cicero: *On the Nature of the Gods* iii. 22. 56; Tzetzes: *On Lycophron* 772, quoting Duris the Samian.

*

1. Odysseus's assassination of the suitors belongs to the Ulysses allegory: one more instance of the sacred king's refusal to die at the close of his reign. He intervenes, that is to say, in the archery contest held to decide his successor (see 135. 1), and destroys all the candidates. One primitive archery test of the candidate for kingship seems to have consisted in shooting through a ring placed on a boy's head (see 162. 10).

2. The *Odyssey* nowhere directly suggests that Penelope has been unfaithful to her husband during his long absence, though in Book xviii. 281–3 she bewitches the suitors by her coquetry, extorts tribute from them, and shows a decided preference for Amphinomus of Dulichium (*Odyssey* xvi. 394–8). But Odysseus does not trust her well enough to reveal himself until he has killed his rivals; and his mother Anticleia shows that there is something to conceal when she says not one word to him about the suitors (*Odyssey* xi. 180 ff.). The archaic account that makes Penelope the mother of Pan by Hermes, or alternatively by all the suitors,

refers, it seems, to the Goddess Penelope and her primitive spring orgies, (see 26. 2). Her cuckolding of Odysseus and eventual return to Mantinea, another archaic story, are a reminder of his insolence in forcing her to come with him to Ithaca, against ancient matrilocal custom (see 160. e). But Nausicaa, the authoress, tells the story in her own way, white-washing Penelope. She accepts the patriarchal system into which she has been born, and prefers gentle irony to the bitter satire found in the *Iliad*. The goddess is now displaced by Almighty Zeus, kings are no longer sacrificed in her honour, and the age of myth has ended – very well! That need not greatly disturb Nausicaa, while she can still joke and play ball with her good-natured servant girls, pull the hair of those who displease her, listen to old Eurycleia's tales, and twist Father Alcinous around one finger.

3. So the *Odyssey* breaks off with Laertes, Odysseus, and Telemachus, a patriarchal male triad of heroes, supported by Zeus-born Athene and triumphing over their foes; while the serving wenches hang in a row for their lack of discretion, to show that Nausicaa disapproves of pre-marital promiscuity as cheapening the marriage-market.

The end has been preserved by other mythographers. Odysseus is banished to Thesprotia, and Telemachus to Cephallenia, whereas Penelope stays contentedly at the palace, ruling in the name of her son Poliporthis. Teiresias's prophecy remains, of course, to be fulfilled: Odysseus will not die comfortably of old age, like the respected and garrulous Nestor. Death must strike him down in the traditional style which he thought to abolish: the New Year Child riding on dolphin-back will run him through with a sting-ray spear. Much the same fate overtook Catreus of Rhodes: his son Althaemenes accidentally speared him on the beach (see 93. 2). Sting-ray spears, also used by the Polynesians, cause inflamed wounds, which the Greeks and Latins held to be incurable (Aelian: *Nature of Animals* i. 56); the sting-ray (*trygon pastinaca*) is common in the Mediterranean. Heracles is said to have been wounded by one (see 123. 2).

4. Telemachus's marriage to Circe, and Telegonus's to Penelope, are surprising at first sight. Sir James Frazer (*Apollodorus* ii. p. 303, Loeb) connects these apparently incestuous unions with the rule by which, in polygamous societies, a king inherited all his father's concubines, except his own mother (2 *Samuel* xvi. 21 ff.). But polygamy never became a Greek institution, and neither Telemachus, nor Telegonus, nor Oedipus, a New Year Child, 'born of the swelling wave', who killed his father and married the widowed Iocaste (see 105. e), nor Heracles's son Hyllus, who married his step-mother Iole (see 145. e), was polygamous. Each merely killed and succeeded the King of the Old Year in the ancient mythic style, and was thereafter called his son. This explains why Telemachus prepares to string the bow – which would have given him Penelope

as his wife – but Odysseus frowns at him, and he desists; it is a detail surviving from the Ulysses story, uncritically retained in the *Odyssey*.

5. Who knows whether Odysseus's red hair has any mythic significance (see 133. 8), or whether it is an irrelevant personal peculiarity, like his short legs, belonging to some adventurer in Sicily whom Nausicaa has portrayed as Odysseus? Autolycus, of course, named him 'the angry one' at birth (see 160. *c*), and red hair is traditionally associated with ill temper. But though masquerading as an epic, the *Odyssey* is the first Greek novel; and therefore wholly irresponsible where myths are concerned. I have suggested the possible circumstances of its composition in another novel: *Homer's Daughter*.*

*London and New York, 1955

INDEX

Many of the meanings are doubtful. Names in italics refer to characters in non-Hellenic mythology. References are to paragraph numbers, not page numbers.

Abas – lizard, 24.*e*,9; 72.3; 73.a

Abderus – ? son of battle, 71. *1*; 130.*b,c*; 168.6

Abraham, 169.5,6

Acacallis – without walls, 90.*a,b*,2

Academus – of a silent district, 104.*b*

Acamas – unwearying, 86.*a*; 101.*a*; 131.*11*; 167.*c*; 168.*d,e,j*; 169.*j*

Acarnan – thistle, 107.*g*

Acastus – ? *acatastatos,* unstable, 80.*b*; 81 *passim*; 148.*i*; 155 *passim*; 162.*d*,8; 169.*f*

Acca – she who fashions, 141.*1*

Acco – she who fashions, 141.*1*

Acesidas – averter from Mt Ida, 53.*b*,2; 164.6

Achaeus – griever, 43.*b*,*1*; 44.*a*

Achates – agate, 162.*b*

Achelois – she who drives away grief, 142.3

Achelous, R. – ? he who drives away grief, 7.4; 67.4; 107.*e*; 127.2; 134.8; 142 *passim*; 170.*q*,7

Achilles – lipless, 31.*c*; 81.*r, s, 1*; 126.*g*, 2; 138.4; 157.*c*; 160 *passim*; 162 *passim*; 163 *passim*; 164 *passim*; 165.*a,b*; 166.*a,g*; 168.*j,k,l*; 169.*g*; 170.*p*

Achish, 159.4

Acidusa – barbed being, 137.*t*

Acmon – anvil, or pestle, 53.*c*; 136.*c*

Acrisius – ill-judgement, 21.8; 38.8; 69.*1*; 72.*g*; 73 *passim*; 81.7; 109.*c*; 148.*i*

Actaeon – shore dweller, 22.*i*,*1*; 28.2; 31.3; 32.*1*; 54.*b*; 82.*e,j*; 138.4

Actaeus – of the coast, 25*d*

Actis – beam of light, 42.*c*,4

Actor – leader, 81.*f*,8; 138.*a,b*; 148.*i*; 166.*b*

Adam, 4.3; 28.6; 51.2; 145.5; 146.2

Adanus – he of the acorns, 1.*d*; 159.3

Admete – untamed, 131.*a,j*,*1,3*

Admetus – untamed, 10.*b*; 21.*n*,7; 69 *passim*; 80.*c*; 130.*b*; 148.*i*; 155.*j*

Adonis – lord, 18.*h,i,j*,2,6,7; 25.5,11; 27.10; 58.*d*; 77.2; 101.*g*; 126.1; 132.4; 136.1; 141.3

Adrasteia – inescapable, 7.*b*,3; 32.3

Adrastus – he who stands his ground, 102.*c*; 106 *passim*; 107.*b,c*; 138.*g*; 158.*l*

Adymnus – unsetting, 89.*d*,9

Aeacus – bewailing, or earth-born, 31.*b*; 66 *passim*; 81 *passim*; 88.*i*; 91.*a,f*; 92.*j*; 94.*e*; 96.*g*; 112.*b*; 158.*l*,8,9; 165.*a,k*; 167.2

Aeanes – wearisome, 160.*m*

Aechmagoras – warlike spirit of the market-place, 141.*h*

Aëdon – nightingale, 108.*g*

Aedos – shame, 32.*1*

Aeëtes – mighty, or eagle, 70.*l*; 129.*1*; 148 *passim*; 152 *passim*; 153 *passim*; 154 *passim*; 157.*b*; 170.*i*

Aegaeon – goatish, 3.*1*; 132.*h*

Aegaeus, R. – goatish, 146.*i*

Aegeia – bright, 106.*a,c*

Aegesta – pleasing goat, 137.*g*

Aegestes, or Acestes – pleasing he-goat, 137.*g*; 169.*m*

Aegeus – goatish, 88.*d*; 90.*h*; 94 *passim*; 95 *passim*; 97 *passim*; 98.*a,d,v*,7; 99.*a*; 152.*d*; 156.*e*; 157.*a*

Aegialeia – of the seashore, 162.*t*; 169.*k*

Aegialeius – of the seashore, 107.*b,c*

Aegimius – ? *aigiminos,* acting the part of a he-goat, 78.*a*; 143.*d*,3; 146.*d,e*

Aegina – goat strength, 66.*b*,*1*; 67.*f*; 138.*b*

Aegisthus – goat strength, 111 *passim*; 113 *passim*; 114 *passim*; 116.1; 117.*a*; 162.*t*

Aegle – dazzling light, 33.*d*; 98.*n*

377

Aegleis – bright, 91.*g*.

Aegyptus – ? supine he-goat, 56.3; 60 *passim*

Aelinus – dirge, 100.*c*

Aëllopus – storm foot, 150.*j*

Aeneas, or Aeneus – praiseworthy, 18.*g*,*3*; 50.2; 51.6; 98.3; 103.1; 158.3; 159.*q*; 162 *passim*; 163.*c*; 166.*j*,*m*; 167.*j*; 168 *passim*

Aeolus – ? earth destroyer, 1.3; 26.1; 43 *passim*; 45.*a*,*d*,2; 67.*e*; 68.*a*; 148.*a*; 170.*g*,10

Aerope – sky face, 93.*a*,*c*; 111.*c*,*e*,*f*, 3,4; 140.*b*

Aesacus – myrtle branch, 158.*m*,*n*,6; 159 *passim*

Aesculapius – ? *ex aesculeo apiens*, hanging from an esculent oak, 50.*i*,2

Aeson – ? *aesymnaon*, ruler, 68.*e*,*f*; 148.*a*,*b*,*e*; 155.*a*,*h*

Aethiolas – ? destroyed by fire, 159.*d*

Aethra – bright sky, 95 *passim*; 97.*b*; 104.*e*; 159.*s*; 168.*d*.*e*

Aethylla – kindling timber, 162.*e*,11

Aetius – originator, 95.*b*,6

Aetolus – ? cause of destruction, 64.*c*,*3*

Agamede – very cunning, 138.6

Agamedes – very cunning, 51.*i*; 84 *passim*; 121*f*; 169.2

Agamemnon – very resolute, 92.4; 93.*c*; 111.*f*,*j*,*n*; 112 *passim*; 113 *passim*; 116.*i*,1,2; 131.11; 159 *passim*; 160 *passim*; 161 *passim*; 162 *passim*; 163 *passim*; 164.*e*; 165 *passim*; 166 *passim*; 167 *passim*; 168 *passim*; 169 *passim*; 170.*p*

Aganippe – mare who kills mercifully, 73.*c*

Aganus – gentle, 159.*v*

Agapenor – much distress, 169.*n*

Agathyrsus – much raging, 132.*v*

Agave – high-born, 27.*f*,9; 59.*d*

Agelaus – herdsman, 136. *q*; 159 *passim*; 171.*h*

Agenor – very manly, 56.*b*,*3*; 57.*a*,1; 58 *passim*; 60.3; 73.*l*; 142.5; 150.*j*

Aglaia – bright, 73.*a*; 105.5

Aglauros – dewfall, 25 *passim*

Aglaus – splendid, 111.*g*

Agraulos – rustic one, 25 *passim*

Agreus – wild, 82.*d*

Agriope – savage face, 28.*b*,4

Agrius – wild (*the Centaur*), 35.*g*; 126.*b*; 164.*a*; 170.*k*

Agyieus – he of the street, 51.*b*

Aidoneus – Hades, 103.*e*

Aissa – swift, 160.*j*

Ajax, Great – of the earth, 66.*i*; 81.*e*; 110.*e*; 137.*i*; 159.*a*; 160.*k*,*n*,*p*,2; 162.*m*; 163 *passim*; 164 *passim*; 165 *passim*; 168 *passim*; 170.*p*

Ajax, Little, 160.*p*,2,6; 163.*h*; 164.*m*; 165.5; 168 *passim*

Ajuna, 135.1

Alalcomeneus – guardian, 5.*a*,1

Alastor – avenger, 111.*p*,5

Alcaeus – mighty one, 88.*h*; 118.*d*,3; 119.*b*; 131.*e*; 136.*g*

Alcaids – sons of the mighty one, 122.*a*,2

Alcathous – impetuous might, 67.1; 109.*e*,*o*; 110.*c*,*d*,*e*,2; 120.*c*

Alcestis – might of the home, 69 *passim*; 106.6; 134.4,8; 155 *passim*

Alcidice – mighty justice, 68.*b*

Alcimede – mighty cunning, 148.*b*

Alcimedes – mighty cunning, or mighty genitals, 156.*e*

Alcimedon – mighty ruler, 141.*h*

Alcinous – mighty mind, 148.9; 154 *passim*; 170.2; 171.2

Alcippe – mighty mare, 19.*b*,2; 25.2; 74.*e*; 92.*a*; 94.*b*

Alcis – might, 121.*c*,*3*

Alcithoë – impetuous might, 27.*g*

Alcmaeon – mighty endeavour, 85.1; 107 *passim*; 113.6; 115.4; 137.*m*

Alcmena or Alcmene – might of the moon, or mighty in wrath, 74. 1; 88.*i*,9; 110.*c*; 118 *passim*; 119 *passim*; 138.*d*; 145.*e*,*h*; 146 *passim*

Alcon – mighty, 119.*f*,4

Alcyone – queen who wards off [storms], 45 *passim*; 95.*b*; 110.*c*; 125.*c*; 126.*d*; 149.5; 160.12

Alcyoneus – *alceoneus*, mighty ass, 35.*c*,4,5; 67.1; 132.*w*

Alecto – unnameable, 6.*a*; 31.*g*; 115.2

Aletes – wanderer, 113.*e*; 117.*a*

Aleus – grinder, 140.*b*; 141 *passim*

Alexander – he who wards off men, 146.*c*

Alexirrhoë – averting the flow, 136.*b*,*f*

Alexiares – warding off war, 145.*i*

Aleyn, 73.2

Aloeides – children of the threshing floor, 35.2; 36.4; 36 *passim*

Aloeus – of the threshing floor, 19.*b*; 37.*a*,1

Alope – *alopecodis*, sly as a vixen, 49 *passim*, 96.*j*,5

Alopecus – fox, 116.*l*,4

Alpheius, R. – whiteish, 22.*g*,2

Alphesiboea – bringing many oxen, 58.*d*,2

Alphito – white goddess, 22.2; 52.7; 61.1; 113.7

Althaea – marshmallow, 80.*a*,1; 142.*a*

Althaemenes – strength of growth, 93 *passim*; 171.3

Alxion – war-like native, 109.*b*

Amaltheia – tender, 7.*b*,3,4; 26.*b*; 30.3; 108.*e*; 142.*d*

Amarynceus – swift darting, 138.*a*,*b*, 5; 139.*e*,*f*

Amathaon, 103.1; 108.8; 148.*f*

Amazons – moon-women, 27.*d*; 39. 5, 6; 75.*d*; 100 *passim*; 131 *passim*; 132.*f*; 134.2; 151.*d*,*e*; 152.*j*; 164 *passim*

Ameinius – unpausing, 85.*b*,1

Ammon – sandy, 27.*b*; 51.1; 97.*a*,1

Amnisian Nymphs – of the she-lambs 22.*f*

Amphiaraus – doubly cursed, 51.*g*; 80.*c*,*e*,*g*; 106 *passim*; 107.*a*; 148.*i*

Amphictyon – fastener together, 24.5; 38.*h*.8

Amphictyonis – fastener together; 38.8

Amphidamas – taming all about him, 108.*b*; 127.*a*; 133.*k*; 160.*m*

Amphilochus – double ambush, 51.*g*, 8; 107.*d*,*i*; 169.*c*,*e*

Amphimarus – ? ambidextrous, 147.*b*

Amphinome – grazing all about, 148.*b*; 155 *passim*

Amphinomus – grazing all about, 171.*l*,2

Amphion – native of two lands, 76.*a*,*b*, *c*,2; 77 *passim*; 109.*j*.6

Amphissa – double strength, 43.*h*

Amphissus – double strength, 21.*j*

Amphitrite – the third one who encircles, i.e. the sea, 16.*b*,1,2; 47.*c*; 87.*c*; 91.2; 98.*j*

Amphitryon – harassing on either side, 74.1; 89.*h*,*i*; 111.*b*; 118 *passim*; 119 *passim*; 120.*a*; 121.*d*; 122.*e*; 135.*e*; 146.*g*; 167.*b*

Amyclas – very lustful, 77.*b*; 125.*c*

Amycus – loudly bellowing, 131.*e*,*h*; 150 *passim*; 151.*c*

Amymone – blameless, 16.*e*,5; 60. *g*,0

Amyntor – defender, 142.*e*; 143.*i*; 160.*l*

Amythaon – unspeakably great, 112.*b*, 138.*m*

Anakim, 88.3; 117.3

Anatha, 9.4; 41.4; 61.1; 82.4; 98.7; 114.4; 133.10; 141.1; 169.5

Anax – king, 88.*b*,3

Anaxagoras – king of the market-place, 72.*k*

Anaxandrides – son of the kingly man, 117.*d*,7

Anaxibia – queenly strength, 111.*f* or Eurydice, 164.*e*

Anaxo – queen, 104.*i*; 118.*a*

Ancaeus – of the glen, 18.7; 80.*c*,*d*,*g*; 148.*i*; 151.*c*; 154.*i*; 157.*e*.2

Anchiale – close to the sea, or sea-girt, 53.*a*

Anchinoë – quick wit, 60.*a*

Anchises – living with Isis, 18.*f,g,3*; 137.*g*; 158.*l,r*; 159.4; 162.*k*; 168 *passim*

Ancius – of the dell, 126.*b*

Androclea – glory of men, 121.*c,3*

Androgeneia – mother of men, 89.*a*

Androgeus – man of the earth, 66.*h*; 90 *passim*; 91.*a,f*; 98.*a,c,p*; 131.*i,6*

Androgyne – man-woman, 18.*8*

Andromache – battle of men, 158.*8*; 168.*h*

Andromeda – ruler of men, 73 *passim*; 137.2

Andron – man's apartment, 160.*u*

Androphonos – man-slayer, 18.4

Andrus – manly, 88.*h*

Angitia – snake-goddess, 157.*a*

Anicetus – unconquerable, 145.*i*

Anippe – queenly mare, 133.*k*

Anius – troublous, 88.*h*; 160.*t,u,v*

Annwm, 31.3

Antaeus – besought with prayers, 53.3; 109.*f*; 132.*f*; 133 *passim*; 134.6,8,9

Antagoras – facing the market-place, 137.*q*

Anteia – precedence, 70.2; 73.*a*; 75.*a,e,1*

Antenor – instead of a man, 158.*r*; 150.*q*; 162.*n*; 166.*j,l*; 167.*e,l,1*; 168 *passim*

Ante-vorta, 154.3

Anthas – flowery, 95.*b*

Anthea – flowery, 95.1

Anthedon – rejoicing in flowers, 90.*j,7*

Antheis – flowery, 91.*g*

Antheus – 85.2; 159.*q,4*

Antibia – confronting strength, 110.*c*

Anticleia – false key, *or* in place of the famous one, 67.*c*; 96.*a*; 160.*c*; 170.*n,0*; 171.2

Antielus – near the marshland, 167.*k,2*

Antigone, in place of a mother, 105.*k*; 106.*m*

Antileon – bold as a lion, 120.*b*

Antilochus – lying in ambush against, 164.*e,f,m*

Antinous – hostile mind, 171 *passim*

Antiochus – driver against, 143.*b*

Antiope – with face confronting, 43.*a*; 68.2; 76 *passim*; 100 *passim*; 101.*b*; 106.7; 131.*e,g*; 151.*f*; 154.*a*; 167.*h*; 170.0

Antiphas – speaking in the name of, 167.*i,3*

Antiphates – spokesmen, 170.*h*

Antiphus – contrary, 158.0

Antipoenus – vicarious penalty, 121.*c*

Anu, 6.6

Anubis, 17.2; 31.3; 34.1; 170.9

Apemosyne – unknowingness, 93 *passim*

Apesantus – ? he who lets loose against, 123.*e,5*

Aphaea – not dark, *or* vanisher, 89.*b,4*

Aphareus – unclothed, 74.*b,c,g,k*; 94.*f*; 141.*f*

Apheidas – lavish, 141.*a*

Aphidamas – ? *amphidamas*, taming all about him, 141.*a*

Aphidnus – shrinking away until he bends backwards, 103.*b*; 104.*e*

Aphrodite – foam-born, 6.6; 11 *passim*; 13.6; 15.*b,1*; 18 *passim*; 19.*a*; 23.1; 28.*f*; 32.4; 33.7; 65.*a,1*; 67.2; 71.*a*; 80.*l*; 83.1; 91.2; 92.*j*; 98.*g,k*; 101.*b,5*; 108.*f*; 126.1; 137.*s*; 152.*a.2*; 154.*d*; 159 *passim*; 162.4; 163.*c,n*; 167.4; 169.1; 170.*q*

   Comaetho – bright-haired, 91.1

   Cyprian, 18.*8*

   Eldest of the Fates, 10.3; 18.4

   Epitragia – turned into a he-goat, 98.*g*

   Epitymbria – of the tombs, 18.4

   Erycina – of the heather, 18.*3*; 132.*r*

   Federal, 99.*d*

   the Fish, 36.*a*

   Melaenis – black, 18.4

   Peeping, 101.*c*

   Schoenis – of the rush-basket, 80.4

   Scotia – of darkness, 18.4

   Stranger, 159.*v*

   Temnian, 109.*g*

Aphrodite – *continued*
  Trojan, 160.*8*
  Uniter, 159.*s*
  Urania – queen of the mountains,
    10.*c,3*
  Victorious, 60.*k*
  Wolfish, 81.*9*
Apis – long ago, 56.*b*; 64.*c, 3,4*; 75.5
Apollo – destroyer, *or* apple-man,
    13.*c*; 14 *passim*; 17 *passim*; 18.*j*; 20
    passim; 22.*b*; 28.*f.3*; 40.*3*; 42.*1*;
    43.*h*; 44.*a*; 50.*c,d,e,4*; 51.*d,4*; 52.*8*;
    66.*i*; 69.*a,c*; 74.*e,f*; 76.*c*; 77.*a,b*;
    82.*a,b,c,1*; 83.*g*; 84.*b*; 91.*b*; 95.*h,5*;
    97.*1*; 98.*t,u,10*; 107.*f*; 113.*f*; 114.
    f.n; 115.*4*; 116.*a*; 135.*d,2,3*; 137.*a*;
    139.*f*; 143.*f*; 154.*i*; 158 *passim*; 161
    passim; 163.*j,p,3*; 164.*j*; 167.*j*; 169
    passim
  Cillaean, 109.*g,2*
  of the Dawn, 151.*b*
  Distraught, 169.*m*
  the Dolphin, 97.*a*; 99.*2*
  of the Embarcations, 149.*a*
  the Hunter, 110.*d*; 133. *l*
  Hyperborean, 21.*3*; 113.*7*
  Lycian, 60.*8*
  Phygian, 158.*d*
  Pure, 82.*b*
  Pythian, 28.*3*; 99.*c*; 100.*b*
  Smintheus – mousy, 14.*2*; 21.*3*;
    90.*3*; 158.*a,j,2*; 161.*i*
  Solar, 109.*2*
  Thymbraean, 158.*p*; 161.*l*; 163.*a*;
    164.*k*; 166.*g*; 167.*h,i*
  of the White Rock, 89.*j*
Apsu, 36.*2*
Apsyrtus, *or* Aegialeus – swept down-
    stream, 148.*9*; 152.*c*; 153 *passim*
Aqhat, 41.*4*
Arachne – spider, 25.*h,6*
Arawn, 108.*8*
Arcas – bear, 64.*c*; 132.*r*
Archelaus – ruler of the people, 117.*g*;
    169.*5*
Archemorus – beginner of doom, *or*
    original olive-stock, 106.*h,3*

Archias – eminent, 142.*g*
Archippe – dominant mare, 110.*c*
Architeles – plenipotentiary, 142.*g*
Ardalus – dirty, 95.*c*
Areia – warlike, 88.*b*
Arene – man-like, 74.*c*
Ares – male warrior, 1.*3*; 12.*c,2*;
    15.*b*; 18.*b,c,d,j*; 19 *passim*; 35.*d*;
    37.*b,d,3*; 40.*b*; 46.*a*; 48.*d*; 58.*g*;
    59.*a,e*; 67.*g*; 70.*m*; 80.*l,1*; 102.*e*;
    106.*j,1*; 109.*b,d*; 130.*a*; 133.*d*; 139.
    b,1; 143.*g*; 151.*f,4*; 152.*h,i*; 159.*h*;
    164.*a*
  Colchian, 148.*g*
Aresthanas – strength of prayer,
    50.*d*
Arëte – unspeakable, 154 *passim*, 170.*z*
Arethusa – *ardusa*, the waterer, 22.*a*;
    82.*g*
Argeius – whited, 110.*c*; 144.*a*
Arge – brightness, 3.*b,2*; 22.*d*
Argeus – bright, 151.*f*
Argiope – bright face, 58.*a,2*; 96.*j,5*;
    141.*e*
Argonauts, 28.*b*; 70.*e*; 126.*f*; 128.*b*;
    133.*f*; 134.*6*; 137.*e*; 148 *passim*; 149
    passim; 150 *passim*; 151 *passim*; 152
    passim; 153 *passim*; 154 *passim*; 155
    passim; 156 *passim*
Argus – bright
  hound, 171.*d*
  son of Medea, 156.*e*
  Panoptes – the bright one, all eyes,
    33.*e*; 56.*a*
  the Thespian, 148.*h,i*; 152.*i*
Aria – oak tree, 21. *i,7*
Ariadne – *ariagne*, most pure; *or* high
    fruitful mother of the barley,
    27.*i,8*; 38.*h,3*; 79.*2*; 88.*h,10*;
    90.*a,b,1*; 92.*12*; 98 *passim*; 101.*d*;
    104.*4*; 114.*6*; 160.*a*; 170.*0*
Aridela – the very manifest one,
    98.*s,5*;
Arion – lofty native, 16.*f,5*; 33.*4*;
    75.*3*; 106.*l*; 138.*g,7*
  King of Miletus, 137.*l*
  the Musician, 87 *passim*

Arisbe – ? from *aristo* and *baino*, she who travels best, 158.*m*; 166.*f*

Aristaeus – the best, 21.*i*; 28.*c*; 82 *passim*; 154.*b*

Aristeus – *see* Aristaeus

Aristippe – best of mares, 27.*g*

Aristo – good, 117.*d*,*7*

Aristomenes – best strength, 74.*o*; 146.*6*

Armenus – union, 154.*l*

Arnacia – sheepskin, 160.*d*

Arnaea – ewe, 160.*d*

Arne – ewe-lamb, 43 *passim*; 91.*a*; 148.*b*

Arrhippe – best of mares, 136.*b*

Arsinoë – male-minded
daughter of Minyas, 27.*g*
daughter of Phegeus, 107.*f*,*g*
nurse of Orestes, 113.*a*

Arsippe – ? *arsipous*, she who raises the foot, 27.*g*

Artemis – ? high source of water, 14 *passim*; 21.*b*,*d*; 22 *passim*; 37.*c*; 41.*d*,*e*,*4*; 43.*c*; 50.4; 69.2; 72.*i*; 77.*a*,*b*; 80 *passim*; 81.9; 89.*a*,*2*; 98.*s*,*u*,*7*; 100.2; 101.*b*,*k*,*l*; 108.*k*; 111.*c*; 116 *passim*; 117. 2;125 *passim*; 126.1; 142.*a*,*l*; 145.*j*; 161.*d*

Alpheia – whiteish, 22.2

Anäeitis – of the planet Venus, 116.*j*

Aphaea – not dark, 89.4

Arician, 101.*l*

Brauronian, 116.5

Carian, 57.2

Caryatis – of the walnut, 86.*b*

Cat, 36.*a*

Cordax – of the rope dance, 109.*p*

Cydonian, 109.*i*

Dictynna – of the net, 116.*c*

Eileithyia – she who comes to the aid of women in childbed, 15.*a*,*1*

Elaphios – hindlike, 125.*1*

Ephesian, 22.1; 100.*f*; 116.5; 131. *d*,*3*,*5*

Famous, 121.*c*,*e*

the Hanged One, 88.*10*; 91.3; 98.5

the Hind, 125.*1*,*3*

the Huntress, 110.*d*

Hyacinthropos – nurse of Hyacinthus, 91.*3*

Hyperborean, 155.*d*,*e*

Lady of the Lake, 89.*b*

Lady of the Wild Things, 22.*1*,*6*

Laphria – despoiling, 22.*6*; 89.*b*,*4*

Lygodesma – bound with willows, 116.*l*

Metapontinan, 43.*e*

Olympian, 22.*1*

Orthia – upright, 103.*b*; 116.*c*,*k*,*l*,*4*

Orthosian, 141.*h*

Persuasive, 60.*k*

Saronian, 101.*g*

Saviour, 98.*x*; 134.*g*

Stymphalian, 128.*d*

Taurian, 100.*1*; 116.*b*,*c*,*j*; 117.*a*

Tauropole – bull-killer, 116.*c*,*i*,*j*; 131.*c*

Thoantea – of Thoas, 116.*c*

Tridaria – threefold assigner of lots, 72.5

Trivia – of the three ways, 116.*c*

Wolfish, 114.*h*

Arthur, King, 31.3; 82.2; 95.5; 98.3; 103.1; 154.3

Aruru, 4.2,5; 39.8

Ascalaphus – short-eared owl, 24.*j*,*l*, 12; 134.*d*

the Orchomenan, 148.*i*

Ascalus, untilled, 169.6

Ascanius – tentless, 168.*o*

Asclepius – unceasingly gentle, 3.*b*; 21.*i*,*n*,*9*; 41.*d*,*3*; 50 *passim*; 51.*g*; 74.*b*,*k*; 90.4; 101.*k*,*m*; 133.11; 140.*a*; 166.*i*

Agnitas – purifier, 50.*h*

Cotylaean – hollow-of-the-hand, 140.*d*,*1*

Ash-nymphs – *see* Meliae

Ashtar, 30.4

Ashtaroth, 11.1

Asius – merry, 158.*m*

Asopus, R. – ? *asiapaos*, never silent, 66 *passim*; 67.*f*,*i*,*4*; 76.*b*; 81.*d*; 109.*b*; 151.*d*

Assaracus – ? *assaros*, disdainful, 158.*g*

Astarte, 56.2; 58.2; 68.4; 73.7; 164.2

Asterië – of the starry sky, *or* of the sun, 88.1; 109.*b*,*3*; 130.*a*

Asterion, R. – of the sun, 16.*e*

Asterius, on – of the starry sky, *or* of the sun

  giant, 88 *passim*; 98.*c*,*2*

  son of Cometes, 148.*i*

  the Lesser, 89.*a*

Asterodeia – goddess of the sun, 152.*c*

Asterope – sun-face, 109.*b*; 158.*n*

Astrabacus – sure-sighted remedy, 116.*l*

Astraeus – starry, 40.*b*,*2*

Astyanax, *or* Scamandrius – king of the city, 168 *passim*

Astydameia – tamer of cities, 110.*c*; 138.*h*; 142.*e*; 143.*i*

Astynome – lawgiver of the city, 162.*l*

Astyocha, Astyoche – possessor of the city, 110.*g*; 141.*g*; 142.*e*; 158.*g*,*l*; 160.*z*; 162.*e*; 166.*i*

Astypalaea – ancient city, 137.*p*

Asvins, 16.6

Atabyrius – (*non-Greek word*), 67.1; 93.1

Atalanta – unswaying, 80 *passim*; 141.*d*; 148.*i*; 152.*i*

Athamas – reaper on high, 24.*3*; 27.*a*; 70 *passim*; 151.*f*; 157.*d*; 169.5

Athene – ? *inversion of* Anatha, Sumerian – Queen of Heaven, 4.*b*; 5.*a*; 8 *passim*; 9.*d*,1,2,4,5,6; 16.*c*,*d*,*e*,3,4; 17.3; 18.*l*; 19.*b*; 21.*e*,9; 22.7; 23.1; 25 *passim*; 30.*b*; 33.*b*,5; 35.*b*; 39.*g*,1,10; 50.*e*,2,3,6,7; 58.*g*; 66.*g*; 70.7; 73.*f*,*h*; 75.*c*,3; 89.4; 97.4; 105.*g*; 106.*j*; 114.*b*,*m*,*n*,2,4; 115 *passim*; 116.*h*,*i*,1; 119.*a*; 124.*d*; 128.1; 134.*c*,*g*; 139.*b*,*e*,1; 141.*b*,*c*,1; 142.1; 143.*g*; 145.*h*; 148.*h*; 158.*e*,*i*,*k*; 159 *passim*; 160 *p*; 165.*c*; 167 *passim*; 168.*f*,*g*,2; 170 *passim*; 171 *passim*

Alalcomeneïs – guardian, 5.1

Alea – she who grinds, 141.*a*,1

Apaturia – guardian of deceits, 95.*d*

Chryse – golden, 161.*j*

Colocasia – of the red water-lily, 111.*h*

Coronis – of the raven, *or* crow, 25.5

Girder-on-of-Arms, 121.*e*,5

Goatish, 50.6

Itone – of the willow, 88.7

of the Just Deserts, 140.*d*

Laphria – despoiler, 9.2

Mother, 138.*g*,6

Narcaea – benumbing, 110.*b*,1

Onga – (*Phoenician word*), 58.*f*

Polias – of the city, 47.4; 48.*b*,1

Sciras – of the parasol, 96.*i*

Warlike, 115.*a*

Atlas – he who dares, *or* suffers, 1.*d*; 7.*d*,*e*; 33.*d*,7; 39 *passim*; 41.*e*; 73.*i*; 77.1; 108.*b*,4; 125.1; 130.*a*; 133 *passim*

Atreus – fearless, 106.2; 109.*q*; 110.*c*,*g*,*h*; 111 *passim*; 112.*a*,*b*,*e*,*g*; 117.*a*.2; 118.*a*; 146.*d*; 161.*d*

Atropos – she who cannot be turned, 10 *passim*; 60.2; 66.*k*

Atthis – ? *actes thea*, goddess of the rugged coast, 94.*f*,1

Attis – (*non-Greek word*), 79.1; 105.6

Atymnius – insatiate of heroic praise, 88.*b*; 89.9

Atys – ? short for *atchyes*, luckless, 136.*g*

Auge – radiance, 141 *passim*

Augeias – bright ray, 90.3; 122.*c*; 127 *passim*; 134.9; 138 *passim*; 139.*e*; 141.*b*; 148.*i*; 152.*b*,*d*

Autolycus – very wolf, 17.*j*; 67.*b*,*c*,1; 119.*f*; 135.*b*; 151.*d*; 160.*c*; 167.*d*; 170.10; 171.5

Autolyte – stampede, 43.*g*

Automedon – independent ruler, 16*a*.

Automedusa – cunning itself, 101.*e*

Autonoë – with a mind of her own, 82.*e*

Auxo – increase, 13.3

Avanc, 148.5

Ay-Mari, 131.3; 151.3

Azan – land of Zeus, 64.*c*
Azeus – temple servant, 121.*f*

Baal, 30.4; 60.1; 170.3
Bacche – raging, 27.*b*
Balius – piebald, 81.*m*,4; 163.*m*
Banbha, 24.3
Bateia – of the bramble, 158.*c*
Baton – blackberry, 106.*k*,5
Battus – tongue-tied, 82.1
Baubo – soother, 24.*d*,*g*
Baucis – over-modest, 41.5
Bel, 1.3; 4.5; 60.1; 73.7; 103.1,2
Belili, 4.5; 60.1; 86.2
Bellerophon – ? *beleëphoron*, bearing
    darts, 67.4; 70.2; 73.5; 75 *passim*;
    95.*d*
Beltis, 1.3
Belus – *baal*, lord, 56.*b*,3; 58.*a*; 60 *pas-
    sim*; 61.*a*; 65.*a*; 165.*k*
Benthesicyme – wave of the deep,
    16.*b*,1; 47.*c*
Beroe – ? *pheroë*, she who brings eggs,
    18.*k*
Bia – force, 8.3
Biadice – justice by force, 70.*d*,*f*,2
Bias – force, 68.*f*; 72 *passim*; 94.*c*
Biton – *bison*, wild ox, 84 *passim*
Blathnat, 91.1
Blodeuwedd, 91.1; 112.1
Boeotus – herdsman, 43 *passim*
Boreas – North Wind, *or* devouring,
    1.*a*,2; 12.5; 25.5; 47.*c*,4; 48 *passim*;
    63.3; 96.6; 109.*d*; 137.*m*,*o*,5; 138.5;
    150.*j*,4; 154.*e*
Borimus, 150.*e*,1
Bormus – plaintive, 150.*e*,*f*,1
Bran, 6.2; 28.1,6; 50.1; 57.1; 120.1;
    134.1; 138.4; 146.2; 170.8
Branchus – hoarse, 96.*j*,5
Branwen, 25.5
Breseus – he who prevails, 162.*j*
Brian, 24.3; 132.5
Briareus – strong, 3.*b*,1; 13.*c*,1; 131.
    g.2; 132.*h*
Brigit, 21.4; 23.1

Brimo – raging one, 24.6; 105.1; 105.1
Brimus – raging one, 24.6; 150.1
Briseis – she who prevails, 162.*h*,*j*,6,8;
    163 *passim*
Britomartis – good maiden, 89.*a*,*b*,2
Brizo – charmer, *or* soother, 21.4
Bromie – roaring, 27.*b*
Brontes – thunderj 3.*b*,2; 21.*d*; 22.*d*,5
Broteas – gory, 108 *passim*
Budeia – goddess of oxen, 121.*a*
Bunomus – ox-grazing, 159.*v*
Bunus – hill, 156.*b*
Busiris – grave of Osiris, 132.*f*; 133.*k*;
    134.6
Butes – herdsman, 18.*k*; 46.*a*,3; 47.
    a,*b*,1,4; 50.5; 102.*c*; 132.*q*; 148.*i*;
    154.*d*
Buzyge – ox yoker, 121.*a*

Cabeiri – (*non-Greek word*), 149.*d*,*e*,3
Cacus – bad, 132.*l*,*m*,6; 134.7,8
Cadmus – from the east, 14.*c*,5; 24.*a*;
    27.6; 36.*d*; 52.*a*,*c*; 58 *passim*; 59 *pas-
    sim*; 67.6; 76.*c*; 105.*i*; 106.*m*; 132.*o*;
    152.*e*,*g*
Caeneus – new, 78 *passim*; 80.*c*; 102.
    c,*e*; 143.*d*,4; 148.*k*
Caenis – new, 78 *passim*
Calais – of changeful hue, 48.*c*; 148.*i*;
    150 *passim*; 155.*i*
Calchas – brazen, 160 *passim*; 161 *pas-
    sim*; 162.*h*; 163.*b*; 165 *passim*; 166.
    a,*g*; 167 *passim*; 168 *passim*; 169
    passim
Cale – fair, 13.3; 105.*h*
Caleb, 88.3
Callidice – fair justice, 171.*k*
Callileon – handsome lion, 11.*g*
Calliope – fair face, 18.*i*,7; 28.*a*; 147.*b*;
    160.*i*; 163.*g*
Callipolis – fair city, 110.*e*,*z*
Callirrhoë – fair flowing, 107 *passim*;
    132.*a*; 158.*g*; 169.*k*
Callisto – fairest, 22.*h*,4; 72.*i*
Calus – fair, 92.*c*
Calybe – cabin, 158.*l*

Calyce – rosebud, *or* ear-ring, 64.*a*; 161.*g*

Calypso – hidden, *or* hider, 170 *passim*

Cameira – sharer out, 42.4; 54.1; 60.2; 93.2

Cameiro – sharer-out, 108.*f*,9

Campe – crooked, 7.*e*

Canache – barking, 43.*h*,4

Candaon – ? shining, 41.*d*

Canethus – [dedicated to] the Basket-goddess, 96.*f*

Canthus – pack ass, 148.*i*; 154.*f*

Capaneus – charioteer, 50.*f*; 106 *passim*; 160.*r*

Caphaurus – camphor, 154.*f*,7

Capys – gulper, *or* snatcher, 137.*g*; 158.*l*; 167.*e*

Car – (non-Greek word), 1.5; 7.4; 57.*a*.2; 82.6; 86.1,2; 95.5

Cardea, 34.3

Cardis – ? Cardian Zeus, 138.*m*

Carius, 57.2

Carmanor – servant of the Moon-goddess Car, 18.7; 21.*b*; 90.*b*; 136.*b*,1

Carmenta – Car the wise, 52.*a*,5; 86.2; 132.0,6

Carnus – trumpet, 146.*k*

Carpo – withering, 13.2

Carya – nut-tree, 86 *passim*

Caryatis – of the nut-tree, 57.2

Cassandra – she who entangles men, 90.5; 112 *passim*; 158 *passim*; 166.*i*; 167 *passim*; 168 *passim*

Cassiopeia – cassia-juice, 73 *passim*; 88.*b*

Castor – beaver, 62.*c*,1; 74 *passim*; 80.*c*; 84.1; 103.*a*,3; 113.*d*; 119.*f*; 148.*i*

Catreus – *catarrhoös*, down-flowing, 90.*a*,*b*,1; 93 *passim*; 111.*f*; 159.*j*; 171.3

Caucon – ? croaker, 138.*h*

Cecrops – *cercops*, face with a tail, 16.*c*; 24.4; 25.*c*,*d*,5; 38.1; 43.*b*; 47.*b*; 94 *passim*

Cedalion – he who takes charge of sailors, 41.*b*

Celaeno – swarthy, 159.*q*

Celeus – caller; *hence*: sorcerer, *or* woodpecker, 24.*e*,*l*,5,10; 47.*c*; 56.2

Celmis – smelting, 53.*c*,2

Cenchrias – spotted serpent, 67.4

Centaurs – (*see* Centaurus), 7.7; 50.5; 63.3; 81.*h*,*l*,4; 92.10; 102 *passim*; 126 *passim*; 134.*a*,8; 143.3

Centaurus – ? one hundred strong, 63.*d*,3

Cephalus – head, 23.1; 25.*d*; 40.*b*,2; 47.*b*; 89 *passim*; 118.*b*

Cepheus – *cepeus*, gardener, 60.*a*; 73 *passim*; 80.*c*,*d*; 140.*b*,*c*; 141.*a*; 148.*i*

Cephissus, R. – river of gardens, 16.*e*; 24.*l*; 85.*a*

Cer – fate, *or* doom, 82.6

Cerambus – horned beetle, 38.*e*,11

Cerberus – ? *ker berethrou*, demon of the pit, 28.*c*; 31.*a*,3,7; 34 *passim*; 97.*c*; 103.*c*; 108.7; 132.4; 134 *passim*; 139.*c*; 151.*c*

Cercopes – faces with tails, 136 *passim*

Cercyon – boar's tail, 49.*a*,*b*; 96.*j*,3,5

Cercysera – distaff wielder, 160.*j*

Cerdo – gain, *or* weasel, *or* vixen, 24.7; 57.*a*,1; 118.5

Ceryz – herald, 25.*d*; 47.*f*

Ceto – sea monster, 33.*b*,*g*,2,7; 133.*b*

Ceuthonymus – hidden name, 134.*d*

Ceyz – sea-mew, 45 *passim*; 142.*g*; 143 *passim*, 144.*a*; 146.*a*

Chaerias – welcomer, 142.*g*

Chalciope – brazen face, 95.*a*; 137.*p*,*r*; 151.*f*; 152.*c*,*d*,*f*

Chalcodon – brazen path, 100.*d*; 104.*f*; 137.*p*

Chalion – ? *chaliphron*, thoughtless, 164.*e*

Chaos – yawning, 1.*a*; 3.*a*; 4.*a*,*c*; 11.1

Chariboea – grace of cattle, 167.*i*

Charis – grace, 13.3

Charites – graces, 13.*a*,3; 105.*h*,5

Charon – fierce brightness, 28.*c*; 31.*a*; 134.*c*

Charybdis – sucker down, 148.*1,9*; 154.*11*; 170.*t,v,1,9*

Cheimarrhus – torrent, 75.*d,6*

Cheiron – hand, 43.*c*; 50.*c,e,g,5*; 63.*d*; 81 *passim*; 82 *passim*; 126 *passim*; 133.*l*; 148.*b,e,2*; 151.*g,5*; 156.*e*; 160.*i,l*

Chem, 73.*8*

Chiade – snowflakes, 77.*1*

Chimaera – she-goat, 17.*j*; 34 *passim*; 73.*5*; 75 *passim*; 105.*e*; 123.*b,1*

Chimaerus – he-goat, 159.*q*

Chione – snowqueen, 47.*c*; 48.*c*; 67.*b*

Chlidanope – delicate face, 82.*a*

Chloris – greenish, 68.*f*; 77.*b*; 110.*a*; 170.*o*

Chnas, 58.*1*

Choere – sow, 24.*7*

Chon, 118.*2*

Chromia – embellisher, 64.*a*

Chrysaor – golden falchion, 33.*b,5*; 73.*h*; 132.*a,f,4*

Chryse – golden, 158.*b*; 161.*j*

Chryseis – golden, 116.*h*; 162.*l,6,8*; 163.*b*

Chryses – golden, 116.*h*; 131.*e*; 148.*j*; 153.*3*; 162.*l,8*; 163.*b,f*; 166.*g*

Chrysippus – golden horse, 29.*1*; 105.*e,2*; 110 *passim*; 111.*a*

Chrysothemis – golden order, 112.*d,1*; 113.*e,n,3,7*; 160.*t,7*

Chthonia – of the soil, 47.*b*

Chthonius – of the soil, 58.*g,5*

Chylus – juice of a plant, *or* berry, 50.*c,2*

Cilix – ? *cillix*, an ox with crooked horns, 58.*a,d,1*; 88.*d*

Cilla – she-ass, *or* dice made from ass's bone, 158.*l*; 159.*g,5*; 168.*d*

Cillus, Cillas, Cellas – ass, 109.*g,i,7*

Cinyras – plaintive cry, 18.*h,5,7*; 65.*a,1*; 77.*2*; 160.*g,11,12*

Circe – falcon, 28.*5*; 42.*3*; 56.*2*; 89.*e,5*; 132.*p*; 148.*3,9*; 152.*b*; 153 *passim*; 154.*b*; 170 *passim*; 171.*k.4*

Circinus – the circular, 92.*c,9*

Cisseis – ivy woman, 168.*3*

Cisseus – of the ivy, 158.*0*; 168.*3,5*

Cissia – ivy, 164.*c,2,3*

Cleia – famous, 27.*2*

Cleisithyra – locker of the door, 169.*l*

Cleite – renowned, 149.*f,g*

Cleitonymus – famous name, 160.*m*

Cleitus – renowned, 40.*b*

Cleobis – *cleo-bios*, famous life, 84 *passim*, 159.*4*

Cleobule – famous counsel, 109.*f*; 160.*l*

Cleodaeus – famous warrior, 136.*g*

Cleodice – famous justice, 125.*c*

Cleola – wholly famous, 111.*f*

Cleolaus – famous people, 136.*g*

Cleomenes – famous strength, 159.*4*

Cleon – famous, 110.*c*

Cleopatra – glory to her father, 45.*2*; 48.*c*; 74.*a*; 80.*d,i*; 150.*l*; 158.*g*

Cleothera – noble beauty, 108.*f*

Clete – chosen, *or* invoked, 164.*b,1*

Clio – proclaimer, 147.*b*

Clotho – spinner, 10 *passim*, 60.*2*; 108.*h*

Clymene – famous might, 39.*a*; 42.*d*; 80.*c*; 93.*a,c*; 109.*f*; 111.*f*; 112.*f*; 170.*o*

Clymeneus, *or* Clymenus – famous might, 64.*a*; 111.*p,5*; 121.*a*; 138.*m*

Clytaemnestra – ? praiseworthy wooing, 62.*c*; 74.*b*; 112 *passim*; 113 *passim*; 114 *passim*; 117.*5*; 159.*c*; 160.*z*; 161 *passim*; 162.*t*

Clytia – famous, 108.*b*

Clytië – famous, 108.*f*

Clytius – famous, 35.*e*; 135.*b*; 158.*l*

Cocalus – spiral shell, 92.*h,12*

Coeus – intelligent, 1.*d*; 14.*a,2*; 133.*3*

Comaetho – bright hair, 72.*5*; 89.*1.7*; 91.*1*

Cometes – long-haired, 117.*h*; 148.*i*; 162.*t*; 169.*k*

Connidas – knowing man from Mt Ida, 95.*f*

Copreus – dung man, 110.*c*; 123.*g*; 127.*d,i*; 135.*e*; 163.*h*

Cordelia, 73.*2*

Core – maiden, 24 *passim*; 27.*11*; 76.*1*
    78.*1*; 96.*i*; 132.*s*; 134.*b*; 136.*4*;
    170.*q*

Corinthius – club man, 110.*c*

Corinthus – club man, 96.*b*; 148.*6*;
    156.*b*,*4*

Coroebus – ? feaster on ox chine,
    147.*a*,*3*

Coronea – of the crows, 70.*i*

Coronis – crow, *or* raven
    mother of Asceplius, 21.*i*,*9*; 47.*4*;
    50.*p*,*m*
    the Hyad, 27.*2*

Coronus – crow, *or* raven, 50.*1*; 78.*a*;
    143.*d*; 148.*i*

Corunetes – cudgel man, 96.*a*

Corybantes – crested dancers, 20.*i*,*5*;
    30.*a*,*1*

Corythus – helmeted, 141.*d*; 158.*f*;
    159.*v*; 160.*w*

Cottus – son of Cotytto, 3.*b*,*1*

Cotytto – (*non-Greek word*), 3.*1*; 27.*2*,*3*

Cranaë – rocky, 94.*1*

Cranaechme – rocky point, 94.*1*

Cranaus – rocky, 94.*f*

Cratus – strength, 8.*3*

Creiddylad, 73.*2*

Creon – ruler, 105.*k*; 106.*k*,*l*,*m*,*7*;
    107.*i*; 118.*b*,*3*; 121.*c*; 122.*a*; 135.*e*;
    156 *passim*

Cresphontes – stronger slayer, 146.*k*

Cressida – *chryseis*, golden, 162.*8*

Cresus – Cretan, 100.*g*,*1*

Crete – *crataie*, strong, *or* ruling, god-
    dess, 88.*e*,*1*

Creteus – ruler, 88.*1*

Cretheis – ruler, 70.*2*; 81.*g*,*q*,*5*

Cretheus – ruler, 68.*e*,*f*; 70.*d*; 88.*a*,*1*;
    148.*a*

Creusa – sovereign being
    mother of Ion, 43.*b*; 44.*a*,*1*; 47.*b*
    Naiad, 82.*a*
    daughter of Priam, 158.*o*

Crimissus, R. – ? (*Cretan word*), 137.*g*

Cristinobyl, *Empress of*, 148.*5*

Cronus – crow, 1.*d*; 6 *passim*; 7 *passim*;
    11.*b*; 12.*a*; 16.*a*,*f*; 25.*4*; 28.*1*;

30.*a*,*3*; 31.*c*,*2*,*6*; 39.*e*; 51.*k*,*6*; 53.
    5,*6*; 54.*a*; 57.*1*; 84.*2*; 105.*5*; 108.*a*;
    109.*2*; 111.*4*; 118.*c*; 129.*2*; 132.*e*.*4*,
    5,*6*; 134.*1*; 138.*i*,*0*,*4*; 139.*1*; 151.*g*;
    164.*5*; 170.*5*,*8*

Croton – dog tick, 132.*t*

Crotopus – thumping foot, 147.*a*,*1*

Crotus – rhythmic beat, 26.*d*; 126.*g*

Cteatus – he who gains possession,
    138.*a*

Ctesippus – possessor of horses, 142.*l*;
    143.*i*

Cuchulain, 63.*3*; 75.*5*; 91.*1*; 103.*1*;
    132.*1*; 162.*8*; 164.*3*

Curetes – young men who have
    shaved their hair, 7.*c*,*1*,*4*; 22.*6*;
    30.*a*,*1*,*3*; 53.*b*; 90.*d*; 95.*5*; 97.*1*;
    158.*b*

Curissia – dirge, 167.*l*

Curoi, 63.*2*; 91.*1*; 162.*8*

Cyamites – son of a bean, 24.*l*

Cyathus – wine-cup, 142.*h*,*4*

Cybele, she of the hair, *or* she with the
    axe, 18.*3*; 21.*e*,*f*; 29.*3*; 80.*l*; 158.*4*

Cybosurus – square bucket, 110.*c*

Cychreus – ? *cichoreus*, of the endive,
    81.*c*,*d*,*6*

Cyclopes – ring-eyed, 3.*b*,*2*; 6.*a*,*b*;
    7.*e*; 21.*n*; 22.*d*; 31.*e*; 41.*2*; 73.*b*,*p*,*r*;
    170 *passim*

Cycnus – swan
    son of Apollo, 123.*t*,*1*
    son of Ares, 133.*d*; 134.*7*; 143 *pas-
    sim*; 161.*4*
    son of Poseidon, 161 *passim*; 162.*f*;
    164.*j*

Cydon – glory, 90.*a*

Cylarabes – ? *cyclarabes*, with rattling
    chariot wheels, 122.*a*; 117.*c*

Cyllene – crooked queen, 17.*a*,*b*

Cyllenius – devoted to the crooked
    queen, 131.*9*

Cyrene – sovereign queen, *or* mistress
    of the bridle, 21.*i*; 82 *passim*; 130.*a*;
    155.*4*

Cyrianassa – queen of the chieftains,
    72.*g*

Cytisorus – clover season, 70.*m*; 148.*8*; 151.*f*; 152.*d,f*; 157.*d*

Cyzicus – exalted, 82.4; 149 *passim*

Dactyls – fingers, 53 *passim*; 131.9; 132.4; 164.6

Daedalus – bright, *or* cunningly wrought, 18.3; 81.*h*; 82.*j*; 88.*e,f,1,7*; 92 *passim*; 94.*b*; 96.*1,3*; 98.*k,r,u,3,5*; 122.*c*

Damarmenus – subduer of sails, 166.2

Damasen – subduer, 90.8

Dam-kina, 60.3; 93.1; 146.4

Damnameneus – compeller, *i.e.* hammer, 53.*c,2*

Damysus – conqueror, 81.*r*; 160.*h*

Dan, 60.3

Danaë – she who judges, *or* parched, 42.4; 43.2; 60.3; 73 *passim*; 93.1; 146.4

Danaids, 16.*e*; 54.1; 60 *passim*, 68.1; 124.*b,3*

Danaus – *Dan*, judge, *or* son of Danaë, 1.2; 53.3; 56.3; 60 *passim*; 73.*a*; 109.*b*; 124.*b*; 146.4

Daphne – laurel, 21.*k,l,b*; 107.*c,1*

Daphnis – laurel, 17.*j*,5; 51.*b,2*; 136.*e*

Daphoene – bloody one, 21.6

Daphoenissa – bloody one, 51.2

Dardanus – ? from *dar-daio*, burner-up, 24.*a*; 48.*e*; 158 *passim*

Dascylus – little pointer, 131.*e,h,9*; 151.*c*

Daunus – sleeper, 169.*k*

David, 82.4; 110.2

Dechtire, 162.8

Deianeira – stringer-together of spoil, 118.2; 134.*c*; 138.*c*; 142 *passim*; 144.*a*; 145 *passim*

Deidameia – taker of spoil, 53.7; 102.*c*; 160.*j,y*

Deileon – spoil-taking lion, 151.*d*

Deimachus – battle spoil, 137.*h,n*

Deimas – fearful, 158.*b*

Deimus – fearful, 18.*a*

Deino – terrible, 33.*c*.5

Deinus – terrible, 130.*a*

Deion – despoiler, 148.*i*

Deione – queen of spoil, 88.*b*

Deioneus – son of the queen of spoil, 63.1; 96.*c*

Deiphilus – lover of spoil, 149.*c*; 168.*l*

Deiphobus – scaring the spoiler, 135.*c*; 158.0; 159.0; 164.*k*; 166.*f*; 167.*k*; 168.*b*

Deipyla, *or* Deipyle – hostile gates, 106.*a,c*; 160.*r*

Deliades – son of Delian Apollo, 75.*a*

Delilah, 91.1; 145.4

Delphinus – dolphin, 16.*b,1*

Delphyne – womb, 21.*a,3*; 36 *passim*

Demeter – barley-mother, 7.*a,8*; 14.*b,4*; 16.*f,5,6*; 24 *passim*; 31.6; 33.4; 51.*e*; 60.*f*; 72.4; 81.*d*; 85.1; 88.9; 94.*f*; 96.*i*; 97.2; 102.*f*; 108.*c,h,5,6*; 121.3; 134 *passim*; 143.1; 154.1; 157.1; 170.*q*

   Eleusinian, 140.*a*

   Erinnys – the fury, 16.6

   Europe – broadfaced, 51.*i*

   Lernaean, 124.*b*

   Mare-headed, 16.5; 19.2; 46.3; 48.2; 75.3; 108.5

   Subterrene, 28.*h*

Demonassa – queen of the people, 145.*f*

Demophon – voice of the people, 86.1; 131.*11*; 146.*b*; 168.*e,j*; 169 *passim*

Demophoön – light of the people, 24.*d,e,10*; 100.*h*; 101.*a*; 114.*l*

Dendrites – tree youth, 27.2

Derceto – (*non-Greek word,*) 89.2; 154.6

Dercynus – *decreynus*, sleeping with open eyes, 132.*k*

Desmontes – *desmentes*, gaoler, 43.*c,d,f*

Despoena – mistress, 16.*f*,5

Deucalion – new-wine sailor

   father of Idomeneus, 160.*n*

   son of Minos, 98.3; 100.*h*; 104.*f*

   husband of Pyrrha, 27.6; 38 *passim*; 39.2

Dexamenus, entertainer, 127.*f*; 131.*b,c*

Dia – of the sky, 63.*a,1,2*; 102.*a,3*; 143.*c*

Diana, 7.1

Diarmuid, 18.7

Dias – bright, 110.*c*

Dictynna – she of the fishing-nets, 89.*b*,2,4; 154.6; 160.10

Dictys – net, 73.*c,o,p*

Didaeon – ? experienced, 135.*b*

Dinah, 60.3

Diocles – glory of Zeus, 24.*l*,5

Diodorus – gift of Zeus, 133.*i*

Diomedes – god-like cunning
of Argos, 70.1; 109.*f*; 159.*a*; 160.*n,r*,2; 162 *passim*; 163 *passim*; 164 *passim*; 166 *passim*; 167 *passim*; 168 *passim*; 169 *Passim*

(Jason), 148 *passim*; 152.1

King of Thrace, 82.*c*; 121.4; 130 *passim*; 134.8; 153.*e*

Dione – divine queen, 1.*d*; 7.1; 11.*b*,2; 14.*b*,4; 108.*b*

Dionysius – lame god, 14 *passim*; 18.*e*,8; 27 *passim*; 28.*d*,2,3; 30.3; 35.*e,h*,1; 38.*h*,3; 70.*g,h*,4; 72.*g*,5; 76.*b*; 79.*a*,2; 82.*k*; 83 *passim*; 86.*b*; 87.*a*; 88.7; 90.*b*; 98.*n,o,s,w*,6,9; 110.*b*; 123.1; 126.*b*; 134.*b*,2,4; 136.*j*; 142.*a*; 148.6; 160.*u*

Bromius – raging, 27.7,9

Cretan, 98.6

of the Marshes, 99.*c*

Plutodotes – giver of wealth, 129.1,2

Sabazius – breaker in pieces, 27.7,9

Saviour, 124.*b*

Dioscuri – sons of Zeus, 74 *passim*; 103.*a,b*; 112.*c*; 113.7; 114.4; 116.*e*; 150.*a*; 159 *passim*

Dirce – *dicre*, cleft, *or* double, 68.2; 76 *passim*; 135.*e*

Dog-star – *see* Orthrus, Sirius

Dolon – ensnarer, 163.*g*

Dolophion – cunning native snake, 166.*b*

Dorippe – gift mare, 160.*u*,7

Doris – bountiful, 33.*a*,2

Dorus – gift, 21.*i*; 43.*b*,1; 64.*c*; 88.*a*,1

Drapaudi, 135.1

Dryads – oak-nymphs, 82.*i*; 86.2

Dryas – oak, 27.*e*,3; 46.*c,d*,2

Dryope – woodpecker, 21.*j*; 26.5; 56.2; 150.*b*,1

Dryops – oak face, 21.7; 143 *passim*

Dylan, 105.1

Dymas – ? *dynamis*, powerful, 158.*o*

Dysaules – of the unlucky house, 24.*e*

Dysponteus – rough sea, 109.*c*

Ea, 6.6; 39.8

Eabani, 4.2

Earth, Mother, 3.*a*,1; 4.*a*; 6.*a*; 7.*a,e*; 13.4; 15.*a*; 20.2; 21 *passim*; 25,*b,d*; 33.*d,g*; 36.*a*; 41.*d,f*; 43.2; 51.*b,f*,2,4; 78.1; 83,3; 88.*b*; 99.*c*; 100.*f*; 113.*g*; 115.*d*; 133.*a,b,g,h*; 143.*g*; 154.3; 170.*t*

Echedemus – he who holds the people, 104.*b*

Echemus – ? *echemythos*, taciturn, 146.*e*

Echenus – rein holder, 132.*o*

Echephron – possessed of intelligence, 132.*r*

Echetus – man of substance, 154.*a*

Echidne – she-viper, 33.*b,e*,1; 34 *passim*; 60.*h*; 75.*b*; 96.*e*; 105.*e*; 124.*a*; 132.*a*; 133.*b,l*; 170.*t*

Echion – viper, 17.*j*,3; 58.*g*,5; 148.*i*; 149.*b*; 167.*m*

Echo – echo, 26.*d*; 56.*a*; 85 *passim*

Eëtion – terrible native, 162.*i,l*,7

Egeria – *aegeiria*, of the black poplar, 101.*l*,1

Eidothea – divine shape, 169.*a*

Eidyia – knowledgeable, 152.*c,d*

Eileithyia – she who comes to aid women in childbed, 15.*a*; 118.*e,g*; 138.*o*; 141.*c*

Eioneus – with high banks, 63.*a*,1; 102.*a*,3; 163.*g*

Eire, 24.3

El, 27.12

Elais – of the olive, 160.*u*

Elaphios – hindlike, 125.1

Elate – fir-tree, 26.2; 78.1

Elatus – of the fir, *or* lofty, 50.b,5; 78.a,1; 126.c; 148.i

Electra – amber
daughter of Agamemnon, 122.d,1; 113 *passim*; 114 *passim*; 166.i,1; 117.a,b,5; 168.l
wife of Corythus, 158.f
Ocean-nymph, 33.g,2
daughter of Oedipus, 59.b
Pleiad, 41.6; 158.b,i,k

Electryo – beaming, 42.c,4

Electryon – beaming, 118.a,b

Eleius – the Elean, 127.a,1

Elpenor – man's hope
son of Chalcodon, 104.f
comrade of Odysseus, 170 *passim*

Elphame, Queen of, 170.2

Elphenor – man's deceit, 169.n

Elymus – quiver, 137.g

Empusae – forcers-in, 55 *passim*; 61.a,1; 64.2

Enalus – child of the sea, 87.c,2

Enarephorus – spoil winner, 103.b

Enarete – virtuous, 43.h,4; 68.a

Enceladus – buzzing, 35.f,h

Endeis – entangler, 66.h; 81.a,1; 96.g

Endor, Witch of, 51.2

Endymion – seduced native, 40.c; 64 *passim*, 138.m

Enkidu, 118.2; 132.1; 142.3

Ennomus – lawful, 142.g

Entella – commanding, 137.g

Enyo – war-like, 33.c,5

Enyues – war-like, 88.h

Eos – dawn, 29.c,1; 35.b; 40 *passim*; 41.b,c,d; 42.a; 89.c,d,f,j; 164.g,h,4; 170.6

Epaphus – a touching, 56.b,c,3; 133.k

Epeius – successor, *or* assaulter, 64.b,3; 89.10; 109.n; 163.n; 167 *passim*

Epheseus – appetite, 100.g

Ephialtes – he who leaps upon, i.e. nightmare, 35.d,3; 37 *passim*

Ephron, 88.3

Epicaste – ? worn-down form of *epi-*

catastrephomene, upsetting over, 111.p

Epidaurus – ? *epidaulos*, shaggy, 110.c

Epigoni – those born afterwards, 107 *passim*; 169.k

Epimedes – he who thinks too late, 53.b,1

Epimetheus – afterthought, 38.c; 39 *passim*; 169.3

Epistrophus – tacking, 162.j

Epopeus – he who sees all, 156.4

Erato – passionate, 27.b

Ercwlf, 132.3

Erebus – the covered [pit], 4.a; 10.a

Erechtheus – ? he who hastens over the heather, *or* shatterer, 25.2,7; 43.b; 44.b; 46.a,3; 47 *passim*; 49.a,1,3; 92.a,1; 94.a; 95.3; 96.i,4; 99.b

Erginus – confiner, 84.b; 121 *passim*; 148.i

Eriboea – rich in cattle, 37.b,d; 98.i

Eriecpaius – feeder upon heather, 2.b,2

Erichthonius – wool on the earth, *or* much earth, *or* from the land of the heather, 25.c,d,e,1,2; 48.e,3; 50. e,1,6; 105.g; 158.g,h,2

Erigone – child of strife, *or* plentiful offspring, 79 *passim*; 88.10; 92.12; 98.5; 106.2; 114.m, n, 6; 117.a,b,2

Erinnyes – angry one, 4.a; 6.a,3; 18.4; 31.g; 32.3,4; 33.g; 80.i; 85.1; 103.e; 105.k,6; 107.d,f; 108.f; 113.f,5,7; 114 *passim*; 115 *passim*; 116.a,e,1; 117.1; 137.m; 164.a; 165.e; 169.g

Eriopis – large-eyed, *or* very rich, 156.e,2; 160.q.

Eripha – kid, 109.e

Eriphus – kid, 27.2

Eriphyle – tribal strife, 106.e; 107 *passim*; 113.6; 115.4; 170.0

Eris – strife, 12.c,2; 19.a; 81.n,d; 102 c.e; 111.e,2; 159.e

Eros – erotic love, 2.b; 15 *passim*; 35.d,1; 152.a,e,2; 159.m,q

Erymanthus – divining by lots, 126. a.1

Erysichthon – earth-tearer, 24.b,4

Erytheia – red land, 132.5

Erytheis – crimson, 33.d

Erythrus – red, 88.h,2

Eryx – heather, 18.k; 132.q.6

Esau, 73.2

Esmun – (Semitic word), he whom we evoke, 21.3; 133.11

Etana, 29.2

Eteocles – true glory, 69.1; 105.k; 106 passim

Eteoclus – true glory, 106.f

Euachme – goodly spear, 110.d

Euanthes – flowering, 27.i,8; 88.h

Euarete – most virtuous, 109.c

Eubule – good counsel, 97.h,2

Eubuleus – good counsel, 24.f,7; 96. 2.4; 97.2

Eudore – generous, 27.2

Eueres – ? well-fitted, 141.c

Euippe – goodly mare, 43.c,2; 50.g; 169.k

Euippus – goodly stallion, 100.d,f

Eumaeus – of good endeavour, 24.7; 171 passim

Eumelus – sweet melody, 163.g; 164.

Eumenides – kindly ones, 31.g

Eumolpus – good melody, 24.f,l,5,7; 47 passim; 48.c; 100.d; 119.g; 134.a

Euneus – of the couch, 100.b; 148.12; 149.c,e,1; 162.i; 166.b

Eunoë – good intelligence, 158.o

Eunomus – orderly, 142.g,4

Eupalamus – inventor, 94.b

Eupheme – religious silence, 26.d

Euphemus – religious silence, 143.a; 148.i; 149.1; 151.a; 154.g; 155.i

Euphorbus – good pasture, 162.b; 163.j,k

Euphrosyne – good cheer, 105.h,5

Europe – broad face, or well watered (Aerope), 111.f
  sister of Cadmus, 58 passim; 88.a; 89.2; 90.3; 101.d; 160.a

Eurotas – fair flowing, 125.c,3

Euryle – wide wandering, or of the broad threshing floor, 33.b,3; 73.f,h

Eurylas – wide wanderer, 148.i; 160.r

Euryanassa – wide-ruling queen, 108. b,j

Eurybatus – wide walker, 136.c

Eurybia – wide strength, 33.g,1,2

Eurybius – long life, 134.i; 146.c

Eurybius – broad fame, 171 passim

Eurydamas – wide taming, 148.i

Eurydice – wide justice
  daughter of Adrastus, 158.l
  sister of Hyacinthus, 125.c
  wife of Orpheus, 28 passim; 33.1; 82.h,i
  daughter of Pelops, 110.c

Eurygyes – wide-circling, 90.1

Eurylochus – extensive ambush, 81.d
  comrade of Odysseus, 170 passim

Eurymachus – wide battler, 171 passim

Eurymedon – wide rule, 1.d; 39.a; 131.e

Eurymedusa – the being of wide cunning, 66.g

Eurynome – wide wandering, or wide rule, 1.a.1; 2.1; 13.a,3; 23.a,1; 33.1; 40.2; 47.2; 48.1; 66.a,1; 93.1

Eurynomus – wide wandering, or wide rule, 142.g

Euryphaessa – wide shining, 42.a,1

Eurypylus – broad cuirass, or wide gate, 72.5; 134.i; 137.p
  son of Telephus, 160.x; 163.h; 164.a; 166.i

Eurysaces – broad shield, 165 passim

Eurysthenes – wide strength, 146.k

Eurystheus – forcing strongly back far and wide, 28.6; 104.j; 110.c; 118. e,3; 122.e; 123.f,g; 124.a,g; 125.b; 126.d,f; 127.a,d,e; 129 passim; 130. a,c; 131.a,j; 133.f; 134.i; 135.a; 138.d,f,j; 143.b; 146 passim

Eurythemista – wide ordering, 108.b

Eurthoë – of wide activity, 109.b

Eurytion – widely honoured, 80.c,g; 81.f,p; 102.d,e,2; 126.c; 127.f; 132 a,d; 142.5
  Centaur, 138.c,1

Eurytus – full-flowing, 35.*e*; 102.*d*;
119.*f*; 135 *passim*; 136.*a*,1; 138.*a*;
144 *passim*; 171.*h*
son of Augeias, 138.*e*

Euterpe – rejoicing well, 163.*g*

Evadne – ? *euanthe*, blooming, 69.2;
74.*a*; 106.*l*,6; 155 *passim*

Evander – good for men, 52.*a*; 132
passim

Eve, 4.2,3; 145.5

Evenus – controlling the reins, 74.*e*,3;
109.*f*; 162.*j*

Fates, Three, 4.*a*,1; 10 *passim*; 13.*a*,3;
17.*h*; 18.*l*; 35.*e*,*g*; 36.*e*,3; 52.*a*,2;
60.2; 69.*c*; 73.9; 80.*a*; 81.*l*; 90.6;
101.*k*; 105.*b*; 115.*f*

Faunus – ? *favonius*, he who favours,
56.2; 132.*p*

Fearinus – of the dawn, 57.1

Fenja, 154.1

Finn mac Cool, 18.7

Fionn, 73.9

Flora, 12.2

Fodhla, 24.3

Fortune, 32.1

Furies – see Erinnyes

Gabriel, 31.3

Galahad, 95.5

Galanthis, Galanthias, Galen – weasel,
118.*g*,*h*,5

Galata – Gaul, *or* Galatian, 132.*j*

Galatea – milk white, 65 *passim*

Ganymedes – from *ganuesthai* and
medea, rejoicing in virility, 29 *passim*; 40.*c*; 81.*l*; 137.*c*; 152.*a*; 164.7
son of Tros, 158.*g*

Gara, 1.5

Garamas – people of the Goddess Car,
3.*c*,3; 90.*b*

Garanus – Crane, 132.*n*,6

Gasterocheires – bellies with hands,
23.2; 73.*b*,3

Geilissa – smiler, 113.*a*,*j*,4

Gelanor – laughter, 60.*e*

Gelonius – laughing, 132.*v*

Geraestus – venerable, 91.*g*,3

Geryon – ? *geranon*, crane, 31.6; 34.*a*;
127.2; 132 *passim*; 134.8; 139.*d*

Giants – 4.*a*; 35 *passim*; 36.*a*; 37.1;
145.*i*; 152.*b*

Gilgamesh, 4.2; 41.3; 90.4; 118.2;
122.3; 124.2; 132.1; 142.3

Glauce – owl, 81.*c*,*e*; 156 *passim*; 164.*a*

Glaucia – grey-green, 137.*n*,*t*,3

Glaucippe – grey mare, 158.*o*

Glaucus – grey green
son of Anthedon, 90.*j*,7
son of Hippolochus, 162.*n*; 163.*c*,*i*;
164.*j*; 168.*b*
son of Minos, 50.*f*,*i*; 90 *passim*;
101.*k*,1; 162.*q*
nephew of Sarpedon, 162.9
sea-god, 170.*t*
son of Sisyphus, 42.2; 67.*a*; 71 *passim*; 75.*a*,5; 90.7; 101.1; 155.*i*;
162.9

Glenus – wonder, 142.*l*

Goat-Pan – *see* Pan

Gode, Goda, 18.1; 89.3; 160.10

Godiva, Lady, 89.3

Gog, 131.7

Golgos – ? *gorgos*, grim, 18.*k*

Gordius – ? *grudios*, muttering, *or*
grunting, 83 *passim*

Gorge – grim, 142.*a*

Gorgons – grim ones, 9.*b*,5; 33 *passim*;
39.*d*; 50.3; 73.*f*,*h*,5,9; 81.9; 131.*m*;
132.*f*,3; 140.*b*,1

Gorgophone – Gorgon-death, 73.*t*;
74 *passim*

Gorgopis – grim-faced, 70.7

Gortys – ? *grotys*, of the cavern, *or* from
Carten, Cretan word for 'cow',
88.*h*.7

Graces, 90.*i*,6; 114.*j*

Graeae – grey ones, 33 *passim*; 38.10;
73.*g*,*i*,9

Gras – ? *grasos*, smelling like a goat,
117.*g*

Gration – scratcher, 33.*g*

Great Goddess, 20.2; 23.2; 29.3; 75.2; 145.4

Green Stripper, 56.2

Gronw, 91.1; 112.1

Guneus – fertile land, 138.d; 169.n

Gwydion, 103.1; 160.5

Gwyn, 73.2

Gwythur, 73.2

Gyges – *gegenes*, earth-born, 3.b,1

Hades – sightless,7.a, e,5; 13.a; 16.a; 17.3; 21.n; 24.c,i,j,k,3; 28.c; 30.a; 31 *passim*; 50.f; 67.g,2; 69.e; 73.g; 101.k; 103.c; 124.b; 134.d,e; 139. b,c,l; 164.0; 170 *passim*

Haemon – skilful, *or* making bloody, 105.e; 106.m, 7

Halesus – wander, 112.l

Halia – of the sea, 42.c,4

Haliartus – bread of the sea, 70.i

Halirrhothius – roaring sea, 19.b,2; 25.4

Haliscus – arrested, 122.l

Halys – (non-Greek word now), 28.1

Hamadryads – oak-nymphs, 21.j; 60.b

Harmonia – concord, 18.a,9; 24.a; 59 *passim*; 106.e; 107.a; 131.b

Harmothoë – sharp nail, 108.e

Harpale – grasping, 161.g

Harpalyce – ravening she-wolf, 111. p.5

Harpalycus – ravening wolf, 119.f

Harpies – snatchers, 33.g,5; 108.f; 150. j.2; 170.7

Harpina – ? falcon, 109.b

Hathor, 68.4

Hawwa, 145.5

Hebe – youth, *or* she who removes from sight, *or* Hittite: *Hepa*, earthmother, 12.2; 29.c; 123.2; 145.i,3,5

Hecabe – moving far off, 34.i; 50.6; 79.1; 158 *passim*; 159 *passim*; 163.a; 164.k,1; 167 *passim*; 168 *passim*; 170.1

Hecaerge – working from afar, 110.e

Hecale, Hecalene – worn-down form

of *Hecate Selene*, the far-shooting moon, i.e. Artemis, 98.b,7

Hecate – one hundred, 16.a; 24.g,k,12; 28.h,4; 31 *passim*; 34.1; 35.e; 37.1; 38.7; 42.3; 50.6; 55.a,1; 76.1; 79.1; 89.2; 116.c; 117.1; 118.h,5; 123.1; 124.4; 134.1; 152.c; 168.1; 170.t

the Younger, 117.b

Hector – prop, *or* stay, 158.o,8; 159.o; 162 *passim*; 163 *passim*; 164 *passim*

Hecuba – *see* Hecabe

Hegemone – mastery, 13.3

Heleius – warty, 118.b

Helen – moon, *or* basket used for offerings to the Moon-goddess

Helen Dendritis – Helen of the trees, 88.10; 105.4; 114.6

daughter of Leda, 31.c, 2; 32.b; 58.3; 62.a,b,c,3; 74.b,0; 79.2; 103 *passim*; 104 *passim*; 112.c,e; 114 *passim*; 116.n; 159 *passim*; 160 *passim*; 162 *passim*; 163.c,0; 164 *passim*; 166 *passim*; 167 *passim*; 168 *passim*; 169 *passim*; 170.1

daughter of Paris, 113.e,k; 159.v

Helenus – of the moon, 158.o,p; 159.p; 162.b; 166 *passim*; 169.f

Helicaon – burning sun, 168.b,d

Helice – willow, 28.5; 44.b,1; 58.3

Helius – the Sun, 1.3; 16.e; 18.a; 24.g; 28.d; 35.b; 37.a; 40.a; 42 *passim*; 67.2; 70.e,l; 72.i; 80.b; 88e; 109.2; 111.e; 118.c; 127.a,1; 132.c,w; 148. 3,9,12; 152.b,3; 154.e,4; 155.3; 160.n; 170.1,u,6

Helle – bright, 38.9,10; 43.1; 58.3; 62.3; 70 *passim*; 159.2

Hellen – bright, 38.h,9; 43 *passim*

Hemera – day, 40.a,3; 164.i

Hemithea – half divine, 161.g,h

Henioche – she who holds the reins, 96.f

Hen Wen, 96.2

Hepa, 145.5

Hepatu, 82.4; 145.5

Hephaestus – ? *hemeraphaestos*, he who shines by day, 9.d; 12.c,2,3; 18 *pas*-

Hephaestus – *continued*
  sim; 23 passim; 25.b; 35.e; 39.h,10;
  41.c; 42.a; 51.c; 92.m,1,4,7; 98.0,5;
  108.c; 109.m,q; 128.b; 132.l; 137.0;
  143.f; 163.l; 164.l

Hepit, 145.5

Hepta, 13.4

Hera – protectress, 7.a; 12 and 13
  passim;14.c; 21.3; 23.a,b; 24.11; 27.
  a,b,2,5,10; 35.b,d,e; 43.i,4; 54.a;
  51.f; 53.3; 58.3; 61.a; 64.2; 68.d,4;
  70.b,d,g; 72.6; 84.a; 85.b; 97.4;
  105.h,8; 110.a,1; 113.4; 118 passim;
  119 passim; 122.b,e; 123.d; 124.a,g;
  128.d; 129.b; 132.d,u; 133.a,c,f,4;
  135.e; 137.0; 139.b,1,2; 140.d; 145.
  g.i; 148.d,e,15; 156.d,2,4; 159 passim; 161.k; 163.h
  Argive, 154.k
  Eriboea, 37.3
  Goat-eating, 140.d,1
  Hellotis, 58.3

Heracles – glory of Hera
  son of Alcmene, 24.l; 31.5; 35 passim; 39.d,1; 51.g; 53.6; 58.d; 60.4;
  68.f; 69.c,3; 70.d; 74.1; 75.3; 93.g;
  95.g,h,2; 100.a; 102.b,2; 103.d,e;
  104.j; 109.q; 118 passim; 119 passim;
  120 passim; 121 passim; 122 passim;
  123 passim; 124 passim; 125 passim;
  126 passim; 127 passim; 128 passim;
  129 passim; 130 passim; 131 passim;
  132 passim; 133 passim; 134 passim;
  135 passim; 136 passim; 137 passim;
  138 passim; 139 passim; 140 passim;
  141 passim; 142 passim; 143 passim;
  144 passim; 145 passim; 146 passim;
  148.i; 149.a,d; 051.4; 152.j,3,4;
  153.e; 154.e; 157.a; 161.k,l,6; 166.
  c,1; 170.p,4,10
  Averter of Ills, 137.k
  Bright-eyed, 134.h
  Buphagus – ox-eater, 138.h,3
  Celestial, 132.3
  Cornopion – locust scarer, 145.k
  the Dactyl, 53.b,1,4; 118.2; 119.3;
  125.1; 131.9; 138.l,4; 145.l

Dorian, 119.3
Egyptian, 118.2; 135.c
the Healer, 148.12
Horsebinder, 121.d,3
Ipoctonus – grub-killer, 145.k,4
Melkarth – protector of the city,
  70.5; 96.3,6; 133.11
Melon – of apples, 125.1
Nose-docker, 121.e
Ogmius – of the Oghams, 52.4;
  119.3; 125.1; 132.3
Ophioctonus – serpent-killing,
  145.4
Saviour, 35.3; 103.5; 104.f; 145.4
Scythian, 132.6
Tyrian, *or* Phoenician, 58.d,5; 128.
  4; 133.11; 156.2
Victor, 137.k
of the Wounded Thigh, 140.1

Heraclides – sons of Heracles, 117.h;
  135.3; 138.n; 146 passim

Hercele, 118.2

Hermaphroditus, hermaphrodite, 18.
  d,8

Hermes – cairn, *or* pillar, 1.3; 14 passim; 15.b,1; 17 passim; 21.h; 24.h,j;
  25.d,4; 26.b,2; 31.a; 41.f; 52.a,6;
  62.b; 67.h; 73.9; 76.2; 93.b; 109.0;
  122.g; 132.p,5; 136.a; 159 passim;
  170.k
  Egyptian (son of Zeus), 56.d
  Infernal, 113.g
  Ram-bearer, 82.3

Hermione – pillar-queen, 114 passim;
  117.b,2; 159.d,s; 169.g

Herne, 31.3

Herophile – dear to Hera, 135.3; 159.g

Herophilus – dear to Hera, 18.d

Herse – sprinkled with dew, 25.d,4;
  48.1

Hesione – queen of Asia, 74.7; 81.e;
  131.i; 137 passim; 158.l,r,q; 157.p;
  160.b,p; 165.d; 168.6

Hespera – evening, 40.a

Hespere – evening, 33.d

Hesperides – nymphs of the West,
  4.a,1; 12.b; 33 passim; 39.d; 133

Hesperides – *continued*
   passim; 142.*d,h*; 154.*e*; 159.3
Hesperis – evening, 33.*d*
Hesperus – evening star, 33.*d,7*; 133.2
Hestia – hearth, 7.*a,8*; 13.*c*; 20 *passim*;
   27.*k,5*; 31.8
Hesychus – silent, 115.*e*
Hezekiah, 111.3
Hicetaon – suppliant, 158.*l*
Hiera – priestess, 160.*z*
Hilaeira – shining, 74.*c,p*
Hileus – *see* Oileus
Himera – longing, 164.*i*
Himerus – longing, 125.*c,3*
Hippalcimus, Hippalcmus, Hippalcus
   – horse strength, 110.*c*; 148.*i*
Hippasus – horseman, 27.*g,9*; 110.*c*;
   144.*a*
Hippeus – horse-like, 120.*b*
Hippo – mare, 131.*c,d*
Hippocoön – horse stable, 74.*b*; 103.*b*;
   140 *passim*
Hippodameia – horse tamer, 73.*d,o*;
   102.*c,e,3*; 103.*a*; 109 *passim*; 110
   passim; 143.2
Hippodamus – horse-tamer, 109.*c*
Hippolochus – born from a mare,
   162.*n,9*; 163.*c*
Hippolyte – of the stampeding horses,
   72.4; 100.*c,g*; 131 *passim*; 138.*c*;
   164.*a,b*
Hippolytus – of the stampeding horses
   son of Theseus, 42.2; 50.*f*; 70.2; 71.1
   90.*b*; 99.*a*; 100.*h,2*; 101 *passim*;
   135.*c*; 169.*k*
   giant, 35.*g,4*
Hippomedon – lord of horses, 106.*d*
Hippomenes – horse might, 80.*l*;
   91.*e*
Hipponoë – horse wisdom, 72.*g*
Hipponous – horse wisdom, 158.*o*
Hippothoë – impetuous mare, 110.*c*
Hippothous – impetuous stallion,
   49.*a,b,1,2*; 141.*f*
Hipta, 145.5
Historis – well-informed, 118.*g*
Hodites – wayfarer, 142.*l*

Holle, Frau, 18.1
Homadus – hubbub, 126.*d*
Hoples – weapon man, 95.*a*
Horus, 21.2,3,10; 41.3,4; 42.1; 73.4;
   89.2; 118.6; 123.3; 126.1; 138.1
Hours, 118.*c*
Hu Gadarn, 148.5
Hundred-handed Ones, 3.*c*; 6.*b*; 7.*e*,
   5,7; 131.2
Hyacinthides – daughters ot Hya-
   cinthus, 91.3
Hyacinthus – hyacinth, 21.*m,8*; 85.2;
   91.*g,3*; 125.*c*; 165.2
Hyades – rain-makers, *or* piglets, 27.2;
   39.*d,1*; 41.6
Hybris – shamelessness, 26.*b*
Hydra – water creature, 34 *passim*;
   60.*h,4*; 124 *passim*; 131.1; 133.4;
   134.8; 145.*c*; 166.1
Hygieia – health, 50.*i,2*
Hylaeus – of the woods, 80.*f*; 126.*b*
Hylas – of the woods, 24.5; 126.*f*;
   137.*e*; 139.*d*; 143.*a,1*; 148.*i*; 150
   passim
Hyllus, *or* Hylleios – ? woodsman,
   142.*l*; 145 *passim*; 146 *passim*;
   171.4
Hyperboreans – beyond-the-North-
   Wind-men, 21.12; 83.*b*
Hyperea – being overhead, 95.1
Hyperenor – overbearing, 58.*g*,5
Hyperion – dweller on high, 1.*d*;
   40.*a*; 41.2; 42.*a,1*; 154.4; 170
   passim
Hyperippe – heavenly mare, 64.*a*
Hypermnestra – excessive wooing,
   60.*k,m,7*
Hyperochus – excelling, 109.*b*
Hypseus – high one, 82.*a*
Hypsipyle – of the high gate, 67.2;
   106.*g,3*; 116.*b*; 149 *passim*
Hypsipylon – of the high gate, 67.*c,2*
Hyria – beehive, 123.*i*
Hyrieus – of the beehives, 41.*f*
Hyrmine – ? murmur of the beehives,
   138.*b*
Hyrtacus – (*non-Greek word*), 058.*m*

Iacchus – boisterous shout, 24.*a*

Iahu – exalted dove, 1.1

Ialebion – ? *ialemobion*, hapless life, 132.*k*

Ialysa – wailing woman, 42.4; 54.1; 60.2

Iambe – limping, 24.*d*,9

Iao, 2.2

Iapetus – hurrier, 4,*b*,*c*; 39.*a*,2; 56.*d*; 87.*c*

Iapys – *see* Iapetus

Iasion – healing native, 24.*a*; 158 *passim*

Iasius – healer, 24.*a*.6; 53.*b*,1; 143.1

Iasus – healer, 57.*a*,1; 80.*c*,*j*

Icadius – *eicadios*, twentieth, 87.*c*,3

Icarius – *iocarios*, dedicated to the Moon-goddess Car, *or* of the Icarian Sea

  the Athenian, 79 *passim*; 82.*f*

  King of Caria, 168.1

  father of Penelope, 74.*b*; 159.*b*; 160.*d*; 170.1; 171.*l*

Icarus – (*same meaning as* Icarius), 29.2; 92 *passim*; 109.4; 161.*a*,*b*

Idaea – of Mt Ida, *or* of a wooded mountain, 150.*l*; 158.*a*,*g*

Idaeus – of Mt Ida, *or* of a wooded mountain, 158 *passim*; 159.*v*

Idas – of Mt Ida, 21.*k*; 74 *passim*; 80.*c*,*d*,*l*; 103.*b*,3; 141.*f*; 148.*i*; 151.*c*

Idmon – knowing, 82.*c*,1; 148.*i*; 151.*c*,2; 161.*b*

Idomeneus – ? *idmoneus*, knowing one, 157.*a*; 159.*a*; 160.*n*,6; 162.*t*; 163.*h*; 169.*f*,*l*, 5; 171.*a*

Iliona – queen of Ilium, 188.*l*

Illyrius – ? *ill-ouros*, squinting wild bull, 59.*e*

Illyunka, 36.3

Ilus – troop, *or* he who forces back (Oileus), 18.*f*; 108.*a*; 109.*a*; 168.2

  brother of Erichthonius, 158 *passim*

  the Younger, 158.*i*

Inachus – ? making strong and sinewy, 16.*e*; 56.*a*,*d*; 57.*a*,1; 58.2; 60.*g*

Indra, 7.6; 132.5

Ino – she who makes sinewy, 24.3; 27.6; 51.5; 70 *passim*; 96.6; 156.3; 170.*y*

Io – moon, 7.*b*,3; 14.*b*,4; 52.*a*,2; 56 *passim*; 57.*a*; 68.4; 72.4; 90.3; 154.*c*,1

Iobates – he who goes with the moon, 73.*a*; 75 *passim*

Iocaste – ? *io-cassitere*, shining moon, 105 *passim*, 170.0

Iodama – ? *iodamalis*, heifer calf of Io, 9.*b*,6

Iolaus – the people of the land, *or* land-boulder, 92.*l*; 118.2; 122.*c*.*g*; 124 *passim*; 127.*d*; 131.*a*; 132.*s*; 133.11; 135.*a*; 137.*h*; 138.*d*; 139.*d*; 142.*f*; 143.*g*; 145.*d*,*k*; 146 *passim*; 155.*i*

  (Protesilaus), 162.*c*

Iole – ? *ioleis* land-flock, 144 *passim*; 145.*a*,*e*,2; 146.*d*; 171.4

Ion – land–man, *or* native, 43.*b*,1; 44 *passim*; 47.*g*

Ioxus – ? *ioxus*, of battle din, 96.*c*

Iphianassa – mighty queen, 64.*a*; 72.*g*,*j*,*k*; 112.*d*

Iphiboë – strength of oxen, 127.*a*

Iphicles – famous might

  son of Amphitryon, 74.1; 80.*c*,*g*,*h*; 104.*i*; 118 *passim*; 119 *passim*; 122.*a*; 138.*c*,*d*

  Argonaut, 140.*c*; 148.*i*

Iphiclus – famous might, 72 *passim*; 162.*c*

Iphigeneia – mothering a strong race, 104.*e*; 112.*d*,*h*,1; 113.*a*; 114.0; 116 *passim*; 117 *passim*; 160.*j*; 161 *passim*; 162.6

Iphimedeia – she who strengthens the genitals, 37.*a*,1; 170.0

Iphimedon – mighty ruler, 146.*c*

Iphinoë – mighty intelligence, 72.*g*,*j*,4; 91.*e*; 92.*a*; 94.*b*; 110.*e*

Iphitus – shield strength, 135 *passim*; 136.*a*; 140.*a*; 152.*i*; 171.*h*

  brother of Eurystheus, 148.*i*

Iris – rainbow, 15.*b*; 24.*g*; 81.*j*; 123.*c*; 150.*j*; 160.*a*; 171.*f*

Irus – *masculine form of* Iris, 171.*f*

Isander – impartial, 162.*n*,9

Ischepolis – strong city, 110.*e*,*f*

Ischys – strength, 50 *passim*

Ishtar, 11.1; 24.11; 29.2; 51.1; 73.7; 103.2; 118.2

Isis – she who weeps, 18.3; 21.2; 22.7; 41.3; 42.1; 56.*b*; 68.4; 73.4; 83.2; 89.2; 123.3; 134.4; 138.1

Ismenius, R. – knowledgeable, 119.*g*; 147.*a*

Itonus – willow-man, 9.*b*,4

Itylus – little Itys, 108.*g*

Itys – willow, 46.*a*,*c*,*d*; 47.*a*

Iuchar, 24.3; 132.5

Iucharba, 24.3; 132.5

Ixion – strong native, 50.2; 63 *passim*; 67.2; 70.*a*,*l*; 102.*a*,*f*,1,3; 103.*e*

Iynx – wryneck, 56.*a*

Jacob, 39.8; 67.1; 37.2; 92.2

Janus, 34.3; 37.2

Japhet, 39.2

Jason – healer, 58.5; 68.*e*; 80.*c*,*g*; 98.*r*; 103.2; 129.1; 148 *passim*; 149 *passim*; 150 *passim*; 151 *passim*; 152 *passim*; 153 *passim*; 154 *passim*; 155 *passim*; 156 *passim*; 157 *passim*; 161.*k*

Jehovah, 1.1; 4.3; 9.4; 51.1; 73.7; 83.4; 84.2; 92.9; 141.1

Jephtha, 161.2; 169.5

Jonah, 103.2; 137.2

Jonathan, 169.5

Jordanes – (*Semitic word*), river of judgement, 136.*a*

Joseph, 75.1

Joshua, 133.*i*; 169.6

Juno, 118.2

Juppiter, 1.4; 118.2; 158.3

Kali, 56.2

Karn – son of Car, 95.5

Ker, 1.5; 57.2

Keret, 159.2

Kilhwych, 148.4,5,6; 152.3

Kingu, 46.2; 39.8

Krishna, 92.10

Kumarbi, 6.6; 27.5

Laban, 67.1

Labdacus – ? *lampadōn aces*, help of torches, 105.*a*,1

Labicus – girdled, 90.*g*

Labryadae – men of the axe, 51.2

Lacedaemon – lake demon, 125.*c*,3

Lachesis – measurer, 10 *passim*; 42.*c*; 60.2

Lacinius – jagged, 132.*t*

Lacone – lady of the lake, 125.3

Ladon – he who embraces, 33.*b*,*f*,1; 66.*a*; 133 *passim*

Laelaps – hurricane, 89.*f*,*g*,*h*; 118.*b*

Laertes – ant, 67.*c*; 148.*i*; 160 *passim*; 171 *passim*

Lahamu, 7.5

Lahmu, 7.5

Laidley Worm, 132.6

Laius – ? *lēios*, having cattle, 76.*c*; 105 *passim*; 110.*g*.*h*

Lamia – gluttonous, *or* lecherous, 61 *passim*; 72.4; 135.3

Lampado – torch, 131.*c*

Lampetia—rightness of the year, 42.*b*; 170.*v*

Lampon – beaming, 130.*a*

Lampus – torch, 130.1; 158.*l*

Lamus – gulper, *or* glutton, 136.*g*; 170.*h*

Laocoön – very perceptive, 167 *passim*

Laodameia – tamer of people nurse of Orestes, 113.*a* wife of Protesilaus, 162.*d*,*n*,8,9

Laodice – justice of the people, 112.*d*; 141.*g*; 158.*o*; 160.*z*; 168.*d*

Laomedon – ruler of the people, 13.*c*; 29.1; 81.*e*; 131.11; 136.*g*; 137 *passim*; 141.*g*; 149.*f*; 152.*d*; 153.*e*; 158.*l*

Laonome – law of the people, 138.*d*

Laothoë—rushing stone, 158.8; 162.*m*; 168.*l*

Lapiths – ? *lapicidae*, flint chippers, 102 *passim*

Lat, 14.*a*; 21.12; 22.7; 62.2; 88.3

Latinus – Latin, 132.*p*; 170.*k,w*

Latona – queen Lat, 14.2; 62.2; 88.3

Latromis – wanton, 27.*i,8*

Lear, 73.2

Learchus – ruler of the people, 27.*a*,2; 70 *passim*; 162.9

Leda – lady, 32.2; 62 *passim*; 74.*b.j*; 113.*a*; 159.*a*; 170.0

Leiriope – lily face, 85.*a*,1

Leontophonus – lion killer, 171.*l*

Leonymus – lion name, 164.*m*

Leos – lion
an Athenisnj 97.*g,h*
son of Orpheus, 97.2

Leprea – scabby, 113.7

Lepreus – scabby, 74.2; 138.*h*,2

Lethe, R. – forgetfulness, 14.*b*,4

Leto – ? stone, *or* lady, 14.*a*,2; 21 *passim*; 22.*b*; 32.2; 62.2; 77 *passim*; 88.3; 89.*a*

Leuce – white, *or* white poplar, 31.*d*,5; 134.*f*

Leucippe – white mare, 27.*g*; 141.*h*; 158.*l*; 161 *passim*

Leucippides – white fillies, 74.*c,p,3*; 103.*b*

Leucippus – white stallion, 21.*l*,6; 74.*b,c*; 109.*c*

Leucon – white, 70.*a,i*

Leucophanes – white appearance, 149.1

Leucothea – white goddess, 42.*c*,4; 45.2; 70.*h*,4,8; 88.9; 170.*y*,9

Leucus – white, 162.*t*; 169.*l*

Libya – dripping rain, 56.*d*,2,3; 58.*a*,2; 82.*b,c*; 154.*e*

Lichas – sheer cliff, 117.*d*; 145.*b,d*

Licymnius – *ichymnios*, hymn at winnowing time, 118.*b*; 140.*a*; 144.*a*; 145.*d*; 146 *passim*

Ligys – shrill, 132.*k*

Lilim – children of Lilith, 55.1

Lilith – scritch-owl, 55.1

Linda – binder with linen thread, 42.4; 54.1; 60.2

Linos – linen thread, 108.*b*

Linus – flax, *or* flaxen lyre-string
of Argos, 147 *passim*
son of Ismenius, 24.5; 119.*g*,3; 147.*a*
son of Oeagrus, 147.*b*,4

Lityerses – (non-Greek word), 7.1; 24.5; 136.*e*

Llew Llaw, 29.2; 91.1,4; 112.1; 132.5; 160.5; 164.3

Llyr, 73.2 r

Lud, 73.6

Lugh, 132.5

Lugos, 132.5

Lycaon – deluding wolf
son of Pelasgus, 38 *passim*; 143.*c*; 162.*i*,4; 163.*c*
brother of Polydorus, 162.*m*,1

Lycastus – fellow citizen of the wolves, 88.*h*,5

Lychnus – lamp, 25.1

Lycomedes – wolf-cunning, 104.*g*; 160.*j,k*; 166.*h*

Lycotherses – summer wolf, 59.*d*

Lyctaea – ? *lycotheia*, divine she-wolf, 91.*g*

Lycurgus – wolf work, 27.*e*.3; 50.*f*; 71.1; 106.*g*; 141.*a*
of Nemea, 149.*e*

Lycus – wolf, 76.*a*; 88.*d*; 94 *passim*; 122.*c*; 131.*e,h*; 135.*e*; 151.*c*; 159.*q*; 169.*k*

Lynceus – sharp-eyed as a lynx, 60. *k,m,4,7*; 74 *passim*; 80.*c*; 103.*b,c*; 148.*i*

Lysianassa – queen who delivers, 133.*k*

Lysidice – dispensing with justice, 110.*c*

Lysippe – she who lets loose the horses, 72.*g,j,k*; 131 *passim*

Macareus – happy, 43.*h*,4

Macaria – blessed, 120.3; 141.1; 142.*l*; 146.*b*

Machaerus – butcher, 169.h

Machaon – lancet, 50.i; 163.h; 164.a; 165.f; 166.d,i

Macris – tall, or far off, 27.b,2; 82.e; 146.i; 148.6; 154 passim; 155.h

Maeander – searching for a man, 169.5

Maenads – madwomen, 21.6; 26.1,2; 27 passim; 28.d,e,f,2; 41.1; 44.a; 153.4; 160.10

Maera – glistening, 77 passim; 168.n.1; 170.0.1

Maeve, 111.1

Magnes – Magnesian, 147.b,4

Maia – grandmother, 17.c,a

Malis – whiteish, 136.g

Maneros, 1.1; 136.e; 147.1

Mante – prophetess, 77.a

Manthu, 39.8

Manto – prophetess, 107.c,i; 169.c

Maraphius – ? marathrius, of the fennel, 159.d

Marathon – ? marathron, fennel, 94.b; 104.c; 156.b,4

Marathus – fennel, 104.c,3

Marduk, 1.1; 4.5; 7.5; 35.5; 71.1; 73.7; 92.3; 103.1,2; 137.2; 170.5

Mariamne, 131.3; 151.3

Marian, 131.3; 162.10

Marienna – high fruitful mother of heaven, 131.3; 151.3

Marmaranax – marble king, 109.4

Marmax – marmaranex, marble king, 109.e,8

Maro – ? maris, a liquid measure of three pints, 170 passim

Marpesia – snatcher, 131.c,d

Marpessa – snatcher, 21.k,7; 74.a,e,3

Mars, 27.12; 158.4

Marsyas – ? from marnamai, battler, 21.e,f,5; 83.g

Mecisteus – greatest, 148.i; 160.r

Meda – cunning, 143.b; 162.t; 169.l

Medea – cunning, 67.d; 92.m,8; 95 passim; 97 passim; 98.a; 135.e; 148.6; 152 passim; 153 passim; 154

passim; 155 passim; 156 passim; 157 passim; 160.a; 164.0

Medeius – cunning, 148.2
alias Polyxemus, 156.e; 157.a,b

Medon – ruler, 117.b; 160.q; 161.i; 163.h; 171.i

Medus – cunning, 97.c

Medusa – cunning, 9.a; 33.b, 3,4; 50.e; 73 passim; 75.3; 132.l,4; 134.c

Megaera – grudge, 6.a; 31.g; 115.2

Megamede – great cunning, 120.b

Megapenthes – great grief, 73.q,s; 117.c; 159.d

Megara – oracular cave, 122 passim; 135.a,e

Megareus – of the oracular cave, 91.e; 94.e; 110.d.f

Megarus – cave, or cleft of rock, 38.e

Megera – passing lovely, 122.a

Melaenis – black one, 18.4

Melampus – black foot, 40.b; 68.f; 72 passim; 126.e; 148.i

Melaneus – black one, 14.a,1; 144.b

Melanion – black native
Atalanta's husband, 80.k,l,4
son of Phrixus, 151.f

Melanippe – black mare, 43.c,2; 100.2; 131.e,g; 164.a

Melanippus – black stallion, 72.5; 96.c; 106.b,j,4

Melanius – black, 135.a

Melantheus, or Melanthus, with black blossoms, or swarthy, 171.d,i

Melas – black, 144.a

Meleager – guinea fowl, 45.a; 74.a,i; 80 passim; 134.c; 141.d; 142.a,1; 148.i; 152.i; 155.i; 162.d

Melia – ash-tree, 57.a,1

Meliae – ash-nymphs, 6.4; 32.3; 86.2

Meliboëa – sweet cry, 77.b

Melicertes – melicretes, sweet power, 42.c; 67.1; 70 passim; 71.a,4; 90.7; 92.7; 96.d,3; 109.5; 110.2; 122.2; 156.2,3

Melisseus – honey-man, 7.3

Melite – attention, 95.a; 146.i

Melkarth, 72.3; 92.7; 122.2; 156.2

Memnon – resolute, 91.5; 162.g,2; 164 passim

Menedemus – withstanding the people, 127.d

Menelaus – might of the people, 31.a; 74.k; 93.c; 111.f,j; 112 passim; 114 passim; 116.n,2; 117.c,5; 146.6; 059 passim; 160 passim; 161.d; 162 passim; 163 passim; 165 passim; 166 passim; 167 passim; 168 passim; 169 passim; 171.a

Menestheus – divine strength, 99.e; 104 passim; 131.11; 157.a; 160.o,3; 168.e; 169.n

Menja, 154.1

Menodice – right of might, 143.a

Menoeceus – strength of the house, 105.i,4; 106.j; 121.a

Menoetes – defying fate, 132.d,4; 134.d,1

Menoetius – defying fate, or ruined strength, 39.a,c,11; 130.c; 134.d; 145.k; 160.m

Menos – moon, 52.1

Mentor – ? menetos, patient, 146.c

Meriones – share of payment, 160.n

Mermerus – care-laden, 156.e,f

Merope – eloquent, or bee-eater, 41.a,b; 67.a,h,j,4; 92.a; 108.f

Merops – eloquent, or bee-eater, 108.c; 158.m,n

Mestor – counsellor, 162.j

Metaneira – she who lives among maidens, 24.d,e,5

Metapontus – oversea, 43.e,g

Metharme – change, 65.a,1

Metiadusa – distressingly full of counsel, 94.b

Metion – deliberator, 94 passim

Metis – counsel, 1.d; 4.a; 7.d; 9 passim; 86.1

Metope – metopedon, headlong, or metapon, forefront, 66.a; 154.a,1; 158.o

Mettus Curtius, 105.4

Michael, 4.3; 92.9

Midas – mita, seed, 21.h; 83 passim

Midea – medeia, cunning, 118.b

Miletus – ? milteias, painted with red ochre, 21.i; 88.b,2,4

Mimas – mimicry, 35.e,4

Minos – ? meinos osia, the moon's creature

son of Lycastus, 88.5

son of Zeus, 29.3; 30.1; 31.b; 58.c; 66.i,4; 87.2; 88 passim; 89 passim; 90 passim; 91 passim; 92 passim; 98 passim; 110.d,h; 129.a; 136.e; 160.n; 167.2; 169.6; 170.p

Minotaur – Minos bull, 88.e,f; 91.4; 98 passim; 129.a

Minthe – mint, 31.d,6

Minyas – moon-man, 27.g; 70.9; 148.j,8; 154.12

Mitra, 7.6; 132.5

Mnemon – mindful, 161.h

Mnemosyne – memory, 13.a

Mnesimache – mindful of battle, 127.f; 138.c

Moera – share, or fate, 98.8

Moerae – see Fates

Molione – queen of the moly, or warrior, 138.a,f,6

Moliones – warriors, 138 passim, 139.e,f

Molionides – sons of the warrior queen, 138.b

Moloch, 70.5; 77.2; 92.7; 110.2; 170.3

Molorchus – tree-planter, 123.d,f,h

Molpadia – death song, 100.e,f

Molpus – melody, 161.g

Molus – toil of war, 138.a; 160.n

Mopsus – ? moschos, calf

the Lapith, 51.g,8; 73.i; 78.b; 89.2; 107.i; 131.o,5; 148.i; 149.h; 154.f,6

grandson of Teiresias, 154.6; 169 passim

Morning Star – see Phosphorus

Moses, 88.6; 99.1; 105.1

Mot, 73.2

Mother of the Gods, 131.n,4; 136.f; 158.e

Moxus, 89.2

Mummi, 36.2

Munippu – solitary stallion, 159.
g,4,5; 168.*d*

Munitus – single shield, 168.*e*

Musaeus – of the Muses, 134.*a*

Muses – mountain-goddesses, 13.*a*,4;
17.3; 21.*f*,0; 28.*e*,*f*; 37.*c*,1; 59.*b*;
75.*b*; 81.*l*; 82.*e*; 95.*c*; 105.*e*,z;
126.*g*; 132.0; 147.*c*; 154.*d*,3; 161.4;
164.*l*; 170.*q*

Mygdon – ? *amygdalon*, almond, 131.*e*

Myles – mill, 125.*c*

Myndon – dumb, 136.*f*

Mynes – excuse, 162.*j*

Myrine – sea-goddess, 131 *passim*;
149.1; 151.3

Myrmex – ant, 66.*g*,2; 81.9

Myrmidon – ant, 66.*g*

Myrtilus – myrtle, 71.*b*; 109 *passim*;
111.*c*

Myrtle-nymphs, 82.*c*,*d*,2

Myrto, Myrtea, Myrtoessa – sea-
goddess, 109.*l*,6

Myscelus – ? little mouse, 132.*t*

Naiads – water-nymphs, 60.*b*; 82 *passim*; 111.*g*

Narcaeus – benumbing, 110.*b*,1

Narcissus – benumbing, *or* narcotic,
21.8; 26.*d*; 85 *passim*

Naucrate – ship mistress, 92.*d*,5

Naupiadame – pursuer of ships, 127.*a*

Nauplius–navigator, 60.0;93.*c*;111,*f*;
112.*f*,*h*;141.*c*; 148.*i*; 160.*c*,*d*; 162.*t*;
169 *passim*

Nausicaa – burner of ships, 170.z,1;
171.2,3,5

Nausinous – cunning sailor, 170.*w*

Nausitheus – in the service of the sea-
goddess, 98.*f*,*m*

Nausithous – impetuous sailor
son of Odysseus, 170.*w*
King of Phaeacians, 146.*i*

Neaera – the younger, 141.*a*,*b*

Nebrophonus – death of a kid, 149.*c*

Necessity, 10.*c*

Neis – water-nymph, 64.*a*

Neith, 8.1; 39.2; 61.1; 73.6; 114.4;
131.3; 133.10; 141.1; 154.5

Neleus – ruthless, 7.3; 67.*j*,3; 68.
d.*e*.*f*.3; 72.*b*; 77.*b*; 94.*c*; 135.*c*; 138.
b.*m*; 139 *passim*; 140.*a*; 148.11

Nemea, of the glade, 123.*c*

Nemesis – due enactment, *or* divine
vengeance, 4.*a*; 7.3; 16.6; 32 *passim*; 62 *passim*

Neoptolemus–new war, 81.*s*,*t*;117.*b*;
161.*e*; 164.*j*; 165.*i*; 166 *passim*; 167
passim; 168 *passim*; 169 *passim*;
170.*p*; 171.*j*

Nephalion – sober, 131.*e*

Nephele–cloud, 63.*d*;70 *passim*;126.*b*

Nephthys, 31.3; 42.1; 123.3; 138.1

Nereids – the wet ones, 4.*b*; 33 *passim*;
73.*j*; 81.*l*,1; 98.*f*; 154.*k*; 164.*l*

Nereis – wet one, 16.1; 33.2

Nereus – wet one, 33.*a*,*g*,2; 133.*d*,*e*,5;
141.*f*

Nergal, 1.3

Nessus – ? *neossus*, young bird *or*
animal, 126.*d*; 142 *passim*; 145 *passim*

Nestor – ? *neostoreus*, newly speaking,
27.5; 67.*j*; 68.*f*; 74.*k*; 80.*c*,*g*; 102.*c*;
135.*c*; 139 *passim*; 160 *passim*; 164.
e; 165.*a*; 166.*i*; 169 *passim*

Ngame – 39.11

Niamh of the Golden Hair, 83.6

Nicippe – conquering mare, 24.*b*; 11.
o,*c*; 118.*d*

Nicostrate – victorious army, 132.0

Nicostratus – victorious army, 117.*c*;
159.*d*

Night, 2.*b*,2; 4.*a*; 10.*a*; 33.7; 137.0

Nile, R. – 133.*k*

Ninib, 1.3

Niobe – snowy, 1.3; 76.*c*; 77 *passim*;
108.*b*,*g*,*i*,1,9; 118.*f*

Nisus – brightness, *or* emigrant, 67.1;
91 *passim*; 92.4; 94.*c*,*d*,*e*; 95.5;
110.*d*
son of Hyrtacus, 158.*m*

Noah, 27.6; 38.3; 39.2; 123.1; 154.12

Nomia – grazer, 17.*j*

Nomius – guardian of the flocks, 82.*d*

Norax – ? *norops*, with face too bright to look at, 132.*d*,5

Norns, Three, 6.4

North Wind – *see* Boreas

Nycteu – of the night, 76.*a*; 154.*a*

Nyctimus – of the night, 38.*b*; 108.*c*

Nysa – lame, 27.*b*

Oceanus – of the swift queen, 1.*d*; 2.*a*,1; 4.*a*; 11.*b*; 32.4; 132.*a*,*c*; 136.*c*; 170.8

Ocypete – swift wing, 150.*i*

Odin, 6.4; 35.4; 150.*j*

Odysseus – angry, 67.*c*,2; 123.2; 132.*p*; 154.*d*,11; 159 *passim*; 160 *passim*; 161 *passim*; 162 *passim*; 163 *passim*; 164 *passim*; 165 *passim*; 166 *passim*; 167 *passim*; 168 *passim*; 169 *passim*; 170 *passim*; 171 *passim*

Oeagrus – *oea-agrios*, of the wild sorb-apple, 28.*a*,1; 147.*b*.4

Oeax – ship's helm, 111.*f*; 112.*h*; 114.*b*; 116.1; 117.*a*; 162.*t*

Oebalides – ? sons of the threshold, 84.1

Oebalus – ? from *oebalia*, speckled sheepskin, *or* from *oecobalos*, threshold of the house, 67.4; 74.*a*,*b*

Oedipus – swell-foot, *or perhaps* child of the swelling wave, 67.1; 105 *passim*; 106.*b*,2; 114.1; 163.*p*

Oeneis – vinous, 26.*b*,2

Oeneus – vinous, 79.*a*; 80 *passim*; 106.*b*; 112.*a*; 138.*c*; 142 *passim*; 159.*h*; 169.*k*

Oeno – of wine, 160.*u*

Oenomaus – impetuous with wine, 53.7; 71.1; 109 *passim*; 116.5; 143.2

Oenone – queen of wine, 159 *passim*; 160.*w*; 166.*e*

Oenope – wine face, 91.*e*

Oenopion – wine in plenty, 27.*i*,8; 41 *passim*; 79.*a*; 88.*h*; 98.0,1,2; 123.4

Oeonus – solitary bird of omen, 140.*a*

Oetolinus – doomed Linus, 147.*a*,1

Ogier le Danois, 103.1

Ogma Sunface, 52.4; 132.3,6

Oicles – noble bird, 137.*h*,*j*,*m*

Oileus, or Hileus – gracious (*early form of* Ilus), 148.*i*; 151.*f*; 160.*q*

Oisin, 83.6

Olus – ? *olesypnos*, destroyer of sleep, 136.*c*

Olwen, 148.4,5

Omphale – navel, 108.*a*,9; 131.*j*; 134.6; 135.*d*; 136 *passim*; 137.*a*

Oncë – pear-tree, 74.6

Oncus – hook, 16.*f*; 24.*d*; 138.*g*

Oneaea – serviceable, 87.*a*

Onn, 42.4

Opheltes – benefactor, *or* wound round by a serpent, 106.*g*,*h*,3; 123.*f*.5

Ophion – native snake, 1.*a*,*b*,*c*,2; 2.1; 25.5; 48.1; 62.3

Opis – awe, 41.*d*,4; 110.*e*

Orchomenus – strength of the battle rank, 111.*g*

Orcus – boar, 123.2

Oreithyia – she who rages on the mountains, 25.2; 47.*b*,*c*; 48.*a*,*b*,1,3,4; 100 *passim*; 103.4; 160.*a*

Orestes – mountaineer, 85.1; 112.*d*,*g*,1; 113 *passim*; 114 *passim*; 115 *passim*; 116 *passim*; 117 *passim*; 160.*z*; 169 *passim*

Orestheus – dedicated to the Mountain-goddess, 38.*h*,7; 114.*k*

Oreus – of the mountain, 126.*b*

Orion – dweller on the mountain, 40.*b*; 41 *passim*; 50.*f*; 123.1,4; 132.1; 143.*a*; 170.*p*

Orneus – *orneon*, bird. 94 *passim*

Ornis – bird, 128.*d*

Ornytion – bird-man, 46.5; 67.*a*; 81.*b*

Orpheus – ? *ophruoeis*, of the river bank, 26.2; 28 *passim*; 53.*a*; 82.*i*; 83.*a*; 97.*h*; 103.1; 147.*b*,5,6; 148.*i*; 149.*a*; 150.*a*; 151.*a*; 153.4; 154.*d*,*g*

Orseis – she who stirs up, 43.*a*

Orsiloche – inducing childbirth, 116.*d*

Orthaea – upright, 91.*g*

Orthrus – early, 34 *passim*; 105.*e*; 123.
b.1; 132.*a,d,3,4*

Osiris, 7.1; 18.*3,7*; 36.1; 38.11; 41.*3*;
42.1; 73.4; 83.2,3; 116.*b,6*; 123.*3*;
126.1; 133.8; 134.2,4; 138.1

Othrias – ? impulsive, 158.*m*

Otionia – with the ear-flaps, 47.*b,d,2*

Otrere – nimble, 131.*b*; 164.*a*

Otus – he who pushes back, 37 *passim*

Oxylus – ? *oxylalus*, quick to seize,
146.*k*

Pactolus, R. – ? assuring destruction,
108.*b*

Paeonius – deliverer from evil, 53.*b*

Pagasus – he who holds fast, 51.*b*

Palaemon – wrestler, 70.*h*; 87.1; 122
passim; 148.*i*

Palamedes – ancient wisdom, 9.5; 17.
h; 39.8; 52.*a,6*; 111.*f*; 112.*f*; 116.1;
160 *passim*; 161 *passim*; 162 *passim*;
167.*f*; 168.1

Pallantids – sons of Pallas, 99.*3*; 105.7

Pallas – maiden, *or* youth
  Giant, 9 *passim*; 35.*e,3*; 89.*c,4*
  son of Lycaon, 99.*a*
  son of Pandion, 94.*c,d*; 95.*e*; 97.*g*;
  99.*a*; 158.*b*
  half-brother of Theseus, 99.*a*
  Titan, 8.*3*
  daughter of Triton, 8 *passim*; 21.5;
  158.*i*

Pammon – *pammaen*, full moon, 158.*o*

Pan – pasture, 76.*e,10*; 17.*j,4*; 21.*c,h,5*;
22.*d*; 26 *passim*; 36.*c*; 56.*a,2*; 108.*h*;
111.*c*; 136.*i,j*; 160.10; 171.*l,2*

Pancratis – all strength, 37.1

Pandareus – he who flays all, 24.*b,4*;
108 *passim*

Pandarus – he who flays all, 163.*c*

Pandion – [priest of the] All-Zeus
festival, 46.*a,b*; 47.*a*; 94 *passim*;
114.*l*

Pandora – all-giving
  wife of Epimetheus, 4.*3*; 39.*h,j,8*;
  169.3
  daughter of Erechtheus, 47.*b,d,2*

Pandorus – all-giving, 94 *passim*

Pandrosos – all-dewy, 25.*d*

Panopeus – all-viewing, *or* full moon,
89.*i*; 98.*n*; 167.*b*

Panthous – all-impetuous, 158.*m*;
163.*j*

Paphus – foam, 65.*a*

Paria – ancient one, 89.*a*

Pariae – ancient ones, 90.6

Paris (*or* Alexander) – wallet, 105.5;
112.*e*; 131.11; 158.*o*; 159 *passim*;
160 *passim*; 162 *passim*; 163 *passim*;
164 *passim*; 166 *passim*; 169.1

Parnasus – ? from *paluno*, scatterer, 38.*f*

Parthenia – maiden, 109.*e*

Parthenopaeus – son of a pierced
maidenhead, 80.*l*; 106.*d*; 141.*d,f*

Parthenope – maiden face, 141.*c*

Pasht, 36.2

Pasiphaë – she who shines for all, 16.2;
21.*k*; 51.*h,5*; 88 *passim*; 89.*c,e,4,5*;
90 *passim*; 91.2; 92.*d,g,12*; 98.*c,p*;
101.*d*; 129.*a*; 167.2

Pasithea Cale – goddess beautiful to
all, 13.*3*; 105.*h*

Passalus – gay, 136.*c*

Patroclus – glory of the father, 159.*a*;
160 *passim*; 163 *passim*; 164 *passim*;
168.6

Pedasus – bounder, 162.*l*; 163.*m*

Pegasus – of the wells, 33.*b,4*; 67.4;
73.*h*; 75 *passim*

Peirithous – he who turns around,
78.*b*; 80.*c*; 95.2; 100.*b*; 101.*c*; 102
passim; 103 *passim*; 104.*e,1*; 113.*3*;
126.2; 132.1; 134.*d*; 159.*s*; 168.*e*

Pelagon – of the sea, 58.*f*

Pelasgus – ancient, *or* seafarer, 1.*d,5*;
38.*a*; 57.*a,1*; 77.1

Peleus – muddy, 16.*b,1*; 29.1; 66.*f*;
70.2; 80.*c,g*; 81 *passim*; 131.*a*;
137.*h*; 148.*i*; 155.*i*; 159.*e*; 160 *passim*; 169.*f*

Pelias – black and blue, 47.c; 68 passim; 69.a; 71.a; 82.a; 138.m; 148 passim; 152.3; 155 passim

Pelopia, eia – muddy face, 111 passim

Pelops – muddy face, 42.2; 53.7; 71.b; 77.a,d; 95.b; 108 passim; 109 passim; 110 passim; 111.a; 113.n; 117.f,5; 118.a; 131.h; 138.i,l,m,4; 143.2; 158.k; 166.h,1,2; 169.6

son of Agamemnon, 112.h

Pelorus – monstrous serpent, 58.g,5

Pemon – misery, 96.b

Pemphredo – wasp, 33.c,5

Pempsus – fifth, 164.n,6

Peneius, R. – of the thread, 21.k,6; 82.a

Peneleos – baneful lion, 148.i; 160.x

Penelope – with a web over her face, or striped duck, 26.b,2; 159.b; 160 passim; 162.10; 171 passim

Penthesileia – forcing men to mourn, 163.q; 164 passim

Pentheus – grief, 27.f,5,9; 59.c,d

Penthilus – assuager of grief, 87.c; 117.b,g

Perdix – partridge, 92.b,1,6

Peredur, 142.3; 148.5

Pereus – slave dealer, 141.a

Pergamus – citadel, 169.f

Periboea – surrounded by cattle, 81.e; 98.i,k; 105.c,d,j; 110.e; 137.i; 160.p (Curissia), 167.i

Periclymenus – very famous, 139.c,1; 148.i

Perieres – ? surrounded by entrenchments, 47 passim; 144.b

Perigune – much cornland, 96.c,2,4

Perilaus – surrounded by his people, 114.m

Perimede – very cunning, 118.b; 148.b

Perimedes – very cunning, 134.i; 146.c

Periopis – with much wealth, 160.m

Periphetes – notorious, 96.a,1; 163.h

Pero – leather bag, 66.a,1; 72 passim; 170.o

Perse – destruction, 170.i

Perseis – destroyer, 88.e,6

Persephatta – she who tells of destruc-

tion, or destructive dove, 24.2

Persephone – bringer of destruction, 13.a; 14.b,4; 16.f; 18.h,i,j; 24.c,k,l, 2; 27.a,k,10,11; 30.a; 31 passim; 51. 7; 67.h; 69.d, 3; 85.1; 94.f; 101.i; 103.c,d,3; 108.c; 121.3; 124.b,4; 134.d; 149.s; 170.l,6

Perses – destroyer, 157.b

Perseus – destroyer, 9.a; 27.j,5; 33.b; 39.d; 73 passim; 111.a; 118.a,d,e,1, 5; 137.2

Peteos – ? peteenos, feathered, 104.d

Phaea – shining one, 96.2,5

Phaeax – bright arrival, 98.f,m

Phaedra – bright one, 70.2; 90.a,b,1; 100.h,2; 101 passim; 103.a; 164.a; 170.o

Phaeo – chin, 27.2

Phaestus – made to shine, 145.k

Phaesyle – ? filtered light, 27.2

Phaëthon – shining
son of Eos, 89.d,9
son of Helius, 2.b; 28.5; 29.1; 42. d,2,3; 71.1; 75.3; 89.9

Phaethon (bull) – shining, 127.c

Phaethusa – bright being, 109.f

Phaetusa – bright being, 42.b

Phalanthus – bald, 87.c,2

Phalas – shining helmet-ridge, 164 passim

Phalerus – patched, or streaked with white, 119.f; 131.11; 148.i

Phanes – revealer, 2.b,2; 123.1

Phanus – torch, 148.i

Pharez, 73.2; 159.4

Phegeus – esculent oak, 107.e,f,g

Pheidippus – sparing his horses, 169.n

Phemius – famous, 171.i

Phereboea – she who brings cattle, 98.i,k

Phereclus – bringing glory, 98.f; 159.q

Pheres – bearer, 148.f; 156.e,f

Phialo – bowl, 141.h,4

Philaeus – ? philaemos, bloodthirsty, 165.l

Philammon – lover of the racecourse, 67.b

Philemon – friendly slinger, 41.5

Philoctetes – love of possessions, 92.10; 145 *passim*; 159.a; 166 *passim*; 169.m,n

Philoetius – happy doom, 171.i

Philolaus – beloved of the people, 133.e

Philomela – sweet melody, 46 *passim*; 47.a; 94.1; 95.a

Philomele – sweet melody, 160.m

Philomeleides – dear to the apple-nymphs, 161.f,3

Philonoë – kindly mind, 75.e

Philyra – lime-tree, 151.g,5

Phimachus – muzzler of pain, 106.b

Phineis – sea-eagle, 87.c,2

Phineus – ? *pheneus*, sea-eagle, 48.c; 58.a,d; 150 *passim*; 151.a,f; 153.a; 158.g

Phlegyas – fiery, 50.a,d; 63.a

Phlogius – fiery, 151.d

Phobus – fear, 18.a; 100.d

Phocus – seal, 46.5; 76.b,c; 81 *passim*; 165.k

Phoebe – bright moon, 1.d; 14.a,2; 51.b; 74.c,p

Phoenissa – bloody one, 58.2

Phoenix – palm-tree, *or* blood-red, 18.h; 58.a,d,2; 88.b,2; 105.6
    son of Amyntor, 160.l,n,5; 163.f; 166.h; 169.f

Phoenodamas – restrainer of slaughter, 137.b,g,3

Pholus – read, 126 *passim*; 138.1

Phorbas – fearful, 146.h; 148.i; 170.t

Phorcids – sow's children, 33 *passim*

Phorcis – sow, 24.7; 33.5

Phorcys – boar, 16.b; 33 *passim*; 73.t; 123.2; 133.b; 170.q,t,z,1,7,9

Phormio – seaman's plaited cloak, 74.m

Phoroneus – bringer of a price, *or fearinus*, of the Spring, 27.12; 28.1; 42.3; 50.1; 52.a,1,4; 57 *passim*; 64.c; 77.1; 118.5; 134.1

Phosphorus – Morning Star, 40.b,2; 45.a

Phrasius – speaker, 133.k

Phrixus – bristling, *or* stiff with horror, 70 *passim*; 148 *passim*; 151.f; 152.b, 3; 153.3; 155.2; 157.d

Phronsis – care, 151.f

Phthia – waning, 21.i; 160.l

Phylacus – guardian, 72 *passim*

Phylas – guard, 143.b

Phyleus – tribal chief, 127 *passim*; 138.g; 142.e

Phylius – leafy, 82.4; 123.i,1

Phyllis – leafy
    the Bisaltian, 169 *passim*
    the Thracian, 86 *passim*; 169.j

Phylonome – tribal pasture, 70.2; 161.g

Physcoa – fat paunch, 100.b

Phytalids – the growers, 98.x,8

Phytalus – orchard-keeper, 24.m,13; 97.a

Picus – woodpecker, 56.2

Pielus – plump, 169.f

Pieris – juicy, 159.d

Pimplea – she who fills, 136.J

Piram, 159.4

Pitthea – pine-goddess, 95.1

Pittheus – pine-god, 95 *passim*, 101.a; 110.c

Pityocamptes – pine-bender, 96.b,2,6

Pitys – fir, 26.e,2

Pleiades – sailing ones, *or* flock of doves, 39.d; 41.e,6; 45.3,4; 67.j,5; 111.e

Pleione – sailing queen, 41.e; 45.4

Pleisthenes – strength in sailing, *or* greatest strength, 93.c; 110.c; 111. f,g; 159.d,s; 163.a

Plexippus – braided horse-hair, 80.h

Pluto – wealth
    alias Hades, 24.5; 31.g
    mother of Tantalus, 108.a

Plutus – wealth, 24.a,5,6; 142.d; 143.1

Podaleirius – without lilies where he treads, i.e. discouraging death, 50.i; 165.f; 166.d; 169.c,d

Podarces – bear-foot, 137.k; 153.e; 158.l

Podarge – bright foot, 81.*m*

Podargus – bright foot, 130.*a,1*

Podes – ? *podiaios*, only a foot high, 162.*l*

Poeas – grazier, 92.*10*; 145.*f,2*; 148.*i*; 154.*h*; 166.*c*

Poene – punishment, 147.*a, 3*

Polites – citizen, 158.*o*; 168.*a*

Poltys – porridge, 131.*i*

Polybus – many oxen, 105.*b,c,d,j*

Polybutes – rich in oxen, 25.*f*

Polycaon – much burning, 74.*a*

Polycaste – ? *polycassiterë*, much tin, 92 *passim*

Polydectes – much welcoming, 73.*c,d,e,o,s*

Polydeuces – much sweet wine, 62.*c,1*; 74 *passim*; 80.*c*; 84.*1*; 103.*a,3*; 148.*i*; 150 *passim*; 155.*i*

Polydora – many gifts, 74.*a*; 162.*d*

Polydorus – many gifts
    son of Hecabe, 158.*o*; 168.*l*
    son of Laothoë, 162.*m*; 168 *passim*

Polyeidus – shape-shifter, 75.*b*; 90 *passim*; 141.*h*

Polygonus – with many children, 131.*i*

Polymede – many-wiled, 148.*b*

Polymela – many songs, 81.*f,g*

Polymele – many songs, 148.*b*; 155.*a*; 160.*m*

Polymnestor – mindful of many things, 168.*l,m,n*

Polyneices – much strife, 69.*1*; 74.*i*; 105.*k*; 106 *passim*; 107.*d*; 160.*w*

Polypemon – much misery, 96.*b,k*

Polypheides – exceedingly thrifty, 112.*i*

Polypheme – famous, 148.*b*

Polyphemus – famous
    Argonaut, 148.*i*; 150 *passim*
    Cyclops, 170 *passim*

Polyphontes – murderer of many, 105.*d*

Polypoetes – maker of many things, 171.*k*

Polyporthis – sacker of many cities, 171.*k,3*

Polyxena – many guests, 69.*2*; 158.*o*; 163.*a,o*; 164.*k,3*; 168 *passim*

Polyxenus – many guests, 97.*f*

Polyxo – much itching, 88.*10*; 114.*o*; 149.*b*

Porces – ? *phorces*, fate, 167.*i*

Porphyrion – dark-blue moon-man, 35.*d,3*

Porthaon – plunderer, 170.*q*

Portheus – sacker, 167.*m*

Poseidon – *potidan*, he who gives to drink from the wooded mountain, 7 *passim*; 9.*c*; 13.*c*; 16 *passim*; 18.*d*; 19.*2*; 25.*b,1*; 27.*9*; 22.*b,4*; 39.*b,7*; 43.*i*; 47.*d,e,3*; 49.*a,b*; 54.*a*; 56.*b*; 60.*g*; 66.*i*; 68.*c,2*; 70.*l*; 73.*h,j*; 75.*d*; 78.*a*; 88.*b,e,f*; 90.*7*; 95.*b,d,f*; 97.*1*; 98.*i*; 99.*f*; 101.*f*; 104.*k,2*; 108.*i*; 127.*2*; 133.*g*; 137.*a*; 137.*b,e,1*; 150.*i*; 158.*l*; 162.*f*; 163.*h*; 164.*l*; 167.*h,i,4*; 168.*f*; 169.*l,1*; 170 *passim*; 171.*k*

Erechtheus, 47.*4*

Post-vorta, 154.*3*

Potidan, 127.*2*

Potniae – powerful ones, 71.*2*

Pramanthu, 39.*8*

Prax – doer, 164.*p*

Praxithea – active goddess, 47.*b*; 97.*h,z*

Presbon – right of inheritance, 70.*m*

Priam – redeemed, 112.*e*; 131.*d,11*; 137.*k,l*; 141.*g*; 153.*e*; 158 *passim*; 159 *passim*; 160 *passim*; 161 *passim*; 162 *passim*; 163 *passim*; 164 *passim*; 166 *passim*; 167 *passim*; 168 *passim*

Priapus – pruner of the pear-tree, 15.*1*; 18.*e,k,2*; 20.*b,1*

Priolas – ? from *priein*, to grate out, and *olola*, I am ruined, 131.*h*

Procleia – challenger, 161.*f,g*

Procles – challenger, 146.*k*

Procne – *progonë*, the elder, 46 *passim*, 47.*a*; 94.*1*; 95.*a*

Procnis – *progonë*, the elder, 47.*b*

Procris – preference
    wife of Cephalus, 89 *passim*; 170.*o*
    Thespiad, 120.*b*

Procrustes – stretcher-out, 96.k,6

Proetus – first man, 69.1; 72 passim; 73 passim; 75.a,e; 81.8; 93.1; 118.g; 126.e; 138.6

Promachus – champion, 132.r; 155.a

Prometheus–forethought, orswastika, 4.b,c,3; 83.c; 39 passim; 57.a; 92.9; 126.c; 133 passim; 152.g

Pronomus – forager, 145.i

Proserpina – fearful one, 24.2

Prosymne – addressed with hymns, 124.b,4

Prote – first, 42.d

Protesilaus – first to rush into battle, 74.a; 162 passim; 163.i; 169.n

Proteus – first man, 27.b,7; 33.2; 82 passim; 90.7; 112.0; 131.i,6; 133.5; 159.u,v; 169.a,7

Protogenus Phaëthon – first-born shiner, 2.b,2

Protogonia – first-born, 47.b,d,2

Pryderi, 27.9

Prylis – dance in armour, 167.a

Psamathe – sandy shore, 81.a,p,1; 147.a,1

Psophis – uproar, 13.2,r

Psylla – flea, 109.d

Pteleon – elm grove, or boar-like, 89.c,e,j,5

Pterelas – launcher of feathers, 89 passim

Pterelaus – feathered riddance, 89.i,7; 91.1; 118.a,c; 119.c

Pwyll, 27.9

Pygmalion – shaggy fist, 65 passim

Pylades – ? pylades, gate of Hades, 113 passim; 114 passim; 116 passim; 117 passim

Pylaemenes – strength of the pass, 168.b

Pylas – gate, 94.c

Pylenor – on the threshold of man-hood, 126.e

Pylia – of the gate, 94.c

Pylius, or Pelius – of the gate, 104.e; 134.a; 166.b

Pylon – gate, 94.c

Pyraechmus – point of flame, 122.b,2; 163.i

Pyrene – fiery reins, 132.j; 133.d

Pyrrha – fiery red, 38 passim; (see also Cercysera)

Pyrrhus (later Neoptolemus) – fiery red, 160.j

Python–serpent, 14.a,2; 21.a,b,2,3,12; 32.a; 36.1; 51.b; 58.5; 96.6

Pyttius – ? inquirer, 138.a

Queen of the May, 26.4

Queens, 138.0,4

Q're, 1.5; 57.2; 82.6; 95.5

Ra, 41.3; 42.4; 117.1

Rahab, 33.2

Rama, 135.1

Rarus – abortive child, or womb, 24. m.8

Recaranus – see Trigaranus, 132.n

Remus, 68.3; 80.2

Rhacius – ragged, 107.i

Rhadamanthys – ? ·rhabdomantis, he who divines with a wand, 31.6; 58.c; 66.i,4; 88 passim; 119.g; 146.f

Rhaecus – breaker, 80.f

Rhea–earth, 1.d; 2.b,2; 7 passim; 12.a; 13.a,2; 16.f; 24.k; 27.a,e,7,12; 30. a,3; 39.8; 47.2; 53.a,c,2; 54.a; 86.2; 91.3; 108.a,h,7; 149.h,3,4; 151.g; 164.6; 169.j,3

Rhea Silvia, 68.3

Rhene – ewe, 160.q

Rhesus – breaker, 163.g

Rhexenor – manly deeds, 95.a

Rhiannon, 27.9; 154.3

Rhode – rhodea, rosy, 16.b,1; 42.c,d

Rhodus – rose, 18.d

Rhoeo – pomegranate, 106.t,7

Rigantona – great queen, 26.9

Rimmon, 27.10

Robin Hood, 119.4; 162.10

Romulus, 21.13; 68.3; 80,2; 105.1,5

Sabazius – breaker in pieces, 7.1; 27.3,7,9

Sagaris, R. – single-edged sword, 136.f

Salamis – ? eastern, 81.d

Salmoneus – beloved of the Goddess Salma, 64.c; 67.e,i,3; 68 passim

Samas – 1.3

Samson, 82.4; 83.3; 91.1.5; 110.2; 145.4; 154.i; 164.3

Sangarius, R. – fit for canoes, 158.o

Sarah, 169.6

Saranyu, 16.6

Sarpedon – rejoicing in a wooden ark
    uncle of Glaucus, 162.9
    brother of Minos, 58.c; 88 passim; 94.f; 131.1
    son of Zeus, 162.n,9; 163.i,j; 164.h

Saturn, 7.1

Satyraea – of the satyrs, 87.2

Saul, 169.5

Saurus – lizard, 125.b

Scamander, R. – crooked man, 68.2; 137.n,3; 163.l
    son of Deimachus, 137.n,t; 158.a.g.l.6.9

Scarphe – black hellebore, 148.b

Schoeneus – of the rush basket, 80.l,4

Schoenus – of the rush basket, 111.p

Sciron – of the parasol, 23.1; 70.h,7; 81.a; 94.e; 96 passim; 110.c

Scorpion-men, 41.3

Scotia – dark one, 18.4

Scylla – she who rends
    daughter of Nisus, 91 passim; 92.4; 168.1
    daughter of Phorcys, 16.b,2; 61.a; 90.7; 148.1,9; 154.11; 170.t,1,9

Scyrius – stony, 94.c

Scythes – Aeolic for scyphes, goblet, 119.5; 132.v

Seasons, 11.a; 12.a,4; 13.a,e

Selene – moon, 1.3; 14.5; 26.e,4; 35.b; 42.a; 62.3; 54.a,b; 67.6; 74.3; 123 passim

Semele – moon, 14.c,5; 27.k,2,6,11; 28.4; 124.b,4; 134.g,4

Set, 18.3; 21.2; 36.1; 41.4; 42.1; 73.4;

83.2; 89.2; 123.3; 133.8; 138.1

Sheol, 24.11

Shiva, 135.1

Sicalus – silent, 135.e

Sicyon – cucumber, 94.b

Sidero – starry, 68.b,d,2,4

Silenus – moon-man, 17.2,4; 27.b; 35.h; 83 passim; 126.b,3

Sillus – jeerer, 136.c

Simoeis – snub-nosed, 158.g

Sin, 1.3

Sinis – robber, 96 passim; 97.a

Sinon – plunderer
    the Greek spy, 167 passim
    son of Sisyphus, 67.a

Sinope – moon-face, 151.d

Sipylus, 108.g; 131.o

Sirens – those who bind with a cord, or those who wither, 126.d,3; 128.1; 148.1,9; 154.d,3; 169.4; 170 passim
Names
    Aglaope – beautiful face
    Aglaophonos – beautiful voice
    Leucosia – white being
    Ligeia – shrill
    Molpe – music
    Parthenope – maiden face
    Peisinoë – persuading the mind
    Raidne – improvement
    Teles – perfect
    Thelxepeia – soothing words
    Thelxiope – persuasive face

Sirius – Dog-star (see Orthrus), 31.7; 34.3; 37.2; 82.f,3; 132.3

Sisyphus – ? se-sophos, very wise, 41.e; 67 passim; 68.b,2; 70.h,9; 71.b; 75.a,3; 96.d; 105.7; 108.2; 155.i; 156.d; 160.c; 170.p

Sita, 135.1

Sleep, 4.a; 118.c; 137.o; 163.j

Smyrna – myrrh, 18.h,5,6; 77.2; 131.3; 160.g

Solemn Ones – (see Erinnyes), 105.k; 115 passim; 117.i

Soloön – egg-shaped weight, 100.b,2

Solyma, 75.4

Som, 118.2

Sophax – ? *sophanax*, wise king, 133.*i*

Sosipolis – saviour of the state, 138.*0,4*

Spermo – of the seed, 160.*u*

Sphaerus – boxer, *or* ball, 95.*d*; 109.*i*

Sphinx – throttler, 34.*a,3*; 82.6; 105 *passim*; 106.1; 119.*e*; 121.*3*; 123.1

Spites, 15.1; 39.*j*

Staphylus – bunch of grapes, 27.*i,8*; 88.*h*; 148.*i*; 160.*t,7*

Sterope – stubborn face, *or* lightning. 109.*c*; 170.*q*

Steropes – lightning, 3.*b,2*; 22.*d*

Stheino – strong, 33.*b,3*

Stheneboea – strength of cattle, 72, *g.4*; 73.*a*; 75.*a*

Sthenele – strong light, 160.*m*

Sthenelus – strong forcer back
    son of Capeneus, 160.*r*; 162.*t*; 167.*c*
    father of Eurystheus, 111.*b*; 112.*a*; 118.*a,d*
    of Paros, 131.*e*

Stheno – strong, 73.*f,h*

Stichius – marshal, 135.*e*

Strophius – twisted head-band, 113. *b,i,j*; 114.*e*
    the Second, 117.*b*

Strymo – harsh, 158.*l*

Strymon – harsh, 163.*g*

Stygian Nymphs, 73.*g,9*

Stymphalus – ? priapic member, 66.*h*; 109.*n,7*; 128.*d*; 141.*c*

Styx – hated, 13.*a*; 31.4; 37.*d*

Susannah, 164.2

Sylea – plunderer, 99.*b*

Syleus – plunderer, 136.*e*

Syrian Goddess, 62.*a,3*; 98.7

Syrinx – reed, 26.*e*

Talos – ? sufferer
    bronze man, 23.1; 90.7
    pupil of Daedalus, 12.*c,3*; 92 *passim*; 154 *passim*; 161.7

Talthybius – *tzalthybius*, stormy life, 161.*d*

Tammuz, or *Thamus*, 18.6,7; 24.11; 26.5; 27.10; 91.4

Tanais, R. – long, 131.*b*

Tantalus – lurching, *or* most wretched, 77.*c*; 105.7; 108 *passim*; 109.*a,1,7*; 111.4; 125.3; 136.*b*; 158.6; 170.*p*
    son of Broteas, 108.*k*
    the Second, 111.*g*; 112.*c,h*
    (*see* Talos), 92.*c,1*

Taphius – of the tomb, 110.*c*

Taras – troubler, 87.2

Taraxippus – horse-scarer, 71.*b,3*

Tartarus – (*Cretan word*) ? far west, 4.*a*; 15.*a*; 36.*a*; 103 *passim*; 134 *passim*

Tauropolus – bull slayer, 27.*i,8*

Taurus – bull, 58.4; 88.7; 92.7; 98.*p,2*; 99.*f*

Taygete – ? *tanygennetos*, long-checked, 125.*c,1,3*

Tecmessa – ? from *tecmairesthai*, she who ordains, *or* judges, 162.*m,9*; 165 *passim*

Tectamus – craftsman, 88.*a,1*

Tecton – carpenter, 159.*q*

Tegeates – roof-man, 88.*h*

Tegyrius – beehive coverer, 47.*c,1*

Teiresias – he who delights in signs, 25.*g*; 77.*a*; 85.*a*; 105.*h,i,j,5,8*; 106.*j*; 107.*b,i*; 119.*e,2*; 154.6; 170 *passim*; 171.3

Telamon – he who suffers, supports, *or* dares; *also* baldric, i.e. supporting strap, 66.*e,i*; 80.*c,g*; 81 *passim*; 108.4; 131.*a*; 137 *passim*; 158.*r*; 160.*p*; 165 *passim*; 168.6

Telchines – enchanted, *or* Tyrrhenians, 42.*c*; 54 *passim*; 60.2; 146.4

Telebus – from *telbomai*, ill-treater, 118.*f*

Telecleia – distant fame, 158.*o*

Teledamus – far-tamer, 112.*h*

Telegonus – last-born
    son of Odysseus, 170.*k*; 171 *passim*
    son of Proteus, 56.*b*; 131.*i*

Telemachus – decisive battle, 160.*f,4*; 171 *passim*

Telphassa – far shiner, 58.*a,e,2*

Telephus – suckled by a doe, 141 *passim*; 160.*w,z*; 166.*i*; 168.*d*

Temenus – precinct, 12.a; 128.d; 146.k

Tenes – strip, or tendon, 70.2; 161 passim

Terambus, 38.11

Tereus – watcher, 46 passim

Termerus – ? termios, destined end, 119.j

Terminus, 158.3

Terpsichore – rejoicing in the dance, 170.q

Tesup, 42.1,4; 66.1; 75.3; 93.1; 170.3

Tethys – disposer, 1.d; 2.a,1; 11.b,2; 33.2; ? 66.1

Teucer – teucter, artisan, 81.e; 137.l; 158.9; 159.a; 160.p; 164.m; 165 passim

Teumessian Vixen, 89.h,8; 116.4; 118.5

Teutamides – son of him who repeats himself, 73.p

Teutamus – repeating himself, 164.d

Teutarus – continual practice, 119.f,5

Teuthras – ? of the cuttlefish, 141 passim

Thalia – festive, 21.i,5; 105.5

Thallo – sprouting, 13.2

Thamyris – thick-set, 21.m; 29.3; 110.h; 147.b

Thasius – the Thasian, 133.k

Thasus – ? from thasso, idler, 58.a,d,1

Thaumacus – wonder worker, 148.i

Thaumas – wonderful, 33.g,2

Thea – divine, 43.c

Theagenes – religiously born, 146.j

Theano – goddess, 43.e,f; 164.l; 168 passim

Thebe – admirable, 66.b; 76.c

Theia – divine, 1.d; 40.a; 42.a; 88.b; 136.c

Theias – diviner, 18.h

Theiodamas – divine tamer, 143.a,b,1; 150.h

Theiomenes – divine strength, 143.a

Theisadie – ? from theiazomenai, oracularly inspired, 159.s

Themis – order
Nymph, 132.o

Titaness, 1.d; 11.a; 13.a,2; 16.b; 38.d; 51.b; 81.j; 95.c,1; 101.j; 159.e

Themiste, oracular, 158.l

Themisto – oracular, 70.i,j,k,3

Theobule – divine counsel, 109.f

Theoclymenus – famous as a god, 136.b

Theogone – child of the gods, 136.b

Theonoë – divine intelligence, 161 passim

Theope – divine face, 97.h,2

Theophane – appearance of the goddess, 70.l

Thersander – encourager of men, 107.a.d; 160.w,x

Thersites – son of courage, 164 passim

Theseus – he who lays down, or deposits, 49.b; 80.c,g; 88.f; 90.b; 95 passim; 96 passim; 97 passim; 98 passim; 99 passim; 100 passim; 101 passim; 102 passim; 103 passim; 104 passim; 105.7; 106.l,m; 113.3; 117.3; 129.b; 131.a,g,4,11; 132.1; 134.a,d,2,7; 135.e; 146 passim

Thespius, divinely-sounding, 120 passim; 122.d; 142.f

Thesprotus – first ordainer, 111.h,i

Thessalus – ? dark prayer, 137.r son of Medea, 156.e,f

Thestius – devotee of the Goddess Hestia, 74.b; 120.a,1; 148.i

Thestor – ? from theiazein, inspirer, 161 passim

Thetis – disposer, 11.2; 13.c,1; 16.b,1; 23.a,1; 27.e; 29.1; 23.a,2; 43.c; 81 passim; 98.j,11; 108.5; 124.3,4; 154.k,11; 157.a; 159.e; 160 passim; 161.h; 162.b; 163.b,l; 164 passim; 165.a; 168.f; 169.7; 170.v

Thoas – impetuous, or nimble
King of Calydon, 167.c; 171.l
Giant, 35.g
the Lemnian, 27.i,6; 88.h; 98.o, 12; 116 passim; 149.b
companion of Theseus, 100.b; 106.g the Younger, 149.c

Thomas the Rhymer, 170.2

Thoösa – impetuous being, 158.*l*; 170.*b*

Thoth, 17.2; 36.2; 52.6; 82.3; 128.4; 133.3; 162.6

Thrasius – confident, 133.*k*

Thriae – triad, 17.*g*,3

Thyestes – pestle, 93.*c*; 106.2; 110. *c*,*g*,*h*; 111 *passim*; 112.*a*,*k*; 117.*a*,2; 118.*a*

Thymbraeus, *or* Melanthus – of the bitter herb, 167.*i*

Thymoetes – ? *thymoeides*, courageous, 159.*g*; 167.*e*

Thyone – raging queen, 27.*k*,2,11

Tiamat, 4.5; 7.5; 33.2; 35.5; 36.2; 73.7; 103.2; 137.2; 170.5

Tillage-gods, 24.1

Timalcus – honoured strength, 110. *d*,*f*

Timandra – honoured by man, 159.*c*

Timosthenes – strength of dignity, 146.*j*

Tinga – ? (*non-Greek word*), 133.*i*

Tiphys – from the pool, 148.*i*; 149.*g*; 150.*c*; 151.*c*,2

Tisamenes – vengeful, 146.*k*

Tisamenus – vengeful
son of Orestes, 117.*h*,2
son of Thersander, 160.*x*

Tisander – avenger of men, 156.*e*

Tisiphone – vengeful destruction, 6.*a*; 31.*g*; 107.*i*; 115.2

Titans, Titanesses – lords, 1.3,4; 4.*a*; 6.*a*; 7.*d*,*e*; 27.*a*,4; 30.*a*,*b*,1,3; 35.*a*; 39.*a*; 77.1; 98.4; 156.1

Tithonus – partner of the queen of day, 29.1; 40.*c*,3; 158.*l*; 164 *passim*

Titias – attempter, 131.*h*,9

Titonë – sovereign lady, 40.3

Tityus – ? from *tituscomai*, attempter, 21.*d*,4; 58.1; 131.10

Tlepolemus – battle-enduring, 114.0; 142.*e*; 143.*i*; 146.*e*,*h*; 160.*s*; 169.*n*

Tmolus – (*non-Greek word*), 83.*g*; 108.*a*,3,10; 136.*b*,1

Torone – shrill queen, 131.6

Toxeus – archer, 80.*a*,2; 135.*b*

Tragasus – lustful as a goat, 161.*g*

Trambelus – ? lord of ships, 137.*l*

Triballus – lounger, 136.*c*

Tricarenon – triple crane, 132.4

Trigaranus – triple crane, 132.4

Triops – three-faced, 146.*h*,4

Triptolemus – thrice daring, 24 *passim*; 65.*d*; 116.6

Triton – *tritaon*, being in her third day, 8.1; 16.*b*,1; 154.*g*; 170.*t*

Tritone – third queen, 8.1

Troezen – worn-down form of *trion hezomenon*, [the city] of the three sitters, 95.*b*,6

Troilus – Trojan from Ilium, 158.0; 161.*l*; 162 *passim*; 164 *passim*

Trophonius – increaser of sales, 51. *i*,*k*,6; 84 *passim*; 121.*f*; 169.2

Tros – Trojan, 29.*a*,*b*,1; 158.*g*; 164.7; 168.*d*

Tubal Cain, 151.3

Tyche – fortune, 32 *passim*; 142.*d*; 162.*s*

Tydeus – ? thumper, 106 *passim*; 160.*j*

Tylon, *or* Tylus – knot, *or* phallus, 90.8

Tyndareus – pounder, 50.*f*; 62.*a*,*c*; 74 *passim*; 103.*b*; 112.*a*,*c*,2; 113.*a*,5; 114 *passim*; 117.*c*; 140.*c*; 159 *passim*; 160.*d*; 169.*g*

Typhon – stupefying smoke, hot wind, *or* hurricane, 21.2; 33.*e*; 34 *passim*; 35.4; 36 *passim*; 48.3; 96.*e*; 105.*e*; 123.*b*; 124.*a*; 132.*a*; 133.*b*,*l*,11; 152.*h*; 170.*t*

Tyro – the Tyrian, 67.*e*; 68 *passim*; 148.*a*

Tyrrhenus – of the walled city, 136.*g*

Tyrsenus – of the walled city, 136.*g*

Udaeus – of the earth, 58.*g*,5

Ullikummi, 6.6; 36.4

Ulysses, *or* Ulyxes – wounded in the thigh, 170 *passim*; 171 *passim*

Unial, 118.2

Urana – queen of the mountains, of the winds, of summer, *or* of wild oxen, 3.*1*

Urania,– heavenly, 147.*b*

Uranus – king of the mountains, 2.*b*.2; 3.*a,1*; 6.*a,1,6*; 7.*a*; 11.*b*; 36.*b*; 54.*a*; 88.*b*

Urion – native who makes water, *or* native of the mountains, 41.*f,5*

Varuna, 3.*1*; 7.*6*; 132.*5*

Velchanus – ? from *helcein*, the king who drags [his foot], 92.*1*

Virbius – *heirobios*, holy life, 101.*l,1*

Vivaswat, 16.*6*

Vixen-goddess, 116.*4*

Vulcan, 32.*2*; 92.*1*

West Wind, 15.*b*; 21.*m*; 48.*a*; 81.*m*

Wild Women, 14.*5*; 27.*11*

Winegrowers, 160.*u,7*

Xanthus – yellow, 75.*5*; 81.*m,4*; 130.*a*; 132.*r*; 158.*o,6*
    horse, 163.*m*
    River, 108.*b*

Xenoclea – famous guest, 135.*c,d,3*

Xisuthros, 38.*4*

Xuthus – sparrow, 43 *passim*; 44.*a*; 46.*5*; 75.*6*; 100.*d*

Yatpan, 41.*4*

Zacynthus – ? (*Cretan word,*) 158.*g,2*; 168.*4*

Zagreus – restored to life, 27.*8*; 28.*1*; 30 *passim*; 70.*5*; 90.*4*; 129.*2*; 140.*1*

Zarah, 73.*2*

Zelus – zeal, 8.*3*

Zetes – searcher, 48.*c*; 148.*i*; 150 *passim*; 155.*i*

Zethus – seeker, 76.*a,b,c*; 108.*g*

Zeus – bright sky, 1.*3*; 7 *passim*; 9 *passim*; 11.*a*; 12 *passim*; 13 *passim*; 14.

a,c,1,5; 16.*a*; 17.*c,f*; 20.*a*; 23.*b*; 24.*c,g*; 28.*h*; 29 *passim*; 30.*a,b,3*; 32.*b,2*; 36.*b,e*; 38.*b,c,1*; 39.*e,f,h,i*; 41.*f*; 43.*i*; 45.*a,2*; 47.*3*; 50.*g*; 51.*a,1*; 53.*a,5*; 56.*a*; 58.*b,c*; 62.*a*; 63.*c,2*; 66 *passim*; 68.*a,1*; 70.*2,6*; 73.*c*; 77.*c*; 81.*j*; 88.*9*; 89.*h*; 98.*j*; 102.*a,3*; 105.*h*; 108.*c,e*; 117.*2*; 118 *passim*; 119 *passim*; 125.*c*; 137.*0*; 138.*k*; 145.*g,h,i*; 148.*10*; 156.*d,4*; 160.*11*; 163.*h*; 170.*x*

Acraeus – of the summit, 148.*10*

Actaeus – of the summit, 148.*10*

Agamemnon – very resolute, 112.*o.3*

Ammon, 36.*2*; 73.*j*; 133.*j*; 137.*b*

Arcadian, 82.*3*

Atabyrius, 93.*1*

Averter of Flies, 138.*i*

Cean, 82.*3*

of the Courtyard, 168.*a*

Cretan, 91.*3*; 108.*7*; 151.*2*

Deliverer, 70.*e*

Dodonan, 51.*a*

Gracious, 97.*a*

Green, 138.*4*

Hecaleius – 98.*b*

Heliopolitan, 1.*4*; 42.*4*

Immortal, 82.*b*

Labradian – of the axe, 131.*j,6*

Laphystian, 134.*h*; 146.*a*; 157.*d,2*

Leader of the Fates, 10.*3*

Lycaeus – wolfish, 38.*a,g*; 108.*5*; 128.*3*

Morius – distributor, 82.*6*

Picus – woodpecker, 56.*d,2*

Preserver, 121.*e*

Reliever, 114.*i*

Sabazius – breaker in pieces, 145.*5*

Saviour, 123.*d,f*

Solar, 21.*10*; 109.*2*

Strong, 95.*e,5*

Warlike, 109.*d*

of the White Poplar, 138.*h*

Velchanos – 160.*6*

Zeuxippe – she who yokes horses, 46.*3*; 158.*l*